THE THOUSAND AUTUMNS OF JACOB DE ZOET

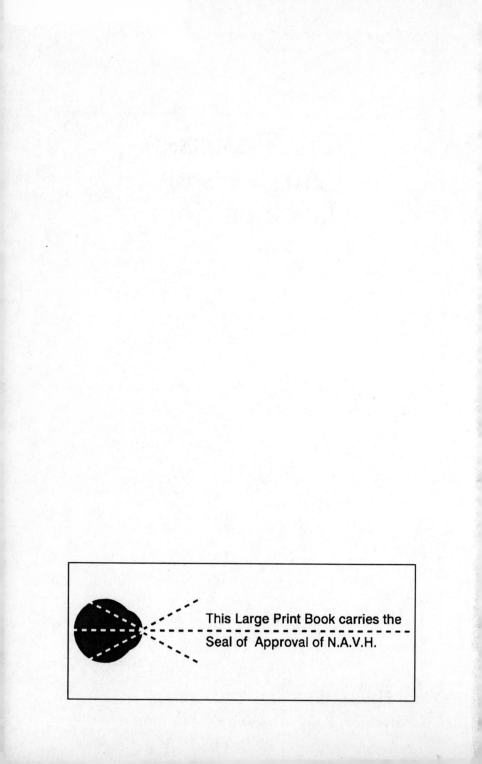

This Large Print Book carries the
Seal of Approval of N.A.V.H.

THE THOUSAND AUTUMNS OF JACOB DE ZOET

DAVID MITCHELL

LARGE PRINT PRESS

A part of Gale, Cengage Learning

CANCELLED

GALE
CENGAGE Learning·

Detroit • New York • San Francisco • New Haven, Conn • Waterville, Maine • London

GALE
CENGAGE Learning·

LIBRARY OF CONGRESS CATALOGING-IN-PUBLICATION DATA

Mitchell, David (David Stephen)
    The thousand autumns of Jacob De Zoet / by David Mitchell.
        p. cm. — (Thorndike Press large print reviewers' choice)
    ISBN-13: 978-1-4104-3312-1
    ISBN-10: 1-4104-3312-9
        1. Deshima (Nagasaki-shi, Japan)—Fiction. 2. Japan—History—
    1787–1868—Fiction. 3. East and West—Fiction. 4. Trading posts—Fiction.
    5. Large type books. I. Title.
    PR6063.I785T47 2011
    823'.914—dc22   2010037623

ISBN 13: 978-1-59413-578-1 (pbk. : alk. paper)
ISBN 10: 1-59413-578-9 (pbk. : alk. paper)

Published in 2012 by arrangement with Random House, Inc.

Printed in the United States of America
    1 2 3 4 5   16 15 14 13 12

FD199

For K, H, & N with love

CONTENTS

AUTHOR'S NOTE

The port of Batavia on the island of Java was the headquarters of the Dutch East Indies Company (*Vereenigde Oost-Indische Compagnie* or VOC in Dutch, literally "United East Indian Company") and the point of embarkation and return for VOC ships sailing the Nagasaki run. During the Japanese occupation of the Indonesian archipelago during World War II, Batavia was renamed Jakarta.

Throughout the novel, the lunar calendar is used to denote Japanese dates. The lunar calendar could be anything from three to seven weeks "behind" the Gregorian calendar, depending on the year. Thus "the first day of the first month" corresponds not to January 1 but to a varying date between the back end of January and the rear middle of February. Years are referred to by their Japanese era names.

Japanese names are ordered throughout with the family name first.

■ ■ ■ ■

Part One:
The Bride for
Whom We Dance

■ ■ ■ ■

The eleventh year of the Era of Kansei

1799

CHAPTER ONE:
THE HOUSE OF
KAWASEMI THE
CONCUBINE,
ABOVE NAGASAKI

The ninth night of the fifth month

"Miss Kawasemi?" Orito kneels on a stale and sticky futon. "Can you hear me?"

In the rice paddy beyond the garden, a cacophony of frogs detonates.

Orito dabs the concubine's sweat-drenched face with a damp cloth.

"She's barely spoken" — the maid holds the lamp — "for hours and hours. . . ."

"Miss Kawasemi, I'm Aibagawa. I'm a midwife. I want to help."

Kawasemi's eyes flicker open. She manages a frail sigh. Her eyes shut.

She is too exhausted, Orito thinks, *even to fear dying tonight.*

Dr. Maeno whispers through the muslin curtain. "I wanted to examine the child's presentation myself, but . . ." The elderly scholar chooses his words with care. "But this is prohibited, it seems."

"My orders are clear," states the chamberlain. "No man may touch her."

13

Orito lifts the bloodied sheet and finds, as warned, the fetus's limp arm, up to the shoulder, protruding from Kawasemi's vagina.

"Have you ever seen such a presentation?" asks Dr. Maeno.

"Yes: in an engraving, from the Dutch text Father was translating."

"This is what I prayed to hear! The *Observations* of William Smellie?"

"Yes: Dr. Smellie terms it," Orito uses the Dutch, " 'Prolapse of the Arm.' "

Orito clasps the fetus's mucus-smeared wrist to search for a pulse.

Maeno now asks her in Dutch, "What are your opinions?"

There is no pulse. "The baby is dead," Orito answers, in the same language, "and the mother will die soon, if the child is not delivered." She places her fingertips on Kawasemi's distended belly and probes the bulge around the inverted navel. "It was a boy." She kneels between Kawasemi's parted legs, noting the narrow pelvis, and sniffs the bulging labia: she detects the malty mixture of grumous blood and excrement, but not the stench of a rotted fetus. "He died one or two hours ago."

Orito asks the maid, "When did the waters break?"

The maid is still mute with astonishment at hearing a foreign language.

14

"Yesterday morning, during the Hour of the Dragon," says the stony-voiced housekeeper. "Our lady entered labor soon after."

"And when was the last time that the baby kicked?"

"The last kick would have been around noon today."

"Dr. Maeno, would you agree the infant is in" — she uses the Dutch term — "the 'transverse breech position'?"

"Maybe," the doctor answers in their code tongue, "but without an examination . . ."

"The baby is twenty days late, or more. It should have been turned."

"Baby's resting," the maid assures her mistress. "Isn't that so, Dr. Maeno?"

"What you say" — the honest doctor wavers — "may well be true."

"My father told me," Orito says, "Dr. Uragami was overseeing the birth."

"So he was," grunts Maeno, "from the comfort of his consulting rooms. After the baby stopped kicking, Uragami ascertained that, for geomantic reasons discernible to men of his genius, the child's spirit is reluctant to be born. The birth henceforth depends on the mother's willpower." *The rogue,* Maeno needs not add, *dares not bruise his reputation by presiding over the stillbirth of such an estimable man's child.* "Chamberlain Tomine then persuaded the magistrate to summon me. When I saw the arm, I recalled your doctor of Scotland and requested your help."

"My father and I are both deeply honored by your trust," says Orito . . .

. . . *and curse Uragami,* she thinks, *for his lethal reluctance to lose face.*

Abruptly, the frogs stop croaking and, as though a curtain of noise falls away, the sound of Nagasaki can be heard, celebrating the safe arrival of the Dutch ship.

"If the child is dead," says Maeno in Dutch, "we must remove it now."

"I agree." Orito asks the housekeeper for warm water and strips of linen and uncorks a bottle of Leiden salts under the concubine's nose to win her a few moments' lucidity. "Miss Kawasemi, we are going to deliver your child in the next few minutes. First, may I feel inside you?"

The concubine is seized by the next contraction and loses her ability to answer.

Warm water is delivered in two copper pans as the agony subsides. "We should confess," Dr. Maeno proposes to Orito in Dutch, "the baby is dead. Then amputate the arm to deliver the body."

"First, I wish to insert my hand to learn whether the body is in a convex lie or concave lie."

"If you can discover that without cutting the arm" — Maeno means "amputate" — "do so."

16

Orito lubricates her right hand with rape-seed oil and addresses the maid: "Fold one linen strip into a thick pad . . . yes, like so. Be ready to wedge it between your mistress's teeth; otherwise she might bite off her tongue. Leave spaces at the sides, so she can breathe. Dr. Maeno, my inspection is beginning."

"You are my eyes and ears, Miss Aibagawa," says the doctor.

Orito works her fingers between the fetus's biceps and its mother's ruptured labia until half her wrist is inside Kawasemi's vagina. The concubine shivers and groans. "Sorry," says Orito, "sorry . . ." Her fingers slide between warm membranes and skin and muscle still wet with amniotic fluid, and the midwife pictures an engraving from that enlightened and barbaric realm, Europe . . .

If the transverse lie is convex, recalls Orito, *where the fetus's spine is arched backward so acutely that its head appears between its shins like a Chinese acrobat, she must amputate the fetus's arm, dismember its corpse with toothed forceps, and extract it, piece by grisly piece. Dr. Smellie warns that any remnant left in the womb will fester and may kill the mother. If the transverse lie is concave, however,* Orito has read, *where the fetus's knees are pressed against its chest, she may saw off the arm, rotate the fetus, insert crotchets into the eye sockets, and extract the whole body, headfirst.* The midwife's index finger locates the child's

17

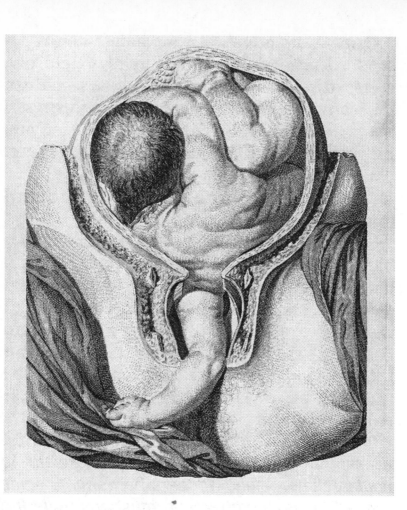

knobbly spine, traces its midriff between its lowest rib and its pelvic bone, and encounters a minute ear; a nostril; a mouth; the umbilical cord; and a prawn-sized penis. "Breech is concave," Orito reports to Dr. Maeno, "but the cord is around the neck."

"Do you think the cord can be released?" Maeno forgets to speak Dutch.

"Well, I must try. Insert the cloth," Orito tells the maid, "now, please."

18

When the linen wad is secured between Kawasemi's teeth, Orito pushes her hand in deeper, hooks her thumb around the umbilical cord, sinks four fingers into the underside of the fetus's jaw, pushes back his head, and slides the cord over his face, forehead, and crown. Kawasemi screams, hot urine trickles down Orito's forearm, but the procedure works first time: the noose is released. She withdraws her hand and reports, "The cord is freed. Might the doctor have his" — there is no Japanese word — "forceps?"

"I brought them along," Maeno taps his medical box, "in case."

"We might try to deliver the child" — she switches to Dutch — "without amputating the arm. Less blood is always better. But I need your help."

Dr. Maeno addresses the chamberlain: "To help save Miss Kawasemi's life, I *must* disregard the magistrate's orders and join the midwife inside the curtain."

Chamberlain Tomine is caught in a dangerous quandary.

"Blame me," Maeno suggests, "for disobeying the magistrate."

"The choice is mine," decides the chamberlain. "Do what you must, Doctor."

The spry old man crawls under the muslin, holding his curved tongs.

When the maid sees the foreign contraption, she exclaims in alarm.

19

" 'Forceps,' " the doctor replies, with no further explanation.

The housekeeper lifts the muslin to see. "No, I don't like the look of *that!* Foreigners may chop, slice, and call it 'medicine,' but it is quite unthinkable that —"

"Do *I* advise the housekeeper," growls Maeno, "on where to buy fish?"

"Forceps," explains Orito, "don't cut — they turn and pull, just like a midwife's fingers but with a stronger grip . . ." She uses her Leiden salts again. "Miss Kawasemi, I'm going to use this instrument" — she holds up the forceps — "to deliver your baby. Don't be afraid, and don't resist. Europeans use them routinely — even for princesses and queens. We'll pull your baby out, gently and firmly."

"Do so . . ." Kawasemi's voice is a smothered rattle. "Do so . . ."

"Thank you, and when I ask Miss Kawasemi to *push* . . ."

"Push . . ." She is fatigued almost beyond caring. "Push . . ."

"How often," Tomine peers in, "have you used that implement?"

Orito notices the chamberlain's crushed nose for the first time: it is as severe a disfigurement as her own burn. "Often, and no patient ever suffered." Only Maeno and his pupil know that these "patients" were hollowed-out melons whose babies were oiled gourds. For the final time, if all goes well, she works her hand inside Kawasemi's womb. Her fingers find the fetus's throat, rotate his head toward the cervix, slip, gain a surer purchase, and swivel the awkward corpse through a third turn. "Now, please, Doctor."

Maeno slides in the forceps around the protruding arm.

The onlookers gasp; a parched shriek is wrenched from Kawasemi.

Orito feels the forceps' curved blades in her palm: she maneuvers them around the fetus's soft skull. "Close them."

Gently but firmly, the doctor squeezes the forceps shut.

Orito takes the forceps' handles in her left hand: the resistance is spongy but firm, like *konnyaku* jelly. Her right hand, still inside the uterus, cups the fetus's skull.

Dr. Maeno's bony fingers encase Orito's wrist.

"What is it you're waiting for?" asks the housekeeper.

"The next contraction," says the doctor, "which is due any —"

Kawasemi's breathing starts to swell with fresh pain.

"One and two," counts Orito, "and — *push, Kawasemi-san!*"

"Push, Mistress!" exhort the maid and the housekeeper.

Dr. Maeno pulls at the forceps; with her

21

right hand, Orito pushes the fetus's head toward the birth canal. She tells the maid to grasp the baby's arm and pull. Orito feels the resistance grow as the head reaches the aperture. "One and two . . . *now!*" Squeezing the glans of the clitoris flat comes a tiny corpse's matted crown.

"Here he is!" gasps the maid, through Kawasemi's animal shrieks.

Here comes the baby's scalp; here his face, marbled with mucus . . .

. . . Here comes the rest of his slithery, clammy, lifeless body.

"Oh, but — oh," says the maid. "Oh. Oh. *Oh . . .*"

Kawasemi's high-pitched sobs subside to moans, and deaden.

She knows. Orito discards the forceps, lifts the lifeless baby by his ankles and slaps him. She has no hope of coaxing out a miracle: she acts from discipline and training. After ten hard slaps, she stops. He has no pulse. She feels no breath on her cheek from the lips and nostrils. There is no need to announce the obvious. Splicing the cord near the navel, she cuts the gristly string with her knife, bathes the lifeless boy in a copper of water, and places him in the crib. *A crib for a coffin,* she thinks, *and a swaddling sheet for a shroud.*

Chamberlain Tomine gives instructions to a

22

servant outside. "Inform His Honor that a son was stillborn. Dr. Maeno and his midwife did their best but were powerless to alter what Fate had decreed."

Orito's concern is now puerperal fever. The placenta must be extracted, *yakumosô* applied to the perineum, and blood stanched from an anal fissure.

Dr. Maeno withdraws from the curtained tent to make space.

A moth the size of a bird enters and blunders into Orito's face.

Batting it away, she knocks the forceps off one of the copper pans.

The forceps clatters onto a pan lid; the loud clang frightens a small creature that has somehow found its way into the room; it mewls and whimpers.

A puppy? wonders Orito, baffled. *Or a kitten?*

The mysterious animal cries again, very near: under the futon?

"Shoo that thing away!" the housekeeper tells the maid. "Shoo it!"

The creature mewls again, and Orito realizes it is coming from the crib.

Surely not, thinks the midwife, refusing to hope. *Surely not . . .*

She snatches away the linen sheet just as the baby's mouth opens.

He inhales once, twice, three times; his crinkled face crumples . . .

. . . and the shuddering newborn boiled-
pink despot howls at Life.

CHAPTER TWO:
CAPTAIN LACY'S
CABIN ON THE
SHENANDOAH,
ANCHORED IN
NAGASAKI HARBOR

Evening of July 20, 1799

"How *else,*" demands Daniel Snitker, "is a man to earn just reward for the daily humiliations we suffer from those slit-eyed leeches? 'The unpaid servant,' say the Spanish, 'has the right to pay himself,' and for once, damn me, the Spanish are right. Why so certain there'll still *be* a company to pay us in five years' time? Amsterdam is on its knees; our shipyards are idle; our manufactories silent; our granaries plundered; The Hague is a stage of prancing marionettes tweaked by Paris; Prussian jackals and Austrian wolves laugh at our borders: and Jesus in heaven, since the bird-shoot at Kamperduin we are left a maritime nation *with no navy.* The British seized the Cape, Coromandel, and Ceylon without so much as a kiss-my-arse, and that Java itself is their next fattened Christmas goose is plain as day! Without neutral bottoms like this" — he curls his lip at Captain Lacy — "Yankee, Batavia would *starve*. In such times, Vorstenbosch, a man's sole insurance is *salable goods in the warehouse*. Why else, for God's sake, are *you* here?"

The old whale-oil lantern sways and hisses.

"That," Vorstenbosch asks, "was your closing statement?"

Snitker folds his arms. "I *spit* on your drumhead trial."

Captain Lacy issues a gargantuan belch. " 'Twas the garlic, gentlemen."

Vorstenbosch addresses his clerk: "We may record our verdict . . ."

Jacob de Zoet nods and dips his quill: ". . . drumhead trial."

"On this day, the twentieth of July, 1799, I, Unico Vorstenbosch, chief-elect of the trading factory of Dejima in Nagasaki, acting by the powers vested in me by His Excellency P. G. van Overstraten, governor-general of the Dutch East Indies, witnessed by Captain Anselm Lacy of the *Shenandoah,* find Daniel Snitker, acting chief of the above-mentioned factory, guilty of the following: gross dereliction of duty —"

"I fulfilled," insists Snitker, "*every duty* of my post!"

" 'Duty'?" Vorstenbosch signals to Jacob to pause. "Our warehouses were burning to cinders whilst *you,* sir, romped with strumpets in a brothel — a fact omitted from that farrago of lies you are pleased to call your day register. And had it not been for the chance remark of a Japanese interpreter —"

"Shit-house rats who blacken my name 'cause I'm wise to their tricks!"

"Is it a 'blackening of your name' that the fire engine was missing from Dejima on the night of the fire?"

"Perhaps the defendant took the engine to the House of Wistaria," remarks Captain Lacy, "to impress the ladies with the thickness of his hose."

"The engine," objects Snitker, "was Van Cleef's responsibility."

"I'll tell your deputy how faithfully you defended him. To the next item, Mr. de Zoet: 'Failure to have the factory's three senior officers sign the *Octavia*'s bills of lading.' "

"Oh, for God's sake. A mere administrative *oversight!*"

"An 'oversight' that permits crooked chiefs to cheat the company in a hundred ways, which is why Batavia in*sists* on triple authorization. Next item: 'Theft of company funds to pay for private cargoes.' "

"Now *that,*" Snitker spits with anger, *"that is a flat lie!"*

From a carpetbag at his feet, Vorstenbosch produces two porcelain figurines in the Oriental mode. One is an executioner, ax poised to behead the second, a kneeling prisoner, hands bound and eyes on the next world.

"Why show me those" — Snitker is shameless — "gewgaws?"

"Two gross were found in your private cargo — 'twenty-four dozen Arita figurines,' let the record state. My late wife nurtured a fondness for Japanese curiosities, so I have a little knowledge. Indulge me, Captain Lacy: estimate their value in, let us say, a Viennese auction house."

Captain Lacy considers. "Twenty guilders a head?"

"For these slighter ones alone, thirty-five guilders; for the gold-leafed courtesans, archers, and lords, fifty. What price the two gross? Let us aim low — Europe *is* at war, and markets unsettled — and call it thirty-five per head . . . multiplied by two gross. De Zoet?"

Jacob's abacus is to hand. "Ten thousand and eighty guilders, sir."

Lacy issues an impressed "*Hee*-haw!"

"Tidy profit," states Vorstenbosch, "for merchandise purchased at the company's expense yet recorded in the bills of lading — unwitnessed, of course — as 'Acting Chief's Private Porcelain,' in *your* hand, Snitker."

"The former chief, God rest his soul" — Snitker changes his story — "willed them to me, before the court embassy."

"So Mr. Hemmij *foresaw* his demise on his

28

way back from Edo?"

"Gijsbert Hemmij was an uncommon cautious man."

"Then you will show us his uncommon cautious will."

"The document," Snitker wipes his mouth, "perished in the fire."

"Who were the witnesses? Mr. van Cleef? Fischer? The monkey?"

Snitker heaves a disgusted sigh. "This is a childish waste of time. Carve off your tithe, then — but not a sixteenth more, else by God I'll dump the blasted things in the harbor."

The sound of carousing washes over from Nagasaki.

Captain Lacy empties his bullish nose into a cabbage leaf.

Jacob's nearly worn-out quill catches up; his hand aches.

"What, I wonder" — Vorstenbosch looks confused — "is this talk of a 'tithe'? Mr. de Zoet, might you shed a little light?"

"Mr. Snitker is attempting to bribe you, sir."

The lamp has begun to sway; it smokes, sputters, and recovers.

A seaman in the lower deck tunes his fiddle.

"You suppose," Vorstenbosch blinks at Snitker, "that my integrity is for sale? Like some pox-maggoty harbormaster on the Scheldt extorting illegal fees from the butter barges?"

"One-ninth, then," growls Snitker. "That's

my last offer."

"Conclude the charge list" — Vorstenbosch snaps his fingers at his secretary — "with 'attempted bribery of a fiscal comptroller' and proceed to sentencing. Roll your eyeballs *this* way, Snitker: this affects you. 'Item the first: Daniel Snitker is stripped of office herewith and all' — yes, all — 'pay backdated to 1797. Second: upon arrival in Batavia, Daniel Snitker is to be imprisoned at the old fort to account for his actions. Third: his private cargo is to be auctioned. Proceeds shall recompense the company.' I see I have your attention."

"You're making" — Snitker's defiance is crushed — "a pauper of me."

"This trial makes an example of you to every parasitic chief fattening himself on the company's dugs: 'Justice found Daniel Snitker,' this verdict warns them, 'and justice shall find you.' Captain Lacy, thank you for your participation in this squalid affair; Mr. Wiskerke, pray find Mr. Snitker a hammock in the fo'c'sle. He shall work his passage back to Java as a landsman and be subject to common discipline. Moreover —"

Snitker upends the table and lunges at Vorstenbosch. Jacob glimpses Snitker's fist over his patron's head and attempts to intercept; flaming peacocks whirl across his vision; the cabin walls rotate through ninety degrees; the floor slams his ribs; and the taste of gunmetal in his mouth is surely blood. Grunts and gasps and groans are exchanged at a higher level. Jacob peers up in time to see the first mate land a pulverizing blow on Snitker's solar plexus, causing the floored clerk to wince with involuntary sympathy. Two more marines burst in, just as Snitker totters and hits the floor.

Belowdecks, the fiddler plays "My Dark-eyed Damsel of Twente."

Captain Lacy pours himself a glass of black-currant whiskey.

Vorstenbosch whacks Snitker's face with his silver-knobbed cane until he is too tired to continue. "Put this cockchafer in irons in your berth deck's foulest corner." The first mate and the two marines drag the groaning body away. Vorstenbosch kneels by Jacob and claps his shoulder. "Thank you for taking that blow for me, my boy. Your noggin, I fear, is *une belle marmelade . . .*"

The pain in Jacob's nose suggests a break-age, but the stickiness on his hands and knees is not blood. Ink, the clerk realizes, hauling himself upright.

Ink, from his cracked inkpot, indigo rivulets and dribbling deltas . . .

Ink, drunk by thirsty wood, dripping be-tween cracks . . .

Ink, thinks Jacob, *you most fecund of liq-uids . . .*

CHAPTER THREE:
ON A SAMPAN
MOORED ALONGSIDE
THE *SHENANDOAH,*
NAGASAKI HARBOR

Morning of July 26, 1799

Hatless and broiling in his blue dress coat, Jacob de Zoet is thinking of a day ten months ago, when a vengeful North Sea charged the dikes at Domburg, and spindrift tumbled along Church Street, past the parsonage where his uncle presented him with an oiled canvas bag. It contained a scarred Psalter bound in deerskin, and Jacob can, more or less, reconstruct his uncle's speech from memory. "Heaven knows, nephew, you have heard this book's history often enough. Your great-great-grandfather was in Venice when the plague arrived. His body erupted in buboes the size of frogs, but he prayed from this Psalter and God cured him. Fifty years ago, your grandfather Tys was soldiering in the Palatine when ambushers surprised his regiment. This Psalter stopped this musket ball" — he fingers the leaden bullet, still in its crater — "from shredding his heart. It is a literal truth that I, your father, and you and

Geertje owe this book our very existences. We are not Papists: we do not ascribe magical powers to bent nails or old rags; but you understand how this Sacred Book is, by our faith, bound to our bloodline. It is a gift from your ancestors and a loan from your descendants. Whatever befalls you in the years ahead, never forget: this Psalter" — he touched the canvas bag — "this is your passport home. David's Psalms are a Bible within the Bible. Pray from it, heed its teachings, and you shall not stray. Protect it with your life that it may nourish your soul. Go now, Jacob, and God go with you."

" 'Protect it with your life,' " Jacob mutters under his breath . . .

. . . *which is,* he thinks, *the crux of my dilemma.*

Ten days ago, the *Shenandoah* anchored off Papenburg Rock — named for martyrs of the true faith thrown from its heights — and Captain Lacy ordered all Christian artifacts placed in a barrel to be nailed shut, surrendered to the Japanese, and returned only when the brig departed from Japan. Not even Chief-Elect Vorstenbosch and his protégé clerk were exempt. The *Shenandoah*'s sailors grumbled that they'd sooner surrender their testicles than their crucifixes, but their crosses and St. Christophers did vanish into hidden nooks when the Japanese inspectors and well-armed guards carried out their search of the

33

decks. The barrel was filled with an assortment of rosary beads and prayer books brought by Captain Lacy for this purpose; the De Zoet Psalter was not among them.

How could I betray my uncle, Jacob frets, *my Church and my God?*

It is buried amid his other books in the sea chest on which he sits.

The risks, he assures himself, *cannot be so very great . . .* There is no marking or illustration by which the Psalter could be identified as a Christian text, and the interpreters' Dutch is too poor, surely, to recognize antique biblical language. *I am an officer of the Dutch East Indies Company,* Jacob reasons. *What is the worst punishment the Japanese could inflict on me?*

Jacob doesn't know, and the truth is that Jacob is afraid.

A quarter hour passes; of Chief Vorstenbosch or his two Malays there is no sign.

Jacob's pale and freckled skin is frying like bacon.

A flying fish scissors and skims itself over the water.

"Tobiuo!" one oarsman says to the other, pointing. *"Tobiuo!"*

Jacob repeats the word, and both oarsmen laugh until the boat rocks.

Their passenger doesn't mind. He watches

the guard boats circling the *Shenandoah;* the fishing skips; a coast-hugging Japanese cargo ship, stocky as a Portuguese carrack but fatter-bellied; an aristocratic pleasure craft, accompanied by several attendant vessels, draped with the ducal black-on-sky-blue colors; and a beak-prowed junk, similar to those of the Chinese merchants of Batavia . . .

Nagasaki itself, wood gray and mud brown, looks oozed from between the verdant mountains' splayed toes. The smells of seaweed, effluence, and smoke from countless flues are carried over the water. The mountains are terraced by rice paddies nearly up to their serrated summits.

A madman, Jacob supposes, *might imagine himself in a half-cracked jade bowl.*

Dominating the shorefront is his home for the next year: Dejima, a high-walled, fan-shaped artificial island, some two hundred paces along its outer curve, Jacob estimates, by eighty paces deep, and erected, like much of Amsterdam, on sunken piles. Sketching the trading factory from the *Shenandoah*'s foremast during the week gone, he counted some twenty-five roofs: the numbered warehouses of Japanese merchants; the chief's and the captain's residences; the deputy's house, on whose roof perches the watchtower; the Guild of Interpreters; a small hospital. Of the four Dutch warehouses — the Roos, the Lelie, the Doorn, and the Eik — only the last two survived what Vorstenbosch is calling "Snitker's Fire." Warehouse Lelie is being rebuilt, but the incinerated Roos must wait until the factory's debts are in better order. The land gate connects Dejima to the shore by a single-span stone bridge over a moat of tidal mud; the sea gate, at the top of a short ramp where the company sampans are loaded and unloaded, is opened only during the trading season. Attached is a customs house, where all Dutchmen except the chief resident and the captain are searched for prohibited items.

A list at whose head, Jacob thinks, *is "Christian Artifacts"* . . .

He turns to his sketch and sets about shading the sea with charcoal.

Curious, the oarsmen lean over; Jacob shows them the page.

The older oarsman makes a face to say, *Not bad.*

A shout from a guard boat startles the pair: they return to their posts.

The sampan rocks under Vorstenbosch's weight: he is a lean man, but today his silk surtout bulges with sections of "unicorn" or narwhal horn, valued in Japan as a powdered cure-all. "It is *this* buffoonery" — the incoming chief raps his knuckles on his garment's sewn-in bumps — "that I intend to eradicate.

'Why,' I demanded of that serpent Kobayashi, 'not simply have the cargo placed in a box, legitimately; rowed across, legitimately; and sold at private auction, legitimately?' His reply? 'There is no precedent.' I put it to him, 'Then why not *create* a precedent?' He stared at me as if I'd claimed paternity of his children."

"Sir?" the first mate calls. "Shall your slaves

accompany you ashore?"

"Send them with the cow. Snitker's black shall serve me meanwhile."

"Very good, sir; and Interpreter Sekita begs a ride ashore."

"Let the mooncalf down, then, Mr. Wiskerke."

Sekita's ample rear juts over the bulwark. His scabbard catches in the ladder: his attendant earns a sharp slap for this mishap. Once the master and servant are safely seated, Vorstenbosch doffs his smart tricorn hat. "A divine morning, Mr. Sekita, is it not?"

"Ah." Sekita nods without understanding. "We Japanese, an island race . . ."

"Indeed, sir. Sea in all directions; deep blue expanses of it."

Sekita recites another rote-learned sentence: "Tall pines are deep roots."

"For why must we waste our scant monies on your obese salary?"

Sekita purses his lips as if in thought. "How do you do, sir?"

If he *inspects my books,* thinks Jacob, *all my worries are for nothing.*

Vorstenbosch orders the oarsmen "Go!" and points to Dejima.

Unnecessarily and unasked, Sekita translates the order.

The oarsmen propel the sampan by "sweeping" their oars in the manner of a water snake, in time to a breathy shanty.

38

"Might they be singing," wonders Vorsten-bosch, " 'Give Us Your Gold, O Stinking Dutchman'?"

"One trusts not, sir, in the presence of an interpreter."

"That's a charitable description of the man. Yet better him than Kobayashi: this may be our last chance to have a private discussion for a little while. Once ashore, my priority must be to ensure as profitable a trading season as our shoddy cargo can afford. Yours, De Zoet, is quite different: piece together the factory accounts, both for company trade and private trade since the year '94. Without knowing what the officers have bought, sold, and exported, and for how much, we cannot know the full extent of the corruption we must deal with."

"I'll do my very best, sir."

"Snitker's incarceration is my statement of intent, but should we mete out the same treatment to every smuggler on Dejima, there would be nobody left but the two of us. Rather, we must show how honest labor is rewarded with advancement, and theft punished with disgrace and jail. Thus, only thus, may we clean out this Augean stable. Ah, and here is Van Cleef, come to greet us."

The acting deputy walks down the ramp from the sea gate.

" 'Every arrival,' " quotes Vorstenbosch, " 'is a particular death.' "

■ ■ ■ ■

Deputy Melchior van Cleef, born in Utrecht forty years ago, doffs his hat. His swarthy face is bearded and piratical; a friend might describe his narrow eyes as "observant," an enemy as "Mephistophelian." "Good morning, Mr. Vorstenbosch; and welcome to Dejima, Mr. de Zoet." His handshake could crush stones. "To wish you a 'pleasant' stay is overly hopeful . . ." He notices the fresh kink in Jacob's nose.

"I am obliged, Deputy van Cleef." Solid ground sways under Jacob's sea legs. Coolies are already unloading his sea chest and carrying it to the sea gate. "Sir, I should prefer to keep my luggage in sight —"

"So you should. Until recently we corrected the stevedores with blows, but the magistrate ruled that a beaten coolie is an affront to all Japan and forbade us. Now their knavery knows no bounds."

Interpreter Sekita mistimes his jump from the sampan's prow onto the ramp and dunks his leg up to the knee. Once on dry land, he smacks his servant's nose with his fan and hurries ahead of the three Dutchmen, telling them, "Go! Go! Go!"

Deputy van Cleef explains, "He means 'Come.' "

Once through the sea gate, they are ushered

into the customs room. Here, Sekita asks the foreigners' names and shouts them at an elderly registrar, who repeats them to a younger assistant, who writes them in his ledger. "Vorstenbosch" is transliterated Bôrusu Tenbôshu, "Van Cleef" becomes Bankureifu, and "De Zoet" is rechristened Dazûto. Rounds of cheese and barrels of butter unloaded from the *Shenandoah* are being poked with skewers by a team of inspectors. "Those damned blackguards," Van Cleef complains, "are known to break open preserved *eggs* lest the chicken sneaked in a ducat or two." A burly guard approaches. "Meet the frisker," says the deputy. "The chief is exempt, but not clerks, alas."

A number of young men gather: they have the same shaven foreheads and topknots as the inspectors and interpreters who visited the *Shenandoah* this week, but their robes are less impressive. "Unranked interpreters," says Van Cleef. "They hope to earn Sekita's favor by doing his job for him."

The frisker speaks to Jacob and they chorus, "Arms rise! Open pockets!"

Sekita silences them and orders Jacob, "Arms rise. Open pockets."

Jacob obeys; the frisker pats his armpits and explores his pockets.

He finds Jacob's sketchbook, examines it briefly, and issues another order.

"Show shoes to guard, sir!" say the quickest

41

house interpreters.

Sekita sniffs. "Show shoes now."

Jacob notices that even the stevedores stop their work to watch.

Some are pointing at the clerk, unabashed and declaring, *"Kômô, kômô."*

"They're talking about your hair," explains Van Cleef. " *'Kômô'* is how Europeans are often dubbed: *kô* signifying 'red,' and *mô,* 'hair.' Few of us, in truth, *do* boast hair of your tint; a genuine 'red-haired barbarian' is worth a good gawp."

"You study the Japanese tongue, Mr. van Cleef?"

"There are rules against it, but I pick up a little from my wives."

"Should you teach me what you know, sir, I would be greatly obliged."

"I'd not be much of a teacher," Van Cleef confesses. "Dr. Marinus chats with the Malays as if he were born black, but the Japanese language is hard won, he says. Any interpreter caught teaching us could feasibly be charged with treason."

The frisker returns Jacob's shoes and issues a fresh command.

"Off clotheses, sir!" say the interpreters. "Clotheses off!"

"Clotheses stay on!" retorts Van Cleef. "Clerks *don't* strip, Mr. de Zoet; the nasty-turdy wants us robbed of another dignity. Obey him today, and every clerk entering

Japan until Doomsday would perforce follow suit."

The frisker remonstrates; the chorus rises, "Clotheses off!"

Interpreter Sekita recognizes trouble and creeps away.

Vorstenbosch hits the floor with his cane until quietness reigns. "No!"

The displeased frisker decides to concede the point.

A customs guard taps Jacob's sea chest with his spear and speaks.

"Open please," says an unranked interpreter. "Open big box!"

The box, taunts Jacob's inner whisperer, *containing your Psalter.*

"Before we all grow old, De Zoet," says Vorstenbosch.

Sick to his core, Jacob unlocks the chest as ordered.

One of the guards speaks; the chorus translates, "Go back, sir! Step behind!"

More than twenty curious necks crane as the frisker lifts the lid and unfolds Jacob's five linen shirts; his woolen blanket; stockings; a drawstring bag of buttons and buckles; a tatty wig; a set of quills; yellowing undergarments; his boyhood compass; half a bar of Windsor soap; the two dozen letters from Anna tied with her hair ribbon; a razor blade; a Delft pipe; a cracked glass; a folio of sheet music; a moth-eaten bottle-green velvet waistcoat; a pewter plate, knife, and spoon; and, stacked at the bottom, some fifty assorted books. A frisker speaks to an underling, who runs out of the customs room.

"Fetch duty interpreter, sir," says an interpreter. "Bring to see books."

"Is not" — Jacob's rib cage contracts — "Mr. Sekita to conduct the dissection?"

A brown-toothed grin appears in Van Cleef's beard. "Dissection?"

"*In*spection, I meant, sir: the inspection of my books."

"Sekita's father purchased his son's place in the guild, but the prohibition against" — Van Cleef mouths "Christianity" — "is too important for blockheads. Books are checked by an abler man: Iwase Banri, perhaps, or one of the Ogawas."

"Who are the" — Jacob chokes on his own saliva — "Ogawas?"

"Ogawa Mimasaku is one of the four interpreters of the first rank. His son, Ogawa Uzaemon, is of the third rank, and" — a young man enters — "ah! Speak of the devil and listen for his feet! A warm morning, Mr. Ogawa."

Ogawa Uzaemon, in his midtwenties, has an open, intelligent face. The unranked interpreters all bow low. He bows to Vorstenbosch, Van Cleef, and lastly the new arrival. "Welcome ashore, Mr. de Zoet." His pronunciation is excellent. He extends his hand for a

44

European handshake just as Jacob delivers an Asian bow: Ogawa Uzaemon reciprocates with an Asian bow as Jacob offers his hand. The vignette amuses the room. "I am told," says the interpreter, "Mr. de Zoet brings many book . . . and here they are" — he points to the chest — "many *many* book. A 'plethora' of book, you say?"

"A few books," says Jacob, nervous enough to vomit. "Or quite a few: yes."

"May I remove books to see?" Ogawa does so eagerly, without waiting for an answer. For Jacob, the world is narrowed to a thin tunnel between him and his Psalter, visible between the two volumes of *Sara Burgerhart.* Ogawa frowns. "Many, many books here. A little time, please. When finish, I send message. It is agreeable?" He misreads Jacob's hesitancy. "Books all safe. I too" — Ogawa places his palm over his heart — "am 'bibliophile.' This is correct word? 'Bibliophile'?"

Out in the weighing yard, the sun feels as hot as a branding iron.

Any minute now, thinks the reluctant smuggler, *my Psalter will be found.*

A small party of Japanese officials is waiting for Vorstenbosch.

A Malay slave bows, waiting for the chief with a bamboo parasol.

"Captain Lacy and I," says the chief, "have a gamut of engagements in the stateroom until luncheon. You look sickly, De Zoet: have Dr. Marinus drain half a pint after Mr. van Cleef has shown you around." He nods a parting at his deputy and walks to his residence.

The weighing yard is dominated by one of the company's tripod scales, as high as two men. "We're weighing the sugar today," says Van Cleef, "for what *that* junk is worth. Batavia sent the very dregs of their warehouses."

The small square bustles with more than a hundred merchants, interpreters, inspectors, servants, spies, lackeys, palanquin bearers, porters. *So these,* thinks Jacob, *are the Japanese.* Their hair color — black to gray — and skin tones are more uniform than those of a Dutch crowd, and their modes of dress, footwear, and hairstyles appear rigidly prescribed according to rank. Fifteen or twenty near-naked carpenters are perched on the frame of a new warehouse. "Idler than a gang of gin-soused Finns . . ." mumbles Van Cleef. Watching from the roof of a customs house is a pink-faced, soot-on-snow-colored monkey, dressed in a sailcloth jerkin. "I see you've spotted William Pitt."

"I beg your pardon, sir?"

"King George's first minister, yes. He answers to no other name. A sailor bought him some six or seven seasons ago, but on the day his owner sailed, the ape vanished, only to reappear the next day, a freedman of

46

Dejima. Speaking of brute apes, over there" — Van Cleef indicates a lantern-jawed and pig-tailed laborer engaged in opening boxes of sugar — "is Wybo Gerritszoon, one of our hands." Gerritszoon places the precious nails in his jerkin pocket. The bags of sugar are carried past a Japanese inspector and a striking foreign youth of seventeen or eighteen: his hair is gold and cherubic, his lips have a Javanese thickness, and his eyes an Oriental slant. "Ivo Oost: somebody's natural son, with a generous glug of mestizo blood."

The bags of sugar arrive at a trestle table by the company tripod.

The weighing is viewed by another trio of Japanese officials, an interpreter, and two Europeans in their twenties. "On the left," Van Cleef points, "is Peter Fischer, a Prussian out of Brunswick" — Fischer is nut-colored, brown-haired but balding — "and an articled clerk — although Mr. Vorstenbosch tells me you are also qualified, giving us an embarrassment of riches. Fischer's companion is Con Twomey, an Irishman of Cork." Twomey has a half-moon face and a sharkish smile; his hair is cropped close and he is roughly tailored in sailcloth. "Don't fret if you forget these names: once the *Shenandoah* departs, we'll have a tedious eternity in which to learn all about one another."

"Don't the Japanese suspect some of our

men aren't Dutch?"

"We account for Twomey's bastard accent by saying he hails from Groningen. When were there ever enough pure-blooded Dutch to man the company? Especially *now*" — the stressed word alludes to the sensitive matter of Daniel Snitker's incarceration — "we must catch as catch can. Twomey's our carpenter but doubles as inspector on weighing days, for the infernal coolies'll spirit away a bag of sugar in a blink without they're watched like hawks. As will the guards — and the merchants are the slyest bastards of all: yesterday one of the whoresons slipped a stone into a bag, which he then 'discovered' and tried to use as 'evidence' to lower the average tare."

"Shall I begin my duties now, Mr. van Cleef?"

"Have Dr. Marinus breathe a vein first, and join the fray once you're settled. Marinus you shall find in his surgery at the end of Long Street — *this* street — by the bay tree. You shan't get lost. No man ever lost his way on Dejima, without he had a bladderful of grog in him."

"Fine thing *I* happened along," says a wheezing voice, ten paces later. "A cove'll lose his way on Dejima faster'n shit through a goose. Arie Grote's my name, an' *you*'ll be" — he thumps Jacob's shoulder — "Jacob de Zoet of Zeeland the Brave an', my oh my, Snitker

48

did put your nose out of joint, didn't he?"

Arie Grote has a grin full of holes and a hat made of shark hide.

"Like my hat, do you? Boa constrictor, this was, in the jungles of Ternate, what slunk one night into my hut what I shared with my three native maids. My first thought was, well, one of my bedmates was wakin' me gentle to toast my beans, eh? But no no no, there's this tightenin' an' my lungs're squeezed tight an' three of my ribs go *pop! snap! crack!* an' by the light o' the Southern Cross, eh, I see him gazin' into my bulgin' eyes — an' *that,* Mr. de Z., was the squeezy bugger's downfall. My arms was locked behind me, but my jaws was free, an' oh I *bit* the beggar's head *that 'ard* . . . A screamin' snake ain't a sound you'll forget in an hurry! Squeezy bugger squeezed me tighter — he weren't done yet — so I went for the worm's jugular an' bit it *clean through.* The grateful villagers made me a robe of its skin and coronated me, eh, Lord of Ternate — that snake'd been the terror of their jungle — but," Grote sighs, "a sailor's heart's the sea's plaything, eh? Back in Batavia a milliner turned my robe to hats what fetched ten rix-dollars a throw . . . but nothing'd splice me from this last one 'cept, mayhap, a favor to welcome a young cove whose need be sharper'n mine, eh? This beauty's yours *not* for ten rix-dollars, no no no, *not* eight but five stuivers. As good

49

a price as none."

"The milliner switched your boa skin for poorly cured shark hide, alas."

"I'll wager *you* rise from the card table," Arie Grote looks pleased, "with a well-fed purse. Most of us hands gather of an evenin' in my humble billet, eh, for a little hazard 'n' companionship, an' as you plainly ain't no stuffed-shirt hoity-toity, why not join us?"

"A pastor's nephew like me would bore you, I fear: I drink little and gamble less."

"Who *ain't* a gambler in the glorious Orient, with his very life? Of every ten coves who sail out, *six*'ll survive to make what hay they may, eh, but four'll sink into some swampy grave an' forty-sixty is damned poor odds. By the by, for every twelve jewels or ducatoons sewn into a coat lining, eleven get seized at the sea gate, and only a one slips through. They're best poked up yer fig hole an' by the by should *your* cavity, eh, be so primed, Mr. de Z., I can get you the best price of all . . ."

At the crossroads, Jacob stops: ahead, Long Street continues its curve.

"That's Bony Alley," Grote points to their right, "goin' to Seawall Lane; an' *that*aways," Grote points left, "is Short Street; and the land gate . . ."

. . . *and beyond the land gate,* thinks Jacob, *is the Cloistered Empire.*

"Them gates'll not budge for us, Mr. de Z., no no no. The chief, deputy, an' Dr. M. pass through from time to time, aye, but not us. 'The shogun's hostages' is what the natives dub us, an' that's the size of it, eh? But listen," Grote propels Jacob forward, "it ain't just gems and coins I deal in, let me tell yer. Just yesterday," he whispers, "I earned a select client aboard the *Shenandoah* a box of purest camphor crystals for some ratty bag-pipes what you'd not fish from a canal back home."

He's dangling bait, Jacob thinks, and replies, "I do not smuggle, Mr. Grote."

"Strike me *dead* afore I'd accuse yer 'f *malpractice,* Mr. de Z.! Just in*formin*' you, eh, as how my commission is one quarter o' the selling price, regular-like: but a smart young cove like *you*'ll keep seven slices per pie o' ten, for I'm partial to feisty Zeelanders, eh? 'Twill be a pleasure to handle your pox powder, too" — Grote has the casual tone of a man masking something crucial — "what with certain merchants who call me 'Brother' beatin' up the price faster an' fatter 'n a stal-lion's stiffy *as we speak,* Mr. de Z., aye, *as we speak,* an' why?"

Jacob stops. "How can you possibly know about my mercury?"

"Hearken to my joyous tidin's, eh? One o' the shogun's numerous sons," Grote lowers his voice, "undertook the mercury cure, this spring. The treatment's been known here twenty years but weren't never trusted, but this princeling's gherkin was so rotted it glowed green; one course o' Dutch pox powder an' praise the Lord, he's cured! The story spread like wildfire; ev'ry apothecary in the land's howlin' f' the miraculous elixir, eh; an' here comes *you* with eight crates! Let *me* negotiate an' yer'll make enough to buy a thousand hats; do it yerself an' they'll skin yer an' make *you* into the hat, my friend."

"How," Jacob finds himself walking again, "do you know about my mercury?"

"Rats," Arie Grote whispers. "Aye, rats. I feed the rats tidbits now an' then, an' the rats tell me what's what an' that's that. *Voilà,* eh? Here's the hospital; a journey shared's a journey halved, eh? So, we're agreed: I'll act as yer agent forthwith, eh? No need for contracts or such stuff: a gentleman'll not break his word. Until later . . ."

Arie Grote is walking back down Long Street to the crossroads.

Jacob calls after him, "But I never *gave* you my word!"

The hospital door opens into a narrow hall. Ahead, a ladder ascends to a trapdoor, propped open; to the right, a doorway gives in to the surgery, a large room ruled over by an age-mottled skeleton crucified on a T-frame. Jacob tries not to think of Ogawa finding his Psalter. An operating table is equipped with cords and apertures and plastered with bloodstains. There are racks for the surgeon's saws, knives, scissors, and chisels; mortars and pestles; a giant cabinet to house, Jacob assumes, *materia medica;* bleeding bowls; and several benches and tables. The smell of fresh sawdust mingles with wax, herbs, and a clayey whiff of liver. Through a doorway is the sickroom, with three vacant beds. Jacob is tempted by an earthenware jar of water: he drinks with the ladle — it is cool and sweet.

Why is nobody here, he wonders, *to protect the place from thieves?*

A young servant or slave appears, swishing a broom: he is barefoot, handsome, and attired in a fine surplice and loose Indian trousers.

Jacob feels a need to justify his presence. "Dr. Marinus's slave?"

"The doctor employs me," the youth's Dutch is good, "as an assistant, sir."

"Is that so? I'm the new clerk, De Zoet; and your name is?"

The man's bow is courteous, not servile. "My name is Eelattu, sir."

"What part of the world do you hail from, Eelattu?"

"I was born in Colombo on the island of Ceylon, sir."

Jacob is unsettled by his suavity. "Where is your master now?"

"At study, upstairs; do you desire that I

53

fetch him?"

"There's no need — I shall go up and introduce myself."

"Yes, sir; but the doctor prefers not to receive visitors —"

"Oh, he'll not object when he learns what I bring him . . ."

Through the trapdoor, Jacob peers into a long, well-furnished attic. Halfway down is Marinus's harpsichord, referred to weeks ago in Batavia by Jacob's friend Mr. Zwaardecroone; it is allegedly the only harpsichord ever to travel to Japan. At the far end is a ruddy and ursine European of about fifty years, with tied-back stony hair. He is sitting on the floor at a low table in a well of light, drawing a flame-orange orchid. Jacob knocks on the trapdoor. "Good afternoon, Dr. Marinus."

The doctor, his shirt unbuttoned, does not respond.

"Dr. Marinus? I am delighted to make your acquaintance at last . . ."

Still, the doctor gives no indication of having heard.

The clerk raises his voice: "Dr. Marinus? I apologize for disturb—"

"From what mouse hole," Marinus glares, "did *you* spring?"

"I just arrived a quarter hour ago, from the *Shenandoah*. My name's —"

"Did I ask for your name? No: I asked for your *fons et origo.*"

"Domburg, sir: a coastal town on Walcheren Island, in Zeeland."

"Walcheren, is it? I visited Middelburg once."

"In point of fact, Doctor, I was educated in Middelburg."

Marinus barks a laugh. "*Nobody* is 'educated' in that nest of slavers."

"Perhaps I may raise your estimate of Zeelanders in the months ahead. I am to live in Tall House, so we are nearly neighbors."

"So propinquity propagates neighborliness, does it?"

"I —" Jacob wonders at Marinus's deliberate aggression. "I — well —"

"This *Cymbidium koran* was found in the goats' fodder: as *you* dither, *it* wilts."

"Mr. Vorstenbosch suggested you might drain some blood —"

"Medieval quackery! Phlebotomy — and the Humoral Theory on which it rests — was exploded by Hunter twenty years ago."

But draining blood, thinks Jacob, *is every surgeon's bread.* "But . . ."

"But but but? But but? *But?* But *but* but but but?"

"The world is composed of people who are convinced of it."

"Proving the world is composed of dunderheads. Your nose looks swollen."

55

Jacob strokes the kink. "Former Chief Snitker threw a punch and —"

"You don't have the build for brawling." Marinus rises and limps toward the trapdoor with the aid of a stout stick. "Bathe your nose in cool water, twice daily, and pick a fight with Gerritszoon presenting the con*vex* side, so he may hammer it flat. Good day to you, Domburger." With a well-aimed whack of his stick, Dr. Marinus knocks away the prop holding up the trapdoor.

Back in the sun-blinding street, the indignant clerk finds himself surrounded by Interpreter Ogawa, his servant, a pair of inspectors: all four look sweaty and grim. "Mr. de Zoet," says Ogawa, "I wish to speak about a book you bring. It is important matter . . ."

Jacob loses the next clause to a rush of nausea and dread.

Vorstenbosch shan't be able to save me, he thinks, *and why would he?*

". . . and so to find such a book astonishes me greatly. . . . Mr. de Zoet?"

My career is destroyed, thinks Jacob, *my liberty is gone, and Anna is lost . . .*

"Where," the prisoner manages to croak, "am I to be incarcerated?"

Long Street is tilting up and down. The clerk shuts his eyes.

"In cancer-*ated?*" Ogawa mocks him. "My poor Dutch is failing me."

56

The clerk's heart pounds like a broken pump. "Is it human to toy with me?"

"Toy?" Ogawa's perplexity grows. "This is proverb, Mr. de Zoet? In Mr. de Zoet's chest I found book of Mr. . . . . Adamu Sumissu."

Jacob opens his eyes: Long Street is no longer tilting. "Adam Smith?"

"Adam Smith — please excuse. *The Wealth of Nations* . . . You know?"

I know it, yes, thinks Jacob, *but I don't yet dare hope.* "The original English is a little difficult, so I bought the Dutch edition in Batavia."

Ogawa looks surprised. "Adam Smith is Englishman?"

"He'd not thank you, Mr. Ogawa! Smith's a Scot, living in Edinburgh. But can it be *The Wealth of Nations* about which you speak?"

"What other? I am *rangakusha* — scholar of Dutch science. Four years ago, I borrow *Wealth of Nations* from Chief Hemmij. I began translation to bring," Ogawa's lips ready themselves, " 'Theory of Political Economy' to Japan. But lord of Satsuma offered Chief Hemmij much money, so I returned it. Book was sold before I finish."

The incandescent sun is caged by a glowing bay tree.

God called unto him, thinks Jacob, *out of the midst of the bush . . .*

Hooked gulls and scraggy kites crisscross

the blue-glazed sky.

*. . . and said, Moses, Moses. And he said,
Here am I.*

"I try to obtain another, but" — Ogawa
flinches — "but difficulties is much."

Jacob resists an impulse to laugh like a
child. "I understand."

"Then, this morning, in your book chest,
Adam Smith I *find.* Very much surprise, and
to speak with sincerity, Mr. de Zoet, I wish
to buy or rent . . ."

Across the street in the garden, cicadas
shriek in ratcheted rounds.

"Adam Smith is neither for sale nor rent,"
says the Dutchman, "but you are welcome,
Mr. Ogawa — very welcome indeed — to
borrow him for as long as ever you wish."

Chapter Four:
Outside the Privy
by Garden House
on Dejima

Before breakfast on July 29, 1799
Jacob de Zoet emerges from buzzing darkness to see Hanzaburo, his house interpreter,
being interrogated by two inspectors. "They'll
be ordering your boy" — Junior Clerk Ponke
Ouwehand appears from thin air — "to open
up your turds to see what you shat. I tor-
mented my first snoop into an early grave
three days ago, so the Interpreters' Guild sent
this hat stand." Ouwehand jerks his head at
the gangly youth behind him. "His name's
Kichibei, but I call him 'Herpes' after how
closely he sticks to me. But I'll defeat him in
the end. Grote bet me ten guilders I can't
wear out five by November. Broken our fast
yet, have we?"

The inspectors now notice Kichibei and
summon him over.

"I was on my way," says Jacob, wiping his
hands.

"We should go before all the hands piss in
your coffee."

The two clerks set off up Long Street, passing two pregnant deer.

"Nice shank of venison," comments Ouwehand, "for Christmas dinner."

Dr. Marinus and the slave Ignatius are watering the melon patch. "Another furnace of a day ahead, Doctor," says Ouwehand, over the fence.

Marinus must have heard but does not deign to look up.

"He's courteous enough to his students," Ouwehand remarks to Jacob, "and to his handsome Indian, and he was gentleness made man, so Van Cleef says, when Hemmij was dying, and when his scholar friends bring him a weed or a dead starfish, he wags his tail off. So why is he Old Master Misery with us? In Batavia, even the French consul — the *French* consul, mark you — called him *un buffalo insufferable.*" Ouwehand squeaks in the back of his throat.

A gang of porters is gathering at the crossroads to bring ashore the pig iron. When they notice Jacob, the usual nudges, stares, and grins begin. He turns down Bony Alley rather than run the gauntlet any farther.

"Don't deny you enjoy the attention," says Ouwehand, "Mr. Red-Hair."

"But I *do* deny it," objects Jacob. "I deny it utterly."

The two clerks turn into Seawall Lane and reach the kitchen.

Arie Grote is plucking a bird under a canopy of pans and skillets. Oil is frying, a pile of improvised pancakes is rising up, and a well-traveled round of Edam and sour apples are divided between two mess tables. Piet Baert, Ivo Oost, and Gerritszoon sit at the hands' table; Peter Fischer, the senior clerk, and Con Twomey, the carpenter, eat at the officers'; today being Monday, Vorstenbosch, Van Cleef, and Dr. Marinus will take their breakfast upstairs in the bay room.

"We was just wond'rin'," says Grote, "where you coves'd got to, eh?"

"Pottage of nightingales' tongues to begin with, maestro," says Ouwehand, poking at the gritty bread and rancid butter, "followed by a quail-and-blackberry pie with artichokes in cream, and, last, the quince-and-white-rose trifle."

"How Mr. O.'s evergreen jests," says Grote, "spice up the day."

"That *is*," Ouwehand peers over, "a *pheasant*'s arsehole your hand is up?"

"Envy," the cook tuts, "is one o' the Seven Deadlies, eh, Mr. de Z.?"

"They say so." Jacob wipes a smear of blood from an apple. "Yes."

"We readied yer coffee." Baert carries over a bowl. "Nice an' fresh."

Jacob looks at Ouwehand, who makes a "told you so" face.

61

"Thank you, Mr. Baert, but I may abstain today."

"But we made it special," protests the Antwerper. "Just for you."

Oost yawns cavernously; Jacob risks a pleasantry. "Bad night?"

"Out smuggling and robbing the company till dawn, weren't I?"

"I wouldn't know, Mr. Oost." Jacob breaks his bread. "Were you?"

"Thought *you* had all the answers afore y'even set foot ashore."

"A civil tongue," cautions Twomey, in his Irish-flavored Dutch, "is —"

"*He*'s the one sittin' in judgment on us all, Con, an' *you* think it, too."

Oost is the only hand rash enough to speak so bluntly to the new clerk's face without the excuse of grog, but Jacob knows that even Van Cleef views him as Vorstenbosch's spy. The kitchen is waiting for his answer. "To man its ships, maintain its garrisons, and pay its tens of thousands of salaries, Mr. Oost, including yours, the company must make a profit. Its trading factories must keep books. Dejima's books for the last five years are a pig's dinner. It is Mr. Vorstenbosch's duty to order me to piece those books together. It is my duty to obey. Why must this make my name Iscariot?"

No one cares to reply. Peter Fischer eats with his mouth open.

Ouwehand scoops up some sauerkraut with his gritty bread.

"Strikes *me,*" Grote says, plucking out the fowl's innards, "that it all rests on what the chief *does* about any . . . *irregularities,* eh, spotted durin' this *piecin' together.* Whether it's a naughty-boy-now-sin-no-more or a firm but fair canin' of one's *derrière,* eh? Or ruination an' a six-by-five-by-four in Batavia jail."

"If —" Jacob stops himself saying *If you did nothing wrong, you have nothing to fear:* everyone present violates the company rules on private trade. "I'm not the —" Jacob stops himself saying *chief's private confessor.* "Have you tried asking Mr. Vorstenbosch directly?"

"Not f' the likes o' *me,*" replies Grote, "to be interrogatin', eh, my superiors?"

"Then you'll have to wait and see what the Chief decides."

A bad answer, realizes Jacob, *implying I know more than I'm saying.*

"Yap yap," mumbles Oost. "Yap." Baert's laughter could be hiccups.

An apple skin slides off Fischer's knife in one perfect coil. "Can we expect you to visit our office later? Or will you be doing more *piecing together* in Warehouse Doorn with your friend Ogawa?"

"I shall *do,*" Jacob hears his voice rise, "whatever the chief *bids.*"

"Oh? Did I touch a rotten tooth? Ouwe-hand and I merely wish to know —"

"Did I" — Ouwehand consults the ceiling — "utter a single word?"

"— to know whether our alleged third clerk shall help us today."

" 'Articled,' " Jacob states, "not 'alleged' or 'third,' just as *you* are not 'head.' "

"Oh? So you and Mr. Vorstenbosch *have* discussed matters of succession?"

"Is this squabblin' *edifyin',*" queries Grote, "for the *lower orders?*"

The warped kitchen door shudders as the servant Cupido enters.

"What d'you want, yer dusky dog?" asks Grote. "You was fed earlier."

"I bring a message for Clerk de Zoet: Chief bids you come to stateroom, sir."

Baert's laugh is born, lives, and dies in his ever-congested nose.

"I'll keep yer breakfast," Grote chops off the pheasant's feet, "good an' safe."

"Here, boy!" whispers Oost to an invisible dog. "Sit, boy! Up, boy!"

"Just a sip o' coffee," Baert proffers the bowl, "to fortify yer, like?"

"I don't think I'd care," Jacob stands to go, "for its adulterants."

"Not a soul's 'cusin' yer 'f a*dult*'ry," says Baert, incomprehending, "just —"

The pastor's nephew kicks the coffee bowl out of Baert's hands.

It smashes against the ceiling; fragments smash on the floor.

The onlookers are astonished; Oost's yaps cease; Baert is drenched.

Even Jacob is surprised. He pockets his bread and leaves.

In the Antechamber of Bottles outside the stateroom, a wall of fifty or sixty glass demi-johns, wired tight against earthquakes, exhibit creatures from the company's once-vast empire. Preserved from decay by alcohol, pig bladder, and lead, they warn not so much that all flesh perishes — what sane adult forgets this truth for long? — but that immortality comes at a steep price.

A pickled dragon of Kandy bears an uncanny resemblance to Anna's father, and Jacob recalls a fateful conversation with that gentleman in his Rotterdam drawing room. Carriages passed by below, and the lamplighter was doing his rounds. "Anna has told me," her father began, "the surprising facts of the situation, De Zoet . . ."

The Kandy dragon's neighbor is a slack-jawed viper of the Celebes.

". . . I have, accordingly, enumerated your merits and demerits."

A baby alligator from Halmahera has a demon's delighted grin.

"In the credit column: you are a fastidious clerk of good character . . ."

The alligator's umbilical cord is attached to its shell for all eternity.

". . . who has not abused his advantage over Anna's affections."

It was a posting to Halmahera from which Vorstenbosch rescued Jacob.

"The debit column. You are not a merchant, not a shipper . . ."

A tortoise from the Island of Diego Garcia appears to be weeping.

". . . or even a warehouse master, but a clerk. I don't doubt your affection is genuine."

Jacob touches the jar of a Barbados lamprey with his broken nose.

"But affection is merely the plum in the pudding: the pudding itself is *wealth*."

The lamprey's O-shaped mouth is a grinding mill of razor-sharp Vs and Ws.

"I am, however, willing to give you a chance to earn your pudding, De Zoet — out of respect for Anna's judge of character. A director at East India House comes to my club. If you wish to become my son-in-law as strongly as you say, he can arrange a five-year clerical post for you in Java. The official salary is meager, but a young man of enterprise may make something of himself. You must give your answer today, however: the *Fadrelandet* is sailing from Copenhagen in a fortnight . . ."

"New friends?" Deputy van Cleef watches him from the stateroom door.

Jacob pulls his gaze from the lamprey's. "I don't have the luxury to pick and choose, Deputy."

Van Cleef hums at his candor. "Mr. Vorstenbosch shall see you now."

"Won't you be joining our meeting, sir?"

"Pig iron won't carry and weigh itself, De Zoet, more's the pity."

Unico Vorstenbosch squints at the thermometer hung by the painting of William the Silent. He is pink with heat and shiny with sweat. "I shall have Twomey fashion me one of those ingenious cloth fans the English brought from India . . . oh, the word evades me . . ."

"Might you be thinking of a punkah, sir?"

"Just so. A punkah, with a punkah-wallah to tug its cord."

Cupido enters, carrying a familiar jade-and-silver teapot on a tray.

"Interpreter Kobayashi is due at ten," says Vorstenbosch, "with a gaggle of officials to brief me on court etiquette during our long-delayed audience with the magistrate. Antique chinaware shall signal that *this* chief resident is a man of refinement: the Orient is all about signals, De Zoet. Remind me what blue blood the tea service was crafted for, according to that Jew in Macao?"

"He claimed it was from the trousseau of the last Ming emperor's wife, sir."

"The last Ming emperor: just so. Oh, and I am desirous that you join us later."

"For the meeting with Interpreter Kobayashi and the officials, sir?"

"For our interview with Magistrate Shirai . . . Shilo . . . Aid me."

"Magistrate Shiroyama, sir — sir, I am to visit Nagasaki?"

"Unless you'd prefer to stay here and record catties of pig iron?"

"To set foot on Japan proper would" — *cause Peter Fischer,* thinks Jacob, *to expire with envy* — "would be a great adventure. Thank you."

"A chief needs a private secretary. Now, let us continue the morning's business in the privacy of my bureau . . ."

Sunlight falls across the escritoire in the small adjacent room. "So," Vorstenbosch settles himself, "after three days ashore, how *are* you finding life on the company's farthest-flung outpost?"

"More salubrious" — Jacob's chair creaks — "than a posting on Halmahera, sir."

"Damnation by dim praise indeed! What irks you most of all: the spies, confinement, lack of liberties . . . or the ignorance of our countrymen?"

Jacob considers telling Vorstenbosch about the scene at breakfast but sees nothing to be gained. *Respect,* he thinks, *cannot be com-*

manded from on high.

"The hands view me with some . . . suspicion, sir."

"Naturally. To decree 'private trade is henceforth banned' would merely make their schemes more ingenious; a deliberate vagueness is, for the time being, the best prophylactic. The hands resent this, of course, but daren't vent their anger on me. You bear the brunt."

"I'd not wish to appear ungrateful for your patronage, sir."

"There's no gainsaying that Dejima is a dull posting. The days when a man could retire on the profit from two trading seasons here are long, long gone. Swamp fever and crocodiles shan't kill you in Japan, but monotony might. But take heart, De Zoet: after one year we return to Batavia, where you shall learn how I reward loyalty and diligence. And speaking of diligence, how proceeds your restoration of the ledgers?"

"The books *are* an unholy mess, but Mr. Ogawa is proving most helpful, and '94 and '95 are in large part reconstructed."

"A shoddy pass that we have to rely on Japanese archives. But come, we must address yet more pressing matters." Vorstenbosch unlocks his desk and takes out a bar of Japanese copper. "The world's reddest, its richest in gold, and, for a hundred years, the bride for whom we Dutch have danced in

Nagasaki." He tosses the flat ingot at Jacob, who catches it neatly. "This bride, however, grows skinnier and sulkier by the year. According to your own figures" — Vorstenbosch consults a slip of paper on his desk top — "in 1790 we exported eight thousand piculs. In '94, six thousand. Gijsbert Hemmij, who displayed good judgment only in dying before being charged for incompetence, suffered the quota to drop under *four* thousand, and during Snitker's year of misgovernance, a paltry three thousand two hundred, every last bar of which was lost with the *Octavia,* wherever her wreck may lie."

The Almelo clock divides time with bejeweled tweezers.

"You recall, De Zoet, my visit to the old fort prior to our sailing?"

"I do, sir, yes. The governor-general spoke with you for two hours."

"It was a weighty discussion about nothing less than the future of Dutch Java. Which you hold in your hands." Vorstenbosch nods at the copper bar. "That's it."

Jacob's melted reflection is captured in the metal. "I don't understand, sir."

"The bleak picture of the company's dilemma painted by Daniel Snitker was not, alas, hyperbole. What he did *not* add, because none outside the Council of the Indies knows, is that Batavia's treasury is starved away to nothing."

Carpenters hammer across the street. Jacob's bent nose aches.

"Without Japanese copper, Batavia cannot mint coins." Vorstenbosch's fingers twirl an ivory paper-knife. "Without coins, the native battalions shall melt back into the jungle. There is no sugarcoating this truth, De Zoet: the High Government can maintain our garrisons on half pay until next July. Come August, the first deserters leave; come October, the native chiefs smoke our weakness out; and by Christmas, Batavia succumbs to anarchy, rapine, slaughter, and John Bull."

Unbidden, Jacob's mind pictures these same catastrophes unfolding.

"Every chief resident in Dejima's history," Vorstenbosch continues, "tried to squeeze more precious metals out of Japan. All they ever received were hand-wringing and unkept promises. The wheels of commerce trundled on regardless, but should *we* fail, De Zoet, the Netherlands loses the Orient."

Jacob places the copper on the desk. "How can we succeed where . . ."

"Where so many others failed? Audacity, pugnacity, and by an historic letter." Vorstenbosch slides a writing set across the desk. "Pray take down a rough copy."

Jacob readies his board, uncorks the inkpot, and dips a quill.

" 'I, Governor-General of the Dutch East Indies, P. G. van Overstraten,' " Jacob looks

71

at his patron, but there is no mistake, " 'on this, the' — was it the *six*teenth of May we left Batavia's roadstead?"

The pastor's nephew swallows. "The fourteenth, sir."

"— 'on this, the . . . ninth day of May, 1799, send cordial salutations to their august excellencies the Council of Elders, as one true friend may communicate his innermost thoughts to another with neither flattery nor fear of disfavor, concerning the venerable amity between the Empire of Japan and the Batavian Republic' — stop."

"The Japanese have not been informed of the revolution, sir."

"Then let us be 'the United Provinces of the Netherlands' for now. 'Many times have the shogun's servants in Nagasaki amended the terms of trade to the company's impoverishment' — no, use 'disadvantage.' Then, 'The so-called flower-money tax is at a usurious level; the rix-dollar has been devalued three times in ten years, while the copper quota has decreased to a trickle' — stop."

Jacob's hard-pressed nib crumples; he takes up another.

" 'Yet the company's petitions are met with endless excuses. The dangers of the voyage from Batavia to your distant empire were demonstrated by the *Octavia*'s foundering, in which two hundred Dutchmen lost their lives. Without fair compensation, the Nagasaki trade is tenable no longer.' New paragraph. 'The company's directors in Amsterdam have issued a final memorandum concerning Dejima. Its substance may be summarized thus . . .' " Jacob's quill skips over an inkblot. " 'Without the copper quota is increased to twenty thousand piculs' — underline the words, De Zoet, and add it in numerals — 'the seventeen directors of the Dutch East Indies Company must conclude that its Japanese partners no longer wish to maintain foreign trade. We shall evacuate Dejima, removing our goods, our livestock, and such materials from our warehouses as may be salvaged with immediate effect.' There. That should set loose the fox in the chicken coop, should it not?"

"A half dozen large ones, sir. But did the governor-general make this threat?"

"Asiatic minds respect *force majeure;* best they are prodded into compliancy."

The answer, then, sees Jacob, *is no.* "Suppose the Japanese call this bluff?"

"One calls a bluff only if one scents a bluff. Thus you are party to this stratagem, as are Van Cleef, Captain Lacy, and myself, and nobody else. Now conclude: 'For a copper quota of twenty thousand piculs, I shall send another ship next year. Should the shogun's council offer' — underline — '*one picul less* than twenty thousand, they shall, in effect, take an ax to the tree of commerce, consign

73

Japan's single major port to rot, and brick over your empire's sole window to the world' — yes?"

"Bricks are not in wide usage here, sir. 'Board up'?"

"Make good. 'This loss shall blind the shogun to new European progress, to the delight of the Russians and other foes who survey your empire with acquisitive eyes. Your own descendants yet unborn beg you to make the correct choice at this hour, as does,' new line, 'Your sincere ally, et cetera, et cetera, P. G. van Overstraten, Governor-General of the East Indies, Chevalier of the Order of the Orange Lion,' and any other titular lilies that occur to you, De Zoet. Two fair copies by noon, in time for Kobayashi; end both with van Overstraten's signature — as lifelike as you may — one to be sealed with this." Vorstenbosch passes him the signet ring embossed with the VOC of the Dutch *Vereenigde Oost-Indische Compagnie*.

Jacob is startled by the last two commands. "*I* am to sign and seal the letters, sir?"

"Here is" — Vorstenbosch finds a sample — "Van Overstraten's signature."

"To forge the governor-general's signature would be . . ." Jacob suspects the true answer would be "a capital crime."

"Don't look so privy-faced, De Zoet! I'd sign it myself, but our stratagem requires Van Overstraten's masterly flourish and not my

74

crabby left-handed smudge. Consider the governor-general's gratitude when we return to Batavia with a threefold increase in copper exports: my claim to a seat on the council shall be irrefutable. Why would *I* then forsake my loyal secretary? Of course, if . . . qualms or a loss of nerve prevents you from doing as I ask, I could just as easily summon Mr. Fischer."

Do it now, thinks Jacob, *worry later.* "I shall sign, sir."

"There is no time to waste, then: Kobayashi shall be here in" — the chief resident consults the clock — "forty minutes. We'll want the sealing wax on the finished letter cool by then, won't we?"

The frisker at the land gate finishes his task; Jacob climbs into his two-bearer palanquin. Peter Fischer squints in the merciless afternoon sunlight. "Dejima is yours for an hour or two, Mr. Fischer," Vorstenbosch tells him from the chief's palanquin. "Return her to me in her current condition."

"Of course." The Prussian achieves a flatulent grimace. "Of course."

Fischer's grimace turns to a glower as Jacob's palanquin passes.

The retinue leaves the land gate and passes over Holland Bridge.

The tide is out: Jacob sees a dead dog in the silt and now . . .

. . . he is hovering three feet over the forbidden ground of Japan.

There is a wide square of sand and grit, deserted but for a few soldiers. This plaza is named, Van Cleef told him, Edo Square, to remind the independent-minded Nagasaki populace where the true power lies. On one side is the shogunal keep: ramped stones, high walls and steps. Through another set of gates, the retinue is submersed in a shaded thoroughfare. Hawkers cry, beggars implore, tinkers clang pans, ten thousand wooden clogs knock against flagstones. The Dutchmen's guards yell, ordering the townspeople aside. Jacob tries to capture every fleeting impression for letters to Anna, and to his sister, Geertje, and his uncle. Through the palanquin's grille, he smells steamed rice, sewage, incense, lemons, sawdust, yeast, and rotting seaweed. He glimpses gnarled old women, pocked monks, unmarried girls with blackened teeth. *Would that I had a sketchbook,* the foreigner thinks, *and three days ashore to fill it.* Children on a mud wall make owl eyes with their forefingers and thumbs, chanting *"Oranda-me, Oranda-me, Oranda-me":* Jacob realizes they are impersonating "round" European eyes and remembers a string of urchins following a Chinaman in London. The urchins pulled their eyes into narrow slants and sang, "Chinese, Siamese, if

76

you please, Japanese."

People pray cheek by jowl before a cramped shrine whose gate is shaped like a π.

There is a row of stone idols; twists of paper tied to a plum tree.

Nearby, street acrobats perform a snonky song to drum up business.

The palanquins pass over an embanked river; the water stinks.

Jacob's armpits, groin, and knees are itchy with sweat; he fans himself with his clerk's portfolio.

There is a girl in an upper window; there are red lanterns hanging from the eaves, and she is idly tickling the hollow of her throat with a goose feather. Her body cannot be ten years old, but her eyes belong to a much older woman.

Wistaria in bloom foams over a crumbling wall.

A hairy beggar kneeling by a puddle of vomit turns out to be a dog.

A minute later, the retinue stops before a gate of iron and oak.

The doors open and guards salute the palanquins passing into a courtyard.

Twenty pikemen are being drilled in the ferocious sun.

In the shade of a deep overhang, Jacob's palanquin is lowered onto its stand.

Ogawa Uzaemon opens its door. "Welcome to magistracy, Mr. de Zoet."

■ ■ ■ ■

The long gallery ends at a shady vestibule. "Here, we wait," Interpreter Kobayashi tells them, and motions for them to sit on floor cushions brought by servants. The right branch of the vestibule ends in a row of sliding doors emblazoned with striped bulldogs boasting luxuriant eyelashes. "Tigers, supposedly," says Van Cleef. "Behind it is our destination: the Hall of Sixty Mats." The left branch leads to a more modest door decorated with a chrysanthemum. Jacob hears a baby crying a few rooms away. Ahead is a view over the magistracy walls and hot roofs, down to the bay, where the *Shenandoah* is anchored in the bleached haze. The smell of summer mingles with beeswax and fresh paper. The Dutchmen's party removed their shoes at the entrance, and Jacob is thankful for Van Cleef's earlier warning about holes in stockings. *If Anna's father could see me now,* he thinks, *paying court to the shogun's highest official in Nagasaki.* The officials and interpreters maintain a stern silence. "The floorboards," Van Cleef comments, "are sprung to squeak, to foil assassins."

"Are assassins," asks Vorstenbosch, "a serious nuisance in these parts?"

"Probably not, nowadays, but old habits die hard."

"Remind me," says the chief, "why one magistracy has *two* magistrates."

"When Magistrate Shiroyama is on duty in Nagasaki, Magistrate Ômatsu resides in Edo, and vice versa. They rotate annually. Should either commit any indiscretion, his counterpart would eagerly denounce him. Every seat of power in the empire is divided, and thereby neutered, in this way."

"Niccolò Machiavelli could teach the shogun very little, I fancy."

"Indeed not, sir. The Florentine would be the novice, *I* credit."

Interpreter Kobayashi shows disapproval at the bandying about of august names.

"Might I direct your attention," Van Cleef changes the subject, "to that antique crow-scarer hanging in the alcove over there?"

"Good God," Vorstenbosch peers closer, "it's a Portuguese harquebus."

"Muskets were manufactured on an island in Satsuma after the Portuguese arrived there. Later, when it was realized that ten muskets wielded by ten steady-handed peasants could slay ten samurai, the shogun curtailed their manufacture. One can imagine the fate of a European monarch who sought to impose such a decree —"

A tiger-emblazoned screen slides open, and a high official with a crushed nose emerges and walks to Interpreter Kobayashi. The interpreters bow low and Kobayashi introduces the official to Chief Vorstenbosch as Chamberlain Tomine. Tomine speaks in a tone as wintry as his demeanor. " 'Gentlemen,' " Kobayashi translates. " 'In Hall of Sixty Mats is magistrate and many advisers. You must show same obeisance to magistrate as to shogun.' "

"Magistrate Shiroyama shall receive," Vorstenbosch assures the interpreter, "exactly the respect he deserves."

Kobayashi does not look reassured.

The Hall of Sixty Mats is airy and shaded. Fifty or sixty sweating, fanning officials — all important-looking samurai — enclose a precise rectangle. Magistrate Shiroyama is identified by his central position and raised dais. His fifty-year-old face looks weathered by high office. Light enters the hall from a sunlit courtyard of white pebbles, contorted pine trees, and moss-coated rocks to the south. Hangings sway over openings to the west and east. A meaty-necked guard announces, *"Oranda Kapitan!"* and ushers the Dutchmen into the rectangle of courtiers, to three crimson cushions. Chamberlain Tomine speaks and Kobayashi translates: " 'Let the Dutchmen now pay respect.' "

Jacob kneels on his cushion, places his clerk's portfolio at his side, and bows. To his right, he is aware of Van Cleef doing the same, but, straightening up, he realizes that

Vorstenbosch is still standing.

"Where," the chief resident turns to Kobayashi, "is my chair?"

This triggers the muted commotion Vorstenbosch intended.

The chamberlain fires a curt question at Interpreter Kobayashi.

"In Japan," Kobayashi tells Vorstenbosch, reddening, "there is no dishonor to seat on floor."

"How laudable. But I am more *comfortable* on a chair."

Kobayashi and Ogawa must pacify an angry chamberlain and placate a stubborn chief.

"Please, Mr. Vorstenbosch," says Ogawa, "in Japan, we have no chairs."

"May one not be improvised for a visiting dignitary? You!"

The pointed-at official gasps and touches the tip of his own nose.

"Yes: bring *ten* cushions. *Ten.* You understand 'ten'?"

In consternation, the official looks from Kobayashi to Ogawa and back.

"*Look,* man!" Vorstenbosch dangles the cushion for a moment, drops it, and holds up ten fingers. "Bring ten cushions! Kobayashi, tell the tadpole what I want."

Chamberlain Tomine is demanding answers. Kobayashi explains why the chief refuses to kneel, while Vorstenbosch wears a smile of tolerant condescension.

The Hall of Sixty Mats falls silent, ahead of the magistrate's reaction.

Shiroyama and Vorstenbosch hold each other's gaze for a magnified moment.

Then the magistrate produces a victor's easy smile and nods. The chamberlain claps: two servants fetch cushions and pile them up until Vorstenbosch glows with satisfaction. "Observe," the Dutch chief tells his compatriots, "the rewards of the resolute. Chief Hemmij and Daniel Snitker undermined our dignity by their kowtowing, and it falls to me," he thumps the unwieldy pile, "to win it back."

Magistrate Shiroyama speaks to Kobayashi.

"Magistrate asks," translates the interpreter, " 'You are comfort now?' "

"Thank His Honor. Now we sit face-to-face, like equals."

Jacob assumes that Kobayashi omits Vorstenbosch's last two words.

Magistrate Shiroyama nods and musters a long sentence. "He says," begins Kobayashi, " 'Congratulate' to new chief resident and 'Welcome to Nagasaki'; and 'Welcome again to magistracy,' to deputy chief." Jacob, a mere clerk, passes unacknowledged. "Magistrate hope voyage not too . . . 'strenuous' and hope sun not too strong for weak Dutch skin."

"Thank our host for his concern," replies Vorstenbosch, "but assure him that, compared to July in Batavia, his Nagasaki summer is child's play."

Shiroyama nods at the translated rendering, as though a long-held suspicion is at last confirmed.

"Ask," Vorstenbosch orders, "how His Honor enjoyed the coffee I presented."

The question, Jacob notices, provokes arch glances between the courtiers. The magistrate considers his reply. "Magistrate says," translates Ogawa, " 'Coffee tastes of no other.' "

"Tell him our plantations in Java can supply enough to satisfy even Japan's bottomless stomach. Tell him future generations shall bless the name Shiroyama as the man who discovered this magical beverage for their homeland."

Ogawa delivers a suitable translation and is met by a gentle rebuttal.

"The magistrate says," explains Kobayashi, " 'Japan is no appetite for coffee.' "

"Stuff! Once, coffee was unknown in Europe, too, but now every street in our great capitals has its own coffeehouse — or ten! Vast fortunes are made."

Shiroyama changes the subject before Ogawa can translate.

"The magistrate gives sympathy," says Kobayashi, "for wreck of *Octavia* on voyage home last winter."

"It's curious, tell him," says Vorstenbosch, "how our discussion turns to the travails suffered by the honorable company in its struggle to bring prosperity to Nagasaki . . ."

Ogawa, who senses trouble he cannot avoid, must nevertheless translate.

Magistrate Shiroyama's face expresses a knowing *Oh?*

"I bear an urgent communiqué from the governor-general on this same topic."

Ogawa turns to Jacob for help: "What is 'communiqué'?"

"A letter," replies Jacob in a low voice. "A diplomat's message."

Ogawa translates the sentence; Shiroyama's hands signal *Give.*

From his tower of cushions, Vorstenbosch nods to his secretary.

Jacob unties his portfolio, removes the freshly forged letter from His Excellency P. G. van Overstraten, and proffers it with both hands to the chamberlain.

Chamberlain Tomine places the envelope before his master.

The Hall of Sixty Mats looks on with undisguised curiosity.

"It is meet, Mr. Kobayashi," says Vorstenbosch, "to warn these good gentlemen — and even the magistrate — that our governor-general sends an ultimatum."

Kobayashi glares at Ogawa, who begins to ask, "What is 'ultim—'?"

" 'Ultimatum,' " says Van Cleef. "A threat; a demand; a strong warning."

"Very bad time," Kobayashi shakes his

head, "for strong warning."

"But surely Magistrate Shiroyama must know as soon as possible," Chief Vorstenbosch's concern is soft with malice, "that Dejima is to be abandoned after the current trading season unless Edo gives us twenty thousand piculs?"

" 'Abandoned,' " repeats Van Cleef, "stopped; ended; finished."

Blood drains from the two interpreters' faces.

Inwardly, Jacob squirms with sympathy for Ogawa.

"Please, sir," Ogawa swallows, "not such news, here, now . . ."

Running out of patience, the chamberlain demands a translation.

"Best not keep His Honor waiting," Vorstenbosch tells Kobayashi.

Word by faltering word, Kobayashi delivers the appalling news.

Questions are fired from all quarters, but Kobayashi's and Ogawa's replies would be drowned out even if they tried to answer. During this mayhem, Jacob notices a man seated three places to the left of Magistrate Shiroyama. His face disturbs the clerk, though he could not say why; neither can Jacob guess his age. His shaven head and water-blue robes suggest a monk or even a confessor. The lips are tight, the cheekbones high, the nose hooked, and the eyes ferocious with intelligence. Jacob finds himself as little able to evade the man's gaze as a book can, of its own volition, evade the scrutiny of a reader. The silent observer twists his head, like a hunting dog listening to the sound of its prey.

CHAPTER FIVE:
WAREHOUSE DOORN
ON DEJIMA

After lunch on August 1, 1799

The cogs and levers of time swell and buckle in the heat. In the stewed gloom, Jacob hears, almost, the sugar in its crates hissing into fused lumps. Come auction day, it shall be sold to the spice merchants for a pittance, or else, as well they know, it must be returned to the *Shenandoah*'s hold for a profitless return voyage back to the warehouses of Batavia. The clerk drains his cup of green tea. The bitter dregs make him wince and amplify his headache but sharpen his wits.

On a bed of clove crates and hempen sacking, Hanzaburo lies asleep.

Mucus from his nostril to his rocky Adam's apple.

The scratch of Jacob's quill is joined by a not dissimilar noise from a rafter.

It is a rhythmic scratting, soon overlain by a tiny, sawing squeak.

A he-rat, the young man realizes, *mounting his she-rat.*

Listening, he becomes enwrapped by memories of women's bodies.

These are not memories he is proud of, or ever discusses . . .

I dishonor Anna, Jacob thinks, *by dwelling on such things.*

. . . but the images dwell on him and thicken his blood like arrowroot.

Concentrate, donkey, the clerk orders himself, *on your work.*

With difficulty, he returns to his pursuit of the fifty rix-dollars fleeing through thickets of forged receipts found in one of Daniel Snitker's boots. He tries to pour more tea into his cup, but the pot is now empty. He calls out, "Hanzaburo?"

The boy does not stir. The rutting rats have fallen silent.

"Hai!" Long seconds later, the boy jolts upright. "Mr. Dazûto?"

Jacob raises his ink-smudged cup. "Tea, please, Hanzaburo."

Hanzaburo squints and rubs his head and blurts, "Huh?"

"More tea, please." Jacob waggles his teapot. *"O-cha."*

Hanzaburo sighs, heaves himself up, takes the teapot, and plods away.

Jacob sharpens his quill, but soon his head is drooping . . .

. . . A hunchback dwarf stands silhouetted in

the white glare of Bony Alley.

Gripped in his hairy hand is a club . . . no, it is a long joint of bony, bloodied pork.

Jacob lifts his heavy head. His stiff neck cricks.

The hunchback enters the warehouse, grunting and snuffling.

The joint of pork is, in fact, an amputated shin, with ankle and foot attached.

Nor is the hunchback a hunchback: it is William Pitt, ape of Dejima.

Jacob jumps up and bangs his knee. The pain is prismatic.

William Pitt clambers up a tower of crates with his bloody prize.

"How in God's name," Jacob rubs his kneecap, "did you *come* by such a thing?"

There is no reply but the calm and steady breathing of the sea . . .

. . . and Jacob remembers: Dr. Marinus was summoned to the *Shenandoah* yesterday, where an Estonian seaman's foot had been crushed by a fallen crate. Gangrenous wounds spoiling faster than milk in a Japanese August, the doctor prescribed the knife. The surgery is being performed today in the hospital so his four students and some local scholars may watch the procedure. However improbably, William Pitt must have forced an entry and stolen the limb: what other explanation is there?

A second figure, momentarily blinded by

89

the warehouse darkness, enters. His willowy chest is heaving with exertion. His blue kimono is covered with an artisan's apron, spattered dark, and strands of hair have escaped from the headscarf that half conceals the right side of his face. Only when he steps into the shaft of light falling from the high window does Jacob see that the pursuer is a young woman.

Aside from the washerwomen and a few "aunts" who serve at the Interpreters' Guild, the only women permitted through the land gate are prostitutes, who are hired for a night, or "wives" who stay under the roofs of the better-paid officers for longer periods. These costly courtesans are attended by a maid: Jacob's best guess is that the visitor is one such companion, who wrestled with William Pitt for the stolen limb, failed to prize it from his grasp, and chased the ape into the warehouse.

Voices — Dutch, Japanese, Malay — clatter down Long Street from the hospital.

The doorway frames their outlines, brief as blinks, running down Bony Alley.

Jacob sifts his meager Japanese vocabulary for any suitable items.

When she notices the red-haired, green-eyed foreigner, she gasps with alarm.

"Miss," implores Jacob in Dutch, "I — I — I — please don't worry — I . . ."

The woman studies him and concludes that

he offers no threat.

"Bad monkey," she regains her composure, "steal foot."

He nods at this, then realizes: "You speak Dutch, Miss?"

Her shrug replies, *A little.* She says, "Bad monkey — enter here?"

"Aye, aye. The hairy devil is up there." Jacob indicates William Pitt up on his crates. Wanting to impress the woman, he strides over. "William Pitt: unhand that leg. Give it to me. *Give!*"

The ape places the leg at his side, grips his rhubarb-pink penis, and twangs it like a harpist in a madhouse, cackling through bared teeth. Jacob fears for his visitor's modesty, but she turns aside to hide her laughter and, in doing so, reveals a burn covering much of the left side of her face. It is dark, blotched, and, close up, very conspicuous. *How can a courtesan's maid,* Jacob wonders, *earn a living with such a disfigurement?* Too late, he is aware that she is watching him gawp. She pushes back her headscarf and thrusts her cheek toward Jacob. *There,* this gesture declares, *drink your fill!*

"I —" Jacob is mortified. "Please forgive my rudeness, Miss . . ."

Fearing she doesn't understand, he holds a deep bow for the count of five.

The woman reties her headscarf and directs

her attention to William Pitt. Ignoring Jacob, she addresses the ape in lilting Japanese.

The thief hugs the leg like a motherless daughter hugs a doll.

Determined to cut a better figure, Jacob approaches the tower of crates.

He jumps up onto an adjacent chest. "Listen to me, you flea-bitten *slave* —"

A warm and liquid whiplash, smelling of roast beef, flays his cheek.

In his effort to deflect the warm stream, he loses his balance . . .

. . . tumbles off the chest, heels over arse, onto the beaten earth.

Mortification, thinks Jacob, as the pain eases, *requires at least a little pride . . .*

The woman is leaning against Hanzaburo's improvised cot.

. . . but I have no pride left, for I am pissed upon by William Pitt.

She is dabbing her eyes and shivering with near-silent laughter.

Anna laughs that way, Jacob thinks. *Anna laughs that very way.*

"I sorry." She inhales deeply and her lips twitch. "Excuse my . . . 'lewdness'?"

" 'Rudeness,' Miss." He goes to the water pail. " 'Rude,' with an R."

" 'Rewdness,' " she repeats, "with an R. It is nothing funny."

Jacob washes his face, but to rinse the monkey urine from his second-best linen shirt he must first remove it. To do so here is out of the question.

"You wish" — she hunts in a sleeve pocket, taking out a closed fan and putting it on a crate of raw sugar, before producing a square of paper — "wipe face?"

"Most kind." Jacob takes it and dabs his brow and cheeks.

"Trade with monkey," she suggests. "Trade thing for leg."

Jacob gives the idea its due. "The beast *is* a slave to tobacco."

"Ta-ba-ko?" She claps her hands once in resolve. "You have?"

Jacob hands her the last of his Javanese leaf in a leather pouch.

She dangles the bait from a broom head, level with William Pitt's aerie.

The ape reaches out; the woman sways it away, mumbling entreaties . . .

. . . before William Pitt lets go of the leg to seize his new prize.

The limb thumps to earth and stops dead at the woman's foot. She gives Jacob a glance of triumph, discards the broom, and takes up the amputated limb as casually as a farmhand picking up a turnip. Its hacked-through bone pokes from the bloody sheath, and its toes are grubby. Up above, the casement rattles: William Pitt has escaped through the window with his bounty, over the roofs of Long Street. "Tobacco is lose, sir," says the woman.

"Very sorry."

"No matter, Miss. You have your leg. Well, not *your* leg . . ."

Shouted questions and answers fly up and down Bony Alley.

Jacob and his visitor take a couple of steps back from each other.

"Forgive me, Miss, but . . . are you a courtesan's maid?"

"Kôchi — zanzu — meido?" This baffles her. "What is?"

"A . . . a" — Jacob grasps for a substitute word — "a whore's . . . helper."

She lays the limb on a square of cloth. "Why horse need helper?"

A guard appears in the doorway; he sees the Dutchman, the young woman, and the lost foot. He grins and shouts into Bony Alley, and within moments more guards, inspectors, and officials arrive, followed by Deputy van Cleef; then Dejima's strutting Constable Kosugi; Marinus's assistant, Eelattu, his apron as bloodied as the burned woman's; Arie Grote and a Japanese merchant with darting eyes; several scholars; and Con Twomey, carrying his carpenter's rule and asking Jacob in English, "What's that *feckin'* smell about ye, man?"

Jacob remembers his half-restored ledger on the table, wide open for all to see. Hastily, he conceals it, just as four youths arrive, each with the shaven heads of medical disciples

94

and aprons like the burned woman's, and commence to fire questions at her. The clerk guesses these are Dr. Marinus's "seminarians," and soon the intruders let the woman recount her story. She indicates the tower of crates where William Pitt clambered up and now gestures toward Jacob, who blushes as twenty or thirty heads look his way. She speaks her language with quiet self-possession. The clerk awaits the hilarity that must greet his dousing in ape piss, but she omits the episode, it seems, and her narrative ends in nods of approval. Twomey leaves with the Estonian's limb, to fashion a wooden substitute of the same length.

"I *saw* you," Van Cleef snatches a guard's sleeve, "you damned *thief!*"

A shower of bright-red nutmeg berries spills across the floor.

"Baert! Fischer! Show these blasted robbers out of our warehouse!" The deputy makes herding motions toward the door, shouting, "*Out! Out!* Grote, frisk whoever looks suspicious — aye, just as they frisk us. De Zoet, watch our merchandise or it'll sprout legs and walk."

Jacob stands on a crate, the better to survey the departing visitors.

He sees the burned maid step into the sunlit alley, assisting a frail scholar.

Contrary to his expectations, she turns and waves her hand.

Jacob is delighted by this secret acknowledgment and waves back.

No, he sees, *she is sheltering her eyes from
the sun . . .*

Yawning, Hanzaburo enters, carrying a pot
of tea.

You didn't even ask her name, Jacob realizes.
Jacob de Bonehead.

He notices that she left behind the closed
fan on the crate of raw sugar.

Storm-faced Van Cleef leaves last, pushing
past Hanzaburo, who stands at the threshold,
holding the pot of tea. Hanzaburo asks,
"Thing happen?"

By midnight, the chief's dining room is foggy
with pipe smoke. The servants Cupido and
Philander play "Apples of Delft" on viol da
gamba and flute.

"President Adams is our 'shogun,' yes, Mr.
Goto." Captain Lacy flicks crumbs of pie
crust from his mustache. "But he was *chosen*
by the American people. This is the point of
democracy."

The five interpreters exchange a look Jacob
now recognizes.

"Great lords," Ogawa Uzaemon clarifies,
"*choose* president?"

"Not lords, no." Lacy picks his teeth.
"Citizens. Every one of us."

"Even" — Interpreter Goto's eyes settle on
Con Twomey — "carpenters?"

"Carpenters, bakers" — Lacy belches — "and candlestick makers."

"Do Washington's and Jefferson's slaves," asks Marinus, "also vote?"

"*No*, Doctor." Lacy smiles. "Nor do oxen, bees, or women."

But what junior geisha, wonders Jacob, *would wrestle an ape for a leg?*

"What if," asks Goto, "people make bad choice and president is bad man?"

"Come the next election, we vote him out of office."

"Old president," Interpreter Hori is maroon with rum, "is *executed?*"

" 'Elected,' Mr. Hori," says Twomey. "When the people choose their leader."

"A better system, surely," Lacy holds his glass for Van Cleef's slave, Weh, to fill, "than waiting for death to remove a corrupt, stupid, or insane shogun?"

The interpreters look uneasy: no informer is fluent enough in Dutch to understand Captain Lacy's treasonous talk, but there is no guarantee that the magistracy has not recruited one of the four to report on his colleagues' reactions.

"Democracy," says Goto, "is not a flower who bloom in Japan."

"Soil in Asia," agrees Interpreter Hori, "is not correct for Europe and America flowers."

"Mr. Washington, Mr. Adams," Interpreter Iwase shifts the topic, "is royal bloodline?"

"Our revolution" — Captain Lacy clicks his fingers to order the slave Ignatius to bring the spittoon — "in which I played my part, when my paunch was flatter, sought to *purge* America of royal bloodlines." He spews out a dragon of phlegm. "A man might be a great leader — like General Washington — but why does it follow that his children inherit their pa's qualities? Are not inbred royals more often dunderheads and wastrels — proper 'King Georges,' one might say — than those who climb the world using God-given talent?" He mumbles an aside in English to Dejima's secret subject of the British monarch. "No offense intended, Mr. Twomey."

"I'd be the *last* fecker," avows the Irishman, "to take offense."

Cupido and Philander strike up "Seven White Roses for My One True Love."

Baert's drunken head droops and settles in a plate of sweet beans.

Does her burn, Jacob wonders, *register touch as heat, cold, or numbness?*

Marinus takes up his stick. "The party shall excuse me: I have left Eelattu rendering the Estonian's shinbone. Without an expert eye, tallow shall be dripping from the ceiling. Mr. Vorstenbosch, my compliments . . ." He bows to the interpreters and limps out of the room.

Captain Lacy's smile is soapy. "Does the law of Japan permit *polygamy?*"

"What is po-ri-ga-mi?" Hori stuffs a pipe.

"Why need permit?"

"You explain, Mr. de Zoet," Van Cleef is saying. "Words are your forte."

"Polygamy is . . ." Jacob considers. "One husband, many wives."

"Ah. Oh." Hori grins, and the other interpreters nod. "Polygamy."

"Mohammedans sanction four wives." Captain Lacy tosses an almond into the air and captures it in his mouth. "Chinese may round up seven under one roof. How many may a Japanese man lock up in his personal collection, eh?"

"In all countries, same," says Hori. "In Japan, Holland, China; all same. I say why. All mans marry first wife. He" — leering, Hori makes an obscene gesture with a fist and finger — "until she" — he mimes a pregnant belly — "yes? After *this*, all mans keep number wives his purse *says* he may. Captain Lacy plans to have Dejima wife for trading season, like Mr. Snitker and Mr. van Cleef?"

"I'd rather," Lacy bites a thumbnail, "visit the famous Maruyama District."

"Mr. Hemmij," recalls Interpreter Yonekizu, "ordered courtesans for his feasts."

"Chief Hemmij," says Vorstenbosch darkly, "partook of many pleasures at the company's expense, as did Mr. Snitker. Hence, the latter dines on hardtack tonight, whilst we enjoy the rewards of honest employees."

Jacob glances at Ivo Oost: Ivo Oost is scowling at him.

Baert lifts his bean-spattered face, exclaims, "But, sir, she ain't really my aunt!" giggles like a schoolgirl, and falls off his chair.

"I propose a toast," declares Deputy van Cleef, "to all our absent ladies."

The drinkers and diners fill one another's glasses. "To all our absent ladies!"

"Especial," gasps Hori, as the gin burns his gullet, "to Mr. Ogawa here. Mr. Ogawa, he marry this year a beauty wife." Hori's elbow is covered with rhubarb mousse. "Each night" — he mimes riding a horse — "three, four, five gallopings!"

The laughter is raucous, but Ogawa's smile is weak.

"You ask a starved man," Gerritszoon says, "to drink to a glutton."

"Mr. Gerritszoon want girl?" Hori is solicitude personified. "My servant fetch. Say you want. Fat? Tight? Tiger? Gentle sister?"

"We'd *all* like a gentle sister," complains Arie Grote, "but what o' the money, eh? A man could buy a brothel in Siam for a tumble with a Nagasaki doxy. Is there no case, Mr. Vorstenbosch, for the company providin' a subsidy, eh, in this quarter? Consider poor Oost: on his *official* wages, sir, a little . . . feminine consolation, eh, would cost him a year's wages."

"A diet of abstinence," replies Vorstenbosch, "never hurt anyone."

"But, sir, what vices might a red-blooded Dutchman be pushed to without a conduit for the, eh, unloosin' o' Nature's urges?"

"You miss your wife, Mr. Grote," Hori asks, "at home in Holland?"

" 'South of Gibraltar,' " quotes Captain Lacy, " 'all men are bachelors.' "

"Nagasaki's latitude," says Fischer, "is, of course, well *north* of Gibraltar."

"I never knew," says Vorstenbosch, "you were a married man, Grote."

"He'd as soon not," Ouwehand explains, "hear the subject raised."

"A mooing West Frieslander slut, sir." The cook licks his brown incisors. "When I consider her at *all*, Mr. Hori, 'tis to pray the Ottomans'll storm West Friesland an' make off with the bitch."

"If not like wife," asks Interpreter Yonekizu, "why do not divorce?"

"Easier said than done, sir," Grote sighs, "in the so-called Christian lands."

"So why marry," Hori coughs out tobacco smoke, "at first place?"

"Oh, 'tis a long an' sorry saga, Mr. Hori, what'd not be of interest to —"

"On Mr. Grote's last trip home," obliges Ouwehand, "he wooed a promising young heiress at her town house in Roomolenstraat who told him how her heirless, ailing papa yearned to see his dairy farm in the hands of a gentleman son-in-law, yet everywhere, she lamented, were thieving rascals *posing* as eligible bachelors. Mr. Grote agreed that the Sea of Courtship seethes with sharks and spoke of the prejudice endured by the young colonial parvenu, as if the annual fortunes yielded by his plantations in Sumatra were less worthy than old monies. The turtledoves were wedded within a week. The day after their nuptials, the taverner presented the bill and each says to the other, 'Settle the account, my heart's music.' But to their genuine horror, neither *could,* for bride and groom alike had spent their last beans on wooing the other! Mr. Grote's Sumatran plantations evaporated; the Roomolenstraat house reverted to a co-conspirator's stage prop; the ailing father-in-law turned out to be a beer porter in rude health, not heirless but hairless, and —"

A belch erupts from Lacy. "Pardon: 'twas the deviled eggs."

"Deputy van Cleef?" Goto is alarmed. "Do Ottomans invade Holland? This news is not in recentest *fusetsuki* report . . ."

"Mr. Grote" — Van Cleef brushes his napkin — "spoke in jest, sir."

" 'In jest'?" The earnest young interpreter frowns and blinks. " 'In jest . . .' "

Cupido and Philander are playing a languid air by Boccherini.

"One grows despondent," ruminates Vorstenbosch, "to think that, unless Edo authorizes an increase in the copper quota, these rooms shall fall forever silent."

Yonekizu and Hori grimace; Goto and Ogawa wear blank faces.

Most of the Dutchmen have asked Jacob whether the extraordinary ultimatum is a bluff. He told each to ask the chief resident, knowing that none of them would. Having lost last season's cargo aboard the doomed *Octavia,* many would be returning to Batavia poorer men than when they left.

"Who *was* that bizarre female," Van Cleef asks, squeezing a lemon into a Venetian glass, "in Warehouse Doorn?"

"Miss Aibagawa," says Goto, "is daughter of doctor and scholar."

Aibagawa. Jacob handles each syllable in turn. *Ai-ba-ga-wa . . .*

"The magistrate give permission," says Iwase, "to study under Dutch doctor."

And I called her a "whore's helper," remembers Jacob, and winces.

"What a bizarre Locusta," says Fischer, "to be at ease in a surgery."

"The fairer sex," objects Jacob, "can show as much resilience as the uglier one."

"Mr. de Zoet *must* publish," the Prussian picks his nose, "his dazzling epigrams."

"Miss Aibagawa," states Ogawa, "is a midwife. She is used to blood."

"But I understood," says Vorstenbosch, "a

woman was forbidden to set foot on Dejima, without she be a courtesan, her maid, or one of the old crones at the guild."

"It *is* forbidden," affirms Yonekizu indignantly. "No precedent. Never."

"Miss Aibagawa," Ogawa speaks up, "work hard as midwife, both for rich customers and poor persons who cannot pay. Recently, she deliver Magistrate Shiroyama's son. Birth was hard, and other doctor renounce, but she persevere and succeed. Magistrate Shiroyama was joyful. He gives Miss Aibagawa one wish for reward. Wish is, study under Dr. Marinus on Dejima. So, magistrate kept promise."

"Woman study in hospital," declares Yonekizu, "is not good thing."

"Yet she held the blood basin steady," says Con Twomey, "spoke good Dutch with Dr. Marinus, and chased an ape while her male classmates looked seasick."

I would ask a dozen questions, Jacob thinks, *if I dared: a dozen dozen.*

"Doesn't a girl," asks Ouwehand, "*arouse* the boys in troublesome places?"

"Not with that slice of bacon" — Fischer swirls his gin — "stuck to her face."

"Ungallant words, Mr. Fischer," says Jacob. "They shame you."

"One cannot pretend it isn't there, De Zoet! We'd call her a 'tapping cane' in *my* town because, of course, only a blind man would touch her."

Jacob imagines smashing the Prussian's jaw with the Delft jug.

A candle collapses; wax slides down the candlestick; the dribble hardens.

"I am sure," says Ogawa, "Miss Aibagawa one day make joyful marriage."

"What's the one sure cure for love?" asks Grote. "*Marriage* is, is what."

A moth careers into a candle flame; it drops to the table, flapping.

"Poor Icarus." Ouwehand crushes it with his tankard. "Won't you ever learn?"

Night insects trill, tick, bore, ring; drill, prick, saw, sting.

Hanzaburo snores in the cubbyhole outside Jacob's door.

Jacob lies awake, clad in a sheet, under a tent of netting.

Ai, mouth opens; *ba,* lips meet; *ga,* tongue's root; *wa,* lips.

Involuntarily, he reenacts today's scene over and over.

He cringes at the boorish figure he cut and vainly edits the script.

He opens the fan she left in Warehouse Doorn. He fans himself.

The paper is white. The handle and struts are made of paulownia wood.

A watchman smacks his wooden clappers to mark the Japanese hour.

The yeasty moon is caged in his half-

Japanese half-Dutch window . . .

. . . Glass panes melt moonlight; paper panes filter it, to dust.

Daybreak must be near. The 1796 ledgers are waiting for him.

It is dear Anna whom I love, Jacob recites, *and I whom Anna loves.*

Beneath his glaze of sweat, he sweats. His bed linen is sodden.

Miss Aibagawa is as untouchable as a woman in a picture . . .

Jacob imagines he can hear a harpsichord.

. . . spied through a keyhole in a cottage happened upon, once . . .

The notes are spidery and starlit and spun from glass.

Jacob *can* hear a harpsichord: it is the doctor, in his attic.

Night silence and a freak of conductivity permit Jacob this privilege: Marinus rejects all requests to play, even for scholar friends or visiting nobility.

The music provokes a sharp longing the music soothes.

How can such a prig, wonders Jacob, *play with such divinity?*

Night insects trill, tick, bore, ring; drill, prick, saw, sting . . .

CHAPTER SIX:
JACOB'S ROOM IN
TALL HOUSE ON
DEJIMA

Very early on the morning of August 10, 1799
Light bleeds in around the casements: Jacob navigates the archipelago of stains across the low wooden ceiling. Outside, the slaves d'Orsaiy and Ignatius are talking as they feed the animals. Jacob recalls Anna's birthday party a few days prior to his departure. Her father had invited half a dozen eminently eligible young men and given a sumptuous dinner prepared so artfully that the chicken tasted of fish and the fish of chicken. His ironic toast was to "the fortunes of Jacob de Zoet, Merchant Prince of the Indies." Anna rewarded Jacob's forbearance with a smile: her fingers stroked the necklace of Swedish white amber he had brought her from Gothenburg.

On the far side of the world, Jacob sighs with longing and regret.

Unexpectedly, Hanzaburo calls out, "Mr. Dazûto want thing?"

"Nothing, no. It's early, Hanzaburo: go

back to sleep." Jacob imitates a snore.

"Pig? Want pig? Ah ah ah, *surîpu!* Yes . . . yes, I like *surîpu . . .*"

Jacob gets up, drinks from a cracked jug, and rubs soap into lather.

His green eyes watch from the freckled face in the speckled glass.

The blunt blade tears his stubble and nicks the cleft in his chin.

A tear of blood, red as tulips, oozes, mixes with soap, and foams pink.

Jacob considers how a beard would save all this trouble . . .

. . . but recalls his sister Geertje's verdict when he returned from England with a short-lived mustache. "Ooh, dab it in lampblack, brother, and polish our boots!"

He touches his nose, recently adjusted by the disgraced Snitker.

The nick by his ear is a memento of a certain dog that bit him.

When shaving, thinks Jacob, *a man rereads his truest memoir.*

Tracing his lip with his finger, he recalls the very morning of his departure. Anna had persuaded her father to take them both to Rotterdam wharf in his carriage. "Three minutes," he had told Jacob as he climbed out of the carriage to speak to the head clerk, "and no more." Anna knew what to say. "Five years is a long time, but most women wait a lifetime before finding a kind and honest

108

man." Jacob had tried to reply, but she had silenced him. "I know how men overseas behave and, perhaps, how they *must* behave — shush, Jacob de Zoet — so all I ask is that you are *careful* in Java, that your *heart* is mine alone. I shan't give you a ring or locket, because rings and lockets can be lost, but this, at least, cannot be lost." Anna kissed him for the first and last time. It was a long, sad kiss. They watched rain stream down the windows, the boats, and the shale-gray sea, until it was time to go . . .

Jacob's shave is finished. He washes, dresses, and polishes an apple.

Miss Aibagawa, he bites the fruit, *is a scholar, not a courtesan . . .*

From the window, he watches d'Orsaiy water the runner beans.

. . . Illicit rendezvous, much less illicit romances, are impossible here.

He eats the core and spits out the pips onto the back of his hand.

I just want to converse, Jacob is sure, *to know her a little . . .*

He takes the chain from his neck and turns the key in his sea chest.

Friendship can exist between the sexes, as with my sister and I.

An enterprising fly buzzes over his urine in the chamber pot.

He digs down, nearly as far as his Psalter,

and finds the bound folio.

Jacob unfastens the volume's ribbons and studies the first page of music.

The notes of the luminous sonatas hang like grapes from the staves.

Jacob's sight-reading skills end with the *Hymnal of the Reformed Church*.

Today, he thinks, *is a day to mend bridges with Dr. Marinus . . .*

Jacob takes a short walk around Dejima, where all walks are short, to polish his plan and hone his script. Gulls and crows bicker on the ridge of Garden House.

In the garden, the cream roses and red lilies are past their best.

Bread is being delivered by provedores at the land gate.

In Flag Square, Peter Fischer sits on the watchtower's steps. "Lose an hour in the morning, Clerk de Zoet," the Prussian calls down, "and you search for it all day."

In Van Cleef's upper window, the deputy's latest "wife" combs her hair.

She smiles at Jacob; Melchior van Cleef, his chest hairy as a bear's, appears. " 'Thou shalt not,' " he quotes, " 'dip thy nib in another man's inkpot.' "

The deputy chief slides shut the *shoji* window before Jacob can protest his innocence.

Outside the Interpreters' Guild, palanquin

bearers squat in the shadows. Their eyes follow the red-haired foreigner as he passes.

Up on the seawall, William Pitt gazes at the whale-rib clouds.

By the kitchen, Arie Grote tells him, "Yer bamboo hat makes yer look like a Chinaman, Mr. de Z. Have yer not considered —"

"No," says the clerk, and walks on.

Constable Kosugi nods at Jacob outside his small house on Seawall Lane.

The slaves Ignatius and Weh argue in Malay as they milk the goats.

Ivo Oost and Wybo Gerritszoon throw a ball to each other, in silence.

"Bowwow," one of them says as Jacob passes: he decides not to hear.

Con Twomey and Ponke Ouwehand smoke pipes under the pines.

"Some blue blood," sniffs Ouwehand, "has died in Miyako, so hammering and music are forbidden for two days. There'll be little work done anywhere, not just here but throughout the empire. Van Cleef swears it's a stratagem to postpone the rebuilding of Warehouse Lelie so we'll be more desperate to sell . . ."

I am not polishing my plan, Jacob admits. *I am losing my nerve . . .*

In the surgery, Dr. Marinus is lying flat on the operating table with his eyes closed. He hums a baroque melody inside his hoggish neck.

111

Eelattu brushes his master's jowls with scented oil and feminine delicacy.

Steam rises from a bowl of water; light is sliced on the bright razor.

On the floor, a toucan pecks beans from a pewter saucer.

Plums are piled in a terra-cotta dish, blue-dusted indigo.

Eelattu announces Jacob's arrival in murmured Malay, and Marinus opens one displeased eye. *"What?"*

"I should like to consult with you on a . . . certain matter."

"Continue shaving, Eelattu. Consult, then, Domburger."

"I'd be more comfortable in private, Doctor, as —"

"Eelattu *is* 'private.' In our little corner of Creation, his grasp of anatomy and pathology is second only to mine. Unless it is the toucan you mistrust?"

"Well, then . . ." Jacob sees he must rely on the servant's discretion as well as Marinus's. "I'm a little curious about one of your students."

"What business have *you*" — his other eye opens — "with Miss Aibagawa?"

Jacob looks down. "None at all. I just . . . wished to converse with her . . ."

"Then why are you here, conversing with me instead?"

". . . to converse with her without a dozen

112

spies looking on."

"Ah. *Ah*. Ah. So you wish me to bring about an *assignation?*"

"That word smacks of intrigue, Doctor, which would not —"

"The answer is, 'Never.' Reason the first: Miss Aibagawa is no rented Eve to scratch *your* itch of Adam, but a gentleman's daughter. Reason the second: even *were* Miss Aibagawa 'available' as a Dejima wife, which, emphatically, she is *not* —"

"I know all this, Doctor, and upon my honor, I didn't come here to —"

"— which she is *not,* then spies would report the liaison within a half hour, whereupon my hard-won rights to teach, botanize, and scholarize around Nagasaki would be withdrawn. So be gone. Deflate your testicles *comme à la mode:* via the village pimp or Sin of Onan."

The toucan taps the dish of beans and utters "Raw!" or a word very similar.

"Sir" — Jacob blushes — "you *grievously* misjudge my intentions. I'd *never* —"

"It is not even Miss Aibagawa after whom you lust, in truth. It is the genus 'The Oriental Woman' who so infatuates you. Yes, yes, the mysterious eyes, the camellias in her hair, what you perceive as meekness. How many *hundreds* of you besotted white men have I seen mired in the same syrupy hole?"

"You are wrong, for once, Doctor. There's no —"

"Naturally, I am wrong: *Domburger*'s adoration for *his* Pearl of the East is based on *chivalry:* behold the disfigured damsel, spurned by her own race! Behold our Occidental knight, who alone divines her *inner* beauty!"

"Good day." Jacob is too bruised to endure any more. "Good day."

"Leaving so soon? Without even offering that bribe under your arm?"

"Not a bribe," he half-lies, "but a gift from Batavia. I had hopes — vain and foolish ones, I now see — of establishing a friendship with the celebrated Dr. Marinus, and so Hendrik Zwaardecroone of the Batavian Society recommended me to bring you some sheet music. But I see now that an ignorant clerk is beneath your august notice. I shall trouble you no more."

Marinus scrutinizes Jacob. "What sort of a gift is it that the giver doesn't offer until he wants something from the intended recipient?"

"I tried to give it to you at our first meeting. You slammed a trapdoor on me."

Eelattu dips the razor in water and wipes it on a sheet of paper.

"Irascibility," the doctor admits, "occasionally gets the better of me. Who is" — Marinus flicks a finger at the folio — "the composer?"

Jacob reads the title page: " 'Domenico Scarlatti's Chefs-d'oeuvre, for the Harpsichord or Piano-Forte; Selected from an Elegant collection of Manuscripts, in the Possession of Muzio Clementi . . . London, and to be had at Mr. Broadwood's Harpsichord Maker, in Great Pulteney Street, Golden Square.' "

Dejima's rooster crows. Noisy feet tromp down Long Street.

"Domenico Scarlatti, is it? He *has* flown a long way to be here."

Marinus's indifference, Jacob suspects, is too airy to be genuine.

"He shall fly a long way back." He turns. "I incommode you no longer."

"Oh, wait, Domburger: sulking doesn't suit you. Miss Aibagawa —"

"— is no courtesan: I *know.* I don't *view* her in that light." Jacob would tell Marinus about Anna, but he doesn't trust the doctor enough to unlock his heart.

"Then in what light," Marinus probes, "*do* you see her?"

"As a . . ." Jacob searches for the right metaphor. "As a book whose cover fascinates, and in whose pages I desire to look a little. Nothing more."

A draft nudges open the creaking door of the two-bed sickroom.

"Then I propose the following bargain: return here by three o'clock and you may have twenty minutes in the sickroom to peruse what pages Miss Aibagawa cares to show you — but the door *remains open throughout,* and should you treat her with one *dram* less respect than you would your own sister, Domburger, my vengeance shall be biblical."

"Thirty seconds per sonata hardly represents good value."

"Then you and your sometime gift know where the door is."

"No bargain. Good day." Jacob leaves and blinks in the steepening sunlight.

He walks down Long Street to Garden House and waits in its shade.

The cicadas' songs are fierce and primal on this hot morning.

Over by the pine trees, Twomey and Ouwehand are laughing.

But dear Jesus in heaven, thinks Jacob, *I am lonely in this place.*

Eelattu is not sent after him. Jacob returns to the hospital.

"We have a deal, then." Marinus's shave is finished. "But my seminarian's spy must be blind-sided. My lecture this afternoon is on human respiration, which I intend to illustrate via a practical demonstration. I'll have Vorstenbosch loan you as a demonstrator."

Jacob finds himself saying, "Agreed . . ."

"Congratulations." Marinus wipes his hands. "Maestro Scarlatti, if I may?"

". . . but your fee is payable upon delivery."

"Oh? My word as a gentleman is not enough?"

"Until a quarter to three, then, Doctor."

Fischer and Ouwehand fall silent as Jacob enters the records office.

"Pleasant and cool," says the newcomer, "in here, at least."

"*I,*" Ouwehand declares to Fischer, "find it heated and oppressive."

Fischer snorts like a horse and retires to his desk: the highest one.

Jacob puts on his glasses at the shelf housing the current decade's ledgers.

He returned the 1793 to 1798 accounts yesterday; now they are gone.

Jacob puts his glasses back on and looks at Ouwehand; Ouwehand nods at Fischer's hunched back.

"Would you know where the '93 to '98 ledgers are, Mr. Fischer?"

"I know where everything is in my office."

"Then would you kindly tell me where to find the '93 to '98 ledgers?"

"Why do you need them" — Fischer looks around — "exactly?"

"To carry out the duties assigned to me by Chief Resident Vorstenbosch."

Ouwehand hums a nervous bar of the *Prinsenlied.*

"Errors," Fischer gnashes his words, "here" — the Prussian thumps the pile of ledgers in front of him — "occur not because we unfrauded the company" — his Dutch deteriorates — "but because Snitker *forbade us* to keep proper ledgers."

Farsighted Jacob removes his glasses to dissolve Fischer's face.

"Who has accused you of defrauding the company, Mr. Fischer?"

"I am sick — do you hear? *Sick!* — of the never-ending inference!"

Lethargic waves die on the other side of the seawall.

"Why does the chief," demands Fischer, "not instruct *me* to repair the ledgers?"

"Is it not logical to appoint an auditor unconnected with Snitker's regime?"

"So *I,* too, am an embezzler now?" Fischer's nostrils dilate. "You admit it! You plot against us all! I *dare* you to deny it!"

"All the chief wants," says Jacob, "is *one* version of the truth."

"My powers of logic," Fischer says, waving an erect index finger at Jacob, "destroy your lie! I warn you, in Surinam I shot more blacks than Clerk de Zoet can count on his abacus. Attack *me,* and I crush you under my foot.

So, *here*." The ill-tempered Prussian deposits the pile of ledgers in Jacob's hands. "Sniff for 'errors.' I go to Mr. van Cleef to discuss — to make a profit for the company this season!"

Fischer rams on his hat and leaves, slamming the door.

"It's a compliment," says Ouwehand. "You make him nervous."

I just want to do my job, Jacob thinks. "Nervous about what?"

"Ten dozen boxes marked 'Kumamoto Camphor' loaded in '96 and '97."

"Were they something other than Kumamoto camphor?"

"No, but page fourteen of our ledgers lists *twelve*-pound boxes; the Japanese records, as Ogawa can tell you, list *thirty-six*-pounders." Ouwehand goes to the water pitcher. "At Batavia," he continues, "one Johannes van der Broeck, a customs officer, sells the excess: the son-in-law of Chairman van der Broeck of the Council of the Indies. It's a swindle as sweet as honey. A cup of water?"

"Yes, please." Jacob drinks. "And this you tell me because . . ."

"Blank self-interest: Mr. Vorstenbosch is here for five whole years, no?"

"Yes." Jacob lies because he must. "I shall serve my contract with him."

A fat fly traces a lazy oval through light and shadow.

"When Fischer wakes up to the fact that

it's Vorstenbosch and not Van Cleef he must wed and bed, he'll stick a knife into *my* back."

"With what knife," Jacob sees the next question, "might he do that?"

"Can you promise" — Ouwehand scratches his neck — "I shan't be Snitkered?"

"I promise" — power has an unpleasant taste — "to tell Mr. Vorstenbosch that Ponke Ouwehand is a helper and not a hinderer."

Ouwehand weighs Jacob's sentence. "Last year's private sales records will show that I brought in fifty bolts of Indian chintz. The Japanese private sales accounts, however, shall show me selling one hundred and fifty. Of the surplus, Captain Hofstra of the *Octavia* commandeered half, though of course I can't prove that, and neither can he, God grant mercy to his drowned soul."

The fat fly settles on Jacob's blotter. "A helper not a hinderer, Mr. Ouwehand."

Dr. Marinus's students arrive at three o'clock precisely.

The sickroom door is ajar, but Jacob cannot see into the surgery.

Four male voices chorus, "Good afternoon, Dr. Marinus."

"Today, seminarians," says Marinus, "we have a practical experiment. Whilst Eelattu and I prepare this, each of you shall study a different Dutch text and translate it into Japanese. My friend Dr. Maeno has agreed to inspect your handiwork later this week. The paragraphs are relevant to your interests: to Mr. Muramoto, our bonesetter-in-chief, I proffer Albinus's *Tabulae sceleti et musculorum corporis humani;* Mr. Kajiwaki, a passage on cancer from Jean-Louis Petit, who lends his name to the *trigonum Petiti,* which is what and where?"

"Muscle hole in back, Doctor."

"Mr. Yano, you have Dr. Olof Acrel, my old master at Uppsala; his essay on cataracts I translated from the Swedish. For Mr. Ikematsu, a page of Lorenz Heister's *Chirurgie* on disorders of the skin . . . and Miss Aibagawa shall peruse the admirable Dr. Smellie. This passage, however, is problematical. In the sickroom awaits the volunteer for today's demonstration, who may assist you on matters of Dutch vocabulary . . ." Marinus's lumpish head appears around the door frame.

"Domburger! I present Miss Aibagawa, and urge you, *Orate ne intretis in tentationem.*"

Miss Aibagawa recognizes the red-haired green-eyed foreigner.

"Good afternoon" — his throat is dry — "Miss Aibagawa."

"Good afternoon" — her voice is clear — "Mr. . . . 'Dom-bugger'?"

" 'Dom*bur*ger' is . . . is the doctor's little joke. My name is De Zoet."

She lowers her writing desk: a tray with

121

legs. " 'Dom-bugger' is funny joke?"

"Dr. Marinus thinks so: I am from a town called 'Domburg.' "

She makes an unconvinced rising *mmm* noise. "Mr. de Zoet is sick?"

"Oh — that is to say — a little, yes. I have a pain in . . ." He pats his abdomen.

"Stools like water?" The midwife assumes control. "Bad smell?"

"No." Jacob is thrown by her directness. "The pain is in my — in my liver."

"Your" — she enunciates the *l* with great care — "*liver*?"

"Just so: my liver pains me. I trust that Miss Aibagawa is well?"

"Yes, I am quite well. I trust that your friend monkey is well?"

"My — oh, William Pitt? My monkey friend is — well, he is no more."

"I am sorry not to understand. Monkey is . . . no more what?"

"No more alive. I" — Jacob mimes breaking a chicken's neck — "killed the rascal, you see; tanned his hide and turned him into a new tobacco pouch."

Her mouth and eyes open in horror.

If Jacob had a pistol, he would shoot himself. "I joke, Miss! The monkey is happy and alive and well, shooling, somewhere — thieving, that is . . ."

"Cor*rect*, Mr. Muramoto." Marinus's voice travels from the surgery. "First one boils away

122

the subcutaneous fat and after injects the veins with colored wax . . ."

"Shall we" — Jacob curses his misfired joke — "open your text?"

She is wondering how this can be done at a safe distance.

"Miss Aibagawa could seat herself *there*." He points to the end of the bed. "Read your text aloud, and when you meet a difficult word, we shall discuss it."

She nods that the arrangement is satisfactory, sits, and begins reading.

Van Cleef's courtesan speaks at a shrill pitch, apparently considered to be feminine, but Miss Aibagawa's reading voice is lower, quieter, and calming. Jacob blesses this excuse to study her part-burned face and her careful lips. " 'Soon after this occ-u-rrence . . .' " She looks up.

"What is, please?"

"An occurrence would be a — a happening, or an event."

"Thank you. '. . . this occurrence, in consulting Ruysch about everything he had writ concerning women . . . I found him exclaiming against the premature extraction of the placenta, and his authority confirmed the opinion I had already adopted . . . and induced me a more natural way of proceeding. When I have separated the funis . . . and given away the child . . . I introduce my finger into the vagina . . .' "

123

In all his life, Jacob has never heard this word spoken aloud.

She senses his shock and looks up, half alarmed. "I mistake?"

Dr. Lucas Marinus, Jacob thinks, *you sadistic monster.* "No," he says.

Frowning, she finds her place again: ". . . to feel if the placenta is at the *os uteri . . .* and if this is the case . . . I am sure it will come down of itself in any rate . . . I wait for some time, and commonly in ten, fifteen, or twenty minutes . . . the woman begins to be seized with some afterpains . . . which gradually separate and force it along . . . but pulling gently at the funis, it descends into the' " — she glances up at Jacob — " 'vagina. Then, taking hold of it, I bring it through the . . . the *os externum.*' There." She looks up. "I finish sentences. Liver is making much pain?"

"Dr. Smellie's language" — Jacob swallows — "is rather . . . direct."

She frowns. "Dutch is foreign language. Words do not have same . . . power, smell, blood. Midwife is my" — she frowns — " 'vacation' or 'vocation' — which?"

" '*Vocation,*' I hazard, Miss Aibagawa."

"Midwife is my *vo*cation. Midwife who fear blood is not helpful."

"Distal phalanx," comes Marinus's voice, "middle and proximal phalanxes . . ."

"Twenty years ago," Jacob decides to tell her, "when my sister was born, the midwife

124

couldn't stop my mother bleeding. My job was to heat water in the kitchen." He is afraid he is boring her, but Miss Aibagawa watches him with calm attention. "*If only I can heat enough water,* I thought, *my mother will live.* I was wrong, I'm sorry to say." Now Jacob frowns, uncertain why he raised this personal matter.

A large wasp settles on the broad foot of the bed.

Miss Aibagawa produces a square of paper from her kimono's sleeve. Jacob, aware of Oriental beliefs in the ascent of the soul from bedbug to saint, waits for her to guide the wasp out through the high window. Instead, she crushes it in the paper, scrunches it into a little ball, and, with perfect aim, tosses it through the window. "Your sister, too, have red hair and green eyes?"

"Her hair is redder than mine, to our uncle's embarrassment."

This is another new word for her. " 'Am-*bass*-a-ment'?"

Remember to ask Ogawa for the Japanese word later, he thinks. " 'Embarrassment,' or shame."

"Why uncle feel shame because sister has red hair?"

"According to common people's belief — or superstition — you understand?"

" '*Meishin*' in Japanese. Doctor call it, 'enemy of reason.' "

"According to superstition, then, Jezebels — that is, women of loose virtue — that is, prostitutes — are thought to have, and are depicted as having, red hair."

" 'Loose virtue'? 'Prostitutes'? Like 'courtesan' and 'whore's helper'?"

"Forgive me for that." Jacob's ears roar. "Now the embarrassment is mine."

Her smile is both nettle and dock leaf. "Mr. de Zoet's sister is honorable girl?"

"Geertje is a . . . very dear sister; she is kind, patient, and clever."

"Metacarpals" — the doctor is demonstrating — "and here, the cunning carpals . . ."

"Miss Aibagawa," Jacob dares to ask, "belongs to a large family?"

"Family was large, is small now. Father, father's new wife, father's new wife's son." She hesitates. "Mother, brothers, and sisters died, of cholera. Much years ago. Much die that time. Not just my family. Much, much suffer."

"Yet your vocation — midwifery, I mean — is . . . an art of life."

A wisp of black hair is escaped from her headscarf: Jacob wants it.

"At old days," says Miss Aibagawa, "long ago, before great bridges built over wide rivers, travelers often drowned. People said, 'Die because river god angry.' People *not* said, 'Die because big bridges not yet invented.' People *not* say, 'People die because we have ignora-

126

tion too much.' But one day, clever ancestors observe spiders' webs, weave bridges of vines. Or see trees, fallen over fast rivers, and make stone islands in wide rivers, and lay from islands to islands. They build such bridges. People no longer drown in same dangerous river, or many less people. So far, my poor Dutch is understand?"

"Perfectly," Jacob assures her. "Every word."

"Nowadays, in Japan, when mother, or baby, or mother *and* baby die in childbirth, people say, 'Ah . . . they die because gods decide so.' Or, 'They die because bad karma.' Or, 'They die because *o-mamori* — magic from temple — too cheap.' Mr. de Zoet understand, it is same as bridge. True reason of many, many death of ignoration. I wish to build bridge *from* ignoration," her tapering hands form the bridge, "to knowledge. This," she lifts, with reverence, Dr. Smellie's text, "is piece of bridge. One day, I teach this knowledge . . . make school . . . students who teach other students . . . and in future, in Japan, many less mothers die of ignoration." She surveys her daydream for just a moment before lowering her eyes. "A foolish plan."

"No, no, no. I cannot imagine a nobler aspiration."

"Sorry . . ." She frowns. "What is 'noble respiration'?"

"*As*piration, Miss: a plan, I mean to say. A

goal in life."

"Ah." A white butterfly lands on her hand. "A goal in life."

She puffs it away; it flies up to a bronze candle on a shelf.

The butterfly closes and opens and closes and opens its wings.

"Name is *'monshiro,'*" she says, "in Japanese."

"In Zeeland, we call the same butterfly cabbage white. My uncle —"

" 'Life is short; the art, long.' " Dr. Marinus enters the sickroom like a limping gray-haired comet. " 'Opportunity is fleeting; experience —' and, Miss Aibagawa? To conclude our first Hippocratic aphorism?"

" 'Experience is fallacious' " — she stands and bows — " 'judgment difficult.' "

"All too true." He beckons in his other students, whom Jacob half-recognizes from Warehouse Doorn. "Domburger, behold my seminarians: Mr. Muramoto of Edo." The eldest, and dourest, bows. "Mr. Kajiwaki, sent by the Chôshu Court of Hagi." A smiling youth not yet grown into his ropy body bows. "Next is Mr. Yano of Osaka." Yano peers at Jacob's green eyes. "And, lastly, Mr. Ikematsu, native son of Satsuma." Ikematsu, pocked by childhood scrofula, gives a cheerful bow. "Seminarians: Domburger is our brave volunteer today; please greet him."

A chorus of "Good day, Domburger" fills

128

the whitewashed sickroom.

Jacob cannot believe his allotted minutes have passed so soon.

Marinus produces a metal cylinder about eight inches in length. It has a plunger at one end and a nozzle at the other. "This is, Mr. Muramoto?"

The elderly-looking youth replies, "It is call glister, Doctor."

"A glister." Marinus grips Jacob's shoulder. "Mr. Kajiwaki: to apply our glister?"

"Insert to rectum, and in-*jure* . . . no, in-*pact* . . . no, *aaa nan'dattaka?* In—"

"—*ject*," prompts Ikematsu, in a comic stage whisper.

"— in*ject* medicine for constipation, or pain of gut, or many other ailment."

"So we do, so we do; and, Mr. Yano, where lies the advantage in *anally* administered medicines over their *orally* administered counterparts?"

After the male students have distinguished "anal" from "oral," Yano responds, "Body more quick absorb medicine."

"Good." Marinus's slight smile is menacing. "Now. Who knows the *smoke* glister?"

The male seminarians confer without including Miss Aibagawa. At length, Muramoto says, "We do not know, Doctor."

"Nor could you, gentlemen: the smoke glister has never been seen in Japan until this hour. Eelattu, if you please!" Marinus's assistant enters, carrying a leather tube as long as a forearm and a deep-bellied lit pipe. The tube he hands to his master, who flourishes it like a wayside performer. "Our *smoke* glister, gentlemen, possesses a valve in its midriff, *here,* into which the leather tube is inserted, *here,* via which the cylinder can be filled with smoke. Please, Eelattu . . ." The Ceylonese inhales smoke from the pipe and exhales it into the leather tube. " 'Intussusception' is the ailment for which this instrument is the cure. Let us speak its name together, seminarians, for who can cure what he cannot pronounce? 'In-tus-sus-*cep*-tion!' " He waves one finger like a conductor's baton. "A-one, a-two, a-three . . ."

" 'In-tus-sus-*cep*-tion.' " The students falter. " 'Intus-sus-*cep*-tion.' "

"A terminal condition where an upper portion of the intestine passes into a lower, *thus*ly . . ." The doctor holds up a piece of sailcloth, stitched like a trouser leg. "This is the colon." He narrows one end in his fist, and feeds it backward inside the cloth tube toward the other end. "*Ouch* and *itai.* Diagnosis is difficult, its symptoms being the classic alimentary triad, namely, Mr. Ikematsu?"

"Abdomen pain, groin swelling . . ." He massages his temples to loosen the third. "Ah! Blood in feces."

"Good: death by intussusception, or," he looks at Jacob, "in the vernacular, 'shitting

130

out your own intestines,' is, as you would expect, a laborious affair. Its Latin name is *miserere mei,* translatable as 'Lord have mercy.' The *smoke* glister, however, can reverse this wrong," he pulls the knotted end of the sailcloth tube out again, "by puffing in such a density of smoke that the 'slippage' is reversed and the intestine restored to its natural state. Domburger, *in guerno* for favors granted, shall loan his *gluteus maximus* to medical science, that I may demonstrate the passage of smoke 'through caverns measureless to man' from anus to esophagus, whence smoke trickles through his nostrils like incense from a stone dragon, though not, alas, so sweet-scented, given its malodorous voyage."

Jacob begins to understand. "Surely, you don't intend —"

"Remove your breeches. We are all servants of medicine."

"Doctor." The sickroom is disagreeably cool. "I never consented to *this.*"

"To treat nerves," Marinus flips Jacob over with an agility belying the doctor's partial lameness, "ignore them. Eelattu: let the seminarians inspect the apparatus. Then we begin."

"A fine joke," wheezes Jacob, under two hundred pounds of Dutch physician, "but —"

Marinus unhooks the now-squirming

clerk's braces.

"*No,* Doctor! No! Your little joke has gone far e*nough . . .*"

CHAPTER SEVEN:
TALL HOUSE, DEJIMA

Early on Tuesday, August 27, 1799
The bed shakes its sleeper awake; two of its
legs snap, tipping Jacob onto the floor,
whacking his jaw and knee. *Merciful Christ* is
his first thought. *The* Shenandoah*'s magazine
is exploded.* But the spasm seizing Tall House
grows stronger and faster. Joists groan; plaster
patters like grapeshot; a window casement
flies from its mount and the lurching room is
lit apricot; the mosquito net enwraps Jacob's
face and the unappeasable violence is magnified threefold, fivefold, tenfold, and the bed
drags itself across the room like a wounded
beast. *A frigate, or a man-of-war, is unloosing a
broadside,* Jacob thinks. A candlestick hops in
dithyrambic circles; sheaves of paper from
high shelves swoop in loops. *Don't let me die
here,* Jacob prays, seeing his skull smashed
under beams and yolky brains dashed in Dejima's dust. Prayer grips the pastor's nephew,
raw-throated prayer, to the Jehovah of the
early Psalms: *O God, Thou hast cast us off,*

Thou hast scattered us, Thou hast been displeased; O turn Thyself to us again! Jacob is answered by roof tiles smashing on Long Street and cows lowing and goats bleating. *Thou hast made the earth to tremble; Thou hast broken it; heal the breaches thereof; for it shaketh.* Glass panes shatter into false diamonds, timber cracks like bones, Jacob's sea chest is tossed by undulating planks, the water jug spills and the chamber pot is upended and Creation herself is being undone and *God God God,* he implores, *bid it cease bid it cease bid it cease!*

The Lord of Hosts is with us; the God of Jacob is our refuge. Selah. Jacob shuts his eyes. Silence is peace. He thanks Providence for subduing the earthquake and thinks, *Dear Christ, the warehouses! My mercury calomel!* He snatches his clothes, steps over the flattened door, and meets Hanzaburo emerging from his nest. Jacob barks, "Guard my room!" but the boy does not understand. The Dutchman stands in the doorway and makes the shape of an X with his arms and legs. "Nobody enter! Understand?"

Hanzaburo nods nervously, as if he must placate a madman.

Jacob clatters down the stairs, unbolts the door, and finds Long Street looking as if an army of British looters just passed through.

134

Shutters lie in pieces, tiles lie in shards, the entire garden wall has collapsed. Dust thickens the air, corroding the sun. On the city's high eastern flank, black smoke billows, and somewhere a woman is wailing out her lungs. The clerk makes his way to the chief's residence but collides with Wybo Gerritszoon at the crossroads. The hand sways and slurs, "Bastard French bastards've landed an' the bastards're everywhere!"

"Mr. Gerritszoon: see to the Doorn and the Eik. I'll check elsewhere."

"You," the tattooed strongman spits, *"parleyin' wi' me, Monsewer Jacques?"*

Jacob steps around him and tests the Doorn's door: it is secure.

Gerritszoon grabs the clerk's throat and roars, "Get yer *filthy French hands* off my house an' take yer *filthy French fingers* off my *sister!"* He relinquishes his grip in order to hurl a jaw-breaker: had its aim been true it could have killed Jacob, but instead its force flings Gerritszoon onto the ground. "French bastards winged me! *Winged* me!"

In Flag Square, the muster bell begins to ring.

"Ig*nore* that bell!" Vorstenbosch, flanked by Cupido and Philander, paces up Long Street. "The jackals would line us up like children even as they reef us!" He notices Gerritszoon. "Is he injured?"

Jacob rubs his aching throat. "By grog, I

fear, sir."

"Leave him be. We must guard ourselves against our protectors."

The damage caused by the earthquake is bad but not disastrous. Of the four Dutch-owned warehouses, the Lelie is still under reconstruction following Snitker's Fire, and its frame held firm; the doors stayed up on the Doorn; and Van Cleef and Jacob were able to guard the damaged Eik against looters until Con Twomey and the *Shenandoah*'s carpenter, a wraithlike Québecois, had rehung the thrown-down doors. Captain Lacy reported that while they didn't feel the earthquake on board the ship, the noise was as loud as war between God and the devil. Some tens of crates, moreover, toppled onto the floor in various warehouses; all must be inspected for breakages and spillages. Dozens of roof tiles must be replaced, new earthenware urns must be procured; the flattened bathhouse must be repaired at the company's expense and the toppled dovecote mended; and the plaster shaken loose from the north wall of Garden House will have to be applied again from scratch. Interpreter Kobayashi reported that the boathouses where the company sampans are stored collapsed and quoted what he called "a superlative price" for repairs. Vorstenbosch shot back, "Superlative for whom?" and swore not to part with a *pen-*

ning until he and Twomey had inspected the damage themselves. The interpreter left in a state of stony anger. From the watchtower, Jacob could see that not every ward in Nagasaki escaped as lightly as Dejima: he counted twenty substantial buildings collapsed and four serious fires pouring smoke into the late August sky.

In Warehouse Eik, Jacob and Weh sort through crates of toppled Venetian mirrors: every last glass is to be unwrapped from its straw and recorded as undamaged, cracked, or smashed. Hanzaburo curls up on a pile of sacking, and soon he is asleep. For most of the morning, the only sounds are mirrors being laid aside, Weh chewing betel nut, the scratch of Jacob's nib, and, over at the sea gate, porters bringing ashore tin and lead. The carpenters who would ordinarily be at work on Warehouse Lelie, across the weighing yard, are engaged, Jacob guesses, on more-pressing jobs in Nagasaki.

"Well, it ain't seven years o' bad luck here, Mr. de Z., but seven *'undred,* eh?"

Jacob hadn't noticed Arie Grote enter.

"Quite pard'nable 'twould be, eh, were a cove to lose count an' enter a few whole mirrors as 'smashed,' wholly in error . . ."

"Is this a thinly veiled invitation" — Jacob yawns — "to commit fraud?"

"May wild dogs chew my head off first!

137

Now, I've arranged a meetin' for us. *You,*" Grote glances at Weh, "can make yerself scarce: a gent's comin' what'd take offense at your shit-brown hide."

"Weh is going nowhere," counters Jacob. "And who is this 'gent'?"

Grote hears something and peers out. "Oh, bloody oath, they're *early.*" He points to a wall of crates and orders Weh, "Hide behind there! Mr. de Z., dispense with yer *sentiments* regardin' our sable brethren, 'cause piles an' piles an' *piles* o' *money* is at stake."

The slave youth looks at Jacob; Jacob, reluctantly, nods; Weh obeys.

"I am here, eh, to play the go-between twixt *you* and —"

Interpreter Yonekizu and Constable Kosugi appear at the door.

Ignoring Jacob altogether, both men usher in a familiar stranger.

Four young, lithe, and grim personal guards appear first.

Next enters their master: an older man who walks as if treading on water. He wears a sky-blue cape and his head is shaven, though a sword hilt shows from his waist sash.

His is the only face in the warehouse not sheathed in sweat.

From what flickering dream, wonders Jacob, *do I know* your *face?*

"Lord Abbot Enomoto of the Domain of Kyôga," announces Grote. "My associate,

Mr. de Zoet."

Jacob bows: the abbot's lips tighten into a smile of recognition.

He speaks to Yonekizu in a burnished, uninterruptible voice.

"Abbot," translates Yonekizu, "says he believed you and he share affinity, on first time he see you at magistracy. Today he know his belief was correct."

Abbot Enomoto asks Yonekizu to teach him the Dutch word "affinity."

Jacob now identifies his visitor: he was the man sitting close to Magistrate Shiroyama in the Hall of Sixty Mats.

The abbot has Yonekizu repeat Jacob's name three times over.

"Da-zû-to," echoes the abbot, and checks: "I say correct?"

"Your Grace," Jacob says, "speaks my name very well."

"The abbot," Yonekizu adds, "translated Antoine Lavoisier into Japanese."

Jacob is duly impressed. "Might Your Grace know Marinus?"

The abbot has Yonekizu translate his reply: "Abbot meet Dr. Marinus at Shirandô Academy often. He has much respect for Dutch scholar, he say. But abbot also have many duties, so cannot devote all life to chemical arts."

Jacob considers the power his visitor must wield to waltz into Dejima on a day turned upside down by the earthquake and mingle with foreigners, free from the usual phalanx of spies and shogunal guards. Enomoto runs his thumb along the crates, as if divining their contents. He encounters the sleeping Hanzaburo and makes a motion in the air above the boy, like a genuflection. Hanzaburo mouths groggy syllables, wakes, sees the abbot, yelps, and rolls onto the floor. He flees from the warehouse like a frog from a water snake.

"Young mans," Enomoto says in Dutch, "hurry, hurry, hurry . . ."

The world outside, framed by the Eik's double doors, dims.

The abbot handles an undamaged mirror. "This is quicksilver?"

"Silver oxide," replies Jacob. "Of Italian manufacture."

"Silver is more truth," remarks the abbot, "than copper mirrors of Japan. But truth is easy to break." He angles the mirror so as to capture Jacob's reflection and puts a question to Yonekizu in Japanese. Yonekizu says, "His Grace ask, 'At Holland also, do dead people lack reflection?' "

Jacob recalls his grandmother saying as much. "Old women believe so, sir, yes."

The abbot understands and is pleased with the answer.

"There is a tribe at the Cape of Good Hope," Jacob ventures, "called the Basutos, who credit a crocodile may kill a man by snapping his reflection in the water. Another tribe, the Zulus, avoid dark pools lest a ghost seize the reflection and devour the observer's soul."

Yonekizu gives a careful translation and explains Enomoto's reply. "The abbot says idea is beautiful and wishes to know, 'Does Mr. de Zoet believe in soul?' "

"To *doubt* the soul," says Jacob, "would strike me as peculiar."

Enomoto asks, "Does Mr. de Zoet believe soul can be taked?"

"Taken not by a ghost or crocodile, no, but by the devil, yes."

Enomoto's *ha* denotes surprise that he and a foreigner could agree so well.

Jacob steps out of the mirror's field of reflection. "Your Grace's Dutch is excellent."

"Listening difficult" — Enomoto turns — "so glad interpreters is here. Once I speak — spoke — Spanish, but now knowledge is decayed."

"It is two centuries," says Jacob, "since the Spaniards walked Japan."

"Time . . ." Idly, Enomoto lifts the lid of a box; Yonekizu exclaims in alarm.

Coiled like a small whip is a *habu* snake. It rears its angry head . . .

. . . its twin fangs glint white; its neck sways back, ready to strike.

Two of the abbot's guards rush up, swords

drawn . . .

. . . but Enomoto makes a pressing motion with his flat hand.

"Don't let it bite him!" exclaims Grote. "He ain't yet paid for the —"

Instead of attacking the abbot's hand, the *habu*'s neck turns limp, and it slumps back on its crate. Its jaws are frozen, wide open.

Jacob's jaws, too, are agape; he glances at Grote, who looks afraid.

"Your Grace, did you . . . charm the snake? Is it . . . is it asleep?"

"Snake is dead." Enomoto orders his guard to take it outside.

How did you do that? Jacob wonders, searching for tricks. "But . . ."

The abbot sees the Dutchman's bafflement and speaks to Yonekizu.

"Lord abbot say," begins Yonekizu, " 'Not trick, not magic.' He says, 'It is Chinese philosophy who scholars of Europe is too clever to understand.' He says . . . excuse, very difficult. He says, 'All life *is* life because possess force of *ki*.' "

"Force of *key?*" Arie Grote mimes turning a key. "What's that?"

Yonekizu shakes his head. "Not key: *ki*. *Ki*. Lord abbot explain that his studies, his order, teach how to . . . what is word? How to *manipule* force of *ki*, to heal sickness, et cetera."

"Oh, Mr. Snaky," mutters Grote, "got his fair share of *et cetera*."

Given the abbot's status, Jacob worries that an apology is due. "Mr. Yonekizu: pray tell His Grace how sorry I am that a snake threatened his well-being in a Dutch warehouse."

Yonekizu does so; Enomoto shakes his head. "Nasty bite, but not very poison."

". . . and say," continues Jacob, "what I just saw shall stay with me all my life."

Enomoto replies with an ambiguous *hnnnnnn* noise.

"In next life," the abbot tells Jacob, "be born in Japan so come to shrine, and — excuse, Dutch is difficult." He addresses several long sentences to Yonekizu in their mother tongue. The interpreter translates them in order. "Abbot says, Mr. de Zoet must not think he is powerful lord like lord of Satsuma. Kyôga Domain is only twenty miles wide, twenty miles long, very many mountains, and has just two towns, Isahaya and Kashima, and villages along road of Sea of Ariake. But," Yonekizu perhaps adds this on his own initiative, "special domain gives lord abbot high rank — in Edo can meet shogun, in Miyako, can meet emperor. Lord abbot's shrine is high on Shiranui Mountain. He say, 'In spring and autumn, very beautiful; in winter, a little cold, but summer, cool.' Abbot say, 'One can breathe and does not grow old.' Abbot say, 'He have two lifes. World above, at Mount Shiranui, is spirit and prayer and *ki*.

143

World below is men and politics and scholars . . . and import drugs and money.' "

"Oh, at flamin' *last,*" mutters Arie Grote.
"Mr. de Z.: this is our cue."

Jacob looks uncertainly at Grote, at the abbot, and back at the cook.

"Raise," sighs Grote, "the subject o' trade."
He mouths the word "mercury."

Jacob, belatedly, understands. "Pardon my
directness, Your Grace," he addresses
Enomoto while glancing at Yonekizu, "but
may we render any service today?"

Yonekizu translates; with a glance, Enomoto
sends the query back to Grote.

"Fact, Mr. de Z., is this: Abbot Enomoto
wishes to pur*chase,* eh, *all* eight chests of our
mercury powder for the sum of *one* hundred
an' six *koban* per crate."

Jacob's first thought is, *"Our" mercury?* His
second is, *One* hundred *and six?*

His third thought is a number: *eight hundred
and forty-eight* koban.

"Twice as much again," Grote reminds him,
"as the Osaka druggist."

Eight hundred and forty-eight *koban* is a
half fortune, at least.

Wait, wait, wait, Jacob thinks. *Why so high a
price?*

"Mr. de Zoet's so 'appy," Grote assures
Enomoto, "he can't speak."

The snake trick dazzled my senses, but keep

a calm head now . . .

"A more de*servin'* cove," Grote says, clapping Jacob's shoulder, "I never knew . . ."

. . . a monopoly, Jacob hypothesizes. *He's after a temporary monopoly.*

"I'll sell six crates," the young clerk announces. "Not eight."

Enomoto understands; he scratches an ear and looks at Grote.

Grote's smile says, *Nothing to worry about.* "A moment, Your Grace."

The cook steers Jacob into a corner, near Weh's hiding place.

"Listen: Zwaardecroone set the sell peg at eighteen per chest."

How can you know, Jacob wonders, astonished, *about my backer in Batavia?*

" 'Tain't no import *how* I know, but I *do.* We're up to *six times* that, yet here you are harpin' for *more?* No better price'll come knockin', an' *six* chests ain't on the table. It's *eight,* see, or nothin' at all."

"In that case," Jacob tells Grote, "I choose nothing at all."

" 'Tis plain we *ain't* makin' ourselfs *clear!* Our client is an *exalted personage,* eh? Irons in every fire: at the magistracy; in Edo; a moneylender's moneylender; a druggist's druggist. Word has it, he's even" — Jacob smells chicken livers on Grote's breath — "lendin' to the magistrate to pay graft till next year's ship from Batavia comes in! So when I promised him the entire supply o' mercury, that's exactly —"

"It appears you shall have to *un*promise him the entire supply."

"No no *no*," Grote almost whinnies. "You ain't under*standin'* what —"

"It was you who hatched a deal on *my* private goods; I refuse to dance to your piper; so now you stand to lose your brokerage fee. What am I not understanding?"

Enomoto is saying something to Yonekizu; the Dutchmen break off their argument.

"Abbot say," Yonekizu clears his throat, "six crates only is sale today. So he buy just six crates today." Enomoto continues. Yonekizu nods, clarifies a couple of points, and translates. "Mr. de Zoet: Abbot Enomoto credits your private account in Exchequer with six hundred thirty-six *koban*s. Magistracy scribe bring proof of payment in company ledger. Then, when you satisfied, his men remove six crates of mercury from Warehouse Eik."

Such speed is unprecedented. "Doesn't Your Grace wish to see it first?"

"Ah," says Grote, "Mr. de Z. bein' such a busy cove, I took the little liberty o' borrowin' the key from Deputy van C. an' showin' our guest a sample —"

"Yes, that *was* a liberty you took," Jacob tells him. "A big one."

"Hundred an' six a box," Grote sighs, "deserves a little *'nitiative,* eh?"

The abbot is waiting. "Do we deal mercury, Mr. Dazûto?"

"Deal he *does,* Your Grace." Grote smiles like a delighted weasel.

"But the paperwork," asks Jacob, "the bribes, documents of sale . . . ?"

Enomoto swats away these difficulties and expels a *pfff* of air.

"Like I say" — Grote bows — " 'a *most* exalted personage.' "

"Then . . ." Jacob has no more objections. "Yes, Your Grace. The deal is agreed."

A sigh of punctured anguish escapes the much-relieved Arie Grote.

Wearing a calm expression, the abbot gives Yonekizu a sentence to translate.

" 'What you not sell today,' " Yonekizu says, " 'you sell soon.' "

"Then the lord abbot" — Jacob remains defiant — "knows my mind better than I."

Abbot Enomoto has the last word: the word is "Affinity." Then he nods at Kosugi and Yonekizu, and his retinue leaves the warehouse without further ado.

"You can come out now, Weh." Jacob is obscurely troubled, despite the likelihood of his going to bed tonight a much richer man than when the earthquake threw him from it this morning. *Provided,* he concedes, *Lord Abbot Enomoto is as good as his word.*

Lord Abbot Enomoto is as good as his word.

147

At half past two, Jacob walks down the steps from the chief's residence in possession of a Certificate of Lodgment. Witnessed by Vorstenbosch and Van Cleef, the document can be redeemed in Batavia or even at the company's Zeeland offices in Vlissingen on Walcheren. The sum represents five or six years' salary from his former job as a shipping clerk. He must repay the friend of his uncle in Batavia who lent him the capital to buy the medicinal mercury — *the luckiest gamble of my life,* Jacob thinks; *how nearly I bought the* bêche-de-mer *instead* — and no doubt Arie Grote has not done badly from the deal, but, by any measure, the transaction made with the enigmatic abbot is an exceptionally lucrative one. *And the remaining crates,* Jacob anticipates, *shall fetch an even higher price, once other traders see the profit that Enomoto earns.* By Christmas of next year he should be back in Batavia with Unico Vorstenbosch, whose star should, by then, be even brighter as a consequence of purging Dejima of its notorious corruption. He could consult with Zwaardecroone or Vorstenbosch's colleagues and invest his mercury money in a yet bigger venture — coffee, perhaps, or teak — to generate an income that might impress even Anna's father.

Back on Long Street, Hanzaburo reappears from the Interpreters' Guild. Jacob returns to

Tall House to deposit his precious certificate in his sea chest. He hesitates before taking out a paulownia-handled fan and putting it in his jacket pocket. Then he hurries to the weighing yard, where, today, lead ingots are being weighed and checked for adulterants before being returned to their boxes and sealed. Even under the supervisors' awning, the heat is sleepy and torrid, but a vigilant eye must be kept on the scales, the coolies, and the numbers of boxes.

"How kind of you," says Peter Fischer, "to report for duty."

News of the new clerk's profit on his mercury is common knowledge.

Jacob cannot think of a reply, so he takes over the tally sheet.

Interpreter Yonekizu watches the adjacent awning. It is slow work.

Jacob thinks about Anna, trying to remember her as she is and not merely as in his sketches of her.

Sun-coppered coolies prize off the nailed-on lids from the crates . . .

Wealth brings our future together closer, he thinks, *but five years is still a long, long time.*

Sun-coppered coolies hammer the lids back on to the crates.

Four o'clock, according to Jacob's pocket watch, comes and goes.

At a certain point, Hanzaburo wanders away without explanation.

At a quarter to five, Peter Fischer says, "That is the two-hundredth box."

At a minute past five, a senior merchant faints in the heat.

Immediately, Dr. Marinus is sent for, and Jacob makes a decision.

"Would you excuse me," Jacob asks Fischer, "for a minute?"

Fischer fills his pipe with provocative slowness. "How long is your minute? Ouwehand's minute is fifteen or twenty. Baert's minute is longer than an hour."

Jacob stands; his legs have pins and needles. "I shall return in ten."

"So your 'one' means 'ten'; in Prussia, a gentleman says what he means."

"I'll go," mutters Jacob, perhaps audibly, "before I do just that."

Jacob waits at the busy crossroads, watching the laborers pass to and fro. Dr. Marinus is not long in coming: he limps past, with a pair of house interpreters carrying his medical box to attend the fainted merchant. He sees Jacob but does not acknowledge him, which suits Jacob. The turd-scented smoke escaping his esophagus at the end of the smoke-glister experiment cured him of any desire for Marinus's friendship. The humiliation he suffered that day has caused him to avoid Miss Aibagawa: how can she — and the other seminarians — ever regard him as anything but a half-naked apparatus of fatty valves and fleshy pipes?

Six hundred and thirty-six kobans, he admits, *salve one's self-esteem, however . . .*

The seminarians leave the hospital: Jacob predicted that their lecture would be cut short by Marinus's summons. Miss Aibagawa is rearmost, half hidden by a parasol. He withdraws a few steps into Bony Alley, as if he is going to Warehouse Lelie.

All I am doing, Jacob assures himself, *is returning a lost item to its owner.*

The four young men, two guards, and one midwife turn into Short Street.

Jacob loses his nerve; Jacob regains his nerve. "Excuse me!"

The retinue turns around. Miss Aibagawa meets his eyes.

Muramoto, the senior student, greets Jacob. "Dombâga-*san!*"

Jacob removes his bamboo hat. "Another hot day, Mr. Muramoto."

He is pleased that Jacob remembers his name; the others join his bow. "Hot, hot," they agree warmly. "Hot!"

Jacob bows to the midwife. "Good afternoon, Miss Aibagawa."

"How" — her eyes betray a droll mischief — "is Mr. Domburger's liver?"

"Much better today, I thank you." He swallows. "I thank you."

"Ah," says Ikematsu, with mock sobriety.

"But how is in-tus-sus-*cep*-tion?"

"Dr. Marinus's magic cured me. What did you study today?"

"*Kan-somu-shan,*" says Kajiwaki. "When cough blood from lungs."

"Oh, con*sum*ption. A terrible disease, and a common one."

An inspector approaches from the land gate: a guard speaks.

"Your pardon, sir," says Muramoto, "but he says we must leave."

"Yes, I shan't detain you. I just wish to return this" — he produces the fan from his jacket and proffers it — "to Miss Aibagawa, who left it at the hospital today."

Her eyes flash with alarm: they demand, *What are you doing?*

His courage evaporates. "The fan you for*got* in the hospital."

The inspector arrives. Glowering, he speaks to Muramoto.

Muramoto says, "Inspector ask, 'What is?' Mr. Dombâga."

"Tell him . . ." *This is a terrible mistake.* "Miss Aibagawa forgot her fan. At Dr. Marinus's hospital. I am returning it."

The inspector is unimpressed. He issues a curt demand and holds out his hand for the fan, like a schoolmaster demanding a schoolboy's note.

"He ask, 'Please show,' Mr. Dombâga," translates Ikematsu. "To check."

If I obey, Jacob realizes, *all Dejima, all Nagasaki, shall learn how I drew her likeness and pasted it, in strips, onto a fan.* This friendly token of esteem, Jacob sees, shall be misconstrued. It may even light the touch paper of a minor scandal.

The inspector's fingers are troubled by the stiff catch.

Blushing in anticipation, Jacob prays for some — for any — deliverance.

Quietly, Miss Aibagawa says something to the inspector.

The inspector looks at her; his grimness softens, just a little . . .

. . . then he snorts with gruff amusement and hands her the fan. She gives a slight bow.

Jacob feels admonished by this narrowest of escapes.

The bright night is raucous with parties, both on Dejima and ashore, as if to frighten away the bad memory of the morning's earthquake. Paper lanterns are strung along Nagasaki's principal thoroughfares, and impromptu drinking parties are taking place at Constable Kosugi's house, Deputy van Cleef's residence, the Interpreters' Guild, and even the land gate's guardroom. Jacob and Ogawa Uzaemon have met on the watchtower. Ogawa brought an inspector to ward off accusations of fraternizing, but he was already drunk, and a flask of *sake* has set him snoring. Hanzaburo is perched a few steps below the platform with Ouwehand's latest much put-upon house interpreter: "I cured myself of herpes," Ouwehand boasted, at the evening mustering. An overladen moon has run aground on Mount Inasa, and Jacob enjoys the cool breeze, despite its soot and smell of effluence. "What are *those* clustered lights," he asks, pointing, "up above the city?"

"More *O-bon* parties, in . . . *how to say?* . . . place where bury corpses."

"Graveyards? You never hold parties in graveyards!" Jacob thinks of *gavottes* in Domburg's graveyard and almost laughs.

"Graveyard is gate of dead," says Ogawa, "so good place to call souls to world of life. Tomorrow night, small fireboats float on sea to guide souls home."

On the *Shenandoah,* the officer of the watch strikes four bells.

"You truly," Jacob asks, "believe souls migrate in such a manner?"

"Mr. de Zoet not believe what he is told when boy?"

But mine is the true faith. Jacob pities Ogawa. *Whilst yours is idolatry.*

Down at the land gate, an officer is barking at an inferior.

I am a company employee, he reminds himself, *not a missionary.*

"Anyway." Ogawa produces a porcelain flask from his sleeve.

154

Jacob is already a little drunk. "How many of those are you hiding?"

"I am not on duty" — Ogawa refills their cups — "so drink to your good profit today."

Jacob is warmed by the thought of his money and by the *sake* roaring down his gullet. "Is there anyone in Nagasaki who *doesn't* know how much profit my mercury yielded?"

Firecrackers explode in the Chinese factory across the harbor.

"There is one monk in very very *very* highest cave," Ogawa says, pointing up the mountainside, "who has not heard, not yet. To speak with sobriety, however: price goes higher, this is good, but sell last mercury to Lord Abbot Enomoto, not another. Please. He is dangerous enemy."

"Arie Grote has the same fearful opinion of His Grace."

The breeze carries over the smell of the Chinamen's gunpowder.

"Mr. Grote is wise. Abbot's domain is small, but he is . . ." Ogawa hesitates. "He is much power. Besides shrine in Kyôga, he has residence here in Nagasaki, house in Miyako. In Edo, he is guest of Matsudaira Sadanobu. Sadanobu-*sama* is much power . . . 'kingmaker,' you say? Any close friend such as Enomoto is also power. Is bad enemy. Please, remember."

Jacob drinks. "Surely, as a Dutchman, I have safety from 'bad enemies.' "

155

When Ogawa makes no reply, the Dutchman feels less safe.

Beach fires dot the shoreline, all the way to the bay's mouth.

Jacob wonders what Miss Aibagawa thinks of her illustrated fan.

Cats tryst on Deputy van Cleef's roof, below the platform.

Jacob surveys the hillsides of roofs and wonders which is hers.

"Mr. Ogawa: in Japan, how does a gentleman propose to a lady?"

The interpreter decodes. "Mr. de Zoet want to 'butter your artichoke'?"

Jacob loses half a mouthful of *sake* in spectacular fashion.

Ogawa is very concerned. "I make mistake with Dutch?"

"Captain Lacy has been enriching your vocabulary again?"

"He give tuition for I and Interpreter Iwase on 'Gentlemanly Dutch.' "

Jacob lets it pass for now. "When *you* asked for your wife's hand in marriage, did you first approach her father? Or give her a ring? Or flowers? Or . . . ?"

Ogawa fills their cups. "I not see wife before wedding day. Our *nakôdo* made match. How to say *nakôdo*? Woman who knows families who want marriage . . ."

"An interfering busybody? No, forgive me: a go-between."

" 'Go-between'? Funny word. 'Go-between' *go between* our families, *achi-kochi*" — Ogawa moves his hand like a shuttle — "describes bride to father. Her father is rich merchant of sappanwood dye in Karatsu, three days' journey. We investigate family . . . no madness, secret debt, et cetera. Her father come in Nagasaki to meet Ogawas of Nagasaki. Merchants lower class than samurai, but . . ." Ogawa's hands become the pans of a weighing scale. "Ogawa stipend is safe, and we involve sappanwood trade via Dejima, and so father agrees. We meet next in shrine on wedding day."

The buoyant moon has freed itself from Mount Inasa.

"What about," Jacob speaks with *sake*-inspired frankness, "what about love?"

"We say, 'When husband love wife, mother-in-law loses her best servant.' "

"What a joyless proverb! Don't you yearn for love, in your hearts?"

"*Yes,* Mr. de Zoet say truth: love is thing of *heart.* Or love is like this *sake:* drink, night of joy, yes, but in cold morning, headache, sick stomach. A man should love concubine, so when love dies he say, 'Goodbye,' easy and no injury. Marriage is different: marriage is matter of *head* . . . rank . . . business . . . bloodline. Holland families are not same?"

Jacob recalls Anna's father. "We are exactly the same, alas."

157

A shooting star lives and dies in an instant.

"Do I not keep you from welcoming your own ancestors, Mr. Ogawa?"

"My father performs rituals at family residence tonight."

The cow lows in the Pine Tree Corner, upset by the firecrackers.

"To speak with sincerity," says Ogawa, "my blood ancestors is not here: I was borned at Tosa Domain, on Shikoku, which is big island" — Ogawa points east — "that way, to father of low retainer of Lord Yamanouchi of Tosa. Lord gave my schooling and sent me in Nagasaki for learn Dutch under Ogawa Mimasaku's house to make bridge between his Tosa and Dejima. But then old Lord Yamanouchi died. His son has no interest in Dutch studies. So I was 'marooned,' you say? But then Ogawa Mimasaku's two sons died in cholera, ten years ago. Much, much death in city that year. So Ogawa Mimasaku adopted me, to continue family name."

"What about your own mother and father back on Shikoku?"

"Tradition says, 'After adoption, do not go back.' So I not go back."

"Didn't you miss them?" Jacob recalls his own bereavement.

"I had new name, new life, new father, new mother, new ancestors."

Does the Japanese race, wonders Jacob, *derive gratification from self-inflicted misery?*

"My study of Dutch," says Ogawa, "is great . . . solace. Is correct word?"

"Yes, and your fluency," the clerk says, quite sincerely, "shows how hard you work."

"To progress is difficult. Merchants, officials, guards not understand how hard. They think, My *work* I *do: why lazy and foolish interpreter cannot do same?*"

"During my apprenticeship" — Jacob unfolds his stiff legs — "to a timber company, I worked at the ports of not only Rotterdam but also London, Paris, Copenhagen, and Gothenburg. I know the vexations of foreign languages, but unlike you, *I* had the advantages of dictionaries and an education populated by French schoolmasters."

Ogawa's "Ah . . ." is full of longing. "So many places, you can go . . ."

"In Europe, yes, but not one toe can I put past the land gate."

"But Mr. de Zoet may pass through *sea* gate and away, over ocean. But I — *all* Japanese" — Ogawa listens to Hanzaburo and his friend's conspiratorial grumbles — "prisoners all life. Who plot to leave is executed. Who leave and return from abroad is executed. My precious wish is one year in Batavia, to speak Dutch . . . to eat Dutch, to drink Dutch, to sleep Dutch. One year, just one year . . ."

These are new thoughts for Jacob. "Do you recall your first visit to Dejima?"

"*Very* well I recall! Before Ogawa Mimasaku adopt me as son. One day, master announce, 'Today, we go Dejima.' I —" Ogawa clutches his heart and mimes awe. "We walk over Holland Bridge and my master says, 'This is longest bridge you ever cross, because this bridge go between two worlds.' We pass through land gate and I see giant from story! Nose big like potato! Clotheses with no tie strings but buttons, buttons, buttons and hair yellow, like straw! Smell bad, too. Just as astonishment, I first see *kuronbô,* black boys who skin like eggplant. Then foreigner opened mouth and say, *'Schffgg-evingen-flinder-vasschen-morgengen!' This* was same Dutch I study so hard? I just bow and bow, and master hits my head and says, 'Introduce self, foolish *baka!'* so I say, 'My name is Sôzaemon *degozaimsu* weather is clement today I thank you very well, sir.' Yellow giant laugh and says, *'Ksssfffkkk schevingen-pevingen!'* and points to marvel white bird who walk like man and tall as man. Master says, 'This is ostrich.' Then much bigger marvel, animal big as shack, blocks out sun; *nyoro-nyoro* nose he dips in bucket and drinks and shoots water! Master Ogawa say, 'Elephant,' and I say, *'Zô?'* and master says, 'No, foolish *baka,* it is *elephant.'* Then we see cockatoo in cage, and parrot who repeat words, strange game with sticks and balls on table-of-walls, called 'billiards.' Bloody tongues lying on ground

160

here, there, here, there: cud of betel juice, spat by Malay servants."

"What," Jacob has to ask, "was an elephant doing on Dejima?"

"Batavia sent for gift for shogun. But magistrate sent message to Edo to say he eat much food so Edo discuss and say, *no, company* must take elephant back. Elephant die of mystery ill very soon —"

Running footsteps thump up the stairs of the watchtower: it is a messenger.

Jacob can tell from Hanzaburo's response that the news is bad.

"We must go," Ogawa informs him. "Thieves in house of Chief Vorstenbosch."

"The strongbox being too heavy to steal," Unico Vorstenbosch says, showing the audience crowded into his private quarters, "the robbers heaved it around and staved in the back with a hammer and chisel — look." He pulls a strip of teak from the iron frame. "When the hole was big enough, they extracted their prize and made good their escape. This was not petty theft. They had the right tools. They knew exactly what they were after. They had spies, spotters, and the skills to smash a strongbox in complete silence. They also had a blind eye at the land gate. In short" — the chief resident glares at Interpreter Kobayashi — "they had help."

Constable Kosugi asks a question. "The

161

headman asks," translates Iwase, "when last time you saw teapot?"

"This morning. Cupido checked it was unscathed by the earthquake."

The constable heaves a weary sigh and issues a flat observation.

"Constable say," Iwase translates, "slave is last who see teapot on Dejima."

"The *thieves,* sir," Vorstenbosch exclaims, "were the last to see it!"

Interpreter Kobayashi tilts his shrewd head. "What was value of teapot?"

"Exquisite craftsmanship, silver leafing on jade — a thousand *koban*s could not buy another. You have seen it yourself. It belonged to the last Ming ruler of China — the 'Chongzhen' emperor, as I gather he is known. It is an irreplaceable antique — as *someone* surely told the thieves, damn their eyes."

"Chongzhen emperor," observes Kobayashi, "hang himself from pagoda tree."

"I did not summon you here for a history lesson, Interpreter!"

"I hope earnestly," Kobayashi explains, "that teapot is not curse."

"Oh, it's cursed for the damned dogs who *stole* it! The company is the owner of the teapot, not Unico Vorstenbosch, and so the Company is the victim of this crime. *You,* Interpreter, shall go with Constable Kosugi to the magistracy *now.*"

"Magistracy is close tonight." Kobayashi wrings his palms. "For *O-bon* festival."

"The magistracy" — the chief hits the desk with his cane — "will have to *open!*"

Jacob knows the look on the Japanese faces: *impossible foreigners.*

"May I suggest, sir," says Peter Fischer, "that you demand searches of the Japanese warehouses on Dejima? Perhaps the sly bastards are waiting until the fuss has died down before smuggling your treasure away."

"Well spoke, Fischer." The chief looks at Kobayashi. "Tell the constable so."

The interpreter's tilted head denotes reluctance. "But precedent is —"

"*Hang* precedent! *I* am the precedent now, and *you,* sir, *you*" — he pokes a chest that, Jacob would wager a sheaf of banknotes, has never been poked before — "are paid *usuriously* to *protect* our interests! Do your job! Some coolie, or merchant, or inspector, or, yes, even an *interpreter* stole the company's property. This act insults the company's honor. And by damn, I shall have the Interpreters' Guild searched, as well! The perpetrators shall be hunted down like pigs, and I shall make them *squeal.* De Zoet — go and tell Arie Grote to make a large jug of coffee. None of us shall be sleeping for some time yet . . ."

CHAPTER EIGHT:
THE STATEROOM IN
THE CHIEF'S HOUSE
ON DEJIMA

Ten o'clock in the morning of September 3, 1799

"The shogun's reply to my ultimatum is a message for *me*," complains Vorstenbosch. "Why must a piece of paper rolled up in a tube spend the night at the magistracy, like a pampered guest? If it arrived yesterday evening, why wasn't it brought to me straightaway?" *Because,* Jacob thinks, *a message from the shogun is the equivalent of a papal edict, and to deny it due ceremony would be capital treason.* He keeps his mouth shut, however; in recent days, he has noticed a growing coolness in his patron's attitude toward him. The process is discreet: a word of praise to Peter Fischer here, a curt remark to Jacob there, but the onetime "Indispensable de Zoet" fears that his halo is dimming. Nor does Van Cleef attempt to answer the chief resident's question. Long ago, he acquired the courtier's knack of distinguishing the rhetorical question from the actual.

Captain Lacy leans back on his groaning chair with his head behind his hands and whistles between his teeth very softly. Waiting on the Japanese side of the state table are Interpreters Kobayashi and Iwase and just two senior scribes. "Magistrate's chamberlain," Iwase offers, "shall bring shogun's message soon."

Unico Vorstenbosch scowls at the gold signet on his ring finger.

"What did William the Silent," wonders Lacy, "say about his moniker?"

The grandfather clock is grave and loud. The men are hot and silent.

"Sky this afternoon is . . ." remarks Interpreter Kobayashi ". . . unstable."

"The barometer in my cabin," agrees Lacy, "promises a blow."

Interpreter Kobayashi's expression is courteous but blank.

"A 'blow' is a storm," explains Van Cleef, "or gale, or typhoon."

"Ah, ah." Interpreter Iwase understands. " 'Typhoon' . . . *tai-fû*, we say."

Kobayashi dabs his shaved forehead. "Funeral for summer."

"Unless the shogun has agreed to raise the copper quota," Vorstenbosch says, folding his arms, "it is Dejima that shall need a funeral: Dejima, and the well-feathered careers of its interpreters. Speaking of which, Mr. Kobayashi, do I take it from your studied silence regarding the company's stolen item of chinaware that not one inch of progress has been made toward its recovery?"

"Investigation is continuing," replies the senior interpreter.

"At the speed of a slug," mutters the chief resident. "Even if we *do* remain on Dejima, I shall report to Governor-General van Overstraten how indifferently you defend the company's property."

Jacob's sharp ears hear marching feet; Van Cleef hears them, too.

The deputy goes to a window and looks down onto Long Street. "Ah, at last."

Two guards stand on either side of the doorway. A bannerman enters first: his pennant displays the three-leafed hollyhock of the Tokugawa Shogunate. Chamberlain Tomine enters, holding the revered scroll tube on a perfect lacquered tray. All the men in the room bow toward the scroll, except Vorstenbosch, who says, "Come in, then, Chamberlain, sit down, and let us learn whether His Highness in Edo has decided to put this damned island out of its misery."

Jacob notices the half-repressed winces on the Japanese faces.

Iwase translates the "sit down" part and indicates a chair.

Tomine looks with distaste at the foreign furniture but has no choice.

He places the lacquered tray before Interpreter Kobayashi and bows.

Kobayashi bows to him, to the scroll tube, and slides its tray to the chief.

Vorstenbosch takes up the cylinder, emblazoned on one end with the same hollyhock insignia, and tries to pull it apart. Failing, he tries to unscrew it. Failing, he tries to find a toggle or catch.

"Pardon, sir," murmurs Jacob, "but it may need a *clockwise* twist."

"Oh, *back to front* and *topsy-turvy,* like this whole blasted country . . ."

Out slides a parchment wound tight around two dowels of cherrywood.

Vorstenbosch unrolls it on the table, vertically, like a European scroll.

Jacob has a good view. The ornate columns of brushstroked *kanji* characters offer, to the clerk's eyes, moments of recognition: the Dutch lessons he gives Ogawa Uzaemon involve a reciprocal aspect, and his notebook now contains some five hundred of the symbols. Here the clandestine student recognizes "Give"; there, "Edo"; in the next column, "ten" . . .

"Naturally," Vorstenbosch sighs, "nobody at the shogun's court writes Dutch. Would either of you prodigies," he looks at the interpreters, "care to oblige?"

The grandfather clock counts off one minute;

two; three . . .

Kobayashi's eyes travel down, up, and across the scroll.

It is not so arduous or long, thinks Jacob. *He is dragging the exercise out.*

The interpreter's ponderous reading is punctuated by thoughtful nods.

Elsewhere in the chief's residence, servants go about their business.

Vorstenbosch refuses to satisfy Kobayashi by voicing his impatience.

Kobayashi growls in his throat enigmatically and opens his mouth . . .

"I read once more, to ensure no mistake."

If looks really could kill, thinks Jacob, watching Vorstenbosch, *Kobayashi would be screaming the agonies of the damned.*

Vorstenbosch tells his slave Philander, "Bring me water."

From his side of the table, Jacob continues to study the shogun's scroll.

Two minutes pass. Philander returns with the pitcher.

"How," Kobayashi turns to Iwase, "may one say *'rôju'* in Dutch?"

Iwase's considered reply contains the words "first minister."

"Then," Kobayashi announces, "I am ready to translate message."

Jacob dips his sharpest quill into his inkpot.

"The message reads: 'Shogun's first minister sends cordialest greetings to Governor-General van Overstraten and chief of Dutchmen on Dejima, Vorstenbosch. First minister asks for' " — the interpreter peers at the scroll — " 'one thousand fans of finest peacock feathers. Dutch ship must carry this order back to Batavia, so fans of peacock feathers will arrive next year trading season.' "

Jacob's pen scratches out a summary.

Captain Lacy belches. " 'Twas my breakfast oysters . . . past their ripest . . ."

Kobayashi looks at Vorstenbosch, as if awaiting his response.

Vorstenbosch drains his glass of water. "Speak to me about copper."

With innocent insolence, Kobayashi blinks and says, "Message says nothing about copper, Chief Resident."

"Do not tell me" — a vein throbs in Vorstenbosch's temple — "Mr. Kobayashi, that *this* is the sum of the message."

"No . . ." Kobayashi peers at the left of the scroll. "First minister also hope autumn in Nagasaki is clement and winter is mild. But I think, 'Not relevant.' "

"One *thousand* peacock-feather fans." Van Cleef whistles.

"*Finest* peacock-feather fans," corrects Kobayashi, unembarrassed.

"Back in Charleston," says Captain Lacy, "we'd call *that* a begging letter."

"Here in Nagasaki," says Iwase, "we call

169

that order of shogun."

"Are those sons of bitches in Edo," asks Vorstenbosch, "*toying* with us?"

"Good news," suggests Kobayashi, "that Council of Elders continues discussions on copper. To not say 'no' is to half say 'yes.' "

"The *Shenandoah* sails in seven or eight weeks' time."

"Copper quota," Kobayashi purses his lips, "complicated matter."

"Contrariwise, it is a simple matter. Should twenty thousand piculs of copper not arrive on Dejima by the middle of October, this benighted country's sole window onto the world is bricked up. Does Edo imagine the governor-general is bluffing? Do they think I wrote the ultimatum myself?"

Well, says Kobayashi's shrug, *it is all beyond my power . . .*

Jacob lets his quill rest and studies the first minister's scroll.

"How reply to Edo on peacock fans?" asks Iwase. " 'Yes' may help copper . . ."

"Why must *my* petitions," Vorstenbosch demands, "wait until kingdom come, yet when the court wants something, we are supposed to act" — he clicks his fingers — "thus? Does this minister suppose peacocks are pigeons? Might not a few windmills please His Elevated Eye?"

"Peacock fan," says Kobayashi, "enough token of esteem for first minister."

"I am sick," Vorstenbosch complains to heaven, "*sick* of these damned" — he thumps the scroll on the table, causing the Japanese to gasp in horror at the disrespect — " 'tokens of esteem'! On Mondays it is 'The magistrate's falconer's guano sweeper asks for a roll of Bangalore chintz'; on Wednesdays, 'The city elders' monkey-keeper requires a box of cloves'; on Fridays it is 'His Lord So-and-so of Such-and-such admires your whalebone cutlery: he is powerful friend of foreigners,' so, hey diddle diddle, it is chipped pewter spoons for me. Yet when *we* need assistance, where are these 'powerful friends of foreigners' to be found?"

Kobayashi savors his victory under an ill-fitting mask of empathy.

Jacob is provoked into a rash gamble. "Mr. Kobayashi?"

The senior interpreter looks at the clerk of uncertain status.

"Mr. Kobayashi, an incident occurred earlier during the sale of peppercorns."

"What in hell," asks Vorstenbosch, "have peppercorns to do with our copper?"

"*Je vous prie de m'excuser, Monsieur,*" Jacob seeks to assure his superior, "*mais je crois savoir ce que je fais.*"

"*Je prie Dieu que vous savez,*" the chief warns him. "*Le jour a déjà bien mal commencé sans pour cela y ajouter votre aide.*"

171

"You see," Jacob speaks to Kobayashi, "Mr. Ouwehand and I argued with a merchant regarding the Chinese ideogram — the *konji,* I believe you call them?"

"Kanji," says Kobayashi.

"Forgive me, the *kanji,* for the number ten. During my stay in Batavia, I learned a small number from a Chinese merchant and, perhaps unwisely, used my limited knowledge instead of sending to the guild for an interpreter. Tempers grew heated, and now I fear a charge of dishonesty may have been made against your countryman."

Kobayashi sniffs fresh Dutch humiliation. "What *kanji* of argument?"

"Well, sir, Mr. Ouwehand said that the *kanji* for 'ten' is" — with a show of clumsy concentration, Jacob inscribes a character on his blotter — "drawn *thus . . .*"

十

"But *I* told Ouwehand, no; the true character for 'ten' is writ . . . *thus . . .*"

百

Jacob fouls the stroke order to exaggerate his ineptitude. "The merchant swore we were *both* wrong. *He* drew" — Jacob sighs and frowns — "a cross, I believe, thus . . ."

X

"I became convinced the merchant was a swindler and may have said as much. Could Interpreter Kobayashi kindly tell me the truth of the matter?"

"Mr. Ouwehand's number," Kobayashi points to the topmost character, "is 'thousand,' not 'ten.' Mr. de Zoet's number, too, is wrong: it mean 'hundred.' *This,*" he indicates the X, "is wrong memory. Merchant wrote *this . . .*" Kobayashi turns to his scribe for a brush. "Here is 'ten.' Two strokes, yes, but one up, one across . . ."

+

Jacob groans with contrition and inserts the numbers 10, 100, and 1,000 beside the corresponding characters. "These, then, are the true symbols for the numbers in question?"

Cautious Kobayashi examines the numbers a final time and nods.

"I am sincerely grateful," Jacob says and bows, "for the senior interpreter's guidance."

The interpreter fans himself. "There are no

more questions?"

"Just one more, sir," says Jacob. "Why did you claim that the shogun's first minister requests one *thousand* peacock-feather fans when, according to the numerals you were just kind enough to teach me, the number in question is a much more modest one *hundred*" — every eye in the room follows Jacob's finger on the scroll, resting on the corresponding *kanji* "hundred" — "as written here?"

Ramifications hatch from the appalling hush. Jacob thanks his God.

"Well, ding-dong bell," says Captain Lacy. "Pussy *is* in the well."

Kobayashi reaches for the scroll. "Shogun's request not for eyes of *clerk.*"

"In*deed* not!" Vorstenbosch pounces. "It is for *my* eyes, sir; *mine!* Mr. Iwase: *you* translate this letter so we may verify *how* many fans we are dealing with — one thousand, or one *hundred* for the Council of Elders and *nine* hundred for Mr. Kobayashi and his cronies? But before we begin, Mr. Iwase, refresh my memory: what *are* the penalties for willfully mistranslating a shogunal order?"

At four minutes to four o'clock, Jacob presses blotting paper over the page on his desk in Warehouse Eik. He drinks another cup of water, of which he shall sweat every last drop. The clerk then lifts the blotter and reads the title: *Sixteenth Addendum: True Quantities of Japanned Lacquerware Exported from Dejima to Batavia Not Declared on the Bills of Lading Submitted Between the Years 1793 and 1799.* He closes the black book, fastens its ties, and puts it into his portfolio. "We stop now, Hanzaburo. Chief Vorstenbosch summoned me to the stateroom for a meeting at four o'clock. Please take these papers to Mr. Ouwehand in the clerks' office." Hanzaburo sighs, takes the files, and drifts disconsolately away.

Jacob follows, locking the warehouse.

Floating seeds fill the sticky air.

The sunburned Dutchman thinks of a Zeeland winter's first snowflakes.

Go via Short Street, he tells himself. *You may catch sight of her.*

The Dutch flag on Flag Square twitches, very nearly lifeless.

If you mean to betray Anna, Jacob thinks, *why chase the unobtainable?*

At the land gate, a frisker sifts a handcart of fodder for contraband.

Marinus is right. Hire a courtesan. You have the money now . . .

Jacob walks up Short Street to the crossroads, where Ignatius is sweeping.

The slave tells the clerk that the doctor's students left some time ago.

One glance, Jacob knows, *would tell me if*

175

the fan charmed or offended.

He stands where she passed, maybe. A couple of spies are watching.

When he reaches the chief's residence, he is accosted by Peter Fischer, who appears from the under way. "Well, well, aren't *you* just the dog who mounted the bitch today?" The Prussian's breath smells of rum.

Jacob can only suppose Fischer is referring to this morning's fans.

"*Three years* in this godforlorn jail . . . Snitker swore I would be Van Cleef's deputy when he left. He swore it! Then you, *you* and your damned mercury, you come ashore, in *his* silk-lined pocket . . ." Fischer looks up the stairs to the chief's residence, swaying uncertainly. "You forget, De Zoet, *I* am not a weak and common clerk. You forget —"

"That you were a rifleman in Surinam? You remind us all daily."

"Rob me of my rightful promotion and I shall break all your bones."

"I bid you a soberer evening than your afternoon, Mr. Fischer."

"Jacob de Zoet! I break my enemy's bones, one by one . . ."

Vorstenbosch ushers Jacob into his bureau with a conviviality not shown for days. "Mr. van Cleef reports you ran the gauntlet of Mr. Fischer's displeasure."

"Unfortunately, Mr. Fischer is convinced

that I devote my every waking minute to the frustration of his interests . . ."

Van Cleef pours a rich and ruby port into three fluted glasses.

". . . but it might have been Mr. Grote's rum making the accusation."

"There's no denying," says Vorstenbosch, "that Kobayashi's interests were frustrated today."

"I never saw his tail," agrees Van Cleef, "so far back between his stumpy legs."

Birds scrat, thud, and issue dire warnings on the roof above.

"His greed trapped him, sir," says Jacob. "I just nudged him."

"*He*'ll not," Van Cleef laughs into his beard, "see it that way!"

"When I met you, De Zoet," begins Vorstenbosch, "I *knew*. Here is an honest soul in a swamp of human crocodiles, a sharp quill among blunt nibs, and a man who, with a little guidance, shall be a chief resident by his thirtieth year! Your resourcefulness this morning saved the company's money and honor. Governor-General van Overstraten shall hear about it, I give my word."

Jacob bows. *Am I summoned here,* he wonders, *to be made head clerk?*

"To your future," says the chief. He, his deputy, and the clerk touch glasses.

Perhaps his recent coolness, Jacob thinks, *was to avert charges of favoritism.*

"Kobayashi's punishment was to be made to tell Edo," gloats Van Cleef, "that ordering goods from a trading factory that may expire in fifty days for want of copper is premature and injudicious. We'll scare more concessions out of him, besides."

Light skitters off the Almelo clock's bearings like splinters of stars.

"We have," Vorstenbosch's voice shifts, "a further assignment for you, De Zoet. Mr. van Cleef shall explain."

Van Cleef drains his glass of port. "Before breakfast, come rain or shine, Mr. Grote receives a visitor: a provedore, who enters with a full bag, in plain view."

"Bigger than a pouch," says Vorstenbosch, "smaller than a pillowcase."

"Then he leaves with the same bag, still full, in plain view."

"What" — Jacob banishes his disappointment that he is not to be promoted on the spot — "is Mr. Grote's story?"

"A 'story,' " says Vorstenbosch, "is precisely what he *would* regale Van Cleef or me with. High office, as you shall one day discover, distances one from one's men. But this morning proves beyond doubt that *yours* is the nose to smoke out a rascal. You hesitate. You think, *Nobody loves an informer,* and, alas, you are right. But he who is destined for high office, De Zoet, as Van Cleef and I divine you are, must not fear a little clambering and

178

elbowing. Pay Mr. Grote a call tonight."

This is a test, Jacob divines, *of my willingness to get dirty hands.*

"I shall redeem a long-standing invitation to the cook's card table."

"You see, Van Cleef? De Zoet never says, 'Must I?' only 'How may I?' "

Jacob indulges in thoughts of Anna reading news of his promotion.

In the after-dinner half dark, swallows stream along Seawall Lane, and Jacob finds Ogawa Uzaemon at his side. The interpreter says something to Hanzaburo to make him disappear and accompanies Jacob to the pines in the far corner. Under the humid trees Ogawa stops, neuters the inevitable spy in the shadows by means of an amiable greeting, and says, in a low voice, "All Nagasaki talks about this morning. About Interpreter Kobayashi and fans."

"Perhaps he won't try to scull us again so shamelessly."

"Recent," says Ogawa, "I warn, do not make Enomoto enemy."

"I take your advice very seriously."

"Here is more advice. Kobayashi is a little shogun. Dejima is his empire."

"Then I am fortunate not to rely on his good offices."

Ogawa frowns at "good offices." "He harms you, De Zoet-*san.*"

179

"Thank you for your concern, but I'm not afraid of him."

Ogawa looks around. "He may search apartment for stolen items . . ."

Seagulls riot in the dusk above a boat hidden by the seawall.

". . . or forbidden items. So if such item in your room . . ."

"But I own nothing," Jacob protests, "that might incriminate me."

A tiny muscle ripples under Ogawa's cheek. "If there is forbidden *book* . . . hide. Hide under floor. Hide very well. Kobayashi wants revenge. For you, penalty is exile. Interpreter who searched your library when you arrive, not so lucky . . ."

I am failing to understand something, Jacob knows, *but what?*

The clerk opens his mouth, but the question expires.

Ogawa knew about my Psalter, Jacob realizes, *all along.*

"I shall do as you say, Mr. Ogawa, before I do anything else."

A pair of inspectors appear from Bony Alley and walk up Seawall Lane.

Without another word, Ogawa walks toward them. Jacob leaves via Garden House.

Con Twomey and Piet Baert rise and their candlelit shadows slide. The impromptu card table is made of one door and four legs. Ivo

Oost stays seated, chewing tobacco; Wybo Gerritszoon spits at, rather than into, the spittoon; and Arie Grote is as charming as a ferret welcoming a rabbit. "We was beginnin' to despair you'd *ever* accept my hospitality, eh?" He uncorks the first of twelve jars of rum lined up on a plank shelf.

"I intended to come days ago," says Jacob, "but work prevented me."

"Buryin' Mr. Snitker's reputation," remarks Oost, "must be a taxing job."

Jacob brushes aside the attack. "To make good falsified ledgers *is* taxing work. How homely your quarters are, Mr. Grote."

" 'F I liked livin' in a tub o' piss," Grote says with a wink, "I'd o' stayed in Enkhuizen, eh?"

Jacob takes a seat. "What is the game, gentlemen?"

"Knave and Devil — our Germanic cousins, eh, play it."

"Ah, Karnöffel. I played it a little in Copenhagen."

"S'prised," says Baert, "*you*'d be familiar with cards."

"The sons — or nephews — of vicarages are less naïve than supposed."

"Each o' these" — Grote picks up a nail from his cache — "is one stuiver off of our wages. We ante up one nail in the pot afore each round. Seven tricks per round, an' who bags most tricks scoops the pot. When the

181

nails is gone, the night's done."

"But how are winnings redeemed, with wages payable only in Batavia?"

"A touch of, eh, legerdemainery: this" — he waves a sheet of paper — "is a record o' who won what off of who, an' Deputy van Cleef records our 'djusted balances in the actual pay book. Mr. Snitker approved this practice, knowin' how his men's *edge* is kept sharp by these convivial, eh, pleasures."

"Mr. Snitker was a welcome guest," says Ivo Oost, "afore losin' his liberty."

"Fischer an' Ouwehand an' Marinus stay aloof, but *you,* Mr. de Z., look cut of gayer cloth . . ."

Nine jars of rum are left on the plank shelf. "So I run away from Pa," says Grote, stroking his cards, "afore he *did* rip out my liver, an' off I tromped to Amsterdam, seekin' fortune an' true love, eh?" He pours himself another glass of urine-colored rum. "But the only love *I* saw was what's paid in cash afore an' clap in arrears, an' not a *sniff* of a fortune. Nah, hunger was all *I* found, snow an' ice an' cutpurses what fed off the weak like dogs . . . *Speculate to 'ccumulate,* thinks I, so I spends my 'inheritance,' eh, on a barrow o' coal, but a pack o' coalmen tipped my cart in the canal — an' me in after it, yellin', *'This is* our *patch, yer West Frieslander mongrel! Come back when it's bath time again!'* Aside from this

182

schoolin' in monopolies, eh, that icy dunkin' give me such a fever I couldn't stir from my lodgin's for a week, an' then my cuddly landlord planted his iron toe in my arse. Holes in my shoes, naught to eat but the stinkin' fog, I sat me down on the steps of Nieuwe Kerk, wonderin' if I should thief a bite while I'd still strength enough to scarper, or jus' freeze to death an' get it over with —"

"Thief an' scarper," says Ivo Oost, "ev'ry time."

"Who should gander along but this gent in a top hat, ivory-knobbed cane, an' a friendly manner. 'Know who I am, boy?' I says, 'I don't, sir.' He says, 'I, boy, am your future prosperity.' Figured he meant he'd feed me f' joinin' his Church, an' so starvin' was I I'd've turned Jew for a bowl o' pottage, but no. 'You have heard of the noble an' munificent Dutch East Indies Company, boy, have you not?' Says I, 'Who ain't, sir?' Says he, 'So you are cognizant of the diamond prospects the company offers stout an' willin' lads in its possessions throughout our Creator's blue an' silver globe, yes?' Says I, catchin' on at last, 'That I do, sir, aye.' Says he, 'Well, I am a master recruiter for the Amsterdam head-quarters, an' my name is Duke van Eys. What d' you say to half a guilder advance on your wages, an' board an' lodgin' till the next company flotilla sets forth on the finny way to the mysterious East?' An' I say, 'Duke van

Eys, you are my savior.' Mr. de Z., does our rum disagree with you?"

"My stomach is dissolving, Mr. Grote, but it is otherwise delicious."

Grote places the five of diamonds: Gerritszoon slaps down the queen.

"Cry havoc!" Baert slams down a five of trumps and scoops up the nails.

Jacob next discards a low heart. "Your savior, Mr. Grote?"

Grote inspects his cards. "The gentleman led me to a tottery house behind Rasphuys, a slanty street, an' his office was poky but dry 'n' warm, an' the smell o' bacon wafted up from belowstairs an', *oh,* it smelled good! I even asked might I have me a rasher or two there 'n' then, an' van Eys laughs an' says, 'Write your name here, boy, and after five years in the Orient you can build a *palace* of smoked hog!' Couldn't read nor write my name back in them days; I just inked my thumb at the foot o' the papers. 'Splendid,' says van Eys, 'and here is an advance on your bounty, to prove I am a man of my word.' He paid me my own new an' shiny half-guilder, an' I was never happier. 'The remainder is payable aboard the *Admiral de Ruyter,* who sails on the thirtieth or thirty-first. One trusts you have no objection to being quartered with a few other stout an' willing lads, future shipmates and partners in prosperity?' Any roof beat no roof, so I pocketed my booty an' said I'd no objection at all."

Twomey discards a worthless diamond. Ivo Oost, the four of spades.

"So two servants," Grote continues, studying his hand, "led me downstairs, but I di'n't rumble what was afoot, eh, till the key was turned in the lock behind me. In a cellar no bigger'n this room was *twenty-four* lads, my age or older. Some'd been there weeks; some was half skel'tons, coughin' up blood . . . Oh, I banged on the door to be freed, but this great scabby grunt strolls over sayin', 'Better give me your half-guilder now for safekeepin'.' Says I, 'What half-guilder?' an' he says I can give it him volunt'ry or else he'll *tenderize* me an' have it anyways. I asks when we're allowed out for exercise an' air. 'We ain't let out,' says he, 'till the ship sails or unless we cark it. Now, the *money.*' Wish I could say I stood my ground, but Arie Grote ain't no liar. He weren't jokin' 'bout carkin' it, neither: *eight* o' them 'stout an' willing lads' left horizontally, two crammed into one coffin. Just an iron grid at street level for air 'n' light, see, an' slops so bad you'd not know which bucket was to eat from an' which to shit in."

"Why didn't you knock down the doors?" asks Twomey.

"Iron doors an' guards with nailed truncheons is why." Grote sweeps head lice from his hair. "Oh, I found ways to live to tell the

185

tale. It's my chief hobby-hawk is the noble art of survivin'. But on the day that we was marched to the tender what'd take us out to the *Admiral de Ruyter,* roped to the others like prisoners, eh, I swore three oaths to myself. First: *never* credit a company gent who says, 'We've yer interests at heart.' " He winks at Jacob. "Second: never be so poor again, come what may, that human pustules like Van Eys could buy 'n' sell me like a slave. Third? To get my half-guilder back off of Scabby Grunt before we reached Curaçao. My first oath I honor to this day; my second oath, well, I have grounds to hope it'll be no pauper's grave for Arie Grote when his time is done; and my third oath — oh, yes, I got my half-guilder back that very same night."

Wybo Gerritszoon picks his nose and asks, "How?"

Grote shuffles the cards. "My deal, shipmates."

Five jars of rum wait on the shelf. The hands are drinking more than the clerk, but Jacob feels a drunken glow in his legs. *Karnöffel,* he knows, *shall not make me a rich man tonight.* "Letters," Ivo Oost is saying, "they taught us at the orphanage, an' arithmetic, an' Scripture: a powerful dose o' Scripture, what with chapel twice daily. We was made to learn the gospels verse by verse, an' one slip'd earn you a stroke o' the cane. What a pastor /

might o' made! But then, who'd take lessons from 'somebody's natural son' on the Ten Commandments?" He deals seven cards to each player. Oost turns over the top card of the remnant pack. "Diamonds is trumps."

"I heard tell," says Grote, playing the eight of clubs, "the company shipped some head-shrinker, black as a sweep, to pastor's school in Leiden. The idea bein' he'll go home to his jungle an' show the cannibals the light o' the Lord an' so render 'em more *pacific,* eh? Bibles bein' cheaper 'n rifles an' all."

"Oh, but rifles make f' better sport," remarks Gerritszoon. "Bang bang bang."

"What good's a slave," asks Grote, "what's full o' bullet holes?"

Baert kisses his card and plays the queen of clubs.

"She's the only bitch on earth," says Gerritszoon, "who'll let yer do *that.*"

"With tonight's winnin's," says Baert, "I may order a gold-skinned Miss."

"Did the orphanage in Batavia give you your name, also, Mr. Oost?" *I would never ask that question sober,* Jacob berates himself.

But Oost, on whom Grote's rum is having a benign effect, takes no offense. "Aye, it did. 'Oost' is from 'Oost-Indische Compagnie,' who founded the orphanage, and who'd deny there's 'East' in my blood? 'Ivo' is 'cause I was left on the steps o' the orphanage on the twentieth o' May, what's the old feast day of

St. Ivo. Master Drijver at the orphanage'd be kind enough to point out, ev'ry now an' then, how 'Ivo' is the male 'Eve' an' a fittin' reminder o' the original sin o' my birth."

"It's a man's conduct that God is interested in," avows Jacob, "not the circumstances of his birth."

"More's the pity it was wolfs like Drijver an' not God who reared me."

"Mr. de Zoet," Twomey prompts, "your turn."

Jacob plays the five of hearts; Twomey lays down the four.

Oost runs the corners of his cards over his Javanese lips. "I'd clamber out o' the attic window, 'bove the jacarandas, an' there, northward, out past the Old Fort, was a strip o' blue . . . or green . . . or gray . . . an' smell the brine 'bove the stink o' the canals; there was the ships layin' hard by Onrust, like livin' things, an' sails billowin' . . . an' 'This ain't my home,' I told that buildin', 'an' you ain't my masters,' I told the wolfs, ' 'cause you're my home,' I told the sea. An' on some days I'd make believe it heard me an' was answering, 'Yeah, I am, an' one o' these days I'll send for you.' Now, I know it *didn't* speak, but . . . you carry your cross as best you can, don't you? So that's how I grew up through them years, an' when the wolfs was beatin' me in the name of rectifyin' my wrongs . . . it was the sea I'd dream of, even though I'd never yet seen its swells an' its rollers . . . even tho', aye, I'd never set my big toe on a boat all my life . . ." He places the five of clubs.

Baert wins the trick. "I may take *twin* gold-skinned Misses for the night."

Gerritszoon plays the seven of diamonds, announcing, "The devil."

"Judas *damn* you," says Baert, losing the ten of clubs, "you damn *Ju*das."

"So how was it," asks Twomey, "the sea *did* call you, Ivo?"

"From our twelfth year — that is, whenever the director *decided* we was twelve — we'd be set to 'fruitful industry.' For girls, this was sewin', weavin', stirrin' the vats in the laundry. Us boys, we was hired out to crate makers an' coopers, to officers at the barracks to go-for, or to the docks, as stevedores. Me, I was given to a rope maker, who set me pickin' oakum out o' tarry old ropes. Cheaper than servants, us; cheaper than slaves. Drijver'd pocket his 'acknowledgment,' he'd call it, an' with above a hundred of us at it 'fruitful industry' it *was,* right enough, for *him.* But what it did do was let us out o' the orphanage walls. We weren't guarded: where'd we run to? The jungle? I'd not known Batavia's streets much at all, save for the walk from the orphanage to church, so now I could wander a little, takin' roundabout ways to work an' back, an' run errands for the rope maker, through the Chinamen's bazaar an' most of all along the wharfs, happy as a granary rat, lookin' at the sailors from far-off lands . . ." Ivo Oost plays the jack of diamonds, winning the trick. "Devil beats the pope, but the knave beats the devil."

"My rotted tooth's hurtin'," says Baert, "hurtin' me frightful."

"Artful play," compliments Grote, losing a card of no consequence.

"One day," Oost continues, "I was fourteen, most like — I was deliverin' a coil o' rope to a chandler's an' a snug brig was in, small an' sweet an' with a figurehead of a . . . a good woman. *Sara Maria* was the brig's name, an' I . . . I heard a voice, *like* a voice, *without* the voice, sayin', 'She's the one, an' it's today.' "

"Well, *that's* clear," mutters Gerritszoon, "as a Frenchman's shit pot."

"You heard," suggests Jacob, "a sort of inner prompting?"

"Whatever it was, up that gangplank I hopped, an' waited for this big man who was doin' the directin' an' yellin' to notice me. He never did, so I summoned my courage an' said, 'Excuse me, sir.' He peered close an' barked, 'Who let *this* ragamuffin on deck?' I begged his pardon an' said that I wanted to run away to sea an' might he speak with the captain? Laughter was the last thing I expected, but laugh he did, so I begged his pardon but said I weren't jokin'. He says,

'What'd your ma 'n' pa think of me for spir-
itin' you away without even a by-their-leave?
And why d'you suppose you'd make a sailor,
with its aches an' its pains an' its colds an' its
hots an' the cargo-master's moods, 'cause
anyone aboard'll agree the man's a very
devil?' I just says that my ma 'n' pa'd not say
nothin', 'cause I was raised in the House of
Bastardy, an' if I could survive *that,* then, no
disrespect, but I weren't afeard o' the sea nor
any cargo-master's mood . . . an' he di'n't
mock or talk snidey like but asked, 'So do
your custodians know you're arranging a life
at sea?' I confessed Drijver'd flay me alive.
So he makes his decision an' says, 'My name
is Daniel Snitker an' I am cargo-master of
the *Sara Maria* an' my cabin boy died o' ship
fever.' They was embarkin' to Banda for
nutmeg the next day, an' he promised he'd
have the captain put me on the ship's book,
but till the *Sara Maria* set sail he bade me
hide in the cockpit with the other lads. I
obeyed sharpish, but I'd been seen boardin'
the brig an' right 'nuff the director sent three
big bad wolfs to fetch back his 'stolen
property.' Mr. Snitker an' his mates pitched
'em in the harbor."

Jacob strokes his broken nose. *I am convict-
ing the lad's father.*

Gerritszoon discards an impotent five of
clubs.

"I b'lieve" — Baert puts nails in his purse

— "the necessessessary house is callin'."

"What yer takin' yer winnin's for?" asks Gerritszoon. "Don't yer trust us?"

"I'd fry my own liver first," says Baert, "with cream an' onions."

Two jars of rum sit on the plank shelf, unlikely to survive the night.

"With the weddin' ring in my pocket," sniffs Piet Baert, "I . . . I . . ."

Gerritszoon spits. "Oh, quit yer blubbin', yer pox-livered pussy!"

"*You* say that" — Baert's face hardens — " 'cause *you*'re a cesspool hog what no'un's ever loved, but my one true love was yearnin' to marry me, an' I'm thinkin', *My evil luck is gone away at long last.* All we needed was Neeltje's father's blessin' an' we'd be sailin' down the aisle. A beer porter, her father was, in St.-Pol-sur-Mer, an' it was there I was headed that night, but Dunkirk was a strange town an' rain was pissin' down an' night was fallin' an' the streets led back where they'd come an' when I stopped at a tavern to ask my way the barmaid's knockers was two juggly piglets an' she lights up all witchy an' says, 'My oh my, ain't *you* just strayed to the wrong side o' town, my poor *lickle* lambkin?' *I* says, 'Please, Miss, I just want to get to St.-Pol-sur-Mer,' so *she* says, 'Why so hasty? Ain't our 'stablishment to your likin'?' an' thrusted them piglets at me, an' *I* says, 'Your 'stablishment is fine, Miss, but my one true love, Neeltje, is waitin' with her father so's I can ask for her hand in marriage an' turn my back on the sea,' an' the barmaid says, 'So you *are* a sailor?' an' I says, 'I *was,* aye, but no more,' an' *she* cries out to the whole house, 'Who'll not drink to Neeltje, the luckiest lass in Flanders?' an' she puts a tumbler o' gin in my hand an' says, 'A little somethin' to warm your bone,' an' promises her brother'll walk me to St.-Pol-sur-Mer, bein' as all sorts o' villains stalk Dunkirk after dark. So I thinks, *Yes, for sure, my evil luck is gone away at long, long last,* an' I raised that glass to my lips."

"Game girl," notes Arie Grote. "What's that tavern named, by the by?"

"It'll be named Smokin' Cinders afore *I* leave Dunkirk again: that gin goes down an' my head swims an' the lamps are snuffed out. Bad dreams follow, then I'm wakin', swayin' this way an' that way, like I'm out at sea, but I'm squashed under bodies like a grape in a wine press, and I think, *I'm dreamin' still,* but that cold puke bungin' up my earhole weren't no dream, an' I cries, 'Dear Jesus, am I dead?' an' some cackly demon laughs, 'No fishy wriggles free o' *this* hook *that* simple!' an' a grimmer voice says, 'You been crimped, friend. We're on the *Venguer du Peuple,* an' we're in the Channel, sailin' west,' an' I says, 'The *Venguer du* What?' an' then I remember

Neeltje an' shout, 'But tonight I'm to be engaged to my one true love!' an' the demon says, 'There's just one engagement *you*'ll see here, matey, an' that's a naval one,' an' I thinks, *Sweet Jesus in heaven, Neeltje's ring,* an' I wriggles my arm to see if it's in my jacket, but it ain't. I despair. I weep. I gnash my teeth. But nothin' helps. Mornin' comes an' we're brought up on deck an' lined along the gunwale. 'Bout a score of us southern Netherlanders there was, an' the captain appears. Captain's an evil Paris weasel; his first officer's a shaggy hulkin' bruiser, a Basque. '*I* am Captain Renaudin, an' *you* are my privileged volunteers. Our orders are to rendezvous,' says he, 'with a convoy bringin' grain from North America an' escort her to Republican soil. The British shall try to stop us. We shall blast them to matchwood. Any questions?" One chancer — a Swissman — pipes up, 'Captain Renaudin: I belong to the Mennonite Church, an' my religion forbids me to kill.' Renaudin tells his first officer, 'We must inconvenience this man o' brotherly love no longer,' an' up the bruiser steps an' shoves the Swissman overboard. We hear him shoutin' for help. We hear him beggin' for help. We hear the beggin' stop. The captain asks, 'Any *more* questions?' Well, my sea legs come back fast 'nough, so when the English fleet is sighted on the first o' June, two weeks later, I was loadin' powder into a twenty-four-pounder. The Third Battle of Ushant, the French call what happened next, an' the Glorious First o' June, the English call it. Well, blastin' lagrange shot through each other's gunports at ten feet off may be 'glorious' to Sir Johnny Roast Beef, but it ain't glorious to me. Sliced-open men writhin' in the smoke; aye, men bigger an' tougher 'n *you,* Gerritszoon, beggin' for their mammies through raggy holes in their throats . . . an' a tub carried up from the surgeon's full o' . . ." Baert fills his glass. "Nah, when the *Brunswick* holed us at the waterline an' we knew we was goin' down, the *Venguer* weren't no ship o' the line no more: we was an abattoir . . . an abattoir . . ." Baert looks into his rum, then at Jacob. "What saved me that terrible day? An empty cheese barrel what floated my way is what. All night I clung to it, too cold, too dead to fear the sharks. Dawn come an' brought a sloop flyin' the Union Jack. Its launch hauls me aboard an' squawks at me in that jackdaw jabber they speak — no offense, Twomey."

The carpenter shrugs. "Irish would be *my* mother tongue, now, Mr. Baert."

"This ancient salt translates for me. 'The mate's askin' where you're from?' an' says I, 'Antwerp, sir: I got pressed by the French an' I damn their bloods.' The salt translates that, an' the mate jabbers some more what the salt translates. Gist was, 'cause I weren't a

Frenchie, I weren't a prisoner. Nearly kissed his boots in gratefulness! But then he told me if I volunteered for His Majesty's Navy as an ordinary seaman I'd get proper pay an' a new set o' slops — well, almost new. But if I di'n't volunteer, I'd be pressed anyhow, and paid salty sod-all as a landsman. To keep from despairin', I asked where we're bound, thinkin' I'd find a way to slip ashore in Gravesend or Portsmouth an' get back to Dunkirk an' darlin' Neeltje in a week or two . . . and the salt says, 'Our next port o' call'll be Ascension Island, for victualin' — not that *you*'ll be settin' foot ashore — and from there it's on to the Bay o' Bengal . . .' an', grown man that I am, I couldn't keep from weepin' . . ."

Not one drop of rum is left. "Lady Luck was passin' indifferent to yer tonight, Mr. de Z." Grote snuffs out all but two candles. "But there's always another day, eh?"

"Indifferent?" Jacob hears the others close the door. "I was shorn."

"Oh, yer mercury profits'll keep famine an' pestilence at bay for a fair while yet, eh? 'Twas a risky stance yer took with the sale, Mr. de Z., but so long as the abbot's willin' to indulge yer, yer last two crates may yet earn a better price. Think what riches *eighty* crates'd fetch, 'stead o' just eight."

"Such a quantity" — Jacob's head steams

with drink — "would violate —"

" 'Twould *bend* company rules on private trade, aye, but the trees what survive cruel winds are those what *do* bend, eh, are they not?"

"A tidy metaphor does not make a wrong thing right."

Grote puts the precious glass bottles back on the shelf. "Five hundred percent profit, you made: word travels, an' yer've two seasons at most 'fore the Chinese flood this market. Deputy van C. an' Captain Lacy both have the capital back in Batavia, an' they ain't men to say, 'Oh, dearie, but I *mayn't,* for my quota is jus' eight boxes.' Or the chief himself'll do it."

"Chief Vorstenbosch is here to eradicate corruption, not aid it."

"Chief Vorstenbosch's interests are as starved by the war as anyone's."

"Chief Vorstenbosch is too honest a man to profit at the company's expense."

"What man *ain't* the honestest cove in his own eyes?" Grote's round face is a bronze moon in the dark. " 'Tain't good intentions what paves the road to hell: it's self-justifyin's. Now, speakin' of honest coves, what's the true reason for the pleasure of yer comp'ny tonight?"

Along Seawall Lane, the guards clap the hour with their wooden clappers.

I am too drunk, thinks Jacob, *to practice cun-*

ning. "I am here about two delicate matters."

"My lips'll be waxed *and* sealed, on my beloved pa's distant grave."

"The truth is, then, the chief suspects a . . . misappropriation is taking place . . ."

"Saints! Not a misappropriation, Mr. de Zoet? Not on Dejima?"

". . . involving a provedore who visits your kitchen every morning —"

"Several provedores visit my kitchen every morning, Mr. de Z."

"— whose small bag is as full when he leaves as when he arrives."

"Glad I am to dispel the misunderstandin', eh? Yer can tell Mr. Vorstenbosch as how the answer's 'onions.' Aye, onions. Rotten, stinkin' onions. That provedore's the rascaliest dog of all. Each mornin' he tries it on, but some blackguards won't listen to 'Begone you shameless knave!' an' that one is one such one I do declare."

Fishermen's voices travel through the warm and salty night.

I'm not too drunk, thinks Jacob, *to miss a calculated insolence.*

The clerk stands. "Well, there's no need to trouble you any further."

"There isn't?" Arie Grote is suspicious.

"There isn't."

"No. Another long day in the yard tomorrow, so I'll bid you good night."

Grote frowns. "You did say *two* delicate

198

matters, Mr. de Z.?"

"Your tale about onions" — Jacob ducks below the beam — "requires the second item to be raised with Mr. Gerritszoon. I'll speak with him tomorrow, in the sober light of day — the news will be an unwelcome revelation, I fear."

Grote blocks the door. "What's this second matter about?"

"Your playing cards, Mr. Grote. Thirty-six rounds of Karnöffel, and of those thirty-six, you dealt twelve, and of those twelve, you won ten. An improbable outcome! Baert and Oost may not detect a deck of cards conceived in sin, but Twomey and Gerritszoon would. That ancient trick, then, I discounted. No mirrors behind us; no servants to tip you the wink . . . I was at a loss."

"A suspicious mind" — Grote's tone turns wintry — "for a God-fearin' cove."

"Bookkeepers acquire suspicious minds, Mr. Grote. I was at a loss to explain your success until I noticed you stroking the top edge of the cards you dealt. So I did the same and felt the notches — those *tiny* nicks: the knaves, sevens, kings, and queens are all notched closer or farther from the corners, according to their value. A sailor's hands, or a warehouseman's, or a carpenter's, are too calloused. But a cook's forefinger or a clerk's is another matter."

"It's custom'ry," Grote says, swallowing,

"that the house be paid for its trouble."

"In the morning we'll find out if Gerritszoon agrees. Now, I really must —"

"Such a pleasant evenin'; what say I reimburse your evening's losses?"

"All that matters is truth, Mr. Grote: one version of the truth."

"Is this how you repay me for makin' you rich? By black*mail?*"

"Suppose you tell me more about this bag of onions?"

Grote sighs, twice. "Yer a bloody ache in the arse, Mr. de Z."

Jacob relishes the inverted compliment and waits.

"Yer know," the cook begins, "yer know o' the ginseng bulb?"

"I know ginseng is valued by Japanese druggists."

"A Chinaman in Batavia — quite the gent — ships me a crate on every year's sailin'. All well an' good. Problem *is,* the magistracy taxes the stuff come auction day: we was losin' six parts in ten till Dr. Marinus one day mentioned a *local* ginseng what grows here in the bay but what's not so prized. So . . ."

"So your man brings in bags of the *local* ginseng . . ."

". . . and leaves" — Grote betrays a flash of pride — "with bags of the Chinese."

"The guards and friskers at the land gate

don't find this odd?"

"They're *paid* not to find it odd. Now, here's my question for you: how's the chief goin' to act on this? On this an' everythin' else you're snufflin' up? 'Cause this is how Dejima works. Stop all these little *perquisites,* eh, an' yer stop Dejima itself — an' *don't* evade me, eh, with your 'That is a matter for Mr. Vorstenbosch.' "

"But it *is* a matter for Mr. Vorstenbosch." Jacob lifts the latch.

"It *ain't* right." Grote clamps the latch. "It *ain't* just. One minute it's 'private trade is killin' the company'; next it's 'I'm not a man to sell my own men short.' Yer can't have a cellar full o' wine *and* yer wife drunk legless."

"Keep your dealings honest," Jacob says, "and there is no dilemma."

"Keep my dealings 'honest' an' my profits is potato peelin's!"

"It's not I who makes the company's rules, Mr. Grote."

"Aye, but yer do its dirty work 'appily enough, though, don't yer?"

"I follow orders loyally. Now, unless you plan on imprisoning an officer, release this door."

"Loyalty looks simple," Grote tells him, "but it ain't."

CHAPTER NINE:
CLERK DE ZOET'S
QUARTERS IN TALL
HOUSE

Morning of Sunday, September 15, 1799
Jacob retrieves the De Zoet Psalter from under the floorboards and kneels in the corner of the room where he prays on his bare knees every night. Placing his nostril over the thin gap between the book's spine and binding, Jacob inhales the damp aroma of the Domburg parsonage. The smell evokes Sundays when the villagers battled January gales up the cobbled high street as far as the church; Easter Sundays, when the sun warmed the pasty backs of boys idling guilt-ily by the lagoon; autumnal Sundays, when the sexton climbed the church tower to ring the bell through the sea fog; Sundays of the brief Zeeland summer, when the season's new hats would arrive from the milliners in Middelburg; and one Whitsunday when Jacob voiced to his uncle the thought that just as one man can be Pastor de Zoet of Domburg *and* "Geertje's and my uncle" *and* "Mother's brother," so God, His Son, and the Holy

Spirit are an indivisible Trinity. His reward was the one kiss his uncle ever gave him: wordless, respectful, and here, on his forehead.

Let them still be there, prays the homesick traveler, *when I go home.*

The Dutch Company professes an allegiance to the Dutch Reformed Church but makes little provision for its employees' spiritual well-being. On Dejima, Chief Vorstenbosch, Deputy van Cleef, Ivo Oost, Grote, and Gerritszoon would also claim loyalty to the Dutch Reformed faith, yet no semblance of organized worship would ever be tolerated by the Japanese. Captain Lacy is an Episcopalian; Ponke Ouwehand a Lutheran; and Catholicism is represented by Piet Baert and Con Twomey. The latter has confided to Jacob that he conducts an "unholy mess of a holy Mass" every Sunday, and is frightened of dying without the ministrations of a priest. Dr. Marinus refers to the Supreme Creator in the same tone he uses to discuss Voltaire, Diderot, Herschel, and certain Scottish physicians: admiring, but less than worshipful.

To what God, Jacob wonders, *would a Japanese midwife pray?*

Jacob turns to the Ninety-third Psalm, known as the "Storm Psalm."

The floods have lifted up, O Lord, he reads, *the floods have lifted up their voice . . .*

The Zeelander pictures the Westerscheldt between Vlissingen and Breskens.

. . . the floods lift up their waves. The Lord on high is mightier than the noise . . .

The Bible's storms, for Jacob, are North Sea storms, where even the sun is drowned.

. . . than the noise of many waters, yea, than the mighty waves of the sea . . .

Jacob thinks of Anna's hands, her warm hands, her living hands. He fingers the bullet in the cover and turns to the Hundred and Fiftieth Psalm.

Praise Him with the sound of the trumpet . . . with the psaltery and harp.

The harpist's slender fingers and sickle-shaped eyes are Miss Aibagawa's.

Praise Him with the timbrel and dance. King David's dancer has one burned cheek.

The sunken-eyed Interpreter Motogi waits under the awning of the guild and notices Jacob and Hanzaburo only when the invited clerk is directly in front of him. "Ah! De Zoet-*san* . . . To summon with little warning causes a great trouble, we fear."

"I'm honored" — Jacob returns Motogi's bow — "not troubled, Mr. Motogi . . ."

A coolie drops a crate of camphor and earns a kick from a merchant.

". . . and Mr. Vorstenbosch has excused me for the entire morning, if need be."

Motogi ushers him into the guild, where

the men remove their shoes.

Jacob then steps onto the knee-high interior floor and passes into the spacious rear office he has never yet ventured into. Sitting at tables arranged in the manner of a schoolroom are six men: Interpreters Isohachi and Kobayashi of the first rank; the pox-scarred Interpreter Narazake and the charismatic, shifty Namura of the second rank; Goto of the third rank, who is to act as scribe, and a thoughtful-eyed man who introduces himself as Maeno, a physician, who thanks Jacob for allowing him to attend, "so you may cure my sick Dutch." Hanzaburo sits in the corner and pretends to be attentive. For his part, Kobayashi takes pains to prove that he bears no grudge over the peacock-fan incident and introduces Jacob as "Clerk de Zoet of Zeeland, Esquire" and "Man of Deep Learning."

The man of deep learning modestly denies this paean.

Motogi explains that, in the course of their work, the interpreters encounter words whose meanings are unclear, and it is to illuminate these that Jacob has been invited. Dr. Marinus often leads these unofficial tutorials, but today he is busy and nominated Clerk de Zoet as his substitute.

Each interpreter has a list of items that evade the guild's collective understanding. These he reads out, one by one, and Jacob explains as clearly as he can, with examples, gestures, and synonyms. The group discusses an appropriate Japanese substitute, sometimes testing it on Jacob, until everyone is satisfied. Straightforward words such as "parched," "plenitude," or "saltpeter" do not detain them long. More abstract items such as "simile," "figment," or "parallax" prove more exacting. Terms without a ready Japanese equivalent, such as "privacy," "splenetic," or the verb "to deserve," cost ten or fifteen minutes, as do phrases requiring specialist knowledge — "Hanseatic," "nerve ending," or "subjunctive." Jacob notices that where a Dutch pupil would say, "I don't understand," the interpreters lower their eyes, so the teacher cannot merely explicate but must also gauge his students' true comprehension.

Two hours pass at the speed of one but exhaust Jacob like four, and he is grateful for green tea and a short interval. Hanzaburo slopes away without explanation. During the second half, Narazake asks how "He has gone to Edo" differs from "He has been to Edo"; Dr. Maeno wants to know when one uses "It neither picks my pocket nor breaks my leg"; and Namura asks for the differences among "If I see," "If I saw," and "Had I but seen"; Jacob is thankful for his tedious hours of schoolboy grammar. The last queries of the morning come from Interpreter Kobayashi.

"Please may Clerk de Zoet explain this word: 'repercussions.' "

Jacob suggests, "A consequence; the result of an action. A repercussion of spending my money is being poor. If I eat too much, one repercussion shall be" — he mimes a swollen belly — "fat."

Kobayashi asks about "in broad daylight." "Each word I understand, but meaning of all is unclear. Can we say 'I visit good friend Mr. Tanaka in broad daylight'? I think no, perhaps . . ."

Jacob mentions the criminal connotations. "Especially when the miscreant — the bad man, that is — lacks both shame and fear of being caught. 'My good friend Mr. Motogi was robbed in broad daylight.' "

" 'Mr. Vorstenbosch's teapot,' " asks Kobayashi, " 'was stolen in broad daylight'?"

"A valid example," agrees Jacob, glad that the chief isn't present.

The interpreters discuss various Japanese equivalents before agreeing on one.

"Perhaps next word," continues Kobayashi, "is simple — 'impotent.' "

" 'Impotent' is the opposite of 'potent' or 'powerful'; that is, 'weak.' "

"A lion," Dr. Maeno proposes, "is strong, but a mouse is impotent."

Kobayashi nods and studies his list. "Next is 'blithely unaware.' "

"A state of ignorance about a misfortune.

Whilst one is unaware of it one is 'blithe,' that is, content. But when one becomes aware, one becomes unhappy."

"Husband is 'blithely unaware,' " suggests Hori, "his wife loves another?"

"Yes, Mr. Hori." Jacob smiles and stretches out his cramped legs.

"Last word," says Kobayashi, "is from book of law: 'lack of proof positive.' "

Before the Dutchman opens his mouth, a grim Constable Kosugi appears at the door; a shaken Hanzaburo is in tow. Kosugi apologizes for the intrusion and delivers a stern narrative that, Jacob sees with mounting unease, includes both Hanzaburo and himself. At one key twist, the interpreters gasp in shock and stare at the bewildered Dutchman. The word for "thief," *dorobô,* is used several times. Motogi verifies a detail with the constable and announces, "Mr. de Zoet, Constable Kosugi bring bad news. Thiefs visit Tall House."

"What?" blurts Jacob. "But when? How did they break in? *Why?*"

"Your house interpreter," confirms Motogi, "believes 'in this hour.' "

"What did they steal?" Jacob turns to Hanzaburo, who looks worried about being blamed. "What *is* there to steal?"

The Tall House stairs are less gloomy than usual: the door to Jacob's upstairs apartment was chiseled off its hinges and, once inside, he finds that his sea chest has suffered the same indignity. The gouged holes on its six sides suggest the burglars were searching for secret compartments. Pained by the sight of his irreplaceable volumes and sketchbooks strewn across the floor, Jacob's first action is to tidy these up. Interpreter Goto helps and asks, "Are some books taken?"

"I can't be sure," Jacob replies, "until they're all gathered up . . ."

. . . but it appears not, and his valuable dictionary is scuffed but safe.

But I can't check my Psalter, Jacob thinks, *until I am left alone.*

There is no sign of this happening soon. As he retrieves his few personal effects, Vorstenbosch, Van Cleef, and Peter Fischer march up the stairs, and now his small room is crowded with more than ten people.

"First my teapot," declares the chief, "now *this* fresh scandal."

"We shall strive great efforts," Kobayashi promises, "to find thiefs."

Peter Fischer asks Jacob, "Where was the house interpreter during the theft?"

Interpreter Motogi puts the question to Hanzaburo, who answers sheepishly. "He go ashore for one hour," says Motogi, "to visit very sick mother."

Fischer snorts derisively. "I know where *I'd* begin my investigations."

Van Cleef asks, "What items did the burglars take, Mr. de Zoet?"

"Fortunately, my remaining mercury — perhaps the thieves' target — is under treble lock in Warehouse Eik. My pocket watch was on my person, as were, thank heaven, my spectacles, and so, on first inspection, it appears that —"

"In the name of God on high." Vorstenbosch rounds on Kobayashi. "Are we not robbed enough by your government during our regular trade without these repeated acts of larceny against our persons and property? Report to the Long Room in one hour, so I may dictate an official letter of complaint to the magistracy, which shall include a *full* list of items stolen by the thieves . . ."

"Done." Con Twomey finishes rehanging the door and lapses into his Irish English. "Feckin' langers'd need to rip out the feckin' wall, like, to get through *that*."

Jacob sweeps up the sawdust. "Who is Feck Inlangers?"

The carpenter raps the door frame. "I'll fix your sea chest tomorrow. Good, like new. This was a bad thing — and in broad daylight, too, yes?"

"I still have my limbs." Jacob is sick with worry about his Psalter.

If the book is gone, he fears, *the thieves will think:* blackmail.

"That's the way." Twomey wraps his tools in oilcloth. "Until dinner."

As the Irishman walks down the stairs, Jacob closes the door and slides the bolt, shifts the bed a few inches . . .

Might Grote have ordered the break-in, he wonders, *as vengeance for the ginseng bulbs?*

Jacob lifts a floorboard, lies down, and reaches for the sack-wrapped book . . .

His fingertips find the Psalter and he gasps with relief. "The Lord preserveth all them that love Him." He replaces the floorboard and sits on his bed. He is safe; Ogawa is safe. *Then what,* he wonders, *is wrong?* Jacob senses he is overlooking something crucial. *Like when I* know *a ledger is hiding a lie or an error, even when the totals appear to balance.*

Hammering starts up across Flag Square. The carpenters are late.

It's concealed in the obvious, Jacob thinks. *"In broad daylight."* Truth batters him like a hod of bricks: *Kobayashi's questions were a coded boast.* The break-in was a message. It declares, *The "repercussions" of crossing me, of which you are "blithely unaware," are being enacted now, "in broad daylight." You are "impotent" to retaliate, for there shall be not a scrap of "proof positive."* Kobayashi claimed authorship of the robbery and placed himself above suspicion: how could a burglar be with his victim at the time of the burglary? If Jacob reported the code words, he would sound delusional.

The broiling day is cooling; its clatter has receded; Jacob feels sick.

He wants revenge, yes, Jacob guesses, *but the gloater wants a prize, too.*

After the Psalter, what is the most damaging thing to have stolen?

The cooling day is broiling; its clatter condenses; Jacob has a headache.

The newest pages of my sketchbook, he realizes, *under my pillow . . .*

Trembling, Jacob throws away the pillow, snatches the sketchbook, fumbles with its ties, turns to the last page, and cannot breathe: here is the serrated edge of a torn-out sheet. It was filled with the drawings of the face, hands, and eyes of Miss Aibagawa, *and somewhere nearby, Kobayashi is contemplating these likenesses in malign delight . . .*

Shutting his eyes against the picture only increases its clarity.

Make this not true, Jacob prays, but this prayer tends to go unanswered.

The street door opens. Slow footsteps drag themselves up the stairs.

The extraordinary fact that Marinus is paying him a call scarcely dents Jacob's adamantine misery. *What if her permission to study on Dejima is revoked?* A stout cane raps on the door. "Domburger."

"I've had enough unwelcome visitors in one day, Doctor."

"Open this door now, you village idiot."

It is easiest for Jacob to obey. "Come to gloat, have you?"

Marinus peers around the clerk's apartment, settles on the window ledge, and takes in the view over Long Street and the garden through the glass-and-paper window. He unties and reties his lustrous gray hair. "What did they take?"

"Nothing . . ." He remembers Vorstenbosch's lie. "Nothing of value."

"In cases of burglary" — Marinus coughs — "I prescribe a course of billiards."

"Billiards, Doctor," Jacob vows, "is the *last* thing I shall be doing today."

Jacob's cue ball sails up the table, rebounds off the bottom cushion, and glides to a halt two inches from the top edge, a hand's length closer than Marinus's. "Take the first stroke, Doctor. To how many points shall we play?"

"Hemmij and I would set our finishing post at five hundred and one."

Eelattu squeezes lemons into cloudy glasses; they scent the air yellow.

A breeze blows through the billiards room in Garden House.

Marinus concentrates hard on his first strike of the game . . .

Why this sudden kindness? Jacob cannot

help but wonder.

. . . but the doctor's shot is misjudged, hitting the red but not Jacob's cue ball.

Easily, Jacob pockets both his and the red. "Shall I tally the score?"

"You are the bookkeeper. Eelattu, the afternoon is your own."

Eelattu thanks his master and leaves, and the clerk shoots a tight series of cannons, quickly taking his score to fifty. The billiard balls' muffled trundling smooths his ruffled nerves. *The shock of the burglary,* he half-persuades himself, *made me go off at half cock: for Miss Aibagawa to be drawn by a foreigner cannot be a punishable offense, even here. It's not as if she posed for me clandestinely.* After accruing sixty points, Jacob lets Marinus on the table. *Nor,* the clerk thinks, *is a page of sketches "proof positive" that I am infatuated with the woman.*

The doctor, Jacob realizes, is a middling amateur at billiards.

Nor is "infatuated," he corrects himself, *an accurate description . . .*

"Time must hang heavy here, Doctor, once the ship departs?"

"For most, yes. The men seek solace in grog, the pipe, intrigues, hatred of our hosts, and in sex. For my part" — he misses an easy shot — "I prefer the company of botany, my studies, my teaching, and, of course, my harpsichord."

Jacob chalks his cue. "How are the Scarlatti sonatas?"

Marinus sits on the upholstered bench. "Fishing for gratitude, are we?"

"Never, Doctor. I gather you belong to a native academy of science."

"The Shirandô? It lacks government patronage. Edo is dominated by 'patriots' who mistrust all things foreign, so, officially, we are just another private school. Unofficially, we are a bourse for *rangakusha* — scholars of European sciences and arts — to exchange ideas. Ôtsuki Monjurô, the director, has influence enough at the magistracy to ensure my monthly invitations."

"Is Dr. Aibagawa" — Jacob pots the red, long distance — "also a member?"

Marinus is watching his younger opponent meaningfully.

"I ask out of mere curiosity, Doctor."

"Dr. Aibagawa is a keen astronomer and attends when his health permits. He was, in fact, the first Japanese to observe Herschel's new planet through a telescope ordered here at wild expense. He and I, indeed, discuss optics more than medicine."

Jacob returns the red ball to the balkline, wondering how not to change the subject.

"After his wife and sons died," continued the doctor, "Dr. Aibagawa married a younger woman, a widow, whose son was to be in-

215

ducted into Dutch medicine and carry on the Aibagawa practice. The young man turned out to be an idle disappointment."

"And is Miss Aibagawa" — the younger man lines up an ambitious shot — "also permitted to attend the Shirandô?"

"There are laws ranged against you: your suit is hopeless."

"Laws." Jacob's shot rattles in the pocket's jaws. "Laws against a doctor's daughter becoming a foreigner's wife?"

"Not constitutional laws. I mean real laws: laws of the *non si fa*."

"So . . . Miss Aibagawa does *not* attend the Shirandô?"

"As a matter of fact, she is the academy's registrar. But as I keep trying to tell you . . ." Marinus pockets the vulnerable red, but his cue ball fails to spin backward. "Women of her class do not become Dejima wives. Even were she to share your *tendresse,* what hopes of a decent marriage after being pawed by a red-haired devil? If you do love her, express your devotion by avoiding her."

He's right, thinks Jacob, and asks, "May I accompany you to the Shirandô? Just the once?"

"Certainly not." Marinus tries to pot both his cue ball and Jacob's but misses.

There are limits, then, Jacob realizes, *to this unexpected détente.*

"You are no scholar," the doctor explains.

216

"Nor am I your pimp."

"Is it fair to berate the less privileged for womanizing, smoking, and drinking" — Jacob pots Marinus's cue ball — "whilst refusing to help their self-betterment?"

"I am not a society for public improvement. What privileges I enjoy, I earned."

Cupido or Philander is practicing an air on a viol da gamba.

The goats and a dog engage in a battle of bleating and barking.

"You spoke of how you and Mr. Hemmij" — Jacob miscues — "used to play for a wager?"

"You're never proposing," the doctor mock-whispers, "gambling on a Sabbath?"

"If I reach five hundred and one first, take me to the Shirandô."

Marinus lines up his shot, looking doubtful. "What is my prize?"

He's not rejecting the idea, Jacob notices, *out of hand.* "Name it."

"Six hours' labor in my garden. Now, pass me the bridge."

"For your question's intents and purposes . . ." Marinus considers his next shot from all angles. "Sentience in this life began in the rainsodden summer of 1757 in a Haarlem garret: I was a six-year-old boy who had been taken to death's door by a savage fever that had seen off my entire family of cloth

217

merchants."

You, too, thinks Jacob. "I'm most sorry, Doctor. I didn't guess."

"The world is a vale of tears. I was passed like a bad *penning* down a chain of relatives, each expecting a slice of an inheritance that had, in fact, been swallowed by debts. My illness made me" — he pats his lame thigh — "an unpromising investment. The last, a great-uncle of dubious vintage named Cornelis, told me I'd one evil eye and one queer one and took me to Leiden, where he deposited me on a canalside doorstep. He told me my 'aunt-in-a-manner-of-speaking' Lidewijde would take me in and vanished like a rat down a drain. Having no other choice, I rang the bell. Nobody answered. There was no point trying to limp after Great-Uncle Cornelis so I just waited on the high doorstep . . ."

Marinus's next shot misses both the red and Jacob's cue ball.

". . . until a friendly constable threatened to thrash me for vagabondage." Marinus drains his lemon juice. "I was dressed in my cousins' castoffs, so my denial fell on deaf ears. Up and down the Rapenburg I walked, just to stay warm." Marinus looks over the water toward the Chinese factory. "A sunless, locked-up, tiring afternoon, and chestnut sellers were out, and canine street urchins watched me, scenting prey, and across the canal, maples shed leaves like women tearing up letters . . . and are you going to play your shot or not, Domburger?"

Jacob achieves a rare double cannon: twelve points.

"Back at the house, the lights were still off. I rang the bell, beseeching the aid of every god I knew, and an old maid's old maid flung the door open, swearing that were *she* the mistress I'd be turned away with no further ado, for tardiness was a sin in her book, but as she wasn't, Klaas would see me in the back garden, though my entrance was the tradesman's, down the steps. She slammed the door. So I made my descent, knocked, and the same wrathful Cerberus in petticoats appeared, noticed my stick, and led me down a dingy basement corridor to a beautiful sunken garden. Play your shot, or we'll still be here at midnight."

Jacob pots both cue balls and lines up the red nicely.

"An old gardener emerged from a curtain of lilac and told me to show him my hands. Puzzled, he asked whether I'd done so much as one day's work as a gardener in my life. No, I said. 'We'll let the garden decide,' said Klaas the Gardener, and very little besides all the livelong day. We mixed hornbeam leaves with horse manure; laid sawdust around the feet of roses; raked leaves in the small apple orchard . . . These were my first pleasant hours for a long, long time. We lit a fire with swept-up leaves and roasted a potato. A robin sat on my spade — it was already *my* spade — and sang." Marinus imitates a robin's *chk-chk-chk*. "It was getting dark when a lady in a satrap's dressing gown and short white hair strode over the lawn. 'My name,' she declared, 'is Lidewijde Mostaart, but the mystery is you.' She had just heard, you see, that the real gardener's boy, due that afternoon, had broken his leg. So I explained who I was and about Great-Uncle Cornelis . . ."

Passing a hundred and fifty points, Jacob misses a shot to let Marinus on the table.

In the garden, the slave Sjako is brushing aphids from the salad leaves.

Marinus leans out the window and addresses him in fluent Malay. Sjako replies and Marinus returns to the game, amused. "My mother, it transpired, was a second cousin of Lidewijde Mostaart, whom she had never met. Abigail, the old maid, huffed, puffed, and complained that anyone would have taken me for the new gardener's boy, given the rags I wore. Klaas said I had the makings of a gardener and retired to the shed. I asked Mrs. Mostaart to let me stay and be Klaas's assistant. She told me it was 'Miss,' not 'Mrs.,' to most, but 'Aunt' to me, and took me inside to meet Elisabeth. I ate fennel soup and answered their questions, and in the morning they told me I could live with them for as long as I wished. My old clothes were sacrificed to the deity in the fireplace."

Cicadas hiss in the pines. They sound like fat frying in a shallow pan.

Marinus misses a side-pocket pot and pockets his own cue ball by mistake.

"Bad luck," commiserates Jacob, adding the foul to his total.

"No such thing, in a game of skill. Well, bibliophiles are not uncommon in Leiden, but bibliophiles made wise by reading are as rare there as anywhere. Aunts Lidewijde and Elisabeth were two such readers, as sagacious as they were rapacious devourers of the written word. Lidewijde had had 'associations' with the stage in her day, in Vienna and Naples, and Elisabeth was what we'd now call a *blauw-stocking,* and their house was a trove of books. To this printed garden, I was given the keys. Lidewijde, moreover, taught me the harpsichord; Elisabeth taught me both French and Swedish, her mother tongue; and Klaas the Gardener was my first, unlettered but vastly learned teacher of botany. Moreover, my aunts' circle of friends included some of Leiden's freest-thinking scholars, which is to say, 'of the age.' My own personal Enlightenment was breathed into being. I bless Great-Uncle Cornelis to this day for abandoning me there."

Jacob pockets Marinus's cue ball and the red alternately three or four times.

A dandelion seed lands on the green baize of the table.

"Genus *Taraxacum.*" Marinus frees it and launches it from the window. "Of the family *Asteraceae.* But erudition alone fills neither belly nor pocketbook, and my aunts survived frugally on slender annuities, so as I reached maturity, it was settled that I should study medicine to support my scientific endeavors. I won a place at the medical school at Uppsala, in Sweden. The choice, of course, was no accident: cumulative weeks of my boyhood had been spent poring through *Species Plantarum* and *Systema Naturae,* and, once ensconced at Uppsala, I became a disciple of the celebrated Professor Linnaeus."

"My uncle says" — Jacob slaps a fly — "he was one of the great men of our age."

"Great men are greatly complex beings. It's true that Linnaean taxonomy underlies botany, but he taught also that swallows hibernate under lakes; that twelve-foot giants thump about Patagonia; and that Hottentots are monorchids, possessing but a single testicle. They have two. I looked. *Deus creavit,* his motto ran, *Linnaeus disposuit,* and dissenters were heretics whose careers must be crushed. Yet he influenced my fate directly by advising me to win a professorship by traveling the East as one of his 'apostles,' mapping the flora of the Indies and trying to gain entry into Japan."

"You are approaching your fiftieth birthday, are you not, Doctor?"

"Linnaeus's last lesson, of which he himself was unaware, was that professorships kill philosophers. Oh, I'm vain enough to want my burgeoning *Flora Japonica* to be published one day — as a votive offering to human knowledge — but a seat at Uppsala, or Leiden, or Cambridge, holds no allure. My heart is the East's, in this lifetime. This is my third year in Nagasaki, and I have work enough for another three, or six. During the court embassy I can see landscapes no European botanist *ever* saw. My seminarians are keen young men — with one young woman — and visiting scholars bring me specimens from all over the empire."

"But aren't you afraid of dying here, so far away from . . . ?"

"One has to die somewhere, Domburger. What are the scores?"

"Your ninety-one points, Doctor, against my three hundred and six."

"Shall we put our finishing post at a thousand points and double the prizes?"

"Are you promising you'll take me to the Shirandô Academy twice?"

To be seen by Miss Aibagawa there, he thinks, *is to be seen in a new light.*

"Provided you are willing to dig horse manure into the beetroot beds for twelve hours."

"Very well, Doctor." The clerk wonders whether Van Cleef might loan him the nimble-fingered Weh to repair the ruff on his best lace shirt. "I accept your terms."

CHAPTER TEN:
THE GARDEN ON DEJIMA

Late in the afternoon of September 16, 1799 Jacob digs the last of the day's horse manure into the beetroot beds and fetches water for the late cucumbers from the tarred barrels. He started his clerical work one hour early this morning so he could finish at four o'clock and begin repaying the twelve hours' garden labor he owes the doctor. *Marinus was a scoundrel,* Jacob thinks, *to hide his virtuosity at billiards, but a wager is a wager.* He removes the straw from around the cucumber plants' stems, empties both gourds, then replaces the mulch to keep the moisture in the thirsty soil. Now and then a curious head appears above the Long Street wall. The sight of a Dutch clerk pulling up weeds like a peasant is worth catching. Hanzaburo, when asked to help, laughed until he saw that Jacob was in earnest, then mimed a back pain and walked away, pocketing a fistful of lavender heads by the garden gate. Arie Grote tried to sell Jacob his shark-hide hat so he could "toil with elegance, like a gentleman farmer"; Piet Baert offered to sell him billiards lessons; and Ponke Ouwehand helpfully pointed out some weeds. Gardening is harder labor than Jacob is used to, *and yet,* he admits to himself, *I enjoy it.* His tired eyes are rested by the living green; rosefinches pluck worms from the ramped-up earth; and a black-masked bunting, whose song sounds like clinking cutlery, watches from the empty cistern. Chief Vorstenbosch and Deputy van Cleef are at the Nagasaki residence of the Lord of Satsuma, the shogun's father-in-law, to press their case for more copper, so Dejima enjoys an unsupervised air. The seminarians are in the hospital: as Jacob hoes the rows of beans, he hears Marinus's voice through the surgery window. Miss Aibagawa is there. Jacob still hasn't seen her, much less spoken to her, since giving her the daringly illustrated fan. The glimmers of kindness the doctor is showing him shall not extend to arranging a rendezvous. Jacob has considered asking Ogawa Uzaemon to take her a letter from him, but if it was discovered, both the interpreter and Miss Aibagawa could be prosecuted for secret negotiations with a foreigner.

And, anyway, Jacob thinks, *what would I even write in such a letter?*

■ ■ ■ ■

Picking slugs from the cabbages with a pair of chopsticks, Jacob notices a ladybird on his right hand. He makes a bridge for it with his left, which the insect obligingly crosses. Jacob repeats the exercise several times. *The ladybird believes,* he thinks, *she is on a momentous journey, but she is going nowhere.* He pictures an endless sequence of bridges between skin-covered islands over voids, and wonders if an unseen force is playing the same trick on him . . .

. . . until a woman's voice dispels his reverie: "Mr. Dazûto?"

Jacob removes his bamboo hat and stands up.

Miss Aibagawa's face eclipses the sun. "I beg pardon to disturb."

Surprise, guilt, nervousness . . . Jacob feels many things.

She notices the ladybird on his thumb. *"Tentô-mushi."*

In his eagerness to comprehend, he mishears: *"O-ben-tô-mushi?"*

"O-ben-tô-mushi is 'luncheon-box bug.' " She smiles. "This" — she indicates the ladybird — "is *O-ten-tô-mushi."*

"Tentô-mushi," he says. She nods like a pleased teacher.

Her deep-blue summer kimono and white

227

headscarf lend her a nun's air.

They are not alone: the inevitable guard stands by the garden gate.

Jacob tries to ignore him. " 'Ladybird.' A gardener's friend . . ."

Anna would like you, he thinks, looking into her face. *Anna would like you.*

". . . because ladybirds eat greenfly." Jacob raises his thumb to his lips and blows.

The ladybird flies all of three feet to the scarecrow's face.

She adjusts the scarecrow's hat as a wife might. "How you call him?"

"A scarecrow, to 'scare crows' away, but his name is Robespierre."

"Warehouse Eik is 'Warehouse Oak'; monkey is 'William.' Why scarecrow is 'Robespierre'?"

"Because his head falls off when the wind changes. It's a dark joke."

"Joke is secret language" — she frowns — "inside words."

Jacob decides against referring to the fan until she does; it would appear, at least, that she is not offended or angered. "May I help you, Miss?"

"Yes. Dr. Marinus ask I come and ask you for *rôzu-meri.* He ask . . ."

The better I know Marinus, thinks Jacob, *the less I understand him.*

". . . he ask, 'Bid Dombâga give you six . . . "sprogs" of *rôzu-meri.*' "

228

"Over here, then, in the herb garden." He leads her down the path, unable to think of a single pleasantry that doesn't sound terminally inane.

She asks, "Why Mr. Dazûto work today as Dejima gardener?"

"Because," the pastor's nephew lies through his teeth, "I enjoy a garden's company. As a boy," he leavens his lie with some truth, "I worked in a relative's orchard. We cultivated the first plum trees ever to grow in our village."

"In village of Domburg," she says, "in province of Zeeland."

"You are most kind to remember." Jacob breaks off a half dozen young sprigs. "Here you are." For a priceless coin of time, their hands are linked by a few inches of fragrant herb, witnessed by a dozen blood-orange sunflowers.

I don't want a purchased courtesan, he thinks. *I wish to earn you.*

"Thank you." She smells the herb. " 'Rosemary' has meaning?"

Jacob blesses his foul-breathed martinet of a Latin master in Middelburg. "Its Latin name is *rosmarinus,* wherein *ros* is 'dew' — do you know the word 'dew'?"

She frowns, shakes her head a little, and her parasol spins slowly.

"Dew is water found early in the morning before the sun burns it away."

The midwife understands. " 'Dew' . . . we say *asa-tsuyu.*"

Jacob knows he shall never forget the word *"asa-tsuyu"* so long as he lives. *"Ros* being 'dew,' and *marinus* meaning 'ocean,' *rosmarinus* is 'dew of the ocean.' Old people say that rosemary thrives — grows well — only when it can hear the ocean."

The story pleases her. "Is it true tale?"

"It may be" — *let time stop,* Jacob wishes — "prettier than it is true."

"Meaning of *marinus* is 'sea'? So doctor is 'Dr. Ocean'?"

"You could say so, yes. Does 'Aibagawa' have meaning?"

"*Aiba* is 'indigo.' " Her pride in her name is plain. "And *gawa* is 'river.' "

"So you are an indigo river. You sound like a poem." *And* you, Jacob tells himself, *sound like a flirty lecher.* "Rosemary is also a woman's Christian name — a given name. My own given name is" — he strains to sound casual — "Jacob."

She swivels her head to show puzzlement. "What is . . . Ya-ko-bu?"

"The name my parents gave me: Jacob. My full name is Jacob de Zoet."

She gives a cautious nod. "Yakobu Dazûto."

I wish, he thinks, *spoken words could be captured and kept in a locket.*

"My pronounce," Miss Aibagawa asks, "is

230

not very good?"

"No no no: you are perfect in every way. Your pronounce is perfect."

Crickets scritter and clirk in the garden's low walls of stones.

"Miss Aibagawa —" Jacob swallows. "What is your given name?"

She makes him wait. "My name from mother and father is Orito."

The breeze twists a coil of her hair around its finger.

She looks down. "Doctor is waiting. Thank you for rosemary."

Jacob says, "You are most welcome," and doesn't dare say more.

She takes three or four paces and turns back. "I forget a thing." She reaches into her sleeve and produces a fruit, the size and hue of an orange but smooth as hairless skin. "From my garden. I bring many to Dr. Marinus, so he ask I take one to Mr. Dazûto. It is *kaki*."

"Then, in Japanese, a persimmon is a *cacky*?"

"Ka-*ki*." She rests it on the crook of the scarecrow's shoulder.

"Ka-*ki*. Robespierre and I shall eat it later; thank you."

Her wooden slippers crunch the friable earth as she walks along the path.

Act, implores the Ghost of Future Regret. *I shan't give you another chance.*

Jacob hurries past the tomatoes and catches her up near the gate.

"Miss Aibagawa? Miss Aibagawa. I must ask you to forgive me."

She has turned and has one hand on the gate. "Why forgive?"

"For what I now say." The marigolds are molten. "You are beautiful."

Her mouth opens and closes. She takes a step back . . .

. . . into the wicket gate. It rattles. The guard swings it open.

Damned fool, groans the Demon of Present Regret. *What have you done?*

Crumpling, burning, and freezing, Jacob retreats, but the garden has quadrupled in length, and it may take a Wandering Jew's eternity before he reaches the cucumbers, where he kneels behind a screen of dock leaves; where the snail on the pail flexes its stumpy horns; where ants carry patches of rhubarb leaf along the shaft of the hoe; and he wishes the earth might spin backward to the moment when she appeared, asking for rosemary, and he would do it all again, and he would do it all differently.

A doe cries for her yearling, slaughtered for the lord of Satsuma.

Before the evening muster, Jacob climbs the watchtower and takes out the persimmon from his jacket pocket. Hollows from the fingers of Aibagawa Orito are indented in her ripe gift, and he places his own fingers there, holds the fruit under his nostrils, inhales its gritty sweetness, and rolls its rotundity along his cracked lips. *I regret my confession,* he thinks, *yet what choice did I have?* He eclipses the sun with her persimmon: the planet glows orange like a jack-o'-lantern. There is a dusting around its woody black cap and stem. Lacking a knife or spoon, he takes a nip of waxy skin between his incisors and tears; juice oozes from the gash; he licks the sweet smears and sucks out a dribbling gobbet of threaded flesh and holds it gently, *gently,* against the roof of his mouth, where the pulp disintegrates into fermented jasmine, oily cinnamon, perfumed melon, melted damson . . . and in its heart he finds ten or fifteen flat stones, brown as Asian eyes and the same shape. The sun is gone now, cicadas fall silent, lilacs and turquoises dim and thin into grays and darker grays. A bat passes within a few feet, chased by its own furry turbulence. There is not the faintest breath of a breeze. Smoke emerges from the galley flue on the *Shenandoah* and sags around the brig's bows. Her gunports are open and the sound of ten dozen sailors dining in her belly carries over the water; and like a struck tuning fork, Jacob reverberates with the parts and the entirety of Orito, with all the *her*-ness of her. The promise he gave to Anna rubs his conscience like a burr. *But Anna,* he thinks uneasily, *is so far away in miles and in years; and she gave her consent, she as good as gave her consent, and she'd never know,* and Jacob's stomach ingests Orito's slithery gift. *Creation never ceased on the sixth evening,* it occurs to the young man. *Creation unfolds around us, despite us, and through us, at the speed of days and nights, and we like to call it "love."*

"Kapitan Bôru-su ten-bôshu," intones Interpreter Sekita, a quarter hour later at the flagpole's foot. Ordinarily, the twice-daily muster is conducted by Constable Kosugi, who requires only a minute to check the foreigners, all of whose names and faces he knows. This evening, however, Sekita has decided to assert his authority by conducting the muster while the constable stands to one side with a sour face. "Where is the" — Sekita squints at his list — "the Bôru-su ten-bôshu?"

Sekita's scribe tells his master that Chief Vorstenbosch is attending the lord of Satsuma this evening. Sekita administers a rebuke to his scribe and squints at the next name. "Where is the . . . the Banku-rei-fu?"

Sekita's scribe reminds his master that Deputy van Cleef is with the chief.

Constable Kosugi clears his throat loudly and unnecessarily.

The interpreter proceeds with the muster list. "Ma-ri-as-su . . ."

Marinus stands with thumbs in his jacket pocket. "*Doctor* Marinus."

Sekita looks up, alarmed. "The Marinus need the doctor?"

Gerritszoon and Baert snort, amused. Sekita senses he has made a mistake and says, "Friend in need is friend indeed." He peers at the next name: "Fui . . . shâ . . ."

"That, I daresay," replies Peter Fischer, "is I, but one says it thus: 'Fischer.' "

"Yes yes, the Fuishâ." Sekita wrestles with the next name. "Ôe-hando."

"Present, for my sins," says Ouwehand, rubbing the ink stains on his hands.

Sekita dabs his brow with a handkerchief. "Dazûto . . ."

"Present," says Jacob. *To list and name people,* he thinks, *is to subjugate them.*

Working down the muster, Sekita butchers the hands' names: the snide quips with which Gerritszoon and Baert respond do not alter the fact that they must, and do, answer. The white foreigners accounted for, Sekita proceeds to the servants and slaves, who stand in two groups to the left and right of their masters. The interpreter begins with the servants: Eelattu, Cupido, and Philander, then squints at the name of the muster list's first slave. "Su-ya-ko."

When there is no reply, Jacob looks around

235

for the missing Malay.

Sekita hammers out the syllables, "Su-ya-ko," but there is no reply.

He fires a foul glare at his scribe, who asks Constable Kosugi a question. Kosugi tells Sekita, Jacob guesses, "This is *your* mustering, so missing names are *your* problem." Sekita addresses Marinus. "Where — are — Su-ya-ko?"

The doctor is humming a bass tune. When the verse ends and Sekita is riled, Marinus turns to the servants and slaves. "Would you be so kind as to locate Sjako and tell him that he is late for muster?"

The seven men hurry to Long Street, discussing Sjako's likely whereabouts.

"*I'll* find where the dog is skulking," Peter Fischer tells Marinus, "faster than that brown rabble. Join me, Mr. Gerritszoon; you are the man for this job."

Peter Fischer emerges from Flag Alley less than five minutes later with a bloodied right hand, ahead of some house interpreters who all speak at once to Constable Kosugi and Interpreter Sekita. Moments later, Eelattu appears and reports to Marinus in Ceylonese. Fischer informs the other Dutchmen, "We found the dung beetle in the crate store down Bony Alley next to Warehouse Doorn. I'd seen him go in there earlier today."

"Why," Jacob asks, "didn't you bring him

here for mustering?"

Fischer smiles. "He shan't be walking for a little while, I daresay."

Ouwehand asks, "What did you *do* to him, in Jesus' name?"

"Less than the slave deserves. He was drinking stolen spirits and spoke to us in an abusive manner unforgivable in an equal, let alone a stinking Malay. When Mr. Gerritszoon made shift to correct this impertinence with a length of rattan, he changed into a black fury, howled like a blood-crazed wolf, and tried to batter our skulls with a crowbar."

"Then why did none of *us*," Jacob demands, "hear this blood-crazed howl?"

"Because," Fischer expostulates, "he closed the door first, Clerk de Zoet!"

"Sjako'd never hurt an ant," says Ivo Oost, "not so far as *I* know."

"Perhaps you are too close," Fischer refers to Oost's blood, "to be impartial."

Arie Grote gently removes a whittling knife from Oost's grip. Marinus gives Eelattu an order in Ceylonese, and the servant runs in the direction of the hospital. The doctor hurries as fast as his lameness allows into Flag Alley. Jacob follows, ignoring Sekita's protestations, ahead of Constable Kosugi and his guards.

The evening light turns the whitewashed warehouses of Long Street dim bronze. Jacob catches up with Marinus. At the crossroads they turn down Bony Alley, pass Warehouse Doorn, and enter the hot, dim, cramped crate store.

"Oh, *you* took yer time," says Gerritszoon, sitting on a sack, "di'n't yer?"

"Where's —" Jacob sees the answer to his question.

The sack is Sjako. His once-handsome head is on the floor in a pond of blood; his lip is slit; one eye is half disappeared; and he gives no sign of life. Splintered crates, a smashed bottle, and a broken chair lie around. Gerritszoon kneels on Sjako's back, binding the slave's wrists.

The others crowd into the crate store behind Jacob and the doctor.

"Jesus, Mary," Con Twomey exclaims, "and Oliver *fecking* Cromwell, man!"

The Japanese witnesses utter expressions of shock in their language.

"Unfasten him," Marinus tells Gerritszoon, "and stay out of my reach."

"Oh, *you* ain't the chief an' y'ain't the deputy, neither, an' I swear by God —"

"Unfasten him now," the doctor commands, "or when that bladder stone of yours is so big that your piss is blood and you are screaming like a terrified child for a lithotomy, then *I* swear by *my* God that my hand shall slip with tragic, slow, and agonizing consequences."

" 'Twas our duty," Gerritszoon growls, "to beat the evil out of him." He stands away.

"It's his *life*," declares Ivo Oost, "you beat out of him."

Marinus hands his stick to Jacob and kneels by the slave's side.

"Were we supposed to look on," Fischer asks, "and let him kill us?"

Marinus works the cord free. With Jacob's help, he turns Sjako over.

"Well, Chief V. ain't goin' to be pleased," sniffs Arie Grote, "at *this* handlin' an' stowage of company property, eh?"

A cry of pain grows from Sjako's chest and fades again.

Marinus bundles his coat under Sjako's head, murmurs to the beaten Malay in his own language, and examines the opened skull. The slave shudders, and Marinus grimaces and asks, "Why is there glass in this head wound?"

"Like I said," replies Fischer, "if you listened, he was drinking stolen rum."

"And attacked himself," asks Marinus, "with the bottle in his hand?"

"I wrestled it off of 'im," says Gerritszoon, "to use on 'im."

"The black dog tried to murder us!" Fischer is shouting. "With a hammer!"

"Hammer? Crowbar? Bottle? You'd better tally your story better than that."

"I shan't tolerate," threatens Fischer, "these

— these insinuations, Doctor."

Eelattu arrives with the stretcher. Marinus tells Jacob, "Help, Domburger."

Sekita taps aside the house interpreters with his fan and looks at the scene in disgust. "That is the Su-ya-ko?"

The first course of the officers' supper is a sweet soup of French onions. Vorstenbosch drinks it in displeased silence. He and Van Cleef returned to Dejima in buoyant spirits, but these were dashed by news of Sjako's beating. Marinus is still at the hospital, treating the Malay's many wounds. The chief even dismissed Cupido and Philander from their musical duties, saying that he was not in the mood for music. It is left to Deputy van Cleef and Captain Lacy to entertain the company with their impressions of the Nagasaki residence of the Satsuma lord and his household. Jacob suspects that his patron doesn't wholly believe Fischer and Gerritszoon's version of events in the crate store, but to say so would place the word of a black slave above a white officer and hand. *What sort of precedent,* Jacob imagines Vorstenbosch thinking, *would that set for the other slaves and servants?* Fischer maintains a cautious reserve, sensing that his hopes of retaining the head clerk's post are in jeopardy. When Arie Grote and his kitchen boy serve up the codfish pie, Captain Lacy dispatches his servant for a half

240

dozen bottles of barley mash, but Vorstenbosch doesn't notice; he mutters, "What in God's name is keeping Marinus?" and sends Cupido to fetch the doctor. Cupido is a long time gone. Lacy recounts a polished narrative about fighting alongside George Washington at the Battle of Bunker Hill and devours three servings of apricot pudding before Marinus limps into the dining room.

"We despaired," says Vorstenbosch, "of your joining us, Doctor."

"A cracked clavicle," Marinus begins, as he sits down, "a fractured ulna; a broken jaw; a splintered rib; three teeth gone; grievous bruising in general, to his face and genitals in particular; and a kneecap part detached from its femur. When he walks again, he shall limp as skillfully as I, and, as you saw, his looks are gone for good."

Fischer drinks his Yankee mash as if this has nothing to do with him.

"Then the slave is not," asks Van Cleef, "in danger of his life?"

"As of now, no, but I don't discount infections and fevers."

"For how long" — Vorstenbosch snaps a toothpick — "should he convalesce?"

"Until he is healed. Thereafter, I recommend his duties be light."

Lacy snorts. "Here, *all* slaves' duties are light: Dejima is a field of clover."

"Have you extracted," asks Vorstenbosch,

"the slave's version of events?"

"I hope, sir," Fischer says, "that Mr. Gerritszoon's and my testimony is more than a mere 'version of events.' "

"Damage to company property must be investigated, Fischer."

Captain Lacy fans himself with his hat. "In Carolina, it would be Mr. Fischer's compensation from the slave's owners we'd be discussing."

"*After,* one trusts, establishing the facts. Dr. Marinus: why did the slave absent himself from the mustering? He's been here years. He knows the rules."

"I'd blame those same 'years.' " Marinus spoons himself some pudding. "They have worn away at him and induced a nervous collapse."

"Doctor, you are —" Lacy laughs and chokes. "You are incomparable! A 'nervous collapse'? What next? A mule too melancholic to pull? A hen too lachrymose to lay?"

"Sjako has a wife and son in Batavia," says Marinus. "When Gijsbert Hemmij brought him to Dejima seven years ago, this family was divided. Hemmij promised Sjako his freedom in return for faithful service when he returned to Java."

"Had I but *one dollar* for every nigger spoiled," Lacy exclaims, "by a rashly promised manumission, I could buy all of Florida!"

"But when Chief Hemmij died," Van Cleef

objects, "his promise died, too."

"This spring, Daniel Snitker told Sjako the oath would be honored after the trading season." Marinus stuffs tobacco into his pipe. "Sjako was led to believe he would be sailing to Batavia as a free man in a few weeks' time and had fixed his heart on laboring for his family's liberty upon the *Shenandoah*'s arrival."

"Snitker's word," says Lacy, "isn't worth the paper it wasn't written on."

"Just yesterday," Marinus continues, pausing to light a taper from the candle and suck his pipe into life, "Sjako learned this promise is reneged and his freedom is dashed to pieces."

"The slave is to stay here," says the chief, "for my term of office. Dejima lacks hands."

"Then why profess surprise" — the doctor breathes out a cloud of smoke — "at his state of mind? Seven plus five equals twelve when last *I* looked: twelve years. Sjako was brought here in his seventeenth year: he shan't be leaving until his twenty-ninth. His son shall be sold long before then, and his wife mated to another."

"How can *I* 'renege' on a promise *I* never made?" Vorstenbosch objects.

"That is an acute and logical point, sir," says Peter Fischer.

"My wife and daughters," says Van Cleef, "I haven't seen in *eight* years!"

"You are a deputy." Marinus picks at a scab of blood on his cuff. "Here to make yourself rich. Sjako is a slave, here to make his masters comfortable."

"A slave is a slave," Peter Fischer declaims, "because he does a slave's work!"

"What about," Lacy says, cleaning his ear with a fork prong, "a night at the theater, to lift his spirits? We could stage *Othello,* perhaps?"

"Are we not in danger," asks Van Cleef, "of losing sight of the principal point? That today a slave attempted to murder two of our colleagues?"

"Another excellent point, sir," says Fischer, "if I may say so."

Marinus places his thumbs together. "Sjako denies attacking his assailants."

Fischer leans back on his chair and declares to the chandelier, *"Fa!"*

"Sjako says the two white masters set about him quite unprovoked."

"The would-be cutthroat," Fischer states, "is a liar of the blackest dye."

"Blacks *do* lie." Lacy opens his snuffbox. "Like geese shit slime."

Marinus places his pipe on its stand. "Why would Sjako attack you?"

"Savages don't need motives!" Fischer spits in the spittoon. "Your type, Dr. Marinus, sit at your meetings, nod wisely at wind about 'the true cost of the sugar in our tea' from an

244

'improved Negro' in wig and waistcoat. I, *I,* am not a man created by Swedish gardens but by Surinam jungles, where one sees the Negro in his natural habitat. Earn yourself one of *these*" — Peter Fischer unbuttons his shirt to display a three-inch scar above his collarbone — "and *then* tell me a savage has a soul just because he can recite the Lord's Prayer, like any parrot."

Lacy peers close, impressed. "How did you pick up *that* souvenir?"

"Whilst recuperating at Goed Accoord," Fischer answers, glowering at the doctor, "a plantation on the Commewina, two days up-river from Paramaribo. My platoon had gone to cleanse the basin of runaway slaves who attack in gangs. The colonists call them 'rebels'; I call them 'vermin.' We had burned many of their nests and yam fields, but the dry season overtook us, when hell has no worse hole. Not one of my men was free from beriberi or ringworm fever. The house blacks of Goed Accoord betrayed our weakness, and on the third dawn, they slithered up to the house and attacked. Hundreds of the vipers crawled out of the dry slime and dropped from the trees. With musket, bayonet, and bare hands, my men and I made a valiant defense, but when a mace struck my skull, I collapsed. Hours must have passed. When I awoke, my arms and feet were bound. My jaw was — how do you say? — mislocated. I lay in a row of wounded men in the drawing room. Some begged for mercy, but no Negro understands the concept. The slave leader arrived and bidded his butchers extract the men's hearts for their victory feast. This they did" — Fischer swills his mash around his glass — "slowly, without first killing their victims."

"Such barbarity and wickedness," Van Cleef declares, "beggars belief!"

Vorstenbosch sends Philander and Weh downstairs for bottles of Rhenish.

"My unluckier comrades, Swiss Fourgeoud, DeJohnette, and my bosom friend, Tom Isberg, they suffered the agonies of Christ. Their screams shall haunt me until I die, and so shall the blacks' laughter. They stored the hearts in a chamber pot, just inches from where I lay. The room stunk of the slaughterhouse; the air was black with flies. It was darkness when my turn came. I was the last but one. They slung me on the table. Despite my fear, I played dead and prayed God to take my soul quickly. One then uttered, '*Son de go sleeby caba. Mekewe liby den tara dago tay tamara.*' Meaning, the sun was sinking, they'd leave these last two 'dogs' for the following day. The drumming, feasting, and fornication had begun, and the butchers were loath to miss the fun. So, a butcher impaled me to the table with a bayonet, like a but-

246

terfly collector's pin, and I was left without a guard."

Insects dirty the air over the candelabra like a malign halo.

A rust-colored lizard sits on the blade of Jacob's butter knife.

"Now I prayed to God for strength. By twisting my head, I could seize the bayonet's blade between my teeth and slowly work it loose. I lost pints of blood but refused to succumb to weakness. My freedom was won. Under the table was Joosse, my platoon's last survivor. Joosse was a Zeelander, like Clerk de Zoet . . ."

Well, now, thinks Jacob, *what an opportune coincidence.*

". . . and Joosse was a coward, I am sorry to say. He was too afraid to move until my reason conquered his fear. Under the coat of darkness, we left Goed Accoord behind. For seven days, we beat a path through that green pestilence with our bare hands. We had no food but the maggots breeding in our wounds. Many times, Joosse begged to be allowed to die. But honor obliged me to protect even the frail Zeelander from death. Finally, by God's grace, we reached Fort Sommelsdyck, where the Commewina meets the Cottica. We were more dead than alive. My superior officer confessed later that he had expected me to die within hours. 'Never underestimate a Prussian again,' I told him.

The governor of Surinam presented me with a medal, and six weeks later I led two hundred men back to Goed Accoord. A glorious revenge was extracted on the vermin, but I am not a man who brags of his own achievements."

Weh and Philander return with the bottles of Rhenish.

"A most edifying history," says Lacy. "I salute your courage, Mr. Fischer."

"The passage where you ate the maggots," remarks Marinus, "rather over-egged the *brûlée*."

"The doctor's disbelief," Fischer addresses the senior officers, "is caused by his sentimental attitudes to savages, I am very sorry to say."

"The doctor's disbelief" — Marinus peers at the label on the Rhenish — "is a natural reaction to vainglorious piffle."

"Your accusations," Fischer retorts, "deserve no reply."

Jacob finds an island chain of mosquito bites across his hand.

"Slavery may be an injustice to some," says Van Cleef, "but no one can deny that all empires are founded upon the institution."

"Then may the devil," Marinus says, twisting in the corkscrew, "take all empires."

"What an extraordinary utterance," declares Lacy, "to hear from the mouth of a colonial officer!"

"Extraordinary," agrees Fischer, "not to say *Jacobinical.*"

"I am no 'colonial officer.' I am a physician, scholar, and traveler."

"You hunt for fortune," says Lacy, "courtesy of the Dutch Empire."

"My treasure is botanical." The cork pops. "The fortunes I leave to you."

"How very 'Enlightened,' *outré,* and French, which nation, by the by, learned the perils of abolishing slavery. Anarchy set the Caribbean alight; plantations were pillaged; men strung up from trees; and by the time Paris had its Negroes back in chains, Hispaniola was lost."

"Yet the British Empire," Jacob says, "is embracing abolition."

Vorstenbosch looks at his onetime protégé like an evaluator.

"The British," Lacy warns, "are engaged in some trickery or other, as time shall tell."

"And those citizens in your own northern states," says Marinus, "who recognize —"

"Those Yankee leeches grow fat on *our* taxes!" Captain Lacy wags his knife.

"In the animal kingdom," says Van Cleef, "the vanquished are eaten by those more favored by Nature. Slavery is merciful by comparison: the lesser races keep their lives in exchange for their labor."

"What use," the doctor says, pouring himself a glass of wine, "is an eaten slave?"

The grandfather clock in the stateroom

strikes ten times.

Vorstenbosch arrives at a decision. "Displeased as I am about the events in the crate store, Fischer, I accept that you and Gerritszoon acted in self-defense."

"I swear, sir" — Fischer tilts his head — "we had no other choice."

Marinus grimaces at his glass of Rhenish. "Atrocious aftertaste."

Lacy brushes his mustache. "What about *your* slave, Doctor?"

"Eelattu, sir, is no more a slave than your first mate. I found him in Jaffna five years ago, beaten and left for dead by a gang of Portuguese whalers. During his recovery, the boy's quickness of mind persuaded me to offer him employ as my chirurgical assistant, for pay, from my own pocket. He may quit his post when he wishes, with wages and character. Can any man on the *Shenandoah* say as much?"

Lacy walks over to the chamber pot. "Indians, I'll admit, ape civilized manners well enough; and I've entered Pacific Islanders and Chinamen into the *Shenandoah*'s books, so I know of what I speak. But for Africans . . ." The captain unbuttons his breeches and urinates into the pot. "Slavery's the best life: were they ever turned loose, they'd starve before the week was out, without they murdered white families for their larders. They know only the present moment; they cannot

250

plan, farm, invent, or imagine." He shakes free the last drops of urine and tucks his shirt into his breeches. "To condemn slavery" — Captain Lacy scratches beneath his collar — "is, moreover, to condemn Holy Scripture. Blacks are descended from Noah's bestial son Ham, who bedded his own mother; Ham's lineage were thereby accursed. It's there in the ninth book of Genesis, plain as day. 'Cursed be Canaan; a servant of servants shall he be to his brethren.' The white race, however, is descended from Japheth: 'God shall enlarge Japheth, and Canaan shall be his servant.' Or do I lie, Mr. de Zoet?"

All the assembled eyes turn to the nephew of the parsonage.

"Those particular verses are problematical," says Jacob.

"So the clerk calls God's word," taunts Peter Fischer, " 'problematical'?"

"The world would be happier without slavery," replies Jacob, "and —"

"The world would be happier," sniffs Van Cleef, "if golden apples grew on trees."

"Dear Mr. Vorstenbosch," Captain Lacy says, raising his glass, "this Rhenish is a superlative vintage. Its aftertaste is the purest nectar."

CHAPTER ELEVEN: WAREHOUSE EIK

Before the typhoon of October 19, 1799
The noises of battening, nailing, and herding are gusted in through the warehouse doors. Hanzaburo stands on the threshold, watching the darkening sky. At the table, Ogawa Uzaemon is translating the Japanese version of Shipping Document 99b from the trading season of 1797, relating to a consignment of camphor crystals. Jacob records the gaping discrepancies in prices and quantities between it and its Dutch counterpart. The signature verifying the document as "An Honest and True Record of the Consignment" is Acting Deputy Melchior van Cleef's: the deputy's twenty-seventh falsified entry Jacob has so far uncovered. The clerk has told Vorstenbosch of this growing list, but the chief resident's zeal as a reformer of Dejima is dimming by the day. Vorstenbosch's metaphors have changed from "excising the cancer of corruption" to "best employing what tools we have to hand," and, perhaps the clearest

indicator of the chief's attitude, Arie Grote is busier and more cheerful by the day.

"It is soon too dark," says Ogawa Uzaemon, "to see clear."

"How long," Jacob asks, "before we should stop working?"

"One more hour, with oil in lantern. Then I should leave."

Jacob writes a short note asking Ouwehand to give Hanzaburo a jar of oil from the office store, and Ogawa instructs him in Japanese. The boy leaves, his clothes tugged by the wind.

"Last typhoons of season," says Ogawa, "can attack Hizen Domain worst. We think, *Gods save Nagasaki from bad typhoon this year,* and then . . ." Ogawa mimes a battering ram with his hands.

"Autumn gales in Zeeland, too, are quite notorious."

"Pardon me" — Ogawa opens his notebook — "what is 'notorious'?"

"Something that is notorious is 'famous for being bad.' "

"Mr. de Zoet say," recalls Ogawa, "home island is below level of sea."

"Walcheren? So it is, so it is. We Dutch live beneath the fishes."

"To stop the sea to flood the land," Ogawa imagines, "is ancient war."

" 'War' is the word, and we lose battles sometimes." Jacob notices dirt underneath

253

his thumbnail from his last hour in Dr. Marinus's garden this morning. "Dikes break. Yet whilst the sea is the Dutchman's enemy, it is also his provider and the — the 'shaper' of his ingenuity. Had Nature blessed us with high, fertile ground like our neighbors, what need to invent the Amsterdam Bourse, the Joint Stock Company, and our empire of middlemen?"

Carpenters lash the timbers of the half-built Warehouse Lelie.

Jacob decides to broach a delicate subject before Hanzaburo returns. "Mr. Ogawa, when you searched my books, on my first morning ashore, you saw my dictionary, I believe?"

"*New Dictionary of Dutch Language.* Very fine and rare book."

"It would, I assume, be of use to a Japanese scholar of Dutch?"

"Dutch dictionary is magic key to open many lock doors."

"I desire . . ." Jacob hesitates. ". . . to give it to Miss Aibagawa."

Wind-harried voices reach them like echoes from a deep well.

Ogawa's face is stern and unreadable.

"How do you think," probes Jacob, "she might respond to such a gift?"

Ogawa's fingers pluck at a knot around his sash. "Much surprise."

"Not, I hope, an unpleasant surprise?"

"We have proverb." The interpreter pours himself a bowl of tea. " 'Nothing more costly than item that has no price.' When Miss Aibagawa receive such a gift, she may worry, 'What is true price if I accept?' "

"But there is no obligation. Upon my honor, none whatsoever."

"So . . ." Ogawa sips his tea, still avoiding Jacob's eyes. "Why Mr. de Zoet give?"

This is worse, thinks Jacob, *than speaking with Orito in the garden.*

"Because," the clerk swallows, "well, *why* I wish to present her with the gift, I mean, the *source* of that urge, what motivates the puppet master, as it were, is, as Dr. Marinus might express it, that is . . . one of the great imponderables."

What inchoate garble, replies Ogawa's expression, *are you spouting?*

Jacob removes his spectacles, looks out, and sees a dog cocking its leg.

"Book is . . ." Ogawa peers at Jacob under an invisible frame. "Love gift?"

"I *know*" — Jacob feels like an actor obliged to go onstage without a glimpse of the script — "that she — Miss Aibagawa — is no courtesan, that a Dutchman is not an ideal husband, but nor am I a pauper, thanks to my mercury. But none of that matters, and doubtless some would consider me the world's greatest fool . . ."

A twisted ribbon of muscle ripples under

Ogawa's eye.

"Yes, perhaps one *could* call it a love gift, but if Miss Aibagawa cares nothing for me, it doesn't matter. She may keep it. To think of her using the book would . . ." *Bring me happiness,* Jacob cannot quite add. "Were *I* to give the dictionary to her," he explains, "spies, inspectors, and her classmates would notice. Nor may I stroll over to her house of an evening. A ranked interpreter, however, carrying a dictionary, would raise no alarums. Nor, I trust, would it be smuggling, for this is a straightforward gift. And so . . . I would like to ask you to deliver the volume on my behalf."

Twomey and the slave d'Orsaiy dismantle the great tripod in the weighing yard.

Ogawa's lack of surprise suggests that he anticipated this request.

"There is no one else on Dejima," says Jacob, "whom I can trust."

No, indeed, agrees Ogawa's clipped *hmm* noise, *there is not.*

"Inside the dictionary, I would — I have inserted a . . . well, a short letter."

Ogawa lifts his head and views the phrase with suspicion.

"A letter . . . to say that the dictionary is hers for always, but if" — *now I sound,* Jacob thinks, *like a costermonger honey-talking housewives at the market* — "were she . . .

ever . . . to consider me a patron, or let us say a protector, or . . . or . . ."

Ogawa's tone is brusque. "Letter is to propose marriage?"

"Yes. No. Not unless . . ." Wishing he had never begun, Jacob produces the dictionary, wrapped in sailcloth and tied with twine, from under his table. "Yes, damn it. It is a proposal. I beg you, Mr. Ogawa, cut short my misery and just give her the damned thing."

The wind is dark and thunderous; Jacob locks the warehouse and crosses Flag Square, shielding his eyes against dust and grit. Ogawa and Hanzaburo have returned to their homes while it is still safe to be out. At the foot of the flagpole, Van Cleef is bellowing up at d'Orsaiy, who is, Jacob sees, having difficulty shimmying up. "You'd do it for a coconut sharp enough, so you'll damned well do it for our flag!"

A senior interpreter's palanquin is carried by; its window is shut.

Van Cleef notices Jacob. "Blasted flag's knotted and can't be lowered — but I'll not have it ripped to shreds just because this sloth's too afeared to untangle it!"

The slave reaches the top, grips the pole between his thighs, untangles the old United Provinces tricolor, and slides down with the prize, his hair waving in the wind, and hands

257

it to Van Cleef.

"Now run and see what use Mr. Twomey can put your damned hide to!"

D'Orsaiy runs off between the deputy's and captain's houses.

"Mustering is canceled." Van Cleef folds the flag in his jacket and shelters under a gable. "Snatch a bowl of whatever Grote has cooked and go home. My latest wife predicts the wind'll turn twice as fierce as this before the typhoon's eye passes over."

"I thought I'd just" — Jacob points up the watchtower — "take in the view."

"Keep your sightseeing short! You'll be blown to Kamchatka!"

Van Cleef shambles up the alley to the front of his house.

Jacob climbs up the stairs, two at a time. Once he's above roof level, the wind attacks him; he grips the rails tight and lies flat against the platform's planks. From Domburg's church tower, Jacob has watched many a gale gallop down from Scandinavia, but an Oriental typhoon possesses a sentience and menace. Daylight is bruised; woods thrash on the prematurely twilit mountains; the black bay is crazed by choppy surf; gobbets of sea spray spatter Dejima's roofs; timber grunts and sighs. The men of the *Shenandoah* are lowering her third anchor; the first mate is on the quarterdeck, bellowing inaudibly. To the east, the Chinese merchants and sailors are likewise busy securing their property. The interpreter's palanquin crosses an otherwise empty Edo Square; the row of plane trees bends and whiplashes; no birds fly; the fishermen's boats are dragged high up the shorefront and lashed together. Nagasaki is digging itself in for a bad, bad night.

Which of those hundreds of huddled roofs, he wonders, *is yours?*

At the crossroads, Constable Kosugi is tying up the bell rope.

Ogawa shan't deliver the dictionary tonight, Jacob realizes.

Twomey and Baert hammer shut the door and casements of Garden House.

My gift and letter are clumsy and rash, Jacob admits, *but a subtle courtship is impossible.*

Something cracks and shatters, over in the garden . . .

At least now, I can stop cursing myself for cowardice.

Marinus and Eelattu are struggling with trees in clay pots and a handcart . . .

. . . and twenty minutes later, two dozen apple saplings are safe in the hospital's hallway.

"I . . . *we*" — panting, the doctor indicates the young trees — "are in your debt."

Eelattu ascends through the darkness and vanishes through the trapdoor.

"I watered those saplings." Jacob catches

his breath. "I feel protective toward them."

"I didn't consider damage from sea salt until Eelattu raised the matter. Those saplings I brought all the way from Hakine: unbaptized in Latin binomials, they might have all perished. There's no fool like an old fool."

"Not a soul shall know," Jacob promises, "not even Klaas."

Marinus frowns, thinks, and asks, "Klaas?"

"The gardener," Jacob replies, brushing his coat, "at your aunts' house."

"Ah, Klaas! Dear Klaas reverted to compost many years ago."

The typhoon howls like a thousand wolves; the attic lamp is lit.

"Well," says Jacob, "I'd best run home to Tall House while I still can."

"God grant it may still be tall in the morning."

Jacob pushes open the hospital door: it is struck with a great blow that knocks the clerk back. Jacob and the doctor peer outside and see a barrel bounding down Long Street toward Garden House, where it smashes into kindling.

"Take refuge upstairs," Marinus proposes, "for the duration."

"I'd not want to intrude," Jacob replies. "You value your privacy."

"What use would your corpse be for my seminarians were your body to share the fate of that barrel? Lead the way upstairs, lest I fall and crush us both . . ."

The wheezing lantern reveals the unburied treasure on Marinus's bookshelves. Jacob twists his head and squints at the titles: *Novum Organum* by Francis Bacon; Von Goethe's *Versuch die Metamorphose den Pflanzen zu erklären;* Antoine Galland's translation of *The Thousand and One Nights.* "The printed word is food," says Marinus, "and you look hungry, Domburger." *The System of Nature* by Jean-Baptiste de Mirabaud: the pseudonym, as any Dutch pastor's nephew knows, of the atheist Baron d'Holbach; and Voltaire's *Candide, ou l'Optimisme.* "Enough heresy," remarks Marinus, "to crush an Inquisitor's rib cage." Jacob makes no reply, encountering next Newton's *Philosophiae Naturalis Principia Mathematica;* Juvenal's *Satires;* Dante's *Inferno* in its original Italian; and a sober *Kosmotheeros* by their countryman Christiaan Huygens. This is one shelf of twenty or thirty, stretching across the attic's breadth. On Marinus's desk is a folio volume: *Osteographia* by William Cheselden.

"See who's waiting inside for you," says the doctor.

Jacob contemplates the details, and the devil plants a seed.

What if this *engine of bones* — the seed germinates — *is a man's entirety . . .*

261

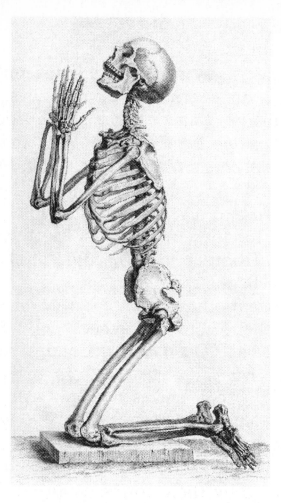

Wind wallops the walls like a dozen tree trunks tumbling.

. . . and divine love is a mere means of extracting baby *engines of bones?*

Jacob thinks about Abbot Enomoto's questions at their one meeting. "Doctor, do you believe in the soul's existence?"

Marinus prepares, the clerk expects, an erudite and arcane reply. "Yes."

"Then where" — Jacob indicates the pious, profane skeleton — "*is* it?"

"The soul is a verb." He impales a lit candle on a spike. "Not a noun."

Eelattu brings two beakers of bitter beer and sweet dried figs.

Each time Jacob is certain the wind cannot rampage more maniacally without the roof tearing free, the wind does, but the roof doesn't, not yet. Joists and beams strain and clunk and shudder like a windmill rattling at full kilter. *A terrifying night,* Jacob thinks, *yet even terror can pale into monotony.* Eelattu darns a sock while the doctor reminisces about his journey to Edo with the late Chief Hemmij and Head Clerk van Cleef. "They bemoaned the lack of buildings to compare to St. Peter's or Notre Dame, but the genius of the Japanese race is manifest in its roads. The Tôkaido Highway runs from Osaka to Edo — from the empire's belly to the head, if you will — and knows of no equal, *I* assert, anywhere on earth, in either modernity or antiquity. The road is a city, fifteen feet in width, but three hundred well-drained, well-maintained, and well-ordered German miles in length, served by fifty-three way stations where travelers can hire porters, change horses, and rest or carouse for the night. And the simplest, most commonsensical joy of all? All traffic proceeds on the left-hand side, so the numerous collisions, seizures, and stand-offs that so clog Europe's arteries are here unknown. On less populated stretches of the road, I unnerved our inspectors by slipping out of my palanquin and botanizing along the verges. I found more than thirty new species for my *Flora Japonica,* missed by Thunberg and Kaempfer. And then, at the end, is Edo."

"Which no more than, what, a dozen Europeans alive have seen?"

"Fewer. Seize the head clerk's chair within three years, you'll see it yourself."

I shan't be here, hopes Jacob, and then, uneasily, thinks of Orito.

Eelattu snips a thread. The sea writhes, just one street and a wall away.

"Edo is a million people in a grid of streets that stretches as far as the eye can travel. Edo is a tumultuous clatter of clogs, looms, shouts, barks, cries, whispers. Edo is a codex of every human demand and Edo is the means of supplying them. Every *daimyo* must keep a residence there for his designated heir and principal wife, and the largest such compounds are de facto walled towns. The Great Edo Bridge — to which every milestone in Japan refers — is two hundred paces across. Would that I could have slipped into a native's skin and roamed that labyrinth, but, naturally, Hemmij, Van Cleef, and I were confined to our inn 'for our own protection,' until the appointed day of our interview with the shogun. The stream of scholars and sightseers was an antidote to monotony, especially those with plants, bulbs, and seeds."

"Upon what matters were you consulted?"

"The medical, the erudite, the puerile: 'Is electricity a fluid?'; 'Do foreigners wear boots because they have no ankles?'; 'For any real number ϕ does Euler's formula universally guarantee that the complex exponential function satisfies $e^{i\phi} = \cos\phi + i\sin\phi$?'; 'How may we construct a Montgolfier balloon?'; 'Can a cancerous breast be removed without killing the patient?'; and once, 'Given that the Flood of Noah never submerged Japan, do we conclude Japan is a more elevated country than others?' Interpreters, officials, and innkeepers all charged admittance to the Delphic Oracle, but, as I intimated —"

The building shudders, as in the earthquake: its timbers shriek.

"I find a certain comfort," confesses Marinus, "in humanity's helplessness."

Jacob cannot agree. "What of your meeting with the shogun?"

"Our costume was the deposited pomp of a century and a half: Hemmij was bedecked in a pearl-buttoned jacket, a Moorish waistcoat, an ostrich-feathered hat, and white *tapijns* over his shoes, and with Van Cleef and I in like mishmash, we were a true trio of decayed

French pastries. We rode in palanquins to the castle gates, thereafter proceeding on foot for three hours down corridors, across courtyards, through gates to vestibules where we swapped stilted pleasantries with officials, councillors, and princes until, at last, we gained the throne room. Here the pretense that the court embassy *is* a court embassy, and not a ten weeks' tributary arse-licking pilgrimage, becomes impossible to maintain. The shogun — half hidden by a screen — sits on the raised rear of the room. When his interlocutor announces, *'Oranda Kapitan,'* Hemmij scuttled, crabwise, shogun-ward, knelt at a designated spot, forbidden even to look at the lofty personage, and waited in silence until the barbarian-quelling generalissimo lifted a single finger. A chamberlain recited a text unrevised since the 1660s, forbidding us to proselytize the wicked Christian faith or to accost the junks of the Chinese or the Ryûkyû Islanders, and commanding us to report any designs against Japan that came to our ears. Hemmij scuttled backward, and the ritual was complete. That evening, I recorded in my journal, Hemmij complained of stomach gripes, which turned into dysenteric fever — an uncertain diagnosis, I confess — on the way home."

Eelattu has finished his darning; he unrolls the bedding.

"A foul death. The rain was incessant. The

place was called Kakegawa. 'Not here, Marinus, not like this,' he groaned, and died . . ."

Jacob imagines a grave in pagan soil, and his own body lowered there.

". . . as if *I*, of all people, had powers of divine intercession."

They are aware of a change in the timbre of the typhoon's roar.

"Its eye," Marinus glances upward, "is above us. . . ."

CHAPTER TWELVE:
THE STATEROOM IN
THE CHIEF'S HOUSE
ON DEJIMA

Minutes after ten o'clock on October 23, 1799
"We are all busy men." Unico Vorstenbosch stares at Interpreter Kobayashi over the state table. "Pray discard the garnish for once and tell me the number."

Drizzle hisses on the roofs. Jacob dips his quill in ink.

Interpreter Iwase translates for Chamberlain Tomine, who arrived with the hollyhock-crested scroll tube delivered this morning from Edo.

Kobayashi's Dutch translation of Edo's message is half unrolled. "Number?"

"What" — Vorstenbosch's patience is exaggerated — "is the shogun's offer?"

"Nine thousand six hundred piculs," announces Kobayashi. "Best copper."

The nib of Jacob's quill scratches: *9,600 piculs copper.*

"This offer," affirms Iwase Banri, "is a good and big increase."

A ewe bleats. Jacob fails to guess what his

patron is thinking.

"We request twenty thousand piculs," assesses Vorstenbosch, "and we are offered less than ten? Does the shogun mean to insult Governor van Overstraten?"

"To triple quota in single year is not insult." Iwase is no fool.

"Such generosity" — Kobayashi uses the weapon of offense — "is no precedent! I strive earnestly for many weeks to achieve result."

Vorstenbosch's glance at Jacob means, *Do not record this.*

"Copper can arrive," says Kobayashi, "in two or three days, if you send."

"Warehouse is in Saga," says Iwase, "castle town of Hizen, is near. I amaze Edo, release so much copper. As high councillor say in message" — he indicates the scroll — "most warehouses are empty."

Unimpressed, Vorstenbosch takes up the Dutch translation and reads.

The clock's pendulum scrapes at time like a sexton's shovel.

William the Silent looks into a future that became past long ago.

"Why does this letter," Vorstenbosch addresses Kobayashi over his half-moon glasses, "omit any mention of Dejima's impending closure?"

"I was not present," Kobayashi says innocently, "at Edo when reply made."

"One wonders whether your translation of Governor van Overstraten's original letter was enhanced *à la mode* of your notorious peacock feathers?"

Kobayashi looks at Iwase as if to say, *Can you make sense of this remark?*

"Translation," declares Iwase, "had seals of all four senior interpreters."

"Ali Baba," mutters Lacy, "had forty thieves: did they make him honest?"

"Our question, gentlemen, is this." Vorstenbosch stands. "Shall nine thousand six hundred piculs buy Dejima a twelve-month stay of execution?"

Iwase translates this for the benefit of Chamberlain Tomine.

Eaves drip; dogs bark; an angry rash itches against Jacob's stockings.

"The *Shenandoah* has space for Dejima's stock." Lacy fishes in his jacket for a jeweled box of snuff. "We can begin loading this afternoon."

Vorstenbosch taps the barometer. "Shall we incur the wrath of our masters in Batavia by accepting this paltry increase and keep Dejima open? Or" — Vorstenbosch strolls to the grandfather clock and scrutinizes its venerable dial — "abandon this unprofitable factory and deprive a backward Asian island of its single European ally?"

Lacy snorts a huge pinch of snuff. "Jesus have mercy: a fine kick!"

Kobayashi keeps his gaze on the chair Vorstenbosch vacated.

"Nine thousand six hundred piculs," states Vorstenbosch, "purchases a year's reprieve for Dejima. Send a message to Edo. Send to Saga for the copper."

Iwase's relief is apparent as he informs Tomine of the news.

The magistrate's chamberlain nods, as if no other decision was viable.

Kobayashi gives his sinister and sardonic bow.

Chief Resident Unico Vorstenbosch, writes Jacob, *accepted this offer . . .*

"But Governor van Overstraten," warns the chief, "shall not be rebuffed twice."

. . . but warned interpreters, adds the clerk's quill, *settlement is not final.*

"We must redouble our efforts to earn the company just recompense for the dreadful risks and inflated expenses of this factory. But for today let us adjourn."

"A moment, Chief Resident, please," says Kobayashi. "More good news."

Jacob feels something malign entering the stateroom.

Vorstenbosch leans on the back of his chair. "Oh?"

"I exhort at magistracy very much about stolen teapot. I say, 'If we do not find teapot, great dishonor falls on our nation.' So, chamberlain sends many . . ." He asks for

Iwase's help. ". . . yes, 'constables,' many constables, to find teapot. Today, at guild, when I finish" — Kobayashi gestures at his translation of the shogun's reply — "messenger arrive from magistracy. Jade teapot of Chongzhen emperor is found."

"Oh? Good. What . . ." Vorstenbosch looks for a trap. "What is its condition?"

"Perfect condition. Two thiefses confessed to crime."

"One thief," Iwase continues, "make box in Constable Kosugi's palanquin. Other thief put teapot into box in palanquin, and so smuggled through land gate. Without Constable's knowledge, of course."

"How," asks Van Cleef, "were the thieves captured?"

"I advise," says Kobayashi, while Iwase explains to the chamberlain the matter now in hand, "Magistrate Ômatsu offer reward, so thiefses were betrayed. My plan worked. Teapot shall deliver later today. There is better news: Magistrate Ômatsu grant permission to execute thieves in Flag Square."

"Here?" Vorstenbosch's satisfaction clouds over. "On Dejima? When?"

"Before *Shenandoah* departs," Iwase answers, "after morning muster."

Kobayashi's smile is saintly. "Dutchmen can see Japanese justice."

The shadow of a bold rat trots along the oiled paper pane.

You demanded blood, is Kobayashi's challenge, *for your precious teapot . . .*

The watch bell on the *Shenandoah* rings.

. . . are you now man enough, the interpreter waits, *to accept delivery?*

The hammering on the roof of Warehouse Lelie stops.

"Excellent," says Vorstenbosch. "Convey my thanks to Magistrate Ômatsu."

In Warehouse Doorn, Jacob dips his quill into the ink and writes across the hitherto-blank title page: *True and Complete Investigation into the Misgovernance of Dejima Factory during the Residences of Gijsbert Hemmij and Daniel Snitker, including Rectifications to those False Ledgers Submitted by the Above-named.* For a moment he considers adding his name, but the rash idea passes. As his patron, Vorstenbosch has every right to pass off his underling's work as his own. *And maybe,* Jacob thinks, *it is safer this way.* Any councillor in Batavia whose illicit profits Jacob's *Investigation* curtails could erase a lowly clerk's prospects with a single stroke of a pen. Jacob places a sheet of blotting paper on the page and evenly presses it down.

It is finished, thinks the tired-eyed clerk.

Red-nosed Hanzaburo sneezes and wipes his nose on a fistful of straw.

A pigeon trills on the high window ledge.

273

Ouwehand's penetrating voice hurries past, along Bony Alley.

However widely Dejima was or wasn't believed to be on the brink of closure, the morning's news has roused the factory from lethargy. The copper — many hundreds of crates — shall arrive within four days. Captain Lacy wants it loaded in the *Shenandoah*'s hold within six and to be leaving Nagasaki in a week, before winter turns the China Sea wild and mountainous. Questions that Vorstenbosch has equivocated upon all summer long shall be resolved in the next few days. Shall the men be given the paltry official quota for private goods in the *Shenandoah* or what they grew used to under Vorstenbosch's predecessors? Deals with merchants are being negotiated with keen urgency. Is Peter Fischer or Jacob de Zoet to be the next head clerk, with the greater salary and control over the shipping office? *And shall Vorstenbosch use my* Investigation, Jacob wonders, putting his report into his portmanteau, *to condemn Daniel Snitker alone, or shall other scalps be claimed?* The cabal of smugglers that operates from Batavia's warehouses has friends as high up as the Council of the Indies, but Jacob's report gives enough evidence for a reform-minded governor-general to shut them down.

Obeying a whim, Jacob clambers up the

tower of crates.

Hanzaburo makes a *heh?* noise and sneezes again.

From William Pitt's roost, Jacob sees fiery maples in the tired mountains.

Orito was absent from yesterday's seminar in the hospital . . .

Nor has Ogawa come to Dejima since the day of the typhoon.

But one modest gift, he assures himself, *cannot have had her banished. . . .*

Jacob secures the shutters, climbs down, takes up his portmanteau, ushers Hanzaburo into Bony Alley, and locks the warehouse door.

Jacob emerges at the crossroads in time to meet Eelattu walking up Short Street. Eelattu is supporting a gaunt young man dressed in an artisan's loose trousers, tied at the ankles, a padded jacket, and a European hat last in style fifty years ago. Jacob notes the youth's sunken eyes, lunar complexion, and lethargic gait and thinks, *Consumption.* Eelattu bids Jacob a good morning but does not introduce his charge, who, the clerk now sees, is not a pure-blood Japanese but a Eurasian, with hair browner than black and eyes as round as his own. The visitor doesn't notice him in the alley's mouth and continues down Long Street toward the hospital.

Filaments of rain drift across the walled-in scene.

"In the midst of life we are in death, eh?"

Hanzaburo jumps and Jacob drops his portmanteau.

"Sorry 'f we startled yer, Mr. de Z." Arie Grote does not look sorry.

Piet Baert appears beside Grote, with a bulky sack on his shoulders.

"No harm done, Mr. Grote." Jacob picks up his bag. "I shall recover."

"More'n that," Baert nods at the Eurasian, "poor half-an'-half will."

As if on cue, the shuffling youth coughs the unmistakable cough.

Hanzaburo is summoned across the street by an idle inspector.

Jacob watches the Eurasian crouch and cough. "Who is he?"

Grote spits. "Shunsuke Thunberg, beggin' the query, '*Whose* is he, eh?' His daddy, so I hear tell, was one Carl Thunberg from Sweden, what was quack here twenty years back for a couple o' seasons. Like Dr. M., he was an educated gent an' one for the botanizin' by all accounts, but as yer see, he di'n't just harvest seeds hereabouts, eh?"

A three-legged dog licks up the bald cook's phlegm.

"Did Mr. Thunberg make no provision for his son's future?"

" 'F he did or no," Grote sucks through his

teeth, " 'provision' needs upkeep, an' Sweden's far as Saturn, eh? The company treats its men's bastards, out o' pity, but they ain't allowed out of Nagasaki without a pass; an' the magistrate has the final say-so on their lives 'n' marriages an' all. Girls earn a fair clip, while their looks last; the 'Corals o' Maruyama,' the pimps call 'em. But for boys, it's harder: Thunberg Junior's a goldfish breeder, I hear, but he'll be a worm breeder by an' by, an' no mistake."

Marinus and an older Japanese scholar approach from the hospital.

Jacob recognizes Dr. Maeno from the Interpreters' Guild.

Shunsuke Thunberg's coughing fit is, at last, easing.

I should have helped, Jacob thinks. "Does the poor fellow speak Dutch?"

"Nah. He was still a babe-in-arms when his daddy sailed away."

"What about his mother? A courtesan, one presumes."

"Long dead. Well, 'scuse us, Mr. de Z., but three dozen chickens're waitin' at the customs house f' loadin' on the *Shenandoah* what need inspectin', 'cause last year half of 'em was half dead, half of 'em *was* dead, an' three was pigeons what the provisioner called 'rare Japanese hens.' "

"*Worm* breeder!" Baert starts laughing. "I just smoked yer, Grote!"

277

Something in Baert's sack kicks, and Grote looks anxious to leave. "Off we go, then, Greasy Lightnin'." They hurry off up Long Street.

Jacob watches Shunsuke Thunberg being helped into the hospital.

Birds are notched on the low sky. Autumn is aging.

Halfway up two flights of steps to the chief's residence, Jacob encounters Ogawa Mimasaku, the father of Ogawa Uzaemon, coming down.

Jacob stands aside. "Good day, Interpreter Ogawa."

The older man's hands are hidden in his sleeves. "Clerk de Zoet."

"I haven't seen the younger Mr. Ogawa for . . . it must be four days."

Ogawa Mimasaku's face is haughtier and stonier than his son's.

An inky growth is spreading out from near his ear.

"My son," says Ogawa Mimasaku, "is very busy outside of Dejima at this time."

"Do you know when he shall be back at the guild?"

"No, I do not." The tone of rebuff is intentional.

Have you discovered, Jacob wonders, *what I asked your son to do?*

From the customs house comes the noise

278

of outraged hens.

A carelessly tossed stone, he frets, *can sometimes result in a rock fall.*

"I was concerned he might be sick, or . . . or unwell."

Ogawa Mimasaku's servants are staring at the Dutchman with disapproval.

"He is well," says the older man. "I report your kind concern. Good afternoon."

"You find me" — Vorstenbosch is peering at a bloated cane toad in a specimen jar — "enjoying a quiet discourse with Interpreter Kobayashi."

Jacob looks around before realizing the chief means the toad. "I left my sense of humor in bed this morning, sir."

"But not, I see" — Vorstenbosch looks at Jacob's portmanteau — "your report."

What lies behind, Jacob wonders, *this shift from "our" to "your"?*

"The gist, sir, you know from our periodic meetings —"

"Law requires *details,* not gist." The chief resident holds out his palm for the black book. "Details beget facts, and facts, judiciously sent forth, become assassins."

Jacob removes the *Investigation* and delivers it to the chief.

Vorstenbosch balances it in his hands, as if determining its weight.

"Sir, if you'd forgive me, I'm curious about —"

"— the post you are to hold in the forth-coming year, yes, but you shall wait, young De Zoet, with everyone else, until the officers' supper tonight. The copper quota was the penultimate component of my future plans, and this" — he holds up the black book — "this is the last."

During the afternoon Jacob works with Ouwehand in the clerks' office, copying this season's bills of lading for the archives. Peter Fischer makes restless exits and entrances, radiating even more hostility than usual. "A sign," Ouwehand tells Jacob, "that he thinks the head clerkship is as good as yours." Evening brings steady rain and the coolest air of the season, and Jacob decides to bathe before supper. Dejima's small bathhouse is attached to the guild's kitchen: the pans of water are heated on copper-plated hobs jutting through the stone wall, and precedent permits the ranked interpreters to treat the facility as their own, despite the exorbitant price the company is obliged to pay for charcoal and faggots. Jacob undresses in the outer changing room and crouches to enter the steamy enclosure, little larger than a big cupboard. It smells of cedarwood. Damp heat fills Jacob's lungs and unplugs the clogged pores on his face. A single storm lamp, steam-fogged, provides enough light for him to recognize Con Twomey soaking in one of the two tubs. "So it *is* the sulfur of Jean Calvin," says the Irishman, in English, "making war on my nostrils."

Jacob ladles lukewarm water over himself. "Why, it's the popish heretic, first in the bath again. Not enough work, is it?"

"The typhoon gave me all I could wish for. 'Tis daylight I lack."

Jacob scrubs himself with a wad of sailcloth. "Where's your spy?"

"Drowned under my fat arse, he is. Where's your Hanzaburo?"

"Stuffing his face in the guild's kitchen."

"Well, with the *Shenandoah* leaving next week, he must fatten himself up whilst he may." Twomey sinks up to his chin like a dugong. "Come a twelve-month, my five years' service'll be finished . . ."

"Are you fixed" — Jacob turns away to scrub his groin — "on going home?"

They hear the cooks talking in the Interpreters' Guild.

"A new start in the New World might suit better-like, I'm thinking."

Jacob removes the wooden lid from the bathtub.

"Lacy tells," says Twomey, "the Indians're being cleared west of Louisiana . . ."

Warmth sinks into every muscle and bone in Jacob's body.

281

". . . and no man afraid of hard work need go without. Settlers need carts to get where they're going and houses once they're there. Lacy reckoned I could work my passage to Charleston from Batavia as ship's carpenter. I've no appetite for war or being pressed into fighting for the British. Would you go back to Holland in the present weather?"

"I don't know." Jacob thinks of Anna's face by a rainy window. "I do not know."

"A coffee king you'll be, sure, with a plantation up in Buitenzorg, or else a merchant prince with new warehouses along the Ciliwung . . ."

"My mercury didn't fetch *so* high a price, Con Twomey."

"Aye, but with *Councillor* Unico Vorstenbosch pulling strings for you . . ."

Jacob climbs into the second tub, thinking of his *Investigation.*

Unico Vorstenbosch, the clerk wants to say, *is a fickle patron.*

Heat soaks into his joints and robs him of the urge to speculate aloud.

"What we need, De Zoet, is a smoke. I'll fetch us a couple of pipes."

Con Twomey rises like a stocky King Neptune. Jacob sinks until only a small island of lips, nostrils, and eyes remains above the water.

When Twomey returns, Jacob is in a warm

trance with his eyes shut. He listens to the carpenter rinse and reimmerse himself. Twomey makes no mention of smoking. Jacob mumbles, "Not a shred of leaf to be had, then?"

His neighbor clears his throat. "I am Ogawa, Mr. de Zoet."

Jacob lurches and water spills. "Mr. Ogawa! I — I thought . . ."

"You so peaceful," says Ogawa Uzaemon, "I do not wish disturb."

"I met your father earlier, but . . ." Jacob wipes his eyes, but with the steamy dark and his farsightedness, his vision is no better. "I've not seen you since before the typhoon."

"I am sorry I could not come. Very many things happen."

"Were you able to — to fulfill my request, regarding the dictionary?"

"Day after typhoon, I send servant to Aibagawa residence."

"Then you didn't deliver the volume yourself?"

"Most trusted servant delivered dictionary. He did not say, 'Parcel is from Dutchman de Zoet.' He explained, 'Parcel is from hospital on Dejima.' You see, it was misappropriate for me to go. Dr. Aibagawa was ill. To visit at such hour is bad . . . *breeding?*"

"I am sorry to hear it. Is he recovered now?"

"His funeral was conducted a day before yesterday."

283

"Oh." *Everything,* Jacob thinks, *is explained.* "Oh. Then Miss Aibagawa . . ."

Ogawa hesitates. "There is bad news. She must leave Nagasaki . . ."

Jacob waits and listens, as droplets of condensed steam fall.

". . . for long time, for many years. She shall not return more to Dejima. Of your dictionary, of your letter, of how she thinks, I have no news. I am sorry."

"The dictionary be damned — but . . . where is she going, and why?"

"It is domain of Abbot Enomoto. Man who bought your mercury."

The man who kills snakes by magic. The abbot looms in Jacob's memory.

"He want her to enter temple of" — Ogawa falters — "female monks. How say?"

"Nuns? *Pray* don't tell me Miss Aibagawa's going to a *nunnery.*"

"Species of nunnery, yes . . . on Mount Shiranui. There she is going."

"What use is a midwife to a pack of nuns? Does she *want* to go?"

"Dr. Aibagawa had great debts with money-lenders, to purchase telescopes, et cetera." Pain strains Ogawa's voice. "To be scholar is costly. His widow must now pay these debts. Enomoto makes contract, or deal, to widow. He pays debts. She gives Miss Aibagawa for nunnery."

"This is tantamount," Jacob protests, "to

selling her into slavery!"

"Japanese custom," Ogawa sounds hollow, "is different to Dutch —"

"What say her late father's friends at the Shirandô Academy? Shall they stand by doing nothing whilst a gifted scholar is sold, like a mule, into a life of servitude up some bleak mountain? Would a son be sold to a monastery in such manner? Enomoto is a scholar, too, is he not?"

Cooks in the Interpreters' Guild can be heard laughing through the wall.

Jacob sees another implication. "But *I* offered her sanctuary here."

"Nothing can be done." Ogawa stands up. "I must go now."

"So . . . she prefers incarceration to living here, on Dejima?"

Ogawa steps out of the bathtub. His silence is blunt and reproachful.

Jacob sees how boorish he must appear in the interpreter's eyes: at no small risk, Ogawa tried to help a lovesick foreigner, who now rewards him with resentment. "Forgive me, Mr. Ogawa, but surely if —"

The outer door slides open and a cheerful whistler enters.

A shadow parts the curtain and asks, in Dutch, "Who goes there?"

"It is Ogawa, Mr. Twomey."

"Good evening to you, Mr. Ogawa. Mr. de Zoet, our pipe must wait. Chief Vorstenbosch wishes to discuss an important matter with you in his bureau. Straightaway. My bones tell me there is good news waiting."

"Why the glum face, De Zoet?" *Investigation into the Misgovernance of Dejima Factory* sits in front of Unico Vorstenbosch. "Lost in love, have we?"

Jacob is appalled that his secret is known even to his patron.

"A quip, De Zoet! Nothing more. Twomey says I interrupt your ablutions?"

"I was just finishing in the bathhouse, sir."

"Cleanliness being next to godliness, I am told."

"I make no claims on godliness, but bathing wards off the lice, and the evenings are a little cooler now."

"You *do* look drawn, De Zoet. Did I drive you too long, too exactingly, on" — Vorstenbosch drums his fingers on the *Investigation* — "your assignment?"

"Exacting or not, sir, my work is my work."

The chief resident nods, like a judge hearing evidence.

"May I hope that my report does not disappoint your expectations, sir?"

Vorstenbosch unstoppers a decanter of ruby Madeira.

Servants are setting the table in the dining room.

The chief fills his own glass but offers nothing to Jacob. "We have gathered painstaking, merit-worthy, and undeniable proof of Dejima's shameful misrule in the nineties, proof that shall justify, amply, my punitive measures against ex–Acting Chief Daniel Snitker . . ."

Jacob notices the "we" and the omission of Van Cleef's name.

". . . *assuming* our proof is presented to Governor van Overstraten with the necessary vigor." Vorstenbosch opens the cabinet behind him and takes out another glass.

"Nobody can doubt," Jacob says, "that Captain Lacy shall do a good job."

"Why should an American care about company corruption, so long as he makes his profits?" Vorstenbosch fills a glass and hands it to Jacob. "Anselm Lacy is no crusader but a hired hand. Back in Batavia he would dutifully deliver our *Investigation* to the governor-general's private secretary and never give it a second thought. The private secretary would, like as not, deposit it in a quiet canal and warn the men you name — and Snitker's cronies — who would grind their long knives in preparation for our return. No. The whys and wherefores of Dejima's crisis, its correctives, and the justice of Daniel Snitker's punishment must be explicated by one whose future is bonded with the company's. Therefore, De Zoet, *I*" — the pronoun is voiced significantly — "shall return to Batavia on

287

the *Shenandoah,* alone, to prosecute our case."

The Almelo clock is loud against the drizzle's hush and the lamp's hiss.

"And," Jacob keeps his voice flat and steady, "your plans for me, sir?"

"You are my eyes and ears in Nagasaki, until next trading season."

Without protection, Jacob considers, *I shall be eaten alive in a week . . .*

"I shall, therefore, appoint Peter Fischer as the new head clerk."

The clatter of consequences tramples over the Almelo clock.

Without status, Jacob thinks, *I shall indeed be a lapdog, thrown into a bear pit.*

"The sole candidate for chief," Vorstenbosch is saying, "is Mr. van Cleef . . ."

Dejima is a long, long way, Jacob is afraid, *from Batavia.*

". . . but what say you to the sound of *Deputy* Chief Resident Jacob de Zoet?"

CHAPTER THIRTEEN:
FLAG SQUARE,
DEJIMA

Morning mustering on the last day of October, 1799

"Little miracle, it is." Piet Baert looks at the sky. "The rain's drained away . . ."

"Forty days an' forty nights," says Ivo Oost, "we was in for, I thought."

"Bodies was washed down the river," Wybo Gerritszoon remarks. "I saw the boats haulin' 'em in with big hooks on poles."

"Mr. Kobayashi?" Melchior van Cleef calls louder. "Mr. Kobayashi?"

Kobayashi turns around and looks in Van Cleef's direction.

"We have a lot of work before the *Shenandoah* is loaded: why this delay?"

"Flood broke convenient bridges in city. There is much lateness today."

"Then why," asks Peter Fischer, "did the party not leave the prison earlier?"

But Interpreter Kobayashi has turned back and watches Flag Square. Converted to an execution ground, it holds the biggest assembly Jacob has seen in Japan. The Dutch-men, their backs to the flagpole, stand in a half-moon. An oblong is drawn in the dirt where the teapot thieves are to be decapi-tated. Opposite ascend three steps under an awning: on the topmost row sit Chamberlain Tomine and a dozen senior officials from the magistracy; the middle row is filled with other dignitaries of Nagasaki; on the lowest step sit all sixteen ranked interpreters, barring Koba-yashi, who is on duty at Vorstenbosch's side. Ogawa Uzaemon, whom Jacob has not met since the bathhouse, looks tired. Three Shintô priests in white robes and ornate headpieces conduct a purification ritual involving chants and the throwing of salt. To the left and right stand servants; eighty or ninety unranked interpreters; coolies and day laborers, happy to be enjoying the sport at the company's expense; and assorted guards, friskers, oars-men, and carpenters. Four men in ragged clothing wait by a handcart. The executioner is a hawkeyed samurai, whose assistant holds a drum. Dr. Marinus stands to one side with his four male seminarians.

Orito was a fever, Jacob reminds himself. *Now the fever is lifted.*

"Hangin's're more of a holiday'n this in Antwerp," notes Baert.

Captain Lacy looks at the flag, thinking of winds and tides.

Vorstenbosch asks, "Shall we be needing

tugboats later, Captain?"

Lacy shakes his head. "We'll have puff enough if this breeze holds."

Van Cleef warns, "The tugs' skippers'll try to attach the ropes regardless."

"Then the pirates'll have a lot of sliced ropes to replace, 'specially if —"

Toward the land gate, the crowd stirs, hums louder, and parts.

The prisoners are conveyed in large rope nets suspended on poles, carried by four men each. They are paraded past the grandstand and dumped on the oblong, where the nets are opened. The younger of the two is only sixteen or seventeen; he was probably handsome until his arrest. His older accomplice is broken and shivering. They wear only long cloths wrapped around their loins and a carapace of dried blood, welts, and gashes. Several fingers and toes are scabby maroon lumps. Constable Kosugi, the stern master of today's grisly ceremony, opens a scroll. The crowd falls silent. Kosugi proceeds to read a Japanese text.

"It is statement of accuse," Kobayashi tells the Dutch, "and confessment."

When Constable Kosugi finishes, he proceeds to the awning, where he bows as Chamberlain Tomine delivers a statement. Constable Kosugi then walks to Unico Vorstenbosch to relay the chamberlain's message. Kobayashi translates with marked brevity: "Do Dutch chief grant pardon?"

Four or five hundred eyes fix themselves on Unico Vorstenbosch.

Show mercy, Deputy-elect de Zoet prays in the rotating moment. *Mercy.*

"Ask the thieves," Vorstenbosch instructs Kobayashi, "whether they knew the likely punishment for their crime."

Kobayashi addresses the question to the kneeling pair.

The older thief cannot speak. The defiant younger one declares, *"Hai."*

"Then why should I interfere in Japanese justice? The answer is *no.*"

Kobayashi delivers the verdict to Constable Kosugi, who marches back to Chamberlain Tomine. When it is delivered, the crowd mutters its disapproval. The young thief says something to Vorstenbosch, and Kobayashi asks, "Do you wish for me to translate?"

"Tell me what he says," says the chief resident.

"The criminal say, 'Remember my face when you drink tea.' "

Vorstenbosch folds his arms. "Assure him that twenty minutes from now I shall forget his face forever. In twenty days, few of his friends shall recall his features with clarity. In twenty months, even his mother shall wonder how her son looked."

Kobayashi translates the sentence with stern relish.

Nearby spectators overhear and watch the Dutchmen ever more balefully.

"I translate," Kobayashi assures Vorsten-bosch, "very faithful."

Constable Kosugi asks the executioner to ready himself for duty, while Vorstenbosch addresses the Dutchmen. "There are those among our hosts, gentlemen, who hope to see us choke on this dish of rightful vengeance; I pray you deprive them of the pleasure."

"Beggin' yer pardon, sir," says Baert, "I ain't graspin' yer meanin'."

"Don't puke an' swoon," says Arie Grote, "afore the yellow host."

"Precisely, Grote," says Vorstenbosch. "We are ambassadors for our race."

The older thief is first. His head is in a cloth bag. He is knelt down.

The drummer drums a dry rhythm: the executioner unsheathes his sword.

Urine darkens the ground beneath the quivering victim.

Ivo Oost, next to Jacob, draws a cross in the dirt with his shoe.

Two or more dogs across Edo Square let loose a frenzy of barking.

Gerritszoon mutters, "Well, here it comes, my pretty . . ."

The executioner's raised sword is bright with polishing but dark with oil.

Jacob hears a chord, always present but

rarely audible.

The drummer strikes his drum for the fourth or fifth time.

There is the noise of a spade cutting through soil . . .

. . . and the thief's head thuds onto the sand, still in its bag.

Blood ejaculates from the shorn stump with a thin, whistling sound.

The gaping stump slumps forward and settles on the thief's knees, vomiting blood.

Gerritszoon mutters, "Bravo, my pretty!"

I am poured out like water, recites Jacob, shutting his eyes, *my tongue cleaveth to my jaws and thou hast brought me into the dust of death.*

"Seminarians," directs Marinus, "observe the aorta; the jugular and spinal cord; and how the venous blood is, in tone, a rich plum color, while the arterial blood is the scarlet of ripe hibiscus. They differ in taste, moreover: the arterial blood has a metallic tang, whilst venous blood is fruitier."

"For the love of God, Doctor," complains Van Cleef. "Must you?"

"Better that *someone* benefit from this futile act of barbarity."

Jacob watches Unico Vorstenbosch remain aloof.

Peter Fischer sniffs. "The safeguarding of company property is a 'futile act of barbarity'? What if the stolen item were your treasured harpsichord, Doctor?"

"Better bid it farewell." The headless body is slung onto the cart. "Spilled blood would clog up its levers, and its tone would never recover."

Ponke Ouwehand asks, "What happens to the bodies, Doctor?"

"The bile is harvested for druggists, and then the remains are pawed apart for the gratification of a paying audience. Such are the difficulties the native scholars face in establishing surgery and anatomy."

The younger thief appears to be refusing his hood.

He is brought to the dark stains where his friend was beheaded.

The drummer strikes his drum a first time . . .

"It's a rare art," Gerritszoon tells nobody in particular, "is choppin': executioners'll mind the client's weight an' the season, 'cause come summer there's more fat on the neck than at winter's end, an' if the skin be wet in the rain or no . . ."

The drummer strikes his drum a second time . . .

"A philosopher of Paris," the doctor tells his students, "was sentenced to the guillotine during the recent Terror . . ."

The drummer strikes his drum the third time . . .

". . . and he conducted an intriguing experiment: he arranged with an assistant that he would begin blinking as the blade fell . . ."

The drummer strikes his drum a fourth time.

". . . and continue blinking thereafter for as long as he might. By counting the blinks, the assistant could measure the brief life of a severed head."

Cupido intones words in Malay, perhaps to ward off the evil eye.

Gerritszoon turns and says, "Stop that darkie jabberin', boy."

Deputy-elect Jacob de Zoet cannot bring himself to watch again.

He inspects his shoes and finds a splash of blood on one toe.

The wind passes through Flag Square, soft as a robe's hem.

"Which brings us," says Vorstenbosch, "almost to the end of things . . ."

It is eleven o'clock by the Almelo clock in the departing chief's bureau.

Vorstenbosch slides the last sheaf of paperwork aside, produces the papers of commission, dips his pen in its well, and signs the first document. "May fortune smile on your tenure, Chief Resident Melchior van Cleef of the Dejima Factory . . ."

Van Cleef's beard shrugs as its owner smiles. "Thank you, sir."

". . . and last but not least," Vorstenbosch

signs the second document, "Deputy Chief Resident Jacob de Zoet." He replaces the pen. "To think, De Zoet, back in April, you were a lesser clerk bound for a swampy pit in Halmahera."

"An open grave." Van Cleef puffs out air. "Escape the crocs, swamp fever shall do for you. Escape the swamp fever, a poison blow dart ends your days. You owe Mr. Vorstenbosch not only a bright future but your very life."

You, you embezzler, Jacob thinks, *owe him your freedom from Snitker's fate.* "My gratitude to Mr. Vorstenbosch is as profound as it is sincere."

"We have time for a brief toast. Philander!"

Philander comes in, balancing three glasses of wine on a silver tray.

Each man takes one of the long-stemmed glasses; they clink rims.

His glass drained, Vorstenbosch presents Melchior van Cleef with the keys to Warehouses Eik and Doorn and to the safe box that houses the trading pass issued fifteen decades ago by the great shogun. "May Dejima flourish under your custodianship, Chief van Cleef. I bequeathed you an able and promising deputy. Next year I desire you both surpass my achievement and wring twenty thousand piculs of copper out of our miserly slit-eyed hosts."

"If it is humanly possible," promises Van

Cleef, "we shall."

"I shall pray for your safe voyage, sir," says Jacob.

"Thank you. And now the matter of succession is settled . . ."

Vorstenbosch takes an envelope from his coat and unfolds a document. "Dejima's three senior officers may sign the summation of exported goods, as Governor van Overstraten now insists we must." He writes his own name in the first space beneath the three-page index of company commodities stowed in the *Shenandoah*'s hold, divided into "Copper," "Camphor," and "Other," and subdivided into lot numbers, quantities, and qualities.

Van Cleef signs the record he compiled, without a second glance.

Jacob takes the proffered pen and, by dint of professional habit, studies the figures: this is the morning's single document not prepared by his own hand.

"Deputy," chides Van Cleef, "surely you shan't oblige Mr. Vorstenbosch to *wait?*"

"The company desires me, sir, to be thorough in all things."

This remark, Jacob notices, is greeted by a frosty silence.

"The sun," says Van Cleef, "is winning the battle for the day, Mr. Vorstenbosch."

"So it is." Vorstenbosch finishes his wine. "Were it Kobayashi's intention to conjure a

Jonah with the executions this morning, his plan is another failure."

Jacob finds a surprising error. *Total Copper Export: 2,600 piculs.*

Van Cleef clears his throat. "Is aught amiss, Deputy?"

"Sir . . . here, in the total column. The 'nine' looks like a 'two.' "

Vorstenbosch states: "The summation is quite in order, De Zoet."

"But, sir, we are exporting *nine* thousand six hundred piculs."

Van Cleef's levity is infused with threat. "Just sign the paper, De Zoet."

Jacob looks at Van Cleef, who stares at Jacob, who turns to Vorstenbosch. "Sir: one unfamiliar with your reputation for integrity *might* see this summation and" — he struggles for a diplomatic phrase — "might be forgiven for supposing that seven thousand piculs of copper have been omitted from the tally deliberately."

Vorstenbosch's face is that of a man resolved to let his son beat him at chess no longer.

"Do you," Jacob's voice has a slight shake, "intend to *steal* this copper?"

" 'Steal' is for Snitker, boy: I claim my rightful perquisites."

"But 'rightful perquisites,' " Jacob blurts, "might be a phrase which Daniel Snitker minted!"

"For your career's sake, don't compare me to *that* wharf rat."

"*I* don't, sir." Jacob taps the summation of exports. "*This* does."

"The lurid beheadings we witnessed this morning," says Van Cleef, "muddied your wits, Mr. de Zoet. Luckily, Mr. Vorstenbosch does not bear grudges, so apologize for your hotheadedness, ink your name on this scrap of paper, and let us forget this disharmony."

Vorstenbosch is displeased but does not contradict Van Cleef.

Feeble sunshine lights the paper panes of the bureau window.

What De Zoet of Domburg, thinks Jacob, *ever prostituted his conscience?*

Melchior van Cleef smells of eau de cologne and pork fat.

"Whatever happened," says Van Cleef, "to 'My gratitude to Mr. Vorstenbosch is as profound as it is sincere,' hey?"

A bluebottle is drowning in his wine. Jacob has torn the summation in two . . .

. . . and again, into four. His heart is pounding, like a murderer's after the kill.

I shall be hearing that tearing sound, Jacob knows, *until I die.*

The Almelo clock taps at time with its tiny hammers.

"I had De Zoet down," Vorstenbosch addresses Van Cleef, "as a young man of sound judgment."

"I had *you* down," Jacob tells Vorstenbosch, "as a man worthy of emulation."

Vorstenbosch takes up Jacob's paper of commission and tears it in two . . .

. . . and again, into four. "I hope you like life on Dejima, De Zoet: you shall know no other for five years. Mr. van Cleef: do you choose Fischer or Ouwehand for your deputy?"

"A poor choice. I desire neither. But let it be Fischer."

In the stateroom, Philander says, "Pardon, but masters all busy."

"Leave my sight," Vorstenbosch tells Jacob, without looking at him.

"Suppose Governor van Overstraten," Jacob wonders aloud, "were to learn —"

"Threaten *me*, you pious Zeelander shitweasel," responds Vorstenbosch calmly, "and where Snitker is plucked, you shall be butchered. Tell me, Chief van Cleef: what are the penalties for forging a letter from His Excellency the Governor-General of the Dutch East Indies?"

Jacob feels a sudden weakness in his thighs and calves.

"That would depend on the motives and circumstances, sir."

"What about an unconscionable clerk who sends a counterfeit letter *to none other than the shogun of Japan,* threatening to abandon the company's venerable outpost unless twenty thousand piculs of copper are sent to Nagasaki, copper that he *manifestly intended* to sell himself — or why else conceal his misdeed from his colleagues?"

"Twenty years in jail, sir," says Van Cleef, "would be the most lenient sentence."

"This" — Jacob stares — ". . . entrapment you planned as early as July?"

"One insures oneself against disappointments. I told you to be gone."

I shall return to Europe, Jacob sees, *no richer than when I left.*

As Jacob opens the bureau door, Vorstenbosch calls, "Philander!"

The Malay pretends not to have been listening at the keyhole. "Master?"

"Fetch me Mr. Fischer. We have welcome news for him."

"*I'll* tell Fischer!" Jacob calls over his shoulder. "Why, he can finish my wine!"

"Fret not thyself because of evildoers, neither be thou envious against the workers of iniquity." Jacob studies the Thirty-seventh Psalm. "For they shall soon be cut down like the grass, and wither as the green herb. Trust in the Lord, and do good; so shalt thou dwell in the land, and verily thou shalt be fed . . ."

Sunshine rusts the upstairs apartment in Tall House.

The sea gate is closed now until next trading season.

Peter Fischer shall be moving in to the deputy's spacious residence.

After fifteen weeks at anchor, the *Shenandoah* shall be unfurling her sails, her sailors yearning for the open sea and a fat purse in Batavia.

Don't pity yourself, thinks Jacob. *Maintain your dignity, at least.*

Hanzaburo's footsteps come up the stairs. Jacob closes the Psalter.

Even Daniel Snitker must be looking forward to the voyage beginning . . .

. . . at least, in Batavia jail, he can enjoy the company of his friends and wife.

Hanzaburo busies himself in his cubbyhole in the anteroom.

Orito preferred incarceration in a nunnery, his loneliness whispers . . .

A bird in the bay tree sings an ambling, musical doodle.

. . . *to a Dejima marriage with you.* Hanzaburo's footsteps go down the stairs.

Jacob worries about his letters home to Anna, to his sister and uncle.

Vorstenbosch shall post them, he fears, *through the* Shenandoah's *privy.*

Hanzaburo is gone, the clerk realizes, without even a goodbye.

One-sided news of his disgrace shall travel: first to Batavia, then Rotterdam.

The Orient, Anna's father shall opine, *tests*

303

a man's true *character.*

Jacob calculates she shan't hear from him until January of 1801.

Every rich, horny, eligible son of Rotterdam shall pay her court . . .

Jacob reopens his Psalter but is too agitated even for David's verses.

I am a righteous man, he thinks, *but see what righteousness has done.*

Going outside is intolerable. Staying inside is intolerable.

The others will think you are afraid to show your face. He puts on his jacket.

On the bottom stair, Jacob steps in something slippery, falls backward . . .

. . . and bangs his coccyx on the edge of a step. He sees, and smells, that the mishap was caused by a large human turd.

Long Street is deserted but for two coolies who grin at the red-haired foreigner and make goblin horns on their heads in the way the French denote a cuckold.

The air swims with insects, born of damp earth and autumn sun.

Arie Grote trots down the steps of Chief van Cleef's residence.

"Mr. de Z. was conspicuous by his absence, eh, at Vorstenbosch's farewell."

"He and I had said our goodbyes" — Jacob finds his path blocked — "earlier."

"My jaw dropped *this* far" — Grote demonstrates — "when I heard the news!"

"Your jaw, I see, has since recovered its customary altitude."

"So yer'll be servin' out yer sentence in Tall House an' not the deputy's. 'A Difference of Opinion over the Deputy's Role,' I understand, eh?"

Jacob has nowhere to look but walls, gutters, or Arie Grote's face.

"Meanin', the rats tell me, you'd not sign off on that crooked summation, eh? Expensive habit is *honesty.* Loyalty ain't a simple matter. Di'n't I warn yer? Y'know, Mr. de Z., a nastier-minded cove, smartin' from the loss of his friendly playin' cards, might even be tempted to gloat a little at his, eh, antagonist's misfortunes . . ."

Limping, Sjako walks by, carrying the toucan in its cage.

". . . but I reckon as I'll leave the gloatin' to Fischer." The leathery cook places his hand on his heart. "All's well as ends well, *I* say. Mr. V. let me ship my *whole stock* for ten percent: last year Snitker wanted fifty-fifty for a moldy corner o' the *Octavia,* that graspin' grasper — an' given *her* fate, 'twas a blessin' we di'n't agree! The trusty *Shenandoah*'s" — Grote nods at the sea gate — "leavin' laden with the harvest o' three honest years' toil, eh. Chief V. even cut me a fifth slice of four gross Arita figurines in lieu, eh, o' my brokerage fees."

A night-soil man's buckets, swinging on his pole, stain the air.

"Wonder how close," Grote thinks aloud, "the friskers search them."

"Four gross figurines." Jacob registers the number. "Not two gross?"

"Forty-eight dozen, aye. Tidy packet they'll fetch at auction. Why d'yer ask?"

"No reason." *Vorstenbosch lied,* thinks Jacob, *from the start.* "Now, if there's nothing I can do for you —"

" 'S'matter o' fact," Grote says, producing a bundle from his jerkin, "it's what *I . . .*"

Jacob recognizes his tobacco pouch, given by Orito to William Pitt.

". . . can do f' *you.* This well-sewn item is yours, I do believe."

"Do you intend to charge me for my own tobacco pouch?"

"Just returnin' it to its rightful owner, Mr. de Z., at no price whats*oever . . .*"

Jacob waits for Grote to name his true price.

". . . though it may be an *opportune* time, eh, to remind yer that a wise head'd sell our two last crates o' pox powder to Enomoto sooner an' not later. The Chinese junks'll come back laden low with every ounce o' mercury to be had within their, eh, sphere of commerce, an' *entre nous,* eh, Messrs. Lacy an' V-bosch'll be sendin' a German ton o' the stuff next year, an' when the market floods, the prices turn soggy."

"I shan't be selling to Enomoto. Find another buyer. Any other buyer."

"Clerk de Zoet!" Peter Fischer marches into Long Street from Back Alley. He shines with vengefulness. "Clerk de Zoet. What is this?"

"We call it a 'thumb' in Dutch." Jacob cannot yet muster a *sir.*

"Yes, I know it is a thumb. But what is this *on* my thumb?"

"That would be" — Jacob senses Arie Grote has disappeared — "a dirty smudge."

"The clerks and hands address me," Fischer says, drawing level, "as 'Deputy Fischer' or 'sir.' Do you understand?"

Two years of this, Jacob calculates, *turn into five if he becomes chief.*

"I understand what you say very well, Deputy Fischer."

Fischer wears a triumphant Caesar's smile. "Dirt! Yes. Dirt. It is on the shelves of the clerks' office. So I direct you to clean it."

Jacob swallows. "Ordinarily, *sir,* one of the servants —"

"Ah, yes, but *I* direct *you*" — Fischer prods Jacob's sternum with his dirty thumb — "to clean the shelves *now,* because you dislike slaves, servants, and inequalities."

A ewe, escaped from her paddock, ambles down Long Street.

He wants me to hit him, thinks Jacob. "I shall clean them later."

"You shall address the deputy as Deputy Fischer, at all times."

Years of this ahead, thinks Jacob. "I shall clean them later, Deputy Fischer."

Protagonist and antagonist stare at each other; the ewe squats and pisses.

"Clean the shelves *now,* Clerk de Zoet. If you do not —"

Jacob is breathless with a fury he knows he shan't control: he walks off.

"Chief van Cleef," Fischer calls after him, "and I shall discuss your insolence!"

Ivo Oost smokes in a doorway. "It's a long way down . . ."

"It is *my* signature," Fischer shouts after him, "that authorizes your wages!"

Jacob climbs the watchtower, praying that nobody is on the platform.

Anger and self-pity are lodged in his throat like fish bones.

This prayer, at least — he gains the vacant platform — *is answered.*

The *Shenandoah* is half a mile up Nagasaki Bay. Tugboats trail in her wake like unwanted goslings. The narrowing bay, pouring clouds, and the brig's billowing canvas suggest a model ship being drawn from its bottle's mouth.

Now I understand, thinks Jacob, *why I have the watchtower to myself.*

The *Shenandoah* fires her cannons to salute

the guard posts.

What prisoner wants to behold his prison door slammed shut?

Petals of smoke are plucked by the wind from the *Shenandoah*'s gunports . . .

. . . *the shot reverberates, like the lid of a harpsichord dropped shut.*

The farsighted clerk removes his spectacles in order to see better.

The burgundy blotch on the quarterdeck is certainly Captain Lacy . . .

. . . *so the olive one must be the incorruptible Unico Vorstenbosch.* Jacob imagines his erstwhile patron using *Investigation into Misgovernance* to blackmail company officials. "The company's mint," Vorstenbosch could now argue most persuasively, "requires a director with my experience and discretion."

Landward, citizens of Nagasaki are sitting on their roofs to watch the Dutch ship embark and dream of its destinations. Jacob thinks of his peers and fellow voyagers from home in Batavia; of colleagues in various offices during his days as a shipping clerk; of classmates in Middelburg and childhood friends in Domburg. *Whilst they are out in the wide world, finding their paths and good-hearted wives, I shall be spending my twenty-sixth, twenty-seventh, twenty-eighth, twenty-ninth, and thirtieth years — my last best years — trapped in a dying factory with whatever flotsam and jetsam happen to wash up.*

Below, out of sight, a reluctant window of the deputy's house is opened.

"Be *careful* with that upholstery," commands Fischer, "you mule . . ."

Jacob looks in his tobacco pouch for a shred of leaf, but there is none.

". . . or I shall use your shit-brown skin to repair it: you savvy?"

Jacob imagines returning to Domburg to find strangers in the parsonage.

In Flag Square, priests conduct purification rites on the execution ground.

"If you not pay priest," Kobayashi warned Van Cleef yesterday, when Jacob's future was silver if not golden, "ghosts of thiefses not find rest and become demon, so no Japanese enter Dejima again."

Hook-beaked gulls duel above a fishing skiff hauling up its nets.

Time passes, and when Jacob looks down the bay, he is just in time to see the *Shenandoah*'s bowsprit vanish behind Tempelhoek . . .

Her fo'c'sle is eaten by the rocky headland, then her three masts . . .

. . . until the bottle's mouth is blue and vacant as the third day of Creation.

A woman's strong voice rouses Jacob from his half doze. She is nearby and sounds angry or frightened or both. Curious, he looks around for the source of the commotion. In Flag Square, the priests are still chanting prayers for the executed men.

The land gate is open to let the water vendor's ox off Dejima.

Standing outside the gate, Aibagawa Orito is arguing with the guards.

The watchtower lurches: Jacob finds he has lain flat on the platform, out of her line of vision.

She is brandishing her wooden pass and pointing up Short Street.

The guard examines her pass with suspicion; she looks over her shoulder.

The ox, an empty urn hanging from each shoulder, is led over Holland Bridge.

She was a fever. Jacob hides behind his eyelids. *The fever is lifted.*

He looks again. The captain of the guard is inspecting the pass.

Can she be here, he wonders, *to seek sanctuary from Enomoto?*

His proposal of marriage now returns like a risen golem.

I did *want her, yes,* he fears, *when I knew I could never have her.*

The water vendor flicks his switch on his ox's lumbering shanks.

She may just be here — Jacob tries to calm himself — *to visit the hospital.*

He notices her disarray: a sandal is missing;

her neat hair is awry.

But where are the other students? Why won't the guards admit her?

The captain is questioning Orito in sharp tones.

Orito's clarity is fraying; her despair is growing; this is no ordinary visit.

Act! Jacob commands himself. *Show the guards she is expected; fetch Dr. Marinus; fetch an interpreter: this is a balance that you may still tip.*

The three priests walk in a slow circle around the bloodstained dirt.

It's not you she wants, whispers Pride. *It's incarceration she wants to avoid.*

Thirty feet away, the captain turns Orito's pass over, unimpressed.

Suppose she were Geertje, asks Compassion, *seeking sanctuary in Zeeland?*

In the captain's resonant string of words Jacob hears the name "Enomoto."

Across Edo Square, a shaven-headed figure appears in a sky-blue robe.

He catches sight of Orito and calls over his shoulder, motioning, *Hurry!*

A sea-gray palanquin appears; it has eight bearers, denoting an owner of the highest rank.

Jacob has a sense of entering a theater well into the play's final act.

I love her, comes the thought, as true as

sunlight.

Jacob is flying down the stairs, barking his shin on a corner post.

He leaps the last six or eight steps and runs across Flag Square.

Everything is happening too slow and too fast and all at once.

Jacob clips an astonished priest and reaches the land gate as it closes.

The captain is brandishing his pike, warning him not to take another step.

Jacob's rectangle of vision is narrowing as the gate closes.

He sees Orito's back as she is led away over Holland Bridge.

Jacob opens his mouth to call out her name . . .

. . . but the land gate slams shut.

The well-oiled bolt slides home.

■ ■ ■ ■

PART TWO:
A MOUNTAIN
FASTNESS

■ ■ ■ ■

The tenth month in the eleventh year of the Era of Kansei

CHAPTER FOURTEEN:
ABOVE THE VILLAGE
OF KUROZANE IN
KYÔGA DOMAIN

Late on the twenty-second day of the tenth month

Twilight is cold with the threat of snow. The forest's edges dissolve and blur. A black dog waits on an outcrop. He scents a fox's hot stink.

His silver-haired mistress struggles up the twisted path.

A dead branch cracks under a deer's hoof across the loud stream.

An owl cries, in this cedar or that fir . . . once, twice, near, gone.

Otane carries a twentieth of a *koku* of rice, enough for a month.

Her youngest niece tried hard to persuade her to winter in the village.

The poor girl needs allies, thinks Otane, *against her mother-in-law.*

"She's pregnant again, too, did you notice?" she asks her dog.

The niece had charged her aunt with the crime of making the entire family worry about her safety. "But I *am* safe," the old woman repeats her answer to the root-truckled steps. "I'm too poor for cutthroats and too withered for bandits."

Her niece then argued that patients could consult her more readily down in the village. "Who wants to trek halfway up Mount Shiranui in midwinter?"

"My cottage is *not* 'halfway up' anything! It's less than a mile."

A song thrush in a mountain ash speaks of endings.

A childless crone, Otane concedes, *is lucky to have relatives to house her . . .*

But she also knows that leaving her hut would be easier than returning.

"Come spring," she mutters, "it'll be, 'Aunt Otane can't go back to *that* ruin!' "

Higher up, a pair of raccoons snarl murderous threats.

The herbalist of Kurozane climbs on, her sack growing heavier with each step.

Otane reaches the gardened shelf where her cottage stands. Onions are strung below the deep eaves. Firewood is stacked below. She puts her rice down on the raised porch. Her body aches. She checks the goats in their stall and tips in a half bale of hay. Last, she peers into the chicken coop. "Who laid an egg for Auntie today, I wonder?"

In the ripe murk she finds one, still warm.

"Thank you, ladies."

She bolts the cottage door against the night, kneels before her hearth with her tinderbox, and coaxes a fire into life for her pot. In this she makes a soup of burdock root and yams. When it is hot, she adds the egg.

The medicine cabinet calls her into the rear room.

Patients and visitors are surprised to see such a beautiful cabinet reaching nearly to the ceiling of her humble cottage. Back in her great-great-grandfather's day, six or eight strong men had carried it up from the village, though as a child it was simpler to believe that it had grown here, like an ancient tree. One by one, she slides out the well-waxed medicine drawers and inhales their contents. Here is *toki* parsley, good for colicky infants; next, acrid *yomogi* shavings, ground to a powder for moxibustion; last in this row, *dokudami* berries, or "fish mint," to flush out sickness. The cabinet is her livelihood and the depository of her knowledge. She sniffs soapy mulberry leaves and hears her father telling her, "Good for ailments of the eye . . . and used with goat wort for ulcers, worms, and boils . . ." Then Otane reaches the bitter motherwort berries.

She is reminded of Miss Aibagawa and withdraws to the fire.

She feeds the lean fire a fat log. "Two days

319

from Nagasaki," she says, "to 'request an audience with Otane of Kurozane.' Those were Miss Aibagawa's words. I was digging manure into my pumpkin patch one day . . ."

Dots of firelight are reflected in the dog's clear eyes.

". . . when who appears at my fence but the village headman and priest."

The old woman chews a stringy burdock root, recalling the burned face. "Can it truly be three whole years ago?"

The dog rolls onto his back, using his mistress's foot as a pillow.

He knows the story well, thinks Otane, *but shan't mind indulging me again.*

"I thought she'd come for treatment, seeing her burned face, but then the headman introduced her as 'the celebrated Dr. Aibagawa's daughter' and 'practitioner of Dutch-style midwifery' — as if *he* knew what such words mean! But then she asked if I might advise her on herbal treatments for childbirth and, well, I thought my ears were liars."

Otane rolls a boiled egg to and fro on her wooden platter.

"When she told me that amongst druggists and scholars in Nagasaki, the name 'Otane of Kurozane' is a guarantee of purity, I was horrified that *my* lowly name was known by such elevated folk . . ."

The old woman picks off the fragments of eggshell with her berry-dyed fingernails and remembers how gracefully Miss Aibagawa dismissed the headman and priest, and how attentively she wrote down Otane's observations. "She wrote as well as any man. *Yakumosô* interested her. 'Smear it over torn loins,' I told her, 'and it prevents fevers and heals the skin. It soothes nipples inflamed by breastfeeding, too . . .'" Otane bites into the boiled egg, warmed by the memory of the samurai's daughter acting quite at home in this commoner's cottage while her two servants rebuilt a goat pen and repaired a wall. "*You* remember the headman's eldest son bringing up lunch," she tells the dog. "Polished white rice, quail eggs, and sea bream, steaming in plantain leaves . . . Well, we thought we were in the Palace of the Moon Princess!" Otane lifts the kettle's lid and drops in a fistful of coarse tea. "I spoke more in a single afternoon than I had done all year. Miss Aibagawa wanted to pay me 'tuition money' — but how could I charge her a single *sen?* So she bought my stock of motherwort but left three times the usual price."

The darkness opposite stirs and quickens into the form of a cat.

"Where were you hiding? We were talking about Miss Aibagawa's first visit. She sent us dried sea bream the following New Year. Her servant delivered it all the way from the city." The sooty kettle begins to wheeze, and Otane thinks about the second visit during the sixth month of the following year, when the butterbur was in flower. "She was in love that summer. Oh, I didn't ask, but she couldn't refrain from mentioning a young Dutch interpreter from a good family named Ogawa. Her voice altered" — the cat looks up — "when she said his name." Outside, night stirs the creaking trees. Otane pours her tea before the water boils and embitters the leaves. "I prayed that, once they were married, Ogawa-*sama* would still let her visit Kyôga Domain to gladden my heart and that her second visit would not be her last." She sips her tea, recalling the day when the news reached Kurozane, passed up a chain of relatives and servants, that the head of the Ogawas had denied his son permission to marry Dr. Aibagawa's daughter. Then, in the New Year, Otane learned that Ogawa the Interpreter had taken another bride. "Despite this unfortunate turn" — Otane pokes the fire — "Miss Aibagawa didn't forget me. She sent me my shawl made out of the warmest foreign wool, as a New Year's gift."

The dog wriggles on his back to scratch his flea bites.

Otane recalls this summer's visit as the strangest of Miss Aibagawa's three excursions to Kurozane. Two weeks before, when the azaleas were in flower, a salt merchant had brought news to the Harubayashi Inn about how Dr. Aibagawa's daughter had performed "a Dutch miracle" and breathed life into Magistrate Shiroyama's stillborn child. "So when she visited, half the village walked up to Otane's cottage, hoping for more Dutch miracles. 'Medicine is knowledge,' Miss Aibagawa told the villagers, 'not magic.' " She gave advice to the small crowd, and they thanked her but left disappointed. When they were alone, the young woman confided that it had been a trying year. Her father had been ill, and the careful way she avoided any mention of Ogawa the Interpreter indicated a badly bruised heart. Brighter news, however, was that the grateful magistrate had given her permission to study on Dejima under the Dutch doctor. "Well, I must have looked worried." Otane strokes her cat. "You hear such stories about foreigners. But she assured me that this Dutch doctor was a great teacher, known even to Lord Abbot Enomoto."

Wings beat by the chimney flue. The owl is out hunting.

Then, six weeks ago, came the most shocking news of Otane's recent life.

Miss Aibagawa was to become a sister at Mount Shiranui Shrine.

Otane tried to visit Miss Aibagawa at the Harubayashi Inn the night before she was taken up the mountain, but neither their existing friendship nor Otane's twice-yearly delivery of medicines to the shrine convinced the monk to ignore the prohibition. She could not even leave a letter. She was told that the newest sister could have nothing to do with the world below for twenty years. *What sort of a life,* Otane wonders, *shall she have in that place?* "Nobody knows," she mutters to herself, "and that is the problem."

She turns over the few known facts about Mount Shiranui Shrine.

It is the spiritual seat of Lord Abbot Enomoto, *daimyo* of Kyôga Domain.

The shrine's goddess ensures the fertility of Kyôga's streams and rice fields.

None but the masters and acolytes of the order enter and leave.

These men number about sixty in total, and the sisters, about a dozen. The sisters live in their own house, within the shrine walls, and are governed by an abbess. Servants at the Harubayashi Inn report blemishes or defects that, in most cases, would doom the girls to lives as freaks in brothels, and Abbot Enomoto is praised for giving these unfortunates a better life . . .

. . . *but surely not,* Otane frets, *the daughter of a samurai and doctor?*

"A burned face makes marriage harder," she mumbles, "but not impossible."

The scarcity of facts leaves holes where rumors breed. Many villagers have heard how former sisters of Shiranui receive lodgings and a pension for the rest of their lives, but as the retired nuns never stop in Kurozane, no villager has ever spoken with one face-to-face. Buntarô, the blacksmith's son, who serves at the halfway gate up Mekura Gorge, claims that Master Kinten trains the monks to be assassins, which is why the shrine is so secretive. A flirty chambermaid at the inn met a hunter who swore he had seen winged monster women dressed as nuns flying around Bare Peak at the summit of Shiranui. This very afternoon, the mother-in-law of Otane's niece in Kurozane observed that monks' seeds are as fertile as any other men's and asked how many bushels of "angel-making" herbs the shrine ordered. Otane denied, truthfully, supplying medicines to cause abortions to Master Suzaku and realized that discovering this had been the mother-in-law's goal.

The villagers speculate, but they know better than to hunt for answers. They are proud of their association with the reclusive monastery and are paid for provisioning it; to ask too many questions would be to bite the hand of a generous donor. *The monks probably* are *monks,* Otane hopes, *and the sisters live as nuns . . .*

She hears the ancient hush of falling snow.

"No," Otane tells her cat. "All we can do is ask Our Lady to protect her."

■ ■ ■ ■

The wooden box niche set into the mud-and-bamboo wall resembles an ordinary cottage altar alcove, housing the death-name tablets of Otane's parents and a chipped vase holding a few green sprigs. After checking the bolt on the door twice, however, Otane removes the vase and slides up the back panel. In this small and secret space stands the true treasure of Otane's cottage and bloodline: a white-glazed, blue-veiled, dirt-cracked statuette of Maria-*sama,* the mother of Iesu-*sama* and empress of heaven, crafted long ago to resemble Kannon, the goddess of mercy. She holds an infant in her arms. Otane's grandfather's grandfather, the story goes, received her from a holy saint named Xavier, who sailed to Japan from paradise on a magical flying boat pulled by golden swans.

Otane kneels on painful knees with an acorn rosary around her hands.

" 'Holy Maria-*sama,* mother of Adan and Ewa, who stole Deusu-*dono's* sacred persimmon; Maria-*sama,* mother of Pappa Maruji, with his six sons in six canoes, who survived the great flood that cleansed all lands; Maria, mother of Iesu-*sama,* who was crucified for four hundred silver coins; Maria-*sama,* hear my —' "

Was that a twig snapping under a man's foot?

Otane holds her breath.

Most of Kurozane's oldest ten or twelve families are, like Otane's, Hidden Christians, but vigilance must be constant. Her silver hair would grant her no clemency if her beliefs were ever exposed; only apostasy and the naming of other followers might transmute death into exile, but then San Peitoro and San Pauro would turn her away from the gates of paradise, and when seawater turns to oil and the world burns, she would fall into that hell called Benbô.

The herbalist is confident that nobody is outside. "Virgin Mother, it's Otane of Kurozane. Once again, this old woman begs Her Ladyship to watch over Miss Aibagawa in the Shiranui Shrine, and keep her safe from illness, and ward off bad spirits and . . . and dangerous men. Please give back what has been taken from her."

Not one rumor, Otane thinks, *ever told of a young nun being set free.*

"But if this old woman is asking too much of Maria-*sama* . . ."

The stiffness in Otane's knees is spreading to her hips and ankles.

". . . please tell Miss Aibagawa that her friend, Otane of Kurozane, is thinking —"

Something strikes the door. Otane gasps. The dog is on his feet, growling . . .

Otane slides down the wooden screen as a second blow strikes.

The dog is barking now. She hears a man's voice. She arranges the alcove.

At the third knock, she walks to the door and calls out, "There is nothing to steal here."

"Is this," a frail man's voice replies, "the house of Otane the herbalist?"

"May I ask my honorable visitor to name himself, at this late hour?"

"Jiritsu of Shiranui," says the visitor, "is how I was called . . ."

Otane is surprised to recognize the name of Master Suzaku's acolyte.

Might Maria-sama, she wonders, *have a hand in this?*

"We meet at the shrine's gatehouse," says the voice, "twice a year."

She opens the door to a snow-covered figure wrapped in thick mountain clothing and a bamboo hat. He stumbles over her threshold, and snow swirls in. "Sit by the fire, Acolyte." Otane pushes the door shut. "It's a bad night." She guides him to a log stool.

With effort, he unfastens his hat, hood, and mountain boot bindings.

He is exhausted, his face is taut, and his eyes are not of this world.

Questions can come later, Otane thinks. *First, he must be warmed up.*

She pours some tea and closes his frozen fingers around the bowl.

She unclasps the monk's damp robe and wraps her woolen shawl around him.

His throat muscles make a grinding noise as he drinks.

Perhaps he was gathering plants, Otane wonders, *or meditating in a cave.*

She sets about heating the remains of the soup. They do not speak.

"I fled Mount Shiranui," announces Jiritsu, coming abruptly to. "I broke my oath."

Otane is astonished, but a wrong word now might silence him.

"My hand, this hand, my brush: they knew, before I did."

She grinds some *yogi* root, waiting for words that make sense.

"I accepted the — the deathless way, but its truer name is 'evil.' "

The fire snaps, the animals breathe, the snow is falling.

Jiritsu coughs, as if winded. "She sees so *far!* So very, very far . . . My father was a tobacco hawker, and gambler, around Sakai. We were just a rung above the outcasts . . . and one night the cards went badly and he sold me to a tanner. An untouchable. I lost my name and slept over the slaughterhouse. For years, for years, I slit horses' throats to earn my board. Slit . . . slit . . . slit. What the tanners' sons did to me, I . . . I . . . I . . . longed for someone to slit *my* throat. Come winter, boiling bones into glue was the only warmth. Come summer, the flies got into

329

your eyes, your mouth, and we scraped up the dried blood and oily shit to mix it with Ezo seaweed, for fertilizer. Hell shall smell of that place . . ."

The roof timbers of the cottage creak. Snow is piling up.

"One New Year's Day I climbed over the wall closing the *eta* village and ran away to Osaka, but the tanner sent two men to fetch me back. They underestimated my skill with knives. No man saw, but *she* saw. *She* drew me . . . day by rumor by crossroads by dream by month by hook, *she* urged me west, west, west . . . across the straits to Hizen Domain, to Kyôga Domain . . . and up . . ." Jiritsu looks at the ceiling, perhaps toward the summit of the mountain.

"Does Acolyte-*sama,*" Otane asks, grinding her pestle, "refer to someone at the shrine?"

Jiritsu stares through her. "They are all as a saw is to a carpenter."

"This foolish old crone doesn't understand who 'she' may be."

Tears sprout in Jiritsu's eyes. "Are we no more than the totality of our acts?"

Otane decides to be direct. "Acolyte-*sama:* in the shrine on Mount Shiranui, did you see Miss Aibagawa?"

He blinks and sees more clearly. "The newest sister. Yes."

"Is she . . ." Now Otane wonders what to ask. "Is she well?"

330

He makes a deep sad purr. "The horses knew I was going to kill them."

"How is Miss Aibagawa" — Otane's mortar and pestle fall still — "treated?"

"If *she* hears," Jiritsu says, drifting away again, "*she* shall poke his finger through my heart. . . . Tomorrow, I shall . . . speak of . . . of that place — but her hearing is sharper at night. Then I am bound for Nagasaki. I . . . I . . . I . . . I . . ."

Ginger for his circulation. Otane goes to her cabinet. *Feverfew for delirium.*

"My hand, my brush: they knew before I did." Jiritsu's wan voice follows her. "Three nights ago, but it may be three ages, I was in the scriptorium, at work at a letter from a gift. The letters are a lesser wrong, 'acts of compassion,' Genmu says . . . but . . . but I left myself, and upon my return, my hand, my brush, had written . . . had written *out . . .*" he whispers and cringes ". . . *I had written out the Twelve Creeds.* Black ink on white parchment! Merely to *utter* them is a profanity, except for Master Genmu and the lord abbot, but to *record* them, so a layman's eyes might read . . . *She* must have been occupied elsewhere, or she would have killed me on the spot. Master Yôten passed by, inches behind me . . . Not moving, I read the Twelve Creeds and saw, for the first time . . . the slaughterhouses of Sakai are a pleasure garden in comparison."

Otane understands little, grates ginger, and her heart feels cold.

Jiritsu slides out a dogwood scroll tube from his inner clothing. "Some few men of power in Nagasaki, Enomoto does not own. Magistrate Shiroyama may yet prove a man of conscience . . . and abbots of rival orders shall be eager to know the worst, and *this*" — he frowns at the scroll tube — "is worse than the worst."

"Then Acolyte-*sama* intends," Otane asks, "to go to Nagasaki?"

"East." The aged young man struggles to locate her. "Kinten shall follow."

"To persuade Acolyte-*sama*," she hopes, "to come back to the shrine?"

Jiritsu shakes his head. "The creeds are clear about those who . . . turn away."

Otane glances at her unlit *butsudan* alcove. "Hide here."

Acolyte Jiritsu looks through his hand at the fire. "Stumbling in the snow, I thought, *Otane of Kurozane will shelter me . . .*"

"This old woman is glad" — rats scrat in the thatch — "glad you thought so."

"*. . . for one night.* But if I stay here two, Kinten shall kill us both."

He says this without drama, as one stating a simple fact.

Fire consumes wood, thinks Otane, *and time consumes us.*

"Father called me 'boy,' " he says. "The

tanner called me 'dog.' Master Genmu named his new acolyte 'Jiritsu.' What is my name now?"

"Do you remember," she asks, "what your mother called you?"

"At the slaughterhouse, I'd dream of a . . . motherly woman who named me Mohei."

"That was surely her." Otane mixes tea with the powders. "Drink."

"When Lord Enma asks my name," the fugitive receives the cup, "for the register of hell, that's what I shall tell him: Mohei the Apostate."

Otane's dreams are of scaly wings, roaring blindness, and distant knocks. She wakes in her bed of straw and feathers stitched between sheets of hemp. Her exposed cheeks and nose are pinched by the cold. By cracks of snow-blue daylight, she sees Mohei, lying curled by the dying fire, and remembers everything. She watches him for a while, uncertain whether he is sleeping or awake. The cat emerges from the shawl and pads over to Otane, who sifts their conversation for delirium, delusion, clues, and truth. *Why he ran away,* she understands, *is what threatens Miss Aibagawa . . .*

It is written in that dogwood scroll. It is still in his hand.

. . . and perhaps, Otane thinks, *he is Maria-*

sama*'s answer to my prayers.*

He could be persuaded to stay a few days until the hunters give up.

There's room to hide in the under-roof, she thinks, *if anyone comes . . .*

She sighs out a plume of white in the cold air. The cat puffs littler clouds.

Praise Deusu in heaven, she recites soundlessly, *for this new day.*

Pale clouds uncoil, too, from the wet nose of the dreaming dog.

But wrapped in the warm foreign shawl, Mohei is stiller than still.

Otane realizes he is not breathing.

Chapter Fifteen:
The House of Sisters, Mount Shiranui Shrine

Sunrise on the twenty-third morning of the tenth month

The three bronze booms of the bell of the first cause reverberate over roofs, dislodge pigeons, chase echoes around the cloisters, sluice under the door of the newest sister's cell, and find Orito, who keeps her eyes shut and begs, *Let me imagine I am elsewhere for a moment longer.* But the smells of sour *tatami,* greasy candles, and stale smoke deny her any illusion of release. She hears the *tap, tap, tap* of the women's tobacco pipes.

During the night, fleas or lice feasted on her neck, breast, and midriff.

In Nagasaki, she thinks, *just two days away, the maples will still be red . . .*

The manju *flowers pink and white, the* sanma *saury fat and in season.*

A two-day journey, she thinks, *which may as well be twenty years . . .*

Sister Kagerô walks past the cell. Her voice stabs, "Cold! Cold! Cold!"

335

Orito opens her eyes and surveys the ceiling of her five-mat room.

She wonders which rafter the last newest sister used to hang herself.

The fire is dead. The twice-filtered light has a bluish whiteness.

First snow, Orito thinks. *The gorge down to Kurozane may be impassable.*

With her thumbnail, Orito makes a nick in the wood skirting the wall.

The house may own me, she thinks, *but it shan't own time.*

She counts the notches: *one day, two days, three days . . .*

. . . forty-seven days, forty-eight days, forty-nine days . . .

This morning, she calculates, is the fiftieth since her abduction.

You'll still be here, Fat Rat mocks, *after ten* thousand *notches.*

Its eyes are black pearls and it vanishes in a furry blur.

If there was *a rat,* Orito tells herself, *it* didn't *speak, because rats* don't. She hears her mother humming in the passageway, as on most mornings. She smells her servant Ayame's toasted *onigiri* rice balls rolled in sesame.

"Ayame isn't here, either," Orito says. "Stepmother dismissed her."

These "slippages" of time and senses, she is sure, are caused by the medicine Master Suzaku concocts for each sister before supper. Hers the master calls "solace." She knows the pleasure it brings is harmful and addictive, but unless she drinks it she shan't be fed, and what hope has a starving woman of escaping from a mountain shrine in the middle of winter? Better to eat.

Harder to tolerate are thoughts of her stepmother and stepbrother waking up in the Aibagawa residence in Nagasaki. Orito wonders what of her and her father's belongings remains and what has been sold off: the telescopes, their apparatus, books, and medicines; Mother's kimonos and jewelry . . . It is all her stepmother's property now, to sell to the highest bidder.

Just like she sold me, thinks Orito, feeling anger in her stomach . . .

. . . until she hears Yayoi, next door: vomiting; groaning; and vomiting again.

Orito struggles out of bed and puts on her padded over-kimono.

She ties her headscarf over her burn and hurries into the passageway.

I am no longer a daughter, she thinks, *but I am still a midwife . . .*

. . . where was I going? Orito stands in the musty corridor partitioned from the cloisters by the rows of sliding wooden screens.

337

Daylight enters through a lattice carved along the top. She shivers and she sees her breath, knowing she was going somewhere, but where? Forgetfulness is another trick of Suzaku's solace. She looks around for clues. The night lamp at the corner by the privy is extinguished. Orito places her palm on the wooden screen, stained dark by countless winters. She pushes, and the screen yields a stubborn inch. Through the gap she sees icicles hanging from the cloisters' eaves.

An old pine's branches sag under snow; snow encrusts the seated stones.

A film of ice covers Square Pond. Bare Peak is streaked by veins of snow.

Sister Kiritsubo emerges from behind the pine's trunk, walking along the cloisters opposite, trailing her withered arm's fused fingers along the wooden screen. She circumnavigates the courtyard one hundred and eight times daily. Upon reaching the gap, she says, "Sister is up early this morning."

Orito has nothing to say to Sister Kiritsubo.

Third Sister Umegae approaches up the inner corridor. "This is just the beginning of the Kyôga winter, Newest Sister." In the snow light, Umegae's dappled stains are berry purple. "A gift in your womb is like a warm stone in your pocket."

Orito knows Umegae says this to frighten her. It works.

The stolen midwife hears the noise of

vomiting and remembers, *Yayoi* . . .

The sixteen-year-old woman bends over a wooden bucket. Gastric fluid dangles from her lips, and a slop of fresh vomit is pumped out. Orito breaks the ice on the water bowl with a ladle and carries it to her. Yayoi, glassy-eyed, nods at her visitor to say, *The worst is over.* Orito wipes Yayoi's mouth with a square of paper and gives her a cup of the numbingly cold water. "Most of it," Yayoi says, hiding her fox's ears with her headband, "went into the bucket this morning, at least."

"Practice" — Orito wipes the splashes of vomit — "*does* make perfect, then."

Yayoi dabs her eyes with her sleeve. "Why am I still sick so often, Sister?"

"The vomiting can sometimes continue right up to the birth."

"Last time, I yearned for *dango* candy; this time, even the *thought* of it . . ."

"Each pregnancy is different. Now lie down for a little while."

Yayoi lies back, puts her hands on her bulge, and withdraws into concern.

Orito reads her thoughts. "You still feel your baby kicking, yes?"

"Yes. My gift" — she pats her belly — "is happy when he hears you . . . but . . . but last year Sister Hotaru was vomiting late into *her* fifth month and then miscarried. The gift had died several weeks before. I was there and

339

the stench was . . .”

“Sister Hotaru had not, then, felt the child kick for several weeks?”

Yayoi is both reluctant and eager to agree. “I . . . suppose not.”

“Yet yours *is* kicking, so what conclusions can you draw?”

Yayoi frowns, allows Orito’s logic to pacify her, and cheers up. “I bless the Goddess for bringing you here.”

Enomoto bought me, Orito thinks, biting her tongue, *my stepmother sold me . . .*

She begins rubbing goat fat into Yayoi’s distended belly.

. . . I curse them both and shall tell them so at the next opportunity.

Here is a kick, below Yayoi’s inverted navel; below the lowest rib, a thump . . .

. . . adjacent to the sternum, a kick; over to the left, another stirring.

“There is a chance,” Orito decides to tell Yayoi, “you are carrying twins.”

Yayoi is worldly enough to know the dangers. “How sure are you?”

“Reasonably sure, and it would explain the prolonged vomiting.”

“Sister Hatsune had twins at *her* second gifting. She climbed two ranks with one labor. If the Goddess blessed me with twins —”

“What can *that* lump of wood,” Orito snaps, “know about human pain?”

340

"*Please,* Sister!" Yayoi begs, afraid. "It's like insulting your own mother!"

Here come fresh cramps in Orito's intestines; here is the breathlessness.

"You see, Sister? She can hear. Say you're sorry, Sister, and she'll stop it."

The more solace my body absorbs, Orito knows, *the more it needs.*

She takes Yayoi's foul-smelling pail around the cloisters to the slop barrow.

Crows perch along the ridge of the steep roof, eyeing the prisoner.

Of all the women you could acquire, she would ask Enomoto, *why rob* me *of my life?*

But in fifty days, the Abbot of Shiranui has not once visited his shrine.

"In time," Abbess Izu answers all her questions and entreaties, "in time."

In the kitchen, Sister Asagao is stirring soup over a huffing fire. Asagao's disfigurement is one of the more arresting in the house: her lips are fused into a circle that also deforms her speech. Her friend Sadaie was born with a misshapen skull, giving her head a feline shape that makes her eyes appear unnaturally large. When she sees Orito, she stops speaking in mid-sentence.

Why do those two watch me, Orito wonders, *like squirrels watch a hungry cat?*

Their faces inform her that she is uttering her thoughts aloud again.

341

This is another mortifying trick of solace and the house.

"Sister Yayoi is sick," says Orito. "I wish to take her a bowl of tea. Please."

Sadaie indicates the kettle with her eyes: one is brown, one is gray.

Beneath her gown, Sadaie's own pregnancy is becoming visible.

It's a girl, thinks the doctor's daughter, pouring the bitter brew.

When Acolyte Zanô's stuffed-nose shout rings out, "Gates opening, Sisters!" Orito hurries to a point in the inner corridor midway between Abbess Izu's and Housekeeper Satsuki's rooms and slides open the wooden screen. From this position, just once, in her first week here, she saw through both sets of gates into the precincts and glimpsed steps, a cluster of maples, a blue-cloaked master, and an acolyte in undyed hemp . . .

. . . but this morning, as usual, the acolyte on sentry duty is more careful. Orito sees nothing but the closed outer gates, and a pair of acolytes bring in the day's provisions by handcart.

Sister Sawarabi swoops from the stateroom. "Acolyte Chûai! Acolyte Maboroshi! This snow hasn't frozen your bones, I hope? Master Genmu's a heartless one, starving his young mustangs into skeletons."

"We find ways," Maboroshi flirts back, "to

keep warm, Sister."

"Oh, but how can I forget?" Sawarabi brushes her middle breast with her fingertips. "Isn't Jiritsu provisioning us this week, that shameless slugabed?"

Maboroshi's levity vanishes. "The acolyte has fallen into sickness."

"My, my. Sickness, you say. Not just . . . early-winter sneezes?"

"His condition" — Maboroshi and Chûai begin carrying supplies into the kitchen — "is grave, it seems."

"We hope," cleft-lipped Sister Hotaru adds, appearing from the stateroom, "that poor Acolyte Jiritsu is not in danger of death?"

"His condition is grave." Maboroshi is terse. "We must prepare for the worst."

"Well, the newest sister was a famous doctor's daughter, in her previous life, so Master Suzaku could do worse than ask for her. She'd come, and gladly, because" — Sawarabi cups her mouth to her hand and calls across the courtyard to Orito's hiding place — "she'd *die* to see the precincts, so as to plan her escape, *wouldn't* you, Sister Orito?"

Blushing, the exposed observer beats a tearful retreat to her cell.

All the sisters except Yayoi, along with Abbess Izu and Housekeeper Satsuki, kneel at the low table in the long room. The doors to

343

the prayer room, where the gold-leafed statue of the pregnant Goddess is housed, are open. The Goddess watches the sisters over the head of Abbess Izu, who strikes her tubular gong. The Sutra of Gratitude begins.

"To Abbot Enomoto-*no-kami*," the women chorus, "our spiritual guide . . ."

Orito pictures herself spitting on the illustrious colleague of her late father.

". . . whose sagacity guides the shrine of Mount Shiranui . . ."

Abbess Izu and Housekeeper Satsuki notice Orito's motionless lips.

". . . we, the Daughters of Izanazô, render the gratitude of the nurtured child."

It is a passive protest, but Orito lacks the means of more active dissent.

"To Abbot Genmu-*no-kami*, whose wisdom protects the House of Sisters . . ."

Orito glares at Housekeeper Satsuki, who looks away, embarrassed.

". . . we, the Daughters of Izanazô, render the gratitude of the justly governed."

Orito glares at Abbess Izu, who absorbs her defiance kindly.

"To the Goddess of Shiranui, Fountainhead of Life and Mother of Gifts . . ."

Orito looks above the sisters opposite at the hanging scrolls.

". . . we, the Sisters of Shiranui, render the fruits of our wombs . . ."

The scrolls display seasonal paintings and

lines from Shintô texts.

". . . so that fertility cascades over Kyôga, so famine and drought are banished . . ."

The center scroll shows the sisters' precedence, ranked by numbers of births.

Exactly like, Orito thinks with disgust, *a stable of sumo wrestlers.*

". . . so that the wheel of life shall turn through eternity . . ."

The wooden tablet inscribed ORITO is on the far right position.

". . . until the last star burns out and the wheel of time is broken."

Abbess Izu strikes her gong once to indicate the sutra's conclusion. Housekeeper Satsuki closes the doors to the prayer room, while Asagao and Sadaie bring rice and miso soup from the adjacent kitchen.

When Abbess Izu strikes the gong again, the sisters begin breakfast.

Speech and eye contact are forbidden, but friends pour one another's water.

Fourteen mouths — Yayoi is excused — chew, slurp, and swallow.

What fine foods is Stepmother eating? Hatred churns Orito's insides.

Every sister leaves a few grains of rice to feed the spirits of their ancestors.

Orito does the same, reasoning that in this place, any and all allies are needed.

Abbess Izu strikes the tubular gong to indicate the end of the meal. As Sadaie and

Asagao clear the dishes, pink-eyed Hashihime asks Abbess Izu about the sick acolyte, Jiritsu.

"He is being nursed in his cell," replies the abbess. "He has a trembling fever."

Several of the sisters cover their mouths and murmur in alarm.

Why such pity, Orito burns to ask, *for one of your captors?*

"A porter in Kurozane died from the disease: poor Jiritsu may have breathed in the same vapors. Master Suzaku asked us to pray for the acolyte's recovery."

Most of the sisters nod earnestly and promise to do so.

Abbess Izu then assigns the day's housekeeping. "Sisters Hatsune and Hashihime, continue yesterday's weaving. Sister Kiritsubo is to sweep the cloisters; and Sister Umegae, twist the flax in the storeroom into twine, with Sisters Minori and Yûgiri. At the Hour of the Horse, go to the great shrine to polish the floor. Sister Yûgiri may be excused this, if she wishes, on account of her gift."

What ugly, twisted words, thinks Orito, *for malformed thoughts.*

Every head in the room looks at Orito. She spoke aloud again.

"Sisters Hotaru and Sawarabi," continues the abbess, "dust the prayer room, then attend to the latrines. Sisters Asagao and Sa-

346

daie are on kitchen duty, of course, so Sister Kagerô and our newest sister" — the crueler eyes turn to Orito, saying, *See the fine lady, working like one of her old servants* — "are to work in the laundry. If Sister Yayoi is feeling better, she may join them."

The laundry, a long annex to the kitchen, has two hearths to heat water, a pair of large tubs for washing linen, and a rack of bamboo poles where laundry is hung. Orito and Kagerô carry buckets of water from the pool in the courtyard. To fill each tub costs forty or fifty trips, and the two do not talk. At first the samurai's daughter was exhausted by the work, but now her legs and arms are tougher, and the blisters on her palms are covered with calloused skin. Yayoi tends the fires to heat the water.

Soon, Fat Rat taunts, balancing on the slop barrow, *your belly shall look like hers.*

"I shan't let the dogs touch me," mutters Orito. "I shan't be here."

Your body isn't yours anymore. Fat Rat smirks. *It's the Goddess's.*

Orito loses her footing on the kitchen step and spills her bucket.

"I don't know how," says Kagerô coolly, "we coped without you."

"The floor needed a good wash, anyway." Yayoi helps Orito mop the spillage.

When the water is warm enough, Yayoi stirs

in the blankets and nightshirts. With wooden tongs, Orito transfers them, dripping and heavy, onto the laundry vise, a slanted table with a hinged door that Kagerô closes to squeeze out the water from the linen. Kagerô then hangs the damp laundry on the bamboo poles. Through the kitchen door, Sadaie is telling Yayoi about last night's dream. "There was a knocking at the gate. I left my room — it was summer — but it didn't feel like summer, or night, or day. . . . The house was deserted. Still, the knocking went on, so I asked, 'Who is it?' And a man's voice replied, 'It's me, it's Iwai.' "

"Sister Sadaie was delivered of her first gift," Yayoi tells Orito, "last year."

"Born on the fifth day of the fifth month," says Sadaie, "the Day of Boys."

The women think of carp streamers and festive innocence.

"So Abbot Genmu," Sadaie continues, "named him Iwai, as in 'celebration.' "

"A brewer's family in Takamatsu," Yayoi says, "called Takaishi adopted him."

Orito is hidden by a cloud of steam. "So I understand."

Asagao says, "*Ph*ut you *uu*r s*ph*eaking a'*out* your drea*n*, Sister . . ."

"Well," Sadaie says, scrubbing at a crust of burned-on rice, "I was surprised that Iwai had grown up so quickly and worried that he'd be in trouble for breaking the rule that bans gifts from Mount Shiranui. But" — she looks in the direction of the prayer room and lowers her voice — "I had to unbolt the inner gate."

"The '*olt*," Asagao asks, " '*as* on the *in*side o*ph* the inner gate, you say."

"Yes, it was. It didn't occur to me at the time. So the gate opened —"

Yayoi provides a cry of impatience. "What did you see, Sister?"

"Dry leaves. No gift, no Iwai, just dry leaves. The wind carried them away."

"*That,*" Kagerô leans hard on the vise's handle, "is an ill omen."

Sadaie is unnerved by Kagerô's certainty. "Do you really think so, Sister?"

"How could your gift turning into dead leaves be a good omen?"

Yayoi stirs the cauldron. "Sister Kagerô, you'll upset Sadaie."

"Just speaking the truth," Kagerô replies, squeezing out the water, "as I see it."

"Could you tell," Asagao asks Sadaie, "I'ai's *pha*ther *phon* his *pho*ice?"

"That's it," says Yayoi. "Your dream was a clue about Iwai's father."

Even Kagerô shows interest in the theory: "Which monks were your engifters?"

Housekeeper Satsuki enters, carrying a new box of soap nuts.

The rarefied sunset turns the snow-veined

349

Bare Peak a bloodied fish pink, and the evening star is as sharp as a needle. Smoke and smells of cooking leak from the kitchen. With the exception of the week's two cooks, the women's time is their own until Master Suzaku's arrival prior to supper. Orito embarks on her anticlockwise walk around the cloisters to distract her body from its clamorous longing for her solace. Several sisters are gathered in the long room, whitening one another's faces or blackening their teeth. Yayoi is resting in her cell. Blind Sister Minori is teaching a *koto* arrangement of "Eight Miles Through a Mountain Pass" to Sadaie. Umegae, Hashihime, and Kagerô are also taking exercise, clockwise, around the cloisters. Orito is obliged to stand aside as they pass. For the thousandth time since her kidnapping, Orito wishes she had the means to write. Unauthorized letters to the outside world, she knows, are forbidden, and she would burn anything she wrote for fear of her thoughts being exposed. *But an ink brush, she thinks, is a skeleton key for a prisoner's mind.* Abbess Izu has promised to present her with a writing set after her first gifting is confirmed.

How could I endure that act, Orito shudders, *and live afterward?*

When she turns the next corner, Bare Peak is no longer pink but gray.

She considers the twelve women in the

house who do endure it.

She thinks about the last newest sister, who hanged herself.

"Venus," Orito's father once told her, "follows a clockwise orbit. All her sister and brother planets circle the sun in an anticlockwise manner . . ."

. . . but the memory of her father is chased away by jeering *ifs*.

Umegae, Hashihime, and Kagerô form a shuffling wall of padded kimonos.

If Enomoto had never seen me or chosen to add me to his collection . . .

Orito hears the *chop chop chop* of knives in the kitchen.

If Stepmother was as compassionate a woman as she once pretended . . .

Orito must press herself against the wooden screen to let them pass.

If Enomoto hadn't guaranteed Father's loans with the moneylenders . . .

"*Some* of us are so well bred," Kagerô remarks, "they think rice grows on trees."

If Jacob de Zoet had seen me at Dejima land gate, on my last day . . .

The three women drift by, hems traipsing along the wooden planks.

A Dutch alphabet V of geese crosses the sky; a forest monkey shrieks.

Better a Dejima wife, Orito thinks, *protected by a foreigner's money . . .*

A mountain bird on the old pine sings in

intricate stitches.

*. . . than what happens to me in the engifting
week, if I don't escape.*

The walled stream enters and leaves the
courtyard under the raised cloister floor, feeding the pool. Orito presses herself against the
wooden screen.

"She supposes," says Hashihime, "a magic
cloud shall whisk her away."

Stars pollinate the banks of Heaven's River,
germinate and sprout.

Europeans, Orito remembers, *call it the Milky
Way.* Her soft-spoken father is back. "Here is
Umihebi, the sea snake; there Tokei, the
clock; over here, Ite, the archer" — she can
smell his warm smell — "and above, Ran-
shinban, the compass . . ."

The bolt of the inner gate screeches open:
"Opening!"

Every sister hears. Every sister thinks, *Master Suzaku.*

The sisters gather in the long room, wearing
their finest clothes, save for Sadaie and Asagao, who are still preparing supper, and
Orito, who owns only the work-kimono in
which she was abducted, a warm quilted
hakata jacket, and a couple of headscarves.
Even lower-ranked sisters like Yayoi already
have a choice of two or three kimonos of fair
quality — one for every child born — with

352

simple necklaces and bamboo hair combs. Senior sisters, like Hatsune and Hashihime, have acquired, over the years, as rich a wardrobe as that of a high-ranking merchant wife.

Her hunger for solace is now an incessant pounding, but Orito also has the longest wait: one by one, in order of the list of precedence, the sisters are summoned to the square room, where Suzaku holds his consultations and administers his potions. Suzaku spends two or three minutes with each patient; for some sisters, the minutiae of their ailments and the master's thoughts on the same are a fascination second only to the New Year letters. First Sister Hatsune returns from her consultation with the news that Acolyte Jiritsu's fever is worsening, and Master Suzaku doubts he shall survive the night.

Most of the sisters express shock and dismay.

"Our masters and acolytes," swears Hatsune, "are so very rarely ill . . ."

Orito catches herself wondering what febrifuges have been administered, before thinking, *He is no concern of mine.*

The women swap memories of Jiritsu, using the past tense.

Sooner than expected, Yayoi is touching her shoulder. "Your turn."

"How do we find the newest sister this

evening?" Master Suzaku gives the impression of a man perpetually on the brink of laughter that never comes. The effect is sinister. Abbess Izu occupies one corner and an acolyte another.

Orito answers her usual answer: "Alive, as you see."

"Do we know" — Suzaku indicates the young man — "Acolyte Chûai?"

Kagerô and the meaner sisters nickname Chûai "the Swollen Toad."

"Certainly not." Orito does not look at the acolyte.

Suzaku clicks his tongue. "The first snow is not sapping our constitution?"

Don't plead for solace. She says, "No." *He loves you to plead.*

"We have no symptoms to report, then? No aches or bleedings?"

The world, she guesses, *is his own vast private joke.* "Nothing."

"Or constipation? Diarrhea? Hemorrhoids? Thrush? Migraines?"

"What I am suffering from," Orito is goaded into saying, "is incarceration."

Suzaku smiles at Acolyte Chûai and the abbess. "Our ties to the world below cut us, like wire. Sever them, and be as happy as your dear sisters."

"My 'dear sisters' were rescued from brothels and freak shows, and perhaps, for them,

354

life here is better. I lost more, and Enomoto"
— Abbess Izu and Acolyte Chûai flinch to
hear the abbot named with such contempt —
"hasn't even faced me since he bought me;
and don't *dare*" — Orito stops herself pointing at Suzaku like an angry Dutchman —
"spout your platitudes about destiny and divine balance. Just give me my solace. *Please.*
The women want their supper."

"It scarcely behooves you," begins the abbess, "to address —"

Suzaku interrupts her with a respectful
hand. "Let us show her a little indulgence,
Abbess, even if undeserved. Contrariness
often is best tamed by kindness." The monk
decants a muddy liquid into a thimble-sized
stone cup.

See how painstakingly he moves, she thinks,
to sharpen your hunger . . .

Orito stops her hand from snatching the
cup from the proffered tray.

She turns away to conceal with her sleeve
the vulgar act of drinking.

"Once you are engifted," promises Suzaku,
"your sense of belonging shall grow, too."

Never, Orito thinks, *never.* Her tongue
absorbs the oily fluid . . .

. . . and her blood pumps louder, her arteries widen, and well-being soothes her joints.

"The Goddess didn't choose you," says Abbess Izu. "You chose the Goddess."

Warm snowflakes settle over Orito's skin,

whispering as they melt.

Every evening, the doctor's daughter wants to ask Suzaku about the ingredients of solace. Every evening, she stops herself. *The question,* she knows, *would initiate a conversation, and conversation is a step toward acceptance.*

"What's good for the body," Suzaku tells Orito's mouth, "is good for the soul."

Dinner is a festive occasion compared to breakfast. After a brief blessing, Housekeeper Satsuki and the sisters eat tofu in tempura batter, fried with garlic and rolled in sesame; pickled eggplant; pilchards and white rice. Even the haughtiest sisters remember their commoners' origins, when such a fine daily diet could only be dreamed of, and they relish each morsel. The abbess has gone with Master Suzaku to dine with Master Genmu, so the mood in the long room is leisurely. When the table is cleared and the dishes and chopsticks washed, the sisters smoke pipes around the table, swap stories, play mahjongg, reread — or have reread — their New Year letters, and listen to Hatsune play her *koto.* The effects of solace wear out a little earlier every night, Orito notices. She leaves, as usual, without saying good night. *Wait till she's been engifted,* she feels the women think. *Wait till her belly is as big as a boulder, and she needs* us *to help* her *scrub, fetch, and carry.*

Back in her cell, Orito finds that someone has lit her fire. *Yayoi.*

Umegae's spite or Kagerô's hostility encourages her to reject the house.

But Yayoi's kindness, she fears, *makes life here more tolerable . . .*

. . . and ushers closer the day when Mount Shiranui becomes her home.

Who knows, she wonders, *if Yayoi is not acting under Genmu's orders?*

Orito, troubled and shivering in the icy air, wipes herself with a cloth.

Under her blankets, she lies on her side, gazing into the fire's garden.

The persimmon's branches sag with ripe fruit. They glow in the dusk.

An eyelash in the sky grows into a heron; the gawky bird descends . . .

Its eyes are green and its hair is red; Orito is afraid of his clumsy beak.

The heron says, in Dutch, of course, *You are beautiful.*

Orito wishes neither to encourage him nor wound his feelings.

She is in the courtyard of the House of Sisters: she hears Yayoi groan.

Dead leaves fly like bats; bats fly like dead leaves.

How can I escape? Orito asks nobody. *The gate is locked.*

Since when, mocks the moon-gray cat, *do cats need keys?*

There is no time — she is knotted by exasperation — *to speak in riddles.*

First, persuade them, says the cat, *that you are happy here.*

Why, she asks, *should I ever give them that false satisfaction?*

Because only then, answers the cat, *shall they stop watching you.*

CHAPTER SIXTEEN: THE SHIRANDÔ ACADEMY AT THE ÔTSUKI RESIDENCE IN NAGASAKI

Sunset on the twenty-fourth day of the tenth month

"I conclude," says Yoshida Hayato, the still-youthful author of an erudite monograph on the true age of the earth, surveying his audience of eighty or ninety scholars, "this widely held belief that Japan is an impregnable fortress is a pernicious delusion. Honorable Academicians, we are a ramshackle farmhouse with crumbling walls, a collapsing roof, and covetous neighbors." Yoshida is succumbing to a bone disease, and projecting his voice over the large sixty-mat hall drains him. "To our northwest, a morning's voyage from Tsushima Island, live the vainglorious Koreans. Who shall forget those provocative banners their last embassy flaunted? 'Inspectorate of Dominions' and 'We Are Purity,' implying, naturally, 'You Are Not'!"

Some of the scholars grizzle in agreement.

"Northeast lies the vast domain of Ezo, home to the savage Ainu but also to Russians, who map our coastlines and claim Karafuto. They call it Sakhalin. It is a mere twelve years since a Frenchman" — Yoshida prepares his lips — "La Pérouse, named the straits between Ezo and Karafuto after himself! Would the French tolerate the Yoshida Straits off their coast?" The point is well made and well received. "The recent incursions by Captain Benyowsky and Captain Laxman warn us of a near future when straying Europeans no longer request provisions but demand trade, quays, and warehouses, fortified ports, unequal treaties. Colonies shall take root like thistles and weeds. Then we shall understand that our 'impregnable fortress' was a placebo and nothing more; that our seas are no 'impassable moat' but, as my far-sighted colleague Hayashi Shihei wrote, 'an ocean road without frontiers that links China, Holland, and Edo's Nihonbashi Bridge.' "

Some in the audience nod in agreement; others look concerned.

Hayashi Shihei, Ogawa Uzaemon remembers, *died under house arrest for his writings.*

"My lecture is finished." Yoshida bows. "I thank the Shirandô for its gracious attention."

Ôtsuki Monjurô, the academy's bearded director, hesitates to ask for questions, but Dr. Maeno clears his well-respected throat and raises his fan. "First, I wish to thank Yoshida-*san* for his stimulating thoughts. Second, I wish to ask how best the threats he

360

enumerates can be countered."

Yoshida takes a sip of warm water and a deep breath.

A vague and evasive answer, thinks Uzaemon, *would be safest.*

"By the creation of a Japanese navy, by the foundation of two large shipyards, and by the establishment of an academy where foreign instructors would train Japanese shipwrights, armorers, gunsmiths, officers, and sailors."

The audience was unprepared for the audacity of Yoshida's vision.

Awatsu, an algebraist, is the first to recover. "Is that all?"

Yoshida smiles at Awatsu's irony. "Emphatically not. We need a national army based on the French model; an armory to produce the newest Prussian rifles; and an overseas empire. To avoid becoming a European colony, we need colonies of our own."

"But what Yoshida-*san* proposes," objects Dr. Maeno, "would require . . ."

A radical new government, thinks Uzaemon, *and a radical new Japan.*

A chemist unknown to Uzaemon suggests, "A trade mission to Batavia?"

Yoshida shakes his head. "Batavia is a ditch, and whatever the Dutch tell us, Holland is a pawn. France, England, Prussia, or the energetic United States must be our teachers. Two hundred bright, able-bodied scholars — a criterion that," he says, smiling sadly, "excludes *me* — must be sent to these countries to study the arts of industry. Upon their return, let them spread their knowledge freely, to the ablest minds of all classes, so we may set about constructing a *true* 'impregnable fortress.'"

"But," Haga the ape-nosed druggist raises the obvious objection, "the Separate Nation decree forbids any subject to leave Japan, on pain of death."

Not even Yoshida Hayato dares suggest, thinks Uzaemon, *the decree be annulled.*

"Hence the decree" — Yoshida Hayato is outwardly calm — "must be annulled."

The statement provokes fearful objections and some nervous assent.

Interpreter Arashiyama glances at Uzaemon: *Should someone not save him from himself?*

He's dying, the young interpreter thinks. *The choice is his.*

"Yoshida-*san,*" calls out Haga the druggist, "is naysaying the third shogun . . ."

". . . who is not a debating partner," the chemist agrees, "but a deity!"

"Yoshida-*sama,*" counters Ômori the Dutch-style painter, "is a visionary patriot and he should be heard!"

Haga stands up. "Our society debates natural philosophy —"

"— and not matters of state," agrees an Edo

362

metallurgist, "so —"

"Nothing is outside philosophy," claims Ômori, "unless fear says it is."

"So whoever disagrees with you," asks Haga, "is, therefore, a coward?"

"The third shogun closed the country to prevent Christian rebellions," argues Aodo the historian, "but its result was to pickle Japan in a specimen jar!"

Clamor breaks out, and Director Ôtsuki strikes two sticks together for order.

When relative quietness is reestablished, Yoshida wins permission to address his detractors. "The Separate Nation decree was a necessary measure in the day of the third shogun. But new machines of power are shaping the world. What we learn from Dutch reports and Chinese sources is a grave warning. Peoples who do not acquire these machines of power are, at best, subjugated, like the Indians. At worst, like the natives of Van Diemen's Land, they are exterminated."

"Yoshida-*san*'s loyalty," concedes Haga, "is beyond question. What I doubt is the likelihood of an armada of European warships sailing into Edo or Nagasaki. You argue for revolutionary changes to our state, but why? To counter a phantom. To address a hypothetical what-if?"

"The present is a battleground" — Yoshida straightens his spine as best he can — "where rival what-ifs compete to become the future 'what is.' How does one what-if prevail over its adversaries? The answer" — the sick man coughs — "the answer, 'Military and political power, of course!' is a postponement, for what is it that directs the minds of the powerful? The answer is 'belief.' Beliefs that are ignoble or idealistic; democratic or Confucian; Occidental or Oriental; timid or bold; clear-sighted or delusional. Power is informed by belief that *this* path, and not another, must be followed. What, then, or where, is the womb of belief? What, or where, is the crucible of ideology? Academicians of the Shirandô, I put it to you that *we* are one such crucible. We are one such womb."

During the first interval, the lanterns are lit, braziers are stoked against the cold, and conversations stew and bubble. Interpreters Uzaemon, Arashiyama, and Goto Shinpachi sit with five or six others. The algebraist Awatsu apologizes for disturbing Uzaemon, "but I hoped to hear news of an improvement in your father's health . . ."

"He is still bed-bound," replies Uzaemon, "but finds ways to wield his will."

Those who know Ogawa the Elder of the first rank smile downward.

"What ails the gentleman?" Yanaoka is a *sake*-blushed doctor from Kumamoto.

"Dr. Maeno believes Father suffers from a cancer of the —"

"A difficult diagnosis! Let us hold a consultation tomorrow."

"Dr. Yanaoka is kind, but Father is particular about who —"

"Come, now, I have known your honorable father for twenty years."

Yes, thinks Uzaemon, *and he has despised you for forty.*

" 'Too many captains,' " Awatsu quotes, " 'sail the ship up the mountain.' Dr. Maeno is no doubt doing an excellent job. I shall offer prayers for his swift recovery."

The others promise to do the same, and Uzaemon expresses due gratitude.

"Another missing face," Yanaoka mentions, "is Dr. Aibagawa's burned daughter."

"You didn't hear, then," says Interpreter Arashiyama, "about her happy ending? The late doctor's finances were found to be in so parlous a state, there was talk of the widow losing the house. When Lord Abbot Enomoto was apprised of the family's hardships, he not only paid every last *sen* of the debts — he found space for the daughter in his convent on Mount Shiranui."

"Why is that a 'happy ending'?" Uzaemon regrets opening his mouth already.

"A full rice bowl every day," says Ozono, the squat chemist, "for reciting a few sutras? For a woman with such an unmarriageable blemish, this is a *jubilant* ending! Oh, I know her father encouraged her to play the scholar,

365

but one must sympathize with the widow. What business has a samurai's daughter to be dabbling with midwifery and mingling with sweaty Dutchmen?"

Uzaemon orders himself to say nothing.

Banda is an earthy engineer from marshy Sendai. "During my stay in Isahaya, I overheard some strange rumors about Abbot Enomoto's shrine."

"Without you want," Awatsu warns Banda cheerfully, "to accuse a close friend of Matsudaira Sadanobu and senior academician of the Shirandô of impropriety, then you should ignore any rumors whatsoever about Lord Enomoto's shrine. The monks live their lives as monks and the nuns live their lives as nuns."

Uzaemon wants to hear Banda's rumors, but he doesn't want to hear.

"Where *is* Abbot Enomoto tonight, anyway?" asks Yanaoka.

"In Miyako," says Yanaoka, "settling some abstruse clerical point."

"At his court in Kashima," says Arashiyama. "Exercising justice, I heard."

"I heard he went to the Isle of Tsu," says Ozono, "to meet Korean traders."

The door slides open: a welcoming hubbub sweeps the hall.

Dr. Marinus and Sugita Genpaku, one of the most celebrated living Dutch scholars, stand at the threshold. Half-lame Marinus leans on his stick; elderly Sugita leans on a houseboy. The pair enjoys a verbal tussle over who should enter first. They settle the matter by a game of scissors, paper, stone. Marinus wins but uses his victory to insist that Sugita takes precedence.

"But *look*," asks Yanaoka, his neck craning, "at that foreigner's *hair!*"

Ogawa Uzaemon sees Jacob de Zoet hit the crown of his head on the door frame.

"Just thirty years ago," Sugita Genpaku says, sitting on the lecturer's low plinth, "there were only three of us Dutch scholars in all Japan and a single book: this old man you see before you, Dr. Nakagawa Jun'an, and my dear friend Dr. Maeno, whose more recent discoveries surely include the elixir of immortality, for he has aged not a day." Sugita's fingers loop his stringy white beard.

Dr. Maeno shakes his head with embarrassment and delight.

"The book," Sugita continues, tilting his head, "was Kulmus's *Tafel Anatomia,* printed in Holland. This I had encountered on my very first visit to Nagasaki. I desired it with my whole being, but I could no more pay the asking price than swim to the moon. My clan purchased it on my behalf and, in so doing, determined my fate." Sugita pauses and listens with professional interest to Interpreter Shizuki translate his words for Marinus and

367

De Zoet.

Uzaemon has avoided Dejima since the *Shenandoah* departed and avoids De Zoet's eye now. His guilt about Orito is knotted up with the Dutchman in ways Uzaemon cannot disentangle.

"Maeno and I took the *Tafel Anatomia* to Edo's execution ground," continues Sugita, "where a prisoner named Old Mother Tea had been sentenced to an hour-long strangulation for poisoning her husband." Shizuki stumbles on "strangulation"; he mimes the action. "We struck a bargain. In return for a painless beheading, she gave us permission to conduct the first medical dissection in the history of Japan on her body and signed an oath not to haunt us in revenge. Upon comparing the subject's inner organs with the illustrations in the book, we saw, to our astonishment, the Chinese sources that dominated our learning were grossly inaccurate. There were no 'ears of the lungs'; no 'seven lobes of the kidneys'; and the intestines differed markedly from the descriptions by the ancient sages . . ."

Sugita waits for Shizuki's translation to catch up.

De Zoet looks gaunter, Uzaemon thinks, *than he did in the autumn.*

"My *Tafel Anatomia,* however, corresponded with our dissected body so precisely that Drs. Maeno, Nakagawa, and myself were of one mind: *European medicine surpasses the Chinese.* To say so nowadays, with Dutch medical schools in every city, is a self-evident truth. Thirty years ago, such an opinion was patricidal. Yet, with just a few hundred Dutch words between us, we resolved to translate *Tafel Anatomia* into Japanese. A few of you may have heard of our *Kaitai Shinsho?*"

His audience savors the understatement.

Shizuki renders "patricidal" into Dutch as "great crime."

"Our task was formidable." Sugita Genpaku straightens his tufted white eyebrows. "Hours were spent in pursuit of single words, often to discover that no Japanese equivalent existed. We created words that our race shall use" — the old man is not immune to vanity — "for all eternity. By dint of example, I devised *'shinkei'* for the Dutch 'nerve,' over a dinner of oysters. We were, to quote the proverb, 'The one dog who barks at nothing answered by a thousand dogs barking at something . . .' "

During the final interval, Uzaemon hides in the not-quite-winter garden courtyard from a possible encounter with De Zoet. An unearthly wail from the hall is accompanied by appalled laughter: Director Ôtsuki is demonstrating his bagpipes, acquired earlier this year from Arie Grote. Uzaemon sits under a giant magnolia. The sky is starless, and the young man's mind recalls the afternoon a year and a half ago when he asked his father for his views on Aibagawa Orito as a possible bride. "Dr. Aibagawa's a notable scholar, but not so notable as his debts, I am informed. Worse yet, what if that singed face of his daughter is passed on to my grandsons? The answer must be *no*. If you and the daughter have exchanged any *sentiments*" — his father's expression suggested a bad smell — "disown them, without delay." Uzaemon begged his father at least to consider an engagement a little longer, but Ogawa the Elder wrote an affronted letter to Orito's father. The servant returned with a short note from the doctor, apologizing for the inconvenience his overindulged daughter had caused and assuring him that the matter was closed. That grimmest of days ended with Uzaemon receiving one last secret letter from Orito, and the shortest of their clandestine correspondence. *I could never cause your father,* it ended, *to regret adopting you.*

Uzaemon's parents were prompted by the "Aibagawa incident" into finding their son a wife. A go-between knew of a low-ranking but wealthy family in Karatsu who had thriving business interests in dyes and were eager for a son-in-law with access to sappanwood entering Dejima. *Omiai* interviews were held, and Uzaemon was informed by his father that the girl would be an acceptable Ogawa wife.

They were married on New Year's Day, at an hour judged to be fortunate by the family's astrologer. *The good fortune,* Uzaemon thinks, *is yet to reveal itself.* His wife endured a second miscarriage a few days ago, a misfortune attributed by his mother and father to "wanton carelessness" and "a laxness of spirit," respectively. Uzaemon's mother considers it her duty to make her daughter-in-law suffer in the same way she suffered as a young bride in the Ogawa residence. *I pity my wife,* Uzaemon concedes, *but the meaner part of me cannot forgive her for not being Orito.* What Orito must endure on Mount Shiranui, however, Uzaemon can only speculate: isolation, drudgery, cold, grief for her father and the life stolen from her, and, surely, resentment at how the scholars of the Shirandô Academy view her captor as a great benefactor. For Uzaemon to interrogate Enomoto, the Shirandô's most eminent sponsor, about his shrine's newest sister would be a near-scandalous breach of etiquette. It would imply an accusation of wrongdoing. Yet Mount Shiranui is as shut to inquiries from outside the domain as Japan is closed to the outside world. In the absence of facts about her well-being, Uzaemon's imagination torments him as much as his conscience. When Dr. Aibagawa had seemed close to death, Uzaemon had hoped that by encouraging,

or, at least, by not *dis*couraging, Jacob de Zoet's proposal of temporary marriage to Orito,
he might ensure that she would stay on Dejima. He anticipated, in the longer term, a
time when De Zoet would leave Japan, or
grow tired of his prize, as foreigners usually
do, and she would be willing to accept Uzaemon's patronage as a second wife. *"Feeble*-
headed," Uzaemon tells the magnolia tree,
"cock-headed, *wrong*headed . . ."

"Who's wrongheaded?" Arashiyama's feet
crunch on the stones.

"Yoshida-*sama*'s provocations. Those were
dangerous words."

Arashiyama hugs himself against the cold.
"Snow in the mountains, I hear."

My guilt about Orito shall dog me, Uzaemon
fears, *for the rest of my life.*

"Ôtsuki-*sama* sent me to find you," says
Arashiyama. "Dr. Marinus is ready, and we
are to sing for our supper."

"The ancient Assyrians used rounded glass
to start fires." Marinus sits with his lame leg
at an awkward angle. "Archimedes the Greek,
we read, destroyed the Roman fleet of Mar-
cus Aurelius with giant burning glasses at
Syracuse, and the emperor Nero allegedly
employed a lens to correct myopia."

Uzaemon explains "Assyrians" and inserts
"the island of" before "Syracuse."

"The Arab Ibn al-Haytham," continues the

doctor, "whom Latin translators named Al-hazen, wrote his *Book of Optics* eight centuries ago. The Italian Galileo and the Dutchman Lippershey used al-Haytham's discoveries to invent what we now call microscopes and telescopes."

Arashiyama confirms the Arabic name and delivers a confident rendering.

"The lens and its cousin the polished mirror, and their mathematical principles, have evolved a long way through time and space. By virtue of successive advancements, astronomers may now gaze upon a newly discovered planet beyond Saturn, Georgium Sidium, invisible to the naked eye. Zoologists may admire the true portrait of man's most loyal companion . . .

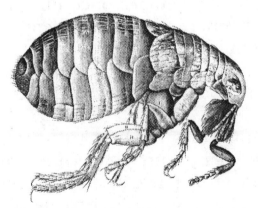

". . . *Pulex irritans.*" One of Marinus's seminarians exhibits the illustration from Hooke's *Micrografia* in a slow arc, while Goto works

373

on the translation. The scholars do not notice his omission of "successive advancements," which Uzaemon can make no sense of, either.

De Zoet is watching from the side, just a few paces away. When Uzaemon took his place on the stage, they exchanged a "good evening," but the tactful Dutchman has detected the interpreter's reticence and not imposed further. *He may have been a worthy husband for Orito.* Uzaemon's generous thought is stained by jealousy and regret.

Marinus peers through the lamplit smoke. Uzaemon wonders whether his discourses are prepared in advance or netted from the thick air extemporaneously. "Microscopes and telescopes are begat by science; their use, by man and, where permitted, by woman, begets further science, and Creation's mysteries are unfolded in modes once undreamed of. In this manner, science broadens, deepens, and disseminates itself — and via its invention of printing, its spores and seeds may germinate even within this Cloistered Empire."

Uzaemon does his best to translate this, but it isn't easy: surely the Dutch word "semen" cannot be related to this unknown verb "disseminate"? Goto Shinpachi anticipates his colleague's difficulty and suggests "distribute." Uzaemon guesses "germinate" means "is accepted" but is warned by suspicious glances from the Shirandô's audience:

If we don't understand the speaker, we blame the interpreter.

"Science moves" — Marinus scratches his thick neck — "year by year toward a new state of being. Where, in the past, man was the subject and science his object, I believe this relationship is reversing. Science itself, gentlemen, is in the early stages of becoming sentient."

Goto takes a safe gamble on "sentience" meaning "watchfulness," like a sentry. His Japanese rendition is streaked with mysticism, but so is the original.

"Science, like a general, is identifying its enemies: received wisdom and untested assumption; superstition and quackery; the tyrants' fear of educated commoners; and, most pernicious of all, man's fondness for fooling himself. Bacon the Englishman says it well: 'The human understanding is like a false mirror, which, receiving rays irregularly, distorts and discolors the nature of things by mingling its own nature with it.' Our honorable colleague Mr. Takaki may know the passage?"

Arashiyama deals with the word "quackery" by omitting it, censors the line about tyrants and commoners, and turns to the straight-as-a-pole Takaki, a translator of Bacon, who translates the quotation in his querulous voice.

"Science is still learning how to talk and

walk. But the days are coming when science shall transform what it is to be a human being. Academies like the Shirandô, gentlemen, are its nurseries, its schools. Some years ago, a wise American, Benjamin Franklin, marveled at an air balloon in flight over London. His companion dismissed the balloon as a bauble, a frivolity, and demanded of Franklin, 'Yes, but what *use* is it?' Franklin replied, 'What use is a newborn child?' "

Uzaemon makes what he thinks is a fair translation, until "bauble" and "frivolity": Goto and Arashiyama indicate with apologetic faces that they cannot help. The audience watches him critically. In a low tone, Jacob de Zoet says, "Toy of a child." Using this substitute, the Franklin anecdote makes sense, and a hundred scholars nod in approval.

"Had a man fallen asleep two centuries ago," Marinus speculates, "and awoken this morning, he should recognize his world unchanged, in essence. Ships are still wooden; disease is still rampant. No man may travel faster than a galloping horse, and no man may kill another out of eyeshot. But were the same fellow to fall asleep tonight and sleep for a hundred years, or eighty, or even sixty, on waking he shall not recognize the planet for the transformations wrought upon it by science."

Goto assumes "rampant" is "deadly" and

must reconstruct the final clause.

Marinus's attention, meanwhile, has drifted away over the scholars' heads.

Yoshida Hayato clears his throat to indicate that he has a question.

Ôtsuki Monjurô looks at Marinus, then nods his consent.

Yoshida writes Dutch more fluently than many interpreters, but the geographer fears making a mistake in public, so he addresses Goto Shinpachi in Japanese. "Please ask Dr. Marinus this, Interpreter: if science is sentient, what are its ultimate desires? Or, to phrase this question another way, when the doctor's imagined sleeper awakens in the year 1899, shall the world most closely resemble paradise or the inferno?"

Goto's fluency is slower in the Japanese-to-Dutch headwind, but Marinus is pleased by the question. He rocks gently to and fro. "I shan't know until I see it, Mr. Yoshida."

CHAPTER SEVENTEEN: THE ALTAR ROOM AT THE HOUSE OF SISTERS, MOUNT SHIRANUI SHRINE

The twenty-sixth day of the eleventh month
Don't let it be me, Orito prays, *don't let it be me.* The Goddess is disrobed for the Annunciation of Engifting: her exposed breasts are ample with milk; and her belly, devoid of a navel, is swollen with a female fetus so fertile, according to Abbess Izu, that the fetus's own tiny womb encloses a still smaller female fetus, which is, in turn, impregnated with a still smaller daughter . . . and so on, to infinity. The abbess watches the nine unengifted sisters during the Sutra of Supplication. For ten days, Orito has acted the part of the penitent sister in hopes of earning access to the precincts and a quiet escape over the wall, but her hopes have come to nothing. She has dreaded this day since she saw Yayoi's pregnant belly and understood what it must mean, and now that day is here. Speculation about the Goddess's choice has been rife. To Orito, it has been unbearable. "One of the two has to be the newest sister," said

Umegae, with cruel satisfaction. "The Goddess will want Sister Orito to feel at home here as soon as possible." Blind Minori, in her eighteenth year here, says that newest sisters are engifted by the fourth month, at the latest, but not always the second. Yayoi suggested that the Goddess may give Kagerô and Minori, neither of whom conceived a gift last month despite being chosen, another chance, but Orito suspects that Yayoi said so to calm her fears, not because it is true.

The prayer room falls silent. The sutra is over.

Don't let it be me. The waiting is unendurable. *Don't let it be me.*

Abbess Izu strikes her tubular gong. The chime rises and falls in waves.

The sisters press their heads against the *tatami* mat in obeisance.

Like criminals, Orito thinks, *waiting for the executioner's sword.*

The abbess's ceremonial clothes rustle. "Sisters of Mount Shiranui . . ."

The nine women all keep their foreheads on the floor.

"The Goddess has instructed Master Genmu that, in the eleventh month —"

A fallen icicle shatters on the cloister walkway, and Orito jumps.

"— in the eleventh month of the eleventh year of the Kansei Era —"

This is not where I belong, Orito thinks. *This*

is not where I belong.

"— the two sisters to be engifted in her name are Kagerô and Hashihime."

Orito smothers a groan of relief but cannot calm her wildly pounding heart.

Won't you thank me, the Goddess asks, *for sparing you this month?*

I can't hear you. Orito clamps her jaw shut. *Lump of wood.*

Next month, the Goddess laughs like Orito's stepmother, *I promise.*

Engiftment days usher a holiday mood into the House of Sisters. Within minutes, Kagerô and Hashihime are being congratulated in the long room. Orito is dumbfounded at the sincerity of the other women's envy. Talk turns to the clothes, scents, and oils the Goddess's choices shall wear to welcome their engifters. Rice dumplings and *azuki* beans sweetened with honey arrive for breakfast; *sake* and tobacco are sent from Abbot Enomoto's storehouse. Kagerô's and Hashihime's cells are decorated with paper ornaments. Orito feels nauseous at this celebration of obligatory impregnation and is grateful when the sun shows its face and Abbess Izu has her and Sawarabi collect, air, and beat the house's bedding. The straw-filled mattresses are folded over a pole in the courtyard and, in rapid turns, struck with a bamboo beater; a faint fog of dust and mites hangs in the cold bright air. Sawarabi is a sturdy daughter of peasants from the Kirishima plateau, but the doctor's daughter soon lags behind. Sawarabi notices and is kind enough to suggest that they have a short rest, and sits on a pile of futons. "I hope you aren't too disappointed that the Goddess overlooked you this month, Newest Sister."

Orito, still catching her breath, shakes her head.

Across the cloisters, Asagao and Hotaru are feeding crumbs to a squirrel.

Sawarabi reads others well. "Don't be afraid of engiftment. You can see for yourself the privileges Yayoi and Yûguri are enjoying: more food, better bedding, charcoal . . . and now the services of a learned midwife! What princess would be so pampered? The monks are kinder than husbands, much cleaner than brothel customers, and there are no mothers-in-law cursing your stupidity for giving birth to daughters but turning into jealousy incarnate when you produce a male heir."

Orito pretends to agree. "Yes, Sister. I see that."

Thawed snow falls from the old pine with a flat thud.

Stop lying. Fat Rat watches from under the cloisters. *Stop fighting.*

Sawarabi hesitates. "Really, Sister, compared to what blemished girls suffer . . ."

The Goddess, Fat Rat says, standing on its

hind legs, *is your gentle, loving mother.*

". . . down there," Sawarabi says, "in the world below, this place is a palace."

Asagao and Hotaru's squirrel darts up a cloister pillar.

Bare Peak is so sharp it might be etched onto glass with a needle.

My burn, Orito cannot add, *doesn't justify the crime of my abduction.* "Let's finish the futons," she says, "before the others think we're idling."

The chores are done by mid-afternoon. A triangle of sunshine still lies over the pool in the courtyard. In the long room, Orito helps Housekeeper Satsuki repair nightgowns: needlework, she finds, numbs her longing for solace. From the training ground across the precincts ebbs the sound of the monks practicing with bamboo swords. Charcoal and pine needles rumble and snap in the brazier. Abbess Izu is seated at the head of the table, stitching a short mantra into one of the hoods worn by the sisters at their engiftment. Hashi-hime and Kagerô, wearing blood-red sashes as a mark of the Goddess's favor, are applying each other's face powder; one of the few objects denied even to the highest-ranked sisters is a mirror. With ill-concealed malevolence, it is Umegae's turn to ask Orito whether she has recovered from her disappointment.

"I am learning," Orito manages to say, "to submit to the Goddess's will."

"Surely the Goddess," Kagerô assures Orito, "shall choose you next time."

"The newest sister," observes blind Minori, "sounds happier in her new life."

"Took her long enough," mutters Umegae, "to come to her senses."

"Getting used to the house," counters Kiritsubo, "*can* take time: remember that poor girl from the Goto Islands? *She* sobbed every night for two years."

Pigeons scuffle and trill in the eaves of the cloisters.

"The sister from Goto found joy in her three healthy gifts," states Abbess Izu.

"But no joy," sighs Umegae, "from the fourth one, which killed her."

"Let us not disturb the dead" — the abbess's voice is sharp — "by digging up misfortunes without reason, Sister."

Umegae's maroon skin hides blushes, but she bows an apology.

Other sisters, Orito suspects, remember her predecessor hanging in her cell.

"Well," says Minori, "*I*, for one, would prefer to ask the newest sister what it was that helped her accept the house as her home."

Orito threads a needle. "Time, and the patience of my sisters."

You're lying, wheezes the kettle, *even I hear*

383

you're lying . . .

The sharper her need for solace, Orito notices, the worse the house's tricks.

"*I* thank the Goddess every single day," Sister Minori says, restringing her *koto,* "for bringing me to the house."

"*I* thank the Goddess" — Kagerô is working on Hashihime's eyebrows — "one hundred and eight times before breakfast."

Abbess Izu says, "Sister Orito, the kettle sounds thirsty to me . . ."

When Orito kneels on the stone slab by the pool to dip the ladle into the ice-cold water, the slanted light creates, just for a moment, a mirror as perfect as a Dutch glass. Orito has not seen her face since she fled her old house in Nagasaki; what she sees shocks her. The face on the pool's silvered skin is hers, but three or four years older. *What about my eyes?* They are dull and in retreat. *Another trick of the house.* She is not so sure. *I saw eyes like those in the world below.*

The song of a thrush in the old pine sounds scattered and half forgotten.

What was it — Orito is sinking — *I was trying to remember?*

Sisters Hotaru and Asagao greet her from the cloisters.

Orito waves back, notices the ladle still in her hand, and remembers her errand. She looks into the water and recognizes the eyes of a prostitute she treated in Nagasaki at a bordello owned by a pair of half-Chinese brothers. The girl had syphilis, scrofula, lung fever, and the Nine Sages alone knew what else, but what had destroyed her spirit was enslavement to opium.

"But, Aibagawa-*san*," the girl had implored, "I don't *need* any other medicine."

Pretending to accept the contract of the house, Orito thinks . . .

The prostitute's once-beautiful eyes stared out of dark pits.

. . . is halfway to accepting the contract of the house.

Orito hears Master Suzaku's carefree laughter at the gate.

Wanting and needing the drugs takes you the rest of the way . . .

The gatekeeping acolyte calls out, "Inner gate opening, Sisters!"

. . . and when it's been done to you once, why resist anymore?

Unless you win your will back, says the girl in the pool, *you'll turn into the others.*

I shall stop taking Suzaku's drugs, Orito resolves, *from tomorrow.*

The stream leaves the pool through mossy grates.

My "tomorrow," she realizes, *is proof that I must stop today.*

■ ■ ■ ■

"How do we find our newest sister this evening?" asks Master Suzaku.

Abbess Izu watches from one corner; Acolyte Chûai sits in another.

"Master Suzaku finds me in excellent health, thank you."

"The sky this evening was a sky from the pure land, was it not, newest sister?"

"In the world below, sunsets were never this beautiful."

Pleased, the man assesses the statement. "You were not aggrieved by the Goddess's judgment this morning?"

I must hide my relief, thinks Orito, *and hide that I am hiding it.* "One learns to accept the Goddess's judgment, does one not?"

"You have come on a long journey in a short time, Newest Sister."

"Enlightenment can occur, I understand, in a single moment."

"Yes. Yes, it does." Suzaku looks at his assistant. "After many years of striving, enlightenment transforms a man in a single heartbeat. Master Genmu is so pleased with your improved spirits that he referred to it in a letter to the lord abbot."

He is watching me, Orito suspects, *for evidence of annoyance.*

"I am unworthy," she says, "of Lord

386

Enomoto's attention."

"Our lord abbot takes a fatherly interest in all our sisters."

The word "fatherly" evokes Orito's father, and recent wounds ache.

From the long room come the sounds and smells of supper.

"We have no symptoms to report, then? No aches or bleedings?"

"Truly, Master Suzaku, I cannot imagine being unwell in the House of Sisters."

"No constipation or diarrhea? Hemorrhoids? Itches? Headaches?"

"A dose of my . . . my daily medicine is all I would ask, if I may."

"With the greatest pleasure." Suzaku decants the muddy liquid into a thimble-sized cup and proffers it to Orito, who turns away and hides her mouth, as women of breeding do. Her body is aching with anticipation of the relief the solace will deliver. But before she can change her mind, Orito tips the contents of the tiny cup into her well-padded sleeve, where the dark-blue hemp soaks it up.

"It has a — a honeyed taste tonight," Orito pronounces. "Or do I imagine it?"

"What's good for the body" — Suzaku looks at her mouth — "is good for the soul."

Orito and Yayoi wash dishes, while Sisters Kagerô and Hashihime are given words of encouragement by their sisters — some shy and some, to judge from the laughter, not at all shy — before being led by Abbess Izu to the altar room to pray to the Goddess. A quarter hour later, the abbess leads them to their rooms, where they await their engifters. After the dishes are washed, Orito stays in the long room, not wanting to be alone with the thought that in one month's time it may be her lying with an embroidered hood over her head for a master or acolyte. Her body is complaining about its denied dose of solace. One minute she is as hot as soup, the next as cold as shaved ice. When Hatsune asks Orito to read the last New Year letter from the first sister's firstborn gift, now a young woman of seventeen, Orito is glad of the distraction.

" 'Dearest Mother,' " Orito reads, peering at the feminine brushstrokes in the lamplight, " 'the berries are red along the verges and one may scarcely credit that another autumn is once more upon us.' "

"She has her mother's elegance with words," murmurs Hatsune.

"My Tarô is a blockhead," sighs Kiritsubo, "compared to Noriko-*chan*."

In their New Year letters, Orito notices, *the "gifts" regain their names.*

"But what hardworking brewer's lad like Tarô," objects proud, modest Hatsune, "has *time* to notice autumn berries? I beg the newest sister to continue."

" 'Once again,' " reads Orito, " 'it is time to

send a letter to my dear mother on distant Mount Shiranui. Last spring, when your First Month letter was delivered to the White Crane Workshop, Ueda-*san* —' "

"Ueda-*san* is Noriko-*chan*'s master," says Sadaie, "a famous tailor in Miyako."

"Is that so?" Orito has been told ten times before. " 'Ueda-*san* gave me a half holiday to celebrate its arrival. Before it slips my mind, Ueda-*san* and his wife send their sincerest compliments.' "

"How lucky," says Yayoi, "to have found such an honorable family."

"The Goddess always takes care of her gifts," avows Hatsune.

" 'Your news, Mother, brought me just as much pleasure as you kindly say my foolish scribblings bring you. How wonderful that you are blessed with another gift. I shall pray that he finds as caring a family as the Uedas. Please give my thanks to Sister Asagao for nursing you during your chest illness, and to Master Suzaku for his daily care.' " Orito pauses to ask, "A chest illness?"

"Oh, the trouble my cough caused! Master Genmu sent Acolyte Jiritsu — may his soul be at rest — down to Kurozane to procure fresh herbs from the herbalist."

A crow, Orito aches, *could reach Otane's chimney in a half hour.*

She recalls this summer's journey to Kurozane and wants to weep.

"Sister?" Hatsune notices. "Is anything the matter?"

"No. 'What with two large court weddings in the fifth month and two funerals in the seventh, the White Crane was inundated with orders. My year has been a lucky one in another respect, Mother, though I blush to write about it. Ueda-*san*'s principal supplier of brocade is a merchant named Koyama-*san,* who visits the White Crane with his four sons every two or three months. For a couple of years the youngest son, Shingo-*san,* would exchange pleasantries with me as I worked. Last summer, however, during the *O-bon* festivities, I was summoned to the garden teahouse where, to my surprise, Shingo-*san,* his parents, Ueda-*san,* and my mistress were drinking tea.' " Orito glances up at the enraptured sisters. " 'You shall have guessed already what was afoot, Mother — but, being a dull-witted girl, I did not.' "

"She isn't dull-*phi*tted," Asagao assures Hatsune, "just *phu*re and innocent."

" 'Small talk was made,' " Orito continues, " 'about Shingo-*san*'s many talents and my own pitiful accomplishments. I did my best to master my shyness, without seeming too forward, and afterward —' "

"Just as you advised her, Sister," clucks Sawarabi, "two years ago."

Orito watches the sister swell with pride. " 'And afterward, my mistress congratulated me on the favorable impression I had made. I returned to my duties, honored by the praise but expecting to hear nothing more about the Koyamas until their next visit to the White Crane. My foolishness was short-lived. A few days later, on the emperor's birthday, Ueda-*san* took all his apprentices to Yoyogi Park to enjoy the fireworks along Kamo River. How magical were the brief-blooming reds and yellows against the night sky! Upon our return, my master summoned me into his office, where my mistress told me that the Koyamas had proposed that I become the wife of their youngest son, Shingo. I knelt there, Mother, as if a fox had put a spell on me! Then Ueda-*san*'s wife mentioned that the proposal had come from Shingo. That such an upstanding young man desired *me* as his bride caused tears to flow down my cheeks.' "

Yayoi hands Hotaru a paper cloth to dab her own eyes.

Orito folds the last page and unfolds the next. " 'I asked Ueda-*san*'s permission to speak frankly. My master urged me to do so. My origins were too obscure for the Koyamas, I said; my loyalties lay with the White Crane Workshop; and that if I entered the Koyama family as a bride, tongues would wag that I had used low cunning to ensnare such a fine husband.' "

"Oh, just grab the lad," Yûgiri cackles, a

little drunk on *sake,* "by his dragon!"

"For shame, Sister," scolds Housekeeper Satsuki. "Let the newest sister read."

" 'Master Ueda replied that the Koyamas were well aware of my origins as the daughter of a shrine but saw no objection. They want a daughter-in-law who is dutiful, modest, resourceful, and not a' " — Orito's voice is joined by sisters who lovingly recite the sobriquet — " 'prissy sherbet-guzzling miss who thinks "hard work" is a town in China. Lastly, my master reminded me that I *am* a Ueda by adoption, and why did I suppose the Uedas to be so *very* far below the Koyamas? Blushing, I apologized to my master for my thoughtless words.' "

"But Noriko-*san* didn't mean that at *all!*" Hotaru protests.

Hatsune warms her hands at the fire. "He is curing her shyness, I believe."

" 'Ueda-*san*'s wife told me that my objections did me great credit, but that the families had agreed that our engagement could last until my seventeenth New Year —' "

"That would be *this* New Year coming," Hatsune explains to Orito.

" '— when, if Shingo-*san*'s feelings are unchanged —' "

"I pray to the Goddess to keep his heart constant," says Sadaie. "Every night."

" '— we shall be married on the first auspicious day in the first month. Ueda-*san* and

392

Koyama-*san* shall then invest in a workshop to specialize in *obi* sashes, where my husband and I can work side by side and train apprentices of our own.' "

"Imagine!" says Kiritsubo. "Hatsune's gift, with apprentices of her own."

"Children of her own, too," says Yûgiri, "if Shingo has his way."

" 'Looking at these lines, my words read like a dreaming girl's. Perhaps, Mother, this is the greatest gift our correspondence gives us: a space in which we can dream. You are in my thoughts every day. Your Gift, Noriko.' "

The women look at the letter, or the fire. Their minds are far away.

Orito understands that the New Year letters are the sisters' purest solace.

Early in the hour of the Boar, the gate opens for the two engifters. Every sister in the long room hears the bolt slide. Abbess Izu's footsteps leave her room and pause at the gate. Orito imagines three silent bows. The abbess leads two sets of male footsteps along the inner passageway, toward Kagerô's room and then to Hashihime's. A minute later, the abbess's footsteps make their return journey past the long room. The candles hiss. Orito expected Yûgiri or Sawarabi to try to catch a glimpse of the chosen engifters in the unlit corridor, but instead they play a sober game of mah-jongg with Hotaru and Asagao. Nobody so much as acknowledges the arrival of the master and acolyte in the chosen sisters' rooms. Hatsune is singing "The Moonlit Castle" very softly to her own accompaniment on the *koto*. Housekeeper Satsuki is repairing a sock. When those carnal negotiations the house terms "engiftment" are actually occurring, Orito sees, the jokes and gossip all cease. Orito also understands that the levity and lewdnesses are not a denial that the sisters' ovaries and wombs are the Goddess's, but a way of making their servitude endurable.

Back in her room, Orito watches the fire through a chink in her blanket. Male footsteps left Kagerô's room some time ago, but Hashihime's engifter is staying longer, as an engifter may when both parties are willing. Orito's knowledge of lovemaking is derived from medical texts and the anecdotes of the women she treated in Nagasaki brothels. She tries not to think of a man under this blanket, pinning her body against this mattress, just one short month from now. *Let me cease to be,* she begs the fire. *Melt what I am into you,* she begs the darkness. She finds her face is wet. Once again, her mind probes the House of Sisters for a means of escape. There are no outside windows to climb through. The ground is stone and cannot be dug through.

394

Both sets of gates are bolted from inside, with a guardroom between them. The eaves of the cloisters jut far over the courtyard and cannot be reached or climbed over.

It's hopeless. She looks at a rafter and imagines a rope.

There is a knock at her door. Yayoi whispers, "It's me, Sister."

Orito jumps out of bed and opens the door. "Is it your waters?"

Yayoi's pregnant shape is fattened further by blankets. "I can't sleep."

Orito bundles her inside, afraid of a man stepping out of the darkness.

"The story goes," Yayoi says, curling Orito's hair around her finger, "that when I was born with these" — Yayoi taps her pointed ears — "the Buddhist priest was called. His explanation was that a demon had crept into my mother's womb and laid his egg there, like a cuckoo. Unless I was abandoned that very night, the priest warned, demons would come for their offspring and carve up the family as a celebratory feast. My father heard this with relief; peasants everywhere 'winnow the seedlings' to rid themselves of unwanted daughters. Our village even had a special place for it: a circle of pointed rocks, high above the tree line, up a dry streambed. In the seventh month, the cold could not kill me, but wild dogs, foraging bears, and hungry spirits were sure to do the job by morning. My father left me there and walked home without regret."

Yayoi takes her friend's hand and places it on her belly.

Orito feels the bulges move. "Twins," she says, "without a doubt."

"Arriving at the village that very night, however" — Yayoi's tone becomes low and droll — "so the story goes, was Yôben the Seer. For seven days and seven nights a white fox had led the holy man, whose halo of starlight lit his path, under mountains and across lakes. His long journey ended when the fox jumped onto the roof of a humble farmhouse above a village that barely warranted a name. Yôben knocked, and at the sight of such a personage, my father fell to his knees. When he heard about my birth, Yôben the Seer pronounced" — Yayoi changes her voice — " 'The fox's ears of the baby girl were no curse but a *blessing* from our Lady Kannon.' By abandoning me, Father had spurned Kannon's grace and invited her wrath. The baby girl had to be rescued, at all costs, before disaster struck . . ."

A door along the passageway is slid open and shut.

"As my father and Yôben the Seer approached the place of winnowing," Yayoi continues her recital, "they heard all the dead babies wailing for their mothers. They heard wolves bigger than horses, howling for fresh meat. My father quivered with fear, but Yôben uttered holy incantations so they could pass through the ghosts and wolves unhurt and enter the circle of pointed rocks, where all was calm and warm as the first day of spring. Lady Kannon sat there, with the white fox, breastfeeding Yayoi, the magical child. Yôben and my father sank to their knees. In a voice like the waves of a lake, Lady Kannon commanded Yôben to travel throughout the empire with me, healing the sick in her holy name. The mystic protested he wasn't worthy, but the baby, who at one day old could speak, told him, 'Where there is despair, let us bring hope; where there is death, let us breathe life.' What could he do but obey the lady?" Yayoi sighs and tries to make her distended abdomen more comfortable. "So whenever Yôben the Seer and the magical fox girl arrived at a new town, that was the story he put about to drum up trade."

Orito lies on her side. "May I ask whether Yôben was your real father?"

"Maybe I say, 'No,' because I don't want it to be true . . ."

The night wind plays a rattling flue like a rank amateur plays *shakuhachi* flute.

". . . but certainly, my earliest memories are of sick people holding my ears as I breathe into their rotten mouths, and of their dying eyes, saying, *Heal me,* of the filthiest inns, of Yôben standing in marketplaces, reading 'testimonials' to my powers from great families."

Orito thinks of her own childhood among scholars and books.

"Yôben dreamed of audiences at palaces, and we spent a year in Edo, but he smelled too much of the showman . . . of hunger . . . and, simply, he smelled too much. During our six or seven years on the road, the quality of our inns never improved. All his misfortunes, of course, were my fault, especially when he was drunk. One day, near the end, after we'd been chased out of a town, a fellow healing trickster told him that where a magical fox *girl* could squeeze money from the desperate and dying, a magical fox *woman* was another matter. That got Yôben to thinking, and within the month he sold me to a brothel in Osaka." Yayoi looks at her hand. "My life there, I try hard to forget. Yôben didn't even say goodbye. Perhaps he couldn't face me. Perhaps he was my father."

Orito wonders at Yayoi's apparent lack of rancor.

"When the sisters tell you, 'The house is far, far better than a brothel,' they don't mean to be cruel. Well, one or two may, but not the others. For every successful geisha with wealthy patrons vying for her favors, there are five hundred chewed-up, spat-out girls

398

dying of brothel diseases. This must be cold comfort for a woman of your rank, and I know you've lost a better life than the rest of us, but the House of Sisters is only a hell, a prison, if you think it is. The masters and acolytes treat us kindly. Engiftment is an unusual duty, but is it so different from the duty any husband demands from his wife? The duty is certainly paid less often — much less."

Orito is frightened by Yayoi's logic. "But twenty years!"

"Time passes. Sister Hatsune is leaving in two years. She can settle in the same town as one of her gifts, with a stipend. Departed sisters write to Abbess Izu, and they are fond and grateful letters."

Shadows sway and coagulate among the low rafters.

"Why did the last newest sister hang herself?"

"Because being parted from her gift broke her mind."

Orito lets time pass. "And it's not too much for you?"

"Of course it hurts. But they haven't died. They are in the world below, well fed and cared for, and thinking about us. After our descent we can even meet them, if we wish it. It's a . . . strange life, I don't deny it, but earn Master Genmu's trust, earn the abbess's trust, and it needn't be a harsh life, or a wasted one . . ."

The day I believe this, Orito thinks, *is the day Shiranui Shrine owns me.*

". . . and you have me here," says Yayoi, "whatever this is worth."

CHAPTER EIGHTEEN: THE SURGERY ON DEJIMA

An hour before dinner on the twenty-ninth day of the eleventh month

"Lithotomy: from the Greek *lithos,* for 'stone,' and *tomos,* for 'cut.' "

Marinus addresses his four pupils. "Remind us, Mr. Muramoto."

"Remove stone from bladder, kidneys, gall-bladder, Doctor."

" 'Till kingdom come . . .' " Wybo Gerritszoon is drunk, senseless, naked between his nipples and his socks, and trussed on the backward-slanting operating table like a frog on a dissection board. " 'Who art unleavened bread . . .' "

Uzaemon takes the patient's words to be a Christian mantra.

Charcoal in the brazier rumbles; snow fell last night.

Marinus rubs his hands. "Symptoms of bladder stones, Mr. Kajiwaki?"

"Blood in urine, Doctor, pain to urine, and wants to urine but cannot."

401

"Indeed. A further symptom is fear of surgery, delaying the sufferer's decision to undergo his stone's removal until he can no longer lie down without aching to piss, notwithstanding that these few" — Marinus peers at Gerritszoon's dribble of pink urine in its specimen dish — "drops are all he can muster. Implying that the stone is now positioned . . . where, Mr. Yano?"

" 'Hello'ed be thy daily heaven . . .' " Gerritszoon belches. "Howz' fockit go?"

Yano mimes a constriction with his fist. "Stone . . . stop . . . water."

"So." Marinus sniffs. "The stone is blocking the urethra. What fate awaits the patient who cannot pass urine, Mr. Ikematsu?"

Uzaemon watches Ikematsu deduce the whole from the parts, "cannot," "urine," and "fate." "Body who cannot pass urine cannot make blood pure, Doctor. Body die of dirty blood."

"It dies." Marinus nods. "The Great Hippocrates warned the phys—"

"Will yer cork yer quack'n' an' do the f'ckin' t' do it yer f'ck'r . . ."

Jacob de Zoet and Con Twomey, here to assist the doctor, exchange glances.

Marinus takes a length of cotton dressing from Eelattu, tells Gerritszoon, "Open, please," and gags his mouth. "The Great Hippocrates warned the physician to 'cut no stones' and leave the job to lowly surgeons;

402

the Roman Ammonius Lithotomos, the Hindoo Susruta, and the Arab Abu al-Qasim al-Zahrawi — who, *en passant,* invented the ancestor of *this*" — Marinus wiggles his blood-encrusted double-sided scalpel — "would cut the perineum" — the doctor lifts the outraged Dutchman's penis and indicates between its root and the anus — "*here,* by the pubic symphysis." Marinus drops the penis. "Rather more than half the patients in those bad old days died — in agonies."

Gerritszoon abruptly stops struggling.

"Frère Jacques, a gifted French quack, proposed a suprapubic incision, above the *corpus ossis pubis*" — Marinus dips his fingernail into an inkpot and marks a line below and to the left of Gerritszoon's navel — "and entering the bladder sideways. Cheselden, an Englishman, perfected the operation, losing less than one patient in ten. I have performed upwards of fifty lithotomies and lost four. Two were not my fault. The two were . . . Well, we live and learn, even if our dead patients cannot say the same, eh, Gerritszoon? Cheselden's fee was five hundred pounds for two or three minutes' work. But luckily," the doctor says, slapping the trussed patient's buttock, "Cheselden taught a student named John Hunter. Hunter's students included a Dutchman, Hardwijke, and Hardwijke taught Marinus, who today performs this operation gratis. So. Shall we begin?"

The rectum of Wybo Gerritszoon releases a hot fart of horror.

"View halloo." Marinus nods at De Zoet and Twomey; they secure a thigh each. "The less movement, the less the accidental damage." Uzaemon sees that the seminarians are uncertain of this pronouncement, so he translates it for them. Eelattu kneels astraddle the patient's midriff, parts Gerritszoon's buttocks, and blocks his view of the knives. Dr. Marinus now asks Dr. Maeno to hold the lamp close to the inked mark and takes up his scalpel. His face changes into the face of a swordsman.

Marinus sinks the scalpel into Gerritszoon's abdomen.

The patient's entire body tenses like a single muscle; Uzaemon shudders.

The four seminarians, peer, transfixed.

"Fat and muscle thickness vary," says Marinus, "but the bladder —"

Still gagged, Gerritszoon releases a loud noise not unlike a man in orgasm.

"— the bladder," continues Marinus, "is about a thumb's width in."

The scalpel inscribes the whole incision mark: Gerritszoon shrieks in pain.

Uzaemon forces himself to watch: lithotomies are unknown outside Dejima, and he must supplement Maeno's report to the academy.

Gerritszoon snorts like a bull, his eyes water, and he groans.

Marinus dips his left forefinger into rapeseed oil and inserts it into Gerritszoon's anus up to its knuckle. "Thus the patient should void his bowels beforehand." There is the smell of rotting meat and sweet apples. "One locates the stone through the rectal *ampulla*" — with his right hand, Marinus inserts the tweezers into the blood-brimming incision — "and pushes it from the *fundus* up toward the incision." Liquid feces ooze out of the patient's rectum around the doctor's hand. "The less one pokes around with the tweezers, the better . . . One puncture is quite enough, and — *ah!* Almost had it . . . and — *aha! Ecco siamo!*" He takes out the stone, retrieves his finger from Gerritszoon's anus, and wipes both on his apron. The stone is as big as an acorn and the yellow of a diseased tooth. "The gash must be stanched before our patient dies of blood loss. Domburger, Corkonian, pray stand aside." Marinus pours another oil over the incision, and Eelattu covers it with a scab-crusty bandage.

Gagged Gerritszoon sighs as the pain lessens from unendurable to grueling.

Dr. Maeno asks, "What is oil, Doctor, if you please?"

"Extract of the bark and leaves of *Hamame-*

lis japonica, which I named myself. It's a local variety of witch hazel, which lessens the risk of fevers — a trick taught me by an unschooled old woman, many lifetimes ago."

Orito, too, remembers Uzaemon, *learned from old mountain herbalists.*

Eelattu changes the dressing, then binds its replacement against Gerritszoon's waist. "The patient should lie down for three days, and eat and drink in moderation. Urine shall leak through the wound in his bladder wall; one must be ready for fevers and swellings; but urine should be appearing by the usual means within two or three weeks." Marinus now unties Gerritszoon's gag and tells him. "About the same time required by Sjako to walk again in the wake of the drubbing you gave him last September, no?"

Gerritszoon unscrews his eyes. "Yer *f'ckin'* yer, yer . . . *f'ckin' f'ckin'* yer . . ."

"Peace on earth." Marinus puts his finger on the patient's lips, badly blotched with cold sores. "Goodwill to all men."

Chief van Cleef's dining room is noisy with six or eight conversations in Japanese and Dutch; silver cutlery clinks on the best tableware; and though it is not yet evening, the candelabra are lighting a battlefield of goat bones, fish spines, bread crusts, crab claws, lobster shells, blancmange gobbets, and holly leaves and berries, fallen from the ceiling. The panels between the dining room and the bay room are removed, affording Uzaemon a view all the way to the distant mouth of the open sea: the waters are slate blue, and the mountains half erased by the cold drizzle turning last night's snow to slush.

The chief's Malay servants finish one song on flute and violin and begin another. Uzaemon remembers it from last year's banquet. It is understood by the ranked interpreters that "Dutch New Year" on the twenty-fifth day of December coincides with the birth of Jesus Christ, but this is never acknowledged in case an ambitious spy one day accuses them of endorsing Christian worship. Christmas, Uzaemon has noticed, affects the Dutch in strange ways. They can become intolerably homesick, even abusive, merry and maudlin, often all at once. By the time Arie Grote brings up the plum pudding, Chief van Cleef, Deputy Fischer, Ouwehand, Baert, and the youth Oost are somewhere between quite drunk and very drunk. Only the soberer Marinus, De Zoet, and Twomey converse with any of the Japanese banqueters.

"Ogawa-*san*?" Goto Shinpachi looks concerned. "Are you ill?"

"No, no . . . I'm sorry. Goto-*san* asked me a question?"

"It was a remark about the beauty of the music."

"I'd rather listen," declares Interpreter Sekita, "to butchered hogs."

"Or a man having his stone cut out," says Arashiyama, "eh, Ogawa?"

"Your description murdered my appetite." Sekita stuffs another deviled egg into his mouth, whole. "These eggs really are very good."

"I'd trust Chinese herbs," says Nishi, the monkey-faced scion of a rival dynasty of Nagasaki interpreters, "before I'd trust a Dutch knife."

"My cousin trusted Chinese herbs," says Arashiyama, "for *his* stone —"

Deputy Fischer laughs his galloping laugh as he bangs on the table.

"— and died in a way that would truly murder your appetite."

Chief van Cleef's current Dejima wife, wearing a snow-patterned kimono and jangling bracelets, slides open the door and bows demurely to the room. Several conversations fall away, and the better-mannered diners stop themselves ogling. She whispers something in Van Cleef's ear that makes his face light up; he whispers back and slaps her buttocks like a farmer slapping an ox. Feigning coquettish anger, she returns to Van Cleef's private chamber.

Uzaemon suspects Van Cleef contrived the scene to show off his possession.

"More's the pity," croons Sekita, "she's not on the menu."

If De Zoet had had his way, thinks Uzaemon, *Orito would be a Dejima wife, too . . .*

Cupido distributes a bottle to each of the two dozen diners.

. . . giving herself to one man — Uzaemon bites — *instead of being given to many.*

"I was afraid," says Sekita, "they'd forgo this pleasant custom."

That's my guilt talking, Uzaemon thinks. *But what if my guilt is right?*

The Malay servant Philander follows, uncorking each bottle.

Van Cleef stands and chimes a spoon on a glass until he has the table's attention. "Those of you who honored the Dutch New Year banquet under Chiefs Hemmij and Snitker shall know of the hydra-headed toast . . ."

Arashiyama whispers to Uzaemon, "What's a hydra?"

Uzaemon knows but shrugs, unwilling to lose more of Van Cleef's sentences.

"We make a toast, one by one," says Goto Shinpachi, "and —"

"— and get drunker and drunker," belches Sekita, "minute by minute."

". . . whereby our joint desires," Van Cleef says, swaying, "forge a . . . a . . . brighter future."

As the custom dictates, each diner fills his neighbor's glass.

"And so, gentlemen, to the nineteenth century!" Van Cleef raises his glass.

409

The room echoes the toast, despite its irrelevance to the Japanese calendar.

Uzaemon notices how unwell he is feeling.

"*I* give you friendship," Deputy Fischer says, "betwixt Europe and the East!"

How often, wonders Uzaemon, *am I doomed to hear these same hollow words?*

Interpreter Kobayashi looks at Uzaemon. "To soon recovery of very dear friends Ogawa Mimasaku and Gerritszoon-*san*." So Uzaemon must stand and bow to Kobayashi the Elder, knowing that he is maneuvering at the Interpreters' Guild to have his son promoted over Uzaemon's head to second rank when Ogawa the Elder accepts the inevitable and retires from his coveted post.

Dr. Marinus's turn is next: "To the seekers of truth."

For the benefit of the inspectors, Interpreter Yoshio proposes in Japanese, "To health of our wise, beloved magistrate." Yoshio also has a son in the third rank with high hopes for the upcoming vacancies. To the Dutch, he says, "To our rulers."

This is the game one must play, thinks Uzaemon, *to rise at the guild.*

Jacob de Zoet swirls his wine. "To all our loved ones, near or far."

The Dutchman happens to catch Uzaemon's eye, and they both avert their gaze while the toast is chorused. The interpreter is still turning his napkin ring moodily when

Goto clears his throat. "Ogawa-*san?*"

Uzaemon looks up to find the entire company looking at him.

"Pardon, gentlemen, the wine stole my tongue."

Goblin laughter sloshes around the room. The diners' faces swell and recede. Lips do not correspond to blurred words. Uzaemon wonders, as consciousness drains away, *Am I dying?*

The steps of Higashizaka Street are slippery with frozen slush and strewn with bones, rags, decayed leaves, and excrement. Uzaemon and bowlegged Yohei climb past a chestnut stall. The smell makes the interpreter's stomach threaten rebellion. Unaware of the approaching samurai, a beggar up ahead is pissing against a wall. Lean dogs, kites, and crows squabble over the street's mean pickings.

From a doorway comes a funerary mantra and tendril of incense.

Shuzai is expecting me for sword practice, Uzaemon remembers . . .

A heavily pregnant girl at a crossroads is selling pig-fat candles.

. . . but to pass out twice in one day would start unhelpful rumors.

Uzaemon bids Yohei buy ten candles; the girl has cataracts in both eyes.

The candle seller thanks her customer.

Master and servant continue climbing.

Through a window, a man shouts, *"I curse the day I married!"*

"Samurai-*sama?*" a lipless fortune-teller calls out from a half-open door. "Someone in the world above needs your deliverance, Samurai-*sama.*"

Uzaemon, irritated by her presumption, walks on.

"Sir," says Yohei, "if you're feeling unsteady again, I could —"

"Don't fuss like a woman: the foreign wine disagreed with me."

The foreign wine, Uzaemon thinks, *on top of the surgical procedure.*

"Reports of my momentary lapse," he tells Yohei, "would worry Father."

"He'll not hear it from my lips, sir."

They pass through the ward gate; the warden's son bows to one of the neighborhood's most important residents. Uzaemon returns a brisk nod and thinks, *Nearly home.* The prospect does not bring much comfort.

"Might Ogawa-sama be generous enough to spare a little time?"

Waiting for his gate to be opened, Uzaemon hears an elderly voice.

A bent-backed mountain woman climbs from the thicket by the stream.

Yohei obstructs her. "By what right do you use my master's name?"

The servant Kiyoshichi opens the Ogawa gates from inside. He sees the mountain woman and explains, "Sir, this feeble-minded creature knocked at the side door earlier, asking to speak with Interpreter Ogawa the Younger. I bade the crazed old crow be gone but, as sir can see . . ."

Her weathered face, framed by a hat and straw coat, lacks the seasoned beggar's cunning. "We have a friend in common, Ogawa-*sama*."

"Enough, Grandmother." Kiyoshichi takes her arm. "Time for you to go home."

He checks with Uzaemon, who mouths, "Gently."

"The ward gate is this way."

"But Kurozane is three days away, young man, on my old legs, and —"

"The sooner you start back home, then, the better, don't you think?"

Uzaemon steps through the Ogawa gate and crosses the sunless stone garden where only lichen thrives on the ailing shrubs. Saiji, his father's gaunt and bird-faced manservant, slides open the door to the main house from inside, a beat before Yohei can open it from the outside. "Welcome home, sir." The servants are jostling for position ahead of the day when their master is not Ogawa Mimasaku but Ogawa Uzaemon. "The senior master is asleep in his room, sir, and sir's wife is suffering from a headache. Sir's

413

mother is nursing her."

So my wife wants to be alone, thinks Uzaemon, *but Mother won't let her.*

The new maid appears with slippers, warm water, and a towel.

"Light a fire in the library," he tells the maid, intending to write up his lithotomy notes. *If I am working,* he hopes, *Mother and my wife may keep their distance.*

"Prepare tea for the master," Yohei tells the maid. "Not too strong."

Saiji and Yohei wait to see whom the master-in-waiting chooses to attend him.

"Attend to" — Uzaemon sighs — "whatever needs attending to. Both of you."

He walks down the cold, waxed corridor, hearing Yohei and Saiji blame each other for the master's bad mood. Their bickering has a marital familiarity, and Uzaemon suspects they share more than a room at night. Gaining the sanctuary of the library, he shuts the door on the cheerless household, the mountain madwoman, the Christmas banquet's babble, and his ignominious exit, and sits at his writing table. His calves ache. He enjoys scraping his inkstone, mixing a few drops of water, and dipping his brush. The precious books and Chinese scrolls sit on the oaken shelves. He remembers his awe at entering the library of Ogawa Mimasaku fifteen years ago, never dreaming then that he might one day be adopted by its master, much less become its master.

Be less ambitious, he warns the younger Uzaemon, *and more content.*

Catching his eye on the nearest shelf is De Zoet's *Wealth of Nations.*

Uzaemon marshals his memories of the lithotomy.

There is a knock: the servant Kiyoshichi slides open the door.

"The weak-witted creature shan't be troubling us again, sir."

Uzaemon needs a moment to make sense of the sentence. "Good. Her family should be told what a nuisance she is making of herself."

"I asked the warden's son to do so, sir, but he didn't know her."

"Then she might be from . . . Kurozaka, was it?"

"Kurozane, begging sir's pardon. I believe it's a small town on the Ariake Sea Road, in Kyôga Domain."

The name sounds familiar. Perhaps Abbot Enomoto mentioned it once.

"Did she say what her business with me was about?"

" 'A private matter' was all she said, and that she is an herbalist."

"Any addled crone able to brew fennel calls herself an herbalist."

"Indeed, sir. Perhaps she heard about the house's ailments and wanted to peddle some miracle cure. She deserves a beating, really, but her age . . ."

The new maid enters with a bucket of coals. Because of the cold afternoon, perhaps, she has put on a white headscarf. A detail from Orito's ninth or tenth letter comes back to Uzaemon. *The herbalist of Kurozane, it read, lives at the foot of Mount Shiranui, in an ancient mountain hut, with goats, chickens, and a dog . . .*

The floor tilts. "Fetch her back." Uzaemon hardly knows his voice.

Kiyoshichi and the maid look at their master in surprise, then at each other.

"Run after the herbalist of Kurozane — that mountain woman. Fetch her back."

The astonished servant is unsure whether to trust his ears.

Uzaemon realizes how oddly he is behaving. *First I faint on Dejima, and now this fickleness over a beggar.* "When I prayed for Father at the temple, a priest suggested that the sickness may be due to a . . . to a want of charity in the Ogawa household, and that the gods would send a . . . an opportunity to make amends."

Kiyoshichi doubts that the gods employ such poor messengers.

Uzaemon claps. "Don't make me ask you again, Kiyoshichi!"

"You are Otane," begins Uzaemon, wondering whether to give her an honorific title,

"Otane-*san,* the herbalist of Kurozane. Earlier, outside, I did not understand . . ."

The old woman sits like a curled-up wren. Her eyes are sharp and clear.

Uzaemon has dismissed the servants. "I apologize for not listening to you."

Otane accepts her due deference but says nothing, yet.

"It is long walk from Kyôga Domain. Did you sleep at an inn?"

"The journey had to be made, and now I am here."

"Miss Aibagawa always spoke of Otane-*san* with great respect."

"On her second visit to Kurozane" — her Kyôga dialect carries an earthy dignity — "Miss Aibagawa spoke about Interpreter Ogawa in a similar fashion."

Her feet may be sore, thinks Uzaemon, *but she knows how to kick.* "The groom who marries according to his heart is a rare man. I had to marry according to the dictates of my family. It is the way of the world."

"Miss Aibagawa's visits are three treasures of my life. Despite our great difference in rank, she was, and remains, a precious daughter to me."

"I understand Kurozane is at the foot of the trail that leads up Mount Shiranui. Is it possible" — Uzaemon can endure hope no longer — "you have met her since she entered the shrine?"

417

Otane's face is a bitter *No.* "All contact is forbidden. Twice yearly I take medicines to the shrine's doctor, Master Suzaku, at the gatehouse. But no layperson is permitted farther, unless invited by Master Genmu or Lord Abbot Enomoto. Least of all —"

The door slides open, and tea is brought in by Uzaemon's mother's maid.

Mother wasted no time, Uzaemon registers, *in sending her spy along.*

Otane bows as she receives the tea on a walnut-wood tray.

The maid departs for a thorough interrogation.

"Least of all," continues Otane, "an old herb gatherer." She wraps her bowl of tea with her medicine-stained bony fingers. "No, it is not a message from Miss Aibagawa I bring, but . . . Well, I will come to this shortly. Some weeks ago, on the night of first snow, a visitor sought shelter in my cottage. He was a young acolyte from Mount Shiranui Shrine. He had run away."

Yohei's blurred outline crosses behind the snow-lit paper window.

"What did he say?" Uzaemon's mouth is dry. "Is she . . . is Miss Aibagawa well?"

"She is alive, but he spoke about cruelties committed by the order against the sisters. He said that if these cruelties were widely known, not even the lord abbot's connections in Edo could defend the shrine. That was the acolyte's plan — to go to Nagasaki and denounce the Order of Mount Shiranui to the magistrate and to his court."

Someone sweeps snow in the courtyard with a stiff-bristled broom.

Uzaemon is cold, despite the fire. "Where is this defector?"

"I buried him the next day between two cherry trees in my garden."

Something scurries at the corners of Uzaemon's vision. "How did he die?"

"There exists a family of poisons that, once ingested, remain in the body, harmlessly, so long as an antidote is taken daily. But without that antidote, the poison will kill its host. This would be my best guess."

"So the acolyte was doomed from the moment he left?"

Down the corridor, Uzaemon's mother is scolding her maid.

"Did the acolyte speak about his order's practices before he died?"

"No." Otane tilts her old head closer. "But he wrote its creeds on a scroll."

"These creeds are the same 'cruelties' endured by the sisters?"

"I am an old woman of peasant stock, Interpreter. I cannot read."

"This scroll." His voice, too, is a whisper. "Is it in Nagasaki?"

Otane stares at him like Time itself, made human. From her sleeve, she withdraws a dogwood scroll tube.

"Are the sisters," Uzaemon makes himself ask, "obliged to lie with the men? Is this the — the cruelty that the acolyte spoke of?"

His mother's sure footsteps approach along the creaking corridor.

"I have grounds to fear," Otane replies, handing the scroll tube to Uzaemon, "that the truth is worse."

Uzaemon hides the dogwood tube in his sleeve just as the door opens.

"But excuse me!" His mother appears in the doorway. "I had no inkling you had company. Shall your . . ." She pauses. "Shall your guest be staying for dinner?"

Otane bows very low. "Such generosity far exceeds what an old grandmother deserves. Thank you, madam, but I must not impose upon your household's charity a minute longer . . ."

Chapter Nineteen:
The House of
Sisters, Mount
Shiranui Shrine

Sunrise on the ninth day of the twelfth month
Sweeping the cloisters is a vexing chore this afternoon: no sooner is a pile of leaves and pine needles gathered than the wind kicks it away again. Clouds unravel on Bare Peak and spill icy drizzle. Orito removes bird lime from the boards with a scrap of sacking. Today is the ninety-fifth day of her captivity: for thirteen days she has turned away from Suzaku and the abbess and tipped her solace into her sleeve. For four or five days she suffered from cramps and fever, but now her mind is her own again: the rats are no longer verbal, and the house's tricks have dwindled away. Her victory is limited, however: she has not won permission to explore the precincts, and although she escaped another engiftment day, a newest sister's chances of being so lucky a fourth time are meager, and a fifth escape would be unprecedented.

Umegae approaches in her lacquered sandals, *click-clack, click-clack.*

She shan't be able to resist, Orito predicts, *making a stupid joke.*

"So diligent, Newest Sister! Were you born with a broom in your hand?"

No reply is expected, none is given, and Umegae walks on to the kitchen. Her jibe reminds Orito of her father praising Dejima's cleanliness, in contrast to the Chinese factory where rubbish is left to rot and rats. She wonders if Marinus misses her. She wonders if a girl from the House of Wistaria is warming Jacob de Zoet's bed and admiring his exotic eyes. She wonders if De Zoet even thinks of her now, except when he needs his lost dictionary.

She wonders the same thing about Ogawa Uzaemon.

De Zoet shall leave Japan never knowing she had chosen to accept him.

Self-pity, Orito reminds herself yet again, *is a noose dangling from a rafter.*

The gatekeeper shouts, "The gates are opening, Sisters!"

Two acolytes push in a cart loaded with logs and kindling.

Just as the gate closes, Orito notices a cat slip through. It is bright gray, like the moon on blurred evenings, and it swerves across the courtyard. A squirrel runs up the old pine, but the moon-gray cat knows that two-legged creatures offer better pickings than four, and it leaps onto the cloisters to try its

luck with Orito. "I never saw you here before," the woman tells the animal.

The cat looks at her and meows, *Feed me,
for I am beautiful.*

Orito proffers a dried pilchard between
finger and thumb.

The moon-gray cat inspects the fish indifferently.

"Someone carried this fish," scolds Orito,
"up this mountain."

The cat takes the fish, jumps to the ground,
and goes beneath the walkway.

Orito lowers herself onto the courtyard, but
the cat has gone.

She sees a narrow rectangular hole in the
foundations of the house . . .

. . . and a voice on the walkway asks, "Has
the newest sister lost anything?"

Guiltily, Orito looks up to see the housekeeper carrying a pile of robes. "A cat pleaded
for a scrap of food, then slunk away when he
got what he wanted."

"Must be a tom." The housekeeper is
doubled over by a sneeze.

Orito helps her pick up the laundry and
carry it to the linen room. The newest sister
feels some sympathy toward Housekeeper
Satsuki. The abbess's rank is clear — below
the masters, above the acolytes — but Housekeeper Satsuki shoulders more duties than
she enjoys privileges. By the logic of the world
below, her lack of disfigurements and freedom

from engiftment make her position an enviable one, but the House of Sisters has its own logic, and Umegae and Hashihime contrive a dozen means a day to remind the housekeeper that her post exists for their convenience. She rises early, retires late, and is excluded from many of the sisters' shared intimacies. Orito notices how red are the housekeeper's eyes, and how poor her color. "Pardon my asking," says the doctor's daughter, "but are you unwell?"

"My health, Sister? My health is . . . satisfactory, thank you."

Orito is sure the housekeeper is concealing something.

"*Truly,* Sister, I'm well enough: the mountain winters slow me down a little . . . That's all."

"How many years have you spent on Mount Shiranui, Housekeeper?"

"This will be my fifth in the shrine's service." She seems happy to talk.

"Sister Yayoi told me you're from a large island in Satsuma Domain."

"Oh, it's a little-known place, a full day's sail from Kagoshima Port, called Yakushima. Nobody's heard of it. A few island men serve the lord of Satsuma as foot soldiers — they bring back stories they spend their lives embroidering, but otherwise very few islanders ever leave. The interior is mountainous and trackless. Only cautious woodsmen, foolish hunters, or wayward pilgrims venture there. The island's *kami* gods aren't used to humans. There is just one notable shrine, halfway up Miura Mountain, two days' journey from the port, with a small monastery, smaller than Shiranui Shrine."

Hatsune passes the linen room's doorway, blowing into her hands.

"How did you come," Orito asks, "to be appointed housekeeper here?"

Yûgiri passes in the other direction, swinging a bucket.

The housekeeper unfolds a sheet to fold again. "Master Byakko visited Yakushima on a pilgrimage. My father, a fifth son of a lesser family of the Miyake clan, was a samurai in name only — he was a rice and millet merchant and owned a fishing boat. As he supplied the Miura monastery with rice, he offered to guide Master Byakko up the mountain. I went to carry and cook; we Yakushima girls are bred sturdy." The housekeeper risks a rare, shy smile. "On the return journey, Master Byakko told my father that the small nunnery attached to Mount Shiranui required a housekeeper who wasn't afraid of hard work. Father jumped at the chance: I was one of four daughters, and the master's offer meant one less dowry to find."

"What were your thoughts about vanishing over the horizon?"

"I was nervous, but excited, too, at the idea

of seeing the mainland with my own eyes. Two days later, I was on a boat, watching my home island shrink until it was small enough to fit into a thimble . . . and then there was no going back."

Sawarabi's spiked laughter carries through from the kitchen.

Housekeeper Satsuki is looking backward through time: her breath is short.

You are more ill, Orito guesses, *than you are admitting.*

"Well, what a gossip I am! Thank you for your help, Sister, but you mustn't let me keep you from your chores. I can finish folding the robes on my own, thank you."

Orito returns to the cloisters and takes up her broom again.

The acolytes knock on the gate to be allowed back into the precincts.

As it opens, the moon-gray cat darts between their legs. It swerves across the courtyard; a squirrel darts up the old pine. The cat heads straight to Orito, slinks against her shins, and looks up at her meaningfully.

"If you've come back for more fish, you rogue, there isn't any."

The cat tells Orito that she is a poor dumb creature.

"In the domain of Hizen," First Sister Hatsune strokes her forever-shut eyelid as the night wind blows around the shrine, "a ravine climbs northward from the San'yôdo High-way to the castle town of Bitchu. At a narrow twist in this ravine, two footsore peddlers from Osaka were overtaken by night and made camp at the foot of an abandoned shrine to Inari, the fox god, underneath a venerable walnut tree draped in moss. Now, the first peddler, a cheerful fellow, sold rib-bons, combs, and suchlike. He'd charm the girls, cajole the young men, and business had been good. 'Ribbons for kisses,' he'd sing, 'from all the young misses!' The second ped-dler was a knife seller. He was a darker-spirited fellow who believed that the world owed him a living, and his handcart was full of unsold merchandise. On the night this tale begins, they warmed themselves at their fire and talked about what they would do on their return to Osaka. The ribbon peddler was set on marrying his childhood sweetheart, but the knife seller planned to open a pawnbro-ker's shop to earn the most money with the least work."

Sawarabi's scissors *snip snip snip* through a band of cotton.

"Before they slept, the knife seller suggested that they pray to Inari-*sama* for his protec-tion through the night in such a lonely spot. The ribbon peddler agreed, but as he knelt before the abandoned altar, the knife seller chopped off his head with a single stroke of his biggest unsold ax."

427

Several of the sisters gasp, and Sadaie gives a little shriek. "No!"

"*Ph*ut, Sister," says Asagao, "you told us the two *n*en were *ph*riends."

"So the poor ribbon seller thought, Sister. But now the knife seller stole his companion's money, buried the body, and fell sound asleep. Surely nightmares, or strange groans, plagued him? Not at all. The knife seller woke up refreshed, enjoyed his victim's food for breakfast, and had an uneventful journey back to Osaka. Setting himself up in business with the murdered man's money, he prospered as a pawnbroker, and soon he was lining his robes and eating the daintiest delicacies with silver chopsticks. Four springs came and four autumns went. Then, one afternoon, a spruce, bushy customer in a brown cloak walked into the pawnbroker's shop and produced a box of walnut wood. From inside, he removed a polished human skull. The pawnbroker said, 'The box may be worth a few copper *mon,* but why are you showing me this old lump of bone?' The stranger smiled at the pawnbroker with his fine white teeth and commanded the skull: 'Sing!' And as I live and breathe, Sisters, sing it did, and here is the song that it sang:

"With beauty shall you sleep, on pleasure shall you dine,

By the crane and the turtle and the goyô
    pine . . ."

A log cracks open in the hearth and half the women jump.

"The three tokens of good fortune," says Minori.

"So thought the pawnbroker," continues Hatsune, "but to the spruce and bushy stranger he complained that the market was flooded with these Dutch novelties. He asked whether the skull would sing for anyone or just the stranger? In his silky voice, the stranger explained that it would sing for its true owner. 'Well,' grunted the pawnbroker, 'here's three *koban:* ask for one *mon* more, and the deal's off.' The stranger said not a word but bowed, placed the skull on its box, took his payment, and left. The pawnbroker lost no time in deciding how best to turn his magical acquisition into money. He clicked his fingers for his palanquin and rode to the den of a certain masterless samurai, a dissolute sort of *ronin* given to strange wagers. Being a cautious man, the pawnbroker tested his new purchase as he rode and ordered the skull, 'Sing!' And sure enough, the skull sang,

"Wood is life and fire is time,
By the crane and the turtle and the goyô
    pine!"

"Once in the samurai's presence, the pawnbroker produced his new acquisition and asked for a thousand *koban* for a song from his new friend, the skull. Quick as a blade, the samurai told the pawnbroker that he'd lose his head for insulting his credulity if it didn't sing. The pawnbroker, who had expected this response, agreed to the wager in return for half the samurai's wealth if the skull *did* sing. Well, the crafty samurai assumed that the pawnbroker had lost his wits — and saw an easy fortune to be had. He objected that the pawnbroker's neck was worth nothing and claimed all his visitor's wealth as a prize. Delighted that the samurai had taken the bait, the pawnbroker raised the stakes again: if the skull sang, his rival must pay *all* his wealth — unless, of course, he was losing his nerve? In reply, the samurai bade his scribe draw up the wager as a blood oath, witnessed by the ward headman, a corrupt fellow well used to such shady goings-on. Then the greedy pawnbroker placed the skull on a box and ordered: 'Sing!' "

The women's shadows are the uneasy shades of slanted giants.

Hotaru is the first to crack. "What happened, Sister Hatsune?"

"Silence was what happened, Sister. The skull uttered not one squeak. So the pawnbroker raised his voice a second time. 'Sing, I command you. Sing!' "

Housekeeper Satsuki's busy needle has

fallen still.

"The skull said not a word. The pawnbroker turned pale. 'Sing! Sing!' But still the skull was mute. The blood oath lay there on the table, its red ink not yet dry. The pawnbroker, in despair, shouted at the skull: 'Sing!' Nothing, nothing, nothing. The pawnbroker expected no mercy, nor received any. The samurai called for his sharpest sword whilst the pawnbroker knelt there, trying to pray. Off came the pawnbroker's head."

Sawarabi drops a thimble: it rolls to Orito, who picks it up and returns it.

"Now," Hatsune continues, nodding ponderously, "too late, the skull chose to sing:

"Ribbons for kisses, from all the young
  misses!
Ribbons for kisses, from all the young
  misses!"

Hotaru and Asagao stare wide-eyed. Umegae's mocking smile is gone.

Hatsune leans backward, brushing her knees. "The samurai knew cursed silver when he saw it. He donated the pawnbroker's money to Sanjusandengo Temple. The spruce and bushy stranger was never heard of again. Who knows that he wasn't Inari-*sama* himself, come to avenge the wickedness committed against his shrine? The skull of the ribbon seller — if his it was — is still housed in

431

a remote alcove in a rarely visited wing of Sanjusandengo. One of the older monks prays for its repose every year on the Day of the Dead. If any of you passes that way after your descent, you may go and see it for yourself . . ."

Rain hisses like swinging snakes and gutters gurgle. Orito watches a vein pulsating in Yayoi's throat. *The belly craves food,* she thinks, *the tongue craves water, the heart craves love, and the mind craves stories.* It is stories, she believes, that make life in the House of Sisters tolerable, stories in all their forms: the gifts' letters, tittle-tattle, recollections, and tall tales like Hatsune's singing skull. She thinks of myths of gods, of Izanami and Izanagi, of Buddha and Jesus, and perhaps the Goddess of Mount Shiranui, and wonders whether the same principle is not at work. Orito pictures the human mind as a loom that weaves disparate threads of belief, memory, and narrative into an entity whose common name is Self, and which sometimes calls itself Perception.

"I can't stop thinking," Yayoi murmurs, "of the girl."

Orito wraps Yayoi's hair around her thumb. "Which girl, sleepyhead?"

"The ribbon seller's sweetheart. The one he planned to marry."

You must leave the house and leave Yayoi,

Orito reminds herself, *soon.*

"So sad." Yayoi yawns. "She'd grow old and die, never knowing the truth."

The fire glows bright and dim as the draft blows strong and weak.

There is a leak over the iron brazier: drips hiss and crackle.

The wind rattles the cloisters' wooden screens like a deranged prisoner.

Yayoi's question comes from nowhere. "Were you touched by a man, Sister?"

Orito is used to her friend's directness, but not on this subject. "No."

That "no" is my stepbrother's victory, she thinks. "My stepmother in Nagasaki has a son. I'd rather not name him. During Father's marriage negotiations, it was settled that he'd train to be a doctor and a scholar. It didn't take long, however, for his lack of aptitude to betray itself. He hated books, loathed Dutch, was disgusted by blood, and was dispatched to an uncle in Saga, but he returned to Nagasaki for Father's funeral. The tongue-tied boy was now a seventeen-year-old man of the world. It was 'Oy, bath!'; it was 'Hey, tea!' He watched me, as men do, with no encouragement. None."

Orito pauses as footsteps in the passageway come and go.

"My stepmother noticed her son's new attitude but said nothing, not yet. Until Father died, she passed as a dutiful doctor's wife, but after the funeral she changed . . . or changed back. She forbade me to leave our residence without her permission, permission that she rarely gave. She told me, 'Your days of playing at scholars are over.' Father's old friends were turned away, until they no longer called. She dismissed Ayame, our last servant from Mother's time. I had to take over her duties. One day my rice was white; from the next, it was brown. What a pampered creature that must make me sound."

Yayoi gasps slightly at a kick in her uterus. "They're listening, and none of us thinks you were a pampered creature."

"Well, then my stepbrother taught me that my troubles had not yet begun. I slept in Ayame's old room — two mats, so it was more of a cupboard — and one night, a few days after Father's funeral, when the whole house was asleep, my stepbrother appeared. I asked him what he wanted. He told me that I knew. I told him to get out. He said, 'The rules have changed, dear stepsister.' He said that as head of the Aibagawas of Nagasaki" — Orito tastes metal — "the household's assets were his. 'This one, too,' he said, and that was when he touched me."

Yayoi grimaces. "It was wrong of me to ask. You don't have to tell me."

It was his crime, Orito thinks, *not mine*. "I tried to . . . but he hit me as I'd never been hit before. He clamped his hand over my

434

mouth and told me" — *to imagine,* she remembers, *he was Ogawa.* "He swore that if I resisted, he would hold the right side of my face over the fire until it matched the left side and do what he wanted to do to me anyway." Orito stops to steady her voice. "Acting frightened was easy. Acting submissive was harder. So I said, 'Yes.' He licked my face like a dog and unfastened himself and . . . then I sank my fingers deep between his legs and squeezed what I found there, like a lemon, with all my strength."

Yayoi looks at her friend in a wholly new way.

"His scream woke the house up. His mother came running and ordered the servants away. I told her what her son had tried to do. He told her *I* had begged him to my bed. She slapped the head of the Aibagawas of Nagasaki once for being a liar, twice for being stupid, and ten times for almost wasting the family's most salable property. 'Abbot Enomoto,' she told him, 'will want your stepsister *intact* when she arrives at his nunnery of freaks.' That was how I learned why Enomoto's bailiff had been visiting. Four days later I found myself here."

The storm pelts the roofs and the fire growls.

Orito remembers how all her fathers' friends refused to shelter her on the night she ran away from her own house.

435

She remembers hiding all night in the House of Wistaria, listening.

She remembers her painful decision to accept De Zoet's proposal.

She remembers her final shaming and capture at Dejima's land gate.

"The monks aren't like your stepbrother," Yayoi is saying. "They're gentle."

"So gentle that when I say, 'No,' they stop and leave my room?"

"The Goddess chooses the engifters, just as she chooses us sisters."

To implant belief, Orito thinks, *is to dominate the believers.*

"At my first engiftment," Yayoi confesses, "I imagined a boy I once loved."

So the hoods, Orito realizes, *are to hide the men's faces, not ours.*

"Might you have known a man" — Yayoi hesitates — "who you could . . . ?"

Ogawa Uzaemon, the midwife thinks, *is no longer my concern.*

Orito banishes all thought of Jacob de Zoet, and recalls Jacob de Zoet.

"Oh," says Yayoi, "I'm as nosy as Hashihime tonight. Pay me no mind."

But the newest sister slips from the warmth of their blankets, goes to the chest given her by the abbess, and takes out a bamboo-and-paper fan. Yayoi sits up, curious. Orito lights a candle and opens the fan.

Yayoi peers at the details. "He was an artist? Or a scholar?"

"He read books, but he was just a clerk in an ordinary warehouse."

"He loved you." Yayoi touches the ribs of the fan. "He loved you."

"He was a stranger from another . . . domain. He scarcely knew me."

Yayoi looks at Orito pityingly and sighs. "So?"

The sleeper knows she is dreaming, because the moon-gray cat pronounces, "Someone carried this fish all the way up this mountain." The cat takes the pilchard, jumps to the ground, and vanishes beneath the walkway. The dreamer lowers herself onto the courtyard, but the cat has gone. She sees a narrow rectangular hole in the foundations of the house . . .

. . . Its breath is warm. She hears children and summer's insects.

A voice up on the walkway asks, "Has the newest sister lost anything?"

The moon-gray cat licks its paws and speaks in her father's voice.

"I know you're a messenger," says the dreamer, "but what is your message?"

The cat looks at her pityingly and sighs. "I left through this hole, beneath us . . ."

The dark universe is packed into one small box that slowly opens.

437

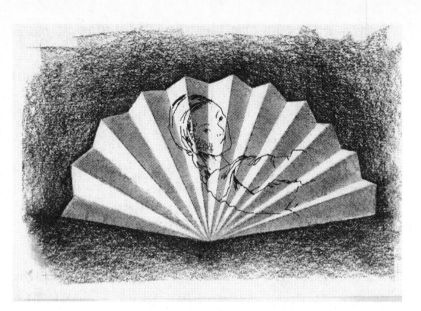

". . . and reappeared at the house gate a minute later. What does that mean?"

The sleeper wakes up in frosted darkness. Yayoi is here, fast asleep.

Orito gropes, fumbles, and understands. *A conduit . . . or a tunnel.*

Chapter Twenty:
The Two Hundred
Steps Leading to
Ryûgaji Temple in
Nagasaki

New Year's Day, the twelfth year of the Era of Kansei
The holiday crowds throng and jostle. Boys are selling warblers in cages dangling from a pine tree. Over her smoking griddle, a palsy-handed grandmother croaks, *"Squiiiiiiiiid on a stick-*oh, *squiiiiiiiiid on a stick-*oh, *who will buy my squiiiiiiiiiid on a stick-*oooh!" Inside his palanquin, Uzaemon hears Kiyoshichi shout, "Make way, make *way!*" less in hope of clearing a path than to insure himself against being scolded by Ogawa the Elder for laziness. "Pictures to as*tound!* Drawings to a*maze!*" hollers a seller of engravings. The man's face appears in the grille of Uzaemon's palanquin, and he holds up a pornographic wood-block print of a naked goblin, who bears an undeniable likeness to Melchior van Cleef. The goblin possesses a monstrous phallus as big as his body. "Might I *proffer* for sir's delecta*tion* a sample of 'Dejima Nights'?" Uzaemon growls, "No!" and the man withdraws, bel-

lowing, "See Kawahara's Hundred and Eight Wonders of the Empire without leaving your house!" A storyteller points to his board about the Siege of Shimabara: "Here, ladies and gentlemen, is the Christian Amakusa Shirô, bent on selling our souls to the king of Rome!" The entertainer plays his audience well: there are boos and yells of abuse. "And so the great shogun expelled the foreign devils, and so the yearly rite of *Fumi-e* continues to the present day, to weed out these heretics feeding off our udders!" A disease-gnawed girl, breastfeeding a baby so deformed that Uzaemon mistakes it for a shaven puppy, implores, "Mercy and a coin, sir, mercy and a coin . . ." He slides open the grille just as the palanquin lurches forward a dozen steps, and Uzaemon is left holding a one-*mon* piece against all the laughing, smoking, joking passersby. Their joy is insufferable. *I am like a dead spirit at* O-bon, Uzaemon thinks, *forced to watch the carefree and the living gorge themselves on Life.* His palanquin tips, and he must grip the lacquered handle as he slides backward. Near the top of the temple steps, a handful of girls on the cusp of womanhood whip their spinning tops. *To know the secrets of Mount Shiranui,* he thinks, *is to be banished from this world.*

A lumbering ox obscures Uzaemon's view of the girls.

The creeds of Enomoto's order shine dark-

ness on all things.
When the ox has passed, the girls are gone.

The palanquins are set down in the Court-yard of the Jade Peony, an area reserved for samurai families. Uzaemon climbs out of his box and slides his swords into his sash. His wife stands behind his mother, while his father attacks Kiyoshichi like the snapping turtle he has come, in recent weeks, to resemble: "Why did you allow us to be buried alive in that" — he jabs his stick toward the thronged steps — "in that human mud?"

Kiyoshichi bows low. "My lapse was unforgivable, Master."

"Yet this old fool," growls Ogawa the Elder, "is to forgive you anyhow?"

Uzaemon tries to intervene. "With respect, Father, I'm sure —"

" 'With respect' is what scoundrels say when they mean the opposite!"

"With sincere respect, Father, Kiyoshichi could not make the crowd vanish."

"So sons now side with menservants against their fathers?"

Kannon, Uzaemon implores, *grant me patience.* "Father, I'm not siding with —"

"Well, doubtless you find this silly old fool *very* behind the times."

I am not your son. The unexpected thought strikes Uzaemon.

"People will start wondering," Uzaemon's

441

mother declares to the backs of her powdered hands, "whether the Ogawas are having doubts about the *fumi-e.*"

Uzaemon turns to Ogawa Mimasaku. "Then let us enter . . . yes?"

"Shouldn't you consult the servants first?" Ogawa Mimasaku walks toward the inner gates. He rose from his sickbed a few days ago only partially recovered, but to be absent from the *fumi-e* ritual is tantamount to announcing one's own death. He slaps away Saiji's offers of help. "My stick is more loyal."

The Ogawas pass a queue of newly wed couples waiting to inhale incense smoke curling from the bronze Ryûgaji dragon's mouth. Local legend promises them a healthy baby son. Uzaemon senses that his wife would like to join them but is too ashamed of her two miscarriages. The temple's cavernous entrance is strung with twists of white paper to celebrate the forthcoming Year of the Sheep. Their servants help them out of their shoes, which they store on shelves marked with their names. An initiate greets them with a nervous bow, ready to guide them to the Gallery of Paulownia to perform the *fumi-e* ritual away from the prying eyes of the lower orders. "The head priest guides the Ogawas," Uzaemon's father remarks.

"The head priest," the initiate apologizes, "is busy with te-te-te —"

Ogawa Mimasaku sighs and stares off to

442

one side.

"— temple duties," the stutterer says, mortified into fluency, "at present."

"Whatever a man is busy with, that is what, or whom, he values."

The initiate leads them to a line of thirty or forty strong. "The wait should" — he takes a deep breath — "n-n-n-nnn-n-n-not be long."

"How, in Buddha's name," asks Uzaemon's father, "do you say your sutras?"

The blushing initiate grimaces, bows, and returns the way he came.

Ogawa Mimasaku is half smiling for the first time in many days.

Uzaemon's mother, meanwhile, greets the family ahead. "Nabeshima-*san!*"

A portly matriarch turns around. "Ogawa-*san!*"

"Another year gone," croons Uzaemon's mother, "in the blink of an eye!"

Ogawa the Elder and the opposing patriarch, a rice-tax collector for the magistracy, exchange manly bows; Uzaemon greets the three Nabeshima sons, all close to him in age and employed in their father's office.

"The blink of an eye," sighs the matriarch, "and *two* new grandsons . . ."

Uzaemon glances at his wife, who is withering away with shame.

"Please accept," says his mother, "our heartfelt congratulations."

"I tell my daughters-in-law," huffs Mrs. Na-

443

beshima, " 'Slow down: it isn't a race!' But young people nowadays won't listen, don't you find? Now the middle one thinks she has another on the way. Between ourselves," she leans close to Uzaemon's mother, "I was too lenient when they arrived. Now they run amok. You three! Where are your manners? For shame!" Her forefinger plucks her daughters-in-law one step forward, each dressed in a seasonal kimono and tasteful sash. "Had *I* worn my mother-in-law down like these three tormentors, *I* would have been sent back to my parents' house in disgrace." The three young wives stare at the ground, while Uzaemon's attention is drawn to their babies, in the arms of wet nurses over to one side. He is assailed, as he has been countless times since the day of the herbalist of Kurozane's visit, by nightmarish images of Orito being "engifted" and, nine months later, of the masters "consuming" the Goddess's gifts. The questions begin circling. *How do they actually kill the newborn? How is it kept secret from the mothers, from the world? How can men* believe *that this depravity lets them cheat death? How can their consciences be amputated?*

"I see *your* wife — Okinu-*san,* isn't it?" — Mrs. Nabeshima regards Uzaemon with a saint's smile and a lizard's eyes — "is a better-bred girl altogether than my three.

'We' are as yet" — she pats her stomach — "unblessed, are we?"

Okinu's face paint hides her blush, but her cheeks quiver slightly.

"My son does his part," Uzaemon's mother declares, "but she is so careless."

"And how," Mrs. Nabeshima tuts, "have 'we' settled into Nagasaki?"

"She still pines for Karatsu," says Uzaemon's mother. "Such a crybaby!"

"Homesickness may be" — the matriarch pats her belly again — "the cause . . ."

Uzaemon wants to defend his wife, but how to combat a painted mud slide?

"Could your husband," Mrs. Nabeshima is asking Uzaemon's mother, "spare you and Okinu-*san* this afternoon, I wonder? We're having a little party at home, and your daughter-in-law may benefit from the advice of mothers her own age. But — oh!" She regards Ogawa the Elder with a dismayed frown. "What *must* you think of such an imposition at so short a notice, given your husband's health —"

"Her husband's health," the old man interrupts, "is excellent. You two," he sneers at his wife and daughter-in-law, "do whatever you wish. I'm going to have sutras recited for Hisanobu."

"Such a devout father," Mrs. Nabeshima says, shaking her head, "is a model for the youth of today. All's settled, then, yes, Mrs.

Ogawa? After the *fumi-e,* come back to our
—" She breaks off her sentence to address a
wet nurse. "Silence that mewling piglet! Have
you forgotten where we are? For shame!"

The wet nurse turns away, bares her breast,
and feeds the baby.

Uzaemon peers at the queue into the gallery, trying to gauge its speed.

The Buddhist deity Fudô Myôô glares from
his candlelit shrine. His fury, Uzaemon was
taught, frightens the impious; his sword slices
their ignorance; his rope binds demons; his
third eye scrutinizes human hearts; and the
rock on which he stands signifies immov-
ability. Seated before him are six officials
from the Inspectorate of Spiritual Purity,
dressed in ceremonial attire.

The first official asks Uzaemon's father,
"Please state your name and position."

"Ogawa Mimasaku, Interpreter of the First
Rank of Dejima Interpreters, head of the
Ogawa household of the Higashizaka Ward."

The first inspector tells a second, "Ogawa
Mimasaku is present."

The second finds the name on a register.
"Ogawa Mimasaku's name is listed."

The third writes the name. "Ogawa Mimasaku hereby registered as present."

A fourth declaims, "Ogawa Mimasaku will
now perform the act of *fumi-e.*"

Ogawa Mimasaku steps onto the well-worn

446

bronze plaque of Jesus Christ and grinds his heel on the image for good measure.

A fifth official calls out, "Ogawa Mimasaku has performed *fumi-e*."

The interpreter of the first rank steps off the idolatrous plaque and is helped by Kiyoshichi to a low bench. Uzaemon suspects he is suffering more pain than he is willing to show.

A sixth official marks his register. "Ogawa Mimasaku is registered as having performed the act of *fumi-e*."

Uzaemon thinks about the foreigner De Zoet's Psalms of David and the narrowness of his own escape when Kobayashi had the Dutchman's apartment burgled. He wishes he had asked De Zoet about his mysterious religion last summer.

Noise washes in from the commoners' ritual in a neighboring hall.

The first official is now addressing him: "Please state your name and profession . . ."

Once the formalities are completed, Uzaemon steps up to the *fumi-e*. He glances down and meets the pained eyes of the foreign god. Uzaemon presses his foot down on the bronze and thinks of the long line of Ogawas of Nagasaki who have stood on this same *fumi-e*. On previous New Year's Days, Uzaemon felt proud to be the latest in this line: some ancestors would, like him, have been adoptive sons. But today he feels like an impostor, and he knows why.

My loyalty to Orito, he phrases it, *is stronger than my loyalty to the Ogawas.*

He feels the face of Jesus Christ against the sole of his foot.

Whatever the cost, Uzaemon vows, *I shall free her. But I need help.*

The walls of Shuzai's *dojo* hall echo with the two swordsmen's shrieks and the crack of bamboo poles. They attack, parry, counter, rout; attack, parry, counter, rout. The sprung wooden floor creaks under their bare feet. Drips of rainwater are caught by buckets, which, when full, are changed by Shuzai's last remaining apprentice. The practice bout comes to an abrupt end when the shorter of the two combatants deals his partner a blow on his right elbow, causing Uzaemon to drop his pole. The concerned victor slides up his mask, revealing a flat-nosed, well-weathered, and watchful man well into his forties. "Is it broken?"

"The fault was mine." Uzaemon is clutching his elbow.

Yohei hurries over to help his master unfasten his mask.

Unlike his teacher's face, Uzaemon's drips with sweat. "There's no breakage . . . look." He bends and straightens his elbow. "Just a well-deserved bruise."

"The light was too poor. I should have lit lamps."

"Shuzai-*san* mustn't waste oil on my account. Let us end here."

"I hope you won't oblige me to drink your generous gift alone?"

"On such an auspicious day, your engagements must be pressing . . ."

Shuzai looks around his empty *dojo* hall and shrugs at Uzaemon.

"Then," the interpreter bows, "I accept your courteous invitation."

Shuzai orders his pupil to light the fire in his private apartment. The men change out of their practice clothes, discussing the New Year promotions and demotions announced earlier by Magistrate Ômatsu. Stepping up into the teacher's quarters, Uzaemon recalls the ten or more young disciples who ate, slept, and studied here when he first took lessons from Shuzai, and the pair of matronly neighborhood women who cajoled and cared for them. The rooms are colder and quieter nowadays, but as the fire comes to life, the two men slip into informal manners and their native Tosa dialect, and Uzaemon is warmed by his and Shuzai's ten-year-old friendship.

Shuzai's boy pours the heated *sake* into a chipped flask, bows, and leaves.

Now is the time, Uzaemon prompts himself, *to say what I have to say.*

The thoughtful host and his hesitant guest

fill each other's cups.

"To the fortunes of the Ogawas of Nagasaki," proposes Shuzai, "and to the speedy recovery of your honorable father."

"To a prosperous Year of the Sheep for the *dojo* hall of Master Shuzai."

The men empty the first cup of *sake,* and Shuzai sighs contentedly. "But prosperity is gone for good, I fear. I pray I'm wrong, but I doubt I am. The old values are decaying, that's the problem. The smell of decadence hangs everywhere, like smoke. Oh, samurai enjoy the notion of wading into battle like their valiant ancestors, but when the storehouse is hungry, it's swordsmanship they say goodbye to, not their concubines and silk linings. Those who do care about the old ways are the very ones who fall foul of the new. Another of my students quit last week, with tears in his eyes: his father's stipend at the armory has been paid at half rate for two years running — and now the gentleman learns that his rank won't be eligible for a New Year payment. This at the end of the twelfth month, when the moneylenders and bailiffs do their rounds, badgering decent people! Have you heard Edo's newest advice to its unpaid officials? 'Cover your indulgences by breeding goldfish.' Goldfish! Who has money to waste on goldfish, other than merchants? Now, if merchants' sons were permitted to carry swords" — Shuzai lowers his voice — "I would have a line of pupils stretching from here to the fish market, but better to plant silver coins in horse shit than wait for Edo to pass *that* edict." He refills his cup and Uzaemon's. "Ah, so much for my woes: your mind was on other things during sword practice."

Uzaemon is no longer surprised by Shuzai's perspicacity. "I don't know if I have the right to involve you."

"To a believer in Fate," replies Shuzai, "it's not you who is involving me."

Damp twigs on the weak fire crackle as if trodden upon.

"Some disturbing news came into my possession, some days ago . . ."

A cockroach, shiny as lacquer, crawls along the base of the wall.

". . . in the form of a scroll. It concerns the Order of the Shrine of Shiranui."

Shuzai, privy to Uzaemon's intimacy with Orito, studies his friend.

"The scroll lists the order's secret precepts. It's . . . disturbing."

"It's a secretive place, Mount Shiranui. You are certain this scroll is genuine?"

Uzaemon produces the dogwood scroll tube from his sleeve. "Yes. I wish it was a forgery, but it was written by an acolyte of the order who was no longer able to bury his conscience. He ran away, and to read the scroll is to understand why . . ."

451

The rain's innumerable hooves clatter on the streets and roofs.

Shuzai holds out his open palm for the scroll tube.

"To read it may implicate you, Shuzai. It could be dangerous."

Shuzai holds out his open palm for the scroll tube.

"But this is" — Shuzai speaks in an appalled whisper — "this is insanity: that *this*" — he gestures at the scroll on his low table — "murderous garble could purchase immortality. The phrases are misshapen but . . . these third and fourth creeds — if the 'engifters' are the initiates of the order and the 'bearers' are the women and their newborn the 'gifts,' then the shrine of Shiranui is a — a — not a harem but . . ."

"A farm." Uzaemon's throat tightens. "The sisters are livestock."

"This sixth creed, about 'extinguishing the gifts in the Bowl of Hands' . . ."

"They must drown the newborn children, like unwanted puppies."

"But the men doing the drowning . . . they must be the fathers."

"The seventh creed orders five 'engifters' to lie with the same 'bearer' over as many nights so no one can know that he is killing his own offspring."

"It — it violates Nature: the women, how

could . . ." Shuzai aborts his sentence.

Uzaemon forces himself to voice his worst fears. "The women are violated when they are most fertile, and when the children are born, they are stolen. The women's consent, I presume, is not a matter of concern. Hell *is* hell because, there, evil passes unremarked upon."

"But might some not prefer to take their own lives to this?"

"Perhaps some do. But look at the eighth creed: 'letters from the extinguished.' A mother who believes that her children are living good lives with foster families may, perhaps, endure what she must — especially if she can nurture hopes of meeting her children again, after her 'descent.' That these reunions can never occur is a truth that, evidently, never reaches the House of Sisters."

Shuzai passes no comment, but squints at the scroll. "There are sentences I cannot decipher . . . See this last line of all: 'The final word of Shiranui is silence.' Your runaway apostate must translate his testimony into plain Japanese."

"He was poisoned. To read the creeds, as I said, is dangerous."

Uzaemon's servant and Shuzai's apprentice talk as they sweep the hall.

"Yet Lord Abbot Enomoto," Shuzai speaks with incredulity, "is known as a . . ."

"A respected judge, yes; a humane lord, yes;

an academician of the Shirandô, a confidant of the great, and a dealer in rare medicines, yes. Yet it appears he is also a believer in an arcane Shintô ritual that buys blood-drenched immortality."

"How could these abominations be kept a secret for so many decades?"

"Isolation, ingenuity, power . . . fear. These achieve most ends."

A clutch of New Year revelers hurries along the street outside.

Uzaemon looks at the alcove where Shuzai's master is honored; a mildewed hanging proclaims, *The hawk may be starving, yet he won't touch corn.*

"The author of this scroll," Shuzai says cautiously, "did you meet him face-to-face?"

"No. He gave the scroll to an old herbalist living near Kurozane. Miss Aibagawa visited her, two or three times, which is how the herbalist knew my name. She sought me out in the hope that I have the will and the means to help the shrine's newest sister."

The two men listen to the percussion of dripping water.

"The will I have; the means are another matter. If a Dutch interpreter of the third rank mounted a campaign against the lord of Kyôga armed with nothing but this scroll of illegitimate provenance . . ."

"Enomoto would have you beheaded for slurring his reputation."

454

This minute, Uzaemon thinks, *is a cross-roads.* "Shuzai, if I had persuaded my father to let me marry Miss Aibagawa, as I once promised, she wouldn't be enslaved in this" — he jabs at the parchment — "farm. Do you understand why I have to free her?"

"What I understand is that if you act alone you'll get sliced like a tuna fish. Give me a few days. I may take a short journey."

Chapter
Twenty-One:
Orito's Room at
the House of
Sisters

The eighth night of the first month in the twelfth year of the Era of Kansei

Orito considers the luck required in the hours ahead: the cat's tunnel must be wide enough to admit a slim woman and not barred at its exit; Yayoi must sleep until morning without checking on her; she must descend an icebound gorge without injury and pass the halfway gate without alerting the guards; and by dawn, she must find Otane's house and trust her friend to give her sanctuary. *All of which,* Orito thinks, *is just the beginning.* Returning to Nagasaki would mean recapture, but escape to the relative safety of Chikugo Domain, or Kumamoto or Kagoshima, would mean arriving in a strange town as a homeless, friendless woman without a *sen* to her name.

Engiftment is next week, Orito thinks. *Next week is your turn.*

Inch by cautious inch, Orito slides open her door.

My first footstep, she thinks, *as a fugitive,* and passes Yayoi's room.

Her heavily pregnant friend is snoring. Orito whispers, "I am sorry."

For Yayoi, Orito's escape will be a brutal abandonment.

It's the Goddess, the midwife reminds herself, *who forces you to do this.*

Orito slides her feet around the passageway to the kitchen, where a screen serves as the curfew exit out onto the cloisters. Here she binds a pair of straw-and-canvas shoes onto her feet.

Outside, icy air soaks into her padded jacket and mountain trousers.

A gibbous moon is grubby. Stars are bubbles, trapped in ice. The old pine is gnarled and malign. Orito navigates the cloisters back to the place the cat showed her a few weeks ago. Watching the shadows, she lowers herself onto the frost-fused stones. She ducks underneath the walkway, bracing herself for a shout of alarm . . .

. . . but there is no shout. Orito crawls under the inner passageway until her groping hand finds the rectangle between the foundation stones. She found it once again after the moon-gray cat showed it to her but in doing so earned the attention of Sisters Asagao and Sawarabi and had to concoct a dubious story about a dropped pin. In the nine days since,

457

she has not risked reconnoitering the tunnel. *If,* she thinks, *it is a tunnel, and not just a few missing blocks in the foundations.* Headfirst, she inserts herself through the black rectangle and crawls forward.

Inside, the "roof" is knee height, the walls a forearm apart. To move, Orito must wriggle laterally, like an eel, less elegantly but as quietly. Soon her kneecaps are scraped, her shins are bruised, and her fingertips hurt as they grapple for traction on the frozen stones. The floor feels smoothed, as if by running water. The darkness is one degree short of absolute. When her probing knuckles slap a stone block, she despairs, thinking she has come to a dead end . . . but then the conduit bends to the left. Twisting her body around the sharp corner, she pushes onward. She shivers uncontrollably and her lungs hurt. She tries not to think of giant rats or entomb-ment. *I must be under Umegae's room,* she supposes, imagining the sister pressed against Hashihime, just two layers of floorboard, a *tatami* mat, and an under-futon above her.

Is the darkness ahead, she wonders, *growing less dark?*

Hope pushes her onward. She makes out another corner.

Rounding it, Orito sees a small triangle of moonlit stone.

A hole in the house's outer wall, she realizes.

458

Please, please let it be big enough.

But after a minute's slow struggle, she finds the hole little bigger than a fist: just the right size for a cat. Years of ice and sun, she guesses, loosened a single lump of stone. *Were the hole any larger,* she thinks, *it would have been noticed from the outside.* Anchoring herself, she places her hand against the stone adjacent to the hole and pushes with all her strength until a painful crick in her bent neck obliges her to stop.

Some objects are potentially movable, she thinks, *but this one, never.*

"That's it, then." Her murmured breath is white. "There's no escape."

Orito considers the next twenty years, the men, and the children removed.

She retreats to the second bend, turns around with difficulty, and propels herself forward, feetfirst, back to the outer wall and wedges herself tight: she plants her heels on the adjacent stone and pushes . . .

I may as well — Orito gasps for breath — *try to shift Bare Peak.*

Then she imagines Abbess Izu announcing her engiftment.

Jackknifing herself, she kicks at the stone with the flat of her feet.

She imagines the sisters' congratulations: gleeful, spiteful, sincere.

Barking her shins, she kicks at the stone again, again, and again . . .

She thinks of Master Genmu pawing and gnawing her.

What was that sound? Orito stops. *Was that a grating sound?*

She imagines Suzaku pulling out her first baby; her third; her ninth . . .

Her feet kick the stone until her calves hurt and her neck throbs.

Grit trickles onto her ankles — and suddenly not one but two blocks tumble away and her feet are sticking out into empty space.

She hears stones thump down a low slope and settle with a thud.

The snow is scabby and ruckled underfoot. *Orient yourself* — Orito is dazed to be outside the house — *and quickly.* The long gully between the ramped foundations of the House of Sisters and the shrine's outer wall is five paces wide, but the wall is as high as three men. To reach its ramparts, she must find the stairs or a ladder. Left, toward the northern corner, is a moon gate in the Chinese style: this, Orito has learned from Yayoi, leads into a triangular courtyard and Master Genmu's fine quarters. Orito hurries in the other direction, toward the eastern corner. Passing the end of the House of Sisters, she enters a small enclosure accommodating the hen coop, dovecote, and stalls for the goats. The birds stir slightly as she passes, but the goats stay asleep.

The eastern corner is connected by a roofed walkway to the Masters' Hall; by a small storehouse, a bamboo ladder is propped against the outer wall. Daring to hope that escape is just a few moments away, Orito climbs up to the rampart. Level with the shrine's eaves, she sees the ancient column of Amanohashira rising from the sacred courtyard. Its spike impales the moon. *Such arresting beauty,* Orito thinks. *Such silent violence.*

She pulls up the bamboo ladder and lowers it over the wall's outer face . . .

The dense pine forest comes to within twenty paces of the shrine.

. . . but the ladder's feet don't reach the ground. Perhaps there is a dry moat.

The thick shadow below the wall obscures the height of the drop.

If I jump and break my leg, she thinks, *I'll freeze to death by sunrise.*

Her numb fingers lose their grip and the ladder falls and shatters.

I need a rope, she concludes, *or the means to fashion one.*

Feeling as exposed as a rat on a shelf, Orito hurries along the rampart toward the great gate in the southern corner, hoping that freedom can be won over the body of a soundly sleeping sentry. She climbs down the next ladder to a gully between the outer wall and the barn-sized kitchen and dining hall.

There is the smell of latrines and soot. Amber light leaks from the kitchen door. Knives are being sharpened by an insomniac cook. To disguise her footfalls, Orito steps in time to the metallic scrape. The next moon gate leads her into the southern courtyard, overlooked by the meditation hall and populated by two giant cryptomeria: Fûjin, the wind god, bent under his sack of the world's winds; and Raijin, the thunder god, who steals navels during thunderstorms, holding up his chain of hand drums. The great gate, like Dejima's land gate, consists of tall double doors for palanquins and a smaller door through the gatehouse. This door, Orito sees, stands slightly ajar . . .

. . . so she creeps closer along the wall, until she smells tobacco and hears voices. She crouches in the shadow of a large barrel. "Any more charcoal?" a voice drawls. "My nuts are nuggets of ice."

A scuttle is rattled empty. "That's the last," says a high voice.

"We'll throw dice," says the drawler, "for the privilege of getting more."

"So what are your chances," says a third voice, "of having those nuggets melted in the House of Sisters during engiftment?"

"Not good," admits the drawler. "I had Sawarabi three months ago."

"I had Kagerô last month," says the third

voice. "I'm at the back of the queue."

"The newest sister's bound to be chosen," says the third voice, "chances are, so we acolytes shan't snatch a peep all week. Genmu and Suzaku are always the first to dig their hoes into virgin soil."

"Not if the lord abbot visits," says the drawler. "Master Annei told Master Nogoro that Enomoto-*dono* befriended her father and guaranteed his loans, so that when the old man crossed the Sanzu, the widow had a stark choice: hand over her stepdaughter to Mount Shiranui or lose her house and everything in it."

Orito has never considered this: here and now, it is sickeningly plausible.

The third voice clucks admiringly. "A master of strategy, our lord abbot."

Orito wishes she could tear the men and their words to pieces, like squares of paper. . . .

"Why go to all the bother to get a samurai's daughter," asks the high voice, "when he can pick and choose from any brothel in the empire?"

"Because this one's a midwife," answers the drawler, "who'll stop so many of our sisters and their gifts dying during labor. Rumor has it she brought the Nagasaki magistrate's newborn son back from the dead. Cold and blue, he was, until Sister Orito breathed life back into him . . ."

That single act is why Enomoto brought me here?

". . . I'd not be surprised," continues the drawler, "if she's a special case."

"Meaning," asks the third voice, "that not even the lord abbot honors her?"

"Not even she could stop herself dying in childbirth, right?"

Ignore this speculation, Orito orders herself. *What if he's wrong?*

"Pity," says the drawler. "If you ignore her face, she's a pretty thing."

"Mind you," adds the high voice, "until Jiritsu is replaced, there's one less —"

"Master Genmu forbade us," exclaims the drawler, "ever to mention that treacherous bastard's name."

"He did," agrees the third voice. "He did. Fill the charcoal bucket as penance."

"But we were going to throw dice for it!"

"Ah. That was prior to your disgraceful lapse. Charcoal!"

The door is flung open: bad-tempered footsteps crunch toward Orito, who crouches into a terrified ball. The young monk stops by the barrel and removes its lid, just inches away. Orito hears his teeth chatter. She breathes into her shoulder to hide her breath. He scoops up charcoal, filling the scuttle lump by lump . . .

Any moment now — she shakes — *any moment now . . .*

. . . but he turns away and walks back to the guardhouse.

Like paper prayers, a year's good luck was burned away in seconds.

Orito abandons all hope of leaving through the gates. She thinks, *A rope . . .*

Her pulse still fast and frightened, she slips from the purple shadows through the next moon gate into a courtyard formed by the meditation hall, the western wing, and the outer wall. The guest quarters are a mirror reflection of the House of Sisters: here the laymen of Enomoto's retinue are housed when the lord abbot is in residence. Like the nuns, they cannot leave their confinement. General supplies, Orito gathers from the sisters, are kept in the western wing, but it is also the living and sleeping quarters of the order's thirty or forty acolytes. Some will be sound asleep, but some will not. In the northwestern quarter is the lord abbot's residence. This building has been vacant all winter, but Orito has heard the housekeeper talk about airing the sheets in its linen cupboards. *And sheets,* it occurs to her, *can be knotted into ropes.*

She creeps down the gully between the outer wall and the guest quarters. . . .

A young man's soft laughter escapes the doors and falls silent.

The fine materials and crest identify the

house as the lord abbot's.

Exposed from three angles, she climbs up to the gabled doors.

Let them open, she prays to her ancestors, *let them open . . .*

The doors are shuttered fast against the mountain winter.

I'd need a hammer and chisel to get inside, Orito thinks. She has nearly walked around the perimeter but is no nearer escaping. *The lack of twenty feet of rope means twenty years of concubinage.*

Across the stone garden of Enomoto's residence is the northern wing. Suzaku, Orito has learned, has his quarters here, next to the infirmary . . .

. . . and an infirmary means patients, beds, sheets, and mosquito nets.

Entering one of the wings is a reckless risk, but what choice is left?

The door slides six inches before emitting a high, singing groan. Orito holds her breath to hear the noise of running footsteps . . .

. . . but nothing happens, and the fathomless night smooths itself.

She squeezes through the gap; a door curtain strokes her face.

Reflected moonlight delineates, dimly, a small entrance hall.

An odor of camphor locates the infirmary through a right-hand door.

There is a sunken doorway to her left, but the fugitive's instinct says, *No . . .*

She slides open the right-hand door.

The darkness resolves itself into planes, lines, and surfaces . . .

She hears the rustling of a straw futon and a sleeper's breathing.

She hears voices and footsteps: two men, or three.

The patient yawns and asks, " 'S anyone there?"

Orito withdraws to the entrance hall, slides the infirmary door shut, and peers around the shrieking door. A lantern bearer is less than ten paces away.

He is looking this way, but the glow of his light impairs his vision.

Now Master Suzaku's voice can be heard in the infirmary.

The fugitive has nowhere to run but the sunken doorway.

This may be the end, Orito thinks, shivering, *this may be the end . . .*

The scriptorium is walled from floor to ceiling with shelves of scrolls and manuscripts. On the other side of the sunken door, someone trips and mutters a curse. Fear of capture pushes Orito into the large chamber before she can be certain that it is unoccupied. A pair of writing tables are illuminated by a double-headed lantern, and a small fire licks a kettle hanging over the brazier. The side aisles provide hiding places, *but hiding places,* she thinks, *are also traps.* Orito walks along the aisle toward the other door, which, she guesses, leads into Master Genmu's quarters, and enters the globe of lamplight. She is afraid to leave the empty room but afraid to stay and afraid to go back. In her indecision, she glances down at a half-finished manuscript on one of the tables: with the exceptions of the wall hangings in the House of Sisters, these are the first written characters the scholar's daughter has seen since her abduction, and despite the danger, her hungry eye is drawn. Instead of a sutra or sermon, she finds a half-composed letter, written not in the ornate calligraphy of an educated monk but in a more feminine hand. The first column she reads obliges her to read the second, and the third . . .

Dear Mother, The maples are aflame with autumn colors and the harvest moon floats like a lantern, just as the words of *The Moonlit Castle* describe. How long ago seems the rainy season, when the lord abbot's servant delivered your letter. It lies in front of me on my husband's table. Yes, Koyama Shingo accepted me as his wife on the auspicious thirtieth day of the seventh month at Shimogamo Shrine, and we are living in the two back rooms of the White

Crane *obi*-sash workshop on Imadegawa Street. After the wedding ceremony, a banquet was held at a famous teahouse, paid for jointly by the Uedas and Koyamas. Some of my friends' husbands turn into spiteful goblins after capturing their bride, but Shingo continues to treat me with kindness. Married life is not a boating party, of course — just as you wrote in your letter three years ago, a dutiful wife must never sleep before her husband or rise after him, and I never have enough hours in the day! Until the White Crane is well established, we economize by making do with just one maid, as my husband brought only two apprentices from his father's workshop. I am happy to write, however, that we have secured the patronage of two families connected with the imperial court. One is a lesser branch of the Konoe—

The words stop, but Orito's head is spinning. *Are the New Year letters,* she wonders, *all written by the monks?* But this makes no sense. Tens of fictional children would have to be maintained until their mothers' descents, and then the subterfuge would be discovered. Why go to so much trouble? *Because* — twin lamps dot Fat Rat's knowing eyes — *the children cannot write New Year letters from the world below for the reason that they never* reach *the world below.* The scriptorium's

469

shadows are watching her react to the implications. Steam rises from the kettle's spout. Fat Rat is waiting. "No," she tells it. *"No."* There is no need for infanticide. *If the gifts were unwanted by the order, Master Suzaku would issue herbs to trigger early miscarriages.* Mockingly, Fat Rat asks her to explain the letter on the table in front of them. Orito seizes on the first plausible answer: *Sister Hatsune's daughter died from disease or an accident.* To save the sister the pain of bereavement, the order must have a policy of continuing the New Year letters.

Fat Rat twitches, turns, and disappears.

The door by which she entered is opening. A man says, "After you, Master . . ."

Orito rushes for the other door; as in a dream, it is both near and far.

"Strange" — Master Chimei's voice follows — "how one composes best at night . . ."

Orito slides the door open three or four hand widths.

". . . but I'm glad of your company at this inhospitable hour, dear youth."

She is through and slides shut the door just as Master Chimei strides into the lamplight. Behind Orito, the passageway to Master Genmu's quarters is short, cold, and unlit. "A story must move," Master Chimei opines, "and misfortune is motion. Contentment is inertia. Hence, into the story of Sister Hat-

470

sune's Miss Noriko, we shall sow the seeds of a modest calamity. The lovebirds must suffer. Either from without, from theft, fire, sickness — or, better yet, from within, from a weakness of character. Young Shingo may grow weary of his wife's devotion, or Noriko may grow so jealous of the new maid that Shingo *does* start tupping the girl. Tricks of the trade, you see? Storytellers are not priests who commune with an ethereal realm but artisans, like dumpling makers, if somewhat slower. To work, then, dear youth, until the lamp drinks itself dry . . ."

Orito slides her feet along the corridor to Master Genmu's quarters, staying close to the wall, where, she hopes, the wood is less likely to squeak. She reaches a paneled door. She holds her breath, listens, and hears nothing. She opens it a tiny crack . . .

The space is empty and unlit; blocks of darkness in each wall indicate doors.

In the middle of the floor lies what might be discarded sacking.

She enters and approaches the sacks, hoping they can be roped together.

She thrusts a hand into the mound and finds a man's warm foot.

Her heart stops. The foot recoils. A limb turns. The blankets shift.

Master Genmu mumbles, "Stay here,

Maboroshi, or I'll . . ." The threat disintegrates.

Orito crouches, not daring to breathe, much less run away . . .

The quilted hills that are Acolyte Maboroshi shift; a snore snags in his throat.

Minutes pass before Orito is even half sure the two men are asleep.

She counts ten slow breaths before carrying on to the door ahead.

Its sliding rumble sounds, to her ears, loud as an earthquake.

The Goddess, lit by a large votive candle and carved in a fine-flecked silver wood, watches the intruder from her plinth in the center of the small, luxurious altar room. The Goddess smiles. *Do not meet her eyes,* an instinct warns Orito, *or she shall know you.* Black robes with blood-maroon silken cords hang along one wall; the other walls are lined with paper, as in the richer Dutchmen's houses, and the mats smell resinous and new. To the right and left of the door on the far wall, large ideograms are written in thick ink on the papered walls. The calligraphic style is clear enough, but when Orito peers at them by the light of the candle, the meanings elude her. Familiar components are arranged in unknown combinations.

After replacing the candle, she opens the door onto the northern courtyard.

472

■ ■ ■ ■

The Goddess, whose paint is peeling, watches the surprised intruder from the center of the mean altar room. Orito is unsure how the shrine's outer walls can accommodate it. Perhaps there is no northern courtyard. She looks behind her, at the Goddess's spine and neck. The Goddess ahead is lit by a vigilant candle. She has aged since the first room, and there is no smile on her lips. *But don't meet her eyes,* insists the same instinct as before. There is a lingering odor of straw, of animals and people. The boarded walls and floors evoke a farmhouse of middling prosperity. Another one hundred and eight ideograms are written on the far wall, this time on twelve mildewed scrolls hanging at either side of the door. Once again, when Orito pauses for a moment to read the characters, they retreat into troubling unintelligibility. *Who cares?* she berates herself. *Go!*

She opens the door onto what must be the northern courtyard . . .

The Goddess in the center of the third altar room is half rotted away: she is unrecognizable from her incarnation in the altar room in the House of Sisters. Her face might be a tertiary syphilitic's, far beyond the salvation of mercury medicine. One of her arms lies

473

on the floor where it fell, and by the glow of the tallow candle Orito sees a cockroach twitching on the rim of a hole in the statue's skull. The walls are bamboo and clay, the floor is straw, and the air is sweet with dung: the room would pass for a peasant's hovel. Orito speculates that the rooms have been hollowed from a spar of Bare Peak, or even hewn out of a series of caves from which the shrine grew as the ages passed. *Better yet,* it occurs to Orito, *it may be an escape tunnel dating from the shrine's military past.* The far wall is caked with something dark — animal blood mixed with mud, perhaps — on which the unreadable characters are daubed in whitewash. Orito raises the poorly made latch, praying that her guess proves accurate . . .

The cold and darkness are from a time before people and fire.

The tunnel is as high as a man and as wide as outstretched arms.

Orito returns for the candle from the last room: it has about an hour's life.

She enters the tunnel, proceeding step by cautious step.

Bare Peak is above you, taunts Fear, *pressing down, pressing down . . .*

Her shoes *click-clack* on rock; her breath is hissed shivers; all else is silence.

The candle's grimy glow is better than nothing, but not by much.

She stands still for a moment: the flame is motionless. *No draft yet.*

The roof stays at the height of a man and the width of outstretched arms.

After thirty or forty steps, the tunnel begins to bend upward.

Orito imagines emerging into starlight through a secret crack . . .

. . . and worries that her escape may cost Yayoi her life.

The crime is Enomoto's, her conscience objects, *Abbess Izu's, and the Goddess's.*

The truth isn't so simple, her confined echo tells her conscience.

Is the air becoming warmer, Orito wonders, *or do I have a fever?*

The tunnel widens into a domed chamber around a kneeling effigy of the Goddess three or four times larger than life. To Orito's dismay, the tunnel ends here. The Goddess is sculpted from a black stone flecked with bright grains, as if the sculptor chiseled her from a block of night sky. Orito wonders how the effigy was carried in: it is easier to believe that the rock has been here since the earth was made and that the tunnel was widened to reach it. The Goddess's back is erect and cloaked in red cloth, but she cups her giantess's hands to form a hollow the size of a cradle. Her covetous eyes gaze at the space. Her predatory mouth opens wide. *If the shrine of Shiranui is a question,* the thought thinks Orito as much as Orito thinks the thought, *then this place is its answer.* Inscribed on the smoothed circular wall at shoulder height are more unreadable ideograms: one hundred and eight, she is quite sure, one for each of the Buddhist sins. Something draws Orito's fingers toward the Goddess's thigh, and when they touch, she nearly drops the candle: the stone is warm as life. The scholar gropes for an answer. *Ducts from hot springs,* she reasons, *in nearby rocks . . .* Where the Goddess's tongue should be, something glints in the candlelight. Ignoring an irrational fear of the stone teeth severing her arm, she reaches in and finds a squat bottle nestling snug in a hollow. It is blown from cloudy glass, or it is full of a cloudy liquid. She removes the cork and sniffs: it has no smell. Both as doctor's daughter and Suzaku's patient, Orito knows better than to taste it. *But why store it in such a place?* She slots the bottle back inside the Goddess's mouth and asks, "What *are* you? What is done here? To what end?"

The Goddess's stone nostrils cannot flare. Her baleful eyes cannot be widening. . . .

The candle is extinguished. Blackness swallows the cavern.

■ ■ ■ ■

Back in the first of the altar rooms, Orito readies herself to pass through Master Genmu's quarters, when she notices the silken cords on the black robes and curses her previous stupidity. Ten of the cords, knotted together, form a light, strong rope as long as the outer wall is high; she attaches another five to make certain. Coiling this up, she slides open the door and skirts the edge of Master Genmu's room to a side door. A screened passageway leads to an outer door and the masters' garden, where a bamboo ladder leans against the ramparts. She climbs up, ties one end of her rope around a sturdy, unobtrusive joist, and throws the other from the parapet. Without a backward glance, she takes her last deep breath in captivity and lowers herself to the dry ditch . . .

Not safe yet. Orito scrambles into a lattice of winter boughs.

She keeps the shrine wall on her right and refuses to think about Yayoi.

Big twins, she thinks, *a fortnight late; a pelvis slimmer than Kawasemi's . . .*

Rounding the western corner, Orito cuts through a swath of firs.

One in ten, one in twelve births in the house ends with a dead woman.

Through stony ice and needle drifts she

finds a sheltered bowl.

With your knowledge and skill — this is no vain boast — *it would be one in thirty.*

The wind's quick sleeves catch on the thorny glassy trees.

"If you turn back," Orito warns herself, "you know what the men will do."

She finds the trail where the slope of *torî* gates begins. Their daylight cinnabar orange is black against the night sky.

Nobody can ask me to submit to enslavement, not even Yayoi.

Then Orito considers the weapon she acquired in the scriptorium.

To doubt one New Year letter — she could threaten Genmu — *is to doubt them all.*

Would the sisters consent to the terms of the house if they weren't sure their gifts were alive and well in the world below?

Bitter hatred, she would add, *does not make for fruitful pregnancies.*

The path turns a sharp corner. The constellation of the Hunter appears.

No. Orito dismisses the half thought. *I shall never go back.*

She concentrates on the steep and icy path. An injury now could ruin her hopes of reaching Otane's cottage by dawn. An eighth of an hour later, Orito turns a high corner above the wood-and-vine bridge called Todoroki and catches her breath. Mekura Gorge plunges down the mountainside, vast as the sky . . .

. . . a bell is ringing at the shrine. It is not the deep time bell but a higher-pitched, insistent bell, rung in the House of Sisters when one of the women goes into labor. Orito imagines Yayoi calling her. She imagines the frantic disbelief prompted by her disappearance, the searches throughout the precincts, and the discovery of her rope. She imagines Master Genmu being woken: *The newest sister is gone . . .*

She imagines knotted twin fetuses blocking the neck of Yayoi's womb.

Clattering acolytes may be dispatched down the path, the halfway gatehouse will be told of her disappearance, and the domain checkpoints at Isahaya and Kashima will be alerted tomorrow, but the Kyôga Mountains are an eternity of forest for fugitives to vanish into. *You shall go back,* Orito thinks, *only if you choose to.*

She imagines Master Suzaku, helpless, as Yayoi's screams scald the air.

The bell could be a trick, she considers, *to lure you back.*

Far, far below, the Ariake Sea is burnished by the moonlight.

What may be a trick tonight will be the truth tomorrow night, or very soon . . .

479

"The liberty of Aibagawa Orito," Orito speaks out loud, "is more important than the life of Yayoi and her twins." She examines the truth of the statement.

CHAPTER TWENTY-TWO: SHUZAI'S ROOM AT HIS DOJO HALL IN NAGASAKI

Afternoon of the thirteenth day of the first month
"I set out early," Shuzai reports. "At Jizo-*sama*'s statue at the marketplace, I lit a three-*sen* candle to ensure against mishap, and I soon had cause to be grateful for the precaution. Trouble found me by Ômagori Bridge. A captain in the shogunal guard on horseback blocked my path: he'd glimpsed my scabbard under my straw cape and wanted to check that I had the rank to carry one. 'Fortune never favors he who wears another's clothes,' so I gave him my true name. Lucky it was I did. He dismounted, removed his own helmet, and called me 'Sensei': I taught one of his sons when I first arrived in Nagasaki. We talked awhile, and I told him I was bound for Saga, for my old master's seventh-year funeral ceremony. Servants wouldn't be appropriate on such a pilgrimage, I claimed. The captain was embarrassed by this attempt to disguise my poverty, so he agreed, bade me good luck, and rode on."

Four students are practicing their best *kendo* shrieks in the *dojo.*

Uzaemon feels a cold blossoming in his sore throat.

"From Oyster Bay — a midden of fishermen's hovels, shells, and rotting rope — I turned north to Isahaya. Low, hilly land, as you know, and on a dismal first-month afternoon, the road is atrocious. By a crooked bend, four porters appeared from behind a shuttered-up tea shack — a leerier pack of wild dogs you never saw. Each carried a hefty bludgeon in his scabby hand. They warned me that robbers would pounce upon a luckless, friendless, helpless traveler like myself and urged me to hire them so I'd arrive at Isahaya unharmed. I drew my sword and assured them I was not as luckless, friendless, or helpless as they believed. My gallant saviors melted away, and I reached Isahaya without further excitement. Here I avoided the bigger, more conspicuous inns and took lodgings in the loft of a talkative tea roaster. The only other guest was a peddler of amulets and charms from holy places as far off as Ezo, so he claimed."

Uzaemon catches his sneeze in a paper square, which he tosses onto the fire.

Shuzai hangs the kettle low over the flames. "I tapped my landlord for what he knew about Kyôga Domain. 'Eighty square miles of mountain with not one town worthy of the name,' save for Kashima. The lord abbot takes a cut from the temples there and harvests rice taxes from the coastal villages, but his real power flows from allies in Edo and Miyako. He feels secure enough to maintain just two divisions of guards: one to keep up appearances when his entourage travels and one barracked in Kashima to quell any local troubles. The amulet peddler told me how he'd once tried to visit the shrine on Mount Shiranui. He'd spent several hours climbing up a steep ravine called Mekura Gorge, only to be turned back at a gatehouse halfway up. Three big village thugs, he complained, told him that Shiranui Shrine doesn't trade in lucky charms. I put it to the peddler that it's a rare shrine that turns away paying pilgrims. The peddler agreed, then told me this story from the reign of Kan'ei, when the harvests failed for three years all across Kyushu. Towns as far off as Hirado, Hakata, and Nagasaki suffered starvation and riots. It was this famine, swore the peddler, that led to rebellion in Shimabara and the humiliation of the shogun's first army. During the mayhem, a quiet samurai begged Shogun Ieyasu for the honor of leading, and financing, a battalion in the second attempt to crush the rebels. He fought so audaciously that after the last Christian head was hoisted on the last pike, a shogunal decree obliged the disgraced Nabeshima clan of Hizen to cede the samurai not only a certain obscure shrine on Mount Shiranui but the entire mountainous region. Kyôga Domain was created by that decree, and the quiet samurai's full title became Lord Abbot Kyôga-no-Enomoto-no-*kami*. The present lord abbot must be his" — Shuzai calculates on his fingers — "his great-great-grandson, give or take a generation."

He pours tea for Uzaemon, and both men light their pipes.

"The sea fog was thick the next morning, and after a mile I struck off east, circling Isahaya from the north, around to the Ariake Sea Road. Better to enter Kyôga Domain, I reckoned, without the guards at the gate seeing my face. I walked along half the morning, passing through several villages with my hood down, until I found myself at the notice board of the village of Kurozane. Crows were at work, unpicking a crucified woman. It stank! Seaward, the fog was dividing itself between weak sky and brown mudflats. Three old mussel gatherers were resting on a rock. I asked them what any traveler would: how far to Konagai, the next village along? One said four miles, the second said less, the third said farther; only the last had ever been, and that was thirty years ago. I made no mention of Otane the herbalist but asked about the crucified woman, and they told me she'd been beaten most nights for three years by her husband and had celebrated the New Year

484

by opening his head with a hammer. The lord abbot's magistrate had ordered the executioner to behead her cleanly, which gave me a chance to ask whether Lord Abbot Enomoto was a fair master. Perhaps they didn't trust a stranger with an alien accent, but they all agreed they'd been born here as rewards for good deeds in previous lives. The lord of Hizen, one pointed out, stole one farmer's son in eight for military duties and bled his villagers white to keep his family in Edo in luxury. In contrast, the lord of Kyôga imposed the rice tax only when the harvest was good, ordered a supply of food and oil for the shrine on Mount Shiranui, and required no more than three guards for the Mekura Gorge gate. In return, the shrine guaranteed fertile streams for the rice paddies, a bay teeming with eels, and baskets full of seaweed. I wondered how much rice the shrine ate in a year. Fifty *koku,* they said, or enough for fifty men."

Fifty men! Uzaemon is dismayed. *We need an* army *of mercenaries.*

Shuzai shows no undue concern. "After Kurozane, the road passes a smart-looking inn, the Harubayashi, as in 'spring bamboo.' A short distance on, an uphill track turns off the coast road and leads up to the mouth of Mekura Gorge. The trail up the mountain is well maintained, but it took me half the day. The guards at the checkpoint don't expect

485

intruders, that much was clear — one well-placed sentinel would have seen me coming — but . . ." Shuzai wrinkles his mouth to indicate an easy climb. "The gatehouse seals a narrow mouth of the gorge, but you'd not need ten years of ninja training to climb up around it, which was what I did. Higher up, patches of snow and ice appeared, and pine and cedar muscled out the lowland trees. The track climbs a couple more hours to a high bridge over the river; a stone marker names the place Todoroki. Not long after, there's a long, steep corridor of *torî* gates, where I left the path and climbed up through a pine forest. I came to the lip of an outcrop midway up Bare Peak, and this drawing" — Shuzai removes a square of paper hidden in a folded book — "is based on the sketches I made on the spot."

Uzaemon surveys Orito's prison for the first time.

Shuzai empties dead ash from his pipe. "The shrine sits in this triangular hollow between Bare Peak above and those two lesser ridges. My guess is that a castle from the Age of Warring States once sat on the site claimed by Enomoto's ancestor in the amulet peddler's tale — note these defensive walls and the dry moat. You'd need twenty men and a battering ram to force those gates, too. But don't be disheartened: any wall is only as strong as the men defending it, and a child

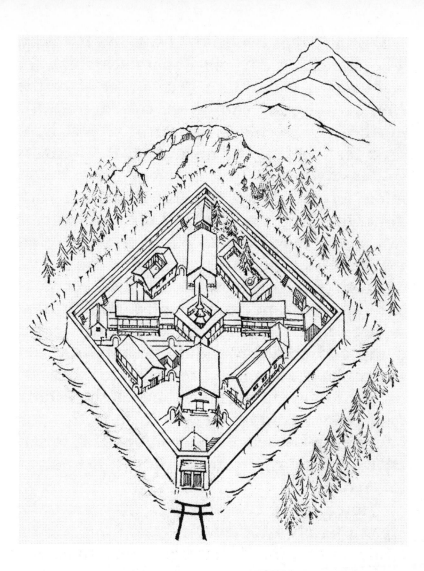

with a grappling hook would be over in a minute. Nor is there any chance of getting lost once we're inside. Now *this*" — Shuzai points his bowstring-calloused forefinger — "is the House of Sisters."

Unguardedly, Uzaemon asks, "Did you see her?"

Shuzai shakes his head. "I was too far away. The remaining daylight I spent searching for ways down from Bare Peak other than the Mekura Gorge, but there are none: this northeast ridge hides a drop of several hundred feet, and to the northwest, the forest is so dense you'd need four hands and a tail to make any headway. At dusk, I headed back down the gorge and reached the halfway gate just as the moon rose. I climbed over a bluff to the lower path, reached the mouth of Mekura Gorge, crossed the rice terraces behind Kurozane, and found a fishing boat to sleep under on the road to Isahaya. It was damp and cold, but I didn't want witnesses coming to share a fire. I returned to Nagasaki by the following evening, but let three days pass before contacting you to hide the link between my absence and your visit. It is safest to assume that your servant is in Enomoto's pay."

"Yohei has been my servant since the Ogawa family adopted me."

Shuzai shrugs. "What better spy than one above suspicion?"

Uzaemon's cold feels worse by the minute. "Do you have solid reason to doubt Yohei?"

"None at all, but all *daimyo* retain informers in neighboring domains, and these informers acquire understandings with major families' servants. Your father is one of only four interpreters of the first rank on Dejima:

the Ogawas are not people of no importance. To spirit away a *daimyo*'s favorite is to enter a dangerous world, Uzaemon. To survive, you must doubt Yohei, doubt your friends, and doubt strangers. Knowing all this, the question is: are you still intent on liberating her?"

"More than ever, but" — Uzaemon looks at the map — "can it be done?"

"Given careful planning, given money to hire the right men, yes."

"How much money and how many men?"

"Less than you'd suppose, is the good news: the fifty *koku* the seaweed gatherers talked about sounds daunting, but a fair portion of that fifty is eaten by Enomoto's entourage. What's more, *that* building" — Shuzai points to the lower right corner — "is the refectory, and when it emptied after dinner, I counted just thirty-three heads. The women I discount. The masters will be past their prime, which leaves at most two dozen able-bodied acolytes. In Chinese legends, monks may shatter rocks with their bare hands, but the goslings of Shiranui are hatched from much frailer eggs. There was no archery range in the shrine, no barracks for lay guards, and no evidence of martial training. Five excellent swordsmen, in my opinion, could rescue Miss Aibagawa. My policy of double insurance calls for ten swords, in addition to yours and mine."

"What if Lord Enomoto and his men appear before we attack?"

"We postpone our venture, disperse, and hide in Saga until he leaves."

Smoke from the struggling fire tastes of salt and bitterness.

"You'll have considered," Shuzai says, raising a delicate point, "that to return to Nagasaki with Miss Aibagawa would be . . . would be . . ."

"Tantamount to suicide. Yes, I have considered little else this last week. I shall" — Uzaemon sneezes and coughs — "I shall abandon my life here, accompany her to wherever she wishes to go, and help her until she orders me to leave. A day, or my lifetime, whichever she chooses."

The swordsman frowns, nods, and watches his friend and student.

Out in the street, dogs run past, barking murderously.

"I worry," admits Uzaemon, "about you being linked to this raid."

"Oh, I assume the worst. I, too, shall move on."

"You are sacrificing your life in Nagasaki in order to help me?"

"I prefer to blame Nagasaki's particularly menacing creditors."

"Won't our hired men also be making fugitives of themselves?"

"Masterless samurai are used to looking after themselves. Make no mistake: the man with the most to lose is Ogawa Uzaemon. You are exchanging a career, a stipend, a bright future . . ." The older man casts around for a tactful phrase.

". . . for a woman — in all likelihood a broken, pregnant woman."

Shuzai's expression replies, *Yes.*

"Or thanking my adoptive father by disappearing without a word?"

My suffering wife, at least, Uzaemon foresees, *can go back to her family.*

"Confucianists would scream 'heresy!' " Shuzai's gaze settles on the urn housing his master's thumb bone, "but there are times when the less loyal son is the better man."

"My 'commission,' " Uzaemon begins, struggling to articulate himself, "feels less a matter of righting a wrong and more a matter of . . . of role, of *This is what I am for.*"

"Now it is you who sounds like the believer in Fate."

"Please make the arrangements for the raid. Whatever the costs, I will pay."

Shuzai says, "Yes," as if there is no other conclusion.

"Raise your elbow *that* high," a sharp-voiced senior disciple in the *dojo* hall tells a junior, "and one well-aimed *uekiri* stroke will pound it to rice powder . . ."

Shuzai changes the subject. "Where is Jiritsu's scroll now?"

Uzaemon resists an urge to touch the scroll

491

tube in an inner pocket. "It is hidden" — *if we are captured,* he thinks, *better not to know the truth* — "under the floor of my father's library."

"Good. Keep it there for now." Shuzai rolls up his own drawing of the Shiranui Shrine. "But bring it when we leave for Kyôga. If all goes well, you and Miss Aibagawa will vanish like two drops of rain, but if Enomoto ever tracks you down, that manuscript could be your sole means of defense. I said earlier that the monks pose little danger; I cannot say the same for the lord abbot's vengeance."

"Thank you," Uzaemon says, and rises, "for your wise advice."

Jacob De Zoet empties the hot water into a cup and stirs in a spoonful of honey. "I had the same cold last week. Sore throat, headache, and I'm still croaking like a frog. During July and August, my body forgot what cold weather felt like — quite a feat for a Zeelander. But now it's that blistering summer heat I can't remember."

Uzaemon misses some words. "Memory is tricks and strangeness."

"That's the truth." De Zoet adds a dash of pale juice. "And this is lime."

"Your room," observes the visitor, "is change." Additions include the low table and cushions, a New Year's *kadomatsu* pine

492

wreath, a competent picture of a monkey drawn in pen and ink, and a folding screen to hide De Zoet's bed. *Which Orito might have shared* — Uzaemon suffers a complicated ache — *and better that she had.* The head clerk has no slave or servant, but the apartment is tidy and swept. "Room is comfort and pleasant."

De Zoet stirs the drink. "Dejima is to be my home for some years."

"You do not wish to take a wife for more comfort life?"

"I don't view such transactions as lightly as do my compatriots."

Uzaemon is encouraged. "Picture of monkey is very beauty."

"That? Thank you, but I'm an incurable beginner."

Uzaemon's surprise is genuine. "*You* draw monkey, Mr. de Zoet?"

De Zoet replies with an embarrassed smile and serves the lime-and-honey drink. He then flouts the laws of small talk. "How may I be of service, Ogawa-*san?*"

Uzaemon looks at the steam rising from the bowl. "I am disturb your office at important period, I fear."

"Deputy Fischer exaggerates. There isn't much to be done."

"Then . . ." The interpreter touches the hot porcelain with his fingertips. "I wish Mr. de Zoet keep — to hide — a . . . a very important thing, safe."

"If you wish to use one of our warehouses, perhaps Chief van Cleef should —"

"No no. This is small thing." Uzaemon produces the dogwood scroll tube.

De Zoet frowns at the item. "I shall oblige, of course, and gladly."

"I know Mr. de Zoet is able to hide items with greatest care."

"I shall hide it with my Book of Psalms, until you want it back."

"Thank you. I — I hoped you say these words." Uzaemon addresses De Zoet's unasked questions with a foreigner's directness. "First, to answer, 'What is the words in this scroll?' You remember Enomoto, I think" — the name causes De Zoet's face to cloud over — "is lord abbot of shrine in Kyôga Domain, where . . . where Miss Aibagawa must live." The Dutchman nods. "This scroll is — how to say? — rules, believings laws of order, of shrine. These laws are —" *This would be hard in Japanese,* the interpreter thinks, sighing, *but in Dutch it is like breaking rocks.* "These rules are . . . are bad, worse, worst than worst wrong, for woman. It is great suffering . . . It is not endurable."

"What rules? What must she endure, Ogawa, for God's sake?"

Uzaemon shuts his eyes. He keeps them shut and shakes his head.

"At least," De Zoet's voice cracks, "tell me

494

if the scroll could be a weapon to attack Enomoto or shame him into releasing her. Or, via the magistracy, could the scroll win Miss Aibagawa justice?"

"I am interpreter of third rank. Enomoto is lord abbot. He has more power than Magistrate Shiroyama. Justice in Japan is justice of power."

"So Miss Aibagawa must suffer — suffer the 'unendurable' for the rest of her life?"

Uzaemon hesitates. "A friend, in Nagasaki, wish to help . . . with directness."

De Zoet is no fool. "You plan a rescue? Can you hope to succeed?"

Uzaemon hesitates again. "Not he and I alone. I . . . purchase assistance."

"Mercenaries are risky allies, as we Dutch know well." De Zoet's mind works an abacus of implications. "But how could you return to Dejima afterward? And she would just be recaptured. You'd have to go into hiding — permanently — and . . . so why . . . why sacrifice so much . . . everything? Unless . . . *oh.*"

Momentarily, the two men are unable to look each other in the eye.

So now you know, the interpreter thinks, *I love her, too.*

"I am a fool." The Dutchman rubs his green eyes. "A boorish fool . . ."

Two of the Malay slaves hurry down Long Street, speaking their language.

"... but why did you help my — my advances toward her, if you, too ..."

"Better she lives here with you than become locked forever in bad marriage or be sent away from Nagasaki."

"Yet still you entrust me with this" — he touches the tube — "unusable evidence?"

"You wish her freedom, too. You will not sell me to Enomoto."

"Never. But what am I to do with the scroll? I am a prisoner here."

"Do nothing. If rescue succeed, I not need it. If rescue ..." The conspirator drinks his honey and lime. "If rescue does not succeed, if Enomoto learns of scroll's existence, he will hunt in my father's house, in friends' houses. Rules of order is very, very secret. Enomoto kill to possess it. But on Dejima, Enomoto has no power. Here he will not search, I believe."

"How will I know whether your mission succeeds or not?"

"If succeeds, I send message when I can, when is safe."

De Zoet is shaken by this interview, but his voice is steady. "You shall be in my prayers, always. When you meet Miss Aibagawa, tell her ... tell her ... just tell her that. You shall both be in my prayers."

CHAPTER
TWENTY-THREE:
YAYOI'S ROOM AT THE
HOUSE OF SISTERS,
MOUNT SHIRANUI
SHRINE

Minutes before sunrise on the eighteenth day of the first month

Housekeeper Satsuki receives Yayoi's milky-lipped baby daughter. By firelight and dawn-light, Satsuki's tears are visible. No fresh snow fell during the night, so the track down Mekura Gorge is passable, and Yayoi's twins are to be taken to the world below this morning. "Now then, Housekeeper." Abbess Izu issues a gentle rebuke. "You've helped with dozens of bestowals. If Sister Yayoi accepts that she isn't losing little Shinobu and Binyô but sending them on ahead into the world below, surely *you* can control your feebler feelings. Today is a parting, not a bereavement."

What you call "feebler feelings," thinks Orito, *I call "compassion."*

"Yes, Abbess." Housekeeper Satsuki swallows. "It's just . . . they're so . . ."

"Without the bestowal of our gifts," Yayoi half-recites, "Kyôga Domain's rivers would dry, its seedlings would wither, and all its mothers would be barren."

Before the night of her escape and voluntary return, Orito would have considered such words to be despicably passive; now she understands that only this belief, that life requires their sacrifice, makes the separation tolerable. The midwife rocks Yayoi's hungry son, Binyô. "Your sister's finished now. Give your mother a little rest."

Abbess Izu reminds her, "We say 'bearer,' Sister Aibagawa."

"You do, Abbess," Orito responds, as expected, "but I am not 'we.' "

Sadaie empties crumbs of charcoal onto the fire; they snap and spit.

We made — Orito holds the abbess's gaze — *firm understandings: remember?*

Our lord abbot — Abbess Izu holds Orito's gaze — *shall have the final word.*

Until that day — Orito holds the abbess's gaze and repeats, "I am not 'we.' "

Binyô's face is damp, pink, velvet; it folds into a prolonged squawk.

"Sister?" Yayoi receives her son for his last feed from her breast.

The midwife scrutinizes Yayoi's inflamed nipple.

"It's much better," Yayoi tells her friend. "The motherwort works."

Orito thinks of Otane of Kurozane, who no doubt supplied the herb, and wonders if she can insist on a yearly meeting among her terms. The newest sister remains the shrine's lowest-ranking captive, but her decision on the Todoroki Bridge to forfeit her escape and her successful delivery of Yayoi's twins have elevated her status in many subtle ways. Her right to refuse Suzaku's drugs is recognized; she is trusted to walk around the shrine's ramparts three times each day; and Master Genmu agreed that the Goddess wouldn't choose Orito for engiftment, in return for Orito's silence about the counterfeit letters. The moral price of the agreement is high: mild friction with the abbess occurs daily, and Lord Abbot Enomoto may undo these advances . . . *but that is a fight,* Orito thinks, *for a future day.*

Asagao appears at Yayoi's door. "Naster Suzaku is arriving, Avhess."

Orito looks at Yayoi, who is determined not to cry.

"Thank you, Asagao." Abbess Izu rises with the suppleness of a girl.

Sadaie reties her headscarf around her misshapen skull.

With the abbess's departure, air and talk flow a little more freely.

"Calm down," Yayoi tells the yowling Binyô. "I have two. Here, greedy one . . ."

Binyô finds his mother's nipple at last and feeds.

Housekeeper Satsuki gazes into Shinobu's face. "A full, happy tummy."

"A full, smelly swaddling band," says Orito. "May I, before she's too sleepy?"

"Oh, let me." The housekeeper lays Shinobu on her back. "It's no trouble."

Orito allows the older woman the sad honor. "I'll fetch some warm water."

"To think," says Sadaie, "how spidery the gifts were just a week ago!"

"We must thank Sister Aibagawa," says Yayoi, reattaching the guzzling Binyô, "that they're sturdy enough for bestowal so soon."

"We must thank her," adds Housekeeper Satsuki, "that they were born at all."

The ten-day-old boy's petal-soft hand clenches and unclenches.

"It is thanks to your endurance," Orito tells Yayoi, mixing hot water from the kettle with a pan of cold water, "your milk, and your mother's love." *Don't talk about love,* she warns herself, *not today.* "Children want to be born; all the midwife does is help."

"Do you think," asks Sadaie, "the twins' engifter might be Master Chimei?"

"This one," Yayoi says, stroking Binyô's head, "is a chubby goblin: Chimei's sallow."

"Master Seiryû, then," whispers Housekeeper Satsuki. "He turns into a goblin king when he loses his temper."

500

On an ordinary day, the women would smile at this.

"Shinobu-*chan*'s eyes," says Sadaie, "remind me of poor Acolyte Jiritsu's."

"I believe they are his," responds Yayoi. "I dreamed of him again."

"Strange to think of Acolyte Jiritsu buried," Satsuki comments, removing the soiled cloth from the baby girl's loins, "but his gifts' lives just beginning." The housekeeper wipes away the pungent paste with a murky cotton rag. "Strange and sad." She washes the infant's buttocks in the warm water. "Could Shinobu have one engifter and Binyô another?"

"No." Orito recalls her Dutch texts. "Twins have just one father."

Master Suzaku is ushered into the room. "A mild morning, Sisters."

The sisters chorus "Good morning" to Suzaku; Orito gives a slight bow.

"Good weather for our first bestowal of the year! How are our gifts?"

"Two feeds during the night, Master," replies Yayoi, "and one more now."

"Excellent. I'll give them a drop of sleep each; they won't wake until Kurozane, where two wet nurses are waiting at the inn. One is the same woman who took Sister Hatsune's gift to Niigata two years ago. The little ones will be in the best hands."

"The master," says Abbess Izu, "has wonderful news, Sister Yayoi."

501

Suzaku shows his pointed teeth. "Your gifts are to be raised together in a Buddhist temple near Hôfu by a childless priest and his wife."

"Think of it!" exclaims Sadaie. "Little Binyô, a priest's son!"

"They'll have a fine education," says the abbess, "as children of a temple."

"They'll have each other," adds Satsuki. "A sibling is the best gift."

"My sincerest thanks" — Yayoi's voice is bloodless — "to the lord abbot."

"You may thank him yourself, Sister," says Abbess Izu, and Orito, washing Shinobu's soiled swaddling, looks up. "The lord abbot is due to arrive tomorrow or the day after."

Fear touches Orito. "I, too," she lies, "look forward to the honor of speaking with him."

Abbess Izu glances at her with triumphant eyes.

Binyô, sated, is slowing down; Yayoi strokes his lips to remind him to slurp.

Satsuki and Sadaie finish wrapping the baby girl for her journey.

Master Suzaku opens his medicine box and unstops a conical bottle.

The first boom of the bell of Amanohashira ebbs into Yayoi's cell.

Nobody speaks; outside the house gate, a palanquin will be waiting.

Sadaie asks, "Where *is* Hôfu, Sister Aibagawa? As far as Edo?"

The second boom of the bell of Amanohashira ebbs into Yayoi's cell.

"Much nearer." Abbess Izu receives the clean, sleepy Shinobu and holds her close to Suzaku. "Hôfu is the castle town of Suô Domain, one domain along from Nagato, and just five or six days away, if the straits are calm . . ."

Yayoi stares at Binyô, and far away. Orito guesses at her thoughts: of her first daughter, Kaho, perhaps, sent last year to candlemakers in Harima Domain; or of the future gifts she must give away before her descent in eighteen or nineteen years' time; or perhaps she is simply hoping that the wet nurses in Kurozane have good, pure milk.

Bestowals are *akin to bereavements,* Orito thinks, *but the mothers cannot even mourn.*

The third boom of the bell of Amanohashira brings the scene nearly to a close.

Suzaku empties a few drops from the conical bottle between Shinobu's lips. "Sweet dreams," he whispers, "little gift."

Her brother, Binyô, still in Yayoi's arms, groans, burps, and farts. His recital does not delight, as it should. The picture is flat and melancholy.

"It is time, Sister Yayoi," states the abbess. "I know you'll be brave."

Yayoi smells his milky neck one last time. "May I feed Binyô his sleep?"

Suzaku nods and passes her the conical bottle.

Yayoi presses the pointed mouth against Binyô's; his tiny tongue slurps.

"What ingredients," Orito asks, "does Master Suzaku's sleep contain?"

"One midwife." Suzaku smiles at Orito's mouth. "One druggist."

Shinobu is already asleep: Binyô's eyelids are sinking . . .

Orito cannot help guessing: *Opiates? Arisaema? Aconite?*

"Here is something for brave Sister Yayoi." Suzaku decants a muddy liquid into a thimble-sized stone cup. "I call it 'fortitude': it helped at your last bestowal." He holds it to Yayoi's lips, and Orito resists the urge to slap the glass away. As the liquid drains down Yayoi's throat, Suzaku lifts her son off.

The dispossessed mother mutters, "But . . ." and stares cloudily at the druggist.

Orito catches her friend's drooping head. She lays the numbed mother down.

Abbess Izu and Master Suzaku each carry out a stolen child.

CHAPTER TWENTY-FOUR: OGAWA MIMASAKU'S ROOM AT THE OGAWA RESIDENCE IN NAGASAKI

Dawn on the twenty-first day of the first month Uzaemon kneels by his father's bed. "You look a little . . . brighter today, Father."

"Leave those flowery fibs to the women: to lie is their nature."

"Truly, Father, when I came in, the color in your face —"

"My face has less color than the skeleton in the Dutch hospital."

Saiji, his father's stick-limbed servant, tries to coax the fire back to life.

"So, you're making a pilgrimage to Kashima, to pray for your ailing father, in the depths of winter, alone, without a servant — if 'serve' is what the oafs sponging off the Ogawa storehouse do. How impressed Nagasaki shall be with your piety."

How scandalized Nagasaki shall be, thinks Uzaemon, *if the truth is ever known.*

A hard brush is scrubbing the stones of the

entrance hall.

"I don't make this pilgrimage to earn acclaim, Father."

"Scholars, you once informed me, disdain 'magic and superstition.' "

"These days, Father, I prefer to keep an open mind."

"Oh? So I am now —" He is interrupted by a scraping cough, and Uzaemon thinks of a fish drowning on a plank and wonders if he should sit his father upright. That would require touching him, which a father and son of their rank cannot do. The servant Saiji steps over to help, but the coughing fit passes and Ogawa the Elder bats him away. "So I am now one of your 'empirical tests'? Do you intend to lecture the academy on the efficacy of the Kashima cure?"

"When Interpreter Nishi the Elder was ill, his son made a pilgrimage to Kashima and fasted for three days. By his return, his father had not only made a miraculous recovery but walked all the way to Magome to meet him."

"Then choked on a fish bone at his celebration banquet."

"I shall ask you to exercise caution with fish in the year ahead."

The reeds of flames in the brazier fatten and spit.

"Don't offer the gods years off your own life just to preserve mine."

Uzaemon wonders, *A thorny tenderness?* "It

shan't come to that, Father."

"Unless, un*less,* the priest swears I'll have my vigor restored. One's ribs shouldn't be prison bars. Better to be with my ancestors and Hisanobu in the pure land than be trapped here with fawners, females, and fools." Ogawa Mimasaku looks at the *butsudan* alcove, where his birth son is commemorated with a funeral tablet and a sprig of pine. "To those with a head for commerce, Dejima is a private mint, even with the Dutch trade as bad as it is. But to those dazzled by" — Mimasaku uses the Dutch word "enlightenment" — "the opportunities are wasted. No, it shall be the Iwase clan who dominates the guild. They already have five grandsons."

Thank you, Uzaemon thinks, *for helping me turn my back on you.* "If I disappoint you, Father, I'm sorry."

"How gleefully" — the old man's eyes close — "life shreds our well-crafted plans."

"It's the very worst time of year, husband." Okinu kneels at the edge of the raised hallway. "What with mud slides and snow and thunder and ice . . ."

"Spring," Uzaemon counters, sitting down to bind his feet, "will be too late for Father, wife."

"Bandits are hungrier in winter, and hunger makes them bolder."

"I'll be on the main Saga highway. I have my sword, and Kashima is only two days away. It's not Hokurikurô, or Kii, or anywhere wild and lawless."

Okinu looks around like a nervous doe. Uzaemon cannot recall when his wife last smiled. *You deserve a better man,* he thinks, and wishes he could say so. His hand presses his oilcloth pack; it contains two purses of money, some bills of exchange, and the love letters Aibagawa Orito sent him during their courtship. Okinu is whispering, "Your mother bullies me terribly when you're away."

I am her son, Uzaemon thinks with a groan, *your husband, and not a mediator.*

Utako, his mother's maid and spy, approaches, an umbrella in hand.

"Promise me," Okinu attempts to conceal her true concerns, "not to risk crossing Omura Bay in bad weather, husband."

Utako bows to them both; she passes into the front courtyard.

"So you'll be back," Okinu asks, "within five days?"

Poor, poor creature, Uzaemon thinks, *whose only ally is me.*

"Six days?" Okinu presses him for a reply. "No more than seven?"

If I could end your misery, he thinks, *by divorcing you now, I would . . .*

"Please, husband, no longer than eight

days. She's so . . . so . . ."

. . . but it would bring unwanted attention on the Ogawas. "I don't know how long the sutras for Father are going to take."

"Would you bring back an amulet from Kashima for brides who want —"

"Hnn." Uzaemon finishes binding his feet. "Goodbye, then, Okinu."

If guilt were copper coins, he thinks, *I could buy Dejima.*

Crossing the small courtyard denuded by winter, Uzaemon inspects the sky: it is a day of rain that never quite reaches the ground. Ahead, waiting by the front gate, Uzaemon's mother is standing under an umbrella held by Utako. "Yohei can still be ready to join you in a matter of minutes."

"As I said, Mother," says Uzaemon, "this pilgrimage is not a pleasure trip."

"People may wonder whether the Ogawas can no longer afford servants."

"I rely on you to tell people why your stubborn son went on his pilgrimage alone."

"Who, exactly, is going to be scrubbing your loincloths and socks?"

A raid on Enomoto's mountain stronghold, Uzaemon thinks, *and it is "loincloths and socks" . . .*

"You shan't think the matter so amusing after eight or nine days."

"I'll be sleeping at inns and guest dormitories in temples, not in ditches."

"An Ogawa mustn't joke, not even joke, about living like a vagabond."

"Why don't you go inside, Mother? You'll catch a dreadful cold."

"Because it's a well-bred woman's duty to see her sons or husband off from the gate, however cozy it may be indoors." She glares at the main house. "One can only wonder what my green-pepper-head of a daughter-in-law was whimpering about."

Utako the maid stares at the droplets on the camellia buds.

"Okinu was wishing me a safe journey, as you are."

"Well, plainly they do things differently in Karatsu."

"She is a long way from home, and it has been a difficult year."

"*I* married a long way from home, and if you're implying I'm one of those 'difficulties,' I can assure you the girl has had it easy! *My* mother-in-law was a witch from hell — from hell, was she not, Utako?"

Utako half-nods, half-bows, and half-whispers, "Yes, ma'am."

"No one was calling you a 'difficulty.' " Uzaemon puts his hand on the latch.

"Okinu" — his mother puts her hand on the latch — "is a disappointment . . ."

"Mother, for my sake, would you please be

kind to her, as —"

". . . a disappointment to all of us. I never approved of the girl, did I, Utako?"

Utako half-nods, half-bows, and half-whispers, "No, ma'am."

"But you and your father were so set on her, so how could I voice my doubts?"

This rewriting of history, thinks Uzaemon, *is breathtaking, even by your high standards.*

"But a pilgrimage," she says, "is a fine chance to reconsider one's missteps."

A moon-gray cat, padding along the wall, catches Uzaemon's eye.

"Marriage, you see, is a transaction . . . Is something wrong?"

The moon-gray cat vanishes into the mist as if it never existed.

"Marriage, you were saying, Mother, is a transaction."

"A transaction, yes; and if one buys an item from a merchant and one finds that item to be broken, then the merchant must apologize, refund the money, and pray that the matter ends there. Now: *I* produced three boys and two girls for the Ogawa family, and although all but dear Hisanobu died in childhood, nobody could accuse me of being a broken item. I don't blame Okinu for her weak womb — some might, but I am fair-minded — yet the fact remains, we were sold bad merchandise. Who would blame us for returning it? Many would blame us — the ancestors of the

Ogawa clan — were we not to send her home."

Uzaemon sways away from his mother's magnified face.

A kite swoops low through the drizzle. Uzaemon hears its feathers.

"Many women have more than two miscarriages."

" 'It's a reckless farmer who wastes good seed on barren soil.' "

Uzaemon raises the latch, with her hand still on it, and swings open the door.

"I say all this," she says, smiling, "not from malice, but from duty . . ."

Here it comes, Uzaemon thinks, *the story of my adoption.*

". . . as it was I who advised your father to adopt you, instead of a richer or a nobler disciple, as his heir. This is why I feel a special responsibility in this matter, to ensure the Ogawa line."

Raindrops find the nape of Uzaemon's neck and trickle between his shoulder blades. "Goodbye."

Half Uzaemon's lifetime ago, in his thirteenth year, he made the two-week journey from Shikoku to Nagasaki with his first master, Kanamaru Motoji, the chief Dutch scholar to the Court of the lord of Tosa. After his adoption by Ogawa Mimasaku in his fifteenth year, he visited scholars as far away as Kumamoto with his new father, but since his appointment as interpreter of the third rank four years ago, Uzaemon has rarely left Nagasaki. His boyhood journeys were bright with promise, but this morning the interpreter — if "interpreter," Uzaemon concedes, *is what I still am* — is hounded by darker emotions. Hissing geese flee their cursing gooseherd; a shivering beggar shits at the loud river's edge; and mist and smoke obscure an assassin or spy beneath every domed hat and behind every palanquin's grille. *The road is busy enough to hide informers,* Uzaemon thinks with regret, *but not busy enough to hide me.* He passes the bridges of the Nakashima River, whose names he recites when he cannot sleep: the proud Tokiwabashi Bridge; the Fukurobashi, by the cloth merchants' warehouses; the Meganebashi, whose reflected double arches form round spectacles on bright days; the slim-hipped Uoichibashi; the matter-of-fact Higashishinbashi; upstream, past the execution grounds, Imoharabashi Bridge; the Furumachibashi, as old and frail-looking as its name; the lurching Amigasabashi; and, last and highest, the Ôidebashi. Uzaemon stops by a row of steps disappearing into the mist and remembers the spring day when he first arrived in Nagasaki.

A voice as small as a mouse's says, " 'Scuse, *o-junrei-sama . . .*"

Uzaemon needs a moment to realize that the "pilgrim" is him. He turns . . .

. . . and a wren of a boy with a gash for an eye is opening his cupped palms.

A voice warns Uzaemon, *He's begging for coins,* and the pilgrim walks away.

And you, a voice admonishes him, *are begging for good luck.*

So he turns and returns, but the gash-eyed boy is nowhere to be seen.

I am Adam Smith's translator, he tells himself. *I don't believe in omens.*

After a few minutes he reaches the Magome ward gate, where he lowers his hood, but a guard recognizes him as a samurai and waves him through with a bow.

Lean and rancid artisans' dwellings cluster along the road.

Rented looms *tack-ratta-clack*-ah, *tack-ratta-clack*-ah . . .

Rangy dogs and hungry children watch him pass, incuriously.

Mud splashes from the wheels of a fodder wagon sliding downhill; a farmer and his son pull it from behind, to help the ox in front. Uzaemon stands aside under a ginkgo tree and looks down to the harbor, but Dejima is lost in the thickening fog. *I am between two worlds.* He is leaving behind the politics of the Interpreters' Guild, the contempt of the inspectors and most of the Dutch, the deceits

514

and falsifications. *Ahead is an uncertain life with a woman who may not accept me, in a place not yet known.* In the ginkgo's knotted heart, a brood of oily crows fling insults. The wagon passes by, and the farmer bows as deeply as he can without losing his balance. The false pilgrim adjusts his shin bindings, secures his shoes, and resumes his journey. He mustn't miss his rendezvous with Shuzai.

The Joyful Phoenix Inn stands by a bend in the road, shy of the eight-mile stone from Nagasaki, between a shallow ford and a stone pit. Uzaemon enters, looking for Shuzai but seeing only the usual citizens of the road sheltering from the cold drizzle: palanquin carriers and porters, mule drivers, mendicants, a trio of prostitutes, a man with a fortune-telling monkey, and a bundled-up bearded merchant sitting near, but not with, his gang of servants. The place smells of damp people, steaming rice, and pig lard, but it is warmer and drier than outdoors. Uzaemon orders a bowl of walnut dumplings and enters the raised room, worrying about Shuzai and his five hired swords. He is not anxious about the large sum he has given to his friend to pay for the mercenaries: were Shuzai less honest than Uzaemon knows he is, the interpreter would have been arrested days ago. Rather, it is the possibility that Shuzai's sharp-eyed creditors sniffed out his plans to flee Nagasaki and threw a net around their debtor.

Someone knocks on the post: it is one of the landlord's girls, with his meal.

Uzaemon asks, "Is it already the Hour of the Horse?"

"Well past noon now, Samurai-*sama,* I do believe it is, yes . . ."

Five shogunal soldiers enter and the chatter dies away.

The soldiers look around the roomful of evasive faces.

The captain's eye meets Uzaemon's: Uzaemon looks down. *Don't look guilty,* he thinks. *I am a pilgrim bound for Kashima.*

"Landlord?" calls out one guard. "Where's the landlord of this shit hole?"

"Gentlemen!" The landlord emerges from the kitchen and kneels on the floor. "What an indescribable honor for the Joyful Phoenix."

"Hay and oats for our horses; your stable boy's flown off."

"Straightaway, Captain." The landlord knows he will have to accept a credit note that won't be honored without a bribe of five times its value. He gives orders to his wife, sons, and daughters, and the soldiers are shown into the best room in the rear. Cautiously, the chatter resumes.

"I don't forget a face, Samurai-*san.*" The bearded merchant has sidled over.

516

Avoid encounters, Shuzai warned him, *avoid witnesses.* "We never met."

"But to be sure we did — at Ryûgaji Temple on New Year's Day."

"You are mistaken. I never laid eyes on you. Now, please —"

"We talked about ray skins, Samurai-*san,* an' scabbards . . ."

Uzaemon recognizes Shuzai under the bedraggled beard and patched cloak.

"Aye, now you remember! Deguchi, Samurai-*san* — Deguchi of Osaka. Now, I wonder, might I hope for the honor of joining you?"

The maid arrives with a bowl of rice and pickles.

"I don't forget a face." Shuzai's grin is brown-toothed and his accent different.

The maid's expression tells Uzaemon, *What a tedious old fart.*

"No, Miss," Shuzai drawls. "Names slip away, but a face, never . . ."

"It's lone travelers who stick out." Shuzai's voice comes through the grille of his palanquin. "But a group of six, on the Isahaya Road? We're as good as invisible. To any part-time informers at the Joyful Phoenix, a taciturn pilgrim wearing a sword is worth watching. But when you left, you were just a pitiful bastard having his ear drilled by a human mosquito. By making you bored, I made you boring."

Mist blurs the farmhouses, erases the road ahead, hides the valley walls . . .

Deguchi's porters and servants turned out to be Shuzai's hired men: their weapons are hidden in the modified floor of the palanquin. *Tanuki* — Uzaemon memorizes their false names — *Kuma, Ishi, Hane, Shakke . . .* They avoid speaking to Uzaemon, as befits their disguise as porters. The remaining six men will be at Mekura Gorge tomorrow.

"By the way," asks Shuzai, "did you bring a certain dogwood scroll tube?"

Say no now, fears Uzaemon, *and he'll think you don't trust him.*

"Everything of value," he slaps his midriff, visible to Shuzai, "is here."

"Good. If the scroll had fallen into the wrong hands, Enomoto might be expecting us."

Succeed, and Jiritsu's testimony shan't be needed. Uzaemon is uneasy. *Fail, and it mustn't be captured.* How De Zoet could ever use this weapon is a question the interpreter cannot answer.

The river below is a drunk, charging boulders and barging banks.

"It's like the Shimantogawa Valley," says Shuzai, "in our home domain."

"The Shimantogawa," replies Uzaemon, "is

518

a friendlier river, I think." He has been wondering about applying for a court post back in his native Tosa. Upon adoption by the Ogawas of Nagasaki, all ties with his birth family were severed — *and they'd not be happy to see a third son, a "cold-rice eater," come back with no fortune and a half-burned wife* — but he wonders whether his former Dutch teacher might be willing and able to help. *Tosa is the first place,* Uzaemon worries, *Enomoto would look for us.*

It would be a matter of not just a fugitive nun but the lord of Kyôga's reputation.

His friend the Elder Councillor Matsudaira Sadanobu would issue a warrant . . .

Uzaemon glimpses the enormity of the risk he is taking.

Would they bother with a warrant? Or just dispatch an assassin?

Uzaemon looks away. To stop and think would be to abort the rescue.

Feet splash in puddles. The brown river surges. Pines drip.

Uzaemon asks Shuzai, "Are we to lodge at Isahaya tonight?"

"No. Deguchi of Osaka chooses the best: the Harubayashi Inn at Kurozane."

"Not the same inn where Enomoto and his entourage stay?"

"The very same. Come now, what group of bandits planning to steal a nun from Mount Shiranui Shrine would *dream* of staying there?"

Isahaya's principal temple is celebrating the festival of a local god, and the streets are busy enough with hawkers and floats and spectators for six strangers and a palanquin to slip through without notice. Street musicians vie for customers, petty thieves trawl the holiday crowds, and serving girls flirt in front of their inns to reel in customers. Shuzai stays inside his palanquin and orders his men to proceed directly to the gate into Kyôga Domain on the east side of the town. The guardhouse is overrun by a herd of pigs. One of the soldiers, dressed in the domain's austere livery, gives Deguchi of Osaka's pass a cursory glance and asks why the merchant has no merchandise. "I sent it all by ship, sir," answers Shuzai, his Osaka accent grown almost impenetrable, "every last piece, sir. By the time every customs man in western Honshu's had his nibble, I'd not be left with the wrinkles on my hands, sir." He is waved through, but another, more observant guard notices that Uzaemon's pass is issued via the headman's office on Dejima. "You're an interpreter for the foreigners, Ogawa-*san?*"

"Of the third rank, yes, in the Interpreters' Guild on Dejima."

"I just ask, sir, because of your pilgrim's clothes."

"My father is gravely ill. I wish to pray for

him at Kashima."

"Please" — the guard kicks a squealing piglet — "step into the inspection room."

Uzaemon stops himself from looking at Shuzai. "Very well."

"I'll be with you once we've cleared these porkers away."

The interpreter steps into the small room where a scribe is at work.

Uzaemon curses his luck. *So much for slipping into Kyôga anonymously.*

"Please forgive this inconvenience." The guard appears and orders the scribe to wait outside. "I sense, Ogawa-*san,* you are a man of your word."

"I aspire," Uzaemon answers, worried where this may lead, "to be one, yes."

"Then I" — the guard kneels and bows low — "I aspire to your good offices, sir. My son's skull is growing . . . wrong, lumpen. We — we daren't take him outside, because people call him an *oni* demon. He's clever and a fine reader, so it's not affected his wits, but . . . he has these headaches, these terrible headaches."

Uzaemon is disarmed. "What do the doctors say?"

"The first diagnosed 'burning brain' and prescribed three gallons of water a day to quench the fires. 'Water poisoning,' said the second, and bid us parch our son until his tongue turned black. The third doctor sold us golden acupuncture needles to press into his skull to expel the demon, and the fourth sold us a magic frog, to be licked thirty-three times a day. Nothing worked. Soon he won't be able to lift his head . . ."

Uzaemon recalls Dr. Maeno's recent lecture on elephantiasis.

". . . so I'm asking all the pilgrims who pass through to pray at Kashima."

"Gladly, I'll recite a healing sutra. What is your son's name?"

"Thank you. Lots of pilgrims say they will, but it's only men of honor I can believe in. I'm Imada, and my son's name is Uokatsu, written on this." He passes a folded slip of paper and a lock of his hair. "There'll be a fee, so —"

"Keep your money. I will pray for Imada Uokatsu when I pray for my father."

The shogun's policy of isolation preserves his *power unchallenged . . .*

"May I suppose," the soldier is bowing again, "Ogawa-*san* also has a son?"

. . . but sentences Uokatsu and countless others to futile, ignorant deaths.

"My wife and I" — *more details,* Uzaemon thinks with regret — "are not yet blessed."

"Lady Kannon will reward your kindness, sir. Now, I am delaying you . . ."

Uzaemon stores the name paper in his *inrô* pouch. "I wish I could do more."

CHAPTER
TWENTY-FIVE:
THE LORD ABBOT'S
QUARTERS AT
MOUNT SHIRANUI
SHRINE

The twenty-second night of the first month
The swaying flames are moonflower blue and silent. Enomoto is seated behind a sunken hearth at the far end of a thin room. The roof is vaulted and ill-defined. He knows Orito is there but does not yet look up. Nearby, the two motionless boy aspirants stare at a *go* board; but for the twitching pulses in their necks, they could be cast from bronze. "You look like an assassin, hovering there . . ." Enomoto's sinewy voice reaches her. "Approach, Sister Aibagawa."

Her feet obey. Orito sits across the watery fire from the lord of Kyôga. He is examining the craftsmanship of what may be a bladeless sword hilt. In the strange firelight, Enomoto looks a full decade younger than she remembers.

If I were an assassin, she thinks, *you would already be dead.*

"What would happen to your sisters without my protection and the house?"

It is faces he reads, thinks Orito, *not minds.* "The House of Sisters is a jail."

"Your sisters would die, miserably and early, in brothels and freak shows."

"How is that to justify their captivity here as monks' playthings?"

Click: an aspirant has placed a black counter on the board.

"Dr. Aibagawa, your honorable father, respected facts, not opinions twisted out of shape."

The sword hilt in Enomoto's hand is, Orito sees, a pistol.

"The sisters are not 'playthings.' They dedicate twenty years to the Goddess and are provided for after their descents. Many spiritual orders make similar pacts with their adherents but demand lifelong service."

"What 'spiritual order' harvests infants from its nuns like your private sect does?"

Darkness uncoils and slides around the edges of Orito's vision.

"The fertility of the world below is fed by a river. Shiranui is its spring."

Orito sifts his tone and words for cynicism but finds faith. "How can an academician — a translator of Isaac Newton — speak like a superstitious peasant?"

"Enlightenment can blind one, Orito. Apply all the empirical methodology you desire to time, gravity, life: their genesis and purposes are, at root, unknowable. It is not superstition but reason that concludes the realm of knowledge is finite and that the brain and the soul are discrete entities."

Click: an aspirant has placed a white counter on the board.

"You never treated the Shirandô Academy to this insight, as I recall."

"We are a spiritual order of limited numbers. The way of Shiranui is no more the way of the scholar than it is the way of the common herd."

"What noble words for a squalid truth. You coop women up for twenty years, impregnate them, snatch the infants from their breasts — and forge letters to their mothers from all the dead ones as they grow up!"

"Just three sadly deceased gifts have their New Year letters written: three out of thirty-six — or thirty-eight, including Sister Yayoi's twins. All the others are genuine. Abbess Izu believes this fiction is kinder to the sisters, and experience bears her out."

"Do the sisters thank you for this kindness when they discover that the son or daughter they wish to join after descent died eighteen years ago?"

"This misfortune has never occurred during my abbotship."

"Sister Hatsune *is* intending to join her dead daughter, Noriko."

525

"Her descent is two years away. If her mind is unchanged, I will explain."

The bell of Amanohashira rings for the Hour of the Dog.

"It saddens me," Enomoto says, leaning into the fire, "that you view us as jailers. Perhaps it is a consequence of your relative rank. One birth every two years is a lighter levy than most wives in the world below must endure. To most of your sisters, the masters delivered them from servitude into a pure land on earth."

"Mount Shiranui Shrine is far from *my* imagining of the pure land."

"The daughter of Aibagawa Seian is a rare woman. A singular case."

"I'd prefer not to hear Father's name on your lips."

"Aibagawa Seian was my trusted friend before he was your father."

"A friendship you repay by stealing his orphaned daughter?"

"I brought you home, Sister Aibagawa."

"I had a home, in Nagasaki."

"But Shiranui was your home, even before you heard its name. Learning of your vocation in midwifery, I knew. Watching you at the Shirandô Academy, I knew. Years ago, recognizing the Goddess's mark on your face, I —"

"My face was burned by a pan of hot oil. It was an accident!"

Enomoto smiles like an adoring father. "The Goddess summoned you. She revealed her true self to you, did she not?"

Orito has spoken to no one, not even Yayoi, about the spherical cave and its strange giantess.

Click: an aspirant places a black counter on the board.

There was a secret seal, logic assures her, *entering the tunnel.*

Wings beat in the spaces overhead, but when Orito looks up, she sees nothing.

"When you ran away," Enomoto is saying, "the Goddess called you back . . ."

Once I believe this lunacy, Orito thinks, *I am truly Shiranui's prisoner.*

". . . and your soul obeyed, because your soul knows what your mind is too knowledgeable to understand."

"I came back because Yayoi would have died if I hadn't."

"You were an instrument of the Goddess's compassion. You shall be rewarded."

Her dread of engiftment opens its ugly mouth. "I . . . can't have done to me what is done to the others. I can't." Orito is ashamed of these words, and ashamed of her shame. *Spare me what the others endure,* the words mean, and Orito begins to tremble. *Burn!* she urges herself. *Be angry!*

Click: an aspirant has placed a white clamshell counter on the board.

Enomoto's voice is a caress. "All of us — the Goddess most of all — know what you sacrificed to be here. Look at me with your wise eyes, Orito. We wish to offer you a proposal. No doubt a doctor's daughter like yourself has noticed Housekeeper Satsuki's poor health. It is, sadly, a cancer of the womb. She has asked to die on her home island. My men shall take her there in a few days. Her post as housekeeper is yours, if you want it. The Goddess blesses the house with a gift every five or six weeks: your twenty years at the shrine would be spent as a practicing midwife, helping your sisters and deepening your knowledge. Such a valuable asset to my shrine would never be engifted. In addition, I shall procure books — any books — you wish, so you can follow in your father's scholarly footsteps. After your descent, I shall purchase you a house in Nagasaki, or anywhere else, and pay you a stipend for the rest of your life."

For four months, Orito realizes, *the house has bludgeoned me with fear . . .*

"You'd be less a sister of Shiranui Shrine than a sister of life."

. . . so that this proposal seems not a tether, or a noose, but a rope lowered to a drowning woman.

Four knocks at the door send ripples across the room.

Enomoto glances past Orito and nods once.

528

"Ah, a long-expected friend has arrived to return a stolen item. I must go and present him with a token of gratitude." Midnight-blue silk flows upward as Enomoto stands. "Meanwhile, Sister, consider our offer."

CHAPTER TWENTY-SIX: BEHIND THE HARUBAYASHI INN, EAST OF KUROZANE VILLAGE IN KYÔGA DOMAIN

The twenty-second morning of the first month
Emerging from the rear privy, Uzaemon looks across the vegetable patch and sees a figure watching him from the bamboo grove. He squints through the half-light. *Otane the herbalist?* She has the same black hood and mountain clothes. *She could be.* She has the same bent back. *Yes.* Uzaemon raises a cautious hand, but the figure turns away, with a slow, sad shake of her gray head.

No, he mustn't acknowledge her? Or *No,* the rescue is doomed?

The interpreter puts on a pair of straw sandals left on the veranda and crosses the ruckled vegetable patch to the bamboo. A path of black mud and white frost winds through the grove.

Back at the inn, the rooster crows in the forecourt.

Shuzai and the others, he thinks, *will be wondering where I am.*

Straw shoes offer little protection for a clerical samurai's soft feet.

On a snapped cane at eye level is a waxwing: its mouth opens . . .

. . . its throat vibrates and spatters out a tuneless tune . . .

In short arcs it hops, from perch to perch, through the thick grove.

Uzaemon follows through slanted bars of light dark and dark dark . . .

. . . through the pressing confinement; thin panes of ice shatter underfoot.

Up ahead, the waxwing beckons him onward, or over to one side?

Are two waxwings, Uzaemon wonders, *toying with one human?*

"Is anyone there?" He dares not raise his voice. "Otane-*sama?*"

The leaves shuffle like paper. The path ends at a noisy river, brown and thick like Dutchmen's tea.

The far bank is a wall of gouged rock . . .

. . . rising up beneath splayed boughs and knuckled roots.

A toe of Mount Shiranui, Uzaemon thinks. *At its head, Orito is waking.*

Upriver, or downriver, a man is shouting in a hunchbacked dialect.

■ ■ ■ ■

But the path back to the rear garden of the Harubayashi Inn delivers Uzaemon into a hidden clearing. Here, on a bed of dark pebbles, several dozen head-sized sea-smoothed rocks are enclosed within a knee-high stone wall. There is no shrine, no *torî* gate, no straw ropes hung with paper twists, so it takes the interpreter a little time to recognize that he is in a cemetery. Hugging himself against the cold, he steps over the wall to examine the headstones. The pebbles grind and give beneath his feet.

Numbers, not names, are engraved on the rocks: up to eighty-one.

Invasive bamboo is kept back, and lichen is cleaned from the stones.

Uzaemon wonders if the woman he mistook for Otane is a caretaker.

Perhaps she took fright, he thinks, *at a samurai charging her way . . .*

But what Buddhist sect spurns even desultory death names on its headstones? Without a death name for Lord Enma's Register of the Dead, as every child knows, a soul is turned away at the next world's gates. Their ghosts drift for all eternity. Uzaemon speculates that the buried are miscarried children, criminals, or suicides, but is not quite convinced. Even members of the untouchable caste are buried with some sort of name.

There is no birdsong, he notices, in winter's cage.

"More than likely, sir," the landlord tells Uzaemon back at the inn, "it was a certain charcoal burner's girl you saw. She lives with her father 'n' brother in a tumbledown cottage an' a million starlings in the thatch, up past Twelve Fields. She drifts this-a-way 'n' that-a-way up 'n' down the river, sir. Weak-headed an' stumble-footed, she is, an' she's been with child twice or three times, but they never take root 'cause the daddy was *her* daddy, or else her brother, an' she'll die in that tumbledown cottage alone, sir, for what family'd want such impureness dilutin' its blood?"

"But it was an old woman I saw, not a girl."

"Kyôga mares are fatter-hipped than the princesses o' Nagasaki, sir: a local girl o' thirteen, fourteen'd pass for an old mare, specially in half-light."

Uzaemon is dubious. "Then what about this secret graveyard?"

"Oh, there's no secret, sir: in the hostelers' trade it's what we call our 'long stayers' quarters.' There's many a traveler who falls sick on the road, sir, 'specially on a pilgrims' route, an' sleep their last in inns, an' it costs us landlords a handsome ransom. An' 'ransom' is the word: we can't very well dump the body by the roadside. What if a relative comes along? What if the ghost scares off business? But a proper funeral needs money, same as everythin' else in this world, sir, what with priests for chantin' an' a stonecutter for a nice tomb an' a plot of earth in the temple . . ." The landlord shakes his head. "So, an ancestor of mine cleared the cemetery in the copse for the benefit, sir, of guests who pass away at the Harubayashi. We keep a proper register of the guests lyin' there, an' number the stones proper, too, an' write down the guests' names if they said one, an' if it's a man or woman, an' guess their age, an' whatnot. So if any relatives do come lookin', we can maybe help."

Shuzai asks, "Are your dead guests often claimed by their relatives?"

"Not once in my time, sir, but we do it, anyway. My wife washes the stones every *O-bon*."

Uzaemon asks, "When was the last body interred there?"

The innkeeper purses his lips. "Fewer single travelers pass through Kyôga, sir, now the Omura Road's so much improved . . . Last one was three years ago: a printer gentleman, who went to bed fit as a goat but come mornin' he was cold as stone. Makes you think, sir, doesn't it?"

Uzaemon is unsettled by the innkeeper's tone. "What does it make you think?"

"It's not just the aged an' frail Death bundles into his palanquin."

The Kyôga road follows the Ariake Sea's muddy shore and then inland through a wood, where one of the hired men, Hane, falls behind and another, Ishi, runs on ahead. "A precaution," explains Shuzai, from inside his palanquin, "to make sure we aren't being followed from Kurozane or expected up ahead." Several upward shrugs of the road later, they cross the narrow Mekura River and take a leaf-strewn track turning up toward the gorge's mouth. By a moss-blotched *torî* gate, a notice board turns away casual visitors. Here the palanquin is lowered, the weapons removed from its false floor, and, before Uzaemon's eyes, Deguchi of Osaka and his long-suffering servants turn into mercenaries. Shuzai emits a sharp whistle. Uzaemon hears nothing — unless a twig cracking is something — but the men hear a signal that all is well. They run with the empty palanquin, climbing shallow curves. The interpreter is soon out of breath. A waterfall's clatter and boom grows louder and nearer, and around a recent rock fall the men arrive at the lower mouth of Mekura Gorge: a stepped cutting in a low escarpment as high as eight or nine men, cloaked and choked by long-tongued ferns and throttling creepers. Down this drop the cold river plunges. The pool below churns and boils.

Uzaemon becomes a prisoner of the ever-plunging waterfall . . .

She drinks from this river, he thinks, *where it is a mountain stream.*

. . . until a thrush whistles in a flank of wild camellia. Shuzai whistles back. The leaves part and five men emerge. They are dressed in commoners' clothes, but their faces have the same military hardness as the other masterless samurai. "Let's get this crate on poles" — Shuzai indicates his battered palanquin — "out of sight."

Hidden by the wall of camellia in a hollow where the palanquin is covered with branches and leaves. Shuzai introduces the new men by false names: Tsuru, the moon-faced leader, Yagi, Kenka, Muguchi, and Bara; Uzaemon, still dressed as a pilgrim, is named "Junrei." The new men show him a distant respect, but they look to Shuzai as the leader of the expedition. Whether the mercenaries view Uzaemon as a besotted fool or an honorable man — *and maybe,* Uzaemon considers, *one may be both* — they give no sign. The samurai named Tsuru gives a brief account of their journey from Saga down to Kurozane, and the interpreter thinks of the small steps that gathered this raiding party: Otane the herbalist's accurate guess at the contents of his heart; Jiritsu the acolyte's revulsion at the order's creeds; Enomoto's

536

nefariousness; and more steps; and more twists — some known, and others not — and Uzaemon marvels at the weaverless loom of fortune.

"The first part of our ascent," Shuzai is saying, "we'll make in six groups of two, leaving at five-minute intervals. First, Tsuru and Yagi; second, Kenka and Muguchi; third, Bara and Tanuki; next, Kuma and Ishi; then, Hane and Shakke; and last, Junrei," he looks at Uzaemon, "and me. We'll regroup below the gatehouse" — the men cluster around an inked map of the mountainside, their breaths mingling — "guarding this natural revile. I'll lead Bara and Tanuki, Tsuru and Hane over this bluff, and we'll storm the gate from uphill — the unexpected direction — shortly after the change of guard. We'll bind, gag, and bag them with the ropes and sacks. They're just farm boys, so don't kill them, unless they insist. Bare Peak is another two hours' stiff march, so the monks will be settling down for the night by the time we arrive. Kuma, Hane, Shakke, Ishi: scale the wall here" — Shuzai now unfolds his picture of the shrine — "on the southwest side, where the trees are closest and thickest. First, go to the gatehouse here and let the rest of us in. Then we send for the highest-ranking master. Him we inform that Sister Aibagawa is leaving with us. This will happen peacefully or over a courtyard of slain acolytes. The choice is his." Shuzai looks at Uzaemon. "A threat you aren't willing to carry through is no threat at all."

Uzaemon nods, but, *Please,* he prays, *don't let any life be lost.*

"Junrei's face," Shuzai tells the others, "is known to Enomoto from the Shirandô Academy. Although our obliging landlord informed us that the lord abbot is in Miyako at present, Junrei mustn't risk being identified, even secondhand. That is why you shall take no part in the raid."

It is unacceptable, thinks Uzaemon, *to cower outside like a woman.*

"I know what you're thinking," says Shuzai, "but you are not a killer."

Uzaemon nods, intending to change Shuzai's mind during the day.

"When we leave, I'll warn the monks that I'll cut down any pursuers without mercy. We then withdraw, with the freed prisoner. We'll cut the vines of Todoroki Bridge to win us more time tomorrow. We pass through the halfway gatehouse during the Hour of the Ox, descend the gorge, and arrive back here by the Hour of the Rabbit. We carry the woman in the palanquin as far as Kashima. There we disperse and leave the domain before horsemen can be dispatched. Any questions?"

■ ■ ■ ■

Winter woods are creaking, knitted and knotted. Dead leaves lie in deep drifts. Needle tips of birdsong stitch and thread the thicket's many layers. Shuzai and Uzaemon climb in silence. Here the Mekura River is a bellowing, roiling, echoing thing. The granite sky entombs the valley.

By mid-morning, the arches of Uzaemon's blistered feet are aching.

Here the Mekura River is as smooth and green as foreign glass.

Shuzai gives Uzaemon oil to rub into his aching calves and ankles, saying, "The swordsman's first weapon is his feet."

On a round rock, an immobile heron waits for fish.

"The men you hired," ventures Uzaemon, "seem to trust you entirely."

"Some of us studied under the same master in Imabari; most of us served under a minor lordling of Iyo Domain who provoked some fierce skirmishes with his neighbor. To have relied on a man to stay alive is a bond closer than blood."

A splash punctures the jade pool: the heron is gone.

Uzaemon recalls an uncle teaching him long ago to skim stones. He recalls the old woman he saw at sunrise. "There are times when I suspect that the mind has a mind of its own. It shows us pictures. Pictures of the past, and the might-one-day-be. This mind's mind exerts its own will, too, and has its own voice." He looks at his friend, who is watching a bird of prey high above them. "I am sounding like a drunken priest."

"Not at all," mumbles Shuzai. "Not at all."

Higher up the mountainside, limestone cliffs wall in the gorge. Uzaemon begins to see parts of faces in the weatherworn escarpments. A bulge looks like a forehead, a protruding ridge a nose, and excoriations and rock slides, wrinkles and sags. *Even mountains*, thinks Uzaemon, *were once young, and age, and one day die.* One black rift under a shrub-hairy overhang could be a narrowed eye. He imagines ten thousand bats hanging from its ruckled roof . . .

. . . *all waiting for one spring evening to ignite their small hearts.*

The higher the altitude, the climber sees, the deeper life must hide from winter. Sap is sunk to roots; bears sleep; next year's snakes are eggs.

My Nagasaki life, Uzaemon considers, *is as gone as my childhood in Shikoku.*

Uzaemon thinks of his adoptive parents and his wife conducting their affairs, intrigues, and squabbles, but not guessing that they have lost their adopted son and husband. The process will take many months.

He touches the place over his midriff where he carries Orito's letters.

Soon, beloved, soon, he thinks. *Just a few hours more . . .*

By trying not to remember the creeds of the order, he remembers them.

His hand, he finds, is gripping his sword hilt tight enough to blanch his knuckles.

He wonders whether Orito is already pregnant.

I will care for her, he swears, *and raise the child as my own.*

Silver birches shiver. *Whatever she wishes is all that matters.*

"What was it like," Uzaemon asks a question he's never asked Shuzai before, "the first time you killed a man?" Sycamore roots grip a steep bank. Shuzai leads for another ten, twenty, thirty paces, until the path arrives at a wide and lapping pool. Shuzai checks the steep, surrounding terrain, as if for ambushers . . .

. . . and cocks his head like a dog. He hears something Uzaemon does not.

The swordsman's half smile says, *One of ours.* "Killing depends on circumstances, as you'd expect, whether it's a cold, planned murder, or a hot death in a fight, or inspired by honor or a more shameful motive. However many times you kill, though, it's the first that matters. It's a man's first blood that banishes him from the world of the ordinary." Shuzai kneels at the water's edge and drinks water from his cupped hands. A feathery fish hovers in the current; a bright berry floats by. "That reckless lordling of Iyo I told you about?" Shuzai climbs onto a rock. "I was sixteen and sworn to serve the greedy dolt. The feud's history is too long to explain here, but my role in it had me blundering through a thicket on the flank of Mount Ishizuchi one stewed night in the sixth month, separated from my comrades. The frogs' racket smothered other sound and the darkness was blinding, and suddenly the ground gave way and I fell into an enemy ditch. The scout was as unprepared as I was, and the ditch so stuffed with our two bodies that neither of us could reach our swords. We fumbled and writhed, but neither of us yelled for help. His hands found my throat and clamped and squeezed, tight as Death. My mind was red and shrieking and my throat was crumpling and I thought, *This is it* . . . but Fate disagreed. Long ago, Fate had chosen for the enemy lord's crest a crescent moon. This insignia was attached to my strangler's helmet so poorly that it snapped off in my hand, so I could slip its sharp metal point through the slit of his eye mask, through the softness behind it, and side to side like a knife in a yam until his grip on my windpipe weakened and fell away."

Uzaemon washes his hands and drinks some water from the pool.

"Afterward," says Shuzai, "in marketplaces, cities, hamlets . . ."

The icy water strikes Uzaemon's jawbone like a Dutch tuning fork.

". . . I thought, *I am in this world, but no longer of this world.*"

A wildcat paces along the bough of a fallen elm, bridging the path.

"This lack of belonging, it marks us" — Shuzai frowns — "around the eyes."

The wildcat looks at the men, unafraid, and yawns.

It leaps down to a rock, laps water, and disappears.

"Some nights," Shuzai says, "I wake to find his fingers choking me."

Uzaemon is hiding in a deep, weather-sculpted crater, like a molar's indentation, a wiry-rooted scramble above the track, with the two mercenaries going by the names Kenka and Muguchi. Kenka is a lithe man of many small and fluid motions, while Muguchi is a stockier, cut-lipped miser of words. From their crater, the men have a partial view of the halfway gatehouse, just an arrow shot away. Smoke blows down from the structure's crude vent. Uphill, upwind, and above the bluff, Shuzai and four of the men are waiting for the guards to change. Across the river, something tears through the wood.

"Wild boar," mutters Kenka. "Sounds like a fat old thumper."

They hear a shadowy far-off bell that must belong to the Shrine of Mount Shiranui.

As improbable as a theatrical backdrop, Bare Peak hangs in the sky under clouds massy and crumpling.

"Rain'd be useful," remarks Kenka, "so long as it waits till we're done. It'd wipe our tracks, swell the rivers, make the roads worse for horses, and —"

"Voices?" Muguchi's hand demands quiet. "Listen — three men . . ."

Uzaemon hears nothing for a minute or more, until the embittered voice on the track below is very near. "Before we was married, she was, 'No, after we're married I'm yours but not till then,' but since the wedding she's all, 'No, I ain't in the mood, so paws off.' All I did was knock sense into her, like any husband would, but since then the demon in the blacksmith's wife jumped into mine an' now she won't look at me. Can't even divorce the she-viper, for fear her uncle'd take back his boat, an' then where'd I be?"

"High an' dry," says a second companion, passing below. "That's where."

The three approach the gates. "Open up,

Buntarô," one calls out. "It's us."

"It's 'us,' is it?" The shout is muffled. "An' who might 'us' be?"

"Ichirô, Ubei, and Tôsui," answers one, "and Ichirô's moanin' 'bout his wife."

"We can find room for the first three, but leave the last outside."

Ten minutes later, the three off-duty guards emerge. "So, Buntarô," says one, as they draw into earshot. "Serve us up the juicy bits."

"Those're 'tween me, Ichirô's wife, and his tell-no-lies futon."

"Tight as a turtle's slit, *you* are, you . . ." The voices fade away.

Uzaemon, Kenka, and Muguchi watch the gate, wait, and listen.

Minute follows minute follows minute follows minute . . .

There is no sunset, just a steady fading of the light.

Something's gone wrong. Fear hisses inside Uzaemon.

Muguchi announces, "Done." One of the gatehouse gates swings open. A form appears and waves a hand. By the time Uzaemon has scrambled down to the track, the other men are halfway to the gatehouse. Waiting for the interpreter at the gate is Kenka, who whispers, "Don't speak." Inside, Uzaemon finds a sheltered porch and a long room built on props and stilts over the river. There is a rack for pikes and axes, an upended cooking pot, a smoldering fire, and three large sacks suspended by ropes from a rafter. First one and then another of the sacks moves, and a bulge shifts, betraying an elbow or knee. The nearest sack, however, hangs motionless as a bag of stones.

Bara is wiping a throwing knife on a bloodied rag . . .

The river flowing underneath clamors with human syllables.

Your sword didn't kill him, Uzaemon thinks, *but your presence here did.*

Shuzai leads Uzaemon up through the rear gates. "We told them we meant them no harm. We told them nobody need be hurt. We said that although samurai cannot surrender, farmers and fishermen can. They agreed to be gagged and bound, but one tried to outwit us. There's a trapdoor in the corner, over the river, and he made a lunge for it. He almost reached it, and had he escaped, things would have gone badly for us. Bara's throwing knife opened his throat, and Tsuru only just saved the body from being washed down to Kurozane."

Is Ichirô's wife, Uzaemon wonders, *now both adulteress* and *widow?*

"He didn't suffer." Shuzai grips his arm. "He was dead within a few seconds."

By night, Mekura Gorge becomes a primordial place. The twelve-strong raiding party walks in single file. The track now rises above the river, clinging to the steep side of the gorge. The aches and creaks of beeches and oaks give way to heavy-breathing evergreens. Shuzai has chosen a moonless night, but the clouds are disintegrating, and the starlight is bright enough to gild the darkness.

He didn't suffer, Uzaemon thinks. *He was dead within seconds.*

He places one sore foot in front of the other and tries not to think.

A quiet life of schoolmastering, Uzaemon imagines a future, *in a quiet town . . .*

He places one sore foot in front of the other and tries not to think.

Maybe a quiet life was all the slain guard wanted, as well . . .

His earlier zeal to take part in the raid on the monastery has gone.

His mind's mind shows him the scene of Bara wiping his knife on the bloodied cloth, over and over, until at last the men arrive at Todoroki Bridge.

Shuzai and Tsuru discuss how best to sabotage it later.

An owl cries, in this cedar or that fir . . . once, twice, nearby . . .

The shrine's last chime of the day, loud and close, announces the late Hour of the Rooster. *Before it rings again,* Uzaemon thinks, *Orito will be freed.* The men wrap their faces in black cloth, leaving only a narrow band for their eyes and noses. They proceed stealthily, not expecting an ambush but not discounting the possibility. When Uzaemon snaps a twig underfoot, the others turn around, glaring. The incline lessens. A fox barks. The tunnel-like succession of *torî* gates begins, slicing the crosswind. The men stop and gather around Shuzai. "The shrine is four hundred paces uphill."

"Junrei-*san*." Shuzai turns to Uzaemon. "Here is where you wait. Remember your sage: 'One pays an army for a thousand days to use it for one.' That day is now. Hide away from the path, but stay warm. You've come farther than most 'clients' ever do, so there's no dishonor in waiting here. Once our business in the monastery is accomplished, I'll send for you, but don't approach the shrine until then. Don't worry. We are warriors. They are a handful of monks."

Uzaemon climbs a short distance through stony ice and drifts of pine needles, to a sheltered bowl out of the worst of the wind; he crouches and stands repeatedly until his hamstrings ache but his legs and torso are warmed through. The night sky is an indecipherable manuscript. Uzaemon remembers last studying the stars with De Zoet on Dejima's watchtower, back in the summer, when the world was simpler. He tries to imagine a sequence of pictures entitled *The Bloodless Liberation of Aibagawa Orito:* here are Shuzai and three samurai, scaling the wall; here, three monks in the gatehouse, surprised into submission; and here comes the head monk, hurrying across the ancient courtyard, muttering, "Lord Enomoto will be displeased, but what choice have we?" Orito is woken and ordered to dress for a journey. She ties her headscarf around her beautiful, burned face. The last picture gives her expression when she recognizes her rescuer. Uzaemon shivers and performs some exercises with his sword, but it is too cold to concentrate, so he turns his thoughts to choosing a name for his new life. Unwittingly, Shuzai has selected his given name — Junrei, the pilgrim — but what about a family name? He may discuss this with Orito: perhaps he could adopt her Aibagawa. *I am tempting Fate,* he warns himself, *to snatch my prize away.* He rubs his cold-gnawed hands, wondering how much time has passed since Shuzai led the attack, and finds he has no inkling. *An eighth of an hour? A quarter?* The shrine bell hasn't rung since they crossed Todoroki Bridge, but the monks have no reason to mark the hours of the night. How long should he wait before concluding that the rescue has foundered? Then what? If Shuzai's masterless samurai were overcome by force, what chance would a former interpreter of the third rank have?

Thoughts of death creep through the pine trees toward Uzaemon.

He wishes the human mind were a scroll that could be rolled up . . .

"Junrei-*san*, we have the —"

Uzaemon is so startled by the speaking tree that he falls on his backside.

"Did we startle you?" A boulder's shadow turns into the mercenary Tanuki.

"Just a little, yes." Uzaemon steadies his breathing.

Kenka appears from the tree. "We have the woman, safe and sound."

"That's good," says Uzaemon. "That's very, very good."

A calloused hand finds Uzaemon's and lifts him to his feet. "Was anyone hurt?" Uzaemon meant to ask, "In what state is Orito?"

"Nobody," says Tanuki. "Master Genmu's a man of peace."

"Meaning," adds Kenka, "he shan't have his shrine polluted by bloodshed for the sake of one nun. But he's also a wily old fox, and Deguchi-*san* wants you to come and check that the man of peace isn't fobbing us off with a decoy before we leave and they barricade the gate."

"There are two nuns with burned faces." Tanuki uncorks a small flask and drinks from it. "I went inside the House of Sisters. What a strange menagerie Enomoto's assembled! Here, drink this: it'll protect you from the cold and bolster your strength. Waiting is worse than doing."

"I'm warm enough." Uzaemon shivers. "There's no need."

"You have three days to put a hundred miles between yourself and Kyôga Domain, preferably on Honshu. You won't get that far with a chill in your lungs. Drink!"

Uzaemon accepts the mercenary's gruff kindness. The spirit scalds his throat. "Thank you."

The trio make their way back down to the tunnel of *torî* gates.

"Assuming you saw the correct Aibagawa-*san,* in what state is she?"

The pause is long enough for Uzaemon to fear the worst.

"Gaunt," answers Tanuki, "but well enough, I'd say. Calm."

"Her mind's sharp," adds Kenka. "She's not asking us who we are: she knows her captors might overhear. I can see why a man might go to all this time and expense for a woman like that."

They arrive at the track and begin the climb through the *torî* gates.

Uzaemon notices a strange elasticity in his legs. *Nerves,* he thinks, *are natural.*

But soon the path is undulating like the slow swell of waves.

The last two days have been taxing. He steadies his breathing. *The worst is over.*

Past the *torî* gates, the ground flattens. The shrine of Mount Shiranui rears up.

Roofs hunker behind high walls. Weak light escapes a gap in the gates.

He hears Dr. Marinus's harpsichord. He thinks, *Impossible.*

His cheek presses the frosted leaf mold, soft as a woman's midriff.

Awareness begins in the membranes of his nose and spreads through his head, but his body cannot move. Questions and statements assert themselves like a throng of sickbed visitors: "You fainted again," says one. "You are indoors in Mount Shiranui Shrine," says another, and then they all speak at once: "Were you drugged?"; "You are sitting upright on a cold floor of beaten earth"; "Yes, you *were* drugged: Tanuki's *drink?*"; "Your wrists are bound behind a pillar and your ankles are tied"; "Was Shuzai betrayed by some of his men?"

"He can hear us now, Abbot," says an unknown voice.

The tip of a glass bottle brushes Uzaemon's nostril.

"Thank you, Suzaku," says a voice he knows but cannot yet place.

The smell of rice, *sake,* and pickled vegetables suggests a storehouse.

Orito's letters. There is an emptiness at his midriff. *They're gone.*

Wasps of pain crawl in and out through the stump of his brain.

"Open your eyes, Ogawa the Younger," says Enomoto. "We aren't children."

He obeys. The lord of Kyôga's face rises in lantern-lit darkness.

"You are an estimable scholar," says the face, "but a risible thief."

Three or four human shapes watch from the edges of the storeroom.

"I didn't come here," Uzaemon tells his captor, "to steal anything that is yours."

"Why oblige me to spell out what is obvious? Mount Shiranui Shrine is an organ in the body of the Domain of Kyôga. The sisters belong to that shrine."

"She was neither her stepmother's to sell nor yours to buy."

"Sister Aibagawa is a glad servant of the Goddess. She has no wish to leave."

"Let her tell me so from her own lips."

"No. Some habits of mind from her old life had to be" — Enomoto pretends to search for the right verb — "cauterized. Her scars are healed, but only a negligent lord abbot would allow a dithering onetime sweetheart to pick at them."

The others, thinks Uzaemon. *What about Shuzai and the others?*

"Shuzai is alive, well," says Enomoto, "and

553

drinking soup in the kitchen with my other ten men. Your plot put them all to some trouble."

Uzaemon refuses to believe. *I've known Shuzai for ten years.*

"He is *a* loyal friend." Enomoto tries not to smile. "But not *your* loyal friend."

A lie, Uzaemon's mind insists, *a lie. A key to pick the lock of my mind . . .*

"Why *would* I lie?" Midnight-blue watered silk flows upward as Enomoto reseats himself much closer. "No, the cautionary tale of Ogawa Uzaemon pertains to discontent. Adopted into a once-illustrious family, he climbed by talent to a high rank, enjoying the respect of the Shirandô Academy, a secure stipend, a pretty wife, and enviable trading opportunities with the Dutch. Who could want more? Ogawa Uzaemon wanted more! He was infected with that sickness the world calls true love. In the end, it killed him."

The human forms around the edges bestir themselves.

I shan't beg for my life, Uzaemon avows, *but I shall learn why and how.* "How much did you pay Shuzai to betray me?"

"Come! The lord of Kyôga's favor is worth more than a hunter's bounty."

"There was a young man, a guard, who died at the halfway gate . . ."

"A spy in the pay of the lord of Saga: your

554

adventure gave us a pleasing way to kill him."

"Why bother bringing me all the way up Mount Shiranui?"

"Assassinations in Nagasaki can lead to awkward questions, and the poetry of your dying so very near your beloved — mere rooms away! — was irresistible."

"Let me see her." The wasps swarm in Uzaemon's brain. "Or I will kill you from the other side."

"How gratifying: a dying curse from a Shirandô scholar! Alas, I have empirical proof enough to satisfy a Descartes or even a Marinus that dying curses don't work. Down the ages, many hundreds of men, women, and even quite small children have all vowed to drag me down to hell. Yet, as you see, I am still here, walking this beautiful earth."

He wants to taste my fear. "So you believe your order's demented creeds?"

"Ah, yes. We found some pleasant letters on your person, but not a certain dogwood scroll tube. Now, I shan't pretend you can save yourself: your death became necessary from the hour the herbalist came knocking on your gate. But you can save the Ogawa residence from the ruinous fire that shall incinerate it in the sixth month of this year. What do you say?"

"Two letters," Uzaemon lies, "were delivered to Ogawa Mimasaku today. One removes me from the Ogawa family register. The other divorces my wife. Why destroy a house that has no connection to me?"

"Pure spite. Give me the scroll, or die knowing they die, too."

"Tell me why you abducted Dr. Aibagawa's daughter when you did."

Enomoto decides to indulge him. "I feared I might lose her. A page from a Dutchman's notebook came into my possession, thanks to your colleague Kobayashi's good offices. Look. I brought it."

Enomoto unfolds a sheet of European paper and holds it up.

Retain this, Uzaemon tells his memory. *Show me her, at the end.*

"De Zoet draws a fair likeness." Enomoto folds it up. "Fair enough to worry Aibagawa Seian's widow that a Dutchman had designs on the family's best asset. The dictionary your servant smuggled to Orito settled the matter. My bailiff persuaded the widow to ignore funerary protocol and settle her stepdaughter's future without further delay."

"Did you tell that wretched woman about your demented practices?"

"What an earthworm knows of Copernicus, you know of the creeds."

"You keep a harem of deformities for your monks' pleasure —"

"Can you hear how like a child trying to postpone his bedtime you sound?"

"Why not present a paper to the academy,"

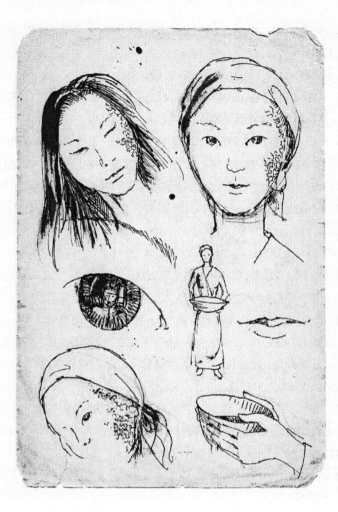

Uzaemon asks, "about —"

"Why do you mortal *gnats* suppose that your incredulity *matters?*"

"— about murdering your 'harvested gifts' to 'distill their souls'?"

"This is your last opportunity to save the Ogawa house from —"

"And then *bottling* them, like perfume, and 'imbibing' them, like medicine, and cheating death? Why not share your magical revelation with the world?" Uzaemon scowls at the shifting figures. "Here's my guess: because there's one small part of you that's still sane, an inner Jiritsu who says, 'This is evil.' "

"Oh, *evil*. Evil, evil, evil. You always wield that word as if it were a sword and not a vapid conceit. When you suck the yolk from an egg, is this 'evil'? Survival is Nature's law, and my order holds — or, better, *is* — the secret of surviving mortality. Newborn infants are a messy requisite — after the first two weeks of life, the enmeshed soul can't be extracted — and a fifty-strong order needs a constant supply for its own use, and to purchase the favors of an elite few. Your Adam Smith would understand. Without the order, moreover, the gifts wouldn't exist in the first place. They are an ingredient we manufacture. Where is your 'evil'?"

"Eloquent lunacy, Lord Abbot Enomoto, is still lunacy."

"I am over six hundred years old. You shall die, in minutes . . ."

He believes his creeds, Uzaemon sees. *He believes every single word.*

". . . so which is stronger? Your reason? Or my eloquent lunacy?"

"Free me," Uzaemon says, "free Miss Aibagawa, and I'll tell you where the scr—"

"No, no, there can be no bargaining. Nobody outside the order may know the creeds and live. You must die, just as Jiritsu did, and that busy old herbalist . . ."

Uzaemon groans with grief. "She was *harmless.*"

"She wanted to harm my order. We defend ourselves. But I want you to look at this — an artifact that Fate, in the guise of Vorstenbosch the Dutchman, sold me." Enomoto exhibits a foreign-made pistol, inches from Uzaemon's face. "A pearl-inlaid handle, and craftsmanship exquisite enough to confound the Confucianists' claim that Europeans lack souls. Since Shuzai told me of your heroic plans, it has been waiting. See — *see,* Ogawa, this concerns you — how one raises this 'hammer' to 'half cock,' loads the gun down the 'muzzle' thus: first, the gunpowder, and then with a lead ball wrapped in paper. One pushes it down with this 'ramrod' stored on the underside of the barrel . . ."

It's now. Uzaemon's heart knocks like a bloodied fist. *It's now.*

". . . then one supplies the 'flashpan,' here, with a little powder, shuts its lid, and now our pistol is 'primed and ready.' Done, in half a Hollander's minute. Yes, a master archer can string another arrow in the blink of an eye, but guns are manufactured more quickly than master archers. Any son of a shit carrier could wield one of these and bring down a mounted samurai. The day is coming — you shan't see it, but I shall — when such firearms transform even our secretive world. When one squeezes the trigger, a flint strikes this 'frizzen' as the flashpan lid opens. The spark ignites the priming powder, sending a flame through this 'touchhole' into the combustion chamber. The main powder ignites, like a miniature cannon, and the lead ball bores through your —"

Enomoto presses the pistol's muzzle against Uzaemon's heart.

Uzaemon is aware of urine warming his thighs but is too scared for shame.

It's now, it's now, it's now, it's now, it's now, it's now, it's now . . .

"— or maybe . . ." The pistol's mouth plants a kiss on Uzaemon's temple.

It's now it's now it's now it's now it's now it's now it's now

"Animal terror," a murmur enters Uzaemon's ear, "has half dissolved your mind, so I shall provide you with a thought. Music, as it were, to die to. The acolytes of the Order of Mount Shiranui are initiated into the twelve creeds, but they stay ignorant of the thirteenth until they become masters — one of whom you met this morning, the landlord at the Harubayashi Inn. The thirteenth creed pertains to an untidy loose end. Were our sisters — and housekeepers, in fact — to descend to the world below and discover that not one of their gifts, their children, is alive or known, questions might be asked. To avoid such unpleasantness, Suzaku administers a gentle drug at their rite of departure. This drug ensures a dreamless death, long before their palanquin reaches the foot of Mekura Gorge. They are then buried in that very bamboo grove into which you blundered this morning. So here is your final thought: your childlike failure to rescue Aibagawa Orito sentences her not only to twenty years of servitude — your ineptitude has, literally, killed her."

The pistol rests on Ogawa Uzaemon's forehead . . .

He expends his last moment on a prayer. *Avenge me.*

A click, a spring, a strangled whimper nothing now but

Now Now Now Now now now now now nownownow —

Thunder splits the rift where the sun floods in.

■ ■ ■ ■

Part Three:
The Master of Go

■ ■ ■ ■

The seventh month of the thirteenth year of the Era of Kansei

August 1800

CHAPTER
TWENTY-SEVEN:
DEJIMA

August 1800

Last trading season, Ignatius whittled a spoon from a bone. A fine spoon, in the shape of a fish. Master Grote saw the fine spoon, and he told Ignatius, "Slaves eat with fingers. Slaves cannot own spoons." Then, Master Grote took the fine spoon. Later, I passed Master Grote and a Japanese gentleman. Master Grote was saying, "This spoon was made by the very hands of the famous Robinson Crusoe." Later, Sjako heard Master Baert tell Master Oost how the Japanese gentleman had paid five lacquer bowls for Robinson Crusoe's spoon. D'Orsaiy told Ignatius to hide his spoon better next time and trade with the coolies or carpenters. But Ignatius said, "Why? When Master Grote or Master Gerritszoon hunt through my straw next time, they find my earnings and take them. They say, 'Slaves do not own. Slaves are owned.' "

Sjako said that masters do not allow slaves

to own goods or money, because a slave with money could run away more easily. Philander said that such talk was bad talk. Cupido said to Ignatius that if he carves more spoons and gives them to Master Grote, Master Grote will value him more and surely treat him better. I said, those words are true if the master is a good master, but for a bad master, it is never true.

Cupido and Philander are favorites of the Dutch officers, because they play music at the dinner parties. They call themselves "servants" and use fancy Dutch words like "wigs" and "laces." They talk about "my flute" and "my stockings." But Philander's flute and Cupido's fat violin and their elegant costumes belong to their masters. They wear no shoes. When the Vorstenbosch left last year, he sold them to the Van Cleef. They say they were "passed on" from the old chief to the new chief, but they were sold for five guineas each.

No, a slave cannot even say, "These are my fingers," or "This is my skin." We do not own our bodies. We do not own our families. Once, Sjako would talk about "my children back in Batavia." He fathered his children, yes. But to his masters they are not "his." To his masters, Sjako is like a horse, who fathered a foal on a mare. Here is the proof: when Sjako complained too bitterly that he had not seen his family for many years,

566

Master Fischer and Master Gerritszoon beat him severely. Sjako walks with a limp now. He talks less.

Once, I thought this question: *Do I own my name?* I do not mean my slave names. My slave names change at the whims of my masters. The Acehnese slavers who stole me named me "Straight Teeth." The Dutchman who bought me at Batavia slave market named me "Washington." He was a bad master. Master Yang named me Yang Fen. He taught me tailoring and fed me the same food as his sons. My third owner was Master van Cleef. He named me "Weh" because of a mistake. When he asked Master Yang — using fancy Dutch words — for my name, the Chinaman thought the question was "From where does he hail?" and replied, "An island called Weh," and my next slave name was fixed. But it is a happy mistake for me. On Weh, I was not a slave. On Weh, I was with my people.

My true name I tell nobody, so nobody can steal my name.

The answer, I think, is yes — my true name is a thing I own.

Sometimes another thought comes to me: *Do I own my memories?*

The memory of my brother diving from the turtle rock, sleek and brave . . .

The memory of the typhoon bending the trees like grass, the sea roaring . . .

The memory of my tired, glad mother rocking the new baby to sleep, singing . . .

Yes — like my true name, my memories are things I own.

Once, I thought this thought: *Do I own this thought?*

The answer was hidden in mist, so I asked Dr. Marinus's servant, Eelattu.

Eelattu answered, yes, my thoughts are born in my mind, so they are mine. Eelattu said that I can own my mind, if I choose. I said, "Even a slave?" Eelattu said, yes, if the mind is a strong place. So I created a mind like an island, like Weh, protected by deep blue sea. On my mind island, there are no bad-smelling Dutchmen, or sneering Malay servants, or Japanese men.

Master Fischer owns my body, then, but he does not own my mind. This I know, because of a test. When I shave Master Fischer, I imagine slitting open his throat. If he owned my mind, he would see this evil thought. But instead of punishing me, he just sits there with his eyes shut.

But I discovered there are problems with owning your mind. When I am on my mind island, I am as free as any Dutchman. There, I eat capons and mango and sugared plums. There, I lie with Master van Cleef's wife in the warm sand. There, I build boats and weave sails with my brother and my people. If I forget their names, they remind me. We speak in the tongue of Weh and drink *kava* and pray to our ancestors. There, I do not stitch or scrub or fetch or carry for masters.

Then I hear, "Are you *listening* to me, idle dog?"

Then I hear, "If you won't move for *me*, here's my whip!"

Each time I return from my mind island, I am recaptured by slavers.

When I return to Dejima, the scars from my capture ache, a little.

When I return to Dejima, I feel a coal of anger glowing inside.

The word "my" brings pleasure. The word "my" brings pain. These are true words for masters as well as slaves. When they are drunk, we become invisible to them. Their talk turns to owning, or to profit, or loss, or buying, or selling, or stealing, or hiring, or renting, or swindling. For white men, to live is to own, or to try to own more, or to die trying to own more. Their appetites are astonishing! They own wardrobes, slaves, carriages, houses, warehouses, and ships. They own ports, cities, plantations, valleys, mountains, chains of islands. They own this world, its jungles, its skies, and its seas. Yet they complain that Dejima is a prison. They complain they are not free. Only Dr. Marinus is free from these complaints. His skin is a white man's, but through his eyes you can see his soul is not a white man's soul. His soul is much older. On Weh, we would call him a *kwaio*. A *kwaio* is an ancestor who does not stay on the island of ancestors. A *kwaio* returns and returns and returns, each time in a new child. A good *kwaio* may become a shaman, but nothing in this world is worse than a bad *kwaio.*

The doctor persuaded Master Fischer that I should be taught to write Dutch.

Master Fischer did not like the idea. He said that a slave who can read might ruin himself with "revolutionary notions." He said he saw this in Surinam. But Dr. Marinus urged Master Fischer to consider how useful I will be in the clerks' office and how much higher a price I will fetch when he wants to sell me. These words changed Master Fischer's mind. He looked down the dining table to Master de Zoet. He said, "Clerk de Zoet, I have the perfect job for a man like you."

When Master Fischer finishes his meal in the kitchen, I walk behind him to the deputy's house. When we cross Long Street, I must carry his parasol so his head stays in the shade. This is not an easy task. If a tassel touches his head, or if the sun dazzles his eyes, he will hit me for carelessness. Today my master is in a bad mood because he lost so much money at Master Grote's card game. He stops here, in the middle of Long Street.

"In Surinam," he yells, "they *know* how to train stinking Negroid dogs like you!" Then he slaps my face, as hard as he can, and I drop the parasol. He shouts at me, "Pick that up!" When I bend down, he kicks my face. This is a favorite trick of Master Fischer's, so my face is turned away from his foot, but I pretend to be in great pain. Otherwise he will feel cheated and kick me again. He says, "That'll teach you to throw my possessions in the dust!" I say, "Yes, Master Fischer," and open the door of his house for him.

We climb the stairs to his bedroom. He lies on his bed and says, "It's too bloody damned hot in this bloody damned prison."

There is much talk about "prison" this summer, because the ship from Batavia has not arrived. The white masters are afraid that it will not come, so there will be no trading season and no news or luxuries from Java. The white masters who are due to return will not be able to. Nor will their servants or slaves.

Master Fischer throws his handkerchief on the floor and says, "Shit!"

This Dutch word can be a curse, or a bad name, but this time Master Fischer is ordering me to put his chamber pot in his favorite corner. There is a privy at the foot of the stairs, but he is too lazy to go down the steps. Master Fischer stands, unfastens his breeches, squats over the pot, and grunts. I hear a slithery thud. The smell snakes its way around the room. Then Master Fischer is buttoning up his breeches. "Don't just stand there, then, you idle Gomorrah . . ." His voice is drowsy because of his lunchtime whiskey. I put the wooden lid on the chamber pot — and go outside to the soil barrel. Master Fischer says he cannot tolerate dirt in his house, so I cannot empty his chamber pot into the privy like other slaves do.

I walk down Long Street to the crossroads, turn into Bony Alley, turn left at Seawall Lane, pass the headman's house, and empty the chamber pot into the soil urn, near the back of the hospital. The cloud of flies is thick and droning. I narrow my eyes like a yellow man's and wrinkle shut my nose to stop any flies laying their eggs there. Then I wash the chamber pot from the barrel of seawater. On the bottom of Master Fischer's chamber pot is a strange building called a windmill, from the white man's world. Philander says that they make bread, but when I asked how, he called me a very ignorant fellow. This means he does not know.

I take the long way back to the deputy's house. The white masters complain about the heat all summer long, but I love to let the sun warm my bones so I can survive the winters. The sun reminds me of Weh, my home. When I pass the pigpens, d'Orsaiy sees me and asks why Master Fischer hit me on

Long Street. With my face, I say, *Does a master need a reason?* and d'Orsaiy nods. I like d'Orsaiy. D'Orsaiy comes from a place called the Cape, halfway to the white man's world. His skin is the blackest I ever saw. Dr. Marinus says he is a Hottentot, but the master hands call him "Knave o' Spades." He asks me if I am going to study reading and writing at Master de Zoet's this afternoon. I say, "Yes, unless Master Fischer gives me more work." D'Orsaiy says that writing is a magic that I should learn. D'Orsaiy tells me that Master Ouwehand and Master Twomey are playing billiards in Summer House. This is a warning to walk briskly so that Master Ouwehand does not report me to Master Fischer for idling.

Back at the deputy's house, I hear snoring. I creep up the stairways, knowing which steps creak and which do not. Master Fischer is asleep. This is a problem, because if I go to Master de Zoet's house for my writing lesson without Master Fischer's permission, he will punish me for being willful. If I do not go to Master de Zoet's house, Master Fischer will punish me for laziness. But if I wake up Master Fischer to ask his permission, he will punish me for spoiling his siesta. In the end, I slide the chamber pot under Master Fischer's bed and go. Perhaps I will be back before he wakes.

The door of Tall House, where Master de

Zoet lives, is ajar. Behind the side door is a large, locked room full of empty crates and barrels. I knock on the lowest step, as usual, and expect to hear Master de Zoet's voice calling, "Is that you, Weh?" But today, there is no reply. Surprised, I climb the stairs, making enough noise to warn him that I am coming. Still there is no greeting. Master de Zoet rarely takes a siesta, but perhaps the heat has overcome him this afternoon. On the landing, I cross the side room where the house interpreter lives during the trading season. Master de Zoet's door is half open, so I peer in. He is sitting at his low table. He does not notice me. His face is not his own today. The light in his eyes is dark. He is afraid. His lips are half mouthing silent words. On my home island, we would say that he has been cursed by a bad *kwaio.*

Master de Zoet is staring at a scroll in front of him.

It is not a white man's book but a yellow man's scroll.

I am too far away to see well, but the letters on it are not Dutch ones.

It is yellow man's writing — Master Yang used such letters.

Next to the scroll on Master de Zoet's table is a notebook. Some Chinese words are written next to Dutch words. I make this guess: Master de Zoet has been translating the scroll into his own language. This has freed a bad curse, and this bad curse has possessed him.

Master de Zoet senses I am here, and he looks up.

CHAPTER TWENTY-EIGHT: CAPTAIN PENHALIGON'S CABIN ABOARD HMS *PHOEBUS*, EAST CHINA SEA

Around three o'clock on October 16, 1800
Indeed it seems, John Penhaligon reads, *that nature purposely designed these islands to be a sort of little world, separate and independent of the rest, by making them of so difficult an access, and by endowing them plentifully, with whatever is requisite to make the lives of their Inhabitants both delightful and pleasant, and to enable them to subsist without a commerce with foreign Nations . . .*

The captain yawns and cricks his jaw. Lieutenant Hovell declares there to be no better text on Japan than Engelbert Kaempfer's and never mind its age; but by the time Penhaligon staggers to the end of one sentence, its beginning has receded into fog. Through the stern window he studies the ominous, busy horizon. His whale's-tooth paperweight rolls off his desk, and he hears

576

Wetz, the sailing master, ordering the topgallants trimmed. *None too soon,* thinks the captain. The Yellow Sea has changed color from this morning's robin's-egg blue to ordure gray, with a sky of scabby pewter.

Where is Chigwin, he wonders, *and where is my damned coffee?*

Penhaligon retrieves his paperweight and pain bites his right ankle.

He squints at his barometer, whose needle is stuck to the "g" of "Changeable."

The captain returns to Engelbert Kaempfer to pick at a knot of illogic: the corollary of the phrase "whatever is requisite" is that man's needs are universal, whereas, in truth, a king's requisites differ radically from a reed cutter's; a libertine's from an archbishop's; and his own from his grandfather's. He opens his notebook and, bracing himself against the swell, writes:

What prophet of commerce in, let us say, the Year 1700 could have foreseen a time when commoners consume tea by the bucket and sugar by the sack? What subject of William and Mary could have predicted the "need" of today's middling multitudes for cotton sheets, coffee, and chocolate? Human requisites are prone to fashion; and, as clamoring new needs replace old ones, the face of the world itself changes . . .

It is too rough to write, but John Penhaligon is pleased and his gout has calmed down again, for now. *A rich vein.* He takes out his shaving mirror from his escritoire. Sweetmeat pies have fattened the fellow in the glass, brandy reddened his complexion, grief sunk his eyes, and bad weather blasted away his thatch, but what restores a man's vigor — and name — better than success?

He sketches his first speech at Westminster. *One recalls that the* Phoebus, he shall inform their enrapt lordships, then decides to amend. *One recalls that* my Phoebus *was no five-decked ship of the line with an auditorium of thunder-spouting guns, but a modest frigate of twenty-four eighteen-pounders. Her mizzen had sprung in the Straits of Formosa, her cordage was tired, her canvas threadbare, half our supplies from Fort Cornwallis were rotted, and her geriatric pump wheezed like my lord Falmouth atop his disappointed whore, and to as little profit* — the chamber shall erupt with laughter as his old enemy flees to die of shame in his stoat hole — *but her* heart, *my lords, was English oak; and when we hammered on the bolted gates of Japan, we did so with that resolve for which our race is justly notorious.* Their lordships' hush shall grow reverential. *The copper we seized from the perfidious Dutch on that October day was but a token. Our truest prize, and the legacy of the* Phoebus, *was a market, sirs, for the fruits of* your *mills, mines, plantations, and manufactories, and the gratitude of the Japanese Empire for rousing her from feudal somnambulance into our modern century. To claim that my* Phoebus *drew the political map of Eastern Asia anew is no hyperbole.* Their lordships will nod their cluttered heads and declare, "Hear, hear!" Lord Admiral Penhaligon continues: *This august chamber is cognizant of history's diverse instruments of change: the diplomat's tongue; treachery's poison; a monarch's mercy; a pope's tyranny . . .*

By God, Penhaligon thinks, *this is good: I must write it down later.*

. . . and it is nothing less than the greatest honor of my life that, in the first year of the nineteenth century, History chose one plucky ship, His Majesty's frigate Phoebus, *to open the doors of the most reclusive empire in the modern world — for the glory of His Majesty and the British Empire!* By now every last bewigged bastard in the place — Whig, Tory, cross-bencher, bishop, general, and admiral alike — shall be jumping to his feet and roaring with applause.

"Cap" — outside his door, Chigwin sneezes — "tain?"

"I trust you disturb me with coffee, Chigwin."

His young steward, the son of a master shipwright at Chatham who overlooked an awkward debt, peers in. "Jones is grinding the beans now, sir: the cook's had Old Harry

579

of a time keeping the stove alight."

"It was *coffee* I ordered, Chigwin, not a mug of excuses!"

"Aye, sir; sorry, sir; it should be just a few minutes more." A slug trail of mucus glistens on Chigwin's sleeve. "But those rocks Mr. Snitker made mention of are sighted to starboard, and Mr. Hovell thought as you may wish to survey them."

Don't chew the boy's head off. "Yes, I should."

"Would there be any instructions for dinner, sir?"

"The lieutenants and Mr. Snitker shall dine with me tonight, so . . ."

They steady themselves as the *Phoebus* plunges down a trough.

". . . bid Jones serve us up those chickens that are laying no more. I have no space for idlers on my ship, not even feathered ones."

Penhaligon hauls himself up the companionway to the spar deck, where the wind slams his face and inflates his lungs like a pair of new bellows. Wetz has the wheel, while lecturing a wobbly cluster of midshipmen on recalcitrant tillers in laboring seas. They salute the captain, who shouts into the wind, "What think you of the weather ahead, Mr. Wetz?"

"Good news is, sir, the clouds're scattering to the west; bad news is, the wind's swung a point northerly and blows a couple of knots harder. Regarding the pump, sir, Mr. O'Loughlan's fashioning a new chain, but he thinks there's a new leak — rats chewed the devil aft of the powder magazine."

When not eating our victuals, thinks Penhaligon, *they eat my ship.*

"Tell the boatswain to hold a miller-hunt. Ten tails buys an extra quart."

Wetz's sneeze sprays a downwind midshipman. "The men'll enjoy the sport."

Penhaligon crosses the rolling quarterdeck. It is in a slutty state: Snitker doubts the Japanese lookouts could distinguish an unkempt Yankee trader from a Royal Navy frigate with gunports blackened, but the captain is taking nothing for granted. Lieutenant Hovell stands at the taffrail, next to the deposed former chief of Dejima. Hovell senses the captain's approach, turns and salutes.

Snitker turns and nods, like an equal. He gestures toward the rocky islet, passing at a fair clip and a safe four or five hundred yards. "Torinoshima."

Torinoshima, Captain, thinks Penhaligon, but inspects the islet. Torinoshima is more a large rock than a little Gibraltar, plastered in guano and raucous with seabirds. It is cliff-bound on all sides, except for a stony scree fall to leeward, where a brave boat might attempt an anchorage. Penhaligon tells Hovell, "Ask

581

our guest if he ever heard of a landing."

Snitker's answer takes up two or three sentences.

What a gagged, mud-slurping thing, thinks Penhaligon, *is the Dutch tongue.*

"He thinks not, sir; he never heard of any attempted landing."

"His reply was more involved than that."

" 'None but a bloody-minded simpleton would chance his longboat,' sir."

"My sensibilities are not so easily wounded, Mr. Hovell. In future, translate in full."

The first lieutenant looks awkward. "My apologies, Captain."

"Ask him if Holland or any nation lays claim to Torinoshima."

Snitker's response to the question contains a sneer and the word "shogun."

"Our guest suggests," explains Hovell, "that we consult with the shogun before planting our Union Jack up in all that bird shit." More follows, with Hovell paying close attention and verifying a detail or two. "Mr. Snitker adds that Torinoshima is referred to as the 'signpost to Japan,' and if this wind keeps up, tomorrow we'll catch sight of the 'garden wall,' the Goto Islands, subject to the lord of Hizen, in whose dominion Nagasaki is located."

"Ask him if the Dutch Company ever landed on the Goto Islands."

This question earns a longer answer.

"He says, sir, that the company's captains never provoked . . ."

The three men grip the taffrail as the *Phoebus* plunges and bucks.

". . . never provoked the authorities so blatantly, sir, because Hidden —"

A cascade of spray falls over the bow; a drenched sailor swears in Welsh.

"— Hidden Christians still live there, so all comings and goings . . ."

One of the midshipmen tumbles down the companionway with a yell.

". . . are watched by government spies, but no bumboats shall approach us lest the crew be executed as smugglers, along with their families."

Rise by plunge, Torinoshima diminishes in stature off the starboard stern. The captain, lieutenant, and traitor sink into their own thoughts. Shearwaters and terns hover, roll, and plunge. The fourth bell of the first dog watch is struck, bringing out the men of the larboard watch without lagging: word has spread that the captain is about. The off-duty men go belowdecks for two hours of make-and-mend.

A narrow amber eye of sky opens on the southern horizon.

"There, sir!" says Hovell, childlike for a moment. "Two dolphins!"

Penhaligon sees nothing but heaving slate-blue waves. "Where?"

"A third! A beauty!" Hovell points, aborts another syllable, and says, "Gone."

"Until dinnertime, then," says Penhaligon to Hovell, moving away.

"Ah, *dinnertime*," repeats Snitker in English, and mimes drinking.

Grant me patience — Penhaligon musters a thin smile — *and coffee.*

The purser leaves the cabin, having worked through the day's subtractions to the pay book. His buzzing voice and charnel-house breath have left Penhaligon with a headache to match the pain in his foot. "The one thing worse than dealing with pursers," his patron Captain Golding advised him many years ago, "is being one. Every company needs a figurehead of hatred: better it be him than you."

Penhaligon drains the silty dregs. *Coffee sharpens my mind,* he thinks, *but burns my guts and strengthens my old enemy.* Since leaving Prince of Wales Island, an unwelcome truth has become irrefutable: his gout is launching a second attack. The first occurred in Bengal last summer: the heat was monstrous, and the pain was monstrous. For a fortnight he could not endure even the light touch of a cotton sheet against his foot. A first attack of the ailment can be laughed away as a rite of passage, but after the second, a man risks being dubbed "a gouty captain," and his prospects with the admiralty can be poleaxed. *Hovell may harbor his suspicions,* thinks Penhaligon, *but daren't air them; the wardrooms of the service are cluttered with first lieutenants orphaned by the premature loss of their patrons.* Worse yet, Hovell may be tempted by a nimbler patron and jump ship, depriving Penhaligon of his finest officer and a future captain's indebtedness. His second lieutenant, Abel Wren, well connected via his marriage to Commodore Joy's ruthless daughter, will smack his lips at the thought of these unexpected vacancies. *I am, then,* Penhaligon concludes, *engaged in a footrace against my gout. If I seize this year's Dutch copper and, please, God, prize open the treasure box of Nagasaki before gout lays me low, my financial and political futures are assured.* Otherwise, Hovell or Wren shall take the credit for bagging the copper and the trading post — or else the mission fails altogether and John Penhaligon retires to West Country obscurity and a pension of, at best, two hundred pounds a year, paid late and begrudgingly. *In my darker hours, I declare, it appears that Lady Luck won me my captaincy eight years ago just for the private pleasure of squatting over me and voiding her bowels.* First, Charlie mortgaged the remains of the family estate, took out debts in his younger brother's name, and disappeared; second, his prize agent and banker absconded to Virginia; third, Meredith, his dear Meredith, died of typhus; and fourth, there was Tristram — vigorous, strident, respected, handsome Tristram — killed at Cape St. Vincent, leaving his father nothing but grief and the crucifix salvaged by the ship's surgeon. *And now comes the gout,* he thinks, *threatening even to wreck my career . . .*

"No." Penhaligon picks up his shaving mirror. "We shall reverse our reverses."

The captain leaves his cabin just as the sentry — Banes or Panes is the man's name — is relieved by another marine, Walker the Scot: the pair salute. On the gundeck, Waldron the gunner's mate crouches by a cannon with a Penzance boy, Moff Wesley. In the gloom and noise of the heavy sea, they do not notice the eavesdropping captain. "Speak it back, then, Moff," Waldron is saying. "First?"

"Mop inside the barrel with the wet swab, sir."

"An' if some sottish cock does a cack-thumbed job o' that?"

"He'll miss embers from the last shot when we puts in the powder, sir."

"And blow a gunner's arms off: I seen it once, an' once'll do. Second?"

"Put in the powder cartridge, sir, or else we

pours it in loose."

"An' is gunpowder brought hither by scamperin' little piskies?"

"No, sir: I fetches it from the aft magazine, sir, one charge at a time."

"So you do, Moff. An' why we don't keep a fat stash to hand is?"

"One loose spark'd blow us all to piss-'n'-sh— pieces, sir. Third" — Moff counts on his fingers — "ram home the powder with a rammer, sir, an' fourth is load up the shot, an' fifth is ram in a wad after the shot, 'cause we may be rollin' an' the shot may roll out again into the sea, sir."

"An' a right crew o' Frenchmen we'd look *then*. Sixth?"

"Roll out the gun, so the carriage front is hard against the bulwark. Seventh, quill down the touchhole. Eighth, it's lit with a flintlock, an' the flintman shouts 'Clear!' an' the primin' powder sets off the powder in the barrel an' fires out the shot, and whatever's in its way it blows to — kingdom come, sir."

"Which causes the gun carriage," interjects Penhaligon, "to do what?"

Waldron is as startled as Moff: he stands to salute too quickly and bangs his head. "Didn't notice you, Captain; beggin' your pardon."

"Which causes the gun carriage," repeats Penhaligon, "to do what, Mr. Wesley?"

"Recoil shoots it back, sir, till the breech ropes an' cascabel stops it."

"What does a recoiling cannon do to a man's leg, Mr. Wesley?"

"Well . . . there'd not be much leg left if it caught it, sir."

"Carry on, Mr. Waldron." Penhaligon continues along the starboard bulwark, recalling his own days as a powder monkey and steadying himself on an overhead rope. At five-foot-eight, he is much taller than the average sailor and must take care not to scalp himself on the deckheads. He regrets his lack of a private fortune or prize money to buy gunpowder for firing practice. Captains who use more than a third of their quota in this way are viewed by the sea lords as imprudent.

Six Hanoverians whom Penhaligon plucked off a whaler at St. Helena are doing their best to wash, wring out, and hang up spare hammocks in the rolling weather. They intone, "Capi*tarn,*" in one chorus, and return to industrious silence. Farther along, Lieutenant Abel Wren has men scrubbing the deck with hot vinegar and holystones. Up above is dirtied for camouflage, but belowdecks needs protection from mildew and bad airs. Wren whacks a sailor with his rattan and bellows, *"Scrub it —* don't *tickle it, you daisy!"* He then pretends to notice the captain for the first time and salutes. "Afternoon, sir."

"Afternoon, Mr. Wren. All well?"

"Never better, sir," says the dashing, ugly second lieutenant.

Passing the canvas-screened galley, Penhaligon peers through a loose flap into the sooty, steamy enclosure, where the messmen help the cook and his mate chop food, keep fires alight, and prevent the coppers overturning. The cook puts chunks of salt pork — Thursday being a pork day — into the bubbling mixture. Chinese cabbage, slabs of yam, and rice are added to thicken the stew. Sons of the gentry may turn up their noses at the starch-and-salt-rich victuals, but ratings eat and drink better than they would ashore. Penhaligon's own cook, Jonas Jones, claps a few times to earn the galley's attention. "The wagers're all in now, boys."

"So let the games," declares Chigwin, "begin!"

Chigwin and Jones each shake one chicken into a state of terror.

The dozen or so men in the galley chant in unison, *"A-one, a-two, a-three!"*

Chigwin and Jones snip off their hens' heads with a pair of shears and set them on the galley deck. The men cheer the blood-spouting headless corpses as they skid and flap. Half a minute later, when Jones's fowl is still kicking on its side, the referee pronounces Chigwin's "One dead fowl, boys." Coins change hands from scowlers to gloaters, and the birds are taken to the benches for plucking and gutting.

Penhaligon could punish the servants with

the feeble charge of disrespect to the officers'
dinner but carries on past the galley to the
sick bay. Its wooden partitions reach not quite
to the ceiling, allowing a little light in and
disease-bearing airs out. "Nay nay *nay,* you
headless tit, it goes like this . . ." The speaker
is Michael Tozer, another Cornishman sent
as a volunteer by the captain's brother Charlie to the *Dragon,* the brig whose second
lieutenancy Penhaligon held eleven years ago.
Tozer's band of ten — now all able seamen
— have followed their patron ever since. His
broken and tuneless voice sings:

> Don't you see the ships a-comin'?
> Don't you see them in full sail?
> Don't you see the ships a-comin'
> With the prizes at their tail?
> Oh, my little rollin' sailor,
> Oh, my little rollin' he;
> I do love a jolly sailor,
> Gay and merry might he be.

" 'Tweren't 'gay,' Michael Tozer," objects a
voice, " 'Twere 'blithe.' "
" 'Gay,' 'blithe' — who humps a hog? What
matters is what's next, so cork it:

> Sailors they get all the money,
> Soldiers they get none but brass;
> Oh, I do love a drink-me-down sailor,
> But soldiers may all kiss my arse.

Oh, my little rolling sailor,
Oh, my little rolling he;
I do love a jolly sailor,
Soldiers may be damned for me.

"*That*'s what the Gosport whores sing, and I'd know, 'cause I had one after the glorious First o' June an' sunk my fork up her figgy-dowdy —"

"Though come mornin'," says the voice, "she'd gone with his prize money."

" 'Tain't the point: the point is, we'll be pluckin' Dutch merchantmen stuffed with the reddest, goldest copper on God's beautiful globe."

Captain Penhaligon stoops through the sick bay's entrance. The half dozen bed-bound inmates stiffen to guilty attention, and the loblolly, a pock-scarred Londoner called Rafferty, stands, putting to one side the tray of tenaculums, ball scoops, and bone rasps he is oiling. "Afternoon, sir. The surgeon's down on the orlop deck. Shall I send for him?"

"No, Mr. Rafferty. I make my rounds, is all. Are you mending, Mr. Tozer?"

"Can't say my chest is better knitted than last week, sir, but I'm grateful to be here at all. 'Twas a fair old fall without a pair of wings. An' Mr. Waldron's been saying as he'll find a space for me on one of his guns, so I look on it as a chance to learn a new trade an' all."

"That's the spirit, Tozer, that's the spirit." Penhaligon turns to Tozer's young neighbor. "Jack Fletcher: do I have it?"

"Jack Thatcher, beggin' your pardon, sir."

"Your pardon, Jack Thatcher. What brings you to the sick bay?"

Rafferty answers for the blushing youth: "Big round of applause, Captain."

"The clap? A souvenir of Penang, no doubt. How far advanced?"

Rafferty answers again: "Mr. Snaky's as scarlet as a Roman bishop's hat, sir, an' oozin' curds, an' Jack's one eye's all blurry, an' widdlin's a torture, is it not, lad? He's been fed his mercury, but there'll be no shuntyin' along the yards for a while yet . . ."

To blame, Penhaligon reflects, is the navy's policy of charging sailors for the treatment of venereal disease, thereby encouraging the men to try every sea-daddy's cure before coming to the ship's surgeon. *When I am made a peer in the lords,* thinks Penhaligon, *I shall rectify this pious folly.* The captain, too, once contracted the French Disease at an officers-only bagnio on St. Kitts and was too scared and too shy to speak to the *Trincomolee*'s surgeon, until passing water was the purest agony. Were he a petty officer still, he'd share this story with Jack Thatcher, but a captain should not dent his authority. "One trusts you learned the true price a doxy's cully must pay, Thatcher?"

"I'll not forget it in a hurry, sir, this I swear."

Yet you'll lie with another, Penhaligon foresees, *and another, and another . . .* He speaks briefly with the other patients: a feverish landsman pressed at St. Ives, whose crushed thumb may or may not have to come off; a luckier Bermudan, glassy-eyed with pain from an abscessed molar; and a Shetlander with more beard than face and a severe case of Barbados leg, which has swollen his testicles to the size of mangoes. "I'm fit as a smashed fiddle," he reports, "God bless you for asking, Captain."

Penhaligon rises to leave.

"Beg pardon, sir," asks Michael Tozer, "might you settle a dispute for us?"

Pain shoots through Penhaligon's foot. "If I may, Mr. Tozer."

"Shall sailors in sick bay still get their rightful slice of the prize, sir?"

"The naval rule book, which I uphold, states that the answer is yes."

Tozer fires an "I told you so" glare at Rafferty. Penhaligon is tempted to quote the proverb about birds in hands and bushes but leaves the *Phoebus*'s rising morale untouched. "There are some miscellaneous matters," he tells the loblolly, "on which I should like to consult Surgeon Nash, after all. He is most likely in his cabin down below, you mentioned?"

■ ■ ■ ■

A mongrel stink smothers the captain as he descends, step by jolting step, to the berth deck. It is dark, cold, and damp in winter, and dark, hot, and airless in the summer: "snug," the ratings call it. In unhappy ships, despised officers are well advised not to venture too far from the companionways, but John Penhaligon has no undue worries. The larboard watch, about a hundred and ten men, are sewing or whittling in the wells of dim light from above, or moaning, shaving, or curling up for a catnap in improvised booths between sea chests, hammocks being unstrung during the day. The captain's shoes and buckles are recognized before the rest of him: a cry rings out, "Captain on deck, lads!" The nearest sailors stand to attention, and the captain is gratified that resentment at his intrusion is concealed, at least. He hides the pain in his feet. "I'm on my way down to the orlop, lads. As you were."

"Shall y' be needin' a lantern or a support, sir?" one of the men asks.

"No need. Blindfolded, I'd find my way around my *Phoebus*'s guts."

He continues down to the orlop deck. It reeks of bilgewater, though not, as on a captured French ship he once inspected, of decayed corpses. Water sloshes, the sea's belly churns, and the pumps clunk and squelp. Penhaligon grunts as he reaches the bottom and half feels his way down the narrow passage. His fingertips identify the powder store; the cheese hold; the grog store, with its heavy padlock; the cabin of Mr. Woods, the boys' careworn tutor; the rope store; the surgeon's dispensary; and, last, a cabin no bigger than his water closet. Bronze light escapes and boxes are shifted. "It is I, Mr. Nash — the Captain."

"Captain." Nash's voice is a husky West Country wheeze. "What a surprise." His lamp-lit face appears, like a fanged mole, betraying no surprise at all.

"Mr. Rafferty said I might find you here, Surgeon."

"Aye, I came down for sulfide of lead." He places a folded blanket on the chest by way of a cushion. "Take the weight off your feet, if you'd care to. Your gout bites back, does it, sir?"

The tall man fills the poky cabin. "Is it so obvious, then?"

"Professional instinct, sir . . . Might I inspect the area?"

Awkwardly, the captain removes his boot and sock and places his foot on a trunk. Nash brings his lamp close, his apron stiff and rustling with dried blood, and frowns at Penhaligon's maroon swellings. "An angry tophus on the metatarsus . . . but no secretions, as yet?"

"None as yet, but it's looking damned similar to this time last year."

Nash pokes at the swelling, and Penhaligon's foot jerks in pain.

"Surgeon, the Nagasaki mission cannot afford for me to be invalided."

Nash polishes his glasses on his grimy cuffs. "I prescribe Dover's remedy. It speeded your recovery in Bengal; it may postpone the attack this time. I want six ounces of blood from you, too, to reduce friction against the arteries."

"Let us waste no more time." Penhaligon removes his coat and rolls up his shirtsleeves, while Nash decants liquids from three different medicine bottles. Nobody could accuse the surgeon of being one of those gentleman physicians one occasionally meets in the service, men who adorn the wardroom with erudition and verve. This steady Devonian can amputate one limb per minute during engagements, pull teeth with a steady hand, bend his accounts no more than is decent, and never blab about officers' complaints to the ratings. "Remind me, Mr. Nash, what goes into this Dover's."

"A variant of ipecacuanha powder, sir, being opium, ipecac, saltpeter, tartar, and licorice." He measures out a spatula of pale powder. "Were you a common Jack, I'd add castoreum — what the medical fraternity call

rancid cod oil — so you'd feel properly phys-
icked. This trick I tend to spare the officers."

The ship rolls, and her timbers creak like a
barn in a gale.

"Have you considered turning apothecary
ashore, Mr. Nash?"

"Not I, sir." Nash does not smile at the
pleasantry.

"I can see Nash's Patented Elixir arrayed in
a row of china bottles."

"Men of commerce, sir" — Nash counts
out laudanum drops into the pewter beaker
— "for the most part, had their consciences
cut out at birth. Better an honest drowning
than slow death by hypocrisy, law, or debt."
He stirs the compound and hands the beaker
to his patient. "Down in a single draft, Captain."

Penhaligon obeys and winces. "Rancid cod
oil may improve it."

"I shall bring a dosage daily, sir. Now for
the bloodletting." He produces a bleeding
dish and a rusty lancet and holds the captain's
forearm. "My sharpest blade: you shan't feel
a —"

Penhaligon bites on his *ouch!*, his oath, and
a shudder of pain.

"— thing." Nash inserts the catheter to
prevent scabbing. "Now . . ."

"Stay still. I know." Slow drips of blood
form a puddle in the dish.

To distract himself, Penhaligon thinks

about dinner.

"Paid informers," avows Lieutenant Hovell, after half-drunk Daniel Snitker has been helped to his cabin to sleep off his mountainous dinner, "serve up that same dish their patrons most wish to" — the ship sways, shudders, and the bulkhead lamps circle in their gimbals — "dine upon. During his ambassadorship at The Hague, my father placed the word of one informer of conscience above the affidavits of ten spies working for lucre. Now, this is not to say that Snitker is *ipso facto* deceiving us, but we are well advised to swallow not a crumb of his 'prize intelligence' without further verification — least of all his sunny prediction that the Japanese shall watch us seize their ancient ally's assets without so much as a murmur."

At a nod from Penhaligon, Chigwin and Jones begin clearing the table.

"The European war is no damned concern of the bloody Asiatics." Major Cutlip, only a shade or two less scarlet than his marines' jacket, sucks a last shred of meat from his chicken drumstick.

"A point of view," says Hovell, "the bloody Asiatics may not share, Major."

"Let them be" — Cutlip snorts — "*taught* to share it, Mr. Hovell."

"Suppose the kingdom of Siam maintained a trading post at Bristol —"

Cutlip glances at Second Lieutenant Wren with a knowing grin.

"— at Bristol," Hovell carries on, undeterred, "for a century and a half, until one fine day a Chinese junk-of-war sailed in, seized our ally's assets with never a by-your-leave, and announced to London that henceforth *they* shall take the place of the Siamese. Would Prime Minister Pitt accept such terms?"

"When next Mr. Hovell's critics," says Wren, "lampoon his humorlessness . . ."

Penhaligon knocks over the salt cellar and throws a pinch over his shoulder.

". . . I shall confound them with his fantasia of a Siamese factory in Bristol!"

"The issue is sovereignty," states Robert Hovell. "The comparison is apt."

Cutlip wags his drumstick. "If eight years in New South Wales taught me anything at all, it's that well-read notions like 'sovereignty' or 'rights' or 'property' or 'jurisprudence' or 'diplomacy' mean one thing to whites but another to the backward races. Poor Phillip at Sydney Cove, he did his damnedest to 'negotiate' with the raggle-taggle backward blacks we found there. Did his fine ideals stop the lazy shit weasels filching our supplies like they owned the place?" Cutlip spits in the spittoon. "It's red-blooded Englishmen and London muskets who lay down the law in the colonies, not any lily-livered 'diplomacy,' and it'll be twenty-four guns and forty well-drilled marines who win the day in Nagasaki, too. One can only hope" — he winks at Wren — "that the first lieutenant's delightful Chinese bedmate in Bengal did not tinge his Caucasian spotlessness a shade yellow, hey?"

What is *it,* Penhaligon groans inwardly, *about the Marine Corps?*

A bottle slides off the table into the young hands of Third Lieutenant Talbot.

"Does your remark," Hovell asks in a deadly calm voice, "impugn my courage as a naval officer, or is it my loyalty to the king that you denigrate?"

"Now, come, Robert: Cutlip knows you" — *there are times,* Penhaligon thinks, *when I am less a captain and more a governess* — "too well to do either. He was just . . . just . . ."

"Dispensing a little affectionate elbowing," says Lieutenant Wren.

"The most trivial quip!" Cutlip protests, all charm. "Affectionate elbowing . . ."

"The wit was sharp," Wren judges, "but wholly lacking in malice."

". . . and I apologize unconditionally," adds Cutlip, "for any offense caused."

The readiest apologies, Penhaligon observes, *carry the littlest worth.*

"Major Cutlip should mind 'his sharp wit,' " says Hovell, "lest he cut himself."

"Is it your plan, Mr. Talbot," Penhaligon asks, "to smuggle that bottle out?"

Talbot takes the question seriously for a moment; then he smiles with relief and fills the company's glasses. Penhaligon orders Chigwin to bring another couple of bottles of the Chambolle Musigny. The steward is surprised by such generosity so late on but goes to fetch them.

Penhaligon senses that a ruling is required. "Were our single objective in Nagasaki to dispossess *Jan Compagnie,* we could be as direct as the major advocates. Our orders, however, urge us also to negotiate a treaty with the Japanese. We must be diplomats as well as warriors."

Cutlip picks his nose. "Guns make the best diplomats, Captain."

Hovell dabs his lips. "Belligerence shan't impress *these* natives."

"Did we subdue the Indians by gentleness?" Wren leans back. "Did the Dutch conquer the Javans by gifts of Edam cheese?"

"The analogy is unsound," argues Hovell. "Japan is *in* Asia but not *of* Asia."

Wren asks, "Another of your Gnostic utterances, Lieutenant?"

"To speak of 'the Indians' or 'the Javanese' is a European conceit: in truth, these are a patchwork of peoples, fissile and divisible. Japan, contrariwise, was unified four hundred years ago and expelled the Spanish and

Portuguese even at the zenith of Iberian might —"

"Pit our artillery, cannonades, and riflemen against their quaint medieval jousters and —" With his lips and hands, the major imitates an explosion.

"Quaint medieval jousters," Hovell replies, "whom you have never even seen."

Better teredo worm in the hull, thinks Penhaligon, *than bickering officers.*

"No more than have you," says Wren. "Snitker, however —"

"Snitker is *with child* to regain his little kingdom and humiliate his usurpers."

In the wardroom below, Mr. Waldron's fiddle strikes up a jig.

Someone, at least, thinks Penhaligon, *is enjoying the evening.*

Lieutenant Talbot opens his mouth to speak but closes it again.

Penhaligon says, "You wish to speak, Mr. Talbot?"

Talbot is unnerved by all the eyes. "Nothing of consequence, sir."

Jones drops a plate of cutlery with an almighty clatter.

"By the by," Cutlip says, transferring his snot to the tablecloth, "I overheard a pair of your Cornishmen, Captain, making a joke about Mr. Hovell's home county. I repeat it without fear of offense, now we know he is man enough to enjoy a little affectionate elbowing: What, pray, is a Yorkshireman?"

Robert Hovell rotates his wedding ring around his finger.

" 'A Scot, by Jove, with the generosity squeezed out!' "

The captain regrets ordering the bottles of '91.

Why must all things, Penhaligon wonders, *go around in stupid circles?*

CHAPTER
TWENTY-NINE:
AN UNCERTAIN
PLACE

An uncertain time

Jacob de Zoet pursues the linkboy's lamp along a putrid canal and into the nave of Domburg church. Geertje sets a roasted goose on the altar table. The linkboy, whose eyes are Asian and hair is copper, quotes, "I will incline mine ear to a parable, Papa; I will open my dark saying upon the harp." Jacob is aghast. *An illegitimate son?* He turns to Geertje but finds the soured landlady of his makeshift lodgings in Batavia. "You don't even know his mother, do you?" Unico Vorstenbosch finds all this inordinately funny and plucks meat from the half-eaten goose. The fowl lifts its crisped head and quotes, "Let them melt away as waters which run continually: when he bendeth his bow to shoot his arrows, let them be as cut to pieces." The goose flies through a bamboo grove, through slanted bars of light dark and dark dark, and Jacob flies, too, until they reach a clearing where the head of John the

Baptist glowers from its Delftware dish. "Eighteen years in the Orient with nothing to show but a bastard half-breed!"

Eighteen years? Jacob notices this number. *Eighteen . . .*

The Shenandoah, he thinks, *embarked less than* one *year ago . . .*

His tether to the netherworld snipped, he wakes, next to Orito.

Praise merciful God in heaven, the waker finds himself in Tall House . . .

. . . where everything is exactly as it appears to be.

Orito's hair is mussed from last night's lovemaking.

Dust is gold in the light of dawn; an insect sharpens its scalpels.

"I am yours, beloved," Jacob whispers, and kisses her burn . . .

Orito's hands, her slim hands, wake, and cup his nipples . . .

So much suffering, Jacob thinks, *but now you are here, I will heal you.*

. . . cup his nipples, and circle his navel, and knead his groin, and —

"As a snail which melteth . . ." Orito's purpled eyes swivel open.

Jacob tries to wake up, but the wire around his neck pulls tight.

". . . let every one pass away," quotes the

corpse, "like the untimely birth . . ."

The Dutchman is covered with snails — bed, room, Dejima, all snails . . .

". . . like the untimely birth of a woman, that they may not see the sun."

Jacob sits up, wide awake, his pulse galloping away. *I am in the House of Wistaria, and last night I slept with a prostitute.* She is here, with a mousy snore caught in her throat. The air is warm and fetid with the smells of sex, tobacco, soiled linen, and overboiled cabbage from the chamber pot. Creation's light is pure on the papered window. Amorous thumps and titters emanate from a nearby room. He thinks about Orito and Uzaemon in various shades of guilt and closes his eyes, but then he sees them more clearly, Orito locked, reaped, and harvested, and Uzaemon hacked to death, and Jacob thinks, *Because of you,* and he opens his eyes. But thought has no eyelids to close or ears to block, and Jacob remembers Interpreter Kobayashi's announcement that Ogawa Uzaemon had been slain by mountain bandits on a pilgrimage to the town of Kashima. Lord Abbot Enomoto had hunted down the eleven outlaws responsible for the atrocity and tortured them to death, but not even vengeance, Kobayashi had opined, can bring the dead to life. Chief van Cleef sent the company's condolences to Ogawa the Elder, but the interpreter never returned to Dejima again, and nobody was surprised when he died shortly after. Any faint doubts in De Zoet's mind that Enomoto had killed Ogawa Uzaemon were dispelled a few weeks later, when Goto Shinpachi reported that the previous night's fire on the eastern slope had begun in the library of the old Ogawa residence. That evening, by lamplight, Jacob retrieved the dogwood scroll tube from under his floorboards and began the most exacting mental labor of his life. The scroll was not long — its title and twelve clauses ran to a little more than three hundred characters — but Jacob had to acquire the vocabulary and grammar entirely in secret. None of the interpreters would risk being caught teaching Japanese to a foreigner, though Goto Shinpachi would sometimes answer Jacob's casual questions about specific words. Without Marinus's knowledge of Chinese, the task would have been impossible, but Jacob dared not show the doctor the scroll for fear of implicating his friend. It took two hundred nights to decipher the creeds of the order of Mount Shiranui, nights that grew darker as Jacob groped closer and closer to its revelations. *And now that the work is done,* he wonders, *how can a closely watched foreigner ever transform it into justice?* He would need the sympathetic ear of a man as powerful as the magistrate to stand the remotest chance of seeing Orito freed and Enomoto brought to justice. *What would happen,* he wonders, *to a Chinaman in Middelburg who sought to prosecute the duke of Zeeland for immorality and infanticide?*

The man in the nearby room is blurting, *"Oh oh Mijn God, Mijn God!"*

Melchior van Cleef: Jacob blushes and hopes his girl doesn't wake.

Prudishness the morning after, he must admit, *is a hypocrite's guilt.*

His condom of goat's intestine lies in a square of paper by the futon.

It is a revolting object, Jacob thinks. *So, for that matter, am I . . .*

Jacob thinks about Anna. He must dissolve their vow.

That honest girl deserves, he thinks unflinchingly, *a truer husband.*

He imagines her father's happiness when she tells him the news.

She may have dissolved her vow to me, he admits, *months ago . . .*

No ship from Batavia this year meant no trade or letters . . .

A water vendor in the street below calls out, *"O-miiizu, O-miiizu."*

. . . and the threat of insolvency for Dejima and Nagasaki looms larger.

Melchior van Cleef arrives at his *"OOOOOOoOoOoOoooo . . ."*

Don't wake, Jacob begs the sleeping woman, *don't wake* . . .

Her name is Tsukinami: "Moon Wave." Jacob liked her shyness.

Though shyness, too, he suspects, *can be applied with paint and powder.*

Once they were alone, Tsukinami complimented his Japanese.

He hopes he did not revolt her. She called his eyes "decorated."

She asked to snip off a lock of his copper hair to remember him by.

Postclimactic Van Cleef laughs like a pirate watching a rival mauled by sharks.

And is this Orito's life, Jacob shudders, *as Ogawa's scroll describes?*

Millstones in his conscience grind, grind, and grind . . .

The bell of Ryûgaji Temple announces the Hour of the Rabbit. Jacob puts on his breeches and shirt, cups some water from the pitcher, drinks and washes, and opens the window. The view is fit for a viceroy: Nagasaki falls away, in stepped alleyways and upthrust roofs, in duns, ochers, and charcoals, down to the arklike magistracy, Dejima, and beyond to the slovenly sea . . .

He obeys an impish urge to shimmy out along the ridge of the roof.

His bare feet grip the still-cool tiles; there is a sculpted carp to hold on to.

Saturday, October 18, in the year 1800 is calm and blue.

Starlings fly in nebulae; like a child in a tale, Jacob longs to join them.

Or else, he daydreams, *let my round eyes become nomadic ovals . . .*

West to east, the sky unrolls and rolls its atlas of clouds.

. . . my pink skin turn dull gold; my freakish hair, a sensible black . . .

From an alleyway, the clatter of a night cart threatens his reverie.

. . . and my boorish body become one of theirs . . . poised and sleek.

Eight liveried horses proceed along a road. Their hoofs echo.

How far would I get, Jacob wonders, *if I ran, hooded, through the streets?*

. . . up through rice terraces, up to the folded mountains, the folds within folds.

Not so far as Kyôga Domain, Jacob thinks. Someone fumbles at a casement.

He readies himself to be ordered inside by a worried official.

"Did gallant Sir de Zoet," hairy and naked Van Cleef taunts, flashing his teeth, "find the golden fleece last night?"

"It was" — *not,* Jacob thinks, *to my credit* — "it was the thing it was."

"Oh, hearken to Father Calvin." Van Cleef puts on his breeches and clambers out of the

610

window to join him, with a flagon hooked on his thumb. *He is not drunk, Jacob hopes, but he is not altogether sober.*

"Our Divine Father made *all* of you, man, in his own image, undertackle included — or do I lie?"

"God *did* make us, yes, but the Holy Book is clear about —"

"Oh, lawful wedlock, awful bedlock, yes, yes, well and good in Europe, but here" — Van Cleef gestures at Nagasaki like a conductor — "a man must improvise! Celibacy is for vegetarians. Neglect your spuds — I quote a medical fact — and they shrivel up and drop off, and what future then —"

"That is *not*" — Jacob almost smiles — "a medical fact, sir."

"— what future then for the Prodigal Son on the Isle of Walcheren, *sans* cods?" Van Cleef swigs from his flagon, wiping his beard on his forearm. "Bachelordom and an heirless death! Lawyers feasting on your estate like crows on a gibbet! This fine house" — he slaps the ridge tile — "is no sink of iniquity but a spa to nourish later harvests — you *did* use the armor urged upon us by Marinus? But who am I talking to? Of course you did."

Van Cleef's girl watches them from the depths of her room.

Jacob wonders what Orito's eyes look like now.

"A pretty little butterfly on the outside . . ."

A sigh heaves Van Cleef, and Jacob fears his superior is drunker than he thought — a fall could end in a broken neck. "But, unwrapped, one finds the same disappointments. 'Tweren't the girl's fault; it's Gloria's fault — the albatross hanging 'round my neck. . . . But why would you want to hear about that, young man, with your heart not yet broken?" The chief stares in the face of heaven, and the breeze stirs the world. "Gloria was my aunt. Batavia-born, I was, but sent to Amsterdam to learn the gentlemanly arts: how to spout bastard Latin, how to dance like a peacock, and how to cheat at cards. The party ended on my twenty-second birthday, when I took passage back to Java with my uncle Theo. Uncle Theo had visited Holland to deliver the governor-general's yearly fictions to East India House — the Van Cleefs were well connected in those days — grease palms, and marry for the fourth or fifth time. My uncle's motto was 'Race Is All.' He'd fathered half a dozen children on his Javanese maids, but he acknowledged none and made dire warnings about God's discrete races mingling into a single pigsty breed."

Jacob remembers the son in his dream. A Chinese junk's sails swell.

"Theo's legal heirs, he avowed, must have 'currency' mothers — white-skinned, rose-cheeked flowers of Protestant Europe — because Batavia-born brides all have orangutans cavorting in the family tree. Alas, his previous wives all expired within months of arriving in Java. The miasma did for them, you see. But Theo was a charming dog, and a rich charming dog, and, lo, it came to pass that between my cabin and my uncle's aboard the *Enkhuizen* was accommodated the latest Mrs. Theo van Cleef. My 'aunt Gloria' was four years my junior and one-third the age of her proud groom . . ."

Below, a rice seller opens up his shop for the day.

"Why bother describing a beauty in her first bloom? None of the bewhiskered nabob hookers on the *Enkhuizen* could compare, and before we'd rounded Brittany, all the eligible men — and many ineligible ones — were paying Aunt Gloria more attention than her new husband would wish. Through my thin cabin wall, I'd hear him warning her against holding X's gaze or laughing at Y's limp jokes. She'd reply, 'Yes, sir,' meek as a doe, then let him exact his marital dues. My imagination, De Zoet, was better than any peephole! Then, afterward, when Uncle Theo was back in his own cot, Gloria would weep, so delicately, so quietly, none but I could hear. She'd had no say in the marriage, of course, and Theo allowed her just one maid from home, a girl called Aagje — a second-class fare would buy five maids at Batavia's slave market. Gloria, you must remember,

613

had rarely gone beyond the Singel Canal. Java was as far off as the moon. Farther, in fact, for the moon is, at least, visible from Amsterdam. Come morning, I'd be kind to my aunt . . ."

In a garden, women drape washing on a juniper tree.

"The *Enkhuizen* took a bad mauling in the Atlantic," Van Cleef went on, pouring the last sunlit drops of beer onto his tongue, "so the captain settled upon a month's stay at the Cape for repairs. To protect Gloria from the common gaze, Uncle Theo took apartments in the villa of the sisters Den Otter, high above Cape Town, up between Lion's Head and Signal Hill. The six-mile track was a quagmire in wet weather and a hoof-twister in dry. Once upon a time the Den Otters were among the colony's grandest families, but by the late seventies the villa's once-famous stuccowork was falling off in chunks, its orchards were reverting to Africa, and its former staff of twenty or thirty reduced to a housekeeper, a cook, a put-upon maid, and two white-haired black gardeners, both called 'Boy.' The sisters kept no carriage but sent for a landau from an adjoining farmstead, and most of their utterances began with 'When dear Papa was alive' or 'When the Swedish ambassador would call.' Deathly, De Zoet — deathly! But young Mrs. van Cleef well knew what her husband wanted to hear and declared the villa to be private, safe, and enchantingly Gothic. The sisters Den Otter were 'a treasure trove of wisdom and improving stories.' Our landladies were defenseless against her flattery, and her sturdiness pleased Uncle Theo, and her brightness . . . her loveliness . . . She pulled me under, De Zoet. Gloria *was* love. Love *was* Gloria."

A tiny girl skips like a skinny frog around a persimmon tree.

I miss seeing children, Jacob thinks, and looks away to Dejima.

"On our first week at the villa, in a grove of agapanthus run amok, Gloria found me and told me to go and tell my uncle that she had flirted with me. Surely I'd misheard. She repeated her injunction: 'If you are my friend, Melchior, as I pray God you are, for I have no other in this wilderness, go to my husband and tell him that I confessed "inappropriate sentiments"! Use those very words, for they could be yours.' I protested that I couldn't besmirch her honor or place her in danger of a beating. She assured me that if I didn't do as she asked, or if I told my uncle about this conversation, *then* she would earn a beating. Well, the light in the grove was orange, and she squeezed my hand and said, 'Do this for me, Melchior.' So I went."

Fingers of smoke appear from the House of Wistaria's chimney.

"When Uncle Theo heard my false witness,

he agreed with my charitable diagnosis of nerves damaged by the voyage. I went for a confused walk along the steep cliffs, afraid of what might befall Gloria back at the villa. But at lunch Uncle Theo made a speech about family, obedience, and trust. After the blessing, he thanked God for sending him a wife and nephew in whom these Christian virtues blossomed. The sisters Den Otter chimed their brandy glasses with their apostle spoons and said, 'Hear, hear!' Uncle Theo gave me a pouch of guineas and invited me to go and enjoy all the pleasures the Tavern of the Two Seas could offer for two or three days . . ."

A man leaves from a brothel's side door. *He is me,* Jacob thinks.

". . . but I'd rather have broken a bone than be separated from Gloria. I begged my donor leave to return his guineas, asking only to keep the empty pouch to encourage me to fill it, and ten thousand more, with the fruits of my own acumen. All Cape Town's tinsel and baubles, I claimed, were not worth an hour of my uncle's company, and, time allowing, perhaps a game of chess? My uncle was silent, and I feared I'd over-sugared the tea, but then he declared that, whilst most young men were rascally popinjays who considered it their birthright to spend their fathers' hard-won fortunes in dissipation, heaven had sent him an exception for a nephew. He toasted the finest nephew in Christendom and, forgetting to conceal his clumsy test of marital fidelity, 'a true little wife.' He enjoined Gloria to raise his future sons with my image in mind, and his true little wife said, 'May they be in our nephew's image, Husband.' Theo and I then played chess, and it taxed my ingenuity, De Zoet, to let the clod outmaneuver me.'"

A bee hovers around Jacob's face, and goes.

"Gloria's and my loyalties now proven, my uncle felt at liberty to enter Cape Town society himself. These pursuits took him out of the villa for most of the day, and sometimes he even slept down in the town. Me, he set to the task of copying paperwork in the library. 'I'd invite you along,' he said, 'but I want the Kaffirs hereabouts to know there's a white man in the villa who can use a flintlock.' Gloria was left to her books, diary, the garden, and the 'improving stories' of the sisters: a spring that ran dry by three o'clock daily, when their lunchtime brandy plunged them into bottomless siestas . . .'"

Van Cleef's flagon rolls down the tiles, falls through the Wistaria frames, and smashes in the courtyard. "My uncle's bridal suite lay down a windowless corridor from the library. Concentrating on correspondence, I'll admit, was harder than usual that afternoon . . . The library clock, in my memory, is silent. Perhaps it is wound down. Orioles are singing like the choirs of Bedlam, and I hear the *click* of a key . . . that pregnant silence, when someone is waiting . . . and here she is in silhouette at the far end. She . . ." Van Cleef rubs his sunburned face. "I was afraid Aagje would find us, and she says, 'Haven't you noticed, Aagje's in love with the eldest son of the next farm?' and it's the most natural thing in the world to tell her I love her, and she kisses me, and she tells me she makes my uncle bearable by imagining he is me, and his is mine, and I ask, 'What if there's a child?' and she says, *Shush . . .*"

Mud-brown dogs race up the mud-brown street.

"Our unlucky number was four. The fourth time Gloria and I lay together, Uncle Theo's horse threw him on his way to Cape Town. He walked back to the villa, so we didn't hear the horse. One moment I was deep inside Gloria, as naked as silk. The next, I was still as naked as silk but lying amongst shards of the mirror my uncle had hurled me against. He told me he'd snap my neck and throw my carcass to the beasts. He told me to go to town, withdraw fifty guilders from his agent, and make sure I was too ill to board the *Enkhuizen* when she sailed on to Batavia. Last, he swore that whatever I'd put inside that whore, his wife, he would be digging out with a spoon. To my shame — or not, I don't know — I went away without saying goodbye to

Gloria." Van Cleef rubs his beard. "Two weeks later I watched the *Enkhuizen* embark. Five weeks later I shipped on a maggoty brig, the *Huis Marquette,* whose pilot spoke with dead spirits and whose captain suspected even the ship's dog of plotting mutiny. Well, you've crossed the Indian Ocean, so I shan't describe it: eternal, sinister, obsidian, mountainous, monotonous . . . After a seven-week crossing, we weighed anchor in Batavia by the grace of God, with little thanks due to the pilot or the captain. I walked along the stinking canal, steeling myself for a thrashing from Father, a duel with Theo, lately arrived on the *Enkhuizen,* disinheritance. I saw no familiar faces and none saw me — ten years is a long time — and knocked on the shrunken door of my boyhood home. My old nurse, wrinkled now like a walnut, opened the door and screamed. I remember Mother hurrying through from the kitchen. She held a vase of orchids. Next thing I knew, the vase had turned into a thousand broken pieces, and Mother was slumped against the wall. I assumed that Uncle Theo had made a *persona non grata* of me . . . but then noticed that Mother was in mourning. I asked if my father was dead. She answered, '*You* are, Melchior: you drowned.' Then there was a sobbing embrace, and I learned that the *Enkhuizen* had been wrecked on a reef just a mile from the Straits of Sunda, in a bright and savage sea, with all hands lost . . ."

"I'm sorry, Chief," says Jacob.

"The happiest ending is Aagje's. She married that farmer's boy and now owns three thousand head of cattle. Each time I'm in the Cape I mean to go and pay my compliments, but never do."

Excited shouts ring out nearby. The two foreigners have been spotted by a gang of carpenters at work on a nearby building. "Gaijin-*sama!*" calls one, with a grin wider than his face. He holds up a measuring rule and offers a service that makes his colleagues howl with laughter. "I didn't catch all of that," says Van Cleef.

"He volunteered to measure the length of your manhood, sir."

"Oh? Tell the rogue he'd need three of those rules."

In the jaws of the bay Jacob sees a fluttering rectangle of red, white, and blue.

No, thinks the head clerk. *It's a mirage . . . or a Chinese junk, or . . .*

"What's wrong, De Zoet? Are your breeches beshatten?"

"Sir — there's a merchantman entering the bay or . . . a frigate?"

"A *frigate?* Who's sending a *frigate?* Whose flag is it, man?"

"Ours, sir." Jacob grips the roof and blesses his farsightedness. "It's Dutch."

CHAPTER THIRTY:
THE ROOM OF THE
LAST
CHRYSANTHEMUM AT
THE MAGISTRACY IN
NAGASAKI

The second day of the ninth month
Lord Abbot Enomoto of Kyôga domain places a white stone on the board.

A way station, sees Magistrate Shiroyama, *between his northern flank . . .*

Shadows of slender maples stripe the board of gold *kaya* wood.

. . . and his eastern groups . . . or else a diversionary attack? Both.

Shiroyama believed he was gaining control, but he was losing it.

Where is the hidden way, he wonders, *to reverse my reverses?*

"Nobody refutes," says Enomoto, "we live in straitened times."

One may *refute,* thinks Shiroyama, *that* your *times are straitened.*

"A minor *daimyo* of the Aso Plateau who sought my assistance —"

Yes, yes, thinks the magistrate, *your discre-*

tion is impeccable.

"— observed that what grandfathers called 'debt' is now called 'credit.' "

"Meaning" — Shiroyama extends his north–south group with a black stone — "that debts no longer have to be repaid?"

With a polite smile, Enomoto removes his next stone from his rosewood bowl. "Repayments remain a tiresome necessity, alas, but the Aso noble's case illustrates the point. Two years ago he borrowed a sizable sum from Numa here" — Numa, one of the abbot's pet moneylenders, bows in his corner — "to drain a marsh. In the seventh month of this year, his shareholders harvested their first rice crop. So in an age when Edo's stipends are tardy and dwindling, Numa's client has well-fed, grateful peasants fattening his storehouses. His account with Numa shall be settled in full . . . when?"

Numa bows again. "A full two years early, Your Grace."

"That same *daimyo*'s lofty neighbor, who swore never to owe a grain of rice to anyone, dispatches ever-more frantic begging letters to the Council of Elders" — Enomoto places an island stone between his two eastern groups — "whose servants use them for kindling. Credit is the seed of wealth. The finest minds of Europe study credit and money within a discipline they call" — Enomoto uses a foreign phrase — " 'political economy.' "

This merely confirms, thinks Shiroyama, *my view of Europeans.*

"A young friend at the academy was translating a remarkable text, *The Wealth of Nations.* His death was a tragedy for us scholars but also, I believe, for Japan."

"Ogawa Uzaemon?" Shiroyama remembers. "A distressing affair."

"Had he but told me he was using the Ariake Road, I would have provided an escort through my domain. But on a pilgrimage for his ailing father, the modest young man wanted to eschew comfort . . ." Enomoto runs a thumbnail to and fro along his lifeline. The magistrate has been told the story by several sources but does not interrupt. "My men rounded up the bandits responsible. I beheaded the one who confessed and hung the others by iron spikes through the feet until wolves and crows had done their work. Then," he sighs, "Ogawa the Elder died, before an heir was chosen."

"The death of a family line," Shiroyama concurs, "is a terrible thing."

"A cousin from a lesser branch is rebuilding the house — I made a donation — but he's a common cutler, and the Ogawa name is gone from Dejima forever."

Shiroyama has nothing to add, but to change the subject is disrespectful.

Doors are slid open to reveal a veranda. Bright clouds bloom.

Over the hilly headland, smoke uncoils from a burning field.

One is here, one is gone, thinks Shiroyama. *Platitudes are profundities.*

The game of *go* reasserts itself. Starched silk sleeves rustle. "It is customary," observes Enomoto, "to flatter a magistrate's skill at *go,* but truly you are the best player I have met these last five years. I detect the influence of the Honinbo School."

"My father" — the magistrate sees the old man's ghost scowling at Enomoto's money-lender — "reached the second *ryu* of the Honinbo. I am an unworthy disciple" — Shiroyama attacks an isolated stone of Enomoto's — "when time permits." He lifts the teapot, but it is empty. He claps once, and Chamberlain Tomine appears in person. "Tea," says the magistrate. Tomine turns around and claps for another servant, who glides to the table, retrieves the tray in perfect silence, and vanishes, with a bow in the doorway. The magistrate imagines the tray descending the ladder of servitude to the toothless crone in the farthest kitchen, who warms the water to the perfect heat before pouring it over perfect leaves.

Chamberlain Tomine has gone nowhere: this is his mild protest.

"So, Tomine: the place is infested with

landowners in boundary disputes, petty officials needing positions for errant nephews, bruised wives begging for divorces, all of whom assail you with offers of coins and daughters, chorusing and imploring, 'Please, Chamberlain-*sama,* speak with the magistrate on my behalf.' "

Tomine makes an awkward *mmf* noise in his crushed nose.

A magistrate is the slave, Shiroyama thinks, *of that many-headed wanting . . .*

"Watch the goldfish," he tells Tomine. "Fetch me in a few minutes."

The circumspect chamberlain withdraws to the courtyard.

"Our game is unfair," says Enomoto. "You are distracted by duty."

A jade-and-ash dragonfly lands on the edge of the board.

"High office," replies the magistrate, "*is* distractions, of all sizes." He has heard that the abbot can remove the *ki* of insects and small creatures through the palm of his hand, and he half-hopes for a demonstration, but the dragonfly is already gone. "Lord Enomoto, too, has a domain to govern, a shrine to maintain, scholarly interests, and" — to accuse him of commercial interests would be an insult — "other matters."

"My days, to be certain, are never idle." Enomoto places a stone in the heart of the board. "But Mount Shiranui rejuvenates me."

An autumn breeze drags its invisible robes around the fine room.

I am powerful enough, the casual reference reminds the magistrate, *to oblige the Aibagawa girl, a favorite of yours, to take vows in my shrine, and you could not intercede.*

Shiroyama tries to concentrate on the game's present and future.

Once, Shiroyama's father taught him, *nobility ruled Japan . . .*

The kneeling servant parts the doors, bows, and brings in the tray.

. . . but now it is deception, greed, corruption, and lust that govern.

The servant brings two new cups and a teapot.

"Lord Abbot," says Shiroyama, "would you care for some tea?"

"You shan't be insulted," he states, "by my preference for my own drink."

"Your" — *what is the tactful word?* — "your caution is known."

Enomoto's indigo-clad aspirant is already there. The shaven-headed youth uncorks a gourd and leaves it with his master.

"Has your host ever . . ." Once again, the magistrate hunts for the right words.

"Been angered by an implicit accusation that he meant to poison me? Yes, upon occasion. But then I pacify him with the story of how an enemy's servant — a woman —

obtained a post at the residence of a famous Miyako family. She worked there as a trusted maid for two years until my next visit. She embellished my meal with a few grains of an odorless poison. Had my order's doctor, Master Suzaku, not been on hand to administer an antidote, I would have died, and my friend's family would have been disgraced."

"You have some unscrupulous enemies, Lord Abbot."

He lifts the neck of the gourd to his mouth, tilts his head, and drinks. "Enemies flock to power" — he wipes his lips — "like wasps to split figs."

Shiroyama threatens Enomoto's isolated stone by placing it in *atari.*

An earth tremor animates the stones; they blur and buzz . . .

. . . but are not dislocated, and the tremor passes.

"Pardon my vulgarity," says Enomoto, "for referring to the business of Numa once again, but that I keep a shogun's magistrate from his duties troubles my conscience. How much credit would it be helpful for Numa to supply in the first instance?"

Shiroyama feels acid in his stomach. "Perhaps . . . twenty?"

"Twenty thousand *ryo?* Certainly." Enomoto does not blink. "Half can be in your Nagasaki storehouse in two nights and half delivered to your Edo residence by the end of the tenth month. Would these times be satisfactory?"

Shiroyama hides his gaze in the board. "Yes." He forces himself to add, "There is a question of guarantees."

"An unnecessary slur," avows Enomoto, "on so illustrious a name . . ."

My illustrious name, thinks its owner, *brings me costly obligations.*

"When the next Dutch ship arrives, money will flow uphill from Dejima through Nagasaki once again, with the largest tributary passing through the magistracy's Exchequer. I am honored to guarantee the loan personally."

Mention of my Edo residence, Shiroyama thinks, *is a faint threat.*

"Interest, Your Honor," Numa bows again, "would amount to one quarter of the total sum paid annually over three years."

Shiroyama is unable to look at the moneylender. "Accepted."

"Excellent." The lord abbot sips from his gourd. "Our host is busy, Numa."

The moneylender bows all the way to the door, bumps it, and is gone.

Enomoto fortifies his north–south wall with his next stone. "Forgive me for bringing such a creature into your sanctuary, Magistrate. Papers must now be prepared for the loan, but these can be delivered to Your Honor tomorrow."

"There's nothing to forgive. Your . . . assistance is . . . timely."

An understatement, Shiroyama admits, and studies the board for inspiration. *Retainers on half pay; desertions imminent; daughters needing dowries; the roof of my Edo residence leaking and walls crumbling; and if my entourage at Edo slips below thirty, jokes about my poverty shall surely begin — and when the jokes reach the ears of my other creditors . . .* His father's ghost may hiss *Shame!* but his father inherited land to sell; nothing remained for Shiroyama but a costly rank and the position of Nagasaki magistrate. Once, the trading port was a silver mine, but in recent years the trade has been haphazard. Graft and wages, meanwhile, must be paid regardless. *If only,* Shiroyama dreams, *human beings were not masks behind masks behind masks. If only this world was a clean board of lines and intersections. If only time was a sequence of considered moves and not a chaos of slippages and blunders.*

He wonders, *Why hasn't Tomine come back to haunt me?*

Shiroyama senses a change in the magistracy's inner weather.

Not quite audible . . . but it *is* audible: a low rumble of agitation.

Footsteps hurry down the corridor. There is a breathless exchange of whispers outside.

Jubilant, Chamberlain Tomine enters. "A

ship is sighted, Your Honor!"

"Ships are entering and leaving all the — the *Dutch* ship?"

"Yes, sir. It's flying the Dutch flag, clear as day."

"But . . ." *A ship arriving in the ninth month is unheard of.* "Are you —"

The bells of every temple in Nagasaki begin to ring out in thanks.

"Nagasaki," observes the lord abbot, "is in no doubt at all."

Sugar, sandalwood, worsted, thinks Shiroyama, *lead, cotton . . .*

The pot of commerce will bubble, and the longest ladle is his.

Taxes on the Dutch, "gifts" from the chief, "patriotic" exchange rates . . .

"May I be the first," asks Enomoto, "to offer congratulations?"

How well you hide your disappointment that I slipped through your net, Shiroyama thinks, breathing properly, it feels, for the first time in weeks. "Thank you, Lord Abbot."

"I shall, of course, tell Numa to darken your halls no longer."

My temporary reverses, Shiroyama dares to believe, *are reversed.*

CHAPTER THIRTY-ONE: THE FORECASTLE TAFFRAIL OF HMS *PHOEBUS*

Ten o'clock sharp on October 18, 1800

"I have the dutch factory." Penhaligon sharpens the image in his telescope, estimating the distance at two English miles. "Warehouses, a lookout post, so we shall assume they know we are here . . . It *is* a poke-hole. Some twenty or thirty junks at anchor, the Chinese factory . . . fishing boats . . . a few grand roofs . . . but where a fat, laden Dutch Indiaman ought to be anchored, gentlemen, I see a stretch of empty blue water. Tell me I am wrong, Mr. Hovell."

Hovell sweeps the bay with his own telescope. "Would that I could, sir."

Major Cutlip whistles between his teeth in lieu of a filthy oath.

"Mr. Wren, do Clovelly's famous eyes spy what ours do not?"

Wren's question — "Do you find our Indiaman?" — is relayed up the foremast.

The answer descends to Wren, who repeats: "No Indiaman sighted, sir."

Then there is no quick killing to be made at Holland's expense. Penhaligon lowers his telescope as the bad news circulates from trestle trees to orlop deck in seconds. In the gundeck below, a Liverpudlian bellows the bad news to a deaf comrade: "No *effin'* ship is what's what, Davy, an' no *effin'* ship equals no *effin'* prize money an' no *effin'* prize money means *we* go home as piss-*effin'*-poor as we was when the *effin'* navy nabbed us!"

Daniel Snitker, under his wide-brimmed hat, needs no translation.

Wren is first to vent his anger at the Dutchman. "Are we too late? Did it sail?"

"Our misfortune is his, too, Lieutenant," Penhaligon warns.

Snitker addresses Hovell in Dutch, while pointing toward the city. "He says, Captain," begins the first lieutenant, "that if our approach was sighted yesterday evening, then the Dutch may be concealing their Indiaman in an inlet behind that high wooded hill with the pagoda atop, east of the river mouth."

Penhaligon senses the crew's hopes revive a little.

Then he wonders whether the *Phoebus* is being lured into a trap.

Snitker's yarn of a daring escape at Macao fooled Governor Cornwallis . . .

"Shall we take her in farther, sir?" Wren asks. "Or cast off in the boat?"

Could such a small-minded lout truly execute

such a complex plot?

Master Wetz calls from the wheel: "Am I to drop the anchors, Captain?"

Penhaligon lines up the questions. "Hold her steady for a minute, Mr. Wetz. Mr. Hovell, pray ask Mr. Snitker why the Dutch would hide their ship from us despite our Dutch colors. Might there be a code signal we have failed to fly?"

Snitker sounds uncertain at first but speaks with increasing confidence. Hovell nods. "He says, sir, that there was no code-signal arrangement when the *Shenandoah* departed last autumn, and he doubts there is one in place now. He says that Chief van Cleef may have hidden the vessel as a precautionary measure."

Penhaligon glances at the sails to gauge the breeze. "The *Phoebus* could reach the inlet in a few minutes, but tacking our way out again would be much slower." Spinach-green waves slurp at cracks between kelp-matted rocks. "Lieutenant Hovell, ask Mr. Snitker this: suppose no ship arrived from Batavia this year, due to shipwreck or the war; would the copper intended for her hold be stored on Dejima?"

Hovell translates the questions: Snitker's *"Ja, ja"* is firm enough.

"And would that copper be Japanese property or Dutch?"

Snitker's reply is less committal: the answer,

Hovell translates, is that the transfer of ownership of the copper depends upon the chief resident's negotiations, which vary year on year.

Deep bells begin ringing in the city and around the bay, and Snitker explains the noise to Hovell. "The bells are to thank the local gods for the safe arrival of the Dutch ship and the money it brings to Nagasaki. We may assume our disguise is working, sir."

A cormorant dives from steep black rocks a hundred yards away.

"Verify once again the procedure that a Dutch ship might observe at this point."

Snitker's reply is accompanied by gestures and pointed fingers.

"A Dutch Company ship, sir," says Hovell, "would sail in another half mile past the fortifications, which are saluted by a round from both bows. The longboat is then rowed out to meet the greeting party, consisting of two company sampans. Then all three boats return to the ship for the customary formalities."

"Exactly when may we expect our greeting party to embark from Dejima?"

The answer, accompanied by a shrug, is, "Perhaps a quarter hour, sir."

"To be clear: the party is composed of Japanese *and* Dutch officials?"

Snitker answers in English: "Japanese and Dutch, *ja*."

"Ask how many swordsmen accompany the party, Mr. Hovell."

The answer is involved, and the first lieutenant must clarify a couple of points. "All the officials on the boat carry swords, but primarily to denote their rank. For the most part, they resemble a country squire at home who talks tough but wouldn't know a sword from a darning needle."

Major Cutlip has no inhibitions. "If you'd like us to bag you a few hostages, sir, we'd have those jabbering monkeys for a second breakfast."

Curse Cornwallis, thinks the captain, *for encumbering me with this* ass.

"*Dutch* hostages," Hovell addresses him, "may strengthen our hand, but —"

"One bloodied Japanese nose," agrees Penhaligon, "may dash any hopes of a treaty for years: yes, I know. Kaempfer's book has impressed upon me the pride of this race, if nothing else. But I judge the risk worthwhile. Our disguise is a short-term expediency, and without better and less-partial intelligence" — he glances at Daniel Snitker, who is studying the city through his telescope — "about conditions ashore, we are blind men trying to outwit the sighted."

"And the possibility of a concealed Indiaman, sir?" asks Lieutenant Wren.

"If there is one, let it wait. She shan't slip past us without our knowledge. Mr. Talbot, bid the coxswain to ready the longboat but not to lower her yet."

"Aye, sir."

"Mr. Malouf," Penhaligon says, turning to a midshipman, "bid Mr. Wetz take us in past those toy fortifications by a half mile, but bid him take his time . . ."

"Aye, sir: in by a half mile, sir." Malouf hurries to Wetz at the wheel, leaping over a coil of crusty rope.

The sooner I can have the deck scrubbed, thinks the captain, *the better.*

"Mr. Waldron." He turns to the bovine master gunner. "Our guns are ready?"

"On both bows, Captain, aye: tampions out, charge in, but no shot."

"Customarily, the Dutch salute the guard posts as they pass those bluffs — see?"

"That I do, sir. Shall I have the lads below do the same?"

"Aye, Mr. Waldron, and though I neither want nor desire action today . . ."

Waldron waits while his captain chooses his words with care.

"Keep your key to the shot lockers to hand. Fortune favors the prepared."

"Aye, sir, we'll be ready." Waldron goes below to the gundeck.

Aloft, the topmen shout to one another as a topgallant is lowered.

Wetz is firing off a volley of orders in all directions.

636

Canvas stiffens, the *Phoebus* moves forward; her timbers and cordage creak.

A cormorant preens its feathers on the frigate's dolphin-spiker.

The leadsman calls, "By the mark nine!" The number is conveyed to Wetz.

Penhaligon studies the shore through his telescope, noting the lack of a castle keep or donjon in Nagasaki. "Mr. Hovell, pray ask Mr. Snitker this: were we to bring the *Phoebus* as close as we dared to Dejima, land forty men in two boats, and occupy the factory, would the Japanese consider Dutch soil to be taken or their own?"

Snitker's brief answer has a matter-of-fact tone. "He says he declines," translates Hovell, "to guess the mind of Japanese authority."

"Ask whether he'd be willing to join such a raid."

Snitker's interpreter translates his reply directly: " 'I am a diplomat and merchant, not a soldier,' sir." His reticence assuages Penhaligon's fears that Snitker is hurrying them into an elaborate trap.

"By the deep ten and a half!" calls the leadsman.

The *Phoebus* is almost level with the guard posts on either shore, upon which the captain now trains his telescope. The walls are thin, the stockades low, and the cannons more dangerous to their gunmen than their targets.

"Mr. Malouf, pray ask Mr. Waldron to give the order to fire our salute."

"Aye, sir: telling Mr. Waldron the order to fire the salute." Malouf goes below.

Penhaligon has his first clear sightings of the Japanese. They are as short as Malays, facially indistinguishable from the Chinese, and their armor brings to mind Major Cutlip's remarks about medieval jousters.

The guns fire through the ports, the noise ricocheting off the steep shores . . .

. . . and the acrid smoke blows over the crew, disinterring memories of battle.

"By the mark nine," calls the leadsman, "and a half nine . . ."

"Two boats embarking," reports the watch in the trestle tree.

Through his telescope, Penhaligon finds blurry images of the two sampans.

"Mr. Cutlip, I want the marines to row the longboat, dressed in landsmen's slops, with cutlasses hidden below the thwarts in sackcloth." The major salutes and goes below. The captain proceeds to the waist to address the coxswain, a cunning Scillies smuggler pressed from the shadow of the Penzance gallows. "Mr. Flowers, lower the longboat but tangle the ropes, so as to buy time. I want the greeting party to meet our longboat closer to the *Phoebus* than to shore."

"A proper Frenchman's fanny I'll make of it, Captain."

Walking back to the bow, Hovell asks permission to air a thought.

"My esteem for your aired thoughts is high, Mr. Hovell."

"Thank you, sir. I posit that the governor-general's and the admiralty's twin orders regarding the present mission — to paraphrase, 'Plunder the Dutch and seduce the Japanese' — do not correspond with the scenario we find here. If the Dutch have nothing to plunder and the Japanese prove loyal to their allies, how are we to carry out our orders? A third strategy, however, may yield a more fruitful result."

"Describe what you have in mind, Lieutenant."

"That the Dutch incumbents of Dejima be viewed not as a barrier to an Anglo-Japanese treaty but, rather, as its *key*. How? In short, sir, instead of smashing the Dutch engine of trade in Nagasaki, we help them repair it and then requisition it."

"By the mark ten," calls out the leadsman, "ten and a third . . ."

"The lieutenant" — Wren heard everything — "has not forgotten that we and the Dutch are at war? Why would they cooperate with their national enemy? If you're still placing your hopes in that scrap of paper from the Dutch King Billy at Kew—"

"Might the second lieutenant be good

639

enough to let the first lieutenant speak, Mr. Wren?"

Wren performs an ironic bow of apology, and Penhaligon wants to kick him . . .

. . . but for your father-in-law admiral and the damage it would cause my gout.

"The Netherlanders' sliver of a republic," continues Hovell, "didn't defy the might of Bourbon Spain without a genius for pragmatism. Ten percent of profits — let us call it the 'brokerage fee' — is a sight better than a hundred percent of nothing. Less than nothing: if no ship arrived from Java this year, then they are ignorant of the Dutch East Indies Company's bankruptcy . . ."

". . . and the loss," realizes the captain, "of their accumulated wages and private trade channeled through the company's books. Poor Jan, Piet, and Klaas are paupers, stranded among heathens."

"With no means," adds Hovell, "of seeing home again."

The captain gazes at the city. "Once we have the Dutch officers aboard, we can reveal their orphaned status and present ourselves not as aggressors but godfathers. We can send one ashore both to convert his countrymen and to act as an emissary to the Japanese authorities, explaining that future 'Dutch sailings' shall come from Prince of Wales Island in Penang rather than Batavia."

"To seize the Dutch copper as prize would

kill the golden goose of trade. But to trade the silks and sugar in our hold and leave with half as a legal cargo would allow us to return each year — to the ongoing enrichment of company and empire."

How Hovell reminds me, Penhaligon thinks, *of my youthful self.*

"The men," Wren says, "would cry havoc at losing their prize money."

"The *Phoebus,*" says the captain, "is His Majesty's frigate, not their privateer." He returns to the coxswain, the pain in his foot now difficult to conceal. "Mr. Flowers, pray untangle your French fanny. Mr. Malouf, ask Major Cutlip to start loading his marines. Lieutenant Hovell, we rely on your skill in the Dutch language to charm a pair of plump Dutch herrings into the longboat without catching a native fish."

The *Phoebus*'s anchor is lowered five hundred yards past the guard posts; the longboat, rowed by marines in sailors' slops, makes leisurely progress toward the greeting party. Coxswain Flowers has the tiller, and Hovell and Cutlip sit at the prow.

"This Nagasaki," notes Wren, "is an anchorage the equal of Port Mahon . . ."

In clear water, a shoal of silver fish changes direction.

". . . a few modern placements would make it impregnable."

Long, curved rice paddies stripe the low and laddered mountains.

"Wasted on a backward race," laments Wren, "too idle to build a navy."

Black smoke rises from the hunchbacked headland. Penhaligon tries to ask Daniel Snitker if the smoke could be a signal, but Snitker fails to make his answer comprehensible so the captain sends for Smeyers, a carpenter's mate who speaks Dutch.

The forests of pines might yield masts and spars.

"The bay presents a lovely prospect," ventures Lieutenant Talbot.

The womanly adjective irritates Penhaligon, and he wonders at the wisdom of Talbot's appointment, necessitated by the death of Sam Smythe at Penang. Then he recalls the loneliness of his own third lieutenancy, caught between the resentment of a frosty captain's cabin and his former comrades in the midshipmen's cockpit. "A fair sight, yes, Mr. Talbot."

A man in the heads, a few feet down and a few feet forward, groans.

"The Japanese, I read," says Talbot, "give florid names to their kingdom . . ."

The unseen sailor issues an almighty orgasmic bellow of relief . . .

" 'The Land of a Thousand Autumns' or 'The Root of the Sun.' "

. . . and a turd hits the water like a cannonball. Wetz rings three bells.

"Seeing Japan," says Talbot, "such poetic names seem precise."

"What *I* see," says Wren, "is a sheltered harbor for an entire squadron."

Never mind a squadron, the captain thinks. *What about a fleet?*

His heart quickens as the vision grows. *A British Pacific fleet.*

The captain imagines a floating city of British men-of-war and frigates . . .

Penhaligon pictures his chart of Northeast Asia, with a British base in Japan . . .

China herself, he dares to think, *could follow India into our sphere . . .*

Midshipman Malouf returns with Smeyers.

. . . and the Philippines, too, would be ours for the taking.

"Mr. Smeyers, be so good as to ask Mr. Snitker about that smoke —"

The toothless Amsterdammer squints at the smoke from the galley stove.

"— that black smoke, there, above that hunchbacked headland."

"Aye, sir." Smeyers points as he translates. Snitker is unworried.

"No bad, he says," translates Smeyers. "Farmers burn fields every autumn."

Penhaligon nods. "Thank you. Stay nearby, in case I need you."

He notices that the flag — the Dutch

tricolor — is tangled around the jibboom.

He looks for someone to right it and sees a half-caste boy with a wiry pigtail picking oakum under the steam grating. "Hartlepool!"

The youth puts down his rope and comes over. "Yessir."

Hartlepool's face speaks of fatherlessness and resilience.

"Pray disentangle that flag for me, Hartlepool."

"Sir." The barefoot boy slips over the main rail, balances on the bowsprit . . .

How many years, wonders Penhaligon, *since I was so nimble?*

. . . and darts up the timber angled at nearly forty-five degrees.

The bereaved captain's thumb finds Tristram's crucifix.

At the spritsail yard, forty yards out and thirty yards up, Hartlepool stops. Gripping the boom between his thighs, he untangles the flag.

"Can he swim, I wonder?" Lieutenant Talbot asks himself aloud.

"I'd not know," says Midshipman Malouf, "but one doubts it . . ."

Hartlepool makes the return trip with the same lithe grace.

"If his mother was a Blackamoor," comments Wren, "his father was a cat."

When Hartlepool jumps onto the deck in

front of him, the captain gives him a new farthing. "Ably done, boy." Hartlepool's eyes widen at the unexpected generosity. He thanks Penhaligon and returns to his oakum-picking.

A lookout shouts: "Greeting party nearly at the longboat!"

Through his telescope, Penhaligon sees the two sampans approaching the longboat. The foremost carries three Japanese officials, two in gray and a younger colleague in black. Three servants sit at the back. The rearmost sampan conveys the two Dutchmen. Their features lack much detail at this range, but Penhaligon can make out that one is tanned, bearded, and rotund, the other is sticklike and pale as chalk.

Penhaligon hands the telescope to Snitker, who reports to Smeyers. "Gray-coats is officials, he says, Captain. Black-coat is translator. The big Dutchman is Melchior van Cleef, chief of Dejima. The thin one is a Prussian. His name is Fischer. Fischer is second in command."

Van Cleef cups his hands to his mouth and hails Hovell, a hundred yards off.

Snitker keeps talking. Smeyers says, "Van Cleef is human rat, he says, sir, a true . . . a damned coat-turn? And Fischer is a sneak, a liar, a cheat whoreson, he says, sir, with big ambition. I don't think Mr. Snitker like them, sir."

"But both men," opines Wren, "sound amenable to our proposal. The last thing we need are incorruptible men-of-principle types."

Penhaligon takes his telescope from Snitker. "Not many of them hereabouts."

Cutlip's marines stop rowing. The longboat glides to a dead stop.

The boat of the three Japanese officials touches the longboat's prow.

"Don't let them board," murmurs Penhaligon to his first lieutenant.

The prows of the two boats nudge each other. Hovell salutes.

The inspectors bow. Via the interpreter, introductions are made.

One inspector and the interpreter now half-stand, as if preparing to transfer.

Delay them, Penhaligon urges Hovell silently, *delay them . . .*

Hovell feigns a coughing fit; he presents one hand in apology.

The second sampan arrives, pulling up to the longboat's port side.

"A disadvantageous position," mutters Wren, "wedged in from both sides."

Hovell recovers from his cough; he doffs his hat at Van Cleef.

Van Cleef stands and leans over the prow to take Hovell's hand.

The spurned inspector and interpreter, meanwhile, half sit down.

Deputy Fischer now stands, clumsily, and the boat rocks.

Hovell swings the large Van Cleef over onto the longboat.

"One in the bag, Mr. Hovell," mutters the captain. "Deftly done."

Faintly comes the rumble of Chief van Cleef's thunderous laughter.

Fischer takes a step toward the longboat, wobbly as a foal . . .

. . . but to Penhaligon's dismay, the interpreter now grips the long boat's lip.

The nearest marine calls to Major Cutlip. Cutlip grapples his way over . . .

"Not yet," mumbles the captain, impotently, "don't let him aboard."

Lieutenant Hovell, meanwhile, is beckoning the deputy over.

Cutlip grips the hand of the unwanted interpreter . . .

Wait wait, the captain wants to yell, *wait for our second Dutchman!*

. . . and Cutlip lets the interpreter go, waving his hand as if it is brutally mangled.

Now, at long last, Hovell has hold of the unsteady deputy's hand.

Penhaligon mumbles, "*Land* the man, Hovell, for Christ's sake!"

The interpreter decides not to wait for further assistance and plants one foot on the longboat's port bulwark just as Hovell swings the Prussian deputy over the starboard . . .

. . . and half of the marines take up their cutlasses, some flashing in sunlight.

The other marines take up their oars and push the sampans away.

The black-coated interpreter flops, like a Pierrot, into the water. The *Phoebus*'s longboat lunges back toward the ship.

Chief van Cleef, realizing that he is being abducted, attacks Lieutenant Hovell.

Cutlip intercepts and falls on him. The boat rocks dangerously.

Let it not capsize, dear God, prays Penhaligon, *not now . . .*

Van Cleef is subdued and the longboat settles. The Prussian is sitting meekly.

Back at the sampans, already three lengths away, the first Japanese to act is an oarsman, who leaps into the water to save the interpreter. The gray-coated inspectors sit and stare in shock at the foreigners' longboat, as it retreats to the *Phoebus.*

Penhaligon lowers his telescope. "The first engagement is won. Strike that Dutch rag, Mr. Wren, and fly the Union Jack, topmast and prow."

"Yes, sir, with the greatest of pleasure."

"Mr. Talbot, have your landsmen rinse the filth from my decks."

The Dutchman van Cleef seizes the rope ladder and clambers up it with an agility belying his bulk. Penhaligon glances up at the quarterdeck, where Snitker remains out of sight, for now, under his floppy-brimmed hat. Batting away proffered hands, Van Cleef leaps onto the *Phoebus* like a Moorish boarder, glares along the line of officers, singles out Penhaligon, points a finger so wrathfully that a pair of marines take a step closer in case of attack, and declares, through his curly, close-cropped beard and tea-brown teeth, *"Kapitein!"*

"Welcome aboard His Majesty's Frigate *Phoebus,* Mr. van Cleef. I am —"

The irate chief's molten invective needs no translation.

"I am Captain John Penhaligon," he says, when Van Cleef next draws breath, "and this is my second officer, Lieutenant Wren. First Lieutenant Hovell and Major Cutlip" — they arrive on deck now — "you have already met."

Chief van Cleef takes a step toward the captain and spits at his feet.

An oyster of phlegm shines on his second-best Jermyn Street shoe.

"Dutch officers for you," declares Wren. "Bereft of breeding."

Penhaligon hands his handkerchief to Malouf. "For the ship's honor . . ."

"Aye, sir." The midshipman kneels by the captain and wipes the shoe.

The firm pressure makes his gouty foot glow with pain. "Lieutenant Hovell. Inform

Chief van Cleef that whilst he behaves like a gentleman, our hospitality shall be accordingly civil, but should he comport himself like an Irish navvy, then that is how he shall be treated."

"Taming Irish navvies," boasts Cutlip, as Hovell translates the warning, "is a labor I am fond of, sir."

"Let us appeal to reason in the first instance, Major."

A high bell is being rung; Penhaligon assumes it is an alarm.

Without looking at Van Cleef, he now extends his greeting to the lesser, second hostage. "Welcome aboard His Majesty's Frigate *Phoebus*, Deputy Fischer."

Chief van Cleef forbids his deputy to speak.

Penhaligon orders Hovell to ask Fischer about this season's Indiaman, but Chief van Cleef claps twice to earn the captain's attention and issues a statement that Hovell translates. "I'm afraid he said, 'I hid it up my arse, you English nancy,' sir."

"A man once spoke to me so in Sydney Cove," recalls Cutlip, "so I searched said hidey-hole with a bayonet and he never came cocky with an officer again."

"Tell our guests this, Mr. Hovell," Penhaligon says. "Tell them we *know* a vessel sailed from Batavia, because I heard from the harbormaster of Macao that she weighed anchor in that port on the twenty-eighth of May."

Hearing this, Van Cleef's anger cools and Fischer looks grave. They consult with each other, and Hovell eavesdrops. "The chief is saying, 'Unless this is English sneakery, another ship is lost . . .'"

A bird in the woods along the shore sounds very like a cuckoo.

"Warn them, Lieutenant, that we shall be searching the bay and that if we discover their Indiaman in any of the coves, they shall both be hanged."

Hovell translates the threat. Fischer rubs his head. Van Cleef spits. The saliva misses the captain's foot, but Penhaligon cannot have his authority eroded in front of the onlooking crew. "Major Cutlip, accommodate Chief van Cleef in the aft rope store: no lamp, no refreshments. Deputy Fischer, meanwhile" — the Prussian blinks like a frightened hen — "may rest awhile in my cabin. Have two of my best men watch him, and tell Chigwin to bring him a half bottle of claret."

Before Cutlip can act on the order, Van Cleef asks Hovell a question.

Penhaligon is curious about the Dutchman's altered tone. "What was that?"

"He wanted to know how we know his and his deputy's names, sir."

It shall profit us, thinks Penhaligon, *to establish that they cannot bluff us.*

"Mr. Talbot, bid our informant to come greet his old friends."

His revenge complete, Daniel Snitker strides up and removes his hat.

Drop-jawed and wide-eyed, Van Cleef and Fischer stare.

Snitker regales the pair with a long-planned speech.

"Some blood-chilling language he's issuing, sir," mutters Hovell.

"Well, this dish *is* best served cold, as they say."

Hovell opens his mouth, closes it again, listens, and translates: "The gist is, 'You thought I'd be rotting in a Batavia jail, didn't you?' "

Daniel Snitker parades up to Fischer and pokes his throat.

"He's saying he's 'captain-in-chief' of Dejima's 'restoration.' "

When Snitker leers into the bearded face of Melchior van Cleef, Penhaligon expects the chief to spit, or hit out, or curse. He certainly does not anticipate the smile of pleasure that overspills into genuine, generous laughter. Snitker is as surprised as the English spectators. Jubilantly, Van Cleef clasps the shoulders of his onetime superior. Cutlip and the marines step forward to intervene, expecting mischief, but Van Cleef speaks, incredulous, delighted, and shaking his head. Hovell reports, "Sir, he's saying that Chief Snitker's appearance is proof that God is just and God is good; that the men ashore want nothing

652

more than to have their old chief back where he belongs . . . that 'Vorstenbosch the viper and his toad Jacob de Zoet' perpetrated a gross travesty."

Van Cleef turns to Deputy Fischer and appears to demand, "Isn't that so?"

Dazed, Deputy Fischer nods and blinks. Van Cleef continues. Hovell follows the next part with difficulty: "There's a lad ashore, it seems, named Oost, who misses Snitker like a son misses a father . . ."

Snitker, at first caught between disbelief and wonder, now begins to soften.

With his giant's hands, Van Cleef indicates Penhaligon.

"He's saying encouraging things for our mission, sir. He's saying . . . that if a man of Mr. Snitker's integrity finds common cause with this gentleman — he means *you,* sir — then he'll gladly clean your shoes himself to apologize for his rudeness."

"Can this about-face be genuine, Lieutenant?"

"I . . ." Hovell looks on as Van Cleef enfolds Snitker in a laughing embrace and says something to Penhaligon. "He's thanking you, sir, from the bottom of his heart . . . for restoring a beloved comrade . . . and hopes that the *Phoebus* may herald the restoration of Anglo-Dutch accord."

"Minor miracles," Penhaligon looks on, "do occur. Ask whether —"

Van Cleef drives a fist into Snitker's belly.

Snitker bends over like a folded jackknife.

Van Cleef seizes his choking victim and flings him over the side.

There is no yell, just an almighty boom of falling body on water.

"Man overboard!" Wren shouts. "*Move, then, you lazy dogs! Fish him out!*"

"Get him out my sight, Major," Penhaligon snarls at Cutlip.

As Van Cleef is led to the companionway, he fires back a statement.

"He expressed surprise, Captain," Hovell translates, "that a British captain allows dog shit on his quarterdeck."

CHAPTER THIRTY-TWO: THE WATCHTOWER ON DEJIMA

A quarter past ten o'clock on the morning of October 18, 1800

When the Union Jack appears on the frigate's Jack staff, Jacob de Zoet knows, *The war is here.* The transactions between the longboat and the greeting party puzzled him, but now the strange behavior is explained. Chief van Cleef and Peter Fischer have been kidnapped. Below the watchtower, Dejima is still in sweet ignorance of the turbulent events being played out across the placid water. A gang of merchants enters Arie Grote's house, and cheerful guards are opening up the long-shuttered customs house at the sea gate. Jacob looks through his telescope one last time. The greeting party is rowing back to Nagasaki as if their lives depend on it. *We must steal this march,* Jacob realizes, *on the magistracy.* He clatters down the zigzag wooden steps, dashes down the alley to Long Street, unties the rope of the fire bell, and rings it with all his strength.

Around the oval table in the stateroom sit Dejima's remaining eight Europeans: the officers Jacob de Zoet, Ponke Ouwehand, Dr. Marinus, and Con Twomey; and the hands Arie Grote, Piet Baert, Wybo Gerritszoon, and young Ivo Oost. Eelattu is seated beneath the engraving of the brothers De Witt. In the last quarter hour, the men have passed from celebration through disbelief to bafflement and gloom. "Until we can secure the release of Chief van Cleef and Deputy Fischer," Jacob says, "I mean to assume command of Dejima. This self-appointment is most irregular, and I shall record objections in the factory's day journal without resentment. But our hosts will want to deal with one officer, not all eight of us, and my rank is now the highest."

"Ibant qui poterant," pronounces Marinus, *"qui non potuere cadebant."*

"Acting Chief de Zoet," Grote clears his throat and says, "has a pleasin' 'nough ring."

"Thank you, Mr. Grote. What of 'Acting Deputy Ouwehand'?"

Glances and nods from around the table confirm the appointment.

"It's the oddest promotion," says Ouwehand, "but I accept."

"We must pray that these posts are temporary, but for now, before the magistrate's inspectors come pounding up those stairs, I wish to establish one guiding principle: namely, that we resist the occupation of Dejima."

The Europeans nod, some defiantly, others less so.

"Is it to seize the factory," Ivo Oost asks, "they've come here?"

"We can only speculate, Mr. Oost. Perhaps they expected a merchantman full of copper. Perhaps they aim to ransack our warehouses. Perhaps they want a fat ransom for their hostages. We suffer from a shortage of hard facts."

"It's our shortage of arms," says Arie Grote, "what worries me. To say 'resist the occupation o' Dejima' is well an' good, but how? My kitchen knives? The doctor's lancets? What's our weapons?"

Jacob looks at the cook. "Dutch guile."

Con Twomey raises his hand in objection.

"I beg your pardon. Dutch and Irish guile — and preparedness. And so, Mr. Twomey, please ensure the fire engines are working properly. Mr. Ouwehand, please draw up an hourly roster for the watchtower during the —"

Urgent footsteps can be heard on the main stairs.

Interpreter Kobayashi enters and glares at the assembly.

A corpulent inspector stands behind him in

the doorway.

"Magistrate Shiroyama sends inspector," says Kobayashi, unsure whom to address, "on business of serious thing . . . happen in bay: magistrate must discuss this thing, no delay. Magistrate sends to higher-ranking foreigner now." The interpreter swallows. "So inspector need know, who is higher-ranking foreigner?"

Six Dutchmen and one Irishman look in Jacob's direction.

Tea is cool lush green in a smooth pale bowl. Interpreters Kobayashi and Yonekizu, Acting Chief Resident Jacob de Zoet's escorts to the magistracy this morning, left him in the vestibule to be watched by a pair of officials. Not realizing that the Dutchman can understand, the officials speculate that the foreigner's eyes are green because his pregnant mother ate too many vegetables. The dignified atmosphere Jacob remembers from last year's visit to the magistracy with Vorstenbosch is overturned by the morning's events: soldiers shout from the barracks wing; blades are being sharpened on flywheels; and servants hurry by, whispering about what might happen. Interpreter Yonekizu appears. "Magistrate is ready, Mr. de Zoet."

"As am I, Mr. Yonekizu, but has any fresh news arrived?"

The interpreter shakes his head ambiguously and leads De Zoet into the Hall of Sixty

Mats. A council of around thirty advisers sits in a horseshoe shape, two or three rows deep, around Magistrate Shiroyama, who occupies a one-mat-high dais. Jacob is ushered into the center. Chamberlain Kôda, Inspector Suruga, and Iwase Banri — the three sent to accompany Van Cleef and Fischer to the Dutch ship — kneel in a row to one side. All three look pale and worried.

A sergeant at arms announces, *"Dejima no Dazûto-sama."* Jacob bows.

Shiroyama says, in Japanese, "Thank you for attending us so quickly."

Jacob meets the clear eyes of the grim man and bows once more.

"I am told," says the magistrate, "that you now understand some Japanese."

To acknowledge the remark would advertise his clandestine studies and may forfeit a tactical advantage. *But to pretend not to understand,* Jacob thinks, *would be deceitful.* "Somehow I understand a little of the magistrate's mother tongue, yes."

The horseshoe of advisers murmurs in surprise at hearing a foreigner speak.

"Moreover," the magistrate says, "I hear you are an honest man."

Jacob receives the compliment with a noncommittal bow.

"I enjoyed dealings," says a voice that chills Jacob's neck, "with the acting chief resident during last year's trading season . . ."

659

Jacob does not want to look at Enomoto, but his eyes are drawn.

". . . and believe that no better leader could be found on Dejima."

Jailer. Jacob swallows as he bows. *Murderer, liar, madman . . .*

Enomoto tilts his head in apparent amusement.

"The opinion of the lord of Kyôga carries much weight," says Magistrate Shiroyama. "And we make a solemn oath to Acting Chief de Zoet: your countrymen *shall* be saved from your enemies . . ."

This unconditional support surpasses Jacob's hopes. "Thank you, Your —"

". . . or the chamberlain, inspector, and interpreter shall die in the attempt." Shiroyama looks at the three disgraced men. "Men of honor," the magistrate states, "do not permit their charges to be stolen. To make amends, they shall be rowed to the intruders' ship. Iwase will win permission for the three men to board and pay a" — Shiroyama's next word must mean "ransom" — "to release the two" — the word must be "hostages." "Once aboard, they will cut the English captain down with concealed knives. This is not the Way of the Bushidô, but these pirates deserve to die like dogs."

"But Kôda-*sama*, Suruga-*sama*, and Iwase-*sama* shall be killed, and —"

"Death shall cleanse them of" — the next

word may be "cowardice."

How shall the de facto *suicides of these three men,* Jacob groans inwardly, *resolve anything?* He turns to Yonekizu and asks, "Please tell His Honor that the English are a vicious race. Inform him that they would kill not only Your Honor's three servants but also Chief van Cleef and Deputy Fischer."

The Hall of Sixty Mats hears this in gravid silence, suggesting that the magistrate's advisers raised this objection or else were too afraid to.

Shiroyama looks displeased. "What action would the acting chief propose?"

Jacob feels like a distrusted defendant. "The best action, for now, is *no* action."

There is some surprise; an adviser leans toward Shiroyama's ear . . .

Jacob needs Yonekizu again: "Tell the magistrate that the English captain is testing us. He is waiting to see whether the Japanese or the Dutch respond and whether we use force or diplomacy." Yonekizu frowns at the last word. "Words, parleying, negotiation. But by not acting, we will make the English impatient. Their impatience will cause them to reveal their intentions."

The magistrate listens, nods slowly, and orders Jacob: "Guess their intentions."

Jacob obeys his instinct to answer truthfully. "First," he begins in Japanese, "they came to take the Batavia ship and its cargo of copper. Because they found no ship, they took hostages. They" — he hopes this makes sense — "they want to harvest knowledge."

Shiroyama's fingers entwine. "Knowledge about Dutch forces on Dejima?"

"No, Your Honor: knowledge about Japan and its empire."

The ranks of advisers mutter. Enomoto stares. Jacob sees a skull wrapped in skin.

The magistrate raises his fan. "All men of honor prefer death by torture over giving information to an enemy." All present — Chamberlain Kôda, Inspector Suruga, and Interpreter Iwase excepted — nod with indignant agreement.

None of you, Jacob thinks, *has been within fifteen decades of a real war.*

"But why," Shiroyama asks, "are the English hungry to learn about Japan?"

I am taking a thing apart, Jacob fears, *that I cannot put back together.*

"The English may wish to trade in Nagasaki again, Your Honor."

My move is made, the acting chief thinks, *and I cannot take it back.*

"Why you use the word," asks the magistrate, " 'again'?"

Lord Abbot Enomoto clears his throat. "Acting Chief de Zoet's statement is accurate, Your Honor. Englishmen traded in Nagasaki long ago, during the time of the first shogun, when silver was exported. One doesn't doubt that the memory of those profits lingers in their land, to this day . . . though naturally, the acting chief would know more about this than I do."

Against his will, Jacob imagines Enomoto pinning Orito down.

Willfully, Jacob imagines bludgeoning Enomoto to death.

"How does kidnapping our allies," Shiroyama asks, "win our trust?"

Jacob turns to Yonekizu. "Tell His Honor the English don't want your trust. The English want fear and obedience. They build their empire by sailing into foreign harbors, firing cannons, and buying local magistrates. They expect His Honor to behave like a corrupt Chinaman or a Negro king, happy to trade the well-being of your own people for an English-style house and a bagful of glass beads."

As Yonekizu translates, the Hall of Sixty Mats crackles with anger.

Belatedly, Jacob notices a pair of scribes in the corner recording every word.

The shogun himself, he thinks, *will soon be reading your words.*

A chamberlain approaches the magistrate with a message.

The announcement, in Japanese too formal for Jacob to understand, seems to heighten the tension. To save Shiroyama the trouble of dismissing him, Jacob turns again to Yonekizu: "Give my government's thanks to the magistrate for his support, and beg his permission for me to return to Dejima and oversee preparations."

Yonekizu provides a suitably formal translation.

The shogun's representative dismisses Jacob with a curt nod.

CHAPTER THIRTY-THREE: THE HALL OF SIXTY MATS AT THE MAGISTRACY

After Acting Chief de Zoet's departure on the second day of the ninth month

"The Dutchman may look like a goblin from a child's nightmare," says Shiroyama, noticing his advisers' sycophantic sneers, "but he is no fool." The sneers quickly turn into wise nods of agreement.

"His manners are polished," approves one city elder, "and his reasoning clear."

"His Japanese was odd," says another, "but I understood much."

"My spies on Dejima," adds a third, "say he studies incessantly."

"But his accent," complains an inspector, Wada, "was like a crow's!"

"And you, Wada, speak Dazûto's tongue," asks Shiroyama, "like a nightingale?"

Wada, who speaks no Dutch at all, is wise enough to say nothing.

"And the three of *you*." Shiroyama waves his fan at the men held responsible for the kidnapping of the two Dutch hostages. "You owe your very lives to his clemency."

The nervous men respond with humble bows.

"Interpreter Iwase, my report to Edo shall note that you, at least, tried to engage the abductors, however ineptly. You are needed at your guild and may go."

Iwase bows deeply and hurries from the hall.

"You two," Shiroyama continues, staring at the hapless inspector and official, "brought disrepute to your rank, and taught the Englishmen that Japan is populated by cowards." *Few of your peers,* the magistrate admits to himself, *would have acquitted themselves any better.* "Stay confined to your houses until further notice."

The two disgraced men crawl backward to the door.

Shiroyama finds Tomine. "Summon the captain of the coastal guards."

The swarthy captain is ushered onto the very mat vacated by De Zoet. He bows before the magistrate. "My name's Doi, Your Honor."

"How soon, with what force, and how best may we retaliate?"

Instead of replying, the man stares at the floor.

Shiroyama looks at Chamberlain Tomine, who is as puzzled as his master.

A half-mute incompetent, Shiroyama wonders, *promoted by a relative?*

Wada clears his throat. "The hall is waiting, Captain Doi."

"I inspected" — the soldier glances up like a rabbit in a snare — "the battle-readiness of both guard posts, north and south of the bay, and consulted with the highest-ranking officers available."

"I want strategies for counterattacks, Doi, not regurgitated orders!"

"It was . . . intimated to me, sir, that — that troop strength is . . ."

Shiroyama notices the better-informed courtiers fanning themselves anxiously.

". . . less than the thousand men stipulated by Edo, Your Honor."

"Are you telling me that the garrisons of Nagasaki Bay are undermanned?"

Doi's cringing bow affirms that this is so. Advisers murmur in alarm.

A small shortage shan't damage me, thinks the magistrate. "By how many?"

"The exact number," Captain Doi swallows, "is sixty-seven, Your Honor."

Shiroyama's guts untwist themselves: not even his most vitriolic rival Ômatsu, with whom he shares the post of magistrate, could portray a lack of sixty-seven men out of one thousand as dereliction. *It could be written off as sickness.* But a glance at the faces around the room tells the magistrate he is missing something . . .

. . . until a fearful thought uproots all things.

"Surely not" — he masters his voice — "sixty-seven men in *total?*"

The weather-beaten captain is too nervous to reply.

Chamberlain Tomine barks: "The magistrate asked you a question!"

"There —" Doi disintegrates and must begin again. "There are thirty guards at the north garrison, and thirty-seven at the south. That is the total, Your Honor."

Now the advisers study Magistrate Shiroyama . . .

Sixty-seven soldiers, he thinks, holding the damning numbers, *in lieu of one thousand.*

. . . the cynical, the ambitious, his appalled allies, Ômatsu's placemen . . .

Some of you leeches knew this, Shiroyama thinks, *and said nothing.*

Doi is still crouching like a prisoner waiting for the sword to fall.

Ômatsu would *blame the messenger . . .* and Shiroyama, too, is tempted to lash out. "Wait outside, Captain. Thank you for dispatching your duty with such speed and . . . accuracy."

Doi glances at Tomine to check he heard correctly, bows, and leaves.

None of the advisers dares be first to violate the awed hush.

Blame the lord of Hizen, Shiroyama thinks. *He supplies the men.*

No: the magistrate's enemies would depict

him as a cowardly shirker.

Plead that the coastal garrisons have been undermanned for years.

To say so implies that he knew of the shortages yet did nothing.

Plead that no Japanese subject has been harmed by the shortage.

The dictate of the shogun deified at Nikko has been ignored. This crime alone is unpardonable. "Chamberlain Tomine," says Shiroyama, "you are acquainted with the standing orders concerning the defense of the Closed Empire."

"It is my duty to be so informed, Your Honor."

"In the case of foreigners arriving at a city without permission, its highest official is commanded to do what?"

"To decline all overtures, Your Honor, and send the foreigners away. If the latter request provisions, a minimal quantity may be supplied, but no payment must be received, so that the foreigners cannot later claim a trading precedent."

"But in the case that the foreigners commit acts of aggression?"

The advisers' fans in the Hall of Sixty Mats have all stopped moving.

"The magistrate or *daimyo* in authority must seize the foreigners, Your Honor, and detain them until orders are received from Edo."

Seize a fully armed warship, Shiroyama thinks, *with sixty-seven men?*

In this room the magistrate has sentenced smugglers, robbers, rapists, murderers, pickpockets, and a Hidden Christian from the Goto Islands. Now Fate, adopting the chamberlain's dense nasal voice, is sentencing him.

The shogun will imprison me for wanton neglect of my duties.

His family in Edo will be stripped of his name and samurai rank.

My precious Kawasemi will have to go back to the teahouses . . .

He thinks of his son, his miraculous son, eking out a living as a pimp's servant.

Unless I apologize for my crime and preserve my family honor . . .

None of his advisers dares hold a condemned man's gaze.

. . . by ritually disemboweling myself before Edo orders my arrest.

A throat behind him is softly cleared. "May I speak, Magistrate?"

"Better that someone says something, Lord Abbot."

"Kyôga Domain is more a spiritual stronghold than a military one, but it is very close. By dispatching a messenger now, I can raise two hundred and fifty men from Kashima and Isahaya to Nagasaki within three days."

This strange man, Shiroyama thinks, *is part of my life and my death.* "Summon them, Lord

Abbot, in the shogun's name." The magistrate senses a glimmer of hope. *The greater glory of seizing a foreign aggressor's warship may,* may, *eclipse lesser crimes.* He turns to the commander-at-arms. "Send riders to the lords of Hizen, Chikugo, and Higo, with orders in the shogun's name to dispatch five hundred armed men apiece. No delay, no excuses. The empire is at war."

CHAPTER THIRTY-FOUR: CAPTAIN PENHALIGON'S BUNK ROOM ABOARD HMS *PHOEBUS*

Around dawn on October 19, 1800
John Penhaligon awakes from a dream of mildewed drapes and lunar forests to find his son at his bedside. "Tristingle, my dear boy! Such horrid dreams I had! I dreamed you'd been killed on the *Blenheim* and" — Penhaligon sighs — "and I even dreamed I'd forgotten what you looked like. Not your hair —"

"Never my hair, Pa," says the handsome lad, smiling. "Not *this* burning bush!"

"In my dream, I sometimes dreamed you were still alive . . . Waking was a — a bitterness."

"Come!" He laughs like Meredith laughed. "Is this a phantom's hand?"

John Penhaligon grips his son's warm hand and notices his captain's epaulets.

"My *Phaeton* is sent to help your *Phoebus* crack this walnut, Father."

Ships of the line hog the glory, Penhaligon's

mentor Captain Golding would say, *but frigates bag the prizes!*

"There's no prize on earth," agrees Tristram, "like the ports and markets of the Orient."

"Black pudding, eggs, and fried bread would be heavenly, my lad."

Why, Penhaligon wonders, *did I answer an unasked question?*

"I'll tell Jones and bring your *Times* of London." Tristram withdraws.

Penhaligon listens to the gentle clatter of cutlery and plates . . .

. . . and sloughs off wasted years of grief, like a snake's skin.

How can Tristram, he wonders, *obtain* The Times *in Nagasaki Bay?*

A cat watches him from the foot of his bed; or perhaps a bat . . .

With a deaf and dumb hum, the beast opens its mouth: a pouch of needles.

It means to bite, thinks Penhaligon, and his thought is the devil's cue.

Agony scalds his right foot; an *Aaaaaaaaagh!* escapes like steam.

Wide awake in closeted dark, dead Tristram's father bites on a scream.

The gentle clatter of cutlery and plates ceases, and anxious steps hurry to his cabin door. Chigwin's voice calls out, "Is all well, sir?"

The captain swallows. "A nightmare ambushed me, is all."

"I suffer them myself, sir. We'll have breakfast served by first bell."

"Very good, Chigwin. Wait: are the native boats still circling us?"

"Just the two guard boats, sir, but the marines watched them all night and they never came within two hundred yards or I'd've woken you, sir. Aside from them, nothing bigger than a duck is afloat this morning. We scared everything off."

"I shall shake my leg shortly, Chigwin. Carry on." But as Penhaligon shifts his swollen foot, thorns of pain lacerate his flesh. "Chigwin, pray invite Surgeon Nash to call on the nonce: my podagra is troubling me, a little."

Surgeon Nash examines the ankle, swollen to twice its usual size. "Steeplechases and mazurkas are, more than like, behind you now, Captain. May I recommend a stick to help you walk? I shall have Rafferty fetch one."

Penhaligon hesitates. *A cripple with a stick, at forty-two.*

Young and agile feet pound to and fro abovedecks.

"Yes. Better to advertise my infirmity with a stick than a fall down stairs."

"Quite so, sir. Now, if I may examine this

674

tophus. This may . . ."

The lancet probes the rupture: a violet agony explodes behind Penhaligon's eyeballs.

". . . hurt just a little, sir . . . but it's weeping nicely — a good abundance of pus."

The captain peers at the frothing discharge. "*That* is good?"

Surgeon Nash unscrews a corked pot. "Pus is how the body purges itself of excessive blue bile, and blue bile is the root of gout. By widening the wound, applying a scraping of murine fecal matter" — he uncorks the pot and extracts a mouse dropping with a pair of tweezers — "we can stimulate the discharge and expect an improvement within seven days. Moreover, I took the liberty of bringing a vial of Dover's remedy, so —"

"I'll drink it now, Surgeon. The next two days are crucial to —"

The lancet sinks in: the stifled scream makes his body go rigid.

"*Damn* it, Nash," the captain gasps finally. "Will you not at least *warn* me?"

Major Cutlip looks askance at the sauerkraut on Penhaligon's spoon.

"Might your resistance," asks the captain, "be weakening, Major?"

"Twice-rotted cabbage shall never conquer *this* soldier, Captain."

Membranous sunlight lends the breakfast table the air of a painting.

675

"It was Admiral Jervis who first recommended sauerkraut to me." The captain crunches his fermented mouthful. "But I told you that story before."

"Never," says Wren, "in *my* hearing, sir." He looks at the others, who concur. Penhaligon suspects them of dainty manners, but summarizes the anecdote: "Jervis had sauerkraut from William Bligh, and Bligh had it from Captain Cook himself. 'The difference between La Pérouse's tragedy and Cook's glory,' Bligh was fond of saying, 'was thirty barrels of sauerkraut.' But when Cook embarked on the first voyage, neither exhortation nor threat would induce the Endeavours to eat it. Thereupon Cook designated the 'twice-rotted cabbage' as officers' food and forbade common tars from touching the stuff. The result? Sauerkraut began to be filched from its own poorly guarded storeroom, until six months later not a single man was buckling under scurvy and the conversion was complete."

"Low cunning," Lieutenant Talbot observes, "in the service of genius."

"Cook is a great hero of mine," avows Wren, "and an inspiration."

Wren's "of mine" irritates Penhaligon like a tiny seed wedged between molars.

Chigwin fills the captain's bowl: a drop splashes on the tablecloth's lovingly embroidered forget-me-nots. *Now is not the time,* thinks the widower, *to remember Meredith.* "And so, gentlemen, to the day's business, and our Dutch guests."

"Van Cleef," says Hovell, "passed an uncommunicative night in his cell."

"Aside," sneers Cutlip, "from demanding to know why his supper was boiled rope."

"News of the VOC's demise," the captain asks, "makes him no less obdurate?"

Hovell shakes his head. "Admission of weakness *is* a weakness."

"As for Fischer," says Wren, "the wretch spent all night in his cabin, despite our entreaties to join us in the wardroom."

"How are relations between Fischer and his former chief, Snitker?"

"They act like perfect strangers," replies Hovell. "Snitker is nursing a head cold this morning. He wants Van Cleef court-martialed for the crime, if you please, of 'battery against a "friend of the court of Saint James's." ' "

"I am sick," says Penhaligon, "heartily sick, of that coxcomb."

"I'd agree, Captain," says Wren, "that Snitker's usefulness has run its course."

"We need a persuasive leader to win the Dutch," says the captain, "and an" — above-deck, three bells are rung — "envoy of gravitas and poise to persuade the Japanese."

"Deputy Fischer wins my vote," says Major Cutlip, "as the more pliable man."

"Chief van Cleef," argues Hovell, "would

be the natural leader."

"Let us interview," Penhaligon suggests, brushing crumbs away, "our two candidates."

"Mr. van Cleef." Penhaligon stands, disguising his grimace of pain as an insincere smile. "I hope you slept well?"

Van Cleef helps himself to burgoo, Seville preserve, and a hailstorm of sugar before replying to Hovell's translation. "He says you can threaten him all you please, sir, but Dejima still has not one nail of copper for you to rob."

Penhaligon ignores this. "I'm pleased his appetite is robust."

Hovell translates and Van Cleef speaks through a mouthful of food.

"He asks, sir, if we have decided what to do with our hostages yet."

"Tell him that we don't consider him a hostage but a guest."

Van Cleef's response to the assertion is a burgoo-spattering "Ha!"

"Ask if he has digested the VOC's bankruptcy."

Van Cleef pours himself a bowl of coffee as he listens to Hovell. He shrugs.

"Tell him that the English East India Company wishes to trade with Japan."

Van Cleef sprinkles raisins on his burgoo as he gives his response.

"His reply, sir, is, 'Why else hire Snitker to

bring you here?' "

He is no novice at this, thinks Penhaligon, *but then, neither am I.*

"We are seeking an old Japan hand to represent our interests."

Van Cleef listens, nods, stirs sugar into his coffee, and says, *"Nee."*

"Ask whether he ever heard of the Kew Memorandum, signed by his own monarch-in-exile, ordering Dutch overseas officers to hand their nations' assets to the safekeeping of the British?"

Van Cleef listens, nods, stands, and lifts his shirt to show a deep, wide scar.

He sits down, tears a bread roll in two, and gives Hovell a calm explanation.

"Mr. van Cleef says he earned that wound at the hands of Scotch and Swiss mercenaries hired by that same monarch-in-exile. They poured boiling oil down his father's throat, he said. On behalf of the Batavian Republic, he begs us to keep both the 'chinless tyrant' and 'British safekeeping' and says that the Kew Memorandum is useful for the privy but nothing else."

"Plainly, sir," declares Wren, "we are dealing with Jacobin."

"Tell him we'd *prefer* to achieve our goals diplomatically, but —"

Van Cleef sniffs the sauerkraut and recoils as at boiling sulfur.

"— failing that we shall seize the factory by

force, and any loss of Japanese and Dutch life shall be on his account."

Van Cleef drinks his coffee, turns to Penhaligon, and insists on Hovell translating his reply line by line so that nothing is missed.

"He says, Captain, that whatever Daniel Snitker has told us, Dejima is sovereign Japanese territory, leased to the company. It is not a Dutch possession.

"He says that if we try to storm it, the Japanese will defend it.

"He says our marines may fire off one round before being cut down.

"He urges us not to throw our lives away, for our family's sakes."

"The man is trying to scare us away," remarks Cutlip.

"More probably," suspects Penhaligon, "he is driving up the price of his help."

But Van Cleef issues a final statement and stands.

"He thanks you for breakfast, Captain, and says that Melchior van Cleef is not for sale to any monarch. Peter Fischer, however, shall be only too delighted to hammer out terms with you."

"My esteem for Prussians," says Penhaligon, "began in my midshipman days . . ."

Hovell translates: Peter Fischer nods, not quite able to believe this wonderful twist of fortune.

"HMS *Audacious* had a Brunswick-born officer named Plessner."

Fischer corrects the pronunciation of "Plessner" and adds a remark.

"Chief Fischer," translates Hovell, "is also a native son of Brunswick."

"Is that so now?" Penhaligon feigns astonishment. "From Brunswick?"

Peter Fischer nods, says *"Ja, ja,"* and drains his small beer.

With a glance, Penhaligon orders Chigwin to fill Fischer's tankard and keep it filled.

"Mr. Plessner was a superb seaman; brave, resourceful . . ."

Fischer's expression signifies, *As one would expect, of course . . .*

". . . and I am overjoyed," the captain continues, "that the first British consul of Nagasaki shall be a gentleman of Germanic stock and values."

Fischer raises his tankard in salute and puts a question to Hovell.

"He's asking, sir, what role Mr. Snitker may have in our plans."

Penhaligon aspirates a tragic sigh, thinks, *I could have walked the boards at Drury Lane,* and says, "To be truthful with you, Envoy Fischer" — Hovell translates the snatch, and Fischer leans in closer — "Daniel Snitker disappoints us as gravely as does Mr. van Cleef."

681

The Prussian nods with co-conspirator's eyes.

"Dutchmen talk large, yet in action they are all piss and vinegar."

Hovell struggles with the idioms but elicits a run of *ja ja ja*s.

"They are too rooted in their Golden Age to notice the changing world."

"This is the . . . *waarheid.*" Fischer turns to Hovell. "How to say, *waarheid?*"

" 'Truth,' " says Hovell, and Penhaligon tries to make his foot more comfortable as he expounds.

"This is why the VOC collapsed and why their much-vaunted Dutch Republic looks set to join Poland in history's dustbin of extinct nations. The British crown needs Fischers, not Snitkers: men of talent, of vision . . ."

Fischer's nostrils widen as he listens to Hovell's rendition, the better to smell his future of wealth and power.

". . . and moral rectitude. In short, we need ambassadors, not whoring merchants."

Fischer completes his metamorphosis from hostage to plenipotentiary with a laborious tale of Dutch lassitude, which Hovell shortens. "Envoy Fischer says that a fire leveled the sea-gate quarter of Dejima last year. Whilst the two biggest Dutch warehouses were burning to the ground, Van Cleef and Snitker were disporting themselves in a brothel at the company's expense."

"Disgraceful dereliction," declares Wren, a connoisseur of bagnios.

"Gross abandonment," agrees Cutlip, Wren's companion of choice.

Seven bells ring. Envoy Fischer shares a new thought with Hovell.

"He says, Captain, that with Van Cleef removed from Dejima, Mr. Fischer is now the acting chief — meaning that the men on Dejima are duty-bound to carry out his instructions. To disobey his orders is a corporal offense."

May his powers of persuasion, thinks the captain, *match his confidence.*

"Snitker shall receive a pilot's fee for guiding us here and a gratis berth to Bengal, but in a hammock, not a cabin."

Fischer's nod agrees, *That is sufficient,* and issues a pronouncement.

"He says," translates Hovell, " 'the Almighty forged this morning's pact.' "

The Prussian drinks from his tankard and finds it empty.

The captain sends Chigwin a tiny shake of his head. "The Almighty," Penhaligon says with a smile, "and His Majesty's Navy, for whom Envoy Fischer agrees to undertake the following . . ." Penhaligon takes up the memorandum of understanding. " 'Article one: Envoy Fischer is to gain the acquiescence of Dejima's men to British patronage.' "

Hovell translates. Major Cutlip rolls a boiled egg on a saucer.

" 'Article two: Envoy Fischer is to broker negotiations with the Nagasaki magistrate to secure a treaty of amity and trade between the British crown and the shogun of Japan. Annual trading seasons are to commence from June of 1801.' "

Hovell translates. Cutlip picks eggshell from the rubbery white.

" 'Article three: Envoy Fischer shall facilitate the transfer of all Dutch-owned copper to His Majesty's Frigate *Phoebus* and a limited trading season in private goods between crew and officers and Japanese merchants.' "

Hovell translates. Cutlip bites into the truffle-soft yolk.

" 'As remuneration for these services, Envoy Fischer is to receive a one-tenth share of all profits from the British Dejima factory for the first three years of his office, which may be renewed in 1803 subject to the consent of both parties.' "

Hovell translates the final clause. Penhaligon signs the memorandum.

The captain then passes the quill to Peter Fischer. Fischer pauses.

He senses the gaze, the captain guesses, *of his future self, watching him.*

"You shall return to Brunswick," Wren assures him, "as rich as its illustrious duke."

Hovell translates, Fischer smiles and signs, and Cutlip sprinkles a little salt onto the remains of his egg.

Today being Sunday, church is rigged, and eight bells summon the ship's company. The officers and marines stand beneath an awning strung between the mizzen and mainmast. All the *Phoebus*'s Christian sailors are expected to toe the line in their best clothes: Hebrews, Mussulmans, Asiatics, and other heathens are excused from prayers and the hymn, but often they watch from the margins. Van Cleef is locked in the sailcloth store for fear of mischief, Daniel Snitker is with the lesser warrant officers, and Peter Fischer stands between Captain Penhaligon — conscious that his walking stick will already be the subject of speculation among the ratings — and Lieutenant Hovell, from whom the newly appointed envoy has borrowed a fresh cotton shirt. Chaplain Wily, a gnarled oboe of a Kentishman, reads from his battered Bible, standing on a makeshift pulpit set before the wheel. He reads line by slow line, allowing the unschooled men time to chew and digest every verse, and giving the captain's thoughts some room to wander: " 'We being exceedingly tossed with a tempest . . .' "

Penhaligon tests his right ankle: Nash's potion is numbing the pain.

" '. . . the next *day* they lightened the ship;

And the third *day* . . .' "

The captain spies the Japanese guard boat, keeping its distance.

" '. . . we cast out with our own hands the tackling of the ship.' "

The seamen grunt in surprise and pay the chaplain close attention.

" 'And when neither sun nor stars in many days appeared . . .' "

The average is either too meek for so unruly a flock . . .

" '. . . and no small tempest lay on us, all hope that we should be saved . . .' "

. . . or else so zealous that the sailors ignore, scorn, or vilify him.

" '. . . was then taken away. But after long abstinence Paul stood forth . . .' "

Chaplain Wily, an oysterman's son from Whitstable, is a welcome exception.

" '. . . in the midst of them and said, Sirs, ye should have hearkened unto me . . .' "

Hands who know the Mediterranean in winter mutter and nod.

" '. . . and not have loosed from Crete, and to have gained this harm and loss.' "

Wily teaches the boys their three Rs and writes illiterate men's letters.

" 'And now I exhort you to be of good cheer: for there shall be no loss . . .' "

The chaplain has a mercantile streak, too, and fifty bolts of Bengali chintz in the hold.

" '. . . of *any man's* life among you but of

the ship. For there stood by me this night . . .' "

Best of all, Wily keeps his readings briny and his sermons pithy.

" '. . . the angel of God, whose I am' " — Wily looks up — " 'and whom I serve, saying . . .' "

Penhaligon lets his gaze wander the lines of his Phoebusians.

" 'Fear not, Paul; . . . lo, God hath given thee all them that sail with thee.' "

There are fellow Cornishmen, Bristolians, Manxmen, Hebrideans . . .

" '. . . About midnight the shipmen deemed that they drew near to some country . . .' "

A quartet of Faroe Islanders; some Yankees from Connecticut.

" '. . . And sounded; and found it twenty fathoms: and when they had gone . . .' "

Freed slaves from the Caribbean, a Tartar, a Gibraltese Jew.

" '. . . further, they sounded again, and found fifteen fathoms . . .' "

Penhaligon considers how land naturally divides itself into nations.

" '. . . Then fearing lest we should have fallen upon rocks, they cast . . .' "

He considers how the seas dissolve human boundaries.

" '. . . four anchors out of the stern, and wished for the day.' "

He looks at the doubloons: men fathered

by Europeans . . .

" 'And as the shipmen were about to flee out of the ship . . .' "

. . . on native women: on girls sold by fathers for iron nails . . .

" 'Paul said . . . Except these abide *in* the ship, ye cannot be saved.' "

Penhaligon locates Hartlepool the half-breed, and remembers his own youthful fornications, and wonders whether any resulted in a coffee-skinned or almond-eyed son who also obeyed the voice of the sea, who thinks the thoughts of the fatherless. The captain remembers this morning's dream, and he hopes so.

" 'Then the soldiers cut the ropes of the boat, and let her fall off.' "

The men gasp at the recklessness. One exclaims, "Madness!"

"Stops deserters," answers another, and Wren calls out: "Hear the chaplain!"

But Wily closes his Bible. "Aye, with the tempest howling, with death a near certainty, Paul says, 'Abandon ship and you'll drown; stay aboard with me and you'll survive.' Would you believe him? Would I?" The chaplain shrugs and puffs. "This wasn't Paul the Apostle speaking with a halo round his head. This was a prisoner in chains, a heretic from a backward ditch of Rome's empire. Yet he persuaded the guards to cut away the boats, and the Book of Acts tells that two hundred and seventy-six were saved by God's mercy. Why did that raggle-taggle crew of Cypriots, Lebanese, and Palestinians heed Paul? Was it his voice, or his face, or . . . something else? Ah, with that secret, I'd be Archbishop Wily by now! Instead, I'm stuck here, with you." Some of the men laugh. "I shan't claim, men, that faith always saves a man from drowning — enough devout Christians have died at sea to make a liar of me. But this I do swear: faith *shall* save your *soul* from death. Without faith, death *is* a drowning, the end of ends, and what sane man wouldn't fear that? But with faith, death is nothing worse than the end of this voyage we call life, and the beginning of an eternal voyage in a company of our loved ones, with griefs and woes smoothed out, and under the captaincy of our Creator . . ."

The cordage creaks as the climbing sun warms the morning dew.

"That's all I have to say this Sunday, men. Our own captain has a few words."

Penhaligon steps up, relying on his stick more than he would like. "So, men, there's no fat Dutch goose waiting to be plucked in Nagasaki. You are disappointed, your officers are disappointed, and I am disappointed." The captain speaks slowly, to allow his words to trickle into other languages. "Console yourselves with the thought of all the unsuspecting French prizes to be netted on our long, long voyage back to Plymouth." Gannets call. The oars of the guard boats drag and splash. "Our mission here, men, is to bring the nineteenth century to these benighted shores. By the 'nineteenth century' I mean the British nineteenth century: not the French, nor Russian nor Dutch. Shall doing so make rich men of us all? In and of itself, no. Shall it make our *Phoebus* the most famous ship in Japan and the toast of the service at home? The answer shall be a resounding *yes.* This is not a legacy you can spend in port. It is a legacy that can never, ever be squandered, stolen, or lost." *The men prefer cash to posterity,* Penhaligon thinks, *but they listen, at least.* "A last word, before — and about — the hymn. The last time a song of praise was heard in Nagasaki was as native Christians were slung off the cliff we passed yesterday for their belief in the true faith. I desire you send a message to the magistrate of Nagasaki, on this historic day, that Britons, unlike the Dutch, shall never trample on Our Savior for the sake of profit. So sing not like shy schoolboys, men. Sing like warriors. One, and two, and three, and —"

CHAPTER THIRTY-FIVE: THE SEA ROOM IN THE CHIEF'S RESIDENCE ON DEJIMA

Morning of October 19, 1800

"Who so beset him round, with dismal stories . . ."

Jacob de Zoet, studying the stock inventory by the viewing window, at first doubts his ears . . .

"Do but themselves confound, His strength the more is."

. . . but, however improbable, a hymn is being sung in Nagasaki Bay.

"No foes shall stay His might; tho' He with giants fight . . ."

Jacob steps out onto the veranda and stares at the frigate.

"He will make good His right to be a pilgrim."

The hymn's odd-numbered lines breathe in: its even-numbered, out.

"Hobgoblin, nor foul fiend, can daunt his spirit,"

Jacob closes his eyes, the better to catch the floating English phrases . . .

"He knows, he at the end shall life inherit."

. . . and lift away each new line from its predecessor's echo.

"Then fancies fly away! He'll fear not what men say."

The hymn is water and sunlight, and Jacob wishes he had married Anna.

"He'll labor night and day to be a pilgrim."

The pastor's nephew waits for the next verse, but it never comes.

"A pleasing ditty," remarks Marinus, from the doorway.

Jacob turns. "You called hymns 'songs for children afraid of the dark.' "

"Did I? Well, one grows less judgmental in one's dotage."

"This was less than a month ago, Marinus."

"Oh. Well, as my friend the dean observes," Marinus says, leaning on the rail, "we have just enough religion to make us hate, but not enough to make us love. Your new habitus suits you very well, if I may say so."

"It's Chief van Cleef's habitus, and I pray he'll be back in it by tonight. I mean it. In my less charitable minutes, I might consider paying the English a ransom to keep Fischer, but Melchior van Cleef is a fair-minded man, by the company's standards — and a Dejima of only four officers is less undermanned than unmanned."

Marinus squints at the sky. "Come and eat. Eelattu and I brought you some poached fish from the kitchen."

They walk through to the dining room, where Jacob makes a point of occupying his usual chair. He asks whether Marinus has had dealings with British naval officers in the past.

"Fewer than you may imagine. I've corresponded with Joseph Banks and some of the English and Scottish philosophers, but I've yet to master their language. Their nation is rather young. You must have met some officers during your London sojourn. Two or three years, was it not?"

"Four years, in total. My employer's principal warehouse was a short walk downriver from the East India docks, so I watched hundreds of ships of the line come and go: the finest ships in the Royal Navy — that is, in the world. But my circle of English acquaintances was confined to warehousemen, scriveners, and bookkeepers. To the grand and the uniformed, a junior clerk from Zeeland with a thick Dutch accent would have been invisible."

The servant d'Orsaiy appears. "Interpreter Goto here, Chief."

Jacob looks around for Van Cleef and remembers. "Show him in, d'Orsaiy."

Goto enters, looking as grave as the situation warrants. "Good morning, Acting Chief"

— the interpreter bows — "and Dr. Marinus. I disturb breakfast, sorry. But inspector at guild send me urgently to discover about war song from English ship. Do English sing such song previous to attack?"

"An attack?" Jacob hurries back to the sea room. He looks at the frigate through his telescope, but its position is the same, and belatedly he sees the misunderstanding. "No, it wasn't a war song that the English were singing, Mr. Goto, it was a hymn."

Goto is puzzled: "What is 'hymn' or who is 'hymn'?"

"A song, sung by Christians to our God. It is an act of worship."

The acting chief continues to watch the frigate: there is activity at the bow.

"Within hailing distance of the Papenburg Rock," observes Marinus. "Whoever claimed that history has no sense of humor died too soon."

Goto does not catch everything, but he understands the shogun's sacrosanct edict against Christianity has been violated. "Very serious and bad," he mutters. "Very" — he searches for another word — "*very* serious and bad."

"Unless I'm mistaken . . ." Jacob is still watching. "Something *is* afoot."

The congregation has disbanded and the church awning lowered.

"Someone in an oat-colored jacket is climbing down . . ."

He is helped into the frigate's boat, moored at her starboard bow.

One of the Japanese guard boats is being called over.

"It appears that Deputy Fischer is being given back his freedom."

Jacob has not set foot on the sea ramp in the fifteen months since his arrival. Soon the sampan shall be in hailing distance. Jacob recognizes Interpreter Sagara next to Peter Fischer in the prow of the boat. Ponke Ouwehand breaks off the tune he is humming. "Being out here whets your appetite for the day when we'll put this jail behind us, doesn't it?"

Jacob thinks about Orito, flinches, and says, "Yes."

Marinus is filling a sack with slimy handfuls of seaweed. "*Porphyra umbilicalis.* The pumpkins shall be delighted."

Twenty yards away, Peter Fischer cups his hands and calls out to his welcoming party: "So I turn my back for twenty-four hours, and 'Acting Chief de Zoet' stages a *coup d'état!*" His levity is stiff and prickly. "Will you be as quick into my coffin, I wonder?"

"We had no notion," Ouwehand calls back, "how long we might be left headless."

"The head is back, 'Acting Deputy Ouwehand'! What a flurry of promotions! Is

695

the monkey now the cook?"

"Good to see you back, Peter," Jacob says, "whatever our titles."

"Fine to be back, Head Clerk!" The boat scrapes the ramp, and Fischer leaps ashore like a conquering hero. He lands awkwardly and slips on the stones.

Jacob tries to help him up. "How is Chief van Cleef?"

Fischer stands. "Van Cleef is well, yes. Very well indeed. He sends his warm regards."

"Mr. de Zoet." Interpreter Sagara is helped out by his servant and a guard. "We have letter from English captain to magistrate. I take now, so no delay. Magistrate summon you later, I think, and he want speak to Mr. Fischer also."

"Oh, yes, indeed," declares Fischer. "Tell Shiroyama I shall be available after luncheon."

Sagara bows vaguely to Fischer, firmly to De Zoet, and turns away.

"Interpreter," calls Fischer after him. "Interpreter Sagara!"

Sagara turns around at the sea gate, a mild *yes?* on his face.

"Remember who is the highest-ranking officer on Dejima."

Sagara's humble bow is not quite sincere. He goes.

"I don't trust that one," says Fischer. "He lacks manners."

"We hope the English treated you and the chief well," says Jacob.

" 'Well'? Better than well, Head Clerk. I have extraordinary news."

"I am touched by your concern," Fischer tells the company assembled in the stateroom, "and you will be eager to learn about my sojourn aboard the *Phoebus*. However, protocol must be respected. Therefore: Grote, Gerritszoon, Baert, and Oost — and you, too, Twomey — you are excused and may return to work for this morning. I have matters of state to discuss with Dr. Marinus, Mr. Ouwehand, and Mr. de Zoet and decisions to make with careful thought and clear heads. When these matters are settled, you shall be informed."

"Yer wrong," states Gerritszoon. "We're stayin', see."

The grandfather clock tocks. Piet Baert scratches his crotch.

"So while the cat's away," Fischer says, pretending to be charmed, "the mice will set up a national convention of the people. Very well, then, I shall keep things as easy to understand as possible. Mr. van Cleef and I spent the night aboard the HMS *Phoebus* as guests of the English captain. His name is John Penhaligon. He is here on the orders of the British governor-general at Fort William in Bengal. Fort William is the principal base of the English East India Company, which —"

"We all know what Fort William is," interjects Marinus.

Fischer smiles for a long second. "Captain Penhaligon's orders are to negotiate a trade treaty with the Japanese."

"*Jan Compagnie* trades in Japan," says Ouwehand. "Not John Company."

Fischer picks his teeth. "Ah, yes, some more news. *Jan Compagnie* is dead as a doornail. Yes. At midnight on the last day of the eighteenth century, while some of *you*" — he happens to glance at Gerritszoon and Baert — "were singing rude songs about your Germanic ancestors on Long Street, the ancient honorable company ceased to exist. Our employer and paymaster is bankrupt."

The men are dumbstruck. "Similar rumors," says Jacob, "have —"

"I read it in the *Amsterdamsche Courant* in Captain Penhaligon's cabin. There: in black and white and plain Dutch. Since January the first we've been working for a phantom."

"Our back wages?" Baert, horrified, bites his hand. "My seven years' wages?"

Fischer nods. "It was clever of you to piss, whore, and gamble most of it away, with hindsight. At least you enjoyed it."

"But our pay's our pay," insists Oost. "Our pay's safe, isn't it, Mr. de Zoet?"

"Legally, yes. But 'legally' implies courts,

compensation, lawyers, and time. Mr. Fischer —"

"I believe the chief resident's books record my promotion to 'Deputy'?"

"Deputy Fischer, did the *Courant* article mention compensation and debt?"

"For the dear Dutch motherland's shareholders, yes, but about the pawns out in the Asian factories, there was not one peep. On the subject of the dear Dutch motherland, I have more news. A Corsican general, Bonaparte, has made himself first consul of the French Republic. This Bonaparte doesn't lack ambition! He conquered Italy, mastered Austria, looted Venice, subdued Egypt, and intends to turn the Low Countries into a *département* of France. I am sorry to report, gentlemen, that your motherland is to be married off and shall lose her name."

"The English are lying!" exclaims Ouwehand. "That's impossible!"

"The Poles said much the same before their country vanished."

Jacob imagines a garrison of French troops in Domburg.

"My brother Joris," says Baert, "served under that Frenchman, that Bonaparte. They said he'd done a deal with the devil at the Bridge of Arcole, an' that's how he crushes whole armies. The deal di'n't cover Boney's men, mind. Joris was last seen on a spike at the Battle o' the Pirrymids, minus his body."

"My sincere condolences, Baert," says Peter Fischer, "but Bonaparte is now your head of state and cares not a tinker's fart about your back wages. So. We have two surprises so far. No more company and no more independent Netherlands. Here is a third surprise, especially interesting for Head Clerk de Zoet, I think. The pilot and adviser who guided the *Phoebus* to Nagasaki Bay is Daniel Snitker."

A stunned silence precedes a volley of surprise — and disbelief.

"But he's in Java," Ouwehand finds his tongue first, "on trial."

Fischer inspects a thumbnail. "Such twists make life much richer."

Aghast, Jacob clears his throat. "You spoke with Snitker? Face-to-face?" He glances at Ivo Oost, who looks pale and perplexed.

"I ate supper with the man. The *Shenandoah* never reached Java, you see. Vorstenbosch — that famous surgeon of the cancer of corruption — and trusty Captain Lacy sold the company's copper — that same copper *you*, Mr. de Zoet, won with such dedication! — to the English East India Company in Bengal for their own personal profit. The irony. The irony!"

This can't be true, thinks Jacob. Jacob thinks, *But, yes, it can.*

"Wait wait wait" — Arie Grote is turning pink — "waity waity waity. What about our private cargoes? What about my lacquerware? What about the Arita figurines?"

"Daniel Snitker does not know their next destination. He escaped at Macao . . ."

"If those *swine*," Arie Grote growls, turning purple, "those *thieving mongrels* —"

". . . and didn't ask, but your goods would fetch a handsome price in Carolina."

"Never mind the damed cargoes," protests Twomey. "How are we to get home?"

Even Arie Grote falls silent as the truth sinks in.

"Mr. Fischer," notes Marinus, "looks immune to the general dismay."

"What ain't y' tellin' us" — Gerritszoon looks dangerous — "*Mister* Fischer?"

"I can speak only as fast as your noble democracy allows! The doctor is right: all is *not* lost. Captain Penhaligon is authorized to propose an Anglo-Dutch entente in these waters. He promises to pay *every last penning* the company owes us and give us passage, gratis, in a comfy side berth, to Penang, Bengal, Ceylon, or the Cape."

"All this," asks Con Twomey, "from the sweetness of an Englishman's heart?"

"In return, we work here for two more trading seasons. For wages."

"Meaning," Jacob intuits, "the English want Dejima and its profits."

"What use is Dejima to *you*, Mr. de Zoet? Where are your ships, your capital?"

"But" — Ivo Oost frowns — "if the English want to trade out of Dejima . . ."

"The interpreters," Arie Grote says, nodding, "speak only *Dutch.*"

Fischer claps his hands. "Captain Penhaligon needs you. You need him. A blissful marriage."

"So it's the same work," Baert asks, "with a new employer?"

"One who won't vanish to Carolina with your private cargoes, yes."

"The day I catch up with Vorstenbosch," vows Gerritszoon, "is the day his brains'll get yanked out of his aristocratic arse."

"Which flag would fly here?" asks Jacob. "Dutch or English?"

"Who cares," demands Fischer, "so long as our wages are paid?"

"What does Chief van Cleef," Marinus asks, "make of the captain's offer?"

"He is negotiating the finer details as we speak."

"He didn't think," asks Jacob, "to send any written orders to us?"

"*I* am his written orders, Head Clerk! But, look, don't accept my word. Captain Penhaligon has invited you — and the doctor, and Mr. Ouwehand — to the *Phoebus* for supper this evening. His lieutenants are a splendid circle. One, named Hovell, speaks fluent Dutch. The leader of his marines, Major Cutlip, has traveled far and wide, and has even lived in New South Wales."

The hands laugh. "Cutlip?" asks Grote. "That's never a real name!"

"If we reject their proposal," asks Jacob, "will the English sail peacefully away?"

Fischer tuts. "The proposal is not yours to accept or reject, is it, Head Clerk? Now Chief van Cleef and I are back, the Republic of Dejima can return to its box of toys and —"

"Ain't so simple," says Grote. "*We* voted Mr. de Zoet as president."

"*President?*" Fischer lifts his eyebrows in mock amazement. "My!"

"We need a man of his word," declares Arie Grote, "lookin' out for us."

"You imply" — Peter Fischer's lips smile — "I am not such a man?"

"Surely you ain't f'gotten a certain bill of lading," says Grote, "what Mr. de Z. would *not* sign but what you was all too happy?"

"Vorstenbosch pokered him," says Piet Baert, "but he'd not poker us."

Jacob is as surprised as Fischer at the strength of the hands' support.

Fischer bristles. "The company oath is clear about obedience."

"The company oath became legally void," notes Marinus, "on January the first."

"But we are all on the same side, men, are we not?" Fischer realizes his miscalculation. "Concerns about flags can be met. What is a flag but a rectangle of cloth? I'll be speaking to the magistrate later — and your 'president' can join me, to show my good faith. In the meantime, your 'Republic of Dejima' . . .''

Naming, thinks Jacob, *even in ridicule, gives what is named substance.*

". . . can debate to its heart's desire. When Jacob and I return to the *Phoebus,* he can tell Captain Penhaligon how things stand ashore. But don't forget, home is twelve thousand miles away. Don't forget, Dejima is a trading post with no trade. Don't forget, the Japanese *want* us to persuade them to work with the English. By making the right choice, we earn money and protect our families against poverty. Who, in God's name, could object to that?"

"So how translate 'stadtholder'?" Tired-eyed Interpreter Goto tests the unshaven shadow around his jaw. "Dutch William Five *is* king or *not* king?"

The Almelo clock in the chief's bureau chimes once. *Titles, titles,* thinks Jacob. *So stupid, so important.* "He is not the king."

"So why William Five use title 'Prince of Orange-Nassau'?"

"Orange-Nassau is — or was — the name of his ancestors' fiefdom, like a Japanese domain. But he was also the head of the Netherlands Army."

"So he is same as Japanese shogun?" ventures Iwase.

The Venetian doge is a better comparison, but that would not help. "The stadtholder was an elected post, but one in the pocket of the House of Orange. Then, after Stadtholder William" — he gestures at the signature on the document — "married the Prussian king's niece, he took on the airs of a monarch, appointed by God. Five years ago, however, we" — the French invasion is still a secret — "the Dutch people changed our government . . ."

The three interpreters look at one another with apprehension.

". . . and Stadtholder William was . . . oh, how to say 'exiled' in Japanese?"

Goto can supply the missing word, and the sentence makes sense to Iwase.

"So with William in London," concludes Jacob, "his old post was abolished."

"So William Five" — Namura must be clear — "has no power in Holland?"

"No, none. All his properties were confiscated."

"Do Dutch people still . . . obey, or respect, stadtholder?"

"Orangists, yes, but Patriots — men of the new government — not."

"Many Dutch people are either 'Orangists' or 'Patriots'?"

"Yes, but most care more about food in their bellies and peace in the land."

"So this document we translate, this 'Kew Memorandum' " — Goto frowns — "is order from William Five to Dutchmen to give Dutch possessions to English for safe protection?"

"Yes, but the question is, do we recognize William's authority?"

"English write, 'All Dutch colonies obey Kew Memorandum.' "

"That's what he writes, yes, but he is probably lying."

There is a hesitant knock. Jacob calls out: "Yes?"

Con Twomey opens the door, removes his hat, and looks at Jacob in an urgent manner. *Twomey wouldn't disturb us now,* Jacob reasons, *with any trifling matter.* "Gentlemen, continue without me. Mr. Twomey and I must speak in the sea room."

"This is about" — the Irishman balances his hat on his thigh — "what we'd call, at home, a 'skeleton in the cupboard.' "

"On Walcheren we say, 'a body in the vegetable patch.' "

"Monster turnips, then, on Walcheren. May I speak in English?"

"Do so. If I need your help, I'll ask."

The carpenter takes a deep breath. "My name is not Con Twomey."

Jacob digests this. "You're not the first pressed man to give a false name."

"My true name is Fiacre Muntervary, an' I wasn't pressed. How I left Ireland's a stranger story altogether. One icy St. Martin's Day, a block of stone slipped from its harness an' crushed my da like a beetle. I did my best to fill his boots, like, but this world's not a merciful place, an' when the harvest failed an' men came to Cork from all over Munster, our landlord trebled our rent. We pawned Da's tools, but soon enough me, Ma, five sisters, an' one little brother, Pádraig, were living in a crumbling barn, where Pádraig caught a chill, an' that's one less mouth to feed. Back in the city I tried the docks, the breweries, I tried feckin' everything, but no luck. So back I went to the pawnbroker an' asked for Da's tools back. Yer man says, 'They're sold, handsome, but it's winter an' folks need coats. I pay shiny shillings for good coats. You understand me?' " Twomey pauses to gauge Jacob's reaction.

Jacob knows not to hesitate. "You had a family to feed."

"One lady's gown, I stole from the theater. Pawnbroker says, 'Gentlemen's coats, my handsome,' an' gives me a clipped threep'nny. Next time I stole a man's coat from a lawyer's office. 'A scarecrow'd not be seen in that,' says yer man. 'Try harder!' Third time, I'm bagged like a partridge. After a fortnight in Cork jail, I appeared in the courthouse, where the one friendly face was the pawnbroker's. He told the English judge, 'Yes, Your Honor, that's the urchin who kept offering me coats.' So I says the pawnbroker's a feckin' liar who *deals* in stolen coats. The judge told me how God forgives everyone who truly repents an' handed down seven years in New South Wales. Five minutes from entry to gavel, like. Now a convict hulk, the *Queen,* was moored in Cork harbor an' it needed filling, an' I helped. Neither Ma nor my sisters can bribe their way aboard to say farewell, so come April — the year '91, this is — the *Queen* joined the third fleet out . . ."

Jacob follows Twomey's gaze over the blue water to the *Phoebus.*

"Hundreds of us, there were, in that dark an' stifling hold; cockroaches, puke, fleas, piss; rats gnawing the quick an' the dead alike, rats as big as feckin' badgers. In cold waters we shuddered. In the tropics, pitch'd drip through the seams an' burn us, an' every waking *and* sleeping minute our one thought was *Water, water, Mother of God, water . . .* Our ration was a half pint a day an' it tasted like sailor's piss, which no doubt much of it was. One in eight died on that passage, by my reck'ning. 'New South Wales' — three dreaded little words back home — changed their meaning to 'deliverance,' an' one old Galway man told us about Virginia, with its wide beaches an' green fields an' Indian girls who'd swap a screw for a nail, an' we're all thinking, *Botany Bay is Virginia, just a little farther . . .*"

Some guards pass beneath the sea room, down Seawall Lane.

"Sydney Cove wasn't Virginia. Sydney Cove was a few dozen patches of hack-an'-peck hoe rows, where the seedlings'd wither if they sprouted at all. Sydney Cove was a dry an' buzzing pit of sting flies an' fire ants an' a thousand starving convicts in torn tents. The marines had the rifles, so the marines had the power, the food, the 'roo meat, an' the women. As a carpenter, I was put to work building the marines' huts, furniture, doors, an' suchlike. Four years went by, Yankee traders began to call, an' if life never got soft, convicts were no longer dying like flies. Half my sentence was up an' I began to dream of seeing Ireland again one day. Then, in '95, a new squadron of marines arrived. My new major wanted a grand new barracks an' house up in Parramatta, so he claimed me an' six or seven others. He'd been garrisoned in Kinsale for a year, so he fancied himself an expert on the Irish race. 'The lassitude of the Gael,' he'd boast, 'is best cured by Dr. Lash,' an' he was liberal with his medicine. You saw the welts on my back?"

Jacob nods. "Even Gerritszoon was impressed."

"For meeting his eye, he'd lash us for insolence. For avoiding his eye, he'd lash us for shiftiness. For crying out, he'd lash us for acting. For not crying out, he'd lash us for stubbornness. Yer man was in paradise. Now, there were six of us Corkmen who looked out for one another an' one was Brophy, the wheelwright. One day the major goaded Brophy into hitting him back. Brophy was slapped in irons, an' the major sentenced him to hang. The major told me, 'High time Parramatta had its own gallows, Muntervary, an' you'll build it.' Well, I refused. Brophy was strung up from a tree an' I was sentenced to a week in the sty an' a hundred lashes. The sty was a cell, four by four by four, so its inmate couldn't stand nor stretch, an' you'll imagine the stink an' flies an' maggots. On my last night, the major visited an' told me he'd be wielding the lash himself and promised I'd be in hell with Brophy by the fiftieth stroke."

Jacob asks, "There was no higher authority to appeal to?"

Twomey's answer is a bitter laugh. "After midnight, I heard a noise. I said, 'Who's there?' an' my reply was a cold chisel, slid beneath the gap under the door, and loaves in a square of sailcloth an' a water bag. Footsteps ran off. Well, with the chisel I made short work of prizing away a couple of planks. Off I ran. The moon was full an' bright as the sun. The encampment has no walls, you understand, 'cause the emptiness is the walls.

Convicts ran off all the time. Many crawled back, beggin' for water. Some were brought back by blacks who were paid in grog. The rest died, I doubt not now . . . But the convicts were mostly unschooled, an' when word spread that by walking north-by-northwest across the red desert you'd reach China — aye, China — hope made it true, so it was China I was bound for that night. I'd not gone six hundred yards when I heard the rifle click. It was him. The major. He had slipped me the chisel and bread, you see. 'You're a runaway now,' he said, 'so I can shoot you dead, no questions asked, you stinking Irish vermin.' He came as close as we are now, an' his eyes were shining, an' I thought, *This is it,* an' he pulled the trigger an' nothing happened. We looked at each other, surprised, like. He lunged the bayonet at my eye socket. I swerved but not fast enough" — the carpenter shows Jacob his torn earlobe — "an' then it all went slow, an' stupid, an' we were pulling at the gun, like two boys arguin' over a toy . . . an' he tripped over an' . . . the rifle swung around an' its butt whacked his skull an' the fecker didn't get up."

Jacob notices Twomey's trembling hands. "Self-defense isn't murder, in either the eyes of God or of the law."

"I was a convict with a dead marine at my feet. I scarpered north, along the shore, an' twelve or thirteen miles later, as day broke, I found a marshy creek to slake my thirst an' slept till the afternoon, ate one loaf, an' carried on walkin', an' so it went for five more days. Seventy, eighty miles, perhaps, I covered, like. But the sun burned me black as toast, an' that land sucks your vigor away, an' some berries made me sick, an' soon I was wishin' the major's rifle *had* gone off, 'cause it was a lingering death I was in for. That evening the ocean changed color as the sun went down, an' I prayed to St. Jude of Thaddeus to end my suffering however he thought fit. You Calvinists may deny saints, but I know you'll agree that all prayers are heard." Jacob nods. "An' when I woke at dawn, on that forsaken coast, uninhabited an' hundreds of miles long, it was to the sound of a rowing shanty. Out in the bay was a scaly-looking whaler flying the Stars an' Stripes. Her boat was coming ashore for water. So I was there to meet the captain an' bade him a pleasant morning. Says he, 'Escaped convict, ain't you?' Says I, 'That I am, sir.' Says he, 'Pray give me a solitary reason why I should kick the balls of the best customer in the Pacific Ocean — the British governor of New South Wales — by shipping one of his runaways?' Says I, 'I am a carpenter who'll work aboard your ship for landsman's pay for one year.' Says he, 'We Americans hold these truths to be self-evident, that all men are created equal, that they are endowed by their Creator with certain unalienable rights, that among these are life, liberty, and the pursuit of happiness, and that'll be *three* years, not one, and your wages are life and liberty, not dollars." The carpenter's pipe has gone out. He rekindles the bowl and takes a deep draft. "Now to why I'm telling you this. Earlier, in the stateroom, Fischer mentioned a certain major who's there, on the British frigate."

"Major Cutlip? Not the luckiest of names in our language, as you know."

"It sticks in this runaway convict's memory for another reason." Twomey looks at the *Phoebus* and waits.

Jacob lowers his pipe. "The marine . . . your tormentor? *He* was Cutlip?"

"You'd think these coincidences'd not happen, not off the stage, not in life . . ."

Repercussions fill the air. Jacob hears them, almost.

". . . yet time and again, the world plays this . . . this same . . .*feckin'* game. It's him! George Cutlip of the marines, late of New South Wales, washes up at Bengal, a hunting chum of the governor's. Fischer let slip the Christian name at lunch, so there's no doubt. Not a shadow." Twomey utters a dry bark in lieu of a laugh. "Your decision about the captain's proposal an' all, it'll be hard enough as it is, but if you do a deal, Jacob . . . if you do a deal, Major Cutlip'd see me an' know me an', by God, he'd settle my outstanding balance, an' unless I killed him first, I'd be feedin' the fish or feedin' the worms."

The autumn sun is an incandescent marigold.

"I would demand guarantees, the protection of the British crown."

"We Irish know about the protection of the British crown."

Alone, Jacob watches the troublesome *Phoebus*. He employs a method of moral bookkeeping: the costs of cooperation with the English would be exposing his friend to Cutlip's revenge and possible charges of collaboration, if a Dutch court ever assembles again. The costs of rejecting the English are years of destitution and abandonment until the war ends and someone thinks to come and relieve them. Might they be forgotten, quite literally, grow sick, grow old, and die here, one by one?

"Knock-knock, eh?" It is Arie Grote, in his stained chef's apron.

"Mr. Grote, please come in. I was just . . . I was just . . ."

"Cogitatin', eh? Lot o' cogitatin' afoot today, Chief de Z . . ."

This born trader, Jacob suspects, *is here to urge me to collaborate.*

". . . but here's a word to the wise." Grote

glances around. "Fischer's lyin.' "

Eyes of sunlight from waves blink and blink on the papered ceiling.

"You have my very closest attention, Mr. Grote."

"Specific'ly, he lied 'bout Van Cleef bein' keen on the deal. Now, I'd not jeopardize our card games by revealin' all, so to speak, but there's a method called the art of lips. Folks reck'n yer know a liar by his eyes, but 'tain't so: 'tis lips what gives a man away. Different liars've diff'rent tellers, but for Fischer, when, say, he's bluffin' at cards, he does *this*" — Grote sucks in his lower lip a fraction — "and the beauty is, *he don't know he does it.* When he spoke o' Van Cleef earlier, he did it: he's lyin', plain as it's writ on his face. Which it is. An' if Fischer's lyin' 'bout specifics, he's bendin' the generalities, too, eh?"

A stray breeze brushes the bedraggled chandelier.

"If Chief van Cleef is not working with the English . . ."

"He's locked up in a hold: which 'splains why Fischer, an' not the chief, comes ashore."

Jacob looks at the *Phoebus.* "Suppose I'm the British captain, hoping to earn the glory of capturing the only European factory in Japan . . . but the locals are known to be prickly in their dealings with foreigners."

"All what's known of 'em is they 'ave no dealin's with foreigners."

"The English need us to effect a transition, that's plain, but . . ."

". . . but give it a year, an' two trading seasons in the bag . . ."

"Nice fat profits; an embassy to Edo; Union Jack fluttering on the pole . . ."

"Interpreters learnin' English: sudd'nwise your Dutch workers . . . well . . . 'Hang on, these Dutch butterboys're prisoners of war!' Why'd they pay us a *shillin'* of our back wages, eh? *I*'d not, if *I* was this Penhaligon, but *oh,* I'd give the butterboys their free passage right 'nough . . ."

"The officers to a jail in Penang, and you hands, you'd be pressed."

" 'Pressed' bein' English for 'enslaved by His Majesty's Navy.' "

Jacob tests each joint of the reasoning for weaknesses, but there are none. *Van Cleef's lack of written orders,* Jacob understands, *was his order.* "Have you spoken about this matter with the other hands, Mr. Grote?"

The cook bends his bald, clever head. "All mornin' long, Chief de Z. If *you* smell this same stinky rat as we do, our vote's to fold up this Anglo-Dutch entente, eh, into pretty little squares for use as privy paper."

Jacob sees two dolphins out in the bay. "What's *my* 'teller' in the art of lips, Mr. Grote?"

"My ma'd never forgive me f' corruptin' a

young gent with cardsharpery."

"We could play backgammon, during future quiet seasons."

"A proper gentl'man's game is gammon. I'll supply the dice . . ."

Tea is cool lush green in a smooth pale bowl. "I'll never know," says Peter Fischer, "how you stomach that spinach water." He flexes and rubs his legs, stiff after twenty minutes of sitting on the floor. "I wish these people would get around to inventing proper chairs." Jacob has little to say to Fischer, who is here to urge the magistrate to allow trade with the British behind a Dutch veneer. Fischer refuses to countenance any opposition from the hands and officers on Dejima, so Jacob has not yet declared it. Ouwehand gave Jacob permission to act in his name, and Marinus quoted Greek. Interpreters Yonekizu and Kobayashi are consulting each other across the anteroom in anxious mutters, conscious now that Jacob might understand. Officials and inspectors enter and leave the Hall of Sixty Mats. The place smells of beeswax, paper, sandalwood, *and* — Jacob inhales — *fear?*

Fischer speaks up. "Democracy is a quaint diversion for the hands, De Zoet."

"If you're implying," Jacob says, putting down the tea bowl, "that *I* somehow —"

"No, no, I admire your cunning: the easiest

way to control others is to give them the illusion of free will. You shan't, of course" — Fischer tests the lining of his hat — "upset our yellow friends with talk of presidents, et cetera? Shiroyama shall be expecting to parley with the deputy chief. That is, with me."

"You are set on recommending Penhaligon's proposal?"

"One must be a scoundrel *and* a fool to do otherwise. We disagree on trivial matters, De Zoet, as friends may. But you, I know, are neither scoundrel nor fool."

"The matter," equivocates Jacob, "is in your hands, it appears."

"Yes." Fischer takes Jacob's compliance at face value. "Of course."

The two men look out over walls and roofs, down to the bay.

"When the English are here," says Fischer, "my influence will rise . . ."

This is counting chickens, thinks Jacob, *before the eggs are even laid.*

". . . and I will remember old friends and old enemies."

Chamberlain Tomine passes, his eyes acknowledging Jacob.

He turns left, through a door decorated with a chrysanthemum.

"A face like his," observes Fischer, "belongs on cathedral gutters."

A gruff official appears and talks to Kobayashi and Yonekizu.

"You understand," Fischer asks, "what they are saying, De Zoet?"

The register is formal, but Jacob gathers that the magistrate is unwell. Deputy Fischer is to consult with his highest advisers in the Hall of Sixty Mats. Moments later, Interpreter Kobayashi confirms the message. Fischer pronounces, "This is acceptable," and tells Jacob, "Oriental satraps are figureheads with no idea of political realities. It is better to speak directly with the marionette masters."

The gruff official adds that, owing to the confusion created by the British warship, one Dutch voice is deemed to be better than two: the head clerk may wait in a quieter area of the magistracy.

Fischer is doubly pleased. "A logical measure. Head Clerk de Zoet" — he claps the Dutchman's shoulder — "may drink spinach water to his heart's content."

CHAPTER THIRTY-SIX: THE ROOM OF THE LAST CHRYSANTHEMUM AT THE MAGISTRACY

Hour of the ox on the third day of the ninth month

"Good afternoon, Magistrate." De Zoet kneels, bows, and with a nod acknowledges Interpreter Iwase, Chamberlain Tomine, and the two scribes in the corner.

"Good afternoon, Acting Chief," replies the magistrate. "Iwase shall join us."

"I will need his talents. Your injury is better, Iwase-*san*?"

"It was a crack, not a fracture." Iwase pats his torso. "Thank you."

De Zoet notices the *go* table, where the game with Enomoto waits.

The magistrate asks, "Is this game known in Holland?"

"No. Interpreter Ogawa taught me the" — he consults with Iwase — "the 'rudiments' during my first weeks on Dejima. We intended to continue playing after the trading season . . . but unfortunate events occurred . . ."

Doves trill, a peaceful sound on this frightened afternoon.

A gardener rakes the white stones by the bronze pond.

"It is irregular," Shiroyama says, turning to business, "to hold council in this room, but when every adviser, sage, and geomancer in Nagasaki is crowded into the Hall of Sixty Mats, it becomes the Hall of Six Mats and Six Hundred Voices. One cannot think."

"Deputy Fischer will be delighted with his audience."

Shiroyama notes De Zoet's courteous distancing. "First, then" — he nods at his scribes to begin — "the warship's name, *Fîbasu*. No interpreter knows the word."

"*Phoebus* is not a Dutch word but a Greek name, Your Honor. Phoebus was the sun god. His son was Phaeton." De Zoet helps the scribes with the strange word. "Phaeton boasted about his famous father, but his friends said, 'Your mother just *claims* your father is the sun god, because she has no real husband.' This made Phaeton unhappy, so his father promised to help his son prove that he was indeed a son of heaven. Phaeton asked, 'Let me drive the chariot of the sun across the sky.' "

De Zoet pauses for the benefit of the scribes.

"Phoebus tried to change his son's mind.

'The horses are wild,' he said, 'and the chariot flies too high. Ask for something else.' But, no, Phaeton insisted, and so Phoebus had to agree: a promise is a promise, even in a myth — especially in a myth. So the following dawn, up, up, up the chariot climbed, from the east, driven by the young man. Too late, he regretted his stubbornness. The horses *were* wild. First, the chariot drove too high, too far, so all the rivers and waterfalls of earth turned to ice. So Phaeton drove closer to earth, but too low, and burned Africa, and burned black the skins of the Ethiopians, and set alight the cities of the ancient world. So in the end the god Zeus, the king of heaven, had to act."

"Scribes: stop." Shiroyama asks, "This Zeus is not a Christian?"

"A Greek, Your Honor," says Iwase, "akin to Ame-no-Minaka-nushi."

The magistrate indicates that De Zoet may continue.

"Zeus shot lightning at the chariot of the sun. The chariot exploded, and Phaeton fell to earth. He drowned in the River Eridanos. Phaeton's sisters, the Heliades, wept so much they became trees — in Dutch we call them 'poplars,' but I do not know whether they grow in Japan. When the sisters were trees, the Heliades wept" — De Zoet consults with Iwase — "amber. This is the origin of amber and the end of the story. Forgive my poor

Japanese."

"Do you believe there is any truth in this story?"

"There is no truth at all in the story, Your Honor."

"So the English name their warships after falsehoods?"

"The truth of a myth, Your Honor, is not its words but its patterns."

Shiroyama stores the remark away and turns to the pressing matter. "This morning, Deputy Fischer delivered letters from the English captain. They bring greetings, in Dutch, from the English King George. The letter claims that the Dutch Company is bankrupt, that Holland no longer exists, and that a British governor-general now sits in Batavia. The letter ends with a warning that the French, Russian, and Chinese are planning an invasion of our islands. King George refers to Japan as 'the Great Britain of the Pacific Ocean' and urges us to sign a treaty of amity and commerce. Please tell me your thoughts."

Drained by his myth-telling, De Zoet directs his answer to Iwase in Dutch.

"Chief de Zoet," Iwase translates, "believes the English wanted to intimidate his countrymen."

"How do his countrymen regard the English proposal?"

This question De Zoet answers directly:

"We are at war, Your Honor. The English break promises very easily. None of us wishes to cooperate with them, except one" — his gaze strays to the passageway leading to the Hall of Sixty Mats — "who is now in the pay of the English."

"Is it not your duty," Shiroyama asks De Zoet, "to obey Fischer?"

Kawasemi's kitten skitters after a dragonfly across the veranda.

A servant looks at his master who shakes his head: *Let it play . . .*

De Zoet considers his answer. "One man has several duties, and . . ."

Struggling, he enlists Iwase's help. "Mr. de Zoet says, Your Honor, that his third duty is to obey his superior officers. His second duty is to protect his flag. But his first duty is to obey his conscience, because God — the god he believes in — gave him his conscience."

Foreign honor, thinks Shiroyama, and orders the scribes to omit the remark. "Is Deputy Fischer aware of your opposition?"

A maple leaf, fiery and fingered, is blown to the magistrate's side.

"Deputy Fischer sees what he wishes to see, Your Honor."

"And has Chief van Cleef communicated any instructions to you?"

"We have heard nothing. We draw the obvious conclusions."

Shiroyama compares the veins in the leaf to

the veins in his hands. "If we wished to prevent the frigate escaping Nagasaki Bay, what strategies would you propose?"

De Zoet is surprised by the question but gives a considered answer to Iwase. "Chief de Zoet proposes two strategies: deception and force. Deception would involve embarking upon protracted negotiations for a false treaty. The merit of this plan is lack of bloodshed. Its demerits are that the English will want to work quickly, to avoid the North Pacific winter, and that they have seen the stratagem in India and Sumatra."

"Force, then," says Shiroyama. "How may one capture a frigate without a frigate?"

De Zoet asks, "How many soldiers does Your Honor have?"

The magistrate first tells the scribes to stop writing. Then he tells them to leave. "One hundred," he confides to De Zoet. "Tomorrow, four hundred; soon, a thousand."

De Zoet nods. "How many boats?"

"Eight guard boats," says Tomine, "used for harbor and coastal duty."

De Zoet next asks whether the magistrate could requisition the fishing boats and cargo ships in the harbor and around the bay.

"The shogun's representative," says Shiroyama, "can requisition anything."

De Zoet delivers a verdict to Iwase, who translates: "It is the acting chief's opinion that while a thousand well-trained samurai

725

would easily subdue the enemy on land or aboard the frigate, the problems of transport are insuperable. The frigate's cannonry would demolish a flotilla before the swordsmen could come close enough to board. The *Phoebus*'s marines, moreover, are armed with the newest" — Iwase uses the Dutch word "rifles" — "but with three times the power, and much faster to reload."

Shiroyama's fingers have dismembered the maple leaf. "So there is no hope of detaining the ship by force?"

"The ship cannot be captured," says De Zoet, "but the bay may be shut."

Shiroyama glances at Iwase, assuming the Dutchman has made a mistake with his Japanese, but De Zoet speaks to his interpreter at some length. His hands mime at various points a chain, a wall, and a bow and arrow. Iwase verifies a few terms and turns to the magistrate. "Your Honor, the acting chief proposes the erection of what the Dutch call a 'pontoon bridge': a bridge made of boats bound together. Two hundred, he thinks, would suffice. The boats should be requisitioned from villages outside the bay, rowed or sailed to the narrowest point of the bay's mouth, and fastened, from shore to shore, to make a floating wall."

Shiroyama pictures the scene. "What stops the warship cutting through?"

The acting chief understands and speaks to

726

Iwase in Dutch. "De Zoet-*sama* says, Your Honor, that to ram through the pontoon bridge, the warship would need to lower her sails. Sailcloth is woven from hemp, and often oiled to make it rainproof. Especially in a season of warm weather, like the present one, oiled hemp is combustible."

"Fire arrows, *yes,*" Shiroyama realizes. "We can hide archers in the boats . . ."

De Zoet looks uncertain. "Your Honor, if the *Phoebus* is burned . . ."

Shiroyama recalls the myth: "Like the chariot of the sun!"

If such a plan succeeds, he thinks, *the lack of guards shall be forgotten.*

"Many sailors," De Zoet is saying, "in the *Phoebus* are not English."

This victory, Shiroyama foresees, *could win me a seat on the Council of Elders.*

De Zoet is anxious. "The captives must be allowed to surrender with honor."

"Surrender with honor." Shiroyama frowns. "We are in Japan, Acting Chief."

CHAPTER
THIRTY-SEVEN:
FROM CAPTAIN
PENHALIGON'S CABIN

Around six o'clock in the evening on October 19, 1800

Dark clouds clot and the dusk is silted with insects and bats. The captain recognizes the European sitting in the prow of the guard boat and lowers his telescope. "Envoy Fischer is being rowed back to us, Mr. Talbot."

The third lieutenant searches for the right reply. "Good news, sir."

The evening breeze, rain-scented, rustles the pages of the pay book.

" 'Good news' is what I hope Envoy Fischer brings us."

A mile over calm water, Nagasaki lights its candles and closes its shutters.

Midshipman Malouf knocks and puts his head around the door. "Lieutenant Hovell's compliments, sir, and Mr. Fischer is being ferried back to us."

"Yes, I know. Tell Lieutenant Hovell to bring Mr. Fischer to my cabin once he is safe on board. Mr. Talbot, send word to Major

728

Cutlip: I want a clutch of marines ready with guns primed, just in case . . ."

"Aye, sir." Talbot and Malouf leave on their agile young feet.

The captain is left with his gout, his telescope, and the fading light.

Torches are lit at the guard posts on shore, a quarter mile astern.

After a minute or two, Surgeon Nash knocks his particular knock.

"Come, Surgeon," says the captain, "and not before time."

Nash enters, wheezing tonight like a broken bellows. "Podagra is an ingravescent cross for sufferers to bear, Captain."

" 'Ingravescent'? Deal in plain English in this cabin, Mr. Nash."

Nash sits by the window bench and helps Penhaligon's leg up. "Gout grows worse before it grows better, sir." His fingers are gentle, but their touch still scalds.

"You think I don't *know* that? Double the dosage of the remedy."

"The wisdom of doubling the quantity of opiates so soon after —"

"Until our treaty is won, double my damned Dover's!"

Surgeon Nash unwraps the bandages and puffs out his cheeks at what he finds. "Yes, Captain, but I shall add henna and aloes before all traffic in your alimentary canal comes to a dead stop . . ."

■ ■ ■ ■

Fischer greets the captain in English, shakes his hand, and nods around the table at Hovell, Wren, Talbot, and Cutlip. Penhaligon clears his throat. "Well, be seated, Envoy. We all know why we are here."

"Sir, one small preliminary matter," says Hovell. "Mr. Snitker has just accosted us, as drunk as Old Noah, demanding to attend our meeting with Envoy Fischer and vowing he'd never allow an interloper to 'siphon off what's rightfully mine.' "

"What's rightfully his," interjects Wren, "is a clog up his arse."

"I told him he'd be called when needed, Captain, and trust I did right."

"You did. It is Envoy Fischer" — he makes a gracious gesture — "who is the man of this hour. Please ask our friend to distill his day's work."

Penhaligon studies the tone of Fischer's replies as Hovell takes notes. The Dutch sentences sound polished. "Well, as per his orders, sir, Envoy Fischer spent the day in consultation with the Dutchmen on Dejima and Japanese officials at the magistracy. He reminds us that Rome was not built in a day but believes the foundation stones of British Dejima are in place."

"We are pleased to learn it — 'British

Dejima' is a fine phrase."

Jones brings in a brass lamp. Chigwin provides beer and tankards.

"Begin with the Dutch: do they, in principle, agree to cooperate?"

Hovell translates Fischer's reply as, " 'Dejima is as good as ours.' "

This "as good as," thinks the captain, *is the first sour note.*

"Do they recognize the legitimacy of the Kew Memorandum?"

The long reply makes Penhaligon wonder about Fischer's "foundation stones." Hovell makes further notes as Fischer speaks. "Envoy Fischer reports that news of the VOC's collapse caused dismay among Dutch and Japanese alike, and without the edition of the *Courant,* the Dutch would not have believed it. He used this dismay to present the *Phoebus* as the Dutchmen's only hope of a profitable homecoming, but one dissenter, a clerk by the name of" — Hovell checks the name with Fischer, who repeats it with distaste — "Jacob de Zoet, dubbed the British race to be 'the cockroaches of Europe' and swore to cut down any 'vermin collaborators.' Objecting to this language, Mr. Fischer challenged him to a duel. De Zoet retreated to his rat hole."

Fischer wipes his mouth and adds a coda for Hovell to translate.

"De Zoet was a lackey of both Chief Vorstenbosch and ex-Chief van Cleef, whose murder he accuses you of, sir. Envoy Fischer recommends his removal, in chains."

Some settling of old scores, Penhaligon thinks, nodding, *is to be expected.* "Very well."

The Prussian next produces a sealed envelope and a checkered box. These he slides across the table with a lengthy explanation. "Mr. Fischer says, sir," explains Hovell, "that thoroughness demanded he tell you of De Zoet's opposition but assures us that the clerk is 'neutered.' While on Dejima, Mr. Fischer was visited by Dr. Marinus, the physician. Marinus had been deputized by all ashore, saving the blackguard De Zoet, to tell Mr. Fischer that the merits of the British olive branch were plain as day and to entrust him with this sealed letter addressed to you. It contains 'the unified will of Dejima's Europeans.' "

"Please congratulate our envoy, Lieutenant. We are pleased."

Peter Fischer's slight smile replies, *Of course you are pleased.*

"Now ask Mr. Fischer about his *tête-à-tête* with the magistrate."

Fischer and Hovell exchange several sentences.

"The Dutch tongue," Cutlip tells Wren, "is the noise of mating pigs."

Insects encrust the cabin's window, drawn by the bright lamp.

Hovell is ready. "Before his return to the *Phoebus* this evening, Envoy Fischer enjoyed a long audience with Magistrate Shiroyama's highest adviser, one Chamberlain Tomine."

"What about his warm relationship with Magistrate Shiroyama?" asks Wren.

Hovell explains, "Envoy Fischer says that Shiroyama is, in fact, a 'lofty castrato' — a figurehead — and that real power lies with this chamberlain."

I prefer a fibbing underling, Penhaligon worries, *to fib consistently.*

"According to Envoy Fischer," Hovell continues, "this powerful chamberlain viewed our proposal for a commercial treaty with great sympathy. Edo is frustrated by Batavia's unreliability as a trading partner. Chamberlain Tomine was astonished at the dismemberment of the Dutch empire, and Envoy Fischer sowed many seeds of doubt in his mind."

Penhaligon touches the checkered box. "This is the chamberlain's message?"

Fischer understands and speaks to Hovell. "He says, sir, that this historic letter was dictated by Chamberlain Tomine, approved by Magistrate Shiroyama, and translated into Dutch by an interpreter of the first rank. He was not shown its contents but has every confidence that it shall please."

Penhaligon examines the box. "Fine workmanship, but how to get inside?"

"There'll be a hidden spring, sir," says Wren. "May I?" The second lieutenant wastes a minute failing. "How damnably Asiatic."

"It would be no match" — Cutlip snorts snuff — "for a good English hammer."

Wren passes it to Hovell. "Picking Oriental locks is your forte."

Hovell slides one end panel and a lid slips off. Inside is a sheet of parchment, folded twice and sealed at the front.

A man's life is made, Penhaligon thinks, *by such letters . . . or unmade.*

The captain slices the seal with his paper-knife and unfolds the page.

The script is Dutch. "I impose once again, Lieutenant Hovell."

"Not at all, sir." Hovell uses a taper to light a second lamp.

" 'To the captain of the English vessel *Phoebus.* Magistrate Shiroyama informs the "Englanders" that changes . . .' " Hovell pauses, frowning. "Pardon, sir, the grammar is homespun — '. . . changes to the rules governing trade with foreigners lie not within the remit of the magistrate of Nagasaki. These matters are the preserve of the shogun's Council of Elders in Edo. The English captain is therefore' — the word is 'commanded' — 'commanded to remain at anchor for sixty days whilst the possibility of a treaty with Great Britain is discussed by the proper authorities in Edo.' "

Hostile silence settles over the table.

"The jaundiced pygmies," declares Wren, "take us for a gaggle of greenhorns!"

Fischer, sensing something badly amiss, asks to see the chamberlain's letter.

Hovell's palm tells him, *Wait*. "There is worse, sir. 'The English captain is commanded to send ashore all gunpowder —' "

"They'll have our *lives*, by all that's holy," swears Cutlip, "before our powder!"

I was a fool, thinks Penhaligon, *to forget that diplomacy is never simple.*

Hovell continues: " '. . . all gunpowder *and* admit inspectors onto his ship to ensure compliancy. The English must not attempt a landing.' That was underlined, sir. 'Doing so without the magistrate's written permission shall be an act of war. Finally, the English captain is warned that the shogun's laws punish smugglers with crucifixion.' The letter is signed by Magistrate Shiroyama."

Penhaligon rubs his eyes. His gout hurts. "Show our 'envoy' the fruits of his cleverness."

Peter Fischer reads the letter with rising incredulity and stammers high-pitched protests at Hovell. "Fischer denies, Captain, that the chamberlain mentioned these sixty days, or the gunpowder."

"One doesn't doubt," says the captain, "Fischer was told what was expedient." Penhaligon slits open the envelope containing the letter from the doctor. He is expecting Dutch but finds neatly written English. "There is a capable linguist ashore. 'To Captain Penhaligon of the Royal Navy: Sir, I, Jacob de Zoet, elected on this day president of the Provisional Dejima Republic —' "

"A 'republic!' " Wren snorts. "That walled-in hamlet of warehouses?"

" '— beg to inform you that we, the undersigned, reject the Kew Memorandum; oppose your goal of illegitimately seizing Dutch trading interests in Nagasaki; reject your bait of gain under the English East India Company; demand the return of Chief Resident van Cleef; and inform Mr. Peter Fischer of Brunswick that he is henceforth exiled from our territory.' "

The four officers look at ex-Envoy Fischer, who swallows and asks for a translation.

"To continue: 'Howsoever Messrs. Snitker, Fischer, *et al.*, assure you otherwise, yesterday's kidnappings are seen by Japan's authorities as a breach of sovereignty. Swift retaliation is to be expected, which I am powerless to prevent. Consider not only your ship's company, innocents in these machinations of states, but also their wives, parents, and children. One appreciates that a captain of the Royal Navy has orders to follow, but *à l'impossible nul n'est tenu.* Your respectful servant, Jacob de Zoet.' It is signed by all the Dutchmen."

Laughter, rakish and rookish, fills the wardroom below.

"Pray share the bones of the matter with Fischer, Mr. Hovell."

As Hovell translates the letter into Dutch, Major Cutlip lights his pipe. "Why did this Marinus feed our Prussian all that donkey manure?"

"To cast him," sighs Penhaligon, "in the role of a prize jackass."

"What was that frog croak," asks Wren, "at the end of the letter, sir?"

Talbot clears his throat. " 'No one is bound to do the impossible.' "

"How I hate a man," says Wren, "who farts in French and expects applause."

"What *is* this" — Cutlip snorts — " 'Republic' buffoonery about?"

"Morale. Fellow citizens make braver fighters than jumpy underlings. This De Zoet is not the fool that Fischer would have us believe."

The Prussian is subjecting Hovell to a volley of outraged denials. "He claims, Captain, that De Zoet and Marinus cooked up the mischief between them — that the signatures must be forged. He says that Gerritszoon and Baert can't even write."

"Hence they inked in their thumbprints!"

Penhaligon resists an urge to hurl his whale's tooth paperweight at Fischer's pasty, sweaty, desperate face. "Show him, Hovell! Show him the thumbprints! *Thumb*prints, Fischer! *Thumbprints!*"

Timbers creak, men snore, rats chew, lamps hiss. Sitting at the fold-down desk in the lamp-lit wooden womb of his sleeping cabin, Penhaligon scratches an itch between the knuckles of his left hand and listens to the twelve sentries relaying the message "Three bells, all well" around the bulwarks. *No it is not, by damn,* thinks the captain. Two blank sheets of paper are waiting to be turned into letters: one to Mr. — *never,* he thinks, *"President"* — Jacob de Zoet of Dejima, and the other to His August Personage, Magistrate Shiroyama of Nagasaki. The uninspired correspondent scratches his scalp, but dandruff and lice, not words, fall onto the blotter.

A wait of sixty days — he tips the detritus into the lamp — *may be justifiable . . .*

Crossing the China Sea in December, Wetz worried, would be a battering voyage.

. . . but to surrender our gunpowder would see me court-martialed.

A cockchafer twitches its twin whiskers in the shadow of his inkpot.

He looks at the old man in his shaving mirror and reads an imaginary article buried deep in the next year's *Times* of London.

"John Penhaligon, former captain of HM Frigate Phoebus, *returned from the first British mission to Japan since the reign of James I. He was relieved of his post and retired without pension, having achieved no military, commercial, or diplomatic success."*

"It'll be the impressment service for you," warns his reflection, "braving outraged mobs in Bristol and Liverpool. There are too many Hovells and Wrens waiting in the wings . . ."

Damn the Dutch eyes, thinks the Englishman, *of Jacob de Zoet . . .*

Penhaligon decrees that the cockchafer has no right to exist.

. . . damn his cheese-weaned health, damn his mastery of my *tongue.*

The cockchafer escapes the *Homo sapiens'* slammed fist.

A disturbance breaks out in his guts; no quarter shall be given.

I must brave the fangs in my foot, Penhaligon realizes, *or shit my breeches.*

The pain, as he hobbles into the next-door privy, is violent . . .

. . . in the black nook, he unbuttons himself and flops on the seat.

My foot — the torture ebbs and flows — *is becoming a calcified potato.*

The agonizing ten-pace journey, however, has quelled his bowels.

Master of a frigate, he ponders, *but not of his own intestines.*

Wavelets lap and nudge the hull, twenty feet below.

Young women, they hide, he hums his shitty ditty, *like birds in the bushes . . .*

Penhaligon twists the wedding ring, embedded in middle-aged plumpness.

Young women, they hide, like birds in the bushes . . .

Meredith died three years ago. His memory of her face is eroded.

. . . and were I but a young man I'd go bang them bushes . . .

Penhaligon wishes he had paid that portraitist his fifteen pounds . . .

To my right fol-diddle-derol, to my right fol-diddle-dee.

. . . but there were his brother's debts to settle, and his own pay was late, again.

He scratches a fiery itch between the knuckles of his left hand.

A familiar acidity burns his sphincter. *Hemorrhoids as well?*

"No time for self-pity," he tells himself. "Letters of state must be written."

The captain listens to the sentries call out, "Five bells, all well . . ." The oil in the lamp is low, but replenishing it will wake his gout, and he is too embarrassed to call Chigwin for so simple a task. His indecision is recorded on the blank sheets of paper. He summons his thoughts, but they scatter like sheep. *Every great captain or admiral,* he considers, *possesses a celebratory location: Nelson has the Nile; Rodney has Martinique* et al.; *Jervis has Cape St. Vincent.* "So why mayn't John Penhaligon have Nagasaki?" *One Dutch clerk named Jacob de Zoet,* he thinks, *is why; damn the wind that blew him this way . . .*

The warning in De Zoet's letter, the captain concedes, *was masterly.*

He watches a teardrop of ink fall from his quill back into the bottle.

To heed the warning would place me in his debt.

Unexpected rain smatters the sea and spatters the deck.

But to ignore the warning could prove reckless . . .

Wetz has the larboard watch tonight: he orders out the awnings and barrels to catch the rain.

. . . and lead not to an Anglo-Japanese accord but an Anglo-Japanese war.

He thinks of Hovell's scenario of Siamese traders in the Bristol Channel.

Sixty days would *be required for Parliament to send an answer, yes.*

He has rubbed a mosquito bite on his knuckle into an angry lump.

He looks into his shaving mirror: his grand-father looks back.

There are "known foreigners," he thinks, *and "foreign foreigners."*

Against the French, Spaniards, or Dutch, one buys intelligence from spies.

The lamp spits, falters, and snuffs out. The cabin is hooded by night.

De Zoet, he sees, *has deployed one of his best weapons.*

"A short sleep," the captain advises himself, "may dispel the fog."

The sentries call, "Two bells, two bells, all well . . ." Penhaligon's sweat-sodden sheet is twisted around him like a spider's cocoon. Down on the berth deck the larboard watch will be asleep, their hammocks strung shoulder to shoulder, with their dogs, cats, and monkeys.

The sheep, two goats, and half dozen chickens are asleep.

The nocturnal rats are probably at work in the provisions holds.

Chigwin, in his cubbyhole shy of the captain's door, is asleep.

Surgeon Nash is asleep, down in his warm snug bunk on the orlop.

Lieutenant Hovell, who has the starboard watch tonight, will be alert, but Wren, Talbot, and Cutlip may sleep through to the morning.

Jacob de Zoet, the captain imagines, is being pleasured by a courtesan: Peter Fischer swears he keeps a harem at the company's expense.

"Hatred eats haters," Meredith told an infant Tristram, "like ogres eat boys."

May Meredith be in heaven now, embroidering cushions . . .

The rhythmic crank of the *Phoebus*'s chain pump starts up.

Wetz must have told Hovell to keep an eye on the bilge.

Heaven is a thorny proposition, he thinks, *best enjoyed at a distance.*

Chaplain Wily is evasive about whether heaven's seas are like earth's.

Would Meredith not be happier, he asks, *with a little cottage of her own?*

Sleep kisses his eyelids. The dreamlight is dappled. He trots up his old mistress's stairs on Brewer Street. The girl's voice shimmers. "You're in the newspaper, Johnny." He takes up today's *Times* and reads: *Admiral Sir John Penhaligon, late of the HM Frigate* Phoebus, *told their lordships how, upon receiving the Nagasaki magistrate's order to surrender his gunpowder, he suspected foul play. "There being no prize to seize* from *Dejima," Admiral Penhaligon avowed, "and Dutch and Japanese alike preventing us trading* via *Dejima, it became necessary to turn our guns* on *Dejima."* In the Commons, Mr. Pitt praised the admiral's bold actions for "ministering the coup de grâce on Dutch mercantilism in the Far East."

Penhaligon sits up in his cabin, bangs his head, and laughs aloud.

The captain struggles onto the spar deck with Talbot's assistance. His stick is no longer an aid but a necessity: the gout is a tight bandage of gorse and nettles. The morning is dry but damp; fat-hulled, barnacled clouds are over-laden with rain. Three Chinese ships slip along the opposite shore, bound for the city. *You're in for a pretty spectacle,* he promises the Chinamen, *as like as not . . .*

Two dozen landsmen sit along the waist under the sailmaker's orders. They salute their captain, noticing his bandaged foot, too swollen and painful to tolerate a boot or shoe. He hobbles to the watch officer's station at the wheel, where Wetz is balancing a bowl of coffee against the *Phoebus*'s gentle rocking. "Good morning, Mr. Wetz. Anything to report?"

"We filled ten butts with rainwater, sir, and the wind's swung north."

Greasy steam and a cloud of obscenities escape the galley vent.

Penhaligon peers at the guard boats. "And

our tireless sentinels?"

"Circling us the whole night through, sir, as they are now."

"I would hear your thoughts, Mr. Wetz, on a speculative maneuver."

"Oh, sir? Then perhaps Lieutenant Talbot might take the wheel."

Wetz walks and Penhaligon limps to the quarterdeck taffrail.

"Could you bring us in to within three hundred yards of Dejima?"

Wetz gestures toward the Chinese junks. "If they can, sir, we can."

"Could you hold us steady for three minutes without anchors?"

Wetz assesses the wind's strength and direction. "Child's play."

"And how soon could we beat down the bay to the open sea?"

"Would we be" — the sailing master squints at the distances in both directions — "fighting our way out, sir, or tacking unimpaired?"

"My pet sybil has a head cold: I can't prize a word from her."

Master Wetz clicks at the panorama like a plowman to a mare. "Conditions unchanged, Captain . . . I'd have us out in fifty minutes."

"Robert." Penhaligon speaks around his pipe. "I disturb your rest. Come in."

The unshaven first lieutenant rolled from his bunk seconds ago. "Sir." Hovell closes the cabin door against the din of a hundred and fifty sailors eating ship's biscuit dipped in ghee. "They do say, 'A well-rested first officer is a neglectful first officer.' May I inquire after your . . ." He looks at Penhaligon's bandaged foot.

"Swollen as a puffball, but Mr. Nash has filled me to my gills with his remedy, so I shall stay afloat for today, which may well be time enough."

"Oh, sir? How so?"

"I authored a couple of missives overnight. Might you peruse them for me? The letters are weighty, for all their brevity. I'd not want them marred by misspellings, and you are the closest to a man of letters the *Phoebus* can offer."

"Honored to oblige, sir, though the chaplain is a better-read —"

"Read them aloud, please, so I may hear how they carry."

Hovell begins: " 'To Jacob de Zoet, Esquire: Firstly, Dejima is not a 'Provisional Republic' but a remote factory whose former owner, the Dutch East Indies Company, is defunct. Secondly, you are not a president but a shopkeeper who, by promoting himself over Deputy Chief Peter Fischer during his brief absence, violates the constitution of the said company.' A strong point, Captain. 'Thirdly, whilst my orders are to occupy Dejima by diplomatic or military means, should these prove impossible, I am obliged to place the trading post beyond use.' " Hovell looks up in surprise.

"We are almost finished, Lieutenant Hovell."

" 'Strike your flag upon receipt of this letter and have yourself transferred to the *Phoebus* by noon, where you shall enjoy the privileges of a gentleman prisoner of war. Ignore this demand, however, and you sentence Dejima to . . .' " Hovell pauses. " '. . . to total demolition. Faithfully, et cetera . . .' "

Sailors with swabs pound dry the quarter-deck over the captain's cabin.

Hovell returns the letter. "There are no errors of grammar or diction, sir."

"We are alone, Robert, so you need not be coy."

"Some may consider such a bluff to be a touch too . . . bold?"

"No bluff. If Dejima is not to be British, it is to be nobody's."

"Were these our original orders from the governor in Bengal, sir?"

" 'Plunder or trade as circumstances permit and your initiative advises.' Circumstances conspire against both plunder and trade. Beating a retreat with our tail between our legs is not an agreeable prospect, so I fall back on my initiative."

Somewhere nearby, a dog barks and a monkey screeches.

"Captain — you will have considered the repercussions?"

"It is a day for Jacob de Zoet to learn about repercussions."

"Sir, as I am invited to speak my mind, I must say that an unprovoked attack on Dejima shall taint Japan's view of Great Britain for two generations."

"Taint" and "unprovoked," notes Penhaligon, *are incautious words.* "Were you insensible to the deliberate offense in the magistrate's letter yesterday?"

"It disappointed, but the Japanese did not invite us to Nagasaki."

One must be wary of understanding one's enemy, Penhaligon thinks, *lest one becomes him.*

"The second letter, sir, is to Magistrate Shiroyama, I presume."

"You presume right." The captain hands over the page.

" 'To Magistrate Shiroyama. Sir: Mr. Fischer extended to you the hand of friendship from the crown and government of Great Britain. This hand was slapped away. No British captain surrenders his gunpowder nor tolerates foreign inspectors in his holds. Your proposed quarantine for HMS *Phoebus* violates common practice between civilized nations. I am, however, willing to overlook the offense, provided that Your Honor meets the following conditions: deliver, by noon, the Dutchman Jacob de Zoet to the *Phoebus;* install Envoy Fischer as the chief resident of Dejima; retract your unacceptable demands regarding our gunpowder and inspections. Without all three conditions are met, the Dutch shall be punished for their intransigence, as the rules of war permit, and incidental damage to property or persons shall be to Your Honor's account. Regretfully, et cetera, Captain Penhaligon of the Royal Navy of the British Crown.' Well, sir, this is . . ."

A throbbing vein in Penhaligon's foot hurts almost exquisitely.

". . . as unambiguous," says the lieutenant, "as the first letter, sir."

Where, thinks the captain, with anger and sorrow, *is my grateful young protégé?* "Translate the magistrate's letter into Dutch, in all haste, then have Peter Fischer rowed to one of the guard boats so he may deliver them."

" 'Soon afterward,' " Lieutenant Talbot, sitting on the window seat of the captain's cabin, reads aloud from Kaempfer's book while Rafferty, the surgeon's mate, scrapes a razor over the captain's jowls, " 'in 1638, this heathen court had no qualms in inflicting upon the Dutch a cursed test to find out whether the orders of the shogun or the love of their fellow Christians had greater power over them. It was a matter of us serving the empire by helping to destroy the native Christians, of whom those remaining, some forty thousand people, in desperation over their martyrdom had moved into an old fortress in the province of' " — Talbot hesitates over the word — " 'of Shimabara and made preparations to defend themselves. The head of the Dutch' " — Talbot falters again — " 'Koekebacker, himself went to the location and in fourteen days treated the beleaguered Christians to four hundred and twenty-six rough cannon salvoes both from land and sea.' "

"I knew as how the Dutch're niggardly bastards." Rafferty tweaks Penhaligon's nasal hair with his surgeon's scissors. "But that they'd slaughter Christians for trading rights nigh on beggars belief, Captain. Why not sell your old mum to a vivisectionist at the same time?"

"They are Europe's most unprincipled race. Mr. Talbot?"

"Aye, sir: 'This assistance resulted neither in surrender nor complete defeat, but broke the strength of the besieged. And because the Japanese had the pleasure to order it, the Dutch factor stripped the vessel of a further six cannons — regardless of the fact that she still had to navigate dangerous seas — so the Japanese might carry out their cruel designs . . .' One wonders whether these cannons could be those same toys adorning the bay's gun placements, sir."

"Possibly so, Mr. Talbot. Possibly so."

Rafferty rubs Pears soap around the captain's cheekbone.

Major Cutlip enters. "The new guard boat is approaching no closer than the old, Captain, and there's no sign of De Zoet. Their flag on Dejima is still flying, cocky as a thumbed nose."

"We shall chop off that thumb," promises Penhaligon, "and slice that nose."

"They're evacuating Dejima, too, carting away what can be carted."

Then their decision is made, he thinks. "The hour, Mr. Talbot?"

"The hour, sir . . . a sliver after half past ten, Captain."

"Lieutenant Wren, tell Mr. Waldron that unless we hear from shore —"

A loud commotion in Dutch breaks out in the passageway.

"*Not* without," Banes or Panes is shouting, "the captain's say-so!"

Fischer's voice shouts a line of angry Dutch ending in "Envoy!"

"The Hanoverian lads may have told him," muses Cutlip, "what's afoot."

"Shall I fetch Lieutenant Hovell, sir?" asks Talbot. "Or Smeyers?"

"If the Japanese refuse our overtures, what need have we of Dutch?"

Fischer's voice reaches them: "Captain Penhaligon! We talk!"

"Sauerkraut may stave off scurvy," says the

captain, "but a sour Kraut —"

Rafferty chuckles noxious fumes through his nose.

"— is more a hindrance than help. Tell him I'm busy, Major. If he doesn't understand 'busy,' then make him understand."

At five minutes to noon, bedecked in his dress coat with gold braiding and tricorn hat, Penhaligon addresses the company on the spar deck. "As in war, men, events move quickly in foreign parts. This morning shall see an engagement. There's no call for a grand eve-of-battle speech, men. I foresee a short, noisy, one-sided affair. Yesterday we extended to the Japanese the hand of friendship. They spat at it. Ungallant? Yes. Unwise? I think so. Punishable under the laws of civilized nations? Alas, no. No, this morning's business is to punish the Dutch" — a ragged cheer comes from some of the older men — "that band of castaways, to whom we offered work and free passage. They responded with an insolence no Englishman can overlook."

Sheets of drizzle tumble through the air down the mountains.

"Were we anchored off Hispaniola or the Malabar coast, we would reward the Dutch by seizing compensation and naming this deep-water bay King George Harbor. The Dutch reckon that I shan't hazard the best crew of my career by raiding Dejima at one

752

o'clock just to yield it by five o'clock, and to this extent they are right: Japan has more warriors, ultimately, than the *Phoebus* has balls of shot."

One of the two guard boats is sculling back toward Nagasaki.

Row as fast as you might, the captain tells it, *you'll not outrun my* Phoebus.

"But by reducing Dejima to rubble, we reduce the myth of Dutch potency to rubble. Once the dust is settled, and lessons drawn, a future British mission to Nagasaki, perhaps as soon as next year, shall not be rebuffed so brusquely again."

"If, Captain," asks Major Cutlip, "the natives attempt to board us?"

"Fire warning shots, but should these be ignored, you may demonstrate the power and precision of British rifles. Kill as few as possible."

Gunner Waldron raises his hand. "Sir, it's likely some shots'll overshoot."

"Our target is Dejima, but should any shots, by accident, fall on Nagasaki —"

Penhaligon senses Hovell at his side, bristling with disapproval.

"— then the Japanese will choose allies more prudently. So let's give this despotic backwater a taste of the coming century." Among the faces in the rigging, Penhaligon sees Hartlepool's, looking down on him like a brown-skinned angel. "Show this pox-blasted pagan port what ruin a British dog of war can inflict upon an enemy when its righteous ire is roused!"

Nearly three hundred men gaze at their captain with fierce respect.

He glances at Hovell, but Hovell is looking toward Nagasaki.

"Gun crews to your posts! Take us in, Mr. Wetz, if you please."

Twenty men turn the windlass; the cable groans; the anchor rises. Wetz shouts orders at the ratings as they swarm up the shrouds.

"A well-run ship," Captain Golding used to say, "is a floating opera . . ."

The spritsails and jibsails drop open; the jibboom enjoys the stretch.

". . . whose director is the captain yet whose *conductor* is the sailing master."

Down come the foremast and main courses; now the topsails . . .

The *Phoebus*'s bones tauten and her joints creak as the strain is taken.

Wetz works the wheel until the *Phoebus* is set to port tack.

Ledbetter, the well-named leadsman, plumbs the depth, clinging to the clew line.

Halfway to the dripping sky, men straddle the topgallant yards . . .

The prow describes an arc of one hundred and forty degrees . . .

. . . and with a tight lurch, the frigate veers

toward Nagasaki.

A smoke-dried Dane makes a Finn's cock of a tangled vang.

"Might you excuse me for a moment, sir?" Hovell indicates the Dane.

"Go," says Penhaligon. His curtness signifies, *And don't hurry back.*

"In fact," he tells Wren, "let us take in the view from the prow."

"An excellent idea, sir," agrees the second lieutenant.

Penhaligon proceeds at a gouty hobble as far as the foremast shrouds. Cutlip and a dozen marines watch the remaining guard boat, just a hundred yards dead ahead: a meager twenty-footer with a small deckhouse, clumsier-looking than a dhow. Its half dozen swordsmen and two inspectors appear to be arguing about the correct response.

"Stand your ground, pretties," murmurs Wren. "We'll slice you in two."

"A gentle peppering," suggests Cutlip, "might clarify their senses, sir."

"Agreed, *but,*" Penhaligon addresses the marines, "don't kill them, men."

"Aye, sir," reply the marines, as they prepare their rifles.

Cutlip waits until the gap is closed to fifty yards. "*Fire,* lads!"

Splinters fly off the guard boat's stanchion; the sea shatters into spray. One inspector crouches; his colleague dives into the deckhouse. Two oarsmen jump to their positions and haul the boat out of the *Phoebus*'s path — and not before time. The prow affords a fine view of the soldiers: they stare up at the Europeans, unflinching and unafraid, but make no move to attack with arrows or spears or to give chase. Their boat lists clumsily in the *Phoebus*'s wake and is lost astern in little time.

"Steady-handed work, men," Penhaligon compliments the marines.

"Load your next round, boys," says Cutlip. "Mind the rain doesn't dampen your powder."

Nagasaki, spilling down the mountainside, is growing closer.

The *Phoebus*'s bowsprit points eight or ten degrees east of Dejima: the Union Jack flies stiff as a board from the jack staff.

Hovell rejoins the captain's intimates without a word.

Penhaligon glimpses a wretched hamlet shat out by a muddy creek.

"You seem pensive, Mr. Hovell," says Wren. "Upset stomach?"

"Your concern, Mr. Wren" — Hovell stares ahead — "is unwarranted."

Spring-heeled Malouf shimmies down the fish davit. "About a hundred native troops are assembled, sir, in a plaza just ashore of Dejima."

"But no boats putting out to meet us?"

"Not a one so far, Captain: Clovelly's watching from the foretop. The factory appears to be abandoned — even the trees have legged it."

"Excellent. I desire the Dutchmen to be seen to be cowards. Back aloft with you, Mr. Malouf."

Ledbetter's soundings, relayed to Wetz, remain comfortable.

The drizzle is heavier, but the wind stays pushy and brisk.

After two or three terse minutes, Dejima's urgent bell can be heard.

Gunner Waldron shouts in the gundeck below: "Open starboard hatches, men!"

The gunport hatches crack like bones against the bows.

"Sir." Talbot has his telescope. "Two Europeans on the watchtower."

"Oh?" The captain finds the pair through his own telescope and eight hundred yards of rainy air. The thinner of the two wears a wide-brimmed hat like a Spanish brigand's. The other is bulkier and appears to wave at the *Phoebus* with a stick as he leans on the railing. A monkey sits on the corner post. "Mr. Talbot, rouse me out Daniel Snitker."

"They fancy," mocks Wren, "we shan't fire so long as they stand there."

"Dejima is their ship," says Hovell. "They are on their quarterdeck."

"They'll scurry away," predicts Cutlip,

"when they know we're in earnest."

The *Phoebus* is seven hundred yards shy of the eastern bend of the bay. Wetz bellows, *"Hard a-port!"* and the frigate rotates through eighty degrees, bringing her starboard bow running parallel to the shorefront, two rifle shots away. They pass a rectangular compound of warehouses: on the roofs, huddling under umbrellas and straw cloaks, are men dressed like the Chinese merchants Penhaligon encountered at Macao.

"Fischer spoke of a Chinese Dejima," recalls Wren. "That must be it."

Gunner Waldron appears. "The starboard guns are to be primed now, sir?"

"All twelve to fire in three or four minutes, Mr. Waldron. Go to it."

"Aye, sir!" Below, he shouts at his men, "Feed the fat boys!"

Talbot arrives with Snitker, who is unsure what attitude to strike.

"Mr. Hovell, lend Snitker your telescope. Bid him identify the men on the watchtower." Snitker's response, when it comes, contains the name *De Zoet.* "He says that the one with the stick is Marinus the physician, the one in the grotesque hat is Jacob de Zoet. The monkey is named William Pitt." Snitker, unprompted, says a few sentences to Hovell.

Penhaligon estimates the distance to be five hundred yards.

Hovell continues: "Mr. Snitker asked me to

758

say, Captain, that had you chosen him as your envoy, the outcome would have been very different, but that had he known you were a Vandal bent on destruction, he'd never have guided you into these waters."

How useful, Hovell, thinks Penhaligon, *to have Snitker utter what you dare not.* "Ask Snitker how the Japanese would treat him were he to be thrown overboard here."

Hovell translates, and Snitker withdraws like a whipped dog.

Penhaligon turns back to the Dutchmen on the watchtower.

At closer range, Marinus, the scholar-physician, looks lumpen and uncouth.

De Zoet is younger and better turned out than expected.

Dutch courage, Penhaligon thinks, *versus English munitions.*

Waldron's torso appears above the hatch. "At your word, Captain."

The Oriental rain is fine as lace on the sailors' leathern faces.

"Give it to them, Mr. Waldron, straight in the teeth."

"Aye, sir." Waldron announces the order below: "Starboard crews, *fire!*"

Major Cutlip, at Penhaligon's side, hums the melody for "Three blind mice, three blind mice . . ."

Out of the gunports, over the bulwarks, fly

the flintmen's cries of *"Clear!"*

The captain watches the Dutchmen staring down the mouths of his guns.

Lapwings fly over stone water: their wingtips kiss, drip, and ripple.

Work for a soldier or madman, Penhaligon thinks, *not a doctor and shopkeeper.*

The first of the guns erupts with a skull-cracking ferocity; Penhaligon's middle-aged heart pulsates as it did in his first fight with an American privateer a quarter century ago; eleven guns follow, over seven or eight seconds.

One warehouse collapses; the seaward wall is smashed in two places; roof tiles spray upward; and, most gratifyingly, the captain is confident as he squints through the smoke and destruction, *De Zoet and Marinus are scuttled to earth with their tails firmly between their Netherlander shanks.*

". . . she chopped off their tails," Cutlip sings, "with a carving knife . . ."

The wind blows the gun smoke back over the deck, bathing the officers.

Talbot sees them first: "They're still on the watchtower, sir."

Penhaligon hurries over to the waist hatch, his foot howling for mercy and his stick striking the deck: *damn you, damn you,* damn *you . . .* The lieutenants follow like nervous spaniels, expecting him to topple. "Ready the guns for a second round," he bellows down the hatch to Waldron. "Ten guineas for the gun crew who cut down the watchtower!"

Waldron's voice shouts back, "Aye aye, sir! You heard the captain, crews!"

Furious, Penhaligon drags himself back to the quarterdeck.

"Hold her steady, Mr. Wetz," he tells the sailing master.

Wetz is engaged in an instinctive algebraic sum involving wind speed, sail yardage, and rudder angle. "Holding her steady, Captain."

"Captain," Cutlip is speaking, "at a hundred and twenty yards my lads could embroider that brassy duo with our Brown Besses."

Tristram, the captain was told by HMS *Blenheim*'s Captain Frederick, *was minced by chain shot on the quarterdeck: he could have thrown himself against the deck and possibly lived, like his lesser warrant officers, but not Tristram, who never blinked at danger . . .*

"I'd not risk grounding us, Major. The day would end badly."

Remember Charlie's bulldog, Penhaligon sighs, *and the cricket bat?*

"The smoke," the captain blinks and mutters, "is wringing out my eyes."

Cowards, like crows, he believes, *consume the courageous dead.*

"This all brings to mind," Wren tells Talbot and the midshipmen, "my Mauritius campaign aboard the *Swiftsure:* three French frigates had the legs of us and, like a pack of baying foxhounds . . ."

"Sir," Hovell says quietly, "might I offer you my cape? The rain . . ."

Penhaligon chooses to bridle. "Am I in my dotage already?"

Robert Hovell retreats into Lieutenant Hovell. "No offense meant, sir."

Wetz shouts; topmen reply; ropes strain; blocks squeak.

A tall, thin warehouse on Dejima belatedly collapses with a shriek and clatter.

". . . so finding myself stranded on the enemy ship," Wren is saying, "in the dusk, smoke, and pell-mell, I pulled down my cap, took a lantern, followed a monkey down to the powder locker — 'twas black as night — slipped into the adjacent cordage locker where I played the firebug . . ."

Waldron reappears. "Sir, the guns're primed for the second round."

Strike the pose of naval officers, thinks Penhaligon, watching De Zoet and Marinus . . .

. . . then you may die as naval officers. "Ten guineas, Mr. Waldron."

Waldron disappears. His bedlamite's yell orders, "Let 'em have it!"

Small cogs of time meet and mesh. The flintmen cry, *"Clear!"*

Explosions hurl the shots in beautiful, terrible, screaming arcs . . .

. . . into a warehouse roof; a wall; and one

762

ball passes within a yard of De Zoet and Marinus. They drop to the platform, but all the other balls fly over Dejima . . .

Damp smoke obscures the view; the wind lifts the damp smoke.

A noise comes like a shrieking trombone, or a great tree, falling . . .

. . . it comes from behind Dejima: an appalling crash of timber and masonry.

De Zoet helps Marinus stand; his stick is gone; they look landward.

Courage in a vilified enemy, Penhaligon thinks, *is a distasteful discovery.*

"Nobody can accuse you, sir," says Wren, "of failing to give due warning."

Power is a man's means, thinks the captain, *of composing the future . . .*

"These medieval Asiatic pygmies," Cutlip assures him, "shan't forget today."

. . . but the composition — he removes his hat — *has a way of composing itself.*

Unearthly screaming boils up through the hatches from the gundeck.

Penhaligon knows, *Someone caught the recoil,* with nauseous certainty.

Hovell hurries to investigate, just as Waldron's head emerges.

The gunner's eyes bear a hideous afterimage. " 'Nother round, sir?"

John Penhaligon asks, "Who was hit, Mr. Waldron?"

"Michael Tozer — the breech rope snapped

clean through, sir."

Stabbed sobs and rasped screams sound in the background.

"Is his leg to come off, do you suppose?"

"It's already off, sir, aye. Poor bastard's bein' taken to Mr. Nash now."

"Sir —" Hovell, Penhaligon knows, wants permission to go with Tozer.

"Go, Lieutenant. Might I have the loan of your cape, after all?"

"Aye, sir." Robert Hovell gives his captain his cape and goes below.

A midshipman helps him into the garment: it has Hovell's warmth.

The captain turns to the watchtower, drunk with venom.

The watchtower still stands, as do the men; and the Dutch flag flies.

"Demonstrate our carronades. Four crews, Mr. Waldron."

The midshipmen look at one another. Major Cutlip hisses with pleasure.

Malouf asks Talbot in a low voice: "Won't carronades lack kick, sir?"

Penhaligon replies: "They *are* built for closer-range smashing, yes, but . . ."

De Zoet, he sees, is watching him through his telescope.

The captain says, "I want that damned Dutch flag torn to rags."

A house on the hill spews oily smoke in the wet and falling air.

The captain thinks, *I want those damned Dutchmen torn to rags.*

The gun crews clamber up from below, grim-faced from Tozer's accident. They remove panels from the quarterdeck's bulwarks and maneuver the short-bore wheeled carronades into position.

Penhaligon orders, "Load up with chain shot, Mr. Waldron."

"If we're aiming at the flag, sir, then . . ." Gunner Waldron indicates the watchtower, just five yards below the top of the flagpole.

"Four cones of whistling, spinning, jagged, broken chains" — Major Cutlip shines like an aroused lecher — "and jagged links of metal will wipe the smiles off their Netherland faces . . ."

". . . and their faces off their heads," adds Wren, "and their heads off their bodies."

The powder monkeys appear from the hatch with their bags of explosives.

The captain recognizes Moff the Penzance urchin. He is pale.

Gunpowder is packed into the short, fat muzzle by a bung of rags.

Chain shot rattles from rusted scuttles tipped inside the carronades' barrels. "Aim at the flag, crews," Waldron is saying. "Not so high, Hal Yeovil."

Penhaligon's right leg is become a pole of scalding pain.

My gout is winning, he knows. *I shall be bed-*

bound within the hour.

Dr. Marinus appears to be remonstrating with his countryman.

But De Zoet, the captain consoles himself, *shall be dead within the minute.*

"Double-tie those breech ropes," orders Waldron. "You saw why."

Might Hovell be right? the captain wonders. *Has my pain been thinking for me these last three days?*

"Carronades ready to fire, sir," Waldron is saying, "at your word."

The captain fills his lungs to pass the death sentence on the two Dutchmen.

They know. Marinus grips the rail, looking away, flinching, but staying put. De Zoet removes his hat; his hair is copper, untamable, bedraggled . . .

. . . and Penhaligon sees Tristram, his beautiful, one-and-only, red-haired son, waiting for death . . .

CHAPTER THIRTY-EIGHT: THE WATCHTOWER ON DEJIMA

Noon on October 20, 1800

William Pitt snorts at the sound of footsteps on the stairs. Jacob de Zoet keeps his telescope trained on the *Phoebus:* the frigate is a thousand yards out, tacking adroitly against the wet northwesterly wind on a course to bring her past the Chinese factory — some inhabitants are sitting on their roofs to watch the spectacle — and alongside Dejima.

"So Arie Grote finally gave you his alleged boa constrictor hat?"

"I ordered all hands to the magistracy, Doctor. Even yours."

"Stay here, Domburger, and you'll be needing a physician."

The frigate opens her gunports, *clack, clack, clack,* hammers on nails.

"Or else" — Marinus blows his nose — "a gravedigger. The rain is in for the day. Look." He rustles something. "Kobayashi sends you a raincoat."

Jacob lowers his telescope. "Did its previous owner die of pox?"

"A little kindness for a dead enemy, so your ghost won't haunt him."

Jacob puts the straw raincoat on his shoulders. "Where's Eelattu?"

"Where all sane men are: at our magistracy quarters."

"Was your harpsichord transported without mishap?"

"Harpsichord and pharmacopoeia alike; come and join them."

Filaments of rain brush Jacob's face. "Dejima is my station."

"If you're supposing the English shan't fire because a jumped-up clerk —"

"I suppose nothing of the sort, Doctor, but —" He notices twenty or more scarlet-coated marines climbing up the shrouds. "They're to repel boarders . . . probably. To take potshots, she'd have to come within . . . a hundred and twenty yards. There'd be too much risk of grounding the ship in waters hostile to British hulls."

"I'd rather a swarm of musket balls than a volley of broadsides."

Grant me courage, Jacob prays. "My life is in the hands of God."

"Oh, the *grief,*" Marinus heaves, "those few pious words can bring about."

"Repair to the magistracy, then, so you won't have to suffer them."

Marinus leans on the railing. "Young Oost

was thinking you must have some secret defense up your sleeve, something to reverse our reverses."

"My defense," Jacob removes his Psalter from his breast pocket, "is my faith."

In the shelter of his greatcoat, Marinus examines the old, thick volume and fingers the musket ball, fast in its crater. "Whose heart was *this* boring into?"

"My grandfather's, but it's been in my family since Calvin's day."

Marinus reads the title page. "Psalms? Domburger, you *are* a two-legged cabinet of wonders! How did you smuggle ashore *this* rattle-bag of uneven translations from the Aramaic?"

"Ogawa Uzaemon turned a blind eye at a crucial moment."

" 'It is *He* that giveth salvation unto kings,' " reads Marinus, " 'who delivereth David His servant from the hurtful sword.' "

The wind carries the sound of orders being relayed about the *Phoebus*.

In Edo Square, an officer shouts at his men; a chorus replies.

A few yards behind them, the Dutch flag flaps and rustles.

"That tricolored tablecloth wouldn't die for *you*, Domburger."

The *Phoebus* bears down: she is sleek, beautiful, and malign.

"Nobody ever died for a flag, only what the

flag symbolizes."

"I'm agog to learn what you *are* risking your life for." Marinus thrusts his hands into his eccentric greatcoat. "It can't just be because the English captain dubbed you a 'shopkeeper.' "

"For all we know, that flag is the last Dutch flag in the world."

"For all we know, it is. But it still wouldn't die for you."

"He" — Jacob notices the English captain watching them through his telescope — "believes we Dutch are cowards. But starting with Spain, every power in our rowdy neighborhood has tried to extinguish our nation. Every power failed. Not even the North Sea has dislodged us from our muddy fringe of the continent, and why?"

"Here's why, Domburger: because you have nowhere else to go!"

"It's because we are stubborn sons of guns, Doctor."

"Would your uncle want you to demonstrate Dutch manliness by dying in a crush of roof tiles and masonry?"

"My uncle would quote Goethe: 'Our friends show us what we *can* do; our enemies teach us what we must do.' Jacob distracts himself by studying the ship's figurehead of the frigate — a mere six hundred yards away now — through his telescope. Its carver endowed Phoebus with a diabolic determination. "Doctor, you must go now."

"But consider Dejima post–De Zoet! We'd be reduced to Chief Ouwehand and Deputy Grote. Lend me your telescope."

"Grote is our best merchant: he could sell sheep shit to shepherds."

William Pitt snorts at the *Phoebus* with a very human defiance.

Jacob takes off Kobayashi's straw coat and puts it on the ape.

"Please, Doctor." Rain wets wooden boards. "Don't add to my debt of guilt."

Gulls vacate the roof ridge of the boarded-up Interpreters' Guild.

"You're absolved! I'm indestructible, like a serial Wandering Jew. I'll wake up tomorrow — after a few months — and start all over again. Behold: Daniel Snitker is on the quarterdeck. It's his hominid walk that betrays him . . ."

Jacob's fingers touch his kinked nose. *Was it only last year?*

The *Phoebus*'s master shouts orders. Sailors on the yards furl the topsails . . .

. . . and the warship drifts to a dead halt, three hundred yards out.

Jacob's fear is the size of a new internal organ, between his heart and his liver.

A gang of the topmen cup their mouths and shout at the acting chief, "Scrub, little Dutch boy, scrub scrub scrub!" and wave the reverse of their index and middle fingers.

"Why" — Jacob's voice is taut and high — "why *do* the English do that?"

"I believe it goes back to archers at the Battle of Agincourt."

A cannon is run through the aft-most port; then another; then all twelve.

Lapwings fly low over the stony water; their wingtips drip.

"They're going to do it." Jacob's voice is not his own. "Marinus! *Go!*"

"As a matter of fact, Piet Baert told me that one winter — near Palermo, I believe — Grote actually *did* sell sheep shit to shepherds."

Jacob sees the English captain open his mouth and bellow . . .

"Fire!" Jacob's eyes clench tight; he puts his hand on the Psalter.

Rain baptizes each second until the cannons explode.

Staccato thunder bludgeoned Jacob's senses. The sky swung sideways. One tardy cannon fired after the others. He has no memory of throwing himself onto the watchtower's decking, but here is where he finds himself. He checks his limbs. They are still there. His knuckles are grazed and, mysteriously, his left testicle is aching, but he is otherwise unharmed.

All the dogs are barking and the crows are crazed.

Marinus is leaning on the railing. "Warehouse number six needs rebuilding; there's a big hole in the seawall behind the guild; Constable Kosugi shall probably" — from Seawall Lane comes an almighty sigh and crash — "shall certainly be lodging elsewhere tonight, and I pissed my thigh from fear. Our glorious flag, as you see, is unhurt. Half of their shots flew over us" — the doctor looks landward — "and caused damage ashore. *Quid non mortalia pectora cogis, Auri sacra fames.*"

The frigate's smoke shroud is being torn by the breeze.

Jacob stands up and tries to breathe normally. "Where's William Pitt?"

"Ran off: one *Macaca fuscata* is cleverer than two *Homines sapientes.*"

"I didn't know you were a veteran of battle, Doctor."

Marinus blows out a mouthful of air. "Did close-range artillery knock any sense into you, or are we staying?"

I can't abandon Dejima, Jacob knows, *and I am terrified of dying.*

"Staying, then." Marinus clicks his tongue. "We have a short interval before the British resume their performance."

Ryûgaji Temple intones the Hour of the Horse, as on any other day.

Jacob watches the land gate. A few uncertain guards venture out.

773

A group runs from Edo Square, over Holland Bridge.

He remembers Orito being led away into the palanquin.

He wonders how she is surviving and prays a wordless prayer.

Ogawa's dogwood scroll tube is snug in his jacket pocket.

If I am killed, let it be found and read by somebody in authority . . .

Some of the Chinese merchants are pointing and waving from their roofs.

Activity in the *Phoebus*'s gunports promises another round.

If I don't keep talking, Jacob realizes, *I shall crack like a dropped dish.*

"I know what you *don't* believe in, Doctor: what *do* you believe?"

"Oh, Descartes's methodology, Domenico Scarlatti's sonatas, the efficacy of Jesuits' bark . . . So little is actually *worthy* of either belief or disbelief. Better to strive to coexist than seek to disprove . . ."

Clouds spill over mountain ridges; rain drips off Arie Grote's hat.

"Northern Europe is a place of cold light and clear lines" — Jacob knows he is spouting nonsense but cannot stop — "and so is Protestantism. The Mediterranean world is indomitable sunshine and impenetrable shade. So is Catholicism. Then this" — Jacob sweeps his hand inland — "this . . . numinous . . . Orient . . . its bells, its dragons, its millions . . . Here, notions of transmigrations, of karma, which are heresies at home, possess a — a —" The Dutchman sneezes.

"Bless you." Marinus splashes rainwater on his face. "A plausibility?"

Jacob sneezes again. "I am making little sense."

"One may make most sense of all when one makes no sense at all."

Up a slope of crowded roofs, smoke hemorrhages from a cleft house.

Jacob tries to find the House of Wistaria, but Nagasaki is a labyrinth. "Do believers in karma, Doctor, believe that one's . . . one's unintentional sins come back to haunt one not in the next life but within this one, within a single lifetime?"

"Whatever your putative crime, Domburger," Marinus says, producing an apple for them each, "I doubt it can be so bad that our current situation is a measured and justified punishment." He puts his apple to his mouth —

The artillery blast this time knocks both men over.

Jacob comes to, curled up like a boy under blankets in a haunted room.

Fragments of tile smash on the ground. *I lost my apple,* he thinks.

"By Christ, Mahomet, and Fhu Tsi Weh,"

says Marinus, "that was close."

I survived twice, thinks Jacob, *but troubles come in threes.*

The Dutchmen help each other up like a pair of invalids.

The land gate's doors are blown away, and the tidy ranks and files of guards in Edo Square are no longer tidy. Two shots tore through the soldiers in two different places: *like marbles,* Jacob recalls a boyhood game, *through wooden men.*

Five or six or seven flesh-and-blood men are down, twitching and screaming.

There is chaos and shouting and running and places of bright red.

More fruits of your principles, mocks an inner voice, *President de Zoet.*

The *Phoebus*'s sailors have stopped taunting them now.

"Look below." The doctor points to the roof underneath. A shot passed first through one side, then out through the other. Half the stairs going down to Flag Square were knocked away. As they watch, the roof ridge collapses into the upper room. "Poor Fischer," remarks Marinus. "His new friends have broken all his toys. Look, Domburger, you've made your stand and there's no dishonor in —"

Timber sings and the watchtower stairs crash to the ground.

"Well," says Marinus, "we could jump into

Fischer's room . . . possibly . . ."

Damn me — Jacob trains his telescope on Penhaligon — *if I run now.*

He sees gunners up on the quarterdeck. "Doctor, the carronades . . ."

He sees Penhaligon training his telescope on him.

Damn you, watch and learn, Jacob thinks, *about Dutch shopkeepers.*

One of the English officers appears to be remonstrating with the captain.

The captain ignores him. Barrels are lifted to the mouths of the ship's deadliest close-range guns. "Chain shot, Doctor," says Jacob. "Hazard that leap."

He lowers his telescope: there is no gain in looking further.

Marinus throws his apple at the *Phoebus*. "*Cras ingens iterabimus aequor.*"

Jacob imagines the dense cones of shrapnel hurtling toward them . . .

. . . about forty feet wide by the time they reach the platform.

The shrapnel will tear through his clothes, skin, and viscera and out again . . .

Don't let death, Jacob reproves himself, *be your final thought.*

He tries to map, backward, the tortuous paths that led to this present . . .

Vorstenbosch, Zwaardecroone, Anna's father, Anna's kiss, Napoleon . . .

"You have no objection if I say the Twenty-third Psalm, Doctor?"

"Provided you have no objection if I join you, Jacob."

Side by side, they grip the platform's rail in the slippery rain.

The pastor's nephew removes Grote's hat to address his Creator.

" 'The Lord *is* my shepherd; I shall not want.' "

Marinus's voice is a seasoned cello's; Jacob's is shaking.

" 'He maketh me to lie down in green pastures: He leadeth me . . .' "

Jacob closes his eyes and imagines his uncle's church.

" '. . . in the paths of righteousness for His name's sake.' "

Geertje is at his side. Jacob wishes she had met Orito . . .

" 'Yea, though I walk through the valley of the shadow of death . . .' "

. . . and Jacob still has the scroll, and *I'm sorry, I'm sorry* . . .

" 'I will fear no evil: for Thou *art* with me; Thy rod and Thy staff . . .' "

Jacob waits for the explosion and the swarm and the tearing.

" '. . . they comfort me. Thou preparest a table before me . . .' "

Jacob waits for the explosion and the swarm and the tearing.

" '. . . in the presence of mine enemies; Thou anointest my head with oil . . .' "

Marinus's voice has fallen away: his memory must have failed him.

" '. . . my cup runneth over. Surely goodness and mercy shall follow me . . .' "

Jacob hears Marinus shake with quiet laughter.

He opens his eyes to see the *Phoebus* tacking away.

Her mainsails are falling, catching the wet wind and billowing . . .

Jacob sleeps fitfully in Chief van Cleef's bed. A habitual maker of lists, he lists the reasons for his fitful sleep: first, the fleas in Chief van Cleef's bed; second, Baert's celebratory "Dejima Gin," so named because gin is the only drink it doesn't taste of; third, the oysters sent from Magistrate Shiroyama; fourth, Con Twomey's ruinous inventory of damage inflicted to the Dutch-owned properties; fifth, tomorrow's meetings with Shiroyama and magistracy officials; and sixth, his mental record of what history shall call the *Phoebus* Incident, and its ledger of outcomes. In the profit column, the English failed to extract one clove from the Dutch or crystal of camphor from the Japanese. Any Anglo-Japanese accord shall be unthinkable for two or three generations. In the debit column, the factory's complement is now reduced to eight

Europeans and a handful of slaves, a roster too lean even to be called "skeletal," and unless a ship arrives next June — unlikely if Java is in British hands and the VOC is no longer extant — Dejima must rely on loans from the Japanese to meet its running costs. How welcome a guest the "ancient ally" will be when reduced to rags remains to be seen, especially if the Japanese view the Dutch as partly responsible for conjuring up the *Phoebus*. Interpreter Hori brought news of damage ashore: six soldiers dead in Edo Square and another six injured, and several townspeople burned in a fire begun when a ball struck a kitchen in Shinmachi Ward. The political consequences, he intimated, were even farther-reaching. *I never heard,* Jacob thinks, *of a twenty-six-year-old chief resident . . .*

. . . or, he turns, *a factory so beset by crises as Dejima.*

He misses Tall House, but the chief must sleep near the safe boxes.

Early the following morning, Jacob is met at the magistracy by Interpreter Goto and Chamberlain Tomine. Tomine apologizes for asking Jacob to perform a distasteful service before meeting the magistrate: the body of a foreign sailor was retrieved yesterday evening by a fishing boat, near the Papenburg Rock.

Would Chief de Zoet examine the corpse and assess the likelihood of its being from the *Phoebus*?

Jacob is not afraid of corpses, having helped his uncle at every funeral in Domburg.

The chamberlain leads him across a courtyard to a storehouse.

He says a word unknown to Jacob; Goto says, "Place dead body wait."

A mortuary, Jacob realizes. Goto asks Jacob to teach him the word.

Outside, an elderly Buddhist priest is waiting with a pail of water.

"To make pure," Goto explains, "when leave . . . 'mortuary.' "

They enter. There is one small window and the smell of death.

The single inmate is a young, pigtailed mestizo sailor on a pallet.

He wears nothing but a sailor's duck trousers and a lizard tattoo.

A cold draft is sucked from the window through the open door.

It tousles the boy's hair, accentuating his motionlessness.

Alive, the boy's slack gray skin must have been bruised gold.

"Were any items," Jacob asks in Japanese, "in his possession?"

The chamberlain produces a tray; on it is a British farthing.

GEORGIVS III REX, reads the obverse; Britannia sits on the reverse.

"I am in no doubt," says Jacob, "he was a sailor from the *Phoebus*."

"*Sa,*" responds Chamberlain Tomine. "But is he an Englishman?"

Only his mother and his Creator could answer, Jacob thinks. He tells Goto, "Please inform Tomine-*sama* that his father was probably European. His mother was probably Negro. Such is my best guess."

The chamberlain is still not satisfied. "But is he English?"

Jacob exchanges a look with Goto: interpreters often have to provide both the answer and the tools to understand it. "If I had a son with a Japanese woman," Jacob asks Tomine, "would he be Dutch or Japanese?"

Involuntarily, Tomine winces at the tasteless question. "A half."

Then so, says Jacob's gesture over the corpse, *is he.*

"But," the chamberlain persists, "does Chief de Zoet say he is English?"

Trilling of doves from under the eaves ruffles the still morning.

Jacob misses Ogawa. He asks Goto in Dutch: "What don't I understand?"

"If foreigner is English," replies the interpreter, "body shall throw in ditch."

Thank you, thinks Jacob. "Otherwise he rests in the foreigners' cemetery?"

The intelligent Goto nods. "Chief de Zoet

782

is correct."

"Chamberlain." Jacob addresses Tomine. "This youth is not English. His skin is too dark. It is my wish that he is buried" — *like a Christian* — "in the cemetery of Mount Inasa. Please place the coin in his grave."

Halfway down the corridor to the Room of the Last Chrysanthemum is a little-visited courtyard where a maple stands over a small pond. Jacob and Goto are asked to wait on the veranda while Chamberlain Tomine consults with Magistrate Shiroyama prior to their audience.

Fallen red leaves drift over a smeared sun held in dark water.

"Congratulations," says a voice in Dutch, "on promotion, Chief de Zoet."

Somehow inevitable. Jacob turns to Ogawa's killer and Orito's jailer.

"Good morning, Lord Abbot," he replies in Dutch, feeling the dogwood scroll tube pressing against his ribs. A long, thin ridge must be visible down his left side.

Enomoto tells Goto, "Some paintings in the vestibule would interest you."

Goto bows. "Lord Abbot, the rules of my guild forbid —"

"You are forgetting who I am. I forgive only once."

Goto looks at Jacob; Jacob nods consent. He tries to turn a little to the left to hide the scroll tube.

One of Enomoto's servants accompanies Goto; another stays nearby.

"Dutch chief was brave against warship." Enomoto practices his Dutch. "News is traveling all over Japan, even now."

Jacob can think only of the Twelve Creeds of the Order of Shiranui. *When members of your order die,* Jacob wonders, *are the creeds not exposed as false commandments? Is your Goddess not proven to be a lump of lifeless wood? Are all the sisters' misery and the drowned infants not shown to be in vain?*

Enomoto frowns, as if trying to catch a distant voice. "At first I saw you, in Hall of Sixty Mats, one year ago, I think . . ."

A slow white butterfly passes within inches of Jacob's face.

". . . I think, *Strange: he is foreigner, but there is affinity.* You know?"

"I remember that day," affirms Jacob, "but I felt no affinity at all."

Enomoto smiles like an adult at a child's harmless lie. "When Mr. Grote say, 'De Zoet sells mercury,' I think, *There: affinity!*"

A black-headed bird watches from the core of the flame-red tree.

"So I buy mercury, but still, I think, *Affinity still exist. Strange.*"

Jacob wonders how Ogawa Uzaemon suffered before he died.

"Then I hear, 'Mr. de Zoet propose to Aibagawa Orito.' I think, *Ohooo!*"

Jacob cannot hide his shock that Enomoto knew. The leaves on the water spin, very slowly. "How did you . . ." and he thinks, *I am confirming it now.*

"Hanzaburo look very stupid; this is why he very good spy."

A heaviness presses down on Jacob's shoulders. His back aches.

He imagines Hanzaburo ripping a page from his sketchbook . . .

. . . and that page, Jacob thinks, *passing up a chain of prurient eyes.*

"What do you do to the sisters at your shrine? Why must you —"

Jacob stops himself from blurting out proof that he knows what Acolyte Jiritsu knew. "Why did you kidnap her, when a man of your position could choose anyone?"

"She and I also — *affinity.* You, I, her. A pleasant triangle . . ."

There is a fourth corner, thinks Jacob, *called Ogawa Uzaemon.*

". . . but now she is content enough." Enomoto is speaking Japanese. "Her work in Nagasaki was important, but her mission on Shiranui is deeper. She serves Kyôga Domain. She serves the Goddess. She serves my order." He smiles pityingly at Jacob's impotence. "So now I understand. Our affinity was

785

not mercury. Our affinity was Orito."

The white butterfly passes within inches of Enomoto's face.

The abbot's hand makes a circular motion over the butterfly . . .

. . . and it drops, lifeless as a twist of paper, into the dark pool.

Chamberlain Tomine sees the Dutchman and the abbot and stops.

"Our affinity is ended, Chief de Zoet. Enjoy a long, long life."

Thin paper screens obscure the fine view of Nagasaki, lending the Room of the Last Chrysanthemum a mournful air like, Jacob thinks, a quiet chapel on a busy city street back home. The pinks and oranges of the flowers in the vase are bleached of half their vigor. Jacob and Goto kneel on the moss-green mat before the magistrate. *You have aged five years,* thinks Jacob, *in two days.*

"It is courteous of the Dutch chief to visit at such a . . . a busy time."

"The honorable magistrate is equally busy, no doubt." The Dutchman instructs Goto to thank the magistrate in suitably formal language for his support during the recent crisis.

Goto performs his job well: Jacob acquires the word for "crisis."

"Foreign ships," the magistrate responds, "visited our waters before. Sooner or later, their guns would speak. The *Phoebus* was prophet and teacher, and next time" — he inhales sharply — "the shogun's servants shall be better prepared. Your 'pontoon bridge' is written in my record for Edo. But this time fortune did not favor me."

Jacob's starched collar scratches his neck.

"I watched you," says the magistrate, "on the watchtower yesterday."

"Thank you for" — Jacob is unsure how to respond — "for your concern."

"I thought of Phaeton, with lightning and thunderbolts flying."

"Luckily for me, the English do not aim as well as Zeus."

Shiroyama opens his fan and closes it again. "Were you frightened?"

"I would like to say, 'No,' but truthfully . . . I was never more afraid."

"Yet when you could have run, you stayed at your post."

Not after the second round, he thinks. *There was no way down.* "My uncle, who raised me, always scolded my —" He asks Goto to translate the word "stubbornness."

Outside, the bamboo winnows the breeze: a sound ancient and sad.

Shiroyama notices the ridge of the scroll tube in Jacob's coat . . .

. . . but he says, "My report to Edo must address a question."

"If I am able answer it, Your Honor, I shall."

"Why did the English sail away before De-jima was destroyed?"

"This same mystery troubled me all night long, Your Honor."

"You must have seen how they loaded the cannons on the quarterdeck."

Jacob has Goto explain how cannons are for punching big holes in ships and walls, whereas carronades are for punching small holes through lots of men.

"Then why did the English not kill their enemy's chief with the 'carronades'?"

"Possibly the captain wanted to limit damage to Nagasaki." Jacob shrugs. "Possibly it was an . . ." He has Goto translate "act of mercy."

A child's voice can be heard, muffled by two or three rooms.

The magistrate's celebrated son, Jacob guesses, *delivered by Orito.*

"Perhaps," Shiroyama muses, examining the joints of his thumb, "your courage made your enemy ashamed."

Jacob, recalling his four years of living with Londoners, doubts the suggestion but bows at the compliment. "Will Your Honor be traveling to Edo to submit your report?"

Pain flashes across Shiroyama's face, and Jacob wonders why. The magistrate addresses his difficult-to-understand answer to Goto. "His Honor says . . ." Goto hesitates. "Edo requires a — the word is a merchant's word, 'settle of accounts'?"

Jacob is being instructed to leave this deliberate vagueness alone.

He notices the *go* board in its corner; he recognizes the same game from his visit two days ago, just a few moves further on.

"My opponent and I," says Shiroyama, "can rarely meet."

Jacob makes a safe guess: "The lord abbot of Kyôga Domain?"

The magistrate nods. "The lord abbot is a master of the game. He discerns his enemy's weaknesses and uses them to confound his enemy's strengths." He considers the board ruefully. "I fear my position is without hope."

"My position on the watchtower," says Jacob, "was also without hope."

Chamberlain Tomine's nod to Interpreter Goto indicates, *It is time.*

"Your Honor." Nervously, Jacob produces the scroll from his inner jacket. "Humbly, I beg you to read this scroll when you are alone."

Shiroyama frowns and looks at his chamberlain. "Precedent would instruct," Tomine tells Jacob, "all letters from Dutchmen to be translated by two members of the Interpreters' Guild of Dejima, and then —"

"A British warship sailed into Nagasaki and opened fire, and what did precedent do about it?" Shiroyama is irritated out of his melancholy. "But if this is a petition for more copper, or any other matter, then Chief de Zoet should know that my star in Edo is not on the rise . . ."

"A sincere personal letter, Your Honor. Please forgive its poor Japanese."

Jacob senses the lie deflate Tomine's and Goto's curiosity.

The innocuous-looking scroll tube passes into the magistrate's hands.

CHAPTER THIRTY-NINE: FROM THE VERANDA OF THE ROOM OF THE LAST CHRYSANTHEMUM, AT THE MAGISTRACY

The ninth day of the ninth month

Gulls wheel through spokes of sunlight over gracious roofs and dowdy thatch, snatching entrails at the marketplace and escaping over cloistered gardens, spike-topped walls, and triple-bolted doors. Gulls alight on white-washed gables, creaking pagodas, and dung-ripe stables; circle over towers and cavernous bells and over hidden squares where urns of urine sit by covered wells, watched by mule drivers, mules, and wolf-snouted dogs, ignored by hunchbacked makers of clogs; gather speed up the stoned-in Nakashima River and fly beneath the arches of its bridges, glimpsed from kitchen doors, watched by farmers walking high, stony ridges. Gulls fly through clouds of steam from laundries' vats; over kites unthreading corpses of cats; over scholars glimpsing truth in fragile patterns;

over bathhouse adulterers; heartbroken slatterns; fishwives dismembering lobsters and crabs; their husbands gutting mackerel on slabs; woodcutters' sons sharpening axes; candlemakers rolling waxes; flint-eyed officials milking taxes; etiolated lacquerers; mottled-skinned dyers; imprecise soothsayers; unblinking liars; weavers of mats; cutters of rushes; ink-lipped calligraphers dipping brushes; booksellers ruined by unsold books; ladies-in-waiting; tasters; dressers; filching page boys; runny-nosed cooks; sunless attic nooks where seamstresses prick calloused fingers; limping malingerers; swineherds; swindlers; lip-chewed debtors rich in excuses; heard-it-all creditors tightening nooses; prisoners haunted by happier lives and aging rakes by other men's wives; skeletal tutors goaded to fits; firemen-turned-looters when occasion permits; tongue-tied witnesses; purchased judges; mothers-in-law nurturing briars and grudges; apothecaries grinding powders with mortars; palanquins carrying not-yet-wed daughters; silent nuns; nine-year-old whores; the once-were-beautiful gnawed by sores; statues of Jizo anointed with posies; syphilitics sneezing through rotted-off noses; potters; barbers; hawkers of oil; tanners; cutlers; carters of night soil; gatekeepers; beekeepers; blacksmiths and drapers; torturers; wet nurses; perjurers; cutpurses; the newborn; the growing; the strong-willed and pliant; the ailing; the dying; the weak and defiant; over the roof of a painter withdrawn first from the world, then his family, and down into a masterpiece that has, in the end, withdrawn from its creator; and around again, where their flight began, over the balcony of the Room of the Last Chrysanthemum, where a puddle from last night's rain is evaporating; a puddle in which Magistrate Shiroyama observes the blurred reflections of gulls wheeling through spokes of sunlight. *This world,* he thinks, *contains just one masterpiece, and that is itself.*

Kawasemi holds up a white under-robe for Shiroyama. She is wearing her kimono decorated with blue Korean morning glories. *The wheel of seasons is broken,* says the spring pattern this autumn day, *and so am I.*

Shiroyama inserts his fifty-year-old arms into the sleeves.

She ducks in front of him, tugging and smoothing the material.

Kawasemi now wraps the *obi* sash above his waist.

She chose a green-and-white design: *Green for life, white for death?*

The expensively trained courtesan ties it in a figure-of-ten cross.

"It always takes me ten times," he used to say, "to get the knot to stay."

Kawasemi lifts the thigh-length *haori* jacket; he takes it and puts it on. The fine black silk is crisp as snow and heavy as air. Its sleeves are embroidered with his family's crest.

Two rooms away he hears Naozumi's twenty-month-old footsteps.

Kawasemi passes him his *inyo* box: it contains nothing, but without it he would feel unprepared. Shiroyama threads its cord through the netsuke toggle; she has chosen him a Buddha carved in hornbill.

Kawasemi's steady hands pass his *tantô* dagger in its scabbard.

Would that I could die in your house, he thinks, *where I was happiest . . .*

He slides its scabbard through his *obi* sash in the prescribed manner.

. . . but decorum must be seen to be observed.

"Shush!" says the maid in the next room. *"Suss!"* laughs Naozumi.

A chubby hand slides the door open and the boy, who looks like Kawasemi when he smiles and like Shiroyama when he frowns, darts into the room, ahead of the mortified maid.

"I beg Your Lordship's pardon," she says, kneeling at the threshold.

"Found you!" singsongs the toothy grinning toddler, and tips over.

"Finish packing," Kawasemi tells her maid. "I'll summon you when it's time."

The maid bows and withdraws. Her eyes

are red from crying.

The small human whirlwind stands, rubs his knee, and totters to his father.

"Today is an important day," says the magistrate of Nagasaki.

Naozumi half-sings, half-asks, " 'Ducky in the duck pond, *ichi-ni-san?*' "

With a look, Shiroyama tells his concubine not to fret.

Better for him now, he thinks, *to be too young to understand.*

"Come here," says Kawasemi, kneeling, "come here, Nao-*kun* . . ."

The boy sits on his mother's lap and loses his hand in her hair.

Shiroyama sits a pace away and circles his hands in a conjuror's flourish . . .

. . . and in his palm is an ivory castle sitting on an ivory mountain.

The man turns it around, inches from the boy's captured eyes.

Tiny steps; cloud motifs; pine trees; masonry grown from rock . . .

"Your great-grandfather carved this," says Shiroyama, "from a unicorn horn."

. . . an arched gate; windows; arrow slits; and, at the top, a pagoda.

"You can't see him," says the magistrate, "but a prince lives in this castle."

You will forget this story, he knows, *but your mother will remember.*

"The prince's name is the same as ours: *shiro* for the castle, *yama* for the mountain. Prince Shiroyama is very special. You and I must one day go to our ancestors, but the prince in this tower never dies: not for so long as a Shiroyama outside — me, you, your son — is alive, and holds his castle, and looks inside."

Naozumi takes the ivory carving and holds it against his eye.

Shiroyama does not gather his son into his arms and breathe in his sweet smell.

"Thank you, Father." Kawasemi angles the boy's head to imitate a bow.

Naozumi leaps away with his prize, from mat to mat to door.

He turns to look at his father, and Shiroyama thinks, *Now.*

Then the boy's footfalls carry him away forever.

Lust tricks babies from their parents, thinks Shiroyama, *mishap, duty . . .*

Marigolds in the vase are the precise shade of summer, remembered.

. . . but perhaps the luckiest are those born from an unthought thought: that the intolerable gulf between lovers can be bridged only by the bones and cartilage of a new being.

The bell of Ryûgaji Temple intones the Hour of the Horse.

Now, he thinks, *I have a murder to commit.*

"It is best that you leave," Shiroyama tells

his concubine.

Kawasemi looks at the ground, determined not to cry.

"If the boy shows promise at *go,* engage a master of the Honinbo School."

The vestibule outside the Hall of Sixty Mats and the long gallery leading to the front courtyard is crammed with kneeling advisers, councillors, inspectors, headmen, guards, servants, exchequer officials, and the staff of his household. Shiroyama stops.

Crows smear rumors across the matted, sticky sky.

"All of you: raise your faces. I want to see your faces."

Two or three hundred heads look up: eyes, eyes, eyes . . .

. . . *dining on a ghost,* Shiroyama thinks, *not yet dead.*

"Magistrate-*sama!*" Elder Wada has appointed himself spokesman.

Shiroyama looks at the irritating, loyal man. "Wada-*sama.*"

"Serving the magistrate has been the deepest honor of my life . . ."

Wada's face is taut with emotion; his eyes are shining.

"We learn from the magistrate's wisdom and example . . ."

All you *learned from me,* thinks Shiroyama, *is to ensure that one thousand men man the coastal defenses at all times.*

"Our memories of you shall dwell in our hearts and minds forever."

As my body and my head, thinks Shiroyama, *molder in the ground.*

"Nagasaki shall never" — his tears stream — "ever recover!"

Oh, supposes Shiroyama, *by next week things will be back to normal.*

"On behalf of *all* who were — *are* — privileged to serve under you . . ."

Even the untouchable, thinks the magistrate, *who empties the shit pot?*

". . . I, Wada, offer our undying gratitude for your patronage!"

Under the eaves, pigeons coo like grandmothers greeting babies.

"Thank you," he says. "Serve my successor as you served me."

So the stupidest speech I ever heard, he thinks, *was the very last.*

Chamberlain Tomine opens the door for his final appointment.

The door rumbles shut on the Hall of Sixty Mats. Nobody may enter now until Chamberlain Tomine emerges to announce Magistrate Shiroyama's honorable death. The near-silent crowd in the gallery is returning to the bright realm of life. Out of respect for the magistrate, the entire wing shall remain vacant until nightfall but for the occasional guard.

One high screen is half open, but the hall is dim and cavernous.

Lord Abbot Enomoto is studying the state of play on the *go* board.

The abbot turns and bows. His acolyte bows low.

The magistrate begins the journey to the center of the room. His body pushes aside drapes of hushed air. His feet swish on the floor. Chamberlain Tomine follows in his master's wake.

The Hall of Sixty Mats might be six hundred wide or six thousand long.

Shiroyama sits across the *go* table from his enemy. "It is unpardonably selfish to lay these last two impositions on such a busy man."

"Your Honor's requests," replies Enomoto, "pay me a singular compliment."

"I had heard of Enomoto-*sama*'s accomplishments as a swordsman, mentioned in low, awed tones, long before I met you in person."

"People exaggerate such stories, but it is true that, down the years, five men have asked me to be a *kaishaku* second at their deaths. I discharged those duties competently."

"Your name came to mind, Lord Abbot. Yours and no other." Shiroyama glances down at Enomoto's sash for his scabbard.

"My acolyte" — the abbot nods at the youth — "has brought it."

The sword, wrapped in black, lies on a

square of red velvet.

On a side table are a white tray, four black cups, and a red gourd.

A white linen sheet, large enough to enfold a corpse, lies at a tactful distance.

"Your wish is still" — Enomoto indicates the game — "to finish what we began?"

"One must do something before one dies." The magistrate drapes his *haori* jacket over his knees and turns his attention to the game. "Have you decided your next move?"

Enomoto places a white stone to threaten black's eastern outpost.

The cautious movement of the stone sounds like the *click* of a blind man's cane.

Shiroyama makes a safe play that is both a bridge to and a bridgehead against white's north.

To win, his father taught him, *purify yourself of the* desire *to win.*

Enomoto secures his northern army by opening an eye in its ranks.

The blind man moves fast: *click* goes his cane; *click,* a stone is placed.

A few moves later, Shiroyama's black takes six white prisoners.

"They were living on borrowed time," Enomoto remarks, "at crippling interest." He plants a spy deep behind black's western frontier.

Shiroyama ignores it and starts a road between his western and central armies.

Enomoto places another strange stone in the southwest of nowhere.

Two moves later, Shiroyama's bold black bridge is only three stones from completion. *Surely,* thinks the magistrate, *he can't allow me to go unchallenged?*

Enomoto places a stone within hailing distance of his western spy . . .

. . . and Shiroyama sees the way stations of a black cordon, curving in a crescent from southwest to northeast.

If white prevents black's main armies conjoining at this late stage . . .

. . . *my empire,* Shiroyama sees, *is split into three paltry fiefdoms.*

The bridge is just two intersections away: Shiroyama claims one . . .

. . . and Enomoto places a white stone on the other: the battle turns.

I go there so he goes there; I go there so he goes there; I go there . . .

But by the fifth move and countermove, Shiroyama forgets the first.

Go *is a duel between prophets,* he thinks. *Whoever sees furthest wins.*

His divided armies are reduced to praying for a white blunder.

But Enomoto, knows the magistrate, *does not make blunders.*

"Do you ever suspect," he asks, "we don't play *go;* rather, *go* plays us?"

"Your Honor has a monastic mind," Enomoto replies.

More moves follow, but the game has passed its perfect ripeness.

Discreetly, Shiroyama counts his territory and the prisoners taken.

Enomoto does the same for white, and waits for the magistrate.

The abbot makes it eight points in white's favor; Shiroyama puts Enomoto's margin of victory at eight and a half points.

"A duel," remarks the loser, "between boldness and subtleties."

"My subtleties very nearly undid me," concedes Enomoto.

The players return the stones to the bowls.

"Ensure this *go* set goes to my son," Shiroyama orders Tomine.

Shiroyama indicates the red gourd. "Thank you for providing the *sake,* Lord Abbot."

"Thank you for respecting my precautions, even now, Magistrate."

Shiroyama sifts Enomoto's tone for glints of irony but finds none.

The acolyte fills the four black cups from the red gourd.

The Hall of Sixty Mats is now as quiet as a forgotten graveyard.

My final minutes, thinks the magistrate, watching the careful acolyte.

A black swallowtail butterfly blunders

across the table.

The acolyte hands one cup of *sake* to the magistrate first, one to his master, one to the chamberlain, and returns to his cushion with the fourth.

So as not to glance at Tomine or Enomoto's cup, Shiroyama imagines the wronged souls — how many tens, how many hundreds? — watching from the slants of darkness, thirsty for vengeance. He raises his cup. He says, "Life and death are indivisible."

The other three repeat the well-worn phrase. The magistrate shuts his eyes.

The volcano-ash glaze of the Sakurajima cup is rough on his lips.

The astringent spirit sluices around the magistrate's mouth . . .

. . . and its aftertaste is perfumed . . . untainted by the additive.

From inside the dark tent of his eyelids, he hears loyal Tomine drink . . .

. . . but neither Enomoto nor the acolyte follows. Seconds pass.

Despair possesses the magistrate. *Enomoto knew about the poison.*

When he opens his eyes, he will be greeted by wry mockery.

Our planning, ingenuity, and Tomine's terrible sacrifice are in vain.

He has failed Orito, Ogawa, and De Zoet, and all the wronged souls.

Did Tomine's procurer betray us? Or the

Chinese druggist?

Should I try to kill the devil with my ceremonial sword?

He opens his eyes to gauge his chances, as Enomoto drains his cup . . .

. . . and the acolyte lowers his own, a moment after his master.

Shiroyama's despair is gone, replaced in a heartbeat by a flat fact. *They will know in two minutes, and we will be dead in four.* "Would you spread the cloth, Chamberlain? Just over there . . ."

Enomoto raises his palm. "My acolyte can perform such work."

They watch the young man unfold the large sheet of white hemp. Its purpose is to absorb blood from the decapitated body and to wrap the corpse afterward, but its role this morning is to distract Enomoto from the magistrate's true endgame while the *sake* is absorbed by their bodies.

"Shall I recite," the lord abbot offers, "a mantra of redemption?"

"What redemption can be won," replies Shiroyama, "is mine now."

Enomoto makes no comment but retrieves his sword. "Is your hara-kiri to be visceral, Magistrate, with a *tantô* dagger, or shall it be a symbolic touch with your fan, after the modern fashion?"

Numbness is encrusting the ends of Shiroyama's fingers and toes. *The poison is safe in our veins.* "First, Lord Abbot, an explanation is owed."

Enomoto lays his sword across his knees. "Regarding what matter?"

"Regarding why the four of us shall be dead within three minutes."

Enomoto studies Shiroyama's face for evidence that he misheard.

The well-trained acolyte rises, reading the silent hall for threat.

"Dark emotions," Enomoto speaks with indulgence, "may cloud one's heart at such a time, but for the sake of your posthumous name, Magistrate, you must —"

"Quiet before the magistrate's verdict!" The crushed-nose chamberlain speaks with the full authority of his office.

Enomoto blinks at the older man. "Addressing *me* in that —"

"Lord Abbot Enomoto-*no-kami*" — Shiroyama knows how little time remains — "*daimyo* of Kyôga Domain, high priest of the shrine of Mount Shiranui, by the power vested in me by the august shogun, you are hereby found guilty of the murder of the sixty-three women buried behind the Harubayashi Inn on the Sea of Ariake Road, of orchestrating the captivity of the sisters of the Shrine of Mount Shiranui, and of the persistent and unnatural infanticide of the issue fathered upon those women by you and your monks. You shall atone for these crimes with your life."

The muffled clatter of horses penetrates the closed-off hall.

Enomoto is impassive. "It grieves me to see a once-noble mind —"

"Do you deny these charges? Or suppose yourself immune?"

"Your questions are ignoble. Your charges are contemptible. Your assumption that you, a disgraced appointee, could punish me — *me!* — is a breathtaking vanity. Come, Acolyte, we must leave this pitiable scene and —"

"Why are your hands and feet so cold on such a warm day?"

Enomoto opens his scornful mouth and frowns at the red gourd.

"It never left my sight, Master," states the acolyte. "Nothing was added."

"First," says Shiroyama, "I offer up my reasons. When, two or three years ago, rumors reached us about bodies being hidden in a bamboo grove behind the Harubayashi Inn, I paid little heed. Rumors are not proof, your friends in Edo are more powerful than mine, and a *daimyo*'s back garden is no one else's concern — ordinarily. But when you spirited away the very midwife who saved the lives of my concubine and son, my interest in the Mount Shiranui Shrine grew. The lord of Hizen produced a spy who told some grotesque tales about your retired nuns. That he was soon killed only confirmed his tales, so when a certain testament in a dogwood scroll tube —"

"Apostate Jiritsu was a viper who turned against the order."

"And Ogawa Uzaemon was, of course, killed by mountain bandits?"

"Ogawa was a spy and a dog who died like a spy and a dog." Enomoto sways as he stands, staggers, falls, and snarls, "What have you — what have you —"

"The poison attacks the body's musculature, beginning at the extremities and ending with the heart and diaphragm. It is extracted from the glands of a tree snake found only in a Siamese delta. This creature is known as the four-minute snake. A learned chemist can guess why. It is unsurpassingly lethal, and unsurpassingly difficult to procure, but Tomine is an unsurpassingly well-connected chamberlain. We tested it on a dog, which lasted . . . how long, Chamberlain?"

"Less than two minutes, Your Honor."

"Whether the dog died of bloodlessness or suffocation, we shall soon discover. I am losing my elbows and knees as we speak."

Enomoto is helped by his acolyte into a sitting position.

The acolyte tumbles and lies struggling, like a cut-string puppet.

"In air," the magistrate continues, "the poison hardens into a thin, clear flake. But a liquid — especially a spirit, like *sake* — dissolves it instantaneously. Hence the coarse Sakurajima cups — to hide the painted-on poison. That you saw through my offensive on the *go* board, but overlooked this simple stratagem, amply justifies my death."

Enomoto, his face distorted by fear and fury, reaches for his sword, but his arm is stiff and wooden and he cannot draw his weapon from its scabbard. He stares at his hand in disbelief and, with a guttural snarl, swings his fist at his *sake* cup.

It skips across the empty floor, like a pebble skimming dark water.

"If you *knew,* Shiroyama, you *horsefly,* what you've done . . ."

"What I know is that the souls of those unmourned women buried behind the Harubayashi Inn —"

"Those disfigured whores were fated from birth to die in gutters!"

"— those souls may rest now. Justice is served."

"The order of Shiranui lengthens their lives, not shortens them!"

"So that 'gifts' can be bred to feed your derangement?"

"We sow and harvest our crop! Our crop is ours to use as we please!"

"Your order sows cruelty in the service of madness and —"

"The creeds *work,* you human *termite!* Oil

of souls *works!* How could an order founded on insanity survive for so many centuries? How could an abbot earn the favor of the empire's most cunning men with quackery?"

The purest believers, Shiroyama thinks, *are the truest monsters.* "Your order dies with you, Lord Abbot. Jiritsu's testimony is gone to Edo and" — his breaths grow sparser as the poison numbs his diaphragm — "and without you to defend it, Mount Shiranui Shrine will be disestablished."

The flung-away cup rolls in a wide arc, trundling and whispering.

Shiroyama, sitting cross-legged, tests his arms. They predecease him.

"Our order," Enomoto gasps, "the Goddess, the ritual, harvested *souls . . .*"

A guppering noise escapes Chamberlain Tomine. His jaw vibrates.

Enomoto's eyes fry and shine. "I cannot die."

Tomine falls forward onto the *go* board. Bowls of stones scatter.

"Senescence undone" — Enomoto's face locks — "skin unmottled, vigor unstolen."

"Master, I'm cold." The acolyte's voice melts. "I'm cold, Master."

"Across the River Sansho," Shiroyama spends his last words, "your victims are waiting." His tongue and lips no longer co-operate. *Some say* — Shiroyama's body turns to stone — *that there is no afterlife. Some say*

809

that human beings are no more eternal than mice or mayflies. But your eyes, Enomoto, prove that hell is no invention, for hell is reflected in them. The floor tilts and becomes the wall.

Above him, Enomoto's curse is malformed and strangled.

Leave him behind, the magistrate thinks. *Leave everything now . . .*

Shiroyama's heart stops. The earth's pulse beats against his ear.

An inch away is a *go* clamshell stone, perfect and smooth . . .

. . . a black butterfly lands on the white stone, and unfolds its wings.

■ ■ ■ ■

PART FOUR:
THE RAINY SEASON

■ ■ ■ ■

1811

CHAPTER FORTY: MOUNT INASA TEMPLE, OVERLOOKING NAGASAKI BAY

Morning of Friday, July 3, 1811

The cortege proceeds across the cemetery, led by two Buddhist priests, whose black, white, and blue-black robes remind Jacob of magpies, a bird he has not seen for thirteen years. One priest bangs a dull drum, and another strikes a pair of sticks. Following behind are four *eta*, carrying Marinus's coffin. Jacob walks alongside his ten-year-old son, Yûan. Interpreters of the First Rank Iwase and Goto walk a few steps behind, with the hoar-frosted, evergreen Dr. Maeno and Ôtsuki Monjurô from the Shirandô Academy ahead of the four guards in the rear. Marinus's headstone and coffin were paid for by the academicians, and Chief Resident de Zoet is grateful: for three seasons Dejima has been dependent upon loans from the Nagasaki Exchequer.

Droplets of mist cling to Jacob's red beard. Some escape down his throat, beneath his least-frayed collar, and are lost in the warm sweat drenching his torso.

The foreigners' enclosure is at the far end of the cemetery, by the edge of the steep forest. Jacob is reminded of the burial place reserved for suicides adjacent to his uncle's church in Domburg. *My late uncle's church,* he corrects himself. The last letter from home reached Dejima three years ago, though Geertje had written it two years before. After their uncle's death, his sister had married the schoolmaster of Vrouwenpolder, a small village east of Domburg, where she teaches the younger children. The French occupation of Walcheren makes life difficult, Geertje admitted — the great church at Veere is a barracks and stables for Napoleon's troops — but her husband, she wrote, is a good man, and they are luckier than most.

The calls of cuckoos haunt the mist-dripping morning.

Within the foreigners' enclosure waits a large group of mourners, half hidden under umbrellas. The slow pace of the cortege allows him to peruse some of the twelve or thirteen dozen headstones: his are the first Dutch feet ever to enter this place, so far as he can determine from his predecessors' day registers. The names of the very earliest dead are lost to frost and lichen, but from the Genroku Era onward — the 1690s, Jacob calculates — inscriptions can be discerned with increasing certainty. Jonas Terpstra, a likely

Frieslander, died in the First Year of Hôei, at the beginning of the last century; Klaas Old-ewarris was summoned to God in the Third Year of Hôryaku, during the 1750s; Abraham van Doeselaar, a fellow Zeelander, died in the Ninth Year of An'ei, two decades before the *Shenandoah* sailed to Nagasaki. Here is the grave of the young mestizo who fell from the English frigate, whom Jacob christened in death "Jack Farthing"; and Wybo Ger-ritszoon, dead of a "ruptured abdomen" in the Fourth Year of Kyôwa, nine years ago: Marinus suspected a burst appendix but kept his promise not to cut open Gerritszoon's body to check his diagnosis. Jacob recalls Gerritszoon's aggression very well, but the man's face has faded from memory.

Dr. Marinus arrives at his final destination.

The headstone reads, in both Japanese and the Roman alphabet, DR. LUCAS MARINUS, PHYSICIAN AND BOTANIST, DIED 7TH YEAR OF THE ERA OF BUNKA. The priests intone a mantra as the coffin is lowered. Jacob removes his snakeskin hat and, by way of counterpoint to the heathen chant, silently recites sections of the Hundred and Forty-first Psalm. " 'Our bones are scattered at the grave's mouth . . .' "

Seven days ago, Marinus was in as hale health as ever.

" '. . . as when one cutteth and cleaveth wood upon the earth. But mine eyes are unto

815

Thee, O God the Lord . . .' "

On Wednesday he announced that he was going to die on Friday.

" '. . . in Thee is my trust; leave not my soul destitute.' "

A slow aneurysm in his brain, he said, was hooding his senses.

" 'Let my prayer be set forth before Thee as incense . . .' "

He looked so unworried — and so well — as he wrote his will.

" '. . . and the lifting up of my hands as the evening sacrifice.' "

Jacob didn't believe him, but on Thursday Marinus took to his bed.

" 'His breath goeth forth,' says the Hundred and Forty-sixth Psalm, 'he returneth to his earth . . .' "

The doctor joked that he was a grass snake, shedding one skin.

" '. . . in that very day his thoughts perish.' "

He took an afternoon siesta on Friday and never woke up.

The priests have finished. The mourners look at the chief resident.

"Father" — Yûan speaks in Dutch — "you may say a few words."

The senior academicians occupy the center; to the left stand fifteen of the doctor's past and present seminarians; to the right stand an assortment of the upper-ranked and curious, a scattering of spies, monks from the temple, and a few others whom Jacob does not examine.

"I must first," he says in Japanese, "express my sincere thanks to everyone . . ."

A breeze shakes the trees and fat drops splash on umbrellas.

". . . for braving the rainy season to bid our friend farewell . . ."

I shan't feel his death, Jacob thinks, *until I return to Dejima and want to tell him about the temple at Mount Inasa, but cannot . . .*

". . . on his final journey. I offer my thanks to the priests here for providing my compatriot with a resting place and for sanctioning my intrusion this morning. Until his final days, the doctor was doing what he loved best: teaching and learning. So when we think of Lucas Marinus, let us remember a . . ."

Jacob notices two women hidden under broad umbrellas.

One is younger — a servant? — and wears a hood that conceals her ears. Her older companion wears a headscarf hiding the left side of her face . . .

Jacob cannot remember what he was saying.

"How kind of you to wait, Aibagawa-*sensei* . . ." There was a donation to offer at the temple, pleasantries to exchange with the scholars, and Jacob was as afraid she would be gone as he was nervous she would not.

Here you are. He looks at her. *The true you,*

truly here.

"It is selfish of me," she begins in Japanese, "to impose on such a busy chief resident whom I knew so briefly, and so long ago . . ."

So many things you are, Jacob thinks, *but never selfish.*

". . . but Chief de Zoet's son conveyed his father's wish with such . . ."

Orito looks at Yûan — who is besotted by the midwife — and smiles.

". . . such courteous persistence that it was impossible to leave."

Jacob's glance thanks Yûan. "I hope he wasn't overly bothersome."

"One doubts such a mannerly boy could ever be bothersome."

"His master — an artist — tries his best to instill discipline into him, but after his mother passed away, my son ran wild, and I am afraid the damage is irreparable." He turns to Orito's companion, wondering whether she is a servant, assistant, or equal. "I'm De Zoet," he says. "Thank you for coming."

The young woman is unperturbed by his foreignness. "My name is Yayoi. I mustn't say how often she talks about you or she'll be cross with me all day."

"Aibagawa-*sensei*," Yûan tells him, "said that she knew Mother long ago, even before you came to Japan."

"Yes, Yûan, Aibagawa-*sensei* was kind enough to treat your mother and her sisters

818

in the Murayama teahouses from time to time. But why, *sensei,* do you happen to be in Nagasaki at this" — he looks toward the cemetery — "at this sad time? I understood you were practicing midwifery in Miyako."

"I still am, but Dr. Maeno invited me here to advise one of his disciples, who plans to establish a school of obstetrics. I hadn't been back to Nagasaki since . . . well, since I left, and so I felt the time was ripe. That my visit coincided with Dr. Marinus's demise is a matter of unhappy chance."

Her explanation makes no mention of a plan to visit Dejima, so Jacob assumes she has none. He senses the curiosity of onlookers and gestures at the long flight of stone steps descending from the temple gates to the Nakashima River. "Shall we walk down together, Miss Aibagawa?"

"With the greatest pleasure, Chief Resident de Zoet."

Yayoi and Yûan follow a few steps behind, and Iwase and Goto bring up the rear, so Jacob and the celebrated midwife may speak in relative privacy. They tread carefully on the wet and mossy stones.

I could tell you a hundred things, thinks Jacob, *and nothing at all.*

"I understand," says Orito, "your son is apprenticed to the artist Shunro?"

"Shunro-*sensei* took pity on the talentless boy, yes."

"Then your son must have inherited his father's artistic gifts."

"I have no gifts! I am a bumbler with two left hands."

"Forgive my contradiction: I carry proof to the contrary."

She still has the fan, then. Jacob cannot quite hide his smile.

"Raising him must have been taxing, after Tsukinami-*sama*'s passing."

"He lived on Dejima until two years ago. Marinus and Eelattu tutored him, and I hired what we call in Dutch a 'nanny.' Now he lives in his master's studio, but the magistrate lets him visit every tenth day. Much as I long for a ship to arrive from Batavia for Dejima's benefit, I dread the prospect of leaving him, also . . ."

An invisible woodpecker works in short bursts on a nearby trunk.

"Maeno-*sensei* told me," she says, "Dr. Marinus died a peaceful death."

"He was proud of you. 'Pupils like Miss Aibagawa justify me, Domburger,' he used to say, and 'Knowledge exists only when it is given. . . .' " *Like love,* Jacob would like to add. "Marinus was a cynical dreamer."

Halfway down, they hear and see the foaming coffee-brown river.

"A great teacher attains immortality," she remarks, "in his students."

"Aibagawa-*sensei* might equally refer to

'her' students."

Orito says, "Your Japanese fluency is most admirable."

"Compliments such as that prove that I still make mistakes. That's the problem with having a *daimyo*'s status: nobody ever corrects me." He hesitates. "Ogawa-*sama* used to, but he was a singular interpreter."

Warblers call and query, higher up the hidden mountain.

"And a brave man." Orito's tone tells Jacob that she knows how he died, and why.

"When Yûan's mother was alive, I used to ask her to correct my mistakes, but she was the worst teacher. She said my blunders sounded too sweet."

"Yet your dictionary is now found in every domain. My own students don't say, 'Pass me the Dutch dictionary,' they say, 'Pass me the Dazûto.' "

The wind musses the long-fingered ash trees.

Orito asks, "Is William Pitt still alive?"

"William Pitt eloped with a monkey on the *Santa Maria,* four years ago. The very morning she sailed, he swam out to her. The guards weren't sure whether the shogun's laws applied, but they let him leave. With him gone, only Dr. Marinus, Ivo Oost, and I were left from your days as a 'seminarian.' Arie Grote has come back twice, but just for the trading season."

Behind them, Yûan says something funny and Yayoi laughs.

"If Aibagawa-*sensei* wished, by chance . . . to visit Dejima, then . . . then . . ."

"Chief de Zoet is most gracious, but I must return to Miyako tomorrow. Several court ladies are pregnant and will need my assistance."

"Of course! Of course. I didn't mean to imply . . . I mean, I didn't . . ." Jacob, stung, dare not say what he didn't mean to imply. "Your duties," he fumbles, "your obligations, are . . . paramount."

At the bottom of the flight of steps, porters around the palanquins are rubbing oil into their calves and thighs for their burdened journeys back to town.

Tell her, Jacob orders himself, *or spend your life regretting your cowardice.*

He decides to spend his life regretting his cowardice. *No, I can't.*

"There is something I must tell you. On that day, twelve years ago, when Enomoto's men stole you away, I was on the watchtower, and I saw you . . ." Jacob dares not look at her. "I saw you trying to persuade the guards at the land gate to let you in. Vorstenbosch had just betrayed me and, like a sulky child, when I saw you I did nothing. I could have run down, argued, fussed, summoned a sympathetic interpreter or Marinus . . . but I didn't. God knows, I couldn't guess the

822

consequences of my inaction . . . or that I'd never set eyes on you again until today — and even that afternoon I came to my senses, but" — he feels as though a fish bone is lodged in his throat — "but by the time I'd run down to the land gate to . . . to . . . help, I was too late."

Orito is listening and treading carefully, but her eyes are hidden.

"A year later, I tried to make amends. Ogawa-*sama* asked me to keep safe a scroll he had been given by a fugitive from the shrine, your shrine, Enomoto's shrine. Days later came the news of Ogawa-*sama*'s death. Month by month, I learned enough Japanese to decipher the scroll. The day I understood what my inaction had exposed you to was the worst day of my life. But despair wouldn't help you. Nothing could help you. During the *Phoebus* incident, I earned the trust of Magistrate Shiroyama, and he earned mine, so I took the grave risk of showing him the scroll. The rumors around his death, and Enomoto's, were so thick that there was no making sense of them . . . but soon after, I learned that the shrine at Shiranui had been razed and Kyôga Domain given to the lord of Hizen. I tell you this . . . I tell you this because — because not to tell you is a lie of omission, and I cannot lie to you."

Irises bloom in the undergrowth. Jacob is blushing and crushed.

Orito prepares her answer. "When pain is vivid, when decisions are keen-edged, we believe that we are the surgeons. But time passes, and one sees the whole more clearly, and now I perceive us as surgical instruments used by the world to excise itself of the Order of Mount Shiranui. Had you given me sanctuary on Dejima that day, I would have been spared pain, yes, but Yayoi would still be a prisoner there. The creeds would still be enforced. How can I forgive you when you did nothing wrong?"

They arrive at the foot of the hill. The river booms.

A stall sells amulets and grilled fish. Mourners revert to people.

Some talk, some joke, some watch the Dutch chief and the midwife.

"It must be hard," says Orito, "not knowing when you can see Europe again."

"I try to think of Dejima as home. My son is here, after all."

Jacob imagines embracing this woman he can never embrace . . .

. . . and imagines kissing her, once, between her eyebrows.

"Father?" Yûan is frowning at Jacob. "Are you unwell?"

How quickly you grow, the father thinks. *Why wasn't I warned?*

Orito says, in Dutch, "So, Chief de Zoet, our steps together is ended."

■ ■ ■ ■

PART FIVE:
THE LAST PAGES

■ ■ ■ ■

Autumn 1817

CHAPTER
FORTY-ONE:
QUARTERDECK OF
THE *PROFETES*,
NAGASAKI BAY

Monday, November 3, 1817

. . . And when Jacob looks again, the morning star is gone. Dejima is falling away by the minute. He waves at the figure on the watchtower, and the figure waves back. The tide is turning but the wind is contrary, so eighteen Japanese boats of eight oars apiece are tugging the *Profetes* out of the long bay. The oarsmen chant the same song in rhythm: their ragged chorus merges with the sea's percussion and the ship's timbers. *Fourteen boats would have done the job,* thinks Jacob, *but Chief Oost drove a fierce bargain on repairs to Warehouse Roos, so perhaps he was well advised to concede this point.* Jacob rubs the fine drizzle into his tired face. A lantern still burns in the sea-room window of his old house. He remembers the lean years when he was forced to sell Marinus's library, volume by volume, to buy lamp oil.

"Morning, Chief de Zoet." A young midshipman appears.

"Good morning, though it's plain old Mr. de Zoet now. You are?"

"Boerhaave, sir. I'm to be your servant on the voyage."

"Boerhaave . . . a fine nautical name." Jacob offers his hand.

The midshipman grips it firmly. "Honored, sir."

Jacob turns to the watchtower, whose observer is now as small as a chessman.

"Pardon my curiosity, sir," begins Boerhaave, "but the lieutenants were talking at supper about how you faced down a British frigate in this bay, all alone."

"All that happened before you were born. And I wasn't alone."

"You mean Providence had a hand in your defense of our flag, sir?"

Jacob senses a devout mind. "Let us say so."

Dawn breathes muddy greens and ember reds through gray woods.

"And afterward, sir, you were marooned on Dejima for seventeen years?"

" 'Marooned' is not quite the word, Midshipman. I visited Edo three times — a most diverting journey. My friend the doctor and I could go botanizing along these headlands, and in later years, I was allowed to visit acquaintances in Nagasaki more or less freely. The regime then more closely resembled that of a strict boarding school than it did a prison island."

A sailor on the mizzen yard shouts in a Scandinavian language.

The delayed reply from the ratline is a long and filthy laugh.

The crew is excited that twelve weeks of anchored idling is at an end.

"You must be eager to see home, Mr. de Zoet, after so long away."

Jacob envies youth its clarities and certainties. "There'll be more strangers' faces than familiar ones on Walcheren, what with the war and the passage of twenty years. Truth be told, I petitioned Edo for permission to settle in Nagasaki as a sort of consul for the new company, but no precedent could be found in the archives." He wipes his misted-over spectacles. "And so, as you see, I must leave." The watchtower is clearer without his glasses, and farsighted Jacob puts them in his jacket pocket. He suffers a lurch of panic to discover his pocket watch is missing, before remembering that he gave it to Yûan. "Mr. Boerhaave, might you know the time?"

"Two bells o' the larboard watch was not so long ago, sir."

Before Jacob can explain that he meant the land time, the bell of Ryûgaji Temple booms for the Hour of the Dragon: a quarter past seven, at this time of year.

The hour of my parting, Jacob thinks, *is*

Japan's parting gift.

The figure on the watchtower is shrunk to a tiny letter i.

He might be me, seen from the quarterdeck of the Shenandoah, though Jacob doubts that Unico Vorstenbosch was a man ever to look back. *Captain Penhaligon, however, probably did . . .* Jacob hopes, one day, to send a letter to the Englishman from the "Dutch shopkeeper" to ask what stayed his hand from firing the *Phoebus*'s carronades that autumn day: was it an act of Christian mercy, or did some more-pragmatic consideration belay the order to fire?

The chances are, he must concede, *Penhaligon, too, is dead by now.*

A black sailor scales a nearby rope, and Jacob thinks of Ogawa Uzaemon telling him how foreign vessels seem manned by phantoms and mirror images who appear and disappear through hidden portals. Jacob says a brief prayer for the interpreter's soul, watching the ship's restless wake.

The figure on the watchtower is an indistinct smudge. Jacob waves.

The smudge waves back, with two smudged arms, in wide arcs.

"A particular friend of yours, sir?" asks Midshipman Boerhaave.

Jacob stops waving. The figure stops waving. "My son."

Boerhaave is unsure what to say. "You're leaving him behind, sir?"

"I have no choice. His mother was Japanese, and such is the law. Obscurity is Japan's outermost defense. The country doesn't *want* to be understood."

"But . . . so . . . when may you meet your son again?"

"Today — this minute — is the last I shall ever see of him . . . in this world, at least."

"I could obtain the loan of a telescope, sir, if you desire it?"

Jacob is touched by Boerhaave's concern. "Thank you, but no. I'd not see his face properly. But might I trouble you for a flask of hot tea from the galley?"

"Of course, sir — though it may take a little while, if the stove isn't yet lit."

"Take as long as it takes. It'll . . . it'll keep the chill from my chest."

"Very good, sir." Boerhaave walks to the main hatch and goes below.

Yûan's outline is losing definition against the backdrop of Nagasaki.

Jacob prays, and shall pray nightly, that Yûan's life will be better than that of Thunberg's tubercular son, but the ex-chief is well versed in Japan's distrust of foreign blood. Yûan may be his master's most gifted pupil, but he shall never inherit his master's title, or marry without the magistrate's permission, or even leave the wards of the city. *He is too*

Japanese to leave, Jacob knows, *but not Japanese enough to belong.*

A hundred wood pigeons scatter from a spur of beech trees.

Even letters must rely upon the fair-mindedness of strangers. Replies will take three or four or five years.

The exiled father rubs an eyelash from his wind-blurry eye.

He stamps his feet against the early cold. His kneecaps complain.

Looking backward, Jacob sees pages from the months and years ahead. Upon his arrival at Java, the new governor-general summons him to his palace in salubrious Buitenzorg, inland and high above the miasmic airs of Batavia. Jacob is offered a plum job in the new governorship, but he declines, citing his desire to return to his fatherland. *If I cannot stay in Nagasaki,* he thinks, *better to turn my back on the Orient altogether.* The following month, he watches nightfall smother Sumatra from a ship bound for Europe, and hears Dr. Marinus, clear as a harpsichord's spindly refrain, remark upon the brevity of life, probably in Aramaic. Naturally, this is a trick of his mind. Six weeks later the passengers see Table Mountain rear up behind Cape Town, where Jacob recalls fragments of a story narrated by Chief van Cleef on the roof of a brothel, long ago. Ship fever, a brutal storm off the Azores, and a brush with a Barbary corsair make the Atlantic leg more arduous, but he disembarks safely in the Texel roadstead in a hailstorm. The harbormaster presents Jacob with a courteous summons to The Hague, where his distant role in the war is recognized by a brief ceremony at the Department for Trade and the Colonies. He proceeds to Rotterdam and stands on the same quay where he once made a vow to a young woman called Anna that within six years he would return from the East Indies, with his fortune made. He has money enough now, but Anna died in childbirth long ago, and Jacob boards the daily packet to Veere on Walcheren. The windmills on his war-bruised native island are rebuilt and busy. Nobody in Veere recognizes the home-coming Domburger. Vrouwenpolder is only half an hour's ride by trap, but Jacob prefers to walk so as not to disturb the afternoon classes at Geertje's husband's school. His sister opens the door when he knocks. She says, "My husband is in his study, sir, would you care to —" then her eyes widen, and she begins to weep and laugh.

The following Sunday, Jacob listens to a sermon in Domburg church, among a congregation of familiar faces as aged as his own. He pays his respects at the graves of his mother, father, and uncle but declines the new pastor's invitation to dine at the parsonage. He rides to Middelburg for meetings with the directors of trading houses and import companies. Positions are proposed, decisions taken, contracts signed, and Jacob is inducted into the Freemasons' Lodge. By tulip-time and Whitsuntide, he emerges from a church arm in arm with the stolid daughter of an associate. The confetti reminds Jacob of the cherry blossoms in Miyako. That Mrs. de Zoet is half her husband's age provokes no disapproval — her youth is an equitable exchange for his money. Man and wife find each other's company agreeable, for most of the time, or, certainly, for some of it; during the earlier years of their marriage, at least. He intends to publish his memoirs about his years as chief resident in Japan, but somehow life always conspires to rob him of the time. Jacob turns fifty. He is elected to the council of Middelburg. Jacob turns sixty, and his memoirs are still unwritten. His copper hair loses its burnish, his face sags, and his hairline retreats until it resembles an elderly samurai's shaven pate. A rising artist who paints his portrait wonders at his air of melancholic distance but exorcises the ghost of absence from the finished painting. One day Jacob bequeaths the De Zoet Psalter to his eldest son — not Yûan, who predeceased him, but his eldest Dutch son, a conscientious boy quite untroubled by curiosity about life beyond Zeeland. Late October or early

November brings a gusty twilight. The day has stripped the elms and sycamores of their last leaves, and the lamplighter is making his rounds as Jacob's family lines the patriarch's bedside. Middelburg's best doctor wears a grave demeanor, but he is satisfied that everything was done for his patient during the short but lucrative illness and that he will be home in time for supper. The clock's pendulum catches the firelight, and in the rattle-breathed final moments of Jacob de Zoet, amber shadows in the far corner coagulate into a woman's form.

She slips between the bigger, taller onlookers, unnoticed . . .

. . . and adjusts her headscarf, the better to hide her burn.

She places her cool palms on Jacob's fever-glazed face.

Jacob sees himself, when he was young, in her narrow eyes.

Her lips touch the place between his eyebrows.

A well-waxed paper door slides open.

ACKNOWLEDGMENTS

First, the author wishes to thank the Netherlands Institute of Advanced Study in the Humanities and Social Sciences and the Dutch Fund for Literature for providing an invaluable residency at NIAS for the first half of 2006.

Second, general thanks to Nadeem Aslam, Piet Baert, Manuel Berri, Evan Camfield, Wayson Choy, Harm Damsma, Walter Donohue, David Ebershoff, Johnny de Falbe, Tijs Goldschmidt, Tally Garner, Trish Kerr, Martin Kingston, Sharon Klein, Tania Kuteva, Hari Kunzru, Henry Jeffreys, Jonny Geller, Jynne Martin, Niek Miedema, Cees Nooteboom, Al Oliver, Hazel Orme, Lidewijde Paris, Jonathan Pegg, Noel Redding, Ruth Tross, Michael Schellenberg, Mike Shaw, Alan Spence, Doug Stewart, Professor Arjo Vanderjagt, Klaas and Gerrie de Vries, Carole Welch my patient editor, Professor Henk Wesselling, Dr. George E van Zanen.

Third, specific thanks to Kees 't Hart, Ship

Manager Robert Hovell of HM Frigate *Unicorn* in Dundee, Archivist Peter Sijnke of Middelburg, and Professor Cynthia Vialle of the University of Leiden for answering a plethora of questions. Research sources were numerous, but this novel is indebted especially to the scholarship of Professor Timon Screech of the School of Oriental and African Studies at the University of London, Beatrice M. Bodart-Bailey's annotated translation of Kaempfer's *Japan: Tokugawa Culture Observed* (as read by Captain Penhaligon), and Annick M. Doeff's translation of her ancestor Hendrik Doeff's memoir, *Recollections of Japan.*

Fourth, thanks to the in-house illustrators Jenny and Stan Mitchell, and in-house translator of Japanese sources Keiko Yoshida.

Lastly, thanks to Lawrence Norfolk and his family.